Brooklyn Jewelry Exchange

By

Meisha C. Holmes

My Lyric's House Press-Brooklyn, New York

ISBN# 0-9761446-0-3

MY Lyric's House Press
593 Vanderbilt Avenue
Suite # 135
Brooklyn, New York 11238
www.Brooklynjewelryexchange.com

To my greatest work of all, Kayla Lyric, thanks for being you. Thanks for working on your computer when mommy couldn't play because she was working on hers. You are my greatest inspiration. Lyric, my life wouldn't be worth singing a song or picking up my pen to write if you weren't here to spend it with me. I love you!

1

That Brooklyn bullshit we on it

"What are you going to wear tonight? I'm so excited. I never get a chance to go out anymore. My kids take up most of my extra time, and between work and their father—"

"You don't have to tell me, Kay. I mean, even though I don't have any kids and shit between school, my job and hunting for a man I never get to go party myself. But this is a milestone, girl. I've got to go shake my ass or something tonight. May fuckin' 15th rolls around again. They should turn this day into a national holiday. Rock Candy Day," Rocky said.

"Rock Candy Day? How would we celebrate? Fuck and shop all day?" Kay asked.

"Exactly," Rocky replied. Both women laughed. "Seriously Kay, we really don't get out much anymore."

"Rocky, please. You're always in Detroit with Mauri, y'all do clubs out there— and didn't you two just come back from the Dominican Republic? Not to mention you're always at a basketball game, or a game after-party. Then there's that nice Thomas guy you keep on dissin'. He takes you out to all the exclusive spots in Manhattan. If I were you I would just stay wi—"

"But you're not me. And don't get it twisted. All that shit you talkin' is business. Mauri pays my rent and my car note so that's why I make my bimonthly trips to Detroit, I'ma hook my ass an NBA player and get married so all my ballgames, trips and parties are necessary, and Thomas is just too fuckin' corny. Besides he's only pulling in about a hundred and forty grand a year. If it wasn't for his big ass dick—"

"One forty? That's about a hundred and ten thousand more than you make. Anyway you know what you're doing, Rocky, you always do. Are you sure this club is gonna to be poppin'? It *is* Thursday."

"Yeah, I'm sure. Nobody throws hot parties on the weekends anymore."

"What should I wear?" Kay asked.

"You have the entire day to think about what you're going to put on," Rocky said.

"I'll call you when I get off of work."

"No, just be ready at ten-thirty. I'll be blowing my horn. Only call me if you are having an extreme outfit emergency. 'Cause your ass will change outfits eight times before tonight, and call me each time you change."

"Alright grandma, call me when you get to work."

"Grandma! Whatever— you ain't but one year behind me. Your ass will be twenty-five before you know it."

"Rocky, I gotta go. I have to be at work for eight and it's already seven-fifteen. I am going to be late fuckin' around with your ass. I'll call you when I get to the job."

Rocky placed her phone on the charger and walked to her closet. She stared at herself through its mirrored doors and began a conversation.

"Well, Rock Candy, you still got it, but why can't you get it? You're educated—" She turned her back towards the mirror, contracted her ass muscles tightly for a second, and quickly released them. Then she jiggled her ass in front of the mirror reassuring herself that it was still firm. "The onion is still there," she said as she rubbed her hand over the curves of her rear end.

She faced the mirror and ran her long, slender fingers through her hair. She stepped closer to the mirror and grinned, revealing two rows of straight, perfect, pearly whites looking for any traces of yesterday's left over goat cheese and spinach wrap that she'd just polished off. Using the tips of her short but tailored fingernails, she removed a small, white chunk from between her two front teeth. Her reflection seemed infatuated by her smile as she continued to stare at it. Her brown almond shaped, eyes marveled at how her deep auburn hair caressed her tan skin. She shook her hair from side to side until it fell on her back. She traced the golden straps of her tan line with two fingers and her smile slowly faded. Without the extra tint of the sun Rocky always felt so pale.

"After I stayed on the beach all weekend? I can't believe my tan is starting to fade already. Nothing a little fakin' bakin' won't fix, I'll make an appointment for twenty minutes at the tanning salon when I get into Detroit next weekend."

Before she opened her closet doors she took one last look at herself. "You're beautiful, no kids, and good in bed. So why don't you have the man that you want?" Rocky opened the closet and rummaged through her clothes. "Should I go for sexy, classy, business like or trashy?"

All of her clothing was arranged by color. Toward the left end of the closet she had red dresses, red blouses, red skirts and one pair of red suede pants. To the right were an array of blue dresses, blue blouses, blue skirts, blue dress pants and different shades of blue jeans. She stopped momentarily when she noticed a pair of navy wool, dress pants in between her faded blue denim jeans. "How did this get here? I must have been really tired when I was hanging up my laundry last weekend." She removed the hanger from the closet and placed the wool pants in their correct place. She passed over a few yellows and even less off-white. Then she looked at her black clothing, which was directly in the middle of her closet. She pulled out an ankle-length dress. It was sheer in the back and slightly see-through. It had a long split up the front that stopped near her inner thigh. It had no sleeves or straps and a sheer diamond patch in the front that stopped about three inches below her navel. She laid it on her bed.

"Now this is hot to death. Just enough to tease the naked eye and be classy, and two steps above slut. This shit will turn heads tonight, and this red fitted suit will turn heads at work all day."

The moment Rocky walked into the office, she heard the phone ringing inside her cubicle. She rushed to her desk to answer it.

"Good morning, College Admissions, Raquel Jones speaking. How may I help you?"

"Happy birthday sweetheart. Why are you breathing so heavy?"

"I just walked in, and thank you, Thomas."

"What time will you be ready for me to pick you up?" Thomas asked.

Fuck, I completely forgot. Why? Why couldn't you just have told him no, she thought.

"Hello— are you there? Can you hear me? Rocky, don't tell me you forgot?" Thomas asked.

"Kind of, sort of. I'm sorry," Rocky said.

"I made dinner reservations for eight o' clock. And—"

She tuned out his voice and looked at the clock. *Let's see*, she thought. *If he can get to my house by seven-fifteen, he can give me my gift, I can eat, probably get some dick and make it to my girls for eleven-thirty.*

"Just be at my house by seven, seven-fifteen. I'll be ready for whatever."

"Alright sweetie. I'll be there at seven. Dress to impress."

"Okay, good-bye." Rocky slammed the phone down and looked at it. "Dress to impress, sweetie" she said in her deepest voice. "Sometimes he makes me so sick. If it wasn't for that thick dick, the thoughtful gifts and the extra cash, I would have dumped his ass a long time ago. He is so muthafuckin' corny. UUUGH."

As she went to pick up her phone it rang again. "Good morning College Admissions Raquel Jon—"

"Yeah, yeah, yeah what up, though? Happy born day, baby girl."

"Not *you* up before noon, thanks for the cash and earrings," Rocky said.

"I wanted to be the first one to wish you a happy born day."

"Thank you, Mauri. The earrings you sent are beautiful," Rocky said.

"You sure you don't want me to fly down there for your special day?" Mauri asked.

"We just came back from celebrating my birthday in the Dominican Republic Sunday, and I'll be out there next weekend."

"I am glad you like your gift. I'll call you later, bye."

Rocky said goodbye to the dial tone. *He's always so abrupt*, she thought as she dialed Kay's number. "Kay, we'll meet at eleven-thirty. I forgot Thomas had something planned. Did you make it on time?"

"You know that's right," Kay replied.

"Good, speak to you later," Rocky said.

"Goodbye."

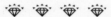

"You better get your butt out of here. It's already seven-fifteen. You're going to be late for school!" Millicent Hendrickson called out.

Tony ignored his mother and swallowed an entire glass of orange juice.

"Ma, it's May 15th, school will be over in—" Tony paused for a second. "— in 43 days, and that's including weekends, stop stressin'," Tony said.

"And I wish you would cut that crap off your head, Tony," Millicent added.

"Bye, Ma. Bye, Malik," Tony replied, letting the kitchen door slam behind him. He walked out the house muttering under his breath. He bent over and checked his reflection in the window of the dusty Saab in the driveway. Small, tight braids zigzagged around Tony's head and rested at the bottom of his shoulders. A thin mustache barely covered his upper lip. His light brown skin glistened from the fresh coat of baby oil he'd just rubbed all over his body. He used his frail fingers to smooth down his thick eyebrows. When he straightened up the reflection of Tony's bony torso moved toward the sidewalk. He tugged up his low hanging jeans on his narrow hips, and was off to school.

"Mom, everybody's wearing braids now leave Tony alone, okay? I'm on my way to work," Malik said.

"You coming in late again? Should I take your dinner out?" Millicent asked sarcastically.

"I'll be home for dinner, Mom. See you later, and you know I'm sorry about last night, but I was detained at work," Malik said.

Millicent smiled and shook her head slowly as she watched Malik walk out of the door. She knew that both of her sons were grown but to her the only way to keep them together was their family dinner at seven-thirty. This way they could gather as one each day and spend quality time. No one was exempt— not her husband, not herself and definitely not her two boys.

"As long as they're under this roof, we eat together," she assured herself firmly. Millicent quickly ran around the kitchen in her white uniform cleaning counter tops, and placing plates and glasses in the dishwasher.

As Malik walked down the street he still heard the sarcasm in his mother's voice. He knew she was upset with him for missing dinner. If he had plans he was expected to call. But yesterday could not be helped.

As he approached the train station and thought about the previous day, he still couldn't believe it . . .

"Mr. Hendrickson. I need you to come upstairs. I have some very important documents that should have gone out yesterday. I want them hand delivered by you, NOW!"

All four men stood at attention. It was not often one of the top attorneys at the firm left their lofty offices to come down to the mailroom requesting special deliveries.

"That won't be a problem ma'am. I will be up in five minutes," Malik said.

"Very well," Susan Eden replied.

As she left eight eyes watched her muscular calves walk out of the door. They used their sight to caress her flat but firm rear end. They relaxed as soon as she was out of view.

"Damn. I would love to hit that," Mike said.

"I second that," a mailroom clerk added.

"Shit, I think we've all had some kind of fantasy about Mrs. Eden. She is the only White woman I would ever think about fuckin', besides Pamela Anderson," Malik said.

"Yo, that's who she reminds me of and shit. But I would never have sex with no White chick," Mike said.

"Yeah, right. Not one?" Malik asked.

"Okay, I wouldn't mind fuckin' Pink and shit, she thinks she's Black. And, I guess I would tap that just because Mrs. Eden has mad dough. Her husband owns the Brooklyn Jewelry Exchanges," Mike said.

"All three of them?" Malik asked

"Yep, all of them," Mike replied.

"I heard she's getting ready to make partner," Malik said.

"What does a partner do, Malik?" Mike asked.

Everyone in the mailroom laughed.

"Well, for starters, partners don't make a salary, they get a percentage of the firm's entire income, they recruit new clients, close deals—"

"You better make your way upstairs. Rumor has it that she is a real bitch," a mailroom clerk put in.

"I could tell by the way she stormed in here," Malik said as he looked at his watch. "And she got me going out like a half an hour before quitting time. I'll see you guys tomorrow."

He straightened his tie and walked out of the mailroom toward the elevator. As he entered the elevator he moistened his lips. Tiny beads of sweat began to cover his forehead and his palms were clammy. Malik punched a button and leaned against the elevator wall as he whispered, "Lord, please don't let anything go wrong. I need this job to get my foot in the door."

The elevator stopped on the 1ˢᵗ floor, and two women dressed in suits walked in.

"Good afternoon," Malik said.

"Hello," one of the women replied smiling at Malik. The women smiled at each other.

"What department are you in?" The second asked.

"I'm the mailroom manager. Why do you ask?"

"No reason. It's just that I've never seen you around before." She leaned next to her co-worker and whispered. "But I would sure like to. He is gorgeous."

The two women giggled and stared at him all the way to the 5ᵗʰ floor where they made their exit. Malik stood 6' tall and had deep dimples. He had a dark tan complexion and his eyes were his most striking feature. They were light brown with small red rings around the pupils. When he smiled, nickel-sized dimples magically appeared on his cheeks and his teeth were straight and white. A slight overbite disguised two chipped teeth on the bottom row.

Malik tried to check his appearance on the metal doors of the elevator, but the reflection was dull and distorted. He wiped his palms on his khakis and waited for the doors to open on the 10th floor. He looked at the cubicles situated behind the reception area. A thick semi-transparent Plexiglas partition separated them. There had to be at least thirty cubicles— they were all empty. He found this quite strange.

"Good afternoon. I am looking for Mrs. Eden's office," Malik said.

The secretary looked up at him and raised one finger motioning for Malik to wait a minute. Her loud, lime green suit was an eyesore in the dull gray office. As she talked on the phone she gave Malik an unpleasant look. After a minute she placed the receiver down and forced a smile.

"And you are?" she asked disapprovingly.

"Malik Hendrickson," he said as he flashed his badge and a smile.

She read it and stared at him with the same disapproving glare. "She doesn't deal in mailroom business. To be quite frank it's very rare mailroom clerks make it past the 5th floor of the building, aside from the twice daily pick ups."

"I am the manager, so I am well aware of what time out going collections are made. Mrs. Eden came down to the mailroom and requested I see her on an urgent matter. So Ms.—" Malik paused to read the metal plate, with her name in white lettering. "—Woods. I'll have her address you once she misses my presence. Good day."

Malik walked toward the elevator doors. As he was about to push the down button he heard her heels. He looked in the direction of the footsteps and smiled.

"Mr. Hendrickson, I was just coming to ask Ms. Woods to call the mailroom. The entire floor is at the monthly staff meeting, including my assistant."

The receptionist's milk white face turned pink like a strawberry shake. Malik didn't say a word. She, however, sighed and nervously ran her fingers through her red hair. "Sorry, Mrs. Eden, I kind of gave him a hard way to go."

"You should have called me and checked first before you asked him off of the floor, Deborah," Mrs. Eden said sternly. She directed her attention to Malik, and said softly, "Mr. Hendrickson, follow me please." As she walked off she frowned over her shoulder at the receptionist. "Don't let it happen again." Once they were a few feet away from the reception area she cleared her throat and made her request. "Now Mr. Hendrickson, I need you to make a personal delivery for me. You can use a company car. Are you a licensed driver?"

"Yes, I am."

"Good. You are to drop off, and bring a package back to me. This has to be kept confidential."

"Yes, ma'am."

At the back of the office there was a small hallway with six doors. She reached into her pocket and removed a slim card. She placed the back of it against a red laser beam, and the door's lock clicked open. Malik studied the definition of her legs, and her backside as he walked close behind her. Susan noticed him looking and she smiled inside. He was surprised by the simplicity of her office. He had thought it would be much more elaborate.

There was a large mahogany and black colored desk, sitting in front of a window that overlooked the New York City skyline. He quit surveying the room, covered his mouth with a cupped fist and coughed. He pointed at the window.

"Do you mind if I— ," Malik said.

"No. Go right ahead," Susan interrupted.

He stared out at the skyline. Despite all the buildings that crowded the post card view it seemed empty to him. He stared at the clear blue sky, searched for the black hole and shook his head.

"I still can't believe they're gone. This is the first time I've been so close. I refuse to go look. This September will make how many years, and I still won't look."

Malik placed two fingers on the window where he figured the World Trade Center should stand. After ten seconds or so he let them glide down leaving long finger smudges on it.

"MaaLick, did you lose anyone in the tragedy?" Mrs. Eden asked.

"It's Malik. Like a leak from a faucet and yeah, my girl worked there."

"Oh, I am so sorry."

Malik sighed heavily. "So am I. I've never looked."

"Are you in school?"

"Yes, I am completing my last year at NYU."

Mrs. Eden rummaged through her drawers, for what she did not know. I can't do this, she thought.

She pulled out a manila folder. "Here we are. Do you have a girlfriend now?"

Malik stared at the empty space in front of him as he spoke. "Nah. I don't want one right now, Mrs. Eden. I am finishing college and will hopefully be starting law school in the fall."

"Please, call me Susan."

She watched him for a moment as he stared out of the window. Susan walked slowly toward him and gently touched his hand. Malik jumped and turned to find his face within inches of hers. Flustered, he stepped back as she leaned forward and kissed his lips gently. Wide-eyed, he balanced himself by placing one arm on the centralized air conditioning unit underneath the window. He used the other hand to push her back. It landed on her firm breasts and he quickly lowered his arm as if he was stung.

"Don't you want to have some unattached fun?" Susan asked.

Every man in the building has fantasized about Susan Eden. Why is she doing this to me? he wondered as he watched her pull a condom from her top drawer.

"I have waited for this moment for a year and a half. I've watched you in the cafeteria. I frequent the reception area on Thursdays when you come up to check the promptness of your carriers. I am so attracted to you— and your body. You are always so pleasant when we speak and your eyes are beautiful."

Speak? She barely says hello, he thought.

She pulled her skirt above her thighs and Malik lost his self-control. She wore garters and her hairless vagina glistened. He felt his dick harden. He grabbed it through his khakis and sat on the top of the air conditioning unit.

"When we speak? I haven't had any formal conversations with you, aside from 'good day' and 'hello'. Are you taping me? What's going on?" Malik asked. Then he snatched the condom from her hand and threw it on the floor.

"Listen Maalick."

"It's Malik."

"This has been really hard for me to do," she said as she placed one leg on the air conditioner next to his thigh. She pulled her skirt higher and fingered the lips of her vagina.

"Oh shit!! It's hard to tell," Malik exclaimed.

"Please don't embarrass me by turning me down." Susan put her leg down and fixed her skirt. Her face turned pink. She took several steps back as her eyes flooded with tears.

Malik stood and countered her actions; he pulled up her skirt, loosened his shirt and unbuckled his belt. When he took a step forward his pants dropped to his knees. He scooped her into his arms and carried her over to one of two chairs that faced her desk. They sat down and he tugged his throbbing dick out of the small opening in his boxers. He went into his wallet and pulled out a condom. He tore it open quickly and rolled it down his penis.

Susan faced Malik then straddled him. The tip of each of her pointy heels barely touched the floor.

Wow! What a cock! I can't believe it's happening. My marriage, job, and reputation are all on the line, she thought. Susan abruptly put her worries aside and guided his penis to her soaked vagina.

If I am being taped they got me already so fuck it, I might as well enjoy this, Malik thought as he cupped one of her plump breasts. He placed it inside of his mouth and slowly pushed her nipple out between his lips. *"No one is going to come in here, right?"* Malik asked.

Susan was breathless. She felt warm and was starting to sweat. She inhaled and spoke softly. *"No."*

"Wait," he said as he pushed her off of him. She was flung to the side like a cowboy at a rodeo. He lightly grabbed her arm to prevent her fall. *"Sorry about that but— is the entire building in on this or something? These two women on the elevator were laughing and looking at me on my way up here."*

"You are definitely a looker, but this is strictly personal business. Now, put it in Maalick," she demanded.

Malik held his penis. Susan sat on it and eased it in as far as it would go. Sharp pains shot through her. She cried out softly.

"You have to be quiet. I don't want anyone to hear us," Malik whispered.

She clutched the back of the chair they were in like it held her last breath. She did not want to loosen her grip for fear that it would provoke more pain. Malik pushed up into her slowly, both of his hands gripping her small waist. He could smell the faint floral aroma of her damp blonde hair— he held his breath to try and savor it. Looking down, at the vanilla legs that straddled his thighs he noticed that the chair's arm left pink blotchy bruises on her skin.

I can't believe I am fucking a White broad. I CAN'T BELIEVE I'M FUCKIN' SUSAN EDEN, his brain screamed. Suddenly Malik swooped Susan up like a rag doll. He grabbed her suit jacket from the back of a chair and laid it on the floor still cradling her in his arms. He placed her down on the tiny jacket as gently as possible then wasted no time. As *soon as her body hit the floor he shoved into her as far he could go and began a fast stroke. Damn this shit is tight, he thought as he felt his dick easing further in with each stroke.*

Susan frantically grabbed the backs of his arms while he pushed into her. Once he was fully penetrated he pounded harder and faster. She moaned loudly. He covered her mouth with his hand. Malik looked into her blue eyes and a surge of energy rushed through his body. Within seconds the condom was filled with his cum. Prudently he pulled out of her, quickly got up and put on his pants, leaving the semen-filled condom on his penis. He helped her off the floor and she rearranged her clothes.

"Please excuse my performance. I still can't believe this. I'm on edge. Having sex with the best looking woman in your place of business isn't as easy as I thought it would be," Malik blushed.

"That was all I imagined it would be and more," Susan sighed.

"That was nothing. Give me another go around and I will give you more than you imagined."

"Do you have the time, sir?"

"Excuse me?"

"Do you have the time?"

"Sure. It's a quarter to eight."

"Thanks," a young girl said, smiling at Malik.

"Damn, I hope I ain't miss my stop. I was so wrapped up in my thoughts and shit," he mumbled to himself.

Malik looked out the window and it was pitch black, darkness, with the exception of an occasional spark or two from the tracks. As the train sped into the station he saw the familiar 'Park Place' sign pass by again and again, until the train came to a screeching halt. He was relieved that he had only two stops left. As he glanced around he noticed the subway car was packed, which usually annoyed him every morning. But this particular morning, it seemed as if he were traveling solo.

I hope this shit ain't on the front of the company newsletter. But Susan has more to lose than I do so I guess I'll be straight, he thought as waited for his stop.

Susan sat at her desk and tapped her pen; she did not know what to think. She was awake in her bed the previous night thinking of an excuse for her actions. *I know I just wanted a one-time fling with a younger man, but I have to have more. Just one more time won't hurt. I'll have him come up again, tomorrow,* she thought.

When Malik got to work it was business as usual. The entire day passed without a phone call or a visit from Mrs. Eden. He was disappointed and relieved. He didn't breathe a word of what happened to his coworkers. When they asked what happened in her office he replied simply,

"She wanted a delivery made and I delivered it."

◈ ◈ ◈ ◈

"Tony, I'm telling you man. I overheard her on her cell phone. This is our ticket into Brooklyn's Finest."

"Kahmelle, how much money is she taking to the bank?" Tony asked.

"She collected more than four thousand dollars cash for the senior trip. She is going to deposit it into the school account today. If we tip Sweat and them off, that could be our first step toward initiation."

"I don't know, Kahmelle," Tony said.

"Yo, come on. Call your older brother and get the number to Sweat's cell. If he snatches her bag, we're in. Let's cut independent study and sneak out the fire exit behind the gym. They usually be hanging out on High Field," Kahmelle said.

"It's too fuckin' early. Besides, I don't want to rob Mrs. Simmons. She's a cool teacher— shit, she's my favorite teacher. And I don't know if my brother still has his number," Tony said.

"Do you want to join the gang or what? You know Latonji ain't going to give you no play if she thinks you a sucker. You know her ex used to hustle, right? Besides, we been talking about this shit all school year. Don't chicken out on me now. Let's end the school year with a bang. Plus, we don't have to rob her, they gonna do it," Kahmelle said.

"I'm sayin' though. I ain't tryin' to rob nobody I know," Tony said.

"See man, you always doing some old sucker shit when it's about to go down. Look, here comes Latonji and them now."

Three young ladies dressed in tightly fitted, black sweaters with gold lettering and short black skirts with big gold pleats walked past the guys. The tallest of the four smiled at Tony. She stood about 5'6", was a dark chocolate complexion and had dark brown eyes. Her breasts seemed to make the gold "B" on her sweater smile. She had a short haircut that tapered off above her ears. Her thighs were of thoroughbred status and her rear-end was so round and plump the back of her skirt rested higher than the front.

"Do you see those fuckin' thighs in that cheerleading outfit? Yo, I definitely want her to be my girl and shit," Tony whispered to Kahmelle. "Hey, what up ladies?" Tony asked. The girls smiled at Tony and Kahmelle as they walked by without stopping their conversation. "Alright, I'll do it. Let's go to our third period classes and then we'll go to High Field after lunch. I got Regents biology after lunch. What about you?" Tony asked.

"I got Spanish 2," Kahmelle said.

"You better pass this time, you fuckin' super senior. You know they won't let you graduate next year if you don't complete your foreign language credits?"

"I know. You sound like my aunt and shit." Kahmelle sucked his teeth.

"I'll see you at lunch," Tony said.

They went off to class with the same thoughts of joining Brooklyn's Finest. After lunch they met up and made their way to the school's track and field.

"I could never figure out why our field is so far from the school, yo. It's too hot to be walkin' out here in this sun," Kahmelle said.

"Our school is almost one hundred years old and the field is only like ten years old, so you figure it out," Tony replied.

"Look, I see them over there underneath the bleachers." Kahmelle pointed at three guys who sat underneath the bleachers drinking Hypnotiq and smoking blunts. "Let me do all the talking."

Kahmelle walked up to where the guys were standing. Tony stopped a couple of feet behind him beside the bleachers.

"Yo, Sweat, what up?" Kahmelle asked.

A tall and lanky, light-skinned man looked up. He had a long keloid scar down the middle of his face. The sun seemed to shine directly on his scar as he stepped out from underneath the bleachers. The skin on his face was tight and ashy, but his scar was shiny and smooth. It seemed to stand off of his face. It started out thin from his hairline, got thicker at the bridge of his nose and stopped above his upper lip where it was thickest. Both his eyes and his tight and kinky low-cut hair were dark brown. He nodded his head slowly several times before he spoke. His voice was deep and raspy.

"Yeah, yeah what up, youngin'?" Sweat replied.

"Me and my boy want into Brooklyn's Finest. We go to the High, and we know that one of our teachers is going to the bank on Flatbush and Fourth Avenue with four thousand dollars cash to deposit into a school account. We could tell you what door she's coming out of and what time, if you let us into the gang." Kahmelle said.

"You know what you got to do to get in, right?" Sweat asked.

"Nah. What?" Tony asked as he stepped closer.

"I ain't even see you over there, son," Sweat said. He squinted his eyes as he peered at Tony. "You Little Tone? LEEKO'S baby brother?" He ran a finger over his scar as he asked the second question. "Yo, I remember when you was yay high and shit. Y'all want in? You got to rob somebody at gunpoint and rob a business establishment. After you hold somebody up, you got six months to put together the other job. You have to come on top with at least three grand. If this shit comes through today, you'll still have two jobs left and you gotta get jumped in. What up with Malik? That nigga still in school and shit?"

"Yeah," Tony said.

"Well, I'm going to let you in on the strength of him, providing we get at least three G's today, but you still have to pull off the two jobs in six months," Sweat said. He looked at Tony and smiled. "The Finest don't do braids, so you have to cut that shit off before Friday. If this broad really has the loot and shit, I'll smash y'all off with a couple of hundred. Give me the times."

"She takes lunch at one o' clock and she is coming out the side entrance on Fourth, cause I saw her park this morning. It's a navy blue Honda Accord, the older models, like a '96," Tony said.

"Meet me here at three and I'll give you your cut, if there's enough to cut," Sweat said.

Tony felt bad inside. He really liked Mrs. Simmons and didn't want her to get hurt. As they walked back to school Tony was silent and his stomach churned.

"Tone, man, we gonna be in and shit," Kahmelle said.

"I don't know, I am kind of having second thoughts and shit. I mean, where are we going to get guns from?" Tony asked.

"Ask your brother. He ain't get rid of everything from his wild days, and I know he can come up with one," Kahmelle said.

"Are you fuckin' nuts? Malik is a fuckin' goodie goodie now, and he would tell my moms, and they would wile out," Tony said.

"Let's just see what happens after school. Tony, did you see that nigga's face? What the fuck is that? You think that shit got pus in it?"

"It's a fuckin' bust down, somebody cut the shit out of that nigga. It wasn't there back when I knew him."

"Word? That's a cut? But why that shit come off his face like that? The shit was following me around when I was talking to him."

"It's a skin condition called keloid. Whenever people with that condition get cut it doesn't heal properly and it stays like that forever. You got that shit yourself, nigga— how you don't know about it?"

"I ain't got that shit," Kahmelle replied with an attitude.

"Yeah, you do. Why you think you got that tittie behind your ear after it was pierced?"

Kahmelle grabbed his ear and squeezed the bottom of the thick round keloid that sat behind his ear lobe. "Oh shit! My aunt never told me that's what this shit is."

Sweat watched as the boys walked away, and continued to stare in that direction way after they were gone. Seeing Tony was like seeing a ghost of his not so distant past. A past that was to stay buried in the depths of his mind.

Officer Joann Nuñez slowly walked her post for the twentieth time that day. Her post was considerably large for one officer to cover. It encompassed four blocks of private homes: Butler Street, Dean Street, Carroll Street and St. Marks Place and they all shared Fourth Avenue as a cross street. Her post also spanned six long blocks along Fourth Avenue, a very busy street with small businesses, bodegas at every other corner, a state building, Brooklyn High School, Brooklyn High's football/track and field and Brooklyn Jewelry Exchange. She patrolled this area at least fifty times a day. She stared at her watch.

"Damn, it's only one! Three o'clock can't come soon enough," she huffed into the air.

She stepped lively down Butler Street, where she'd found boys smoking behind an abandoned private home minutes ago, and made her way back to Fourth Avenue. Loud static blared through her radio as she crossed the street. She could barely believe her ears when the dispatch came through.

"Post two. Post two. There's a 34 at 3787 Fourth Avenue, corner of Second Street. The perps are between sixteen and twenty-five, all male, all Black, all wearing blue jeans, all wearing green T-shirts."

"That's a copy," Officer Joann Nuñez replied into the radio.

Joann ran to the corner where two blocks away she could see the perps fleeing from the scene on foot.

"This is Post Two. There are three perps heading south on Fourth. I am two blocks away," she said.

Joann sprinted up the block at top speed to find a young woman sprawled out on the concrete against the iron bars of Brooklyn High School's gate. She ran to her side and knelt down.

"Ma'am, I'm Officer Nuñez with the New York City Police Department. Can you hear me?"

The woman rolled her head up and looked in the direction of Joann's voice. She winced in pain as she tried to open her eyes, but they burned terribly. Her head fell onto the concrete and she began to sob.

"I can hear you officer. But I can't see. MY EYES!"

"Do you know who did this to you?" Joann asked.

"No. None of them go to this school or looked familiar to me," the victim sobbed.

"Can you give me a brief description?" Joann asked.

"My eyes, officer. I can't think. My head!" She cried.

"What is your name?" Joann asked.

"Simmons. Tina Simmons I am a teacher here at Brooklyn High."

Joann spoke into her radio. "This is Post Two. I've got a 24 and the victim needs a bus. She is coherent, but bleeding heavily."

"4."

Joann looked down at Mrs. Simmons. Beneath a demolished pair of glasses her eyes were swollen shut. There were pieces of the broken lens on her cheeks and small streams of blood ran down her face. One eye was covered in blood, and pus began to appear under her eyelid as Joann stared at her. She gently patted her shoulder.

"Try your best to be calm. Everything will be fine."

Two school safety guards came running out of the building. One opened her mouth wide in horror and clasped her hand over it as she looked down. "Oh my god! Oh my god, its Simmons."

Squad cars sped past, lights flashing and sirens blaring. Joann continued to hold Mrs. Simmons' hand. Her broken glasses still clung to cheek. Blood continued to run down her face covering her eyes, and her cheeks. Joann searched for an open wound, but could not locate one. At the corner, near to the crossing light, one of her shoes laid next to a small tote bag with papers scattered around it. The shoe stood upright, as if was patiently waiting to cross the street. Within three minutes more sirens filled the air.

The ambulance arrived and Mrs. Simmons began speaking. "They took an envelope filled with trip money. There was over four thousand dollars in it."

As the ambulatory technicians mounted her onto the stretcher, Mrs. Simmons did not release her grip on Joann's hand. A crowd began to gather as they placed her into the ambulance. Officer Joann Nuñez released her grip.

"Please officer. Don't leave me as yet," Mrs. Simmons pleaded.

As a technician removed her glasses, Joann recognized Mrs. Simmons as one of the few teachers who arrive at the school early daily. She watched as the technician checked her vitals and took her blood pressure.

She arrives a little after they drop me off at my post, she thought as she climbed out of the ambulance. "Okay Mrs. Simmons, we'll be in touch. You are in good hands now," Joann said.

"Thank you, officer," Mrs. Simmons replied as the technicians closed the ambulance doors.

Damn, Joann thought angrily. *If I stayed at the bodega just a minute longer she would have never been mugged.*

Joann walked over to the bodega and leaned against its window. She looked at her watch; it was one thirty-six p.m. She pulled a thick, black memo book with multicolored rubber bands clinging to its outsides out of her back pocket.

"Let's see I need an Aided and a 61," she said out loud. She placed the rubber bands on her wrist and began filling out two standard police forms.

At three p.m. hundreds of adolescents poured out of Brooklyn High. Kahmelle and Tony eagerly ran to meet Sweat. As they reached the busy field Sweat was exiting the opposite opening from where Tony and

Kahmelle entered. The school's football players and cheerleaders were starting to assemble on the field.

"Yo, Sweat! Wait up!" Kahmelle called.

Sweat looked at his watch and shook his head slowly. "Once shit livens up on the field I'm gone. It's three-fifteen. I said three. Anyway, thanks for tipping a nigga off and shit. It went mad easy, too. Here's a little cash for the both of you."

Sweat handed five, crisp, one hundred dollar bills to Kahmelle and then peeled off twenty-five twenties from a large bankroll and handed them to Tony.

"Five hundred a piece. Here, y'all gonna need these," Sweat said. He handed the boys two black cellular phones and two chargers. "These have a walkie talkie system. If something goes down and I need y'all I'll walkie you."

"How we gonna pay for these?" Tony asked.

"They blow up jacks. You can't make any phone calls on them, only the radio works. All of the Finest have them compliments of me. Keep them charged at all times," Sweat said.

"So, we in?" Kahmelle said.

"Friday under the bleachers, five o' clock. Then you'll know if you're in. Wear green, 'cause Brooklyn's Finest is all about getting that green, ya heard. And Lil' Leek—"

"Tony," Tony said loudly.

Sweat smiled. "Lil' Tone, you need to get rid of them braids by tomorrow. Our clique, don't do that hair-do, son. No braids." Sweat gave them each a pound and left.

"I'm going to buy me a pair of green and white Prada sneakers with this cash right here," Tony said.

"I want a new Phat Farm sweat suit," Kahmelle said.

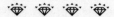

Thomas looked at the clock as he pulled up on Butler Street. It was six fifty-eight. "Good, I'm on time. She is always so upset when I am late," Thomas said.

She might be 'the one'. I'm eight months in this relationship and she's definitely marriage material. No kids, okay job— but she is in school, gorgeous, nice body, sweet as pie, well organized, can cook her ass off, and the sex is no joke either. Yeah, Thomas thought, *this might be her.*

The bright, interior lights of his truck interrupted his thoughts. Rocky quickly glanced at him through the open truck door. She must have stood at least 5'7" in her stiletto heels. She gently climbed into the truck. As she sat she pulled her dress up to her thighs. Her long, auburn hair lay neatly below her bosom. She planted a soft kiss on his cheek.

"Hey Thomas, how are you?" She looked him up and down. "Wow, you look nice. So what do you have planned for tonight?" Rocky asked.

"I have reservations for Jean George's. You look really nice—"

Rocky tuned out his voice, placed it elsewhere and thought hard. *How am I going to get the money to fly down to Vegas next month? Holyfield is fighting and mad ballers will be there. I need to use the two G's Mauri sent me for my birthday on rent and my tuition. I can always hit Thomas up for my car note and insurance— but how am I going to flip this Vegas trip?*

"—Isn't that right, Rocky?" Thomas asked as he gently nudged her side and bust out laughing.

Rocky laughed lightly then cooed, "Soooo, what did you get me, baby?"

"Reach into the back, your gifts are on the seat," Thomas said.

Rocky glanced at the back seat and saw three boxes tied with beautiful red satin ribbons. She grabbed all three.

"OOOH, Godiva chocolates, my favorite!" She opened the golden box, picked out a white-chocolate covered strawberry by its stem and bit into it. "Open wide, sweetie," she said as she placed the half-eaten strawberry into Thomas' mouth. She replaced the ribbon back on the box and gently placed it on the back seat. She unwrapped the second box and gasped.

"Thomas, its La Perla? This is gorgeous! I think I am going to have to model this for you tonight."

She opened the biggest box last. *Wonder what is in here?* She thought. *It's probably a dress or something. I hope it's that cute little Ana Sui number I pointed out when we were in Neiman Marcus. I could take that to Vegas with me.* Rocky unfolded the tissue paper and pulled the dress halfway out of the box. *This isn't Sui?* She raised her hands above her head holding one shoulder of the dress in each and shook it out. *This is better than Su—*

"I hope you like it. I couldn't remember the exact dress you picked out when we were shopping last month, but I thought this one was stunning," Thomas said.

"I love it," Rocky squealed excitedly.

"There's more. Look in the bottom of the box," Thomas said.

She unraveled more paper and discovered a small matching Gucci clutch. She opened the clutch and saw a jewelry box.

Jesus, he really went all out. The Gucci dress and bag has to be well over three grand alone. The La Perla was easily three hundred, the chocolate another forty, and now this, Rocky thought. "Thomas I don't know what to say, I—," she said.

"You haven't even opened it yet," Thomas said.

She opened the box, and then her mouth. She stared at him for a minute before she kissed him. "It's beautiful, Thomas. Could you put it on for me before we eat?" Rocky asked.

It was a thin, shiny, white gold chain dangling a diamond zipper pendant on its end. Rocky held it in her hand and stared at it. She estimated its weight to be at least three-carats total. She examined the diamonds' clarity and smiled. She threw a sidelong glance at Thomas. He was either pleased at his choice in gifts or her reaction. *Damn, he's whipped. I can't believe he spent all this cash. Wait until I talk to Kay*, she thought.

This was their second trip to Jean George's Restaurant, so if it wasn't for the fact that she noticed Jay-Z and Beyoncé sitting across from them she would not have been impressed. They laughed, drank and had a genuinely good time.

While waiting out front for the valet to bring the truck around, Rocky grabbed Thomas' penis. "I had an extremely good time tonight, Thomas. But we'll have real fun when we get back to your house." She unzipped his zipper and searched for his dick. She found his soft penis and squeezed it as she kissed his nose and upper lip.

"Rocky, cool it, there's people out here. I must keep in mind that you cannot hold your liquor," Thomas said. He twisted his mid section away from her hand and quickly zipped up his pants. Thomas looked down at Rocky and couldn't help but chuckle at her current condition.

She looked up into his face and smiled at how devilishly handsome he was. His soft lips were just as brown and thick as everything else on his body. They sat between a long, straight nose and a deeply cleft chin. His low cut kinky fro was always freshly trimmed. He was definitely Rock Candy's eye candy. She thought they made a pretty couple.

As soon as he straightened his clothes a huge black Range Rover pulled up in front of them. Thomas reached into his breast pocket, pulled out a bill and placed it in the valet's hand.

"Thanks, nice ride man," the valet said.

Thomas led Rocky over to the passenger side of the truck and helped her inside. Rocky looked at the green numbers on the digital clock that read nine-fifteen. She felt too horny to hang out with her girls. She reached into her purse for her cell phone.

"Hey, wuzzup, Kay?" Rocky slurred.

"You sound like you've already done a considerable amount of partying. Let me guess, we ain't hangin', huh?" Kay asked.

Rocky let out a loud hiccup, followed by a belch. She could taste and smell her drink again. "You got it. How 'bout tomorrow?" Rocky finally replied.

"Sounds good, I'll call the rest of the girls and let them know," Kay said.

"Later, Kay."

"Enjoy the rest of your day, Rocky."

She flipped the phone closed and shoved it into her purse. Her hiccups continued.

"Are you okay, Rocky?" Thomas asked.

"I'm fine. I'm just going to close my eyes until we get to your place," she replied.

Rocky kept to her promise. She nodded off just two blocks after her statement. She slept with her head against the window and her hands folded on her lap. Thomas looked over at her every chance he got. Before he knew it they were at his home. She was awakened by a soft, wet kiss on her cheek. As soon as he turned to exit the truck, she brusquely wiped her cheek. She hated wet kisses. Thomas grabbed her gifts from the back of his truck, opened the door and steadied her into his house. They carefully ascended a narrow flight of stairs. At the top they heard laughter. Rocky was startled. She stepped back.

"Don't worry. It's my father. He's staying here for a couple of days," Thomas said. "Thomas," he called. "I want you to meet my girlfriend. Raquel, this is my father, Thomas Senior."

Rocky stumbled from the top step and tried to focus on the dark figure sitting in the living room. The blue tint from the television was her only light so she could barely make out his features. He stood and walked toward them. Rocky stumbled and squinted as bright light flooded the room. It gave her a headache. She blinked. "It's very nice to meet you sir," Rocky said.

His father's stare made Rocky uncomfortable. He wore a sheepish grin, and it seemed like his eyes peeled off her dress. He licked his lips and nodded his head before he spoke. "What did you say her name was? I didn't quite catch it."

"Candy. I mean, Rocky. I answer to either one," she slurred.

Thomas' father looked puzzled.

"Her name is Raquel Candace. Rock Candy is a childhood nickname she hasn't been able to shake. So she answers to Raquel, Candy, and Rocky, but I call her Rocky, Thomas. Come on baby, let's go upstairs," Thomas Junior said.

He grabbed her hand and guided her toward more steps. Thomas turned around halfway up and caught his father staring at Rocky's ass.

"I'm going to call you Candy, 'cause you sure look sweet. Boy, you better be glad I ain't twenty years younger, or you would be assed out. You got yourself a dime piece there, boy don't fuck up. Nice to meet you young lady."

"Likewise," Rocky replied a little too loudly.

When they reached Thomas' bedroom she threw herself across his firm waterbed. He dropped the boxes on the bed and ran across the room.

"I have to use the latrine. Get comfortable, mi casa is su casa."

"Okay," she said smiling. With the click of the bathroom door her smile dried up. "You see? He is so corny— mi casa is su casa, what the fuck is that?" She murmured into a pillow.

She shifted her body, sucked her teeth, and continued bickering about his 'casa' remark. The sound of the running water in the bathroom soothed her. She quickly removed her dress and pondered the strange way his father stared at her. She was embarrassed to acknowledge that their eye contact made her hot. *Damn he looked good*, she thought. She inhaled and caught a quick shiver up her spine. *Mmm he was so distinguished.*

She ran over to his walk-in closet carrying her dress and the La Perla box. The lights automatically came on when she opened the door. She dropped her boxes, then hugged and smelled his suits.

"God, I love this fuckin' closet," she whispered. "This shit is almost as big as my fuckin' bedroom."

She hung up her dress and wiggled into the golden lace La Perla set. She lay on the carpeted closet floor pulling each stocking up to her mid-thigh, provocatively staring at her pussy in the mirror as she did so. She strapped each stocking to the garters and slipped into her stilettos. She spread her legs open, gently rubbed her clit, and let out a tiny moan. When she heard the water stop running she got on all fours and pulled in the closet door. The bathroom door swung open. Thomas looked around. He figured Rocky would be sprawled across the bed in a deep sleep.

"Rocky?" he called out. "She must have gone to the bathroom down the hall," he said softly.

Rocky cracked the door wide enough to see half his back facing the closet. He was sitting on the bed undressing. She quietly crawled around the corners of the bed. As she was about to startle him, he turned right into her face.

"You can be so silly," Thomas smiled down at her.

On her knees she was eye level with his dick. She stuck her tongue into his boxers and tried to lick his penis out of the opening. She placed her lips around his now hardening meat and pulled it out. It had a salty taste on its tip, but she still continued to lick.

"Shit," he whispered bewildered.

She made loud slurping noises, but kept her jaws suctioned tightly around his dick. She bobbed her head back and forth, and each movement made her hotter and hotter. His dick was so big she had a hard time deep throating it, but she didn't stop. Never that, she kept on going. When he groaned she moaned and became more aroused. Thomas stumbled back. It felt so good that his knees went weak. He gently pushed her forehead back and collapsed on the bed. He pulled his boxers off as quickly as possible, trying to savor the moment. Rocky crawled onto the bed.

"Damn baby, you're the greatest," Thomas panted, as he watched her crawl toward him. She reached over his body and opened the night table drawer. Without looking she fished out a blue condom. She straddled his stomach and tore the package open with her teeth. She looked down at his nearly flawless body. His Snickers bar complexion looked so good under her creamy butter pecan skin. As she removed the condom from the wrapper she slid her butt down to his upper thighs. She ran her slim fingers over his heaving six pack, and licked her lips. His dark brown eyes followed her every move. She pulled the condom over his penis and placed his dick into her pulsating pussy. She eased down on it in one slow motion. Then she started to ride.

The headboard thumped the wall with each stroke. Thomas looked up into Rocky's face. The ends of her beautiful, long and silky auburn hair were plastered to her chest with sweat. Her bright brown orbs rolled around sexily in their sockets as she took her ride.

Look at her, bite down on her thick ass pretty pink lip. All this pretty skin all over m— Thomas' eyes rolled back into his head after his last thought and he suddenly sat up and thrust harder into her. She wrapped her legs around his waist and hugged him with all her might. She planted kisses all over his face as she rode him like a stallion. When she reached her peak she stopped.

"What's wrong? Am I hurting you again?"

"Not really," Rocky managed to force out. She was winded. "I want you to get on top," she whispered.

Thomas held her in one arm and got on his knees. Without taking his dick out of her, he gently placed Rocky on her back, lay on top of her and slowly began to push. He grabbed her thick calf, which fit perfectly in the palm of his hand, and placed her leg on his shoulder. Her pointy heel near his face made him fuck her harder. Rocky grabbed the sheets and winced in pain. He planted kisses on the inside of her leg as he slid in and out of her pussy. He took another look at her pink-coated toenails tightly curled up in her stilettos and pushed with even more force. He tried to pick up her left leg but her pleasure turned to pain.

"AHHHH!" she yelled. "Put my leg down that hurts."

He slowed down and gently lowered her leg. Then he thrust faster; she followed by tightening her vaginal muscles each time he humped. He screamed, "Oh Rock Candy!"

"Choke me now," she exclaimed as she placed her petite hands around his neck.

Thomas was not surprised, this time. He placed his hands around her neck and applied pressure. As Rocky climaxed she almost lost consciousness, but that made her orgasm feel as no other. It was like an out-of-body experience. Her muffled scream of ecstasy caused Thomas to release his grip. He thrust harder into her body and grunted under his breath. Rocky coughed and shook her head several times before she regained her focus. She felt so light headed— so satisfied.

She tightened her grip around his neck as he let out one more long and hard stroke. Rocky let him go, and he rolled off her body. She slowly sat up, slipped off her sandals and neatly placed them by his bed.

"Rock fuckin' Candy, I love you girl," he said as he stared at the ceiling trying to catch his breath. "This is the best lovemaking I have ever had. It just gets better and better."

She inched up next to him, and nestled under his arm. "You know, you're right. That shit felt so good I could go slap your father," Rocky joked. They both laughed. She felt so good under his arm.

"Baby, how tall are you?" Rocky asked.

"I am 6'1". Why?"

"I feel so tiny laying here."

"You're about 5'3", right?" Thomas asked.

"I am 5'5", thank you very much."

"Rocky— you know I love you."

She hugged him tighter, kissed his chest, but did not say a word. *Rock Candy loves no one*, she thought, as she closed her eyes and quickly fell into a deep sleep. Thomas gazed down at her small but curvy frame, and wondered how she really felt. At the six month point of their relationship he knew he was head over heels, but she never really shared her feelings with him. He placed her hair behind her ear with his forefinger, then traced her side burns, and gently kissed her cheek. Not wanting to wake her, he smoothly maneuvered himself into a more comfortable position without moving the arm she was nestled under. He fell asleep with her in his embrace.

The next day, Tony desperately scanned the hallways for Kahmelle. He'd stopped at all of their hangouts except one, the cafeteria. Kahmelle was coming up the staircase that led to it as Tony made his way to the lunchroom. Tony felt relieved when he spotted his long time friend. He could still remember their first meeting in junior high school. Kahmelle looked exactly the same. He was a few inches shorter than Tony and a year and a half older. Kahmelle was 5'8". He was a dark brown complexion with slanted, deep, dark brown eyes. Although his teeth were straight they were borderline yellow. He was thick. His hands, cheeks stomach and overall physique were meaty, but he was far from fat. His frame was stocky, like he worked out, but he'd never been to a gym in his life. Kahmelle introduced himself to Tony on their first day of junior high and they had remained close friends ever since.

"Yo, Kah, come here, let me holla at you for a second," Tony said. They met up in the middle of the stairwell and Tony lowered his voice. "Mrs. Simmons wasn't in homeroom this morning. You know she ain't never absent."

"She's probably shaken up since they stole her bag and shit. I wouldn't really worry about it. Sweat said that the shit was easy," Kahmelle said.

"You're probably right. I gotta run. I have AP English this period, I can't miss that," Tony said.

Tony took off down the hall, dodging book bags and kids, and Kahmelle strolled in the other direction. Tony made it to the classroom just in time for the morning announcements.

"Good morning. It's time for our daily announcements" The principal's voice boomed through the loud speaker. "I have some very unfortunate news to end this week. Mrs. Simmons was mugged leaving the building yesterday on her way to the bank. As it stands the senior trip is now off. She is in critical condition at a nearby hospital. If anyone has any information on this heinous act, please contact me personally in the main office. That will be all, and let's try to have a good day."

Tony looked down the hallway to see if Kahmelle was around. He saw several teens walking in and out of classrooms, but not Kahmelle. He ran straight down the steps into the main office.

"Mrs. Coolridge, what happened to Mrs. Simmons? Is she alright?" Tony asked out of breath.

"You heard the announcement. She got mugged yesterday and is in the hospital with minor to severe injuries," Mrs. Coolridge said.

"What hospital is she in? I would really like to go and visit her."

Mrs. Coolridge looked over the rims of her glasses at Tony. She looked around the office and stood up behind her desk. "I know how close you are to her, Mr. Hendrickson. I didn't tell you anything. Brooklyn Hospital."

Tony scurried out of the office.

"Hendrickson," the school secretary called out. "Don't tell a soul. Do you understand me?"

"Yes, Mrs. Coolridge— thanks."

Tony sat in class with a heavy heart. *It's all my fault*, he thought. *I can't believe I let Kahmelle talk me into this shit. I hope she's okay.*

At his desk, he palmed his face while his fellow students recited Shakespearean soliloquies from memory during the oral portion of a final examination. He stared at them, but didn't hear one word. Guilt rang loudly in his ears and gave him a headache.

I want out, before I get in too deep, he thought. He looked at his green jersey and his crisp green and white Prada sneakers. Suddenly he didn't feel so tough anymore.

"Mr. Hendrickson." His teachers direct address brought him out of his thoughts. "Would you step in front of the class and recite your soliloquy, please."

"I prefer not to, Mrs. Ruderman," Tony replied.

"Excuse me, Bartelby the Scribner. I think you *would* prefer to, because I am sure you know this is part one of your final."

The entire class laughed at the teacher's joke. That's when it hit Tony.

Look at all these nerds. Your average dude on the street wouldn't understand that joke, he thought as he walked to the front of the classroom.

The class stopped laughing when he reached the blackboard and they all awaited his presentation. Tony stared at his classmates. *I don't belong here. There ain't one live nigga in this whole class*, he thought

Mrs. Ruderman looked at Tony. "We are waiting," she said.

Tony cleared his throat and looked at the class. He spoke loudly, and deepened his tone.

"She should have died hereafter. There would have been time for such a word tomorrow and tomorrow and tomorrow creeps in this petty pace from day to day and all our yesterdays light the road to dusty death. Out, out brief candle!"

Cheers livened up the room. Everyone knew Tony would come through, especially Mrs. Ruderman. He was her star pupil. She smiled from behind her marking book. "Now, what play was that from and what does it mean, Tony?" She asked.

Tony looked at his classmates and ran out of the classroom, muttering under his breath. He ran down three flights of steps, straight to a side door, and exited the school. He walked and talked out loud.

"I don't belong in there. Fuck them nerd ass niggas. There's only four other Blacks in there with me and they all act White and shit. I don't belong there. I don't belong no where."

"Hey kid, where you going?" Officer Joann Nuñez called out. Tony rerouted his steps to where she stood. "Do I need to call a truant van for you, or are you going to cooperate and go back to school, son?"

He looked up at her with water-filled eyes. "Officer, my favorite teacher was robbed yesterday and she's in the hospital. You can send me back if you want, but I am just going to leave again to see her," Tony confessed.

"I was the one who answered that call. She was in pretty bad shape. You have any idea who would do that to her?" Joann asked.

Tony shook his head, and lost the tears he'd tried so hard to hold back. They found themselves seeping down his cheeks, as he stared silently at her. Joann reached into her pocket, and handed him a tissue.

Hundreds of teens passed her every morning— cursing up a storm, smoking weed, walking in the opposite direction of the school— but this particular young man always gave her a warm smile and a good morning. He seemed to be a good kid from a good home. In the year and a half that she has been on this post, she has never had any run-ins with him. With this in mind she put her hand on his shoulder stiffly, as he regained his composure. When he looked up she gave him a reassuring smile. "Go ahead kid, go see your teacher."

"Thanks, officer." He wiped his eyes as he read her nametag. "Nuñez."

She smiled again when he said her name. "Don't mention it, kid. See you tomorrow morning."

He cursed himself the entire ten-block walk to Brooklyn Hospital. As he approached the hospital he subconsciously removed the Celtics Jersey he inadvertently acquired from her mugging and walked over to the information desk.

"Hi. I am here to see Mrs. Tina Simmons," Tony said.

The woman behind the desk punched a couple of keys on her computer and smiled. "Take this pass, go up the escalator and make a right. The elevators will be right there and you need to go to the ninth floor. Room 922."

Please don't let her be too fucked up. Please God, I swear I'll give this shit up if you don't let her be too fucked up. Tony pleaded with God silently until he made it to her room. The door was already open.

When he walked in she was in her bed watching a small TV mounted in front of her face. The television completely blocked her head from his view so she looked fine from the doorway. As he got closer she moved the TV aside. She smiled once she made Tony out through her blurred vision.

"Tony? I figured you would come here to see me."

Tony immediately began to cry. Her entire face was bruised, and her right eye was nearly swollen shut. Her beautiful light-tan skin was covered with swollen, purple knots and whelps from her face to her arms. Her left eye was covered with thick layers of gauze and a little blood seeped through where her eyebrow would be.

"My God. Mrs. Simmons what did they do to you?" Tony asked.

She spoke slowly, in a raspy voice. "Well, they asked for my purse and the envelope I carried. When I refused, they roughed me up a little. They punched my glasses into my face, and pieces of the broken lens scraped my eye. That's why I have this thing on. They punched and kicked me on top of the hood of my car until I released the envelope— boy, stop crying, 'cause you're going to get me all teary-eyed, and that will probably hurt."

"They'll find out who did this to you," Tony sniffled.

"It didn't look like any boys from the school, and if they were, I surely didn't recognize them. Anyway, I should be out of here in a day or two. What time is it?"

"Nine-thirty."

"Tony, you better get your little behind back to school."

"Can I stay here for a while and keep you company?" Tony asked.

"No. I really don't want to be around anyone looking like this. Although I am grateful you came to visit, I want you to go back to school."

Tony touched her bruised arm gently, forced a sad smile, then started to leave the room. Mrs. Simmons noticed Tony putting on a green hat. She couldn't make out what color jeans he was wearing, but after a considerable amount of strain she noticed he had a green shirt hanging out of his back pocket. *I know those aren't green sneakers!* She thought. *None of the kids at Brooklyn High wear more than one green item at a time.* "Tony!" Mrs. Simmons yelled.

He spun around and quickly returned to her bedside before answering. "Yes Mrs. Simmons."

"Are you crazy? How long have I known you?"

"I don't know, Mrs. Simmons, why?"

"Long enough for you to not stand here and lie to me. You're not down with Brooklyn's Finest, are you?"

"You know me better than that," he replied without hesitation.

"Then you must have some kind of death wish. You'd better take off all of that damn green you have on before they come after you. I don't want you lying here next to me. Go home and change those clothes."

"Yes Mrs. Simmons."

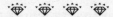

Thomas woke up, reached back, and searched the bed for Rocky with his arm. As he sat up and stretched he noticed the tray that sat at the edge of the bed. "Breakfast in bed," he sighed.

Rocky had cleaned his kitchen, bathroom and washed the clothes that had been scattered on the bottom of his closet before he awoke. When he was finished eating, she sat down on the bed next to him.

"How was breakfast?" Rocky asked.

"Superb, just like you. Who's better than you are, Rocky?"

She smiled. "Nobody. Come give me a ride home."

After making passionate love in the shower, the two dressed and headed to his truck. During the entire ten-minute ride to her apartment he pleaded with her to stay.

"You sure you don't want to hang out today? Now that you've done my laundry, I really don't have much to do. I am not going into the office until late this afternoon."

"No babes, I have to do my Saturday morning cleaning and shopping and I have to work out."

"But it's Friday."

"Yeah, but since I didn't hang with the girls yesterday, I'll probably go out tonight. So I will sleep late Saturday morning instead of doing my chores. Bye, baby, " Rocky said as she kissed his forehead.

She removed her gifts from the back of his car and then gently fingered the chain on her neck. "Thanks again for the lovely gifts," she called as she walked up the steps to her apartment.

"Anything for my queen." Thomas blew her a kiss then sped off. Rocky screwed up her face, rolled her eyes and mimicked his parting statement. She sucked her teeth. "Damn, why does he have to be so fuckin' corny?"

She unlocked the front door and headed up the steps to her apartment. Inside she quickly pulled off her sweats and threw them into her hamper. "I have to remember to bring an additional change of weekend clothes over to his house."

She sat on her bed and looked over at the dress and matching clutch Thomas purchased her. She looked at the tag inside the dress. "Size six, perfect," she said. Rocky slipped into it and despite it being a bit snug around her thighs, it looked good. "If I add fifteen minutes to my morning exercise, this will be extra right in no time."

She took her cell phone out of her purse, and looked at the screen. **6 Missed Calls**.

She scrolled through the numbers. "Let's see who was sweating me, Audrey, Cheryl, Lita, Nacole and Mauri called twice." She picked up her cordless and plopped on her bed. She scrolled through the caller ID and dialed a number on her phone. "Damn, Mauri called me at four in the morning. He knows I don't stay at clubs that late, no matter what. I better get my alibi straight."

"So, what did he get you for your birthday?" Kay asked. "Where did y'all go?"

"Damn, can I say good morning, or get a hello, bitch?" Rocky replied.

"Yeah— hi, whatever, what did you get?"

"This bangin' Gucci dress. It's brown, tan and light blue with off white piping, and the matching clutch."

"Say word, I know which one you're talkin' about. It has big stripes all over it, right? Old girl from "Sex in the City" had it on a couple of weeks ago."

"That's not all. He got me a La Perla lingerie set, and a white gold chain with a diamond, zipper pendant."

Kay let out a high pitched, horror movie cackle. "You lying?" SHUT UP! she said out of breath.

"I swear! This shit is hot I look like I should be the first female rapper in the Cash Money Clique with all this ice. This shit looks like it's holdin' at least three-carats total in weight. You know Mauri mailed me a pair of four-carat, princess cut studs for my birthday, and some money. I got those shits appraised at my spot. Which reminds me, I'm going to pawn my great Nahnan's diamond beetle broach."

Kay shook her head in disgust and looked at her phone.

"You be playin' games, you know that? Last time you did that shit you almost didn't get it back. That piece is irreplaceable and mad valuable, Raquel."

"I know but—"

"But shit. Didn't your great-great grandmother get that from the plantation owner that she was fuckin'? As a matter of fact, your great-great grandfather?"

"Yeah, that's even more a reason—"

"I don't know. What are you pawning it for this time?"

Rocky was almost embarrassed to answer, and when she did it was barely audible. "I need to pay for my trip to Las Vegas," Rocky mumbled.

"What?" Kay snapped.

"I NEED IT FOR MY TRIP TO VEGAS!!" Rocky said loudly.

"Rock Candy, you *are* trippin' all right. You can get that money up another way. Tell Detroit you want to go."

"I can't take Mauri with me. I'm goin' out there to look for my husband. I was going to ask Thomas but he just purchased me all these birthday gifts. He must'a spent at least four thousand dollars."

Kay had an uncontrollable fit of laughter.

"What the fuck is so funny?" Rocky said.

Kay could barely finish her sentence. "Remember when we were in school— ha ha." Kay laughed so hard it was contagious. Rocky began laughing before she could hear the story.

"Stop laughing, come on," Rocky said.

"Okay— remember when you told Too Sweet that you needed money for an abortion so you could buy the new Gucci shoes."

Rocky couldn't help but laugh. "How can I forget that? But I can top that— how about the time I traded in his diamond ring for a tennis bracelet. You know I got jipped, right?"

They both laughed so hard they were crying.

"Listen, Raquel," Kay started in a serious tone. Whenever Kay called Rocky Raquel, she knew the laughter was about to be replaced with a dose of truth. "You do be doin' a lot. But you always have alternative ways of getting what you want. Just think about that before you do it—was that your phone?"

Rocky looked at her cordless, the 313 area code told her it was Mauri.

"Yeah girl, it's Mauri. I have to bounce. We still on for tonight?"

"I guess so, that is, if you don't pawn your girls for more dick," Kay laughed.

"Whatever. I'll call you after my chores." Rocky clicked over to the other line. "Hello?"

"Yo, where the fuck yo ass was all night?" Mauri asked.

"I went out with Kay and them and got so tore back I had to let her drive my car. I spent the night there." The lie came easy.

"I want to see you today, boo," Mauri changed his tone.

Rocky hated when guys called her that. But she just sucked it up.

"I can't. I thought you already purchased my ticket for next Friday."

"I did but I miss that ass. I want to see yo face and hold you and shit."

Rocky forced a smile. "I miss you too, baby. But we'll see each other next Friday. That's only one week away. Plus the more I miss you, the happier I'll be to see you when I get there. That's Memorial Day weekend so I could probably spend an extra day."

"Alright. I'll call you a lil' later. I gotta go take care of somethin'." He hung up the phone before she could say goodbye.

I don't know why I bother, she thought as she lay across her bed and stared at the ceiling. *If I could only take some of Mauri and shove him into Thomas, then I'd have a corporate thug. He'd have just enough edge to hang in the street, but he'd be polished enough to do the opera,* she thought.

Rocky took off her new dress and hung it up. She placed her lingerie in her dresser drawer, pulled out three monogrammed handkerchiefs and quickly slipped into a powder blue jogging suit. She pulled an old-fashioned, large, mahogany wooden jewelry box from underneath her bed. When she opened it the classic Fleur der Lis played, and she jokingly sang the lyrics to Nas' song. "I know I can, be what I want to be. . ."

There were all kinds of jewelry in the box. She pulled out a small gold ring and smiled. Its two hearts had the initials R and T engraved on them. She threw it back in and retrieved the two-carat tennis bracelet she and Kay had just spoke of and snickered.

She lifted the red paneling. Underneath was a tattered, (once black) discolored, brownish yellow velvet sack. She eased out a 24 karat gold ring that held a 12-carat diamond, a stunning bangle with seven rows of diamonds, and perhaps the most stunning piece of all, a black and white diamond beetle broach. The entire broach was covered with black and white diamonds, except the actual pin. These items had been given to her mother by her grandmother, who got them from her mother and so on originating with her great-great grandmother. With each generation and each passing of the jewelry went a story.

Rocky's great-great grandmother, Lucille had been a beautiful indentured servant who worked in the home of the Wentworth family of Columbia, South Carolina. She was admired by all, for her dark striking beauty including her master that she slaved for. They were secretly lovers, and he spent his every spare moment with her. He adorned her with beautiful jewelry and fine clothes. She was kept in the master's house, and never sent to work the fields. In house Lucille was second to none, not even his wife. She bore him two children, and raised them along side the children he had by his wife. When he died, he left her a considerable amount of money, along with his name— and her freedom. Lucille took her two mulatto children and moved north. She used her small fortune to start her own laundry business, and made sure her two children got the best education.

After mentally replaying her great-great grandmother's story, she gently put the ring and bracelet in the pouch. She placed the beetle on her bed and put the box back. She scooped up the broach, delicately wrapped it up in three handkerchiefs and placed it in the pocket of her jogging suit. The phone rang. She looked at her caller ID— it was Thomas. She didn't answer. Rocky walked down the small hallway that joined her bedroom to a narrow kitchen area, and then a small living room. She opened what looked like a linen closet, but there were no sheets in it. There were at least one hundred pocket books hanging on small hooks from the top of the closet to just above the floor. She removed a powder blue Gucci fanny pouch from one of the hooks in the middle. It was surrounded by the same bags in black, brown, and pink. She put the broach in it and fastened it around her waist.

Rocky walked into her spotless living room and looked around. She had a small, off white cloth couch with a dark brown wooden frame and matching recliner. Her floors were hard wood, and shined throughout her apartment. Across from the couch was a fireplace covered with plaster. It had a beautiful mantle over it and a mirror with a dark brown wooden frame. In front of the mantle sat an antique chaise lounge in the same color fabric and wood as the rest of her furniture. There was a small wooden chest with an oval piece of glass over it that served as a coffee table between the couch and the recliner. This was home.

She retrieved her car keys from the mantel then placed them in her pouch. She locked her door and jogged eight blocks straight from her lofty Brooklyn Heights apartment, on Butler Street, to Fourth Avenue where the Brooklyn Jewelry Exchange stood. She stopped in front of the glass and looked inside. They had just opened. She took a swig of water, crossed the street and jogged back toward her home.

She admired the beautiful brownstones that lined her neighborhood. Some were huge and some were small but they were all well constructed and well maintained. The closer she got to her apartment, the more expensive the properties were, which made her happy. At the corner of Bergen and Court she reached into her fanny pouch and pulled out her car keys. Inside the car Rocky combed her hair several times. She drove straight down the block she just jogged, hooked a right onto Fourth Avenue and parked directly in front of the Brooklyn Jewelry Exchange.

Walking in, she held the door for a young girl carrying a screaming baby in her arms.

"Thank you miss, my baby just got her ears pierced," the young girl confessed.

Rocky looked at the beautiful infant the girl held in her arms and smiled. "Enjoy that beautiful bundle of joy," Rocky said.

"Thank you," the young girl replied. "Alright mamacita, it will be okay," She said gently bouncing the baby in her arms. At that moment the young mother looked up and saw a cop approaching her car, equipped with a memo book and pen in hand.

"Please stop officer, I am right here," she shouted as she ran toward the cop clutching her crying baby tightly. Officer Nuñez stopped writing the ticket and watched the young woman run towards her. She was fair skinned with a small upper body. The officer focused in on the wide hips that ran toward her, and the thick that thighs led the way. She just knew a big ass trailed behind her. The young mother slowed down as she neared the officer.

Joann watched as her full lips parted to reveal beautiful straight teeth, when the young mother smiled at her. Her soft wavy hair was pulled back, but the loose strands that wildly framed her face bounced as she ran. When the mother came to a stop Joann looked down at the bawling red-faced baby. The officer kept a stiff exterior, but inside her emotions ran wild.

"Officer, I just stopped for fifteen minutes to get my daughter's ears pierced. PLEASE don't give me a ticket," she panted.

Joann loosened up and smiled. "Can I see the baby? How old is she?"

"She just made three months today. Her name is Seven."

Joann put the memo book away, looked down at the baby, then up into the girl's face. *Damn she's fine*, Joann thought. "What's your name?"

"Yanick."

"I am Jo— Joann Nuñez. Nice to meet you, and I'm not going to give this beautiful baby a ticket."

"Thank you, officer. I really appreciate it."

"Um, what do you feed her? I have a hook up with Similac," Joann said quickly.

"Really?"

"Yeah, I can get it by the case for fifty percent off."

"Oh my God! You're playin' right?" Yanick screeched. The baby cried louder. "Take down my numbers and call me. Shoot, I always need formula— it's so expensive. Plus, her father is trippin' so money is tight. Where do you get the formula from?"

"My father's family business," Joann replied.

"When's the next time you can get it?" Yanick asked.

"When ever you need it. Call me tonight and we'll arrange a time."

"Are you serious?" Yanick asked as she walked to her car door.

"Yeah, whenever. Here, let me get that for you." Joann said, as she opened the door and helped Yanick put the baby into the car seat.

"Thank you, officer."

"Call me Joann."

Joann pulled out a piece of paper from the back of her memo book. She jotted down her number quickly and handed it to her.

"Can you write my number down, too?"

Joann jotted her number into the memo book and closed it up.

"I get off at five today. So give me a holla later and drive safely," Joann said.

Yanick smiled as she strapped into her seat belt. "Okay, later Joann."

Joann watched her ride off. She took off her hat and shook her shoulder length tresses. She wiped the sweat off of her brow and tucked her hair back in. She muttered as she continued along her post.

"I got that right there. That little sexy thing is mine. Now all I have to do is find some New York tags that begin with the letter R so I can make this ticket happen."

Joann walked up the block checking license plates with her memo book opened and ready.

Inside Brooklyn Jewelry Exchange, Rocky walked straight to the rear where the owner stood and smiled. "Good afternoon Mr. Eden how are you?"

Mr. Eden looked down over his glasses and smiled at Rocky. "Rachel, right? How nice to see you back so soon. Let me guess. You have another piece you would like appraised," he said as he looked at the necklace she was wearing.

Smiling she unfastened her necklace, and spoke quickly. "It's Rocky. Yes, Mr. Eden I have another piece for appraisal. I would also like to know how much you could give me if I pawned this?" She handed him her chain. Then she reached into her bag for the broach.

"It's nearly four-carats total in weight. Another beautiful piece for the beautiful birthday girl. Let me see the second piece." Rocky unwrapped the broach, and placed it on the counter. "My God. This is simply breathtaking." He shot a quick head-to-toe look at Rocky. *Where did she get an antique like this,* he thought. *These diamonds are so—* he paused his thoughts and cleared his throat. "You should really— wait one minute."

Mr. Eden went to a small table. He turned on a desk lamp and picked up an eye-shaped plastic coated magnifying glass. He examined the broach for about five minutes. Rocky stared at him as he worked.

Damn, I can't believe this is her husband! He looks all old and shit. He's got to be two inches shorter and at least five years older than her and I mean at least. He's all red with his stomach overhanging his pants. There's nothing to him, and he is so out of shape.

Rocky quickly switched her thoughts to his wife, which she'd met in the park Thursday morning who suggested she bring the earrings here to be appraised and insured. . .

"That's one strenuous workout you have going there. Don't over do it," Rocky said. The woman did not stop her jumping jacks. She just looked at Rocky and smiled. "You mind if I join in? You can never burn too much fat," Rocky added.

"I don't mind at all," the woman panted as she continued to jump.

Rocky guessed the woman's age to be around thirty, thirty- five. She had long, full, blonde hair, pulled back in a ponytail, and the most stunning blue eyes. She was about 5'7". She wore a gray, firmly filled sports bra and small yellow running shorts. She had a feminine but muscular body. Rocky thought her body was banging. Before Rocky started the conversation she had noticed a gleaming, diamond engagement ring under a platinum band on the woman's finger. She pegged it to be about five-carats; she was definitely somebody Rocky felt she should know. As they jumped Rocky smiled inside at the fact that the woman's breasts didn't budge. Exquisite boob job, she thought.

Before she finished giving the woman the once over they had finished their set, and Rocky stopped out of breath.

"Twenty-five isn't bad for a start, but I think you can double that—you want to finish your set?"

Rocky was bent over with her hands on her knees, trying to catch her breath. "That was fifty! I just sprinted four laps around the track, and stopped to stretch when I approached you. I haven't even caught my breath from my run."

Susan extended her arm. "I'm Susan Eden. It's nice to meet you."

"I'm Raquel, but everyone calls me Rocky, for short."

" Maybe we can do some cardio together in the morning?"

"Sure anytime. Wow, that's a beautiful ring you have on." Rocky spoke like it was the first time she noticed it.

"Thanks, your earrings are beautiful as well."

"These old things," Rocky said as she touched her ears. She suddenly placed her hand over her chest and her jaw dropped open. "Oh

goodness, I didn't even realize I had these on. I just got these for my birthday."

"Somebody loves you, huh? That's a real nice gift. Those are about four-carats?"

"I'm not sure. I'm taking them to be appraised."

"Listen, my hubby owns the Brooklyn Jewelry Exchange chain. He's always in his main store down on Fourth Avenue. Take them to him and he will do it for free, just tell him I sent you. You should also get them insured. I have to get to work, honey. I'll see you tomorrow at six?"

"Nah, Monday. Today's my birthday."

Susan picked up a pair of pink arm weights, slid them onto her wrists and began to jog out of the park.

"Okay, see you then. Happy Birthday, honey," she called over her shoulder.

"Thanks! I'm going to stop by the Brooklyn Jewelry Exchange . . ."

"Five thousand is the best I can do, sweet cheeks," Mr. Eden said.

"Excuse me. My mind wandered for a second."

"Five thousand. It's worth a lot more, but I don't give loans over that price." He put the broach on the counter and looked into her eyes, then shook his head. "Listen, I don't usually get into my customer's business but, by the looks of ya, I don't think you need to pawn this heirloom. I'm not going to ask where you got it, but it would be a shame if you lost this priceless piece. I mean hey, I never turn down business, but you should think about it first."

Rocky heard Kay's voice in her head, and thought about the countless romantic stories she'd heard about her great–great Nahnan over the years.

"This piece was my great - great – I won't bore you with the story but believe me, I have no intentions of losing it to you, Mr. Eden," Rocky smiled.

Mr. Eden looked out of his storefront at the black, shiny, brand new, convertible Mercedes Benz coup the young lady pulled up in. He looked down at the broach. He looked into her eyes once more and raised his eyebrows. His facial expression clearly read, 'are you sure?' She nodded her head, and he walked to the back.

Rocky walked around the spacious store. It was painted all white and housed twenty-four large glass cases. She looked at bracelets, rings, chains, charms, charm bracelets and every type of jewelry you could imagine. She mouthed each sign she came across. 'Affordable financing available. Yes, we pawn jewelry. Ear piercing done on premises.'

"Excuse me miss," one of the younger sales men called to Rocky.

Rocky ignored him.

"Excuse me, miss but—"

Rocky sucked her teeth loud enough for him to hear, and turned in the opposite direction. *Oh, please. He has some nerve talking to me— he's way below my level. I don't know what makes these low income niggas think they can talk to anyone they want to,* Rocky thought, as she swung her hair onto her left shoulder. She moved to the next case.

"Miss, I was just trying to tell you that you're about to get a ticket."

"Fuck!!" Rocky ran outside and approached the cop.

"Excuse me, officer. Please don't give me a ticket. I just stopped to—"

"ROCANDY," Joann mouthed her plate number as she continued to write. "Did you read that sign, miss? It's right here in red and white, 'No Standing Anytime'."

"Give me a break, officer, I was—"

"Too late, I already wrote in your plate number." Joann continued to write.

Rocky stood in front of Joann with her arms folded, muttering under her breath. "Fuckin' bitch. She ain't got shit else to do."

Joann ripped the ticket out of the memo book and placed it on Rocky's window. "It takes a bitch to know one. Have a good day miss. And I do have other shit to do."

"You do the same Officer Nuñez." Rocky sucked her teeth. "Damn man. Just my fuckin' luck, one hundred and fifteen dollars. Ain't this a bitch," Rocky said.

She walked back into the store studying her ticket. Rocky looked up at the sales man that had tried to warn her. He gave her a well-deserved smirk, and started to help a customer.

Mr. Eden presented Rocky with several papers. "You sure you want to do this?" he asked.

"Where do I sign?" Rocky smiled.

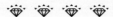

Joann arrived home later that afternoon. She took off her Chukkas and laid her holster across a small coffee table. She unbuttoned her uniform pants, plopped down on her dark gray leather love seat and picked up the remote. She channel surfed and drifted off to sleep. The soft ringing of her phone startled her. She sat up and looked around for the phone. Joann shifted to the side, and the ring became louder. She slid her hands between the cushions of her love seat and removed it.

"Hello," she said groggily.

"Hi, Joann?"

"Yeah, who this?"

"This is Yanick, the girl you met with the baby in front of Brooklyn Jewelry Exchange."

Joann sat up quickly and cleared her throat. "Hey, how are you?"

"I'm fine. Did I catch you at a bad time?"

"Nah, I just fell asleep in front of the TV."

"Is tomorrow okay for the Similac? I can bring you the money now."

"I'll pick it up for you and you can just pay me back when I deliver. I'm off tomorrow. Where do you live?"

"I live at 390 Bushwick Avenue."

"Wow, and you came all the way downtown to get her ears pierced."

"YEAH. I wasn't going to let any old tienda de porqueria pierce my Seven's ears."

"What?"

"You are Latino, aren't you?" Yanick asked.

"Nah."

"With a name like Nuñez."

Her slight Spanish accent turned Joann on. "I know. I know. Yanick, where are you from?"

"I was born here but my parents are Puerto Rican."

"I was born here and my parents are from down south."

"Down south? With a name like Nuñez?"

"Somewhere along the line I am mixed with something, but nobody in the family is quite sure what. How is that precious little thing? She is so gorgeous— evidently she takes after you."

"Thanks, she's fine. She should be waking up for her ten o'clock feeding any minute."

"So who do you live with over there?" Joann asked.

"My mother and father."

"What's with you and Seven's father? You told me he was trippin'."

"Yeah. He doesn't believe Seven is his. He moved to Virginia with his aunt when I was about six months pregnant."

Joann shifted on the couch and sat up. "Don't worry, I'm sure you'll manage as pretty as you are, you won't have a problem finding a man."

"Joann, I don't even want to think about that right now. I am going to finish school, move out and do me."

"I'll meet you around two, is that cool?"

"Yeah. Thanks so much, Joann."

"Don't mention it good bye."

"Bye."

Joann pressed the flash button on her phone and placed a phone call.

"Monique, what's up? It's me. Can I borrow your BJ's card tomorrow? I have to go and buy some Similac."

2

On a canopy my stamina be enough for Pamela Anderson Lee

"T-G-I-F, muthafuckas," Malik said as he sorted through several packages. What do you have planned for the weekend? I'm hitting the books."

"Nothing, but next weekend it is on. Wanna to fly down to Miami with me and my boys for Memorial Day weekend? Last year that shit was off the chain," Mike said.

"Nah, I think I'll pass. Besides, that's next weekend, I'd have to pay a small fortune if I booked my flight now," Malik said.

"You gettin' old before your time. You act like you're forty. How old are you?" Mike asked.

"I feel like it."

"How old are you, Malik?"

"Twenty-seven," Malik answered.

"Dag, twenty-seven, no kids and no nagging-ass baby mamas or girl— what I wouldn't give to be in your shoes."

"Mike, you have two kids, right?"

"You know that you're the first one's godfather. Yep, two kids, two baby muthas and a girl— shit is hectic."

"So why don't you do something with your kids on Memorial Day?" Malik asked.

Mike looked around at the other men in the mailroom before he answered. "Are you kidding me? First of all, neither one of my baby muthas gets along with me or the other baby mother. I rarely get my two girls at the same time, and my girl don't like either one of my exes."

"That's fucked up. When I have kids, I am marrying their mother."

"That's what I said at first, but Cherry got pregnant six months after Mindy and when Cherry found out she left my ass. Mindy was a mistake, but you know how it is when you getting paper and shit, everybody wants some."

The door opened suddenly. A young woman wearing a lavender suit walked inside the mailroom.

"Good afternoon, is Mr. Hendrickson here?" she asked.

"I'm Mr. Hendrickson," Malik answered.

"This is a memo for you. I am Mrs. Eden's assistant." The young woman handed him a parcel and an envelope.

"Okay, thanks," Malik said.

"I need a prompt reply. If you can't deliver this she will have to call in a messenger service, and these documents are very important."

Malik didn't know what to do or say. He hadn't heard from Susan since the 'incident'. He slowly opened the letter and read it silently.

"Sure. I'll hand deliver it."

"The keys are in the envelope. You can find the vehicle in company parking. Thank you." The young woman exited the mailroom.

"That's fucked up, man. They can't treat you like that and shit. If I were you I would complain. You're the mailroom manager, not the mailroom messenger," Mike said, disgruntled.

"It's cool. At least I don't have to be in this boring ass mailroom all day, and I can take my time coming back. With my hour lunch and my twenty-minute break, shit I might not come back. Mike, I want you to get all these packages out, pronto. Be sure everything goes out on time."

"You're leaving right now?" Mike said.

"Yes. The notice says this package has to be delivered by twelve and its is already ten-thirty. The place is in mid-town so I have to hurry up."

Malik shut the door and smiled as he approached the elevator. "I knew she wanted more," he whispered.

Malik stepped onto the elevator and pushed 'P'. He reread the letter and placed it inside his pocket. He looked down at the yellow number markings on the ground and followed them until he reached forty-one. A navy blue Lincoln Town Car occupied the space.

He wheeled up to the parking attendant, gave him the authorization letter, and was on his way. "I wonder where she is sending me? Hmmm 50th and Eight Avenue. When I get back to her office, I hope she has those garters on again."

He thought about how exact the instructions were. *Maybe she doesn't want a second go round? Maybe this is an on the field job. For the past two days all I can picture is her pink cat smiling at me by her desk, and how wet and tight her pussy was. Why hasn't she contacted me? I guess I will see today.*

As written in the instructions, he parked at a lot on the corner of his destination, and paid with a voucher that was in the envelope. It took him a few minutes to realize he was in a hotel. He rode the elevator to the 8th floor, walked to the room and knocked.

Susan leapt off of the bed and tiptoed to the door. She peeped through it without making a sound. Her heart beat with excitement when she saw Malik's face. She opened the door slowly. "Come in," she whispered.

Malik walked in and was almost surprised to see Susan standing there.

"I really thought you had sent me on a delivery. I thought that I was going to see you back in the office, so we could continue where we left off." He looked around the room with an approving nod. "I didn't even know this was a hotel, it's so new wave. What's the name of this place?"

"The Time," Susan answered. She looked him up and down. "You look so, so—"

"Like a thug?" Malik asked.

"No, that's not exactly the term I was looking for. Your jeans and boots make you look like a teen. I have never seen you dress like this."

"Third Friday of the month is 'Dress Down Day'. I see you haven't taken advantage of that," Malik said.

"Are you hungry? We could order room service."

They both sat on the bed and kept up the small talk, until Malik turned the conversation in a different direction.

"You know you are the sexiest thing in that office building. All of the men in that firm would pawn their souls to be in my position right now."

Susan blushed. "Thank you."

Malik took her hand and looked at her rings. "I also heard that you are happily married. Why would you be interested in messing with someone like me?"

"How do you know I'm happily married? You weren't asking around about me, were you?"

"No, the day you came downstairs the fellas in the mailroom said that you were married to a man who owns the Brooklyn Jewelry Exchange."

"This is true. Well, you are quite intelligent. I never thought someone as cute as you would have any brains— why are you in that mailroom?"

Malik put his hand up Susan's skirt. Smooth panties covered her vagina. He pushed the crotch of the panties aside and circled her clitoris with his middle knuckle. He licked his lips and cleared his throat.

"Why me? That's all I want to know. I'm truly flattered, but why me?"

Susan was too flustered to speak; she flashed him a seductive look. Malik kissed her neck softly, cupped her breasts and put one in his mouth. He stopped suddenly and pulled off his jeans and shirt. Susan undressed too.

"Damn, your body is banging, Mrs. Eden."

"Call me Susan." Susan watched as his penis stood straight up.

Malik pulled the last condom from his wallet. *Shit. I have got to re-up*, he thought. He pulled his condom on, crawled besides her and fingered her blonde hair. "So why me? I have to know this," Malik asked.

Susan really did not know why. Aside from the fact that he was gorgeous, there was no reason.

"I am just extremely attracted to you. There is no other reason," she said softly.

"It doesn't have anything to do with me being Black does it?"

Susan sat up and looked at him. "No, not at all," she said as she pushed him down on the bed and straddled his thighs.

"You wanted to see if the Black man myth is true, huh? Be honest."

He grabbed her back and flipped their positions, so that he was on top. He slipped his penis into her vagina, and with one, long, forceful stroke she was fully penetrated. He thrust his penis in her, and gently pulled it out over and over again.

Damn, this shit got a grip on my dick. It's so tight, feels like virgin pussy. He moaned loudly after that thought. "You like this Mrs. Eden?"

He slammed her insides harder and harder. He could feel her pelvic bone slam into him.

"Yes, Malik, this feels good," she blurted out between moans.

"Say my name again, you finally got it right."

"Ma- li- k." She uncontrollably matched her syllables to his strokes.

"Get up for a second." Susan did as she was told. "Turn around." He guided her by her hips to the edge of the bed. She went to lie down and he stopped her. "Nah, on your hand and knees, sexy."

They both knelt in front of the large mirror. He caressed her plump breasts from behind. They stared at their reflection in the mirror. He lifted her hair from her neck and watched himself suck on it. He continued to squeeze and rub her breasts. She welcomed his hands between her legs by opening them wider. He rubbed her clitoris and slid his fingers, two at a time, in and out of her vagina. She loudly moaned his name.

Suddenly Malik felt extremely powerful. He noted the differences in their skin tone, and at how much she seemed to enjoy him. *She's one of the firm's top attorneys, she's White, her husbands a millionaire and I've got my fingers in her pussy right now*, he thought. He pushed her shoulders down towards the bed, and her reflection disappeared. He pulled her waist away from the bed's edge until her blonde hair and balloon breasts filled the mirror. Susan humped the air, awaiting penetration. Finally she felt him poking around, and a sharp pain flooded her body. She screamed out.

"I'm sorry Susan," Malik said. He eased himself out of her and a loud slurpy sound broke the silence in the room. "Shit you are so wet."

He pulled her hair back with one hand and gripped it tightly so it wouldn't obstruct his view of her breasts and face in the mirror. He used his other hand to pull her by her waist it into his groin. Susan gritted her teeth as he thumped away behind her. Her breasts barely jiggled with each stroke. She shivered and moaned as a warm sensation suddenly overtook her body. "Oh my God," she moaned.

Malik pulled out and checked his condom. It was in tact. On her back, she threw her legs in the air and opened them wide to finger her clitoris.

"What's wrong?"

"Oh my God!" Susan exclaimed as a clear liquid dripped out of her vagina. Drops splattered on her inner thighs, wrists and fingertips.

Malik tore his condom off and jerked his penis by her mouth. "Suck it," he said in a coarse whisper.

"What?"

"SUCK IT!"

Just as Susan regained her breath she sat up and took the tip of his penis to her mouth. He pushed her back and exhaled a loud, "FUCK," as his semen shot all over her neck and lips. He pushed her down and rubbed his penis on her fat breasts, letting the last trickles of his cum ooze over her pink nipples. He lay next to her and stroked her hair.

"Damn, Susan, I could get used to this. If you don't want this on the regular, this better be our last encounter."

Susan smiled. She had not had an orgasm since she had been married to her current husband, of twelve years. She has always had to fake them with him. She exhaled and silently weighed her options. *This is fucking unreal. It really is. Sex with Edey is always missionary. I have to have more. Hell, I just had sexual intercourse from the back!!* Susan thought. "Can you handle more? Can I trust you to keep this between you and me?" she asked.

Malik held his limp penis in his hand and wiggled it around as he replied. "You don't know me to trust me, Susan. Do you mind if I ask you a personal question?"

"How long have you been married? Do you always cheat?"

"Twelve years, and the day before yesterday was my fist time."

"Why cheat now? He's not 'turning the other cheeks on you', is he?"

"What?" Susan asked confused.

"Is he gay?"

"No!"

"Is he cheating on you? Are you trying to get back at him?"

"No. It's nothing like that at all. I just want more sexually. Now let me give you the twenty."

"Twenty?"

"Twenty questions." Susan sat up and slid her hands under his 'wife beater' to rub his back. She felt a long, thick scar that traced all the way up his shoulder blade. She also noticed a small thin one right under his ear. "What happened to your back?" she asked.

"I got cut in a fight when I was younger."

"I see. How old are you?"

"Twenty-seven."

"You have any children?"

"No, but I have a little brother. We're really close. What about you?"

"Nope, I never really liked children."

"How old are you?"

"I am forty-three."

"Wow! You look good for your age." He gave her a tight hug. She stayed nestled in his embrace.

"What are you in school for?"

"I am studying law. That's why I took the position in the mailroom at the firm, hoping I could move up but that hasn't happened yet."

"We will see about that. I better get back to the office."

Susan got into the shower. As the water beat down on her she thought about how invigorating her orgasm had been. Five minutes into her 'wet thoughts' Malik invaded the shower. She studied his figure as he entered the stall. The enormous, gross scar he had on his back repulsed her. He kissed the top of her head and rubbed on her breasts. He let the water beat down on his head as he knelt and licked her navel. He kissed her nipples. He stroked her vagina softly. Just as it seemed she was about to lose it, he stopped abruptly.

"You never answered me. Is this going to be the beginning or the ending of our friendship?"

"I really want to see a lot of you. But it can't be on company time."

"Okay," he said as he grabbed her behind and kissed her stomach.

Susan grasped the top of his head with both hands and motioned him to stand. "I'm serious. We can't talk to each other at work, and definitely can't rendezvous like this on work time."

"You call it, baby. That's fine— I just won't look forward to any more special deliveries."

"I really have to go. Maybe we could meet up over the weekend. I will call you. Oh, and order anything you want, and charge it to the room."

"Has anybody ever told you that you look exactly like Pamela Anderson Lee?"

Susan kissed Malik passionately on his lips and smiled. "I have heard that once or twice but not often. Sorry, honey, I have to run. Goodbye."

Malik stayed in the shower for another five minutes. He let his thoughts run wild. *"I should have dicked her ass down again. That bitch can help me move up in the firm, not to mention her pussy is tight. I think I am going to like this."*

Out of the shower he flicked on the TV and ordered up a cheeseburger and fries from room service. In the middle of his meal he stopped chewing. "Shit! She doesn't have any of my personal information. How is she going to get up with me? Fuck!"

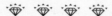

Tony left the school library with three borrowed books under his arm and his book bag hanging from his opposite shoulder. He wasn't surprised to see Kahmelle standing outside.

"I knew I would catch you in here," Kahmelle said as he extended his arm. "How come you didn't return my calls yesterday, Tone? I tried to walkie you but your joint wasn't on. You mad at me, son?" Tony gave him a pound and a leery look. "How does she look man?" Kahmelle wanted to know.

"They fucked her ass up, yo. I can't believe that I had a hand in that shit. Her face was purple and her eyes are swollen shut. The lenses from her frames broke in her eye. Her vision may never be fully restored."

Kahmelle didn't say a word. He just walked with his head down. "Let's go to my house and chill out for the rest of the day. We ain't gotta meet up with Sweat and them until five," Kahmelle said.

"I'm not going. Fuck Brooklyn's Finest, I'm not with it," Tony said.

"Tony, you know if I thought they were going to do all of that I wouldn't have gone through with it either, but it's done. We can't turn back now. Look, it's twelve. I don't feel like going back to class and shit. Let's go to the crib and watch videos. You can decide what you want to do after that."

"She said she wouldn't let it go and they started to stomp on her and shit. Is that what we have to do?"

"Listen, you *that* nigga. You come from a home with two parents. I come from a home with a borrowed aunt and shit. You get good ass grades, and scholarships, I get F's and left back. This is something I want to do. So I can say I finally did something," Kahmelle snapped.

"Whatever. Your ass ain't running a guilt trip on me now."

"Yo, we wanted to do this shit all year. Just try it out with me. Sweat is going to bless us on the strength of you and your brother. He might not take me without you. Just do this six months with me, until final initiation. I promise we won't hit no one up that we know again."

Kahmelle stuck his arm out for a pound. Against his better judgment Tony shook his hand and gave him a quick hug.

"We in together boss?" Kahmelle asked.

"Yeah," Tony said.

"Let's head back to the crib."

"Nah. I'm going back to class. After that I'll grab some lunch, and see if I can catch Latonji. She actually gave a nigga some conversation this morning. I will meet up with you under the bleachers at five."

"Nah, meet me at three-thirty, we have to visit the barber, son. You have some business to take care of, remember?"

Tony ran his hands over his braids, and shook his head. "I was thinking about cutting these things off anyway. My moms has been buggin' me to do it for months— and your aunt be shitin' on me when I need to get them done. So fuck it, I will meet you here at three-thirty."

"One son."

"One."

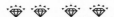

"Yo, is it time yet? Friday always seems to be the longest day of the week," Mike said.

"Nah, we still have forty-five minutes to go," Malik said.

"Yo, by the way, while you were out earlier Human Resources called. They wanted to update addresses, emergency and personal numbers of all employees. I gave them your info," Mike said.

"That's peace," Malik answered.

"What do you have planned for this weekend, nigga?" Mike asked.

"I am going to hit the books. I have finals coming up, and I'm hoping to hear from some law schools," Malik said.

"You really serious about this lawyer shit, huh? Who would have ever thought *you* would be a lawyer."

A cell phone went off and all four men in the room checked their hips.

"It's mine," Malik said. He didn't recognize the number. "Hello?"

"Hey, Malik, it's me Susan. Don't say my name."

"Hey sexy, how are you?"

"Fine. I just called to tell you how much I enjoyed your company today. I am looking forward to seeing you soon."

"So am I. I had a nice time."

"How about tonight?"

"What?"

"I will tell you where to meet me and we could drive out to Jersey, catch a movie, a bite and a quickie."

"You trying to wear me out? Where should I go?"

"Take the A train to Canal Street. Meet me on the corner of Hudson and Canal in front of that big precinct over there at eight, I have to be home before twelve, or I will turn into a pumpkin," Susan chuckled.

"Alright, sexy I'll see you then." Malik flipped the phone closed and smiled. He held it in his hands for a few minutes and gazed straight ahead. Images of their earlier encounter flashed through his mind. He reminisced on how simply she had walked into the mailroom earlier that week. He still couldn't believe it.

"Let me find out you withholding information on a nigga," Mike said.

"What?" Malik was startled. He placed his phone in its clip.

"Sexy? Who was that, playa?" Mike asked.

"Oh, just this chick I've been banging out."

"You ain't tell me about this one. I haven't heard you talk about no broads lately. I thought you was still chillin' with Palma," Mike said as he laughed uncontrollably.

"Who the fuck is Palma?" Malik asked.

"The palm- a your hand, nigga."

All the guys in the mailroom laughed at Mike's joke.

Malik laughed. "You got that one."

Mike continued to pour on the jokes and everyone laughed. Malik wondered how they had stayed friends so long. They had gone to high school together, and hustled in Maryland, together. When Mike blew all of his money and came back to New York, Malik got him a job working in the mailroom with him. They hadn't spoken in a couple of years, but it was as if they were never apart. His deep chocolate brown skin glistened like it was just polished with a coat of Vaseline. His forehead barely reached Malik's eye-level, but the ladies loved Mike. His once-athletic frame now carried a basketball-sized gut. His dark brown eyes have seen a lot, and although he was two years Malik's senior, he wasn't as mature.

"I thought you would be going through your Palm Pilot to find a date."

Malik couldn't help but laugh. "Nah, she's just a chick that I mess around with when I need some action, that's all."

"Is she bad? And does she have any friends?"

"I think you have your share of women right now. And don't forget you have two little girls. You need to mind how you treat women from now on, son."

"I'll start that as soon as I get back from Miami next weekend. It's quitting time. Yo, can we stop at J&R before we get on the train there's a new CD that I want to pick up."

"I'm not going your way today. I 'm hooking up with Palma, after work," Malik said with a smile.

Tony stood in a crowd of about thirteen guys wearing green tops and blue jeans. They talked amongst themselves. He kept his eyes open for Kahmelle and couldn't understand why he was late. Just as he was about to leave, Kahmelle walked in, talking to Sweat. Kahmelle spotted Tony right away. Kahmelle slid his hands over Tony's glistening head and gave him a pound. Sweat walked to the front of the crowd, and everyone got quiet.

"What that green look like, niggas?" Sweat asked. All of the guys responded to the greeting. Tony and Kahmelle just smiled.

"Listen up, we have six people that want to be blessed into Brooklyn's Finest— four bitches and two niggas. Step up."

Tony looked around for females, but he did not see any. He and Kahmelle stepped into the middle of the small crowd.

"When you see these dudes on the streets, know they one of us. The broads, we'll soon see how to deal with them. They around the corner waiting for the 'okay' to come through."

Sweat disappeared for a couple of minutes. A few guys from the neighborhood approached Tony and Kahmelle.

"What up with that green? I'm Spam." He looked at Kahmelle and smiled. "You yeah, but I'm saying *you*— this don't seem like your type of shit, duke. Wasn't you always into your books and shit?" he asked. The other guys from the High agreed and laughed.

"Yeah, and?" Tony asked, annoyed.

One of the older guys extended his hand to Tony. "Hey, I'm Webb. I know your brother, L."

"Leek-o - L?" Spam asked.

"Yeah," Webb said.

"Word?" Spam was shocked. Suddenly all the guys were eager to strike up a conversation with Tony. They bombarded him with questions.

"What's up with that dude? Is he still doing his thing?"

"He still be out in Maryland? He still fuck with Sweat like that?"

Tony was overwhelmed. "Malik is chillin'," he replied simply.

"Yo, your brother was sick out here on these streets, man," Spam said.

"Word," Tony agreed.

"Check it out. Here go the girls who want to be down," Kahmelle said. Sweat walked in with four young girls, two on each side of him.

"Little Tone and Kahmelle make yourselves seen," Sweat called.

They stepped from the middle of the crowd and looked at Sweat. Sweat grabbed two of the girls by their wrists. He pointed toward Tony and Kahmelle then nodded his head.

"Go blaze them," Sweat said firmly.

"What?" One of the girls snapped.

"Blaze them. Suck they dicks and fuck 'em right here. Depending on your performance, you *might* get in," Sweat said.

Kahmelle unzipped his pants and let his jeans fall down to his ankles.

"You buggin! I don't wanna be down *that* bad," the same girl snapped.

"Come on, Shaine, it won't be that bad."

"Fuck, that Camille, I'm out."

Shaine started to walk off, but Sweat grabbed her by the back of her jean jacket and roughly yanked her towards him. "Where you going pretty? Go give my man Tony some head," Sweat said. He wasn't asking. He shoved her into Tony.

Kahmelle stared at the girl as she started to cry. He talked to Tony. "Yo that bitch is bad as hell. I want that one right there." Tony watched as the young lady stood in front of him crying. She leaned her head on his shoulder and sobbed hard.

"You, go over there and service my man Kahmelle," Sweat said shoving another young lady toward Kahmelle. She wasted no time in pulling Kahmelle's limp dick out of his underpants. Dropping to her knees she placed his dick in her mouth. Her head bobbed back and forth, and with in seconds Kahmelle's limp dick was hard as a rock.

Sweat cupped the back of the head of a girl standing next to him and pushed her down to her knees. He looked down at her. "What's your name?" The girl answered with a confident attitude, "Diamond."

"Watch those pretty-ass teeth, Diamond," Sweat said. She willingly unbuckled his belt, pulled down his pants and went to work. The remaining girl stood still. Sweat grabbed her by the ass. "Bring your big ass tits over here. Open your blouse and let your tits say 'what up'. Pull that skirt up and let me touch it," Sweat said.

The girl in front of Tony looked at him and he smiled at her. *Damn, she is a dime,* he thought. Tony pulled his penis through his open zipper and held it in his hands. He turned his back on the group of guys standing around cheering them on. She dropped to her knees and cried harder.

"What's your name?" Tony asked.

"Shaine," The girl said in between sobs.

"Why are you here then?" Tony asked softly.

"I didn't think I would have to do this. I'm sorry I just can't," she cried.

"If she's giving you a problem, just smack the bitch, ya heard?" Sweat snarled. Then he looked back down to his gleaming, spit-shined dick.

Tony stroked her hair and gently pulled her hands away from her face. He rubbed her lips with his penis, and then used it to wipe some tears off of her cheek. "Listen Shaine, if you don't, Sweat might hurt you."

She placed his penis into her mouth. He pushed it in, and she started to suck it. "OUCH," Tony snapped. "You have to open your mouth wider than that. Your teeth just scraped my dick."

She did as she was told, still crying. His dick went limp after the second scrape. He heard commotion and loud laughter behind him. He turned in time to see Kahmelle ejaculating all over the girl's face. Tony felt horrible. He gently pushed her head back and told her to stop.

"Thank you," she said.

"Just stay in this position and maybe they won't notice you're not doing it. Move your head back and forth."

"You know Tony, I never thought you would be trying to join a gang. You have so much going for you," Shaine said bobbing her head slowly back and forth as she whispered.

"How you know who I am?"

"I go to the High, too. I was in your honors English class two years in a row. But my grades dropped and I didn't make this year."

"Oh shit. Now I know who you are. You got thick and tall, girl!"

Tony turned around and shook his head. He saw Kahmelle with his pants in the dirt. His black ass glistened in the sun as it pounded in and out of the ass of the girl he was with. She was bent over and gripping the back of the bleachers. From what he could see Kahmelle was moving fast.

"I hope Kah has a bag on and shit. Alright, I think we've stalled long enough. You can stand." Tony straightened himself out and walked towards the crowd with the girl following closely.

Sweat smiled at the two of them as they approached.

"Now that wasn't that bad was it?" Sweat asked.

Shaine rolled her eyes and stayed silent. "Now fuck him," Sweat demanded.

Tony answered quickly. "Sweat, I just bust off on her, I can't get it back up that quick," Tony lied nervously.

"Whatever," Sweat said.

"Yeah bitch, what's my muthafuckin' name," Kahmelle shouted a few feet away.

"Kahmelle!" she called.

"You like this shit, huh?" Kahmelle smacked the girl on her ass with an open palm as he completed his sentence. He repeated smacking her behind. The laughing, cheering members of Brooklyn's Finest drowned out the loud smacks.

Sweat directed his attention toward Tony and smiled. "Thugglemen ass muthfucka."

"What?" Tony replied.

"That's what my grandmother used to call your brother. He was thugged out but a real gentlemen too. I could tell you are going to do big things with us." Sweat shook the girls off of him. "Fuckfest is over."

"Damn, and I was just getting ready to cum again," Kahmelle said. He yanked the dry condom off of his dick and pulled on his jeans.

"The broads ain't blessed and won't be able to complete initiation," Sweat said. The bleachers were quiet except for the girl who had fucked Kahmelle. "Why?" She yelled as she straightened out her clothes.

"Because *she* ain't fuck," Sweat said pointing at Shaine "and that's that. Get the fuck out of here and don't ask me no more questions."

The girls began to make their way out of the park, except Camille, who had dealt with Kahmelle. She stopped in her tracks. "Yo, Sweat," she said boldly as she stared into his eyes. "I will be back, and you gonna bless me. You feel me?" She rolled her eyes and walked out holding her head high. Shaine followed closely behind her.

Tony caught up to her and grabbed her hand. "Wait for me on Fourth Avenue. I will walk you home," he said. She nodded her head and rushed to catch up to the rest of the girls.

"Now fellas, this is where we hang out when it's warm. When we're discussin' a job, or it's mad cold all meetings are held at the Bat Cave. No one steps foot into the Bat Cave until they've been blessed. And let me take this time to say I'm blessin' y'all. Tony and Kahmelle, you folklore now, y'all in the green. You have six months to become official Brooklyn's Finest members."

Tony and Kahmelle gave each other a pound and a hug. "We did it, son," Kahmelle said.

"Word," Tony said smiling weakly. *But exactly what have I just done?* he thought silently.

"See you in two weeks. Keep your batteries charged just in case anything goes down," Sweat said.

Tony and Kahmelle emerged from beneath the bleachers deep in conversation.

"Yo, Tony. That shit was off the hook. Her pussy smelled a little like fish, but that shit sure did feel good," Kahmelle said.

"Did you throw on a bag?" Tony asked.

"You know that's right. What about the head? How was it?"

Tony sucked his teeth. "She was all crying and shit. She scraped my dick once, and I made her stop. We faked it."

"She was a fuckin' sucker. Not really though." Kahmelle laughed loudly at his own witty humor. "Get it? Not really a sucker."

"I got it the first time. The shit just wasn't funny," Tony said.

"It wasn't funny because you ain't nut off, that's why," Kahmelle said.

"What time is it?" Tony asked.

Kahmelle looked at his new phone. "Seven-thirty."

"Oh shit, my moms is going to flip. I'm out son."

"One, son"

They left park in opposite directions. Tony rushed towards Flatbush Avenue. As he approached the huge intersection he saw Shaine standing under a store's awning with the girls who were trying to get blessed.

"Hey, what up, Shaine?" Tony asked.

She was visibly upset. Her nose was red and her eyes were puffy and swollen. She held a balled up tissue in one hand and a can of soda in the other. They stared at each other in silence.

"Thank you so much," Shaine replied.

"I'm sayin'. You ain't like that. Anyone in honors English, especially a female, don't have no business in Brooklyn's Finest," Tony said.

She sniffled and rolled her eyes. "What about you? Your ass was trying to get down too!" Shaine blurted out.

Tony didn't answer. He spat on the ground and looked at Camille. "Why you hanging out with trash like that?"

"Camille is my friend. I don't know the other girls," Shaine said.

"Let's be out," Tony said.

"Camille, Tony is going to walk me home. I'll call you later on."

Camille walked over toward Tony and poked him on his shoulder. "Yo, you need to tell Sweat that I want into Brooklyn's Finest bad. I ain't fuck your ashy ass boy for nothing," she said.

Tony didn't answer. He grabbed Shaine's hand and they walked away. Camille walked back over to other girls and they all laughed loudly.

"So Shaine, you still ain't tell me why you was trying to get down?"

"Well, I, guess I don't know. I am an only child— well, I was until my pops split on my moms last year and got this young chick pregnant. Now I got a baby sister."

"Word? Me and my brother are ten years apart. He used to treat me like I was his son and shit. We got a good relationship. You should try to be there for the shorty as she grows up."

"My fuckin' moms is dating and shit, her ass is never home. We hardly ever talk anymore. I started hanging out with Camille and shit. All the guys like her and she dresses fly. She be at all the hot spots and shit like that. She wanted me to join with her— it was her idea to try to get into Brooklyn's Finest. I guess I just wanted to belong."

"I know what you mean about belonging and shit, but that shit ain't for you. You are way to pretty and smart for that shit."

The pair strolled down Flatbush Avenue. They laughed, and talked the entire ten-minute walk to her building. They sat down on the stoop.

"Yo, you in the same grade as me?" Tony asked as he took her hand.

"Yep," Shaine replied.

"I'm going to help you with your English and shit. Next year is do or die. If you could score high on your English final, you could get back into honors English, and that shit will look good on your college applications," Tony said firmly.

"I don't think I'm going—"

"Nah, if you going to be my girl you have to go to college."

Shaine looked up at Tony. "You mean that?" she asked with her bright, wide, hope-filled eyes.

"You ain't dating nobody right?" Shaine shook her head. "Then it's settled." Tony took off his chain and placed it around her neck. He leaned over and kissed her lips slowly. He looked at her and kissed her again. This time he added a little tongue.

"You want to come in?" Shaine asked.

"Nah I have to go home. Give me your number and I will call you tonight," Tony said.

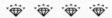

"Jonathan, I can't believe neither one of those boys is home yet," Millicent Hendrickson said to her husband. She looked at the clock that hung over the doorway to the kitchen and rose from the table.

Jonathan Hendrickson cleaned his plate with his fork and smiled at his wife. "Millicent, would you give me some more chicken, and yams, please?" he asked.

Millicent took her husband's plate to the stove. She scooped out a healthy portion of food for Jonathan. She opened the door to the stove, bent down and wrestled out a biscuit that was stuck to the pan. She felt the comforting hands of her husband grab her waistline and she straightened quickly.

"Listen, Millie, the boys are grown now. Malik's finally got his act together and Tony is doing fine. Besides, we aren't getting any younger. We need to start worrying about ourselves," Jonathan said.

Jonathan looked at his wife's petite frame. She stood 5'3"and was just as fine as the day he met her. Her white nurse's uniform clung to her curves. Her hips were wide and her legs were thick down to her calves. Suddenly he longed to squeeze the extra weight that surrounded her mid section, and he did. She despised it, but he loved it. Her dark brown complexion was still smooth and blemish free, except for the two deep dimples that sat in her cheeks. He removed the clamp that held her hair up in a bun and let it unravel down her back.

"God, woman, I love you. You seem to grow more and more beautiful as the years go by."

Millicent put the plate on the stove, turned toward her husband and smiled. "I guess you're right, I am beautiful," she teased.

"And?"

"And the boys are grown but rules are rules."

"You almost bit Malik's head off for coming in late the other night. He is damn near thirty. And Tony graduates next year. I'm surprised he never comes in late. Don't be so hard on them, Millicent," Jonathan said.

"That's just my point, Jonathan. Dinner is the one time we can get together daily as a family. I know Malik is grown and Tony is right behind him. They're so different now. I barely see them anymore. They need to respect that time. After dinner they can come and go as they please."

Jonathan stuck his hands up the bottom of Millicent's uniform.

"Not now baby. One of the boys might come in. Besides, I want you to finish this plate up. Let's save that for tonight. It's Friday, the boys will be out and when they're gone, we can make all the noise we want."

Jonathan smiled and did as he was told. Millicent looked up at the wall; the clock read eight twenty-five. She began to worry.

Officer Joann Nuñez stood with two cases of Similac at her feet outside of Yanick's door. *This shit cost me over one hundred dollars.* Joann thought. *Well, here goes nothing, keep your mack game up, Joann.*

Joann knocked on the door then smoothed out her hair. The door slowly opened revealing Yanick with her index finger over her lips.

"Shhhh, Seven just fell asleep and I don't want to wake her. You look different without that uniform, girl. Come in," Yanick whispered.

Joann dragged the cases into the living room. Seven was fast asleep in a white, whicker bassinet at the living rooms center. Her pacifier moved quickly between her lips.

"Come to my room and I will give you the money," she whispered.

Yanick led Joann through the crowded apartment. It was filled with way too much furniture, large colorful portraits, and cheap and tacky paintings. Joann laughed to herself— *everyone has at least one family member with a home like this*. They reached a small room, went inside and closed the door. Joann looked up at the cracks in the mint green paint on the ceiling, and the huge white chips in the mint green paint on the wall. The room wasn't large enough to hold a bedroom set.

"Go ahead, sit down," Yanick said.

Joann sat on the bed and shifted around a few times in an attempt to get comfortable. The bed was extremely soft, and lumpy, and with every shift she seemed to sink lower. Yanick plopped down on the bed next to Joann and stared at her for a second. Joann had a dark brown complexion with relaxed, shoulder length hair. She wore a Chinese bang across her forehead. She had slanted dark brown eyes. She had no curves, and was very slim with big breasts.

"You really look different officer. You don't look like a cop."

"Why did you go there again? Call me Joann, don't call me officer." Joann shifted her weight so she was closer to Yanick and looked at her. Her mid-drift was bare and revealed a curvaceous waist, with very little to no flab. She stared at her bare stomach and her thick lips.

"You like the way I look, don't you?" Joann asked. She spoke in a very soft tone, much different from the firm, deep voice she regularly used.

Yanick became visibly uncomfortable and inched back. " I ain't gay or nothing, but you're pretty. The uniform makes you look a little rough."

Easy Jo, don't scare her away, Joann thought "The way I wear my hair underneath my hat could have something to do with it. So, what's the deal with you and your old man?" Joann asked.

"I told you, I don't have one. He skipped town a couple of months ago," Yanick said.

"Do you get out much?" Joann asked.

"I could if I had somewhere to go, plus, I don't have that much extra cash. My parents be beggin' me to go out sometimes. I stay in with Seven all the time. Sometimes I go out with my homeboy George."

"Where's the baby's room?"

Yanick turned her palms up and shrugged her shoulders. "You're in it."

"Where's the crib?"

"She's still little so she stays in the bassinet. When the time comes I will get her one. I am going to try and get a summer job."

"How old are you?"

"I'm twenty-one. I have one more semester to finish up my Associates degree."

"Yeah? Where do you go?"

"I go to City Tech, on Jay Street."

"I know exactly where that is."

"I would have graduated next month, with two classes left to take in the summer, but Seven came a little earlier than I expected."

"Really?"

"Yeah, she was born premature in my seventh month, on the seventh of March, at seven minutes after six. That's why I named her Seven. My professors are willing to let me make up my finals over the summer, and all I need after that is seven credits."

"That's really admirable. Don't stop school until you have achieved everything you want. Remember it's just not about you anymore, it's about you and Seven." Joann looked around the room and forced a smile. "Besides you have to get that little princess her own room."

"You have any kids?" Yanick asked.

"Nah, but I have a gang of nieces and nephews. That's all I need."

"How old are you?"

"I'm twenty-nine."

Yanick noticed Joann staring at her lips and licking her own. She became uncomfortable and suddenly sprang off the bed. "So, how much do I owe you?" she asked.

"Listen, I rarely get to hang out anymore. How about you keep your money in your pocket, and let this be my gift to Seven. You can repay me by catching a flick with me. I have Sunday off. I'll call you tomorrow night to confirm."

Yanick smiled and flopped back on the bed next to Joann. "Sounds like a plan. My parents will be happy I'm getting out. I will pick you up around eight. Thanks for the formula. Seven and I really appreciate it."

They stood up simultaneously. Joann stared at Yanick and Yanick turned her head. The young mother's cut-off jeans shorts suctioned her thick thighs, and hugged her hips.

Joann shook her head. *She definitely does not have the body of a new mother. One little advance won't hurt*, she thought. She ran three fingers slowly across Yanick's navel in circular motions. When Yanick did not tense up or pull away, she ran her fingers across her entire midsection. Joann let her fingers pry a little lower, brushing the inside of the waist of her denim shorts. With no resistance, Joann went lower. When her fingers rubbed the coarse pubic hairs underneath her navel she licked her lips slowly and looked into Yanick's eyes.

Yanick was immediately turned on; she was hot but scared. As Joann's fingers touched the elastic on her thong Yanick jumped. Joann cleared her throat loudly.

"I'm sorry, Yanick, I just can't believe you had a baby in that flat stomach only three months ago."

Yanick was too worked up to respond. Joann knew her work was done. After the movies she would definitely get the hundred dollars and change she'd spent on Similac back. Yanick's chest heaved up and down as she spoke in a low voice. "Do you see—" Yanick's words came out husky. She cleared her throat and grabbed her stomach before she continued. "Do you see this shit? It is enormous. My stomach was flat, I'm talkin six pack."

Joann squeezed Yanick's waist gently then walked toward the door. "If that's enormous. Shiiii."

They silently walked back through the apartment.

"Thanks for the formula, Joann. See you Sunday."

Joann stopped at the bassinet and peeked in on Seven. "I have to see about buying this precious baby girl a crib set," she said.

Yanick felt a tingling sensation fluttering around her mid section. Joann walked over to the front door. She turned around and smiled at Yanick. Yanick smiled back and mouthed the words 'thank you'.

"Don't mention it. Make sure you wear that shirt Sunday. Bye," Joann said.

"Bye," Yanick locked the door and stood with her back against it. She sucked her stomach in tightly hugging her waist with a grin. She still felt Joann's soft fingers touching her. Yanick released her self-embrace, ran to the phone and called her closest friend, George.

3

Oh where's my kitty cat
where's my kitty cat at - strokin' me

Rocky looked out the airplane window and watched as several men in gray jump suits packed luggage onto her plane. As she waited for take off, a group of four laughing women, around her age, boarded the plane. The first to board looked at Rocky and stopped laughing. She tapped her girlfriend's shoulder and whispered in her ear. Rocky rolled her eyes and continued to stare out the window. "Did you see that chick in first class? I wonder who she is?"

"I don't know," the friend replied loudly as she directed her attention towards Rocky. "She's pretty though, and her bag and shoes are fly."

"Don't sweat her like that. Come on."

"Shit, you the one who told me to look."

Rocky laughed loud enough for them to hear her and continued looking out of the window. She was used to being looked at with envy when she sat in first class twice a month. That was the only way Mauri sent for her. Rocky continued to watch the men sort through dozens of suitcases, duffel bags, garment bags and boxes. She thought about her luggage, and other passengers' possible destinations.

When she became bored with the luggage she began watching the boarding passengers. A young woman boarded with a little girl who smiled at Rocky as she passed.

"Hi, cutie petutey. How old are you?" Rocky asked.

"I'm seven and a half years old. My mommy and me are going to visit my grandpa. Where are you going pretty lady?"

"Come along, Kayla. Don't bother the lady," the child's mother warned.

Rocky smiled. "Oh she is no bother, and she's beautiful. Bye, bye."

The mother pushed her daughter along and continued toward their seats. Rocky immediately thought about how happy she had been as a child, until her mother sent her away one Sunday by Grey hound, at the age of 8. . .

"Now listen, Rock Candy, you know that mommy loves you, and I'm going to send for you as soon as I get back on my feet."

Rocky stood on the top stairwell step of the bus and stared down at her mother, who stood outside. She dropped her small green and white trimmed duffel bag next to the bus driver, jumped down the steps and hugged her mother by the waist.

"But why do I have to go? Why can't I stay here with you, Roger, and the new baby?" Rocky rubbed her mother's bulging belly and kissed it. That was the closest she'd ever come to holding her younger sibling.

"Girl, if you don't bring your ass on you gonna fuck me up. I have to check my books before the numbers play," Roger snapped.

"Just a minute Roger, I'm coming," her mother called behind her. Rocky looked over at Roger with hot tears burning wildly on her face, and he turned his back on her. Rocky began to scream hysterically.

"Mommy, why does he hate me? You love him more than me! Make him go, please. I don't want to stay with grandma and them, they don't really know me no more. I ain't seen them since we left Shorty and Cess."

Her mother smiled at her. Her long, relaxed, dirty blonde hair blew in the wind and her hazel eyes did not release one tear. She bent down and kissed her daughter's forehead, then wiped the tears off her face with the back of her hand. She gently grabbed her by both shoulders and looked into her eyes.

"Rock Candy, I don't love him more than you—I love no man, shit I don't even know if I love myself. But I love you enough to know that I ain't doin' you right, and I know your grandma can."

"But you're so beautiful. Why don't you love yourself?"

Her mother released her grip and backed away from the bus.

"Young lady, you either have to come have a seat or get off of the bus. You're going to take me off schedule," the bus driver said gently. He felt sorry for the little girl.

Rocky suddenly grabbed her bag and ran off the bus. As the doors closed, the bus hadn't gone two feet before Roger ran from the curb toward Rocky. The bus driver slammed on his brakes.

"You stupid, fuckin' kid! Would you get on the fuckin' bus! I got shit to do," Roger yelled.

Rocky's mother jumped in front of her and shoved Roger before he reached her. "Have you lost your fuckin' mind? Don't you dare yell at my daughter. I'll get on that bus with her and you'll never see me or this fuckin' baby again".

Rocky left her mother and Roger arguing in the small, glass enclosed bus shelter. Rocky stood next to the bus driver and watched as Roger dropped to his knees kissing her mother's stomach. They didn't even notice she was back on the bus until it was too late. Her mother backed away from Roger, covered her mouth with both hands and shook her head as the bus slowly left the stop. Rocky tried to run to the back of the bus so she could get a longer glimpse of her mother. But by the time she reached the middle window the bus was turning the corner.

She timidly walked to the front of the bus and watched the flowered, sequined hats of a dispassionate group of church ladies discussing her *situation. Their faces showed little sympathy for the pretty girl as she continued to mope down the aisle. She heard whisper after whisper. Every passenger thought they knew Rocky's story that day. They each put their own finishing touches on it. Each comment seemed to get worse. It felt like she would never reach the front of that bus.*

"Now that woman know she dead wrong, getting rid of the little girl for a man."

"I swear I don't know why these teenage girls be havin' babies and don't be takin' care of 'em— and that girl is pregnant again."

"You know Junior got some nasty little heathen pregnant, and they tryin' to get me to raise that baby. I said hell no, I ain't laid down to make it so I ain't got to take it!"

Rocky blocked out their comments and walked with her head down to the front of the bus.

"Don't worry, little girl we right outside Philadelphia. New York is only about three hours away," the driver said with a reassuring smile. He seemed to be the only friendly, non-judgmental face on the bus. He smiled over his shoulder at her. His shiny dark face beaded with sweat underneath the brim of his navy blue hat. His big, dark hand reached over to pass her a canned soda and a light blue napkin filled with chocolate chip cookies. She thanked him, quickly bit into a cookie and started to relax as she sipped on the soda.

"Can I interest you in a beverage? Today you will be viewing 'The Water Boy' featuring Adam Sandler. Your head phones are conveniently placed in the seat's back pocket." A flight attendant in a starched gray and red uniform stood smiling down at her. It was now she noticed the plane had already taken off.

"No, thanks. But could you bring me a shot of Hennesy and a side of Coke."

"Yes ma'am" The stewardess placed a can of Coke and two clear cups on the tray in front of Rocky. She poured half the can into one clear plastic cup with ice and the entire contents of the miniature Henessy bottle into the other.

"Thank you," Rocky said. As she took her first sip Rocky remembered how the thump of her mother's headboard beating against the wall would wake her up in the middle of the night. The creaks of the bed and the cries of pleasure were her only company in her dark lonely room. . .

"Damn, Denise, you got some good-ass pussy girl," Thump! Thump! Thump! "Goddamn, girl, you better marry me," Thump! Creak! Thump! "Whose pussy is this?" Creak! Thump!"

"Shhhh, Roger, you gonna wake up my baby girl."

"I thought I was your baby?"

She took the next sip and remembered one of the few times she and Roger spent alone.

"You know, you look just like your daddy— I can't stand that nigga," Roger said.

"I only seen him twice. Momma won't let him around me 'cause he hit her once."

"I can't stand your daddy. Why don't you go in the back and play with some matches until your mother comes back. I'm gonna watch some TV."

Hours passed before her mother came in the next morning. The door slammed at three a.m. Denise swaggered into her daughter's bedroom and switched on the light. Rocky could still remember the hot stench of liquor coating her cheek before her mother leaned down and kissed her on that dark morning. As she stood up and turned around Roger stood directly in her face.

"What the fuck? I look like 'Mr. Mom' to you? You been gone over twelve hours. I sent you out to buy coats for you and your kid, and you come back drunk the next day! You better not have been fuckin' that nigga again or I'll kill both of you."

Rocky's mother staggered over to Roger's face and dropped her shopping bags. She shoved her tongue down his throat, immediately silencing him. Then she pulled him by his zipper out of Rocky's room.

Once they were out of view little, Rock Candy, jumped out of bed and rummaged through the bags on the floor. Rocky loved when her mother purchased her new clothes. There were two dark brown mink coats in the bag. One was just her size. She put it on over her pajamas and rubbed the ultra-soft coat sleeve against her cheek. It felt so good. She raced to thank her mother, but stopped short when she heard the slurping noises and Roger's groaned marriage proposal. Rocky didn't dare look. She got back into the bed wearing her mink coat, and vowed that she would not have sex until she got married.

"Well, I guess that promise was premature, shit, I was only six," she said in a whisper. Rocky picked up the empty cup and placed it to her mouth trying to sip the last drop. She unfastened her seat belt to get up and use the rest room, but she was too queasy. *My mother used to be able to put them away. But if I just smell liquor I get drunk*, she thought, as she sat back in her seat. She immediately fell asleep.

She woke up to light taps on her shoulder.

"Sorry to bother you, ma'am. But we are preparing for landing. You must fasten you seat belt and put your seat in its full upright position."

Rocky adjusted her seat as the flight attendant removed the rubbish off of her tray. She grabbed the soda can before the flight attendant could. "Can I please finish the rest of my soda?"

"I'm sorry, ma'am— I thought you were finished."

Wow, I can't believe I slept the entire flight. That Henny knocked me on my ass. She thought. *Roger used to look at mom with love in his eyes, and so much admiration.* She sighed. *That's the same way Thomas looks*

at me. I wish I could be madly in love with him. He's almost perfect, but
still no cigar. If I could only take Mauri's street edge, money and a
smidgen of his ghetto ways and place them inside Thomas' perfect body,
with his big dick and book brilliance I'd have the perfect man. It seems
like I wish for that everyday bu—

The plane pounded on the runway, sending her soda can flying all over the gray leather seat in front of her. "What the—" Rocky looked out the window to make sure the plane hadn't plunged into water.

Outside the airport, she was burnt with the reality of Detroit. A stretch Cadillac Escalade was parked in front of Exit 9. A chauffeur holding a sign with royal blue lettering that spelled out 'Rock Candy' stood in front of it. The unbearable Detroit heat was a reminder that she had to spend the next four days with Mauri. The chauffeur placed the luggage on the seat next to her, per her request, and closed the door behind her.

"Who are you? Where is Jack or Mauri?" Rocky asked the chauffeur.

"Mauri had a business meeting and Jack drove him there, so I'm dropping you off at Northland Mall. Mauri will meet you there, ma'am."

"Ma'am makes me feel so old— call me Rocky. Could you please roll up the partition? I would like to make some calls."

The chauffeur rolled up the partition and Rocky rolled down her window. She laughed as she watched the four girls who had ridiculed her on the plane shove their luggage into a taxicab. She called out to them and waved from her window. "Have a nice trip ladies."

The girls sourly watched the limo pull off. Rocky called Kay.

"Hey girl, what's up?" Rocky said.

"Not a damn thing. Sitting at my desk trying to get these orders out on time. You in Detroit?"

"I sure am. I just wanted to let you know I made it out here all right. Four days in Detroit, but thank God I only have to spend three with Mauri, today is almost over. He is so much easier to tolerate when I am in Brooklyn. I'm just going to suck it up like I always do, girl," Rocky said.

"Why are you talking so damn low? You are barely audible." Kay said.

"'Cause I'm in the back of one of Mauri's cars," Rocky said.

"I wish you would just get rid of him. You had a good two-year run. You got a Mercedes, beautiful jewelry, vacations and countless shopping sprees out of his ass. The first year was all right. You were so caught up with his money and shit that you really seemed to like him. Year two rolls around and you can't stand his ass. Listen to yourself. Why should you have to 'suck it up' and pretend you like him? You're much better than that, girl."

"I know, I know. It is about time, I do care for him, but I need more. Besides, my car has like seven more payments on it. And as soon as I stash some cash, I think it'll be about that time. You know he asked me to marry him after I graduated?"

"You didn't tell me that. What did you say?"

"I told him I wanted to work on a Masters degree first."

"You just be careful out there, okay? Make sure you call."

"I'll speak to you tomorrow."

Rocky closed her cell and looked out of the window. She rolled it up and leaned back. Her best friend's words rang in her ears. 'You're much better than that'. It was getting so she couldn't stand the sight of Mauri. He stood 5'7". Rocky was taller than he was when she wore her heels, which annoyed her, but did not bother him in the least. He was brown in complexion with a slender face, skinny arms and legs and a round protruding stomach. When they first met he wore a curl and several gold teeth, but Rocky did not stand for that. She had him cut his hair during their first date, and had him remove his gold teeth after one month.

Mauri is a thirty-three year old millionaire. He owns a chain of self-titled businesses throughout the Detroit and Chicago areas. One is a chain of six urban clothing stores called, Mr. Maurice. The second and third are Maurice's Limousine Service, and three locations of Mauri's Hand Car Wash and Detail Centers. Last, but not least, and perhaps one of his biggest moneymakers is a strip club called 'Maur Pussy'.

The partition went down and the limo driver spoke. "Rock Candy? Mauri said you are to meet him right next door to the Baker's on the first floor. He has a surprise for you. I'll take your bags."

"Thanks. And please call me Rocky." *I wonder why he chose this mall? He knows I don't shop in these kinds of stores. Damn, it's hot*, she thought.

In the five seconds it took Rocky to walk from the limo into the mall she broke out in a small sweat. Relief caressed her body in the form of cool, conditioned air. Noise, lights and laughter surrounded her. She steeled herself for the beginning of another long weekend.

Two little boys with ice cream cones ran past her giggling. She walked up to the directory and located her destination. "Bakers is just a couple of stores fronts around this bend."

Some teenage boys blew kisses at Rocky as they passed her. She wore a pair of stretch Seven jeans, a white wife beater and baby blue, high heeled, Chanel mules. She sported the matching clutch underneath her arm. Her tinted baby blue, rhinestone studded Chanel shades sat a top her head pushing her hair back so that her trimmed mane sat neatly above her chest. Rocky licked her lips slowly and smiled at the boys as she passed by. When she turned the corner she giggled quietly as the boys responded with requests for her phone number.

She spotted Mauri standing in front of a vacant store space that neighbored Bakers. He was with two older White gentlemen in business suits. All three stood with their backs toward her. Mauri wore a baby blue, velour, sweat suit and shell toe Adidas with baby blue stripes.

You would have thought we planned this shit!! I can't believe we're wearing the same colors— how corny. Well, he does look cute, but I know he's going to ruin my moment as soon as he opens his damn mouth. Just smile and be nice, Rocky .You only have a few more months on that car. Fifteen more trips out here won't kill you, Rocky thought. She approached him quietly and gently ran the palm of her hand up the back of his leg. "Well, I never thought I would see the day you would be wearing shorts on those legs," Rocky laughed.

"Hey, baby girl. You're right on time," Mauri replied. He faced the two gentlemen with him, pulled Rocky in front of him and hugged her waist from behind. "Marlon, David, I would like you to meet my wife, Rocky."

She extended her arm and beamed a very broad smile. "It's so nice to meet you both."

"Next month this time your husband will have a 'Mr. Maurice' right here in this spot," Marlon said indicating the vacant store.

"Oh honey, I am so happy! You have been trying so hard for this." Rocky squeezed his arms tightly around her waist. She was genuinely happy for him.

"This will be the first store of its kind in this mall so it's bound to make a killing," David said.

"You have your card with you?" Mauri asked.

"Yes, sweetie," Rocky answered.

"Go tear the mall up. Buy anything you want and Jack will meet us outside in an hour and a half. Buy yourself a nice dress, cause we gonna celebrate tonight," Mauri said.

Rocky kissed Mauri passionately and waved goodbye to the two men.

"Have a nice day, gentlemen." As soon as she turned her back the smile left her face.

Tear this mall up? Please. What could I possibly buy in here? He knows I don't shop in places like this, she thought. She walked back to the directory. *Well, I am hungry. Let's see what I can get to eat.*

"Monique, this shorty is a dime," Joann said.

"I don't know why you like to turn them straight ones out like that. Those chicks always get fatal on you when you're ready to bounce. You need to settle down with a classy woman, someone that knows the ropes. I still don't believe you turned Samantha down, she's a trophy piece— so she's right up your alley, and a veterinarian. She's still feeling you. All it would take is a phone call and some flowers."

"After I got the ass I wasn't really interested in Sam anymore. Wait until you see this chick— her body is banging. I had her sweatin' and shit. Monique you have to see her lips they're juicy as hell. I bet you a ten spot I'll have her up in this apartment tonight, and I will pop that thang."

"You are a straight up mess. It's all about the challenge with you. In three to six months you will set her straight again. She will be running straight back to the dick that she ran to you from."

Joann smiled and shook her head.

"You have to be fuckin kiddin' me Yanick, you're really going out with this dyke?"

"She's not a dyke, George. She's too pretty. Besides, if she is one I am just going to tell her that I don't get down like that. We already went to the movies last weekend, and she didn't touch me."

"Yeah right Yanick, your ass called me as soon as she left your spot the other day. You were feeling her then. And I know how your horny ass is. If she pushes the right buttons, you will get down like that, quick fast," George said.

"I gotta go, George."

"Call me if you need me, Yanick."

Yanick clicked the phone off and walked to her bedroom. She lay on her back and imagined Joann's fingers caressing her body. She thought about what George had said. *Will she hit on me? Nah, she knows I don't get down like that.*

🔹 🔹 🔹 🔹

Before Rocky could even sit on the bed, Mauri lifted up her hair and licked the back of her neck.

"Yuck, I've been sweating all day. At least let me get in the shower?"

"Girl, it's been two weeks. I'm about to bust," Mauri said as he grabbed his crotch.

Won't be much of an explosion. Her snide thoughts made her smile. *I know exactly how to get him off my back*, she thought.

Without hesitation Rocky dropped to her knees. Mauri started to breathe heavily before she even touched the ground. She eased his shorts and boxers down with one pull. She grabbed his erect penis and placed it in her mouth. Then she opened her lips wide and began to suck. He grabbed her by the back of her head and pushed it toward his groin whenever her mouth touched the tip of his dick.

"Oh, Rock Candy," he moaned repeatedly.

I wonder where we're going tonight? I could swallow this shit hole; Mauri's shit is half the size of Thomas', she thought as her head bobbed up and down. Within five bobs Mauri let out a loud groan. *Good. I knew this shit wouldn't take long.*

Rocky put on the most seductive look she could possibly muster, looked up into his eyes and quickly moved her face away from his dick. "Yeah, Daddy you liked that, huh?" she said as she jerked his dick three times and semen shot out past her shoulder.

Mauri spoke quickly, out of breath. "You know I can't take it when you do that. That shit feels so good, and it's been so long and all I gotta lie down. But I got something for that ass tonight." Within seconds Mauri was snoring.

She peered around his bedroom and smiled. It seemed like just yesterday he had asked her to redecorate his house, and every touch she had made stayed the same. She had decorated it just six months into their relationship. Everything she would have wanted in her own house she furnished in Marui's spacious 16-room home, which he alone occupied. She walked over to his dresser and pinned all her hair into one bun on top of her head. She looked at him through the reflection and shook her head. He was sprawled across it with his shorts at his ankles and his sneakers still on his feet. "Just like a baby," Rocky whispered to herself.

It was a circular, king-sized bed. The room was off white with hardwood floors, and stainless steel and wood furniture. There were two round night tables with sliding doors that stood on both sides of the huge circular bed. It had no headboard, but a huge chrome piece of artwork that Rocky had bid on at an upscale auction, hung on the wall behind it.

The dresser was right next to the bathroom. Rocky turned both of the bathtub knobs on full blast and walked over to a small closet at the rear of the bathroom. She removed a medium sized, black, satin pouch from out of it, and a bottle of bubble bath. She sat on the tub's edge and squeezed the red soap into the rapidly filling tub. Bubbles quickly started to form and fill up the beige Victorian styled tub. She stood up slowly and daintily stepped out of her mules, she peeled off her jeans— which seemed to be adhesive instead of stretch and pulled her wife beater over her head. She stuck her hand in the water and immediately pulled it out. "Ouch!"

She turned off the hot water knob and let the coldwater gush through the faucet a few moments more. When Rocky climbed in, she slid down into the foamy white bubbles so that they adorned her neck like jewelry. Inhaling deeply, she slid deeper into the luxuriously warm water.

She opened her legs and ran the entire length of her middle finger up and down her clitoris repeatedly. She began to moan softly and the bubbles bobbed around her heaving chest slowly. She stopped abruptly and reached back toward the edge of the tub almost knocking over the satin pouch. She felt blindly around the inside of the pouch and pulled out a clear plastic vibrating dildo, with a small piece extended from the bottom. She flicked on a switch and the penis shaped rod began to twist slowly. She flicked on a second switch and the extension began to vibrate. *Damn, I love this rabbit*, she thought as she stared at it with a sexy smile on her face.

The rabbit took a dive through the churning bubbles and she guided it toward her throbbing vagina. She threw one leg over the tub's edge as she eased it into her. She gradually pushed it further in until the vibrating portion touched her clitoris. Slowly she twisted grinds against the apparatus— making rhythm and blues. She and the rabbit stayed in sync until she crooned a screaming orgasm. She muffled her pleasure quickly in fears that Mauri would hear.

As she eased it out and shut it off she shut her eyes and a satisfying feeling caressed her, body and soul. She felt so relaxed. Rocky cleaned it by squishing it around in the bubbles and smiled as she pulled it out of the water and placed it back in its pouch. Giving head always made her horny.

After fifteen minutes or so she stepped out of the tub and pulled the plug. She placed her bag back into the closet and retrieved a large fluffy cranberry colored towel. She wrapped herself up and walked back into the bedroom.

Damn, I can't believe I've been coming out here for two years. If I don't find what I'm looking for when I go to Vegas, I'm just going to marry Mauri or Thomas. I'm getting too old for this shit.

She sat on the edge of the bed and gently tugged off Mauri's sneakers. Then she removed his boxers and shorts. She kissed him on his cheek and lay beside him. She drifted off running her fingers through Mauri's hair, feeling the ultimate satisfaction after running through her vibrating hare.

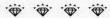

Tony opened the side door of his parents' house, which led into the kitchen. He placed his book bag down and looked at the food on the stove. Before he could open a pot his mother appeared behind him with her arms folded.

"I've already shared your food. It's wrapped in foil inside the fridge."

Her husband came in seconds after she did.

"Mommy, I can explain everything. You see I met this girl named Shaine. She is beautiful, and I have been kicking it with her for a week now. I sort of lost track of time. She's my new girlfriend."

His mother smiled. *Tony isn't much of the girlfriend type. He stays in his books and plays a lot of video games. This must be special—*"And all this time I was thinking you cut off those braids for me. You met yourself a girl?"

"So son, what does she look like," his father asked.

"Well, she is about mom's height and they got the same complexion. She wears her hair back in a ponytail and she has the most beautiful dimples I have ever seen. Yo pop, she is a dime."

Jonathan laughed. "You know she sounds a lot like someone I know."

"Who? Debbie?" Tony asked.

"Nah, your mother," Jonathan replied.

Tony looked at his mother and smiled. "Nah, she ain't as pretty as you, but she comes close."

"Mm hmm. Don't try to charm my uniform off me, boy. I know you're getting older, and I am not excusing you for coming in late, but you should have called or something."

Tony removed the foil off of the plate and placed it in the microwave.

"I am going to let you off easy this time, but you know how I feel about dinner."

"Yes ma."

"What grade is she in and where does she live?" Millicent asked.

"We're in the same grade, we used to have honors together, but I never really noticed her before."

"Make sure you use a rubber boy. The pretty ones get the same thing the ugly ones get."

"JONATHAN!" "DAD!" Tony and Millicent yelled at the same time.

"Well, at least I know where you'll be for the next couple of Friday nights. Just let me know where you are and have your behind in here for seven-thirty."

Millicent looked at the clock. It was eight-thirty. "I know your story Tony, but I wonder where your brother is, and why his black-ass hasn't come home for dinner?" Millicent placed his plate in front of him, and kissed the top of his head.

"Millicent, everyone in this house is getting some lovin' except me. Come on upstairs and show me what you're working with," Jonathan said.

"Jonathan, would you stop talking like that in front of Tony, please?"

"Shoot baby, you heard him, he has a girlfriend and you know what we were doing when we were teens." He looked at his youngest son. "I'm tellin' you, Tony, I ain't ready to be no grandfather yet, and anyone could have the 'monster' boy."

"You sound worse than the kids, Jonathan!"

Tony sat down at the table and listened to his parents disagree about his dad's choice of words. He bit into the chicken and fantasized about Shaine sucking his dick mere minutes ago.

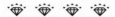

Susan lay underneath Malik's arm. She traced the scar that took up most of his back all the way up to his neck. "You were amazing!"

Malik shook his head and squeezed her tightly. He looked at the small clock radio Motel 6 provided for its guests.

"I've been thinking about you, your body, and last Friday night all week. I could definitely get used to this every Friday at the hotel thing. If we are going to catch a flick we should be getting out of here. It's already eight-thirty."

"I say we stay in here and get to know each other. Plus, you can never be too careful. We could run across the street to IHOP or 7 /Eleven, bring up some junk and watch Pay-Per View until eleven, eleven-thirtyish."

"Susan, can I ask you a question?"

"Sure."

"Why are you cheating on your husband? I need to take notes, just in case I ever jump the broom?"

"What do you mean jump the broom?"

"Back in slavery times, slaves couldn't get married legally. So, they developed their own wedding ceremony in which they jumped a broom into the land of matrimony."

"Ohhhh. Well, we just don't have good sex anymore. And when we do, he won't try anything new. I love him, but I need more. I know he has cheated on me more than once, but that doesn't bother me because he is a loving husband. He just doesn't ever want to do anything kinky."

"So you're freaky, huh?" Malik asked.

"He just lays down, does a couple of quick humps and that's it. I haven't had an orgasm in twelve years, prior to sex with you, that is."

Malik sat up in the bed and said, "Say word. You sure he's not turning the other cheeks?"

Susan gave him a puzzled look. "Word?"

Malik laughed. " I meant you're exaggerating, right?"

"No. Not at all, and I told you he is definitely not a homosexual," Susan said. She traced his hairline to his ear lobe. She gently kissed a tiny diamond stud. "If you treat me right and keep things quiet I will replace these small studs for you."

"Talk is cheap. Come on let's go get something to eat. You worked up my appetite," Malik said.

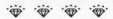

"That southern fried lobster was sinful. The restaurant was superb, Mauri. It's really everything I thought it would be."

"Uh huh, you always braggin' about them restaurants in New York, but the D is where the real food's at, baby."

Rocky looked at the green and white street sign and mouthed 'Monroe Street' as they pulled off. She had been dying for him to take her to this restaurant when she first started to come visit him in Detroit. She looked at the golden pianos that glimmered on the royal blue awnings. The statues of the two golden lions that sat in front of the restaurant looked as if they were guarding their sweet southern recipe secrets.

"Sweet Georgia Browns' is all of that. We have to make this a regular for us, baby. Thanks for having your special night where I wanted to go."

"Aw, that's cool. You know we going to the club, right?"

"Yes."

They sat silently next to each other during the twenty-minute ride in the back of the limo. As they pulled up in front, Mauri squeezed Rocky's hand. "You know I was serious about us getting hitched right?" Mauri asked.

"Not now. How could you talk about such an important matter when we're getting ready to go to the club?"

"You're right. But we gonna talk about this when we get back to the house," Mauri said with a stern look on his face. The limo opened up.

"Dang, look at this shit. The club is packed— you ready, Rock?"

Her face was lit up with excitement. "Yep, let's go," Rocky replied.

As they stepped from the limo everyone stared, whispered and or pointed in their direction. Mauri was the most eligible and tangible bachelor in the Black community. Women loved him. Rocky didn't understand why she didn't. The only time she came close to loving him is when they were out on the town and she realized how many people sweated him. She didn't love being in the limelight; she lived to be in it.

Rocky straightened the hem of her short black dress. Girls smiled and waved at Mauri, then rolled their eyes or flashed fake smiles at Rocky as they walked straight through the crowd and in the front door. Mauri gave pounds and what-ups to several people on the line. Two White bouncers in black suits opened the door for them.

"Mauri, how you doin'? Long time no see," the bouncer on the left said.

"Yeah, long time, man," Mauri replied.

"Kevin is upstairs in the private VIP, I'm sure he'll be glad to see you. Just go right up," the bouncer on the right said.

The club was hot and crammed with people. The dance floor was crowded with young people polished in fresh coats of shining perspiration. The couple entered hand in hand and boarded an elevator near the front of the club. It went up swiftly and opened onto a medium sized room with shapely waitresses and dimly lit tables around it. Each table had a flat TV screen at its center. As soon as they stepped from the elevator a tall, slim, middle aged man approached them. He grabbed Mauri's arm with both hands, and firmly shook his hand.

"Mauri, it's good to see you. Please, why don't you and your lovely girlfriend come and sit at my table. Rock Candy, right?"

"Yes," she smiled. "Call me Rocky."

As they followed him to his corner table, Rocky felt her face get numb when Jalen Chambers and Shawn Tailman from the Chicago Bulls approached them.

"Hey, playa, what's goin' on? Thanks for them bumpin' sweats you sent me, man," Shawn said as he and Mauri embraced.

"Shawn, Jalen, this is my wife Rocky."

"Pleased to meet you," Shawn said.

"How ya' doin'?" Jalen asked.

"Same here— fine thank you," Rocky replied, slightly flustered.

"You ain't send me nothin', nigga!" Jalen playfully pushed Mauri.

"Shit, you ain't ask. Have your people call my people and you know I'll make that happen. Why don't y'all come sit down with us."

"We'll holla at you later. We're going to watch some booty shaking."

Shawn looked at Rocky and smiled. "No disrespect, Rocky."

"None taken."

"Alright then, I'll catch you on the rebound," Mauri acted like he was making a jump shot as he made his last statement. They all laughed, except Rocky. *They couldn't have possibly thought that shit was funny,* she thought.

Rocky shook her head, as she followed Mauri to Kevin's table. *My God! I could shake my ass all night for that fine-ass Shawn Tailman, now that's husband material. Look at how he apologized after making that statement. Shit, Mauri better be happy he's here, or I would have bagged that shorty right here,* she thought.

"Girl you deaf?" Mauri yelled over the music.

"Huh? I'm sorry, I didn't hear you," Rocky said as she sat down.

"What are you drinkin'?"

"I'll have a Hennesy and Coke. Nah, as a matter of fact, I'll have what she's having," she said, pointing to a well-dressed woman seated next to Kevin.

"Two Apple Martinis coming right up." A tall, slender, and big-breasted blonde took their orders and disappeared into the crowd.

Kevin yelled over the music, "Rocky this is Maize."

Rocky shook her hand and smiled. "Nice to meet you, Maize."

"Likewise," Maize answered.

Before the smile left Rocky's face she had already sized Maize up.

"Mauri, I didn't know your girlfriend was so pretty. Where are you from, Rocky?" Maize asked.

"New York," Rocky replied, still smiling.

"I love New York. Do you come out here often?" Maize asked.

"Twice a month," Rocky said.

"We should exchange numbers. Whenever you come out we could hang. If Mauri is as busy as Kevin is, I know you must get bored," Maize said excitedly.

"I'd love that," Rocky lied.

"Ladies, your Apple Martinis," the waitress said as she distributed the drinks.

Rocky immediately began sipping. She smiled at Maize from behind the cold chartreuse liquid. She sat back on the cushioned seat and got lost in her thoughts. *These fuckin' mixed breed bitches make it hard for us regular Black chicks to get a man with money.*

She put her glass down on the table and laughed when everyone else at the table laughed, even though she did not hear a word— her thoughts kept her preoccupied. *Wait until I call Kay. First the fuckin' White broads was takin' all the eligible Black men, then Spanish chicks was in style— well they never really went out of style, especially since J-Lo been dancing her fat ass around and shit. Now it's the Japanese chicks, and this one has the nerve to have a little color.* She picked up her glass and swallowed its entire contents in one gulp. *These fuckin' video type bitches is gettin' all the fuckin' action.* She looked at Mauri who seemed to be enjoying Kevin's conversation, and put her glass on the table. *Shit, I better get my piece of the pie while I still look good. I'm all for that interracial shit, but Black brothers just don't make it easy for us.*

"Here you are, sweetie," the waitress said.

Rocky smiled as she picked up her fresh martini. She made small talk with Maize, and enjoyed schmoozing with all the bigwigs as they came over to check her and her Detroit man.

Later that same morning Rocky was stretched out on Mauri's bed with a dark kerchief covering her eyes. "You know I don't like shit like this baby. It's late, let's just go to sleep," Rocky said.

Mauri reinforced Rocky's blindfold, grabbed her by the shoulders and pulled her back toward the bed. "I'll be right back."

Rocky was stiff. Her hands were cuffed above her head. Her flawless body was smooth and bare. Her legs were sprawled open. Suddenly she felt drops of warm liquid in different spots on her— first her thighs, then her vaginal area. A familiar grip palmed her thighs and worked the oil in. Then Mauri stroked the oil on her vaginal area. It's greasiness, and temperature made her tingle all over. She felt his fingers spread her lips open and she squirmed at the thought of his past botched attempts at oral sex. Then a small rough feeling shot across her clitoris.

"OOOH," she moaned in delight. Moments later she felt it again, this time she noticed it was rough and warm. Her eyes rolled back into her head as it happened again and again. The abrasive feel was pleasing.

She'd never felt anything like this in her life. She opened her eyes, and was startled by the extreme darkness. *Oh the blindfold*, she remembered.

She started to thrust her mid section up and down. The small rough feeling became faster and faster. She humped and moaned forcefully, and Mauri's fingers lost their grip. She came to a complete halt when she felt fur on her vagina. She immediately tensed up. She instinctively closed her legs, and she felt fur brush across her thigh. She listened closely and almost gagged when she heard what she thought was the purring of a cat coming from the bed.

"Mauri!" Rocky screamed. "I know that's' not what I think it is. Take this fuckin shit off of my face right now. "He did not answer. "I'm not fuckin' playin' with you. Take this shit off now!" she half whined.

"Girl, don't trip," Mauri said coolly.

She heard the feline pounce onto the floor and shrieked in horror. "You sick bastard, I am going to need a rabies shot fuckin with you." She sat up and began to work her hands out of the cuffs.

"Wait, don't bruise your shit up. I got the key right here," Mauri said.

As soon as Mauri unlocked the cuffs she tore the blindfold off and smacked him on the side of his head. Tears rolled down her cheeks. She had never felt so low in her life. She covered herself with the bedspread.

"Get outta my face! Get me a hotel and have Jack's 'Fonzworth Bently' ass drive me there right fuckin' now!"

Mauri felt bad. He had never seen Rocky cry before. He didn't think she would be so upset. "Kevin and Maize do that cat shit all the—"

"Don't say a word, Maurice Nixon. Just do as I say. I want to stay at that nice hotel in Birmingham!"

Mauri got up and walked out of the room. Rocky fell forward and cried into the palm of her hand. The tears were a mixture of disgust at the present situation, and the waste of two years of her life. She picked up the bottle of oil from the night table. "Cat nip oil!"

She threw it to the floor. She didn't bother to pack anything that wasn't already in her bags. Dressing quickly, she stormed out of the bedroom and headed straight to the front door. Rocky sat on the front steps of the house, and waited outside. She felt like she owed an apology to herself, but she just looked ahead at the dark Detroit sky. There was no noise, only the silent loudness of bright shining stars. She could never have all of this at home. There was always too much noise in Brooklyn for quiet, and too many streetlights and tall, lit buildings for bright stars, but was it worth this? She closed her legs tightly and rested her elbows on her knees. After five minutes she picked up her cell.

"Kay, you sleep?" Rocky whispered.

"I was. It's damn near three in the morning. What's wrong with you?" Kay said.

"This fuckin' asshole had a kitten eating my pussy. I feel so violated," Rocky confessed.

Kay was silent. She sat up in her bed, looked at her husband, and placed a soft kiss on his cheek. She looked up toward the ceiling and thanked God for him. She took a deep breath, stretched, got out of her bed, walked into the bathroom and closed the door. "You have to be kidding me!"

"No, and I'm on my way to a hotel right now— well in a few. You think I should go get a shot?"

"I don't think it would hurt. Girl, ain't NO fuckin' money worth that shit. Bring your ass home first thing tomorrow," Kay demanded.

"Nah, I'm going to relax in a four star," Rocky said.

"I ain't one of those stupid ass niggas you be fuckin. If you wanted to relax you would bring your ass home. What are you up to? Get that asshole to send you home. It's been two years too long since you met him in Vegas and now—"

"That's it. I don't know what I would do without you. You're a genius. Call me in the morning." Rocky felt a little bit better. *This could be my ticket out of this relationship, and the reasoning behind me going to Vegas*, she thought.

"So you're going to get him to send you home?" Kay said.

"Nope. I'm going to get Mauri to send me to Vegas next month," Rocky said.

"There has to be some method to your madness, but since I can't figure it out, I am going back to bed. Call me tomorrow," Kay yawned. "Bye."

A burgundy Escalade pulled up in front of the house. Jack stepped out and placed Rocky's bags in the trunk. She slowly walked towards the truck. Rocky reluctantly turned around and looked at the house. Mauri stood on the steps looking pitiful. He waved.

"Yo, you do not understand how sorry I am," Mauri called out softly.

Rocky got into the passenger seat of the truck, and did not say a word. She looked at Mauri through tinted windows as she and Jack pulled off. She stared out the back window at Mauri's luxurious sixteen-room home as they drove down his long, winding, stone-paved driveway onto Woodward Street. His home didn't look as intimidating as its top became camouflaged among the roofs of other mansions and large houses. She continued to stare as they exited the posh Palmer Woods Estates and turned onto Eight-Mile Road. They drove a few blocks then turned onto Seven-Mile Road entering the urban streets of Detroit. Rocky noticed that the people on the street corners stopped to watch the Escalade drive by. She looked at the illuminated green numbers over the radio.

Three-thirty.

Why are they out here so late, she thought?

The color of the streets even seemed to change. At Palmer Woods where Mauri lived the pavement was black and smooth. Once they crossed the borders the pavement was tan, with cracks in it and crackheads all over it. There was music and laughter, cussing and horns blowing. In the fifteen minutes they had been driving, the contrast was dramatic. As they hopped on I-94, Jack and Rocky looked at each other. They drove for ten minutes in dead silence until Rocky revived the mood.

"Do you know where I am going?"

"Yes, Mauri made all the arrangements from the house. You will be staying at the Townsend twenty minutes out of Detroit, in Birmingham."

"Jack, you're married right?"

Jack looked at Rocky, not knowing where the conversation was heading. "Yes, I am. Why?"

"How long have you been with your wife?"

"For fifteen years."

"Are you serious? How could you stay with one person so long?" She stared at Jack. "You don't look a day over thirty."

"I'm the same age as Mauri. Me and my wife have been together since our junior year in high school." Jack looked over at Rocky momentarily, and cleared his throat. "Listen, I ain't tryin' to get into y'all business or nothin' but I ain't seen him so upset in a long time. Rocky, he don't be havin' no women up in his house." He hesitated and then sighed. "Never mind. We'll be there in fifteen minutes."

"Go ahead, Jack. Speak your mind."

"Well, don't do nothin' stupid. I mean— I thought— man he wanna marry you, Rocky. Don't tell him I told you but he's been talkin' about it a lot lately. He told me he ran it by you, but you didn't take him seriously." He slowed the car down and smacked the top of the steering wheel with the bottom of both his hands. "He's gettin' boo-koo money, and I hate to see some gold diggin' bitch take your place. At least I know you love my boy. I mean I don't know what y'all fought about but it can't be worth leaving."

"I just need some time to think, Jack. I ain't leaving him." *At least not yet,* she thought.

After a few minutes Jack interrupted the silence. "Rocky, did you see how the ladies looked at him when y'all was going in the club?"

Rocky continued to look out of the window. "Yes."

"Well, they practically throw their draws at him when you ain't around. You keep his big head in its place. I done seen a lot of women come and go but you by far are the classiest and I like you."

"Thank you." Rocky turned her head slowly toward Jack and smiled.

"Fifteen years, huh? You ever disrespected your wife?"

"Not intentionally. But you know how sensitive you females can be."

"Your boy disrespected me something awful today. I don't know if I can forgive him. I've got to reach deep down to do that," Rocky said mournfully.

"We're here. I know that boy feels you somethin' awful. Just keep that in mind. Sit tight for a second and I'll take care of your luggage and your key."

He closed the door softly. Within minutes he was back. Rocky got out of the truck and gave Jack a quick hug. "I'll see you in two weeks," Jack smiled.

As soon as Rocky opened the door to her room the phone rang. There was a box of chocolates on the pillow and an envelope on top of the box. She quickly ran over to the mini fridge and took out a bottled water. She leapt onto the bed, stretched over to the other side and picked up the phone.

"Hello?" Rocky said.

"Hey Rocky just hear me out. I'm sorry. I thought this would be something that you would really like. Don't do nothin' drastic, okay?" Mauri said.

"Would you like it if I stuck a fucking gerbil in your ass?" Rocky snarled.

"You just like to get your sex on and I thought this would take you where I can't. Sometimes I think I just don't do it for you."

You don't say, she thought.

"Kevin's girl loves that shit. He had his cat take a shot and made sure the shit was safe. My kitten went through the same thing. Once I rubbed that cat-nip oil on you— you should have seen your face, it looked like you was feelin' it."

"You should have asked me first, Mauri," Rocky sighed.

"I— love— I love you, Rocky. I want you in my life. I know I don't tell you that often, but I want you to marry me."

Rocky was quiet. She stared at the ceiling as she twirled the white coiled cord around her middle finger.

"I was going to save this secret for when I give you your ring and shit but— I am working on a new store in a mall in Chicago. I want to have a Mr. Maurice's women's chain, and if you become my wife I'll call it Rock Candy."

Rocky shot straight up on the bed. She quickly unraveled the cord from around her finger and covered her mouth. Tears flooded her eyes. She blocked out Mauri's voice, and fantasized. *Rock Candy. I could have one in New York and shit. I've been in college for years and never figured out what I wanted to do. I would be good at that shit. Fashion is my life. I could put this Bachelor in Business and Finance I am about to acquire in January to use.*

"Rocky?" Mauri said.

Rocky tried to conceal her excitement and fall back into her annoyed demeanor. "I'm listening," she said with an over exaggerated attitude.

"You would be the buyer and owner. Everything would be in your name; you would get all the profits. Plus, I want someone to fly back and forth to Milan and be my personal buyer— this is how serious I am, Rocky."

Mauri didn't feel like he was making any progress. He let out a long sigh and flopped on his bed. He placed his hand on his forehead and rested his elbow on his knee. He looked down into the eyes of the kitten that rested at his feet. He gave it a gentle kick and watched as it ran out of the room.

Rocky sat on the edge of the hotel bed with her elbow resting on her knee and her hand covering her mouth. She was ecstatic.

I think I really fucked this one up, damn. I'ma kill Kevin and that ol' freaky ass bitch of his, he thought. He looked on the floor at the bottle of cat-nip and oil he'd rubbed Rocky down with and shook his head.

Mauri's emotions ran rampant. His face felt like pins and needles were pricking it from the inside out. His stomach was now a fifty-pound weight chillin' on his lower abdomen and he suddenly got the urge to take a shit. He didn't know what to say next. He remembered having this feeling only once before, when he lost his first store down on West Seven-Mile. There was an entire minute of silence between him and the phone.

Now is the perfect time to hit him with this Vegas shit, Rocky thought as her emotions exploded, silently. She didn't know whether she should laugh or scream. Tears ran down her cheeks as she smiled. She did a small victory dance on the bed that resembled the running man. She took a deep breath and suppressed her feelings of joy. She shook her head and took several large gulps of her bottled water— this extinguished her smile and she spoke in a serious tone.

"Listen, Maurice. You know how I feel about you, and I don't plan to let this jeopardize our future but I just need time to get my head straight."

Mauri lifted his head and repositioned himself on the bed. "Jack just called me and said you felt disrespected. You know I see a lot of cat in my line of business."

Rocky was more annoyed. She sucked her teeth and spoke firmly. "No pun intended, huh?"

"Fuck," Mauri whispered harshly. "That was a bad choice of words, I apologize. You know I've been through a lot of tail. Women approach me all the time, but you, you do something for me. I want kids and shit, and I want them with you. You smell me?"

"Yes, Mauri.

"I truly apologize, Rocky. You accept?"

"Yes, I do. But I really need some time to think. You threw a lot of shit at me tonight. And I still don't believe you had a cat between my legs—YUCK!" She inhaled deeply. "Listen, I wanted you to take me to the fight July 4th weekend. But now I think you should send me by myself. Get me a ticket to the fight. I already reserved a room for us at the Venetian from the 4th to the 7th. I just want you to pay for the shit, and I am going solo."

"Yeah, whatever. If that's going to fix this shit then whatever it takes, Rocky. Did you read my letter, and get the box of chocolates I sent up to your room?"

"I just got in here when the phone rang. I did see the chocolate though. Thanks baby."

"You ain't say nothing about my idea for your store and shit."

"It's a wonderful idea. I really don't know what to say, but let's discuss that another time."

"Alright. Can I come and talk to you?"

"That's the reason I want to go to Vegas by myself . . . so I can have some time to think about what you mean to me and my future."

"Whose name is the hotel under yours or mine?"

"Mine."

"I'll have my secretary do your Vegas shit. When you come back out here in two weeks, we'll kiss and make up. Since you need time."

"No, baby. I want a timeout until after the fight."

"It's the end of May! Rocky, that's a month and some change. You're taking this shit overboard!" Mauri stood up and walked toward the mirror. He looked at himself and picked up a photo of him and Rocky from his dresser. Looking at it, he smiled as he spoke. "You know I can make everything we spoke about happen, right? Don't do no stupid shit. A month and a half is a long ass time."

"I know you can, and don't worry cheating is the last thing on my mind. I definitely don't want to break up with you. I just want you to have some time to think about things. I want to think about this marriage shit, and that cat shit. Can I marry a man that likes to do things like that? I don't know."

"I ain't talkin' about the marriage shit no more, because when I do propose to you, it is going to be one proposal that will blow your mind."

"Okay, baby, I'm going to get in the shower. I'll speak to you later."

"Later."

Rocky put the phone down and jumped up and down on the bed like an adolescent at a slumber party. "Whooooooo weeeeeee!" she screamed. "I'll have Rock Candies all over the country. My store will be like Filth Mart but jazzier—" Suddenly she stopped jumping, and her thoughts brought her down to reality. *I can't marry Mauri. I barely like him. I refuse to settle for this shit.*

She sat on the edge of the bed and peeled off her clothing. She talked under her breath as she dropped each article to the floor. "Besides, when I meet Mr. Right, and I get my degree, he can finance my stores and I can be the brains and beauty behind them. I do thank Mauri for the idea though."

Rocky picked up the remote and switched on the television. She walked into the bathroom and turned on the shower. She removed a complimentary shower cap from the sink and neatly stuck all the stray ends of her hair underneath it. As soon as she stepped into the shower she vigorously scrubbed her vaginal area with a soapy washrag. She thought of how unusually pleasing the kittens tongue had felt on her clitoris and shuddered at the thought. "I don't care how good it felt, it was still disgusting."

She rubbed harder and harder until she felt herself getting a little sore and stopped. She let the water run across her face and closed her eyes. She thought of Thomas, and decided to give him a call first thing in the morning. She left the shower feeling sore, but cleansed. She pulled back the comforter and jumped into bed. The cold sheets felt smooth against her body and gave her a quick chill. She turned onto her stomach, and slept.

Rocky sprang up suddenly with severe flashes of pain all over her head. She used her arm and instinct to search the end table for her cellular phone. She looked at the clock and grabbed the phone.

"It's almost eleven. I never sleep this late," she mumbled. She stretched her arms over head and cleared her throat. "Damn, I need to turn my ringer down. This shit is entirely too loud. Hello?"

"Tell me you're in New York and not out there with that freak-a-zoid." Kay said.

"No. No. Yes."

"What?"

"I'm right outside of Detroit, in Birmingham, at a four star by myself."

"You just waking up? Cause you sound like shit."

"Yeah."

"Alright. Call me during my lunch hour. Don't forget."

"Okay."

Rocky put her cell phone down, picked up the hotel phone and dialed out. She sat up in the bed and flipped through the channels.

"Good morning, may I please speak with Thomas Rolland please."

"May I ask who is calling?"

"Raquel Jones."

"This is in reference to…"

"It's personal."

"One moment and I'll see if he is available."

Moments later he answered. "Hey, Rocky. I thought you forgot about me."

"Never that. How's my baby doing?"

"Bogged down with work, as usual. We're in the middle of discovery."

"What's that?

"Well, as you know I am working on this big breach of contract action, and it's going to trial. I am doing depositions every day next week, so I am getting all of my paper work together."

"It sounds like an awful lot."

"How is your family down there? Are the books up to par, business running okay?"

"Yeah, everything is just fine," Rocky smiled.

"You need me to pick you up from the airport on Sunday?"

"Yes."

"You got it. Make sure you leave my secretary your flight information some time today."

"I miss you, Thomas," Rocky said softly.

"I miss you too, Rocky. I can't stay on too long. But I am really glad you called, I was becoming a little bit anxious," Thomas said.

"All you had to do was call, you know?"

"I know."

"Don't work too hard. After all, it is Saturday. I was supposed to come back on Monday. But I am changing my flight to tomorrow."

"I'll try not too work to hard baby, but Saturday is just another day of the week to me."

"I'll call your secretary back with my new flight information. Please let her know I am going to call so she can bypass the attitude."

"Was she rude to you?"

"Not at all, just very bland."

"That's just her personality, nothing personal. I'll see you tomorrow."

"Okay, bye."

She placed the phone on the receiver and picked it right back up. She surveyed all the icons on the phone. "Housekeeping, front desk, operator, and room service, ahh, here we go, the Concierge." Rocky pushed the button and a woman answered.

"Good morning, Concierge."

"Yes, I am in Room 112 and I was wondering if there were any appointments at the day spa for a massage before two."

"I'll check availability, Ms. Jones." Rocky heard the swift tapping of keys. It seemed as if the woman was typing eighty words a minute. "We have an opening at twelve-thirty. Shall I lock that in for you?"

"Perfect. I would also like to make an appointment for three o' clock with Carol C. at Bordan's. Just tell her that it's Rock Candy from New York, and she will squeeze me in. Lastly, I would like an appointment for twenty minutes in the tanning salon at two o'clock. Charge all services to my room please."

"If there are any problems with any of your appointments I will call you back. You have a nice day Ms. Jones and thank you for staying at the Birmingham Townsend."

"Thank you." Rocky disconnected the call. Now, let's see— that gives me just enough time to go work out down stairs at the gym." As she rose to go into the shower the phone rang. "It's probably Mauri— hello?"

"Hey, what up though, I called you this morning and you were gone. Where are you?" Mauri asked.

"I was sleep. I am going to the spa, and getting my hair done today."

"You've got your day planned, huh? Just charge everything to the room. I am really sorry about last night. I don't want this to fuck us up."

"It won't. I'm just relaxing and taking some Rocky time. When I come back out here in a month we will iron everything out. I don't want to talk about marriage again until I graduate in January and then we can delve into that. Right now I need to focus on getting my degree."

"No chance I can see you before you leave Monday?"

"Mauri, give me a chance to think things out. I just don't want to make the wrong decisions, besides I want you to change my ticket so I can leave tomorrow."

"You lucky I'm finalizing these two stores or I would come down there and get your ass, no matter what you say."

"I miss you already, sweetie. This is the first time I ever came down here and stayed for such a short period of time, Mauri."

Truth be told she was happy to be away from him. She blocked out his voice with thoughts of new gear she was getting ready to buy for her trip, and what accessories she would wear with her new fits. The only thing she seemed to hear him say was goodbye.

❖ ❖ ❖ ❖

"Monique, hang on, it's my other line— hello?"

"Joann, it's Yanick. I'm outside your apartment building."

Joann looked out the window and spotted Yanick's car.

"I will be right down." She clicked back to the other line. "Well, this is it. She's outside."

"Call me with details. You have been talking about this all weekend. Simone and I are going out to dinner, but we'll be in early."

Yanick fiddled with her hair in the rear view mirror, and moistened her lips with her tongue.

Joann ran down the two flights of steps. She slowed down as she hit the sidewalk not wanting to seem too anxious. She sat in the car and smiled. Yanick's curly mane hung wildly over her breasts and on her shoulders.

"Hey, we look like twins," Yanick said. Joann looked puzzled. "You have on blue jeans and a wife beater, and I have on blue jeans shorts and a white tee. I guess great minds think a like. So what do you want to go and see? It's my treat."

"I'll take care of it, keep your money. Let's see what's playing."

"I haven't repaid you for the Similac yet. What theater do you want to go to?"

"Don't worry about that let's go to 23rd Street and Eighth Avenue."

"Sounds like a plan," Yanick smiled.

They laughed throughout the movie. Yanick caught Joann staring at her during the movie. Joann was pondering how she could make the night last. Yanick got in a couple of brief stares, but was never caught. They discussed their likes and dislikes the entire car ride home. Yanick pulled up in front of Joann's building and leaned back on the headrest.

"I had a really good time," Yanick said.

"I haven't had so much attention in a long time. At least eight different sets of guys came up to us. You definitely look good," Joann confessed.

"Girl you got some of that action, too don't front. And I thought nobody would look at me since I had the baby. I'm all flabby and everything," Yanick said.

"Good niggas like a little something to hold on to," Joann said. *And I am that nigga*, she thought giving Yanick a nod of approval. As they stared awkwardly at each other the nearby music of an ice-cream truck could be heard.

"OOH, I want a popsicle!" Yanick screamed.

"Turn off the car and we'll go grab one," Joann said.

The two ladies hopped out of the car and ran across the street, as the big, white truck drove slowly down the block. Joann flagged it down, and they both stood at the window.

"I'll have vanilla in a cup with chocolate sprinkles," Joann said out of breath.

"I want a rocket."

Joann paid the ice-cream man as Yanick walked toward her car. Joann caught up and pulled her gently by the hand. "It's kind of hot out here. Let's go upstairs and eat these before they melt," Joann suggested.

The two laughed all the way up the steps and into the apartment.

"Wow, this is a nice apartment. How many bedrooms?" Yanick asked.

"Three."

"All this space for yourself?" Yanick was skeptical.

Joann nodded her head, walked into the kitchen, put her ice cream in the freezer, and started to wash the dishes. Yanick looked around the apartment. It was decorated entirely in gray. From the leather couch, to the kitchen appliances, Venetian blinds and the walls.

"You sure do like gray, huh?" Yanick called out.

"It's not hard to tell what my favorite color is. It's not too much, is it?"

"It is a lot of gray, but it looks really nice. It's so modern."

"Thanks. Anytime you need a break from your parents, you and Seven can come and stay for a couple of days. I have plenty of room. I'm going to the bathroom, the remote is on the couch."

Yanick bent over and smelled the flowers. She noticed a note card sitting among them. She looked toward the bathroom door then pulled the card out of the small envelope and read it.

'I really enjoyed dinner. But I really enjoyed after dinner. I can tell you did too. So why haven't you returned my calls? Sam.'

Yanick shoved the card into the envelope quickly and dropped it back into the flowers. Joann walked to the couch, sat down and reached for the remote. "You want to watch some TV?"

Yanick was to busy killing her popsicle to answer, and Joann studied her every lick. Yanick shoved the popsicle in and out of her mouth slowly over and over again. When she realized she had an audience she stopped and wiped her mouth with the wrinkled napkin that was wrapped around the bottom of the popsicle's stick.

"Damn, that popsicle sure looks good. I should have gotten one."

"I used to love these rocket pops. When I was small my brother used to buy me these all the time." Yanick sucked the popsicle from its pointed top to the wooden stick. Joann slid closer to her, until their thighs touched. She reached over and placed her hand over Yanick's, so they were both holding the popsicle. "Can I have a lick?" Joann asked.

Without waiting for a reply, Joann began to suck on the popsicle. Yanick felt uneasy and hot. Yanick licked her lips and sucked on the popsicle directly after her. Joann leaned closer to her holding onto her soft warm hand and the edge of the cold popsicle. She quickly licked Yanick's lips and kissed her passionately. Joann caressed Yanick's small breasts with her free hand. Yanick moaned loudly and released her grip on the popsicle. She wiggled her hand free from Joann's and placed it under her shirt. Her breasts were plump and soft, she gave them a gentle squeeze.

"OH SHIT, OH SHIT— Oh my God, what am I doing?" Yanick shrieked. She jumped up and straightened her clothes as she spoke. "I have to go now."

"Okay, I guess we'll hook up soon. Are you okay?"

The phone rang and Yanick jumped. Joann grabbed her hand and Yanick pulled it away. "Relax, Yanick," Joann said softly.

"I had a wonderful time, Joann, but I don't get down like that."

"That's your fear talking, because your mouth doesn't feel that way. There's nothing to be scared of," Joann said after she licked her lips.

Yanick pushed away from her. "I'm serious. I—," she was interrupted by the answering machine.

'HI THIS IS JOEY CRACK. LEAVE YOUR MESSAGE AT THE TONE' "Hey, Joann, This is SAM, AKA, WHY HAVEN'T YOU RETURNED MY CALLS? HOPE YOU LIKE THE FLOWERS, CALL ME.'

Yanick listened to the message and smirked inside. *I knew Sam was a chick,* she thought. She looked at Joann and continued. "I am not gay, Joann," she said firmly.

Joann shrugged her shoulders, then spoke. "I know that."

"So why would you come on to me like that? I think I better go."

"I didn't mean to make you feel strange. Let me walk you to your car."

"I'm good. I can make it by myself." Yanick walked out the door and Joann locked it behind her.

"She'll be back," Joann whispered, as she walked to the window with no remorse. She sat and waited. Within seconds she watched Yanick's curves switch toward her car. "Damn, look at that ass!" Joann exclaimed. She watched as Yanick got into her car.

Yanick started to call George, but she couldn't tell him. She floored the gas and sped home thinking of nothing else. *What just happened?* The question repeated its self in her mind. When she got home she found Seven was fast asleep in her bassinet. She plopped on her bed and dialed out. "Hello George? It's me."

"What happened?"

"She kissed me."

"GET THE FUCK OUT OF HERE. What did you do?" George said loudly.

"I got scared and left. I told her I don't get down like that."

"Word?"

"But you know what, on the low, that shit felt good and soft. I touched her titties and my chocha was on fire." The line was silent. "George!!"

"I can't believe what you're saying."

"Her apartment is banging, she's cute and I think I can get her to buy Seven a crib. Come by my house."

"I'll call you tomorrow. Later, Yanick."

"Bye." Yanick stared at the cracks in her ceiling for hours thinking about what had taken place between her and the policewoman.

Have I been in the closet all of my life and haven't known it? Am I gay? Why can't I get her off my mind? She felt so soft though. When her thoughts became too much to handle she dialed out again.

The phone rang. Joann looked over at the alarm clock. It was two-thirty in the morning. She turned over and ignored it. She could hear her loud voice blaring over the speaker of answering machine in the kitchen. She turned on her back and sucked her teeth.

"Joey Crack? You're mad funny. It's Yanick. I know you're sleep but—" Joann leapt to the side and grabbed the phone off of the nightstand. She moistened her mouth. "Hi, pretty."

"I'm sorry I left on such a sour note today, but I honestly didn't know how I felt. I never kissed a woman before, and I definitely didn't expect to like it," Yanick said coyly.

"MM, so you liked that."

"Yeah— I did. I have never been kissed like that before."

"That's because you have never been kissed by a woman. I would never treat you like Seven's father. You need to give me a chance. Not only will I treat you better, but I can fuck you better, too."

Yanick became instantly flushed from embarrassment and curiosity.

"Fuck me? How you figure? You ain't got no dick," she said.

"I bet I can make you feel better than your ex. You need somebody that's going to be into Yanick. Not just your looks or your bangin' body, but Yanick. Once someone taps into those things, then you will have the best sex you ever had."

"That popsicle shit was really sexy. Is that how you got Sam hooked?" Yanick asked.

Joann sat up in her bed and scratched her head. "Say word? How you know about her?"

"She left you a message as I was leaving your house, remember? And she gave you those beautiful flowers on your coffee table."

"Let me find out you're sneaky."

"Nah, just very observant."

"When am I going to see you again?" Joann asked.

"When is your next day off?"

"The day after tomorrow. How about we go out then?"

"Sounds like a plan. Call me later on today."

"Okay, and listen Yanick, don't feel strange, there is nothing more natural than two women diggin' on each other. Goodnight."

"Bye."

Joann hung up the phone, tossed and turned a few times and fell fast asleep. Yanick stared at the ceiling. She could still feel the officer's soft touch on her breasts, and her soft kiss. She hadn't felt this excited in months. She walked over to her daughter and looked at her fast asleep in her wicker bassinet. She lay down on her back, licked her index finger and rubbed her clitoris until she was soaking wet. Yanick humped her fingers, closed her eyes and thought about Joann's soft touch. She tried to picture her standing in that very spot, on that first day playing with her stomach as she pulled her finger in and out of her vagina. Her low, moaning orgasm caused Seven to whimper several times, but she did not wake up. Yanick balled up into a fetal position, placed her thumb in her mouth and fell asleep thinking, *this shit just might work out.*

4

And I'm Crooklyn's Finest

Yanick opened the door, only to find both her parents sitting on the couch. She smiled and turned toward Joann. "Ma, Dad, this is Joann."

They smiled at her. Her mother stood up and shook Joann's hand. "It is so nice to finally meet you. Yanick talks about you all the time and we really appreciate what you have done for our granddaughter," the mother said with a strong Latino accent.

"Did they finish painting the room?"

"Yes, they did and again we both thank you," Yanick's father said.

"The furniture will be here on June 6th."

"That's this Friday, no? her mother asked.

"Yes, Ma. Seven and I are going to stay with Joann until the furniture comes and the paint dries."

The smile on Yanick's mother's face faded quickly. "Oh, there is no need for you to leave. You can stay on the couch and Seven can sleep next to you in her bassinet."

"Maaaa, don't worry, I'll be fine. Joann has a three bedroom apartment."

"Yani, you're going to leave just like that? You have no clothes for you and the baby?"

"Yes, I do Ma, I already packed them. They're in Joann's truck."

"Truck? You drive a truck? I thought you were a cop?" the mother asked.

"No ma, not a truck truck, it's like a jeep. Come on Jo, let's go."

Joann looked Yanick up and down. Her eyes stopped at her ass as she walked out of the door. Yanick's mother followed Joann's eyes as Joann watched her daughter walk out the door.

"Again, it's very nice to meet you," Joann said as she walked out the door.

Yanick carried her daughter in a carrier that hung in front of her. The baby's feet dangled and kicked playfully as she walked down the steps. Joann walked directly behind her, watching her ass jiggle down the stairs. Once they were out of sight, Yanick's mother closed the door.

"I really don't trust that girl. Did you see how she looked at Yanick?"

"What are you yapping about?" Yanick's father complained.

"¡Ella es una pata!" Yanick's mother screamed.

"¡Por favor!"

"She was just staring at her butt, she's spending all this money renovating her room, and they spend so much time together. What kind of friend does that for a friend?" Yanick's mother said.

"A friend with money. She just had the room painted and bought the baby a furniture set."

"Ai, yo no sé pero no me gusta. I just don't trust it. . ."

"Your parents are really cute, Yanick." Joann said as they stood in the lobby of Yanick's building. I want you to drop me to work. I only have to go in for a couple of hours. I have no groceries in the house so I guess we can catch a bite to eat after I get off of work."

"Can we go to Applebee's?" Yanick asked.

"Whatever your heart desires. I get off at eight meet me outside Juniors at eight-fifteen."

"But I thought we were going to Applebee's?"

"I know, but it's brighter on that side of the street. Let's be out. I have to been in by eleven. I'm doing some over time to pay for my Seven's new room."

Yanick looked around the lobby of her apartment building. There was no one there but her and Joann. She kissed her lips passionately. "Thank you, Joann. Thank you so much."

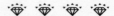

Brooklyn High stood five stories tall and encompassed four city blocks. The entrance was on Fourth Avenue. Students and staff climbed twenty stone steps to reach the school's entrance. It was built in the early 1900's, and aside from a few touch-ups, the structure never needed to be refurbished. The hallways of Brooklyn High were filled with boys and girls rushing to class. Some dragged book-bags on wheels while others carried books in their hands and bags on their backs.

"I hate Wednesdays," Shaine said to Tony.

"It's already fourth period, so Wednesday will be done soon. Meet me after school and we'll walk home together," Tony replied. He kissed Shaine on the lips and watched her walk into the classroom. He turned around to find Latonji and her crew walking toward him.

"What up, ladies?" he said.

"Hey, Tony. You all laced in green. Let me find out you Brooklyn's Finest and shit," Latonji said with a smile.

"I can't call it," Tony replied.

"Sweat blessed you?" Latonji asked.

"Something like that," Tony said.

"Who was that girl I saw you kissin' and shit?" Latonji asked in an annoyed tone.

"Why? What's it to you?" Tony asked smiling.

Latonji stepped so close into Tony's face that her breasts brushed his chest. "Just asking." Latonji gave a light tug on his doo-rag, smiled, and walked off. "I will be seeing you soon."

Excitement welled in him as he rushed to his next class. That's when he noticed he hadn't seen Kahmelle all day. He pulled out his phone and walkied him.

"Hey what up?" came loudly through the speaker on Tony's phone.

"Nada, nigga, where you at?" Tony asked.

"Getting my dick sucked, in my bed."

"By who?"

"Camille and one of them other broads she was with— hold up hold up what's your name, shorty?"

Tony could hear the girl in the background saying her name. "You better bring your ass to school."

"There's always tomorrow, son. One."

"One." Tony laughed and scurried through the empty halls to class.

Later that evening, the Hendrickson family sat around the table. The sound of silverware clanking against plates prevented the room from being completely silent, along with gums smacking and occasional finger licking.

"Mom, this is slamming," Malik said.

"Thank you, son."

"This does taste really good, Ma. Can Shaine come over for dinner Friday night? This is going to be our three-week anniversary. I would like for you guys to meet her."

"She got any older siblings I might know? I need to give this chick a thorough check-out," Malik said.

"Nah, she's an only child."

"Yeah, like I would have been if you wasn't born, punk." Malik said as Tony punched him in the leg underneath the table. Malik swung his knee into Tony's thigh and almost sent him flying out his chair. They laughed.

"Cut all that nonsense out at the table."

"Yes, Mom," Malik said.

"Yes, Ma," Tony said.

As Millicent got up from the table and went into the kitchen Tony's phone suddenly started to beep loudly.

"What's that, son?"

Malik looked over at his brother with a puzzled look on his face.

"That's just my phone beeping, Dad."

He looked at the phone and 'Alert Sweat' appeared across the screen.

"I didn't know you had a phone. Why you ain't give me the number?" Malik asked.

Tony was nervous. The only person to walkie him since he had the phone was Kahmelle. It beeped repeatedly and loudly. He didn't know what to say. He shut it off.

"Cause it ain't really a phone. They walkie-talkie phones, you know I can't afford no cell bill. It's a Nextel without the phone service. Me and Kahmelle got them so we could always talk to each other. Excuse me." Tony sprang up from the table and Malik reached over to grab the phone.

"Let me see it, man."

"Nah," Tony shouted. He ran up the steps to his bedroom, slammed the door, lay across his bed and turned on the phone. As soon as it came on, it beeped again. He answered.

"Yeah, yeah, what up?" Tony said.

Sweat's voice came on loudly. "Be on the corner of Flatbush and Dekalb in an hour. Right in front of Junior's, dig?"

"Yeah."

As soon as he put his phone on his hip it beeped loudly again. Malik came to the door as the beeping ceased.

"Yo, what up? Why you actin' funny?"

"Ain't nobody actin' funny," Tony replied.

The phone beeped again. Tony looked at the screen and 'Alert Kahmelle' appeared. He tossed the phone to his brother who stood between the doorway and the door. Malik looked at the phone and saw Kahmelle's name across the screen. He tossed the phone back.

"Don't nobody want to see your stinking ass phone now. Yo, dig, you know you can always talk to me, right?"

"Yeah."

"Alright, one baby brother."

"One."

As soon as his brother closed the door he looked for the volume button on his phone. He turned the speaker down and then answered.

"Yeah, yeah what up, Kah?"

"Tony, they walkied you?" Kahmelle asked.

"Yep. I am on my way to your house now, one."

Tony went into his drawer and pulled out a green doo-rag and tied it tightly on his head. Then he took off his blue T-shirt and squirmed into a green one. He took his wallet out of his back pocket and placed it on his computer desk. He walked down the steps and his mother and father were sitting at the table drinking coffee.

"Listen, Ma Kahmelle just walkied me. We're going to catch a movie."

"Have your behind in here at a decent hour, it's a school night," Millicent added.

"But Ma, it's June 4th, school will be over in 23 days!"

"You heard your Momma, boy— twelve no later."

"Twelve? You might as well let him stay out until sunrise, Jon."

"Millie please—"

Tony left through the kitchen exit. Once he hit the street an uneasy feeling overtook him. He really did not know what to expect.

Inside the Hendrickson home, Malik sat in the living room with the television blaring. As 'Chapelle's Show' watched him, he thought about his little brother.

I haven't really been paying much attention to him lately. He's been in late for dinner several times and he was acting mad suspect at the table when that phone went off. I need to hang out with him more and put my ears to the street— make sure he's up to good.

His own cell phone interrupted his thoughts. He looked at Susan's name flash across its small screen, and placed the phone back into the clip. "I don't feel like any pussy tonight— you are wearing me out," he said quietly.

Seconds after his cell phone stopped ringing his house phone started. His mother quickly picked it up. "Hello?"

"Hi, is Malik there?"

"Sure, one second please. Leeko, the phone is for you. Sounds like one of those bill collectors."

Malik got up and ran to the phone. "Hello?"

"Hi. How are you?"

Malik rolled his eyes. "I'm fine Susan, what's up with you?"

"Do you think you can take the 30th off? That's the last Monday of the month."

"Yeah. Why?"

"Do you have a passport?"

"Yes."

"I am planning a week long vacation in Jamaica. I would love for you to spend the first weekend with me, if that is all right with you. I also took the liberty of calling a friend of mine at NYU Law School, who is on the board. You're in there."

"Are you serious?"

"Yeah. You were in even before I made the call. You are also eligible for a scholarship that pays 70% of your tuition. The deadline was last month, but I have pulled some strings. If I write you a recommendation, you'll still get it. So let's call this a celebration vacation."

"I really don't know what to say? Can I see you tonight?" Malik asked.

"No, my husband will be in soon, and we have reservations for a late dinner, but maybe tomorrow."

"Thanks a lot, Susan."

"I have my travel agent on the other line. I just wanted to make sure I had the correct spelling of your name. Malik is spelled M-A-L-I-K and Hendrickson is H-E-N-D-R-I-C-K-S-O- N."

"Correct."

"What is your middle initial?"

"M. You sure your travel agent won't say anything to your husband?"

"We are flying in on different flights and different days through different travel agencies. You arrive Friday, June 27[th,] in the evening. I arrive the following afternoon. A car will pick you up from your house and the airport in Jamaica. This must be confidential. I'll see you tomorrow, handsome."

"Okay!" As soon as he hung up the phone he started screaming. "Ma, Dad, guess what? I am in NYU! I made it into their law school!"

"Honey, that is wonderful news. Did you finally get that mail you were looking for?" his mother asked.

"No, but a friend of mine from work just called. She knows some important people at NYU law and she just told me the news. I might even get a scholarship that pays more than half my tuition."

"Son, that is wonderful! You know me and your mom are going to help you out anyway we can," Jonathan said proudly.

"So, this friend from work, is she a love interest? I ain't getting no younger, I am looking forward to some grandbabies around here. From you, and not your little brother," Millicent added.

"No. Just you know— definitely not any one to start looking for grandchildren from".

"You haven't been serious about anyone since—"

"I know, Ma, don't start that again. I am just not ready for another serious relationship."

"But that was over—"

"I'm going out to get a drink. Don't wait up," Malik said annoyed and walked out of the house.

"You see what you did, Millie. You can't rush the boy."

"I know but I am so concerned. He needs to start dating again."

"Let him finish school first. Then we can worry about that. He's a grown-ass man, and he'll start dating again when he's ready. Our son is going to be a lawyer."

The couple engaged in a long embrace. Jonathan let his hands slide down to his wife's rear end.

"Jonathan, don't you ever get tired? You're worse than the boys."

"How you think you trapped me? Aside from your beautiful smile, deep dimples, your good cookin', your witty sense of humor—"

"Don't forget about how smart I am—"

"That, too. Aside from all of that you have the sweetest pussy I have ever had."

"JONATHAN, I swear!"

"That's how you make me feel, Millie, young like the boys. I feel like we just met yesterday. I love you."

"I love you too, Jon. Now, let's go upstairs so you can show me how young you really feel."

"Fuck going upstairs I want to wax that ass on the kitchen counter!"

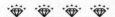

Tony paced around Kahmelle's living room, which doubled as his bedroom and sat on the couch.

"What I tell you about putting your dirty ass jeans where my head rests, nigga? Go sit on the Lazy Boy over there."

Tony sprang off the couch and walked over to the tattered matching chair on the other side of the small living room. "I don't know if I'm ready for this. What do you think is going to happen out there tonight?"

"I don't know, Tone, but I got this shit right here for protection." Kahmelle pulled out a dull black thirty-eight.

"Oh shit, son! Where did you get that from?"

"My aunt's ex-boyfriend got locked up, and he left most of his shit here. Look— it still has two bullets in it."

Kahmelle extended the gun to Tony and Tony shook his head. "I don't want to see that shit."

"These niggas ain't no joke. He said he would call us if anything went down. Well, shit's going down and I ain't tryin' to go out," Kahmelle said.

"Tony inhaled deeply and talked low. "Let's be out."

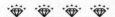

Malik walked out the house and picked up his cell phone.

"What up, Mike? Your boy is in there like swimwear, nigga."

"What the deal?"

"Yo dig, I made it into NYU Law. I can't believe this shit. I am on my way downtown to Junior's to get a drink."

"Fuck Junior's! Didn't they just throw up a new Applebee's across the street from there? Drinks on you big time."

"I am going to walk over there and shit— take in some fresh air. I will be there in about a half. I'll put my name down and wait for you in the spot."

"I'm already so fresh and so clean. I'll be there in forty-five minutes."

Flatbush and Dekalb Avenue was live this Wednesday night. Shoppers hustled and bustled into cabs, subways, buses and parked cars. Loud horns and the sounds of people talking filled the air. Although it was 'Hump Day', it felt like Friday. Shopping bags attached to the hands of beautiful brown, tan, chocolate, pecan and peach-colored people crisscrossed Flatbush at Dekalb Avenue. Young mothers clutched children's hands as they hurried across this huge intersection where traffic can come at you three ways from eight different lanes. White papers, bright green and clear plastic soda bottles, brown paper bags and sweet candy wrappers were scattered along the curbs. Parallel-parked cars covered part of the spectrum of garbage. Teenage boys hollered and whistled at teenage girls. Grandmothers pushed strollers. Businesswomen toting briefcases and cell-phones talked as they rushed across it. Girlfriends, homeboys, and couples talked while they walked into one of two restaurants that stood on diagonally opposite corners, facing each other. One was a Brooklyn landmark, Junior's, the other a brand new trendy restaurant, Applebee's.

Yanick stood in front of Junior's nervously looking at her watch as she watched four teenage males join a crowd of males that already were standing in front of the restaurant. *I told Joann I should have stood across the street, but she wouldn't listen to me.* She could hear Joann's voice in her head. '*Yanick, it's well lit and safer for you to wait across the street.*' She looked at her watch. It was eight-thirty. *This isn't the first time she's been late, and this is only our first month of dating. I better check her on that. Oh my God, I can't believe I just said we're dating. I guess this is really going down*, she thought.

When Kahmelle and Tony reached Junior's, eighteen young males and three females stood outside. They all wore some shade of green. As Kahmelle and Tony crossed the street, two guys approached them. "Yo, son, what that green look like? Long time, man," Webb said.

"Just tryin' to get out of school and shit," Tony said.

The same guy extended his hand to Kahmelle. "Yo, Kah, what the deal, yo?"

"It's all about that green, Webb. Why are we here?" Kahmelle asked.

"I don't really know, dawg. We waiting for Sweat," Webb said.

"Damn, Tone, you see that chick right there? She is bangin', right? I'ma go step to that, son." Kahmelle pointed at Yanick who stood a couple of feet away waiting patiently.

Webb laughed out loud. "That bitch ain't trying to holla back at a nigga. I already tried, and so did Spam, and Spam gets all the pussy," Webb said.

"Fuck that. I got this." Just as Kahmelle made his way over to Yanick, Joann hurried up the street.

"Yo, Kah, come here," Tony said as he instantly made out the approaching woman to be Officer Nuñez.

"No, you come here, Tony, she has a friend, and the friend looks good, too," Kahmelle said.

Kahmelle approached them smiling. He stood in front of Yanick and gently touched her wrist. She quickly pulled it back. "Easy ma, what's your name? If you need some child support for your little baby, I got you," Kahmelle said.

Tony shook his head and dipped into the crowd, so he couldn't be seen. Joann stepped in front of Yanick. "Nah, son. We ain't interested. We're both spoken for," Joann said.

"Your man ain't got nothing to do with me," Kahmelle replied.

Joann looked around the crowd, and then back at Kahmelle. "Don't I know you from somewhere? You go to the High?" she asked.

Kahmelle's eyes opened wide. The woman's second comment rang in his ears. He knew the voice, then he recognized the face. "Nah, you beautiful ladies have a good night." He took two steps back and dipped into the crowd, next to Tony.

"Yo, that was that loud-ass cop that be on the block by our school, yo," Kahmelle said.

"I tried to warn you, but you wouldn't listen," Tony said.

As Malik walked he thought about how his luck had changed. He would soon be in law school, and Susan was the icing on the cake. Up until that phone call he had little to no feelings for her, but now he genuinely liked her. He thought about his parent's comments.

'I ain't getting no younger I want some grandbabies running around.'

Then his thoughts quickly shifted to that of Nyla. He inhaled deeply, and mentally rewound her frantic phone call on that God-awful day.

"I can't feel my back baby!!! I- I- ran but the explosion. Aaahhhh!!" she cried in horror.

"Nyla!! What happened?! Where are you?!"

She cried hoarsely for a minute, and then cried out in an even more hoarse strain. *"Don't think I am going to make it."*

"What happened? Call 911, or an ambulance."

"I will always love you," she cried.

"What are you talking about? CALL AN AMBULANCE NYLA"—the phone went dead.

That was the entire conversation. He remembered running to the television and watching the airplane crash into the first tower where Nyla had worked. He ran outside and jumped into his car. As he approached the Brooklyn Bridge the sky smelled like there was a fire nearby. Malik could not view the Manhattan skyline— it was blocked by a thick, light gray dust cloud. Droves of people covered in thick white ash and soot from head to toe walked and ran across the bridge. He felt like he was living in a black and white world, but those who crossed did so with blood seeping through their thick, chalky, soot filled clothing.

The police would not permit any motorists to drive across the Brooklyn Bridge. Malik made a U-turn and parked across the street from it. He attempted to walk across, but they would not let him. All he could do was wait.

Three days later, he got a call from Nyla's parents. She had been found unconscious and slightly dismembered. She was barely alive. Debris from the first plane had sliced the entire back portion of her body off. It scorched the back of her head, taking off most of her hair and removing most of the skin on her back down to her tail bone. It sliced off her entire behind and the back of her heels. You could see the bottom of her spine and her entire tale bone through a thin layer of cartilage. Plastic surgeons crowded the room and displayed pictures of butts to her parents and Malik. Overwhelmed, he and his fiancés family agreed to make decisions on her cosmetic surgery the next day, but she died that very night.

He had never loved before. He had fucked, but not loved. He had even liked two or three at a time, but had never loved one. Nyla was the one exception. They had just gotten engaged— she was supposed to grow his seeds. He had nightmares for a year and a half following the tragedy. This year was going to be different for him. He finally started to go out and laugh again, but he couldn't imagine himself having feelings for another woman— at least not yet.

As he approached Applebee's, he noticed a crowd of guys across the street, and several cop cars starting to crowd around. He caught a chill, thinking of his not-so-distant past and walked inside the restaurant.

"How long is the wait for a table of two?" Malik asked.

The hostess smiled at Malik and started to blush. "Fifteen minutes. Your name?"

"Malik."

"Just wait for your name to be called. You can sit at the bar or wait in our waiting area."

"Thank you."

He is fine! His eyes are so beautiful, the young hostess thought.

Malik sat by the window and watched the crowd of guys across the street. They looked young from where he sat. *They can't be any older than little Tone. They probably the same age me and Sweat was when we started running the streets and getting money back in the day.* He shook his head, and rubbed the scar on the back of his neck. *I'm glad little Tone is hitting the books instead of that pavement. The streets is no joke,* he thought.

Joann and Yanick walked into the restaurant and headed toward the hostess. Yanick noticed a handsome young man sitting in the waiting area. She smiled at him, and Malik returned gesture. The hostess escorted them to a table with a window seat that overlooked the corner of Dekalb and Flatbush Avenues.

"I wonder what's going on over there in front of Junior's? I should go check it out," Joann said.

"Let me find out you be taking your work home with you. You're off duty. Besides, why check them out when you could be checking me out?" Yanick said.

Joann smiled, looked at Yanick, gently touched her hand and rubbed it. "I can't stop thinking about that kiss today, Yanick."

Yanick smiled. *Neither can I. But I would never tell her that*, she thought.

As Joann stared out the window, Yanick watched Malik walk by with Mike and smiled. Malik stared at Yanick and flashed a quick smile. Mike looked at Yanick and Joann.

"Malik, that girl is checkin' for you. There's two of them. Work your magic on them, son," Mike said.

"Nah. If she ain't have that baby, I would bag that. But you know her baby's daddy is still tappin' that ass."

Mike smiled. "Son, I was starting to worry about you. It seemed like you was pussy-free. I thought you would never be the old Leeko again. The baddest broads be checkin' for your ass, and it's like you don't even see them. I'm glad you're back, nigga."

"Thanks. Look, she's still looking over here, and she's fat assin' it."

"How you know, Leek? She's sittin' down."

"I noticed her when she walked in. What you drinkin'?"

Yanick blushed at the thought of a handsome guy giving her the eye. Ever since she gave birth to her daughter she had been feeling fat and unattractive.

"Look, the cops are breaking them up. They're walking away," Joann said excited.

"What?" Yanick asked.

Joann pointed at Brooklyn's Finest through the window. "Over there, those kids— the cops are moving them from in front of Junior's."

"They're probably just hanging out," Yanick replied.

As the Brooklyn's Finest was dispersed by New York's Finest, Sweat arrived and all the guys followed him to Fort Greene Park. He stood on the base of a monument that stood at the center of the park, and informed the guys that they were going to rob a frat party at Pratt Institute. "The party starts at ten. We will arrive at eleven-thirty."

"What fraternity is it?" Tony asked inquisitively from the middle of the crowd.

"Your Thugglemen ass would ask that question. Some boot-leg local New York frat. But it has over eighteen chapters in New York and this is a rich boy frat. Only cats whose parents have money is going to be up at this spot. We rollin' twenty deep. I want seven niggas outside breakin' in cars. Webb, Kahmelle, Darren, Juice, Skeeter, Spam, and Lil' Tone will do that." Sweat reached behind him and pulled out four, army green, medium sized duffel bags out of one large duffel bag. He threw them down in front of him and they picked them up.

Tony almost pissed himself when he thought he would be separated from Kahmelle. All seven guys walked over to a tree about twenty feet from the monument to talk.

"I want six niggas inside with me to heat up the place," Sweat pulled a gun from the back of his pants and held it in the air as he made that statement. "You already know who you are." Six guys walked up to the base of the monument.

"Now for Brooklyn's Finest ladies. Camille, I want you and Kee-lo to be lookouts and shit. One of you stand by the front entrance and the other by the back entrance. Diamond you're my decoy. Take your pretty ass over to the security booth, and ask for directions. Keep him occupied until I walkie you, then hang around like you're trying to kick it and watch the streets. As soon as any of you see po-po, walkie me. Everyone put your phones on vibrate."

Sweat unhooked his phone and switched it to vibrate. All the gang members did the same. "No one walkies me except the ladies, no matter what. I don't care if you get hit, don't walkie me. Sweat looked menacingly around the crowd. "Duck, you drive my green truck, and Gleason drive the blue one. Monk, you ride with Gleason. I will walkie you on the way out and have the fuckin' doors open so we can split. Niggas on the street stay on the street, and we'll meet at the Bat Cave between twelve and twelve-thirty.

Camille walked over to Kahmelle and tapped him on the shoulder. "I want to go where you go."

"Get the fuck outta here, Camille. You got your assignment. We can hang out later and shit," he said. Kahmelle smacked her on the ass and she walked toward the other girls smiling.

As everyone discussed individual plans of action, the distinct smell of marijuana filled the air. "You know I don't like any of us fuckin around under the influence when we do jobs. We need to be sharp, in and out and focused. Put that shit out now," Sweat ordered.

The smoke immediately stopped, but continued to linger. Sweat looked at his phone. It was a quarter past eleven. "Let's make this happen, baby. My street squad, roll out now. Walk straight down Myrtle." As they exited the park, Sweat called to them and stared directly at Tony and Kahmelle. "Do the damn thing. And remember, go hard or go home. If you can't do it, you ain't Finest. We don't bang for free we bang for a cause. We the last of the stick-up niggas in Brooklyn! Don't nobody be robbin' and stealin' no more but us. Represent Brooklyn's Finest to the fullest, you feel me? "

With the exception of Kahmelle and Tony, who wore green fitteds, they all wore green sleeveless hoodies. Tony's nerves played with him as they walked down Myrtle Avenue. He was hardly able to laugh when his boys laughed, but he kept a smirk on his face.

As the group neared their destination, Webb pulled Tony aside at a street light. "Lil Tone, don't be nervous, duke. We got the easiest jobs and shit. This is your first time out, huh?" Tony shook his head. "Ask your brother about me. We used to get it on out here. I got you, pa."

"Good lookin', Webb." Tony nudged Kahmelle on the arm. "Yo, I look that nervous?"

"Do you? Relax, you know I got heat in my pocket. We gonna be alright," Kahmelle said.

They continued to laugh and talk down the Ave. Tony began to unwind, and even laughed a few times until they got to the corner of Hall and Myrtle. Then he became tense again. They slowed down, got serious and surveyed their surroundings.

"I'm not going to take Willoughby as we originally planned. I am going to take this side of Hall, 'cause it has more cars, and I move faster. I'm going to snag all the air bags I can. I could probably get eight hundred for a pair. Y'all follow me and get whatever else y'all can. You guys take the side with all the driveways. Kahmelle take this hammer. Remember try to look for the red alarm light. If there's an alarm leave it alone. Look for tinted windows, there's always less mess since the glass doesn't fall. Stick your hand into the hole and pop the—"

"Webb, I got this, pa," Kahmelle said.

"When you in there, try to look like you own the shit, too. Always break into the side away from the street, and then sit in the driver's seat like you own the fuckin' car. Everyone else knows the deal so let's go. Oh, Lil' Tone, stand at the intersection, act like you're on the phone and look for 5-0, and any nosey ass bystanders."

They all crossed at the same time, and immediately went to work. Tony leaned against the traffic light at the intersection and watched the guys scatter in different directions. He picked up his phone and put it to his ear. He looked up and down Hall Street. It was long, desolate and dimly lit. One side of the block bordered the fenced-in university. There was nothing to see but the tall black iron fences, bushes, the sides of campus buildings, and Kahmelle and his crew. They stopped at a gold Camry parked near the middle of the block. Kahmelle took the hammer and swung into the window of one of the back doors. The glass cracked instantly, and left a small hole. He used his fist to make a bigger hole. The glass stayed in place with the exception of the hole. He stuck his arm in, pulled up the lock to the door and opened it. To his surprise, no alarm went off. Tony was relieved.

Kahmelle unlocked the front door. As he got in, his man jumped in with him. They rummaged through the car. He removed a cell phone and a digital camera from the glove compartment and put it in his pocket. He pulled the visor down and two crisp twenty-dollar bills and a lieutenant's benevolence card fell out. He placed them in his pocket. He popped the trunk and went through it. Then he moved onto the next car.

Tony scanned the opposite side of the block for Spam and Skeeter. He looked at the back of two apartment buildings then several garages, and a couple of private homes before they came into view. *How the fuck they get down there so fast? They must have started on the other end of the block*, he thought.

He watched Kahmelle punch out the back door window of a Burgundy Navigator, and Tony's stomach dropped as a loud alarm went off. Without hesitation, Kahmelle unlocked the door and opened and closed it. The alarm still blew. As a car drove down the street, Kahmelle stepped off the sidewalk to the driver's side and shook a pair of keys. He opened the door and sat in the front. "Yo, he must be out of his fuckin' mind," Tony said under his breath. The alarm finally stopped. No one came out to look, no cops, nothing, and with in seconds they were out of that car into the next one.

Sweat and his team hopped out of the back of two, dark colored SUVs on Dekalb Avenue. A dozen frat brothers entered the campus as they got out of the truck, and they walked closely behind them. Once they reached the middle of the campus both groups entered the main building. They walked down the steps and loud music greeted them. Sitting behind a card table were three guys, and a campus security guard standing beside them. One guy collected tickets, another collected money and the third collected money for drink tickets. Sweat and his squad rolled tightly behind the twelve frat brothers.

Sweat looked around the small hall they stood in and walkied Diamond. "You good?"

"I'm lost. But this nice security guard is giving me directions," Diamond replied in a sweet voice.

Sweat tapped the guy at his side and shook his head. At that instant they cocked their pistols and shot out the two cameras located on opposite sides of the room. Sweat noticed the security guard reaching for his side. Without hesitation he rammed the handle of his gun into the security guard's head. He dropped to the floor instantly with the blow. Sweat bent over and pistol-whipped him a second time. He saw no weapon besides a Billy club.

Two of the boys behind the card table tried to run for the door. Before they took their second steps Sweat cocked his pistol. Both of the guys froze in their tracks. Sweat grabbed a jar of money and a small green tin safe. He shoved them in a bag he wore hanging off of his shoulder.

The three young men in the lobby stared at Sweat. Two of them whimpered as they stared, the third perspired and breathed heavily.

"Go inside and lay on the ground with your hands behind your heads."

All three guys followed their orders promptly. As the heavy breather made it to the entrance of the gym Sweat grabbed him by his arm. Sweat looked at his team and began to yell, "Move! Move! Move!"

Screams and yells permeated the gym as Sweat's squad entered with their pistols drawn and their hoods over their heads. Sweat shoved the guy toward the table where the DJ's equipment was; the barrel of the gun was pressed into his back. The loud beeper of the late Notorious B.I.G.'s 'Warning' filled the gym. Sweat released his grip to grab the mic, and shifted the gun's barrel to the boy's head.

"Listen up. Stay down on the ground, take out your wallets and nobody gets hurt. If you try to be a super hero, Forrest Gump here will get it in the head."

All six members of his squad ran around the gymnasium with their hoodies on grabbing wallets and placing them in duffel bags. The loud music muffled the whimpers, cries and sniffles that traveled around the gymnasium. Sweat picked up his phone and walkied Camille, keeping his gun steady in his right hand.

"How's it looking out there?"

"Clear."

He looked at the time on the phone. It was eleven forty-five. He walkied Kee-lo. "How's it looking out there?"

"Everything's good."

He walkied Diamond. "Did you find your way, Diamond?"

"There's a group of people getting ready to come down to the party."

"The party's over. Alert the other girls, one."

In one motion he pushed the kid to the ground. The table jumped and the record skipped, but landed right back on the beat. He ran toward an exit door toward the rear of the gym, and his squad followed him. This lead them right to the back entrance of the Main Building, within forty-eight feet of the getaway trucks and thirty feet away from the small security station. As soon as they hit the warm air they walked slowly and calmly. As they approached the security booth they kept quiet. A guard stood smiling in Diamond's face as she gave him a fake number while his partner laid out cold in the lobby and his other partner slept in the booth.

They got into the trucks and peeled off. Tony smiled as he saw both trucks speed by him. Five minutes later he noticed a cop car moving slowly down the block with their lights flashing and their sirens off.

A faint "yo, yo," was heard in the distance.

"Chill, that's Tony," Kahmelle said.

Kahmelle knew his best friend's voice and sank down into the driver's seat of the 325 he just broke into. The rest of the team dropped their duffel bags, pulled their hoods down and continued to walk slowly down the street laughing and talking. Kahmelle looked across the street for Webb and the rest of his squad, but didn't see anyone. The cop car rode slowly down the street and passed them by. Minutes later Webb hopped out of a car and looked around.

"Eighty-six it," Webb yelled.

Tony looked at his phone. It was eleven fifty-one. He walked slowly up to Myrtle as planned. En route, he turned around and saw all the members of his squad walking quickly behind him.

"We splittin' up. You three that way, the four of us this way. Let's move and get back to the Bat Cave— one."

"Webb, you good?" Sweat asked through the walkie.

"Yeah, we're right." Webb replied.

"How quick can you meet me on the corner of Washington and Park?" Sweat asked.

"We just passed there."

"I'm pullin' over on Waverly and Park."

"We split. Skeeter and them went down Myrtle."

"Gleason, got them already. Hurry up."

"One."

They walked faster. Kahmelle and Tony walked several feet behind Webb. Within a minute the green Tahoe, with no plates, pulled up in front to them. "Get in where you fit in and hurry up, Sweat yelled.

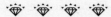

"I'm fuckin' done. We've been in here for hours and shit," Malik said.

"Yeah, well, my dick is in the dirt. I am going home and fuckin' the shit out of my broad. Congratulations, nigga," Mike said.

"Thanks. You good?"

"Yeah."

Mike and Malik staggered out of Applebee's. Malik caught a cab and Mike went down into a subway station located right in front of the restaurant. Malik stared at the bright green numbers of the digital clock— eleven forty-seven. He closed his eyes. They were opened up to the unfamiliar accent of the cab driver in front of his house at eleven fifty-nine. He paid his fare, went inside and fell asleep, fully dressed.

Joann and Yanick walked into the apartment. Joann looked at the clock on her wall it was twelve a.m. Yanick took Seven out of her carrier and placed her in her playpen/bassinet that Joann purchased. The baby was fast asleep. She pulled off the baby's clothes, and placed a onesie on her. Afterwards, she walked into the bedroom and stared at Joann who sat naked on her bed. Yanick stood in the doorway.

"The time we have been spending together has been so fun. After Seven's father, I didn't think I could feel this way about a person again."

"So why don't you come in here and sleep in the bed with me. It's been a couple of weeks. Come here and lay down. Seven is sleep."

"I'm scared Joe," Yanick said in a low tone.

"Scared of what, that you will like it? All this kissing and dry humping isn't getting it. I want you come here, Yanick. " Joann got out of the bed and walked up to Yanick. She placed her hands on Yanick's face, and pushed all of her hair back. Joann stuck her tongue down her throat. The kiss was wet and sloppy and Yanick loved it.

"Go lay down. I'm going to pee," Joann said.

Yanick walked into the bedroom. She quickly stripped and pulled on a large T-shirt. She jumped into Joann's bed, and lay stiff and straight on her back clutching the sheets over her chest. When Joann came in the room Yanick tightened up. Joann lay down next to her and tugged at the covers, but Yanick would not let go.

"Yanick, can I get some of those covers please."

"Oh, of course." Yanick released her grip.

Joann immediately slid close to Yanick. She placed her hand under her T-shirt and caressed her breasts. She began to mount Yanick, but Yanick quickly sat up. "I can't. I'm not ready for this yet. I thought I was but—"

Joann sighed and shook her head. "If you're not ready, I will not press you." She kissed her lips gently and squeezed one of her nipples before moving her hand from underneath her nightshirt. "But you can't expect me to lay next to your sexy behind and behave. I'm going to sleep in the guestroom. I have to wake up really early."

"Are you mad at me?" Yanick asked.

"Nah. Just a little disappointed with the situation, but never with you. Good night."

"Good night Joann, thanks for understanding."

Joann took one of the pillows from bed, kissed Yanick on her cheek, and went into the guest bedroom. She got under the covers, buried her face in the pillow and yelled loud. She released the pillow and sat up in the bed. *It will happen Joey, give it some time. It's only been a second. Good girls make you wait for two months, it will happen soon.*

Tony and Kahmelle weren't surprised when they reached Sweat's house.

"Just as I expected," Kahmelle said. "I thought he would live in a rat and roach infested project or something just like this. Straight up grimy."

"I've been to his house before, back in the day. He used to live with his grandmother in a real nice spot," Tony said.

Kahmelle smirked. "Yeah, well this shit right here smells like a muthafuckin' kennel."

Everybody dumped their bags onto the middle of the floor. Kahmelle went into his pockets and dropped a phone. Then he emptied his bag.

"Yo, I snagged at least ten pairs of air bags. If I take these over to Mook, at his shop, we could get an easy seven grand for these shits yo," Webb said.

"That's what I'm talking about. Just take yours out and bring my cut once you slice that cake, baby," Sweat said.

The guys drank, smoked and listened to music. After an hour Sweat stood up. "Together we nabbed eight G's, and some shit we can sell. I am taking all the electronics and knocking them off. That, plus the money from the air bags, will go toward the rent for this piece of shit right here and the cost of keeping our blow up jacks going. Thugglemen, how much for each of us? We twenty deep."

Everyone turned and looked at Tone. Without thinking he answered him. "That's about four hundred a pop"

"Diamond, give everybody their cut."

"This one dude I robbed in there had 'bout six hundred in his wallet," one guy called out.

"There are some phones, palm pilots and designer wallets down here that ain't worth me trying to knock off. If y'all want them go through them."

Kahmelle was on the floor before anyone else. He grabbed three wallets and an electronic organizer. The other guys standing around the pile laughed at him. "Yo Tony. I grabbed the Louy wallet for you and the Prada Wallet for me."

"Fuck that. I got the Prada sneakers. Let me get that," Tony said.

"You got it."

Tony reached home almost two hours after Malik. He stripped off his clothes and lay with his hands clasped behind his head. He reviewed the night's events and really didn't know how to feel. Part of him felt bad, but for the most part he felt proud. He felt like he belonged.

He stopped for a minute to think about Malik, and began to worry. *If my brother finds out that I'm fuckin' with Sweat, he'll kill me.* He quickly dismissed that thought and smiled. *My brother doesn't have a clue. I've got paper in my wallet, and I am down with Brooklyn's Finest. Not to mention that now that I go with Shaine, she has been labeled the baddest chick in the school. Life is good. I really don't have anything to worry about.*

5

Down in Negril, gettin' ill

Kahmelle and Tony walked slowly by the Brooklyn Jewelry Exchange on their way to school.

"Last day of school, pa, and I'm feeling good. What do you want to get into today?" Kahmelle asked.

"Why don't you fellas speed it up? I'm sure class started, it is already nine," Joann called out.

"I'm sayin', officer, we ain't doing nothing but walking," Kahmelle hissed.

"What he meant to say was that we are walking to school as fast as we can Officer Nuñez. You have a nice day," Tony said.

Joann felt her phone vibrating on her hip, it startled her. She waved at Tony and leaned against the store front of the bodega. As she flipped the phone open she smiled at the sound of Yanick's voice and watched Tony yank Kahmelle up the block.

"What the fuck is wrong with you? Don't you know the cops from that precint are notorius for beating Black people down," Tony said.

"She's Black, too, and we could beat her ass down," Kahmelle snapped as he yanked his arm out of Tony's grasp.

"Man, she's a cool cop, but don't be provoking shit," Tony said.

"Ain't no cool cops. The minute you do something sideways she'll slap cuffs on your ass in a sec."

"Hey, Joann, do you want to go out to eat tonight?"

"I was just thinking about you. If it's food you want, I will feed you. Pick you up at eight?"

"Okay. Can we go to Applebee's?"

"Nah, let me take you somewhere a little more special than that. It's time you give that place a rest."

"Okay, but I love their Caesar salads, and there daquiri's are so good."

"Don't sound so disapointed, you'll like the new spot. How's my litle girl?"

"She's fine. I am dropping her off at my aunt's house, and then I am going to school, I am so happy to finally be going back."

"Okay, sexy. I'll pick you up later."

"Bye."

Tony and Kahmelle continued their conversation as they walked into the school.

"That bitch right there is always mad. She be arresting niggas from our school on the reg."

"She only fucks with people that be fuckin' up or fuck with her. You've been actin' real stupid lately."

"Camille is pregnant."

"WHAT?"

"Yeah. She's pregnant, nigga, and she won't have no abortion either."

"Kah, you jus' met that bitch. You sure it's yours?"

"That's what her mouth say, Tone. Plus I've been beatin' that pussy up like twice a day since I met her."

"You better kick that dirty bitch down the fuckin steps, or stick a hanger in her pussy or something."

"Don't talk about her like that. I love that bitch. Don't no one talk about Shaine like that."

"Look how you met her, Kah!"

"Look how you met HER, Tone."

"Yeah, but, you know we faked it. How pregnant is she?"

"I don't know. It's only been a couple of weeks."

"Damn, man. We have to talk her out of it, Kah!"

"Listen, I got a plan for our next hit," Kahmelle said.

"What you talking about?"

"For initiation and shit, yo. There be mad people jogging around High Field, it closes at eleven. They be out there at night. That could be our gun point hold up, yo."

"I don't know," Tony said reluctantly.

"I'm saying we could do this. Let's set it up."

"I don't know. What if we got caught?"

"Time is winding down if we gonna be full fledged Finest, nigga we got to finish our initiation."

"Shit, we got six months," Tony said loudly.

"Tonight we're gonna go out there and rob somebody."

"What are we going to rob them for? Their fuckin' sneakers, Kah?"

"It doesn't matter. As long as we hold them up. We can take they wallets or those litte bags that they wear on their waist."

Tony shook his head. "Are you sure you want in, Kahmelle? I'm having second thoughts."

"Fuck yeah. We going out of school with a bang this year. Let's walkie Webb. He will probably help us."

"Yeah, I'm sure he will."

"Ma, don't worry about me— I'll be all right. I am only going away for the weekend."

"But I don't even know this girl you're going away with. Why don't you—"

"Millicent, leave him. He is a grown man— just let him go. You want us to pick you up from the airport?"

"Yes, Dad. I left my information on the fridge. If anything comes up I will call. As a matter fact I will call you as soon as I get there. My flight leaves at eleven and it is already minutes after nine. A car has been sitting outside waiting for me for fifteen minutes. I have to go."

"Make sure you take protection with you. Don't buy them rubbers out there. I don't trust that third world shit," Jonathan said.

Malik laughed and shook his head. *Dad will never change*, he thought as he hugged his father tightly. He walked over to his mother and kissed her cheek. "I will see you Monday. Tell Tony I said later."

Malik stared silently out of the window the entire ride. He blankly stared at the cars, signs and people they cruised past on the Belt Parkway. He had a clear head. Nothing was on his mind.

As they pulled up in front of the airline terminal Malik didn't have to pay or sign his name on a voucher. He stepped out of the car with his overnight bag in his hand and walked into the airport. He zipped through check-in and customs and made his way to the plane. When the plane started to taxi down the runway, he exhaled loudly.

◈ ◈ ◈ ◈

"Tonight's the night baby boy," Kahmelle said excitedly.

"We still have one more job to do after this one, you know," Tony said.

"Yep. And we gonna do that one real big, watch," Kahmelle said.

The lunchroom looked like a Sunday afternoon. Normally there would be at least three hundred or so screaming teens in the cafeteria at a time, sitting at long white tables with long white benches attached to them. But on the last day of school the cafeteria only seated about thirty.

"We're going to put on our sleeveless hoodies, and doo-rags. We'll jog around the park until we find the right victim. When we spot them we jog up next to them, pull out the heat, duck under the bleachers and rob them," Kahmelle said.

"Nigga, this ain't 'Boys in the Hood'. That shit only works on TV. We are going to sit underneath the bleachers like we always do, but we are going to sit by an opening. When the mark comes by the opening I'll grab them from behind and we both yank them underneath the bleachers. You cock the pistol, point it at them and shake them down while I hold them. After that, we threaten them. Tell them to count to twenty with their face down in the dirt, if they look up we will bust a shot in the air, and then jet. We run around the corner and away from the block."

Kahmelle sat with an open mouth and an astonished look on his face. "So you really do have a criminal mind. I thought you was soft," he said.

Tony laughed. "All jokes aside, that Camille shit is serious, son. You better talk her ass out of it. Shit beat her ass out of it or something y'all too young to have kids. That shit cost some serious cake."

"I know."

Tony started to get up but Kahmelle tapped his hand lightly. "Don't look now, but here comes Latonji. Sit down, son she's coming this way." Latonji walked over, and sat next to Tony. She smelled sweet, like watermelon. "Hey, Tony. Kahmelle," she said with a wide grin.

"What's up?" Tony said.

"Nothing. How come you haven't called me? I only gave you my number three times," Latonji said.

Tony stared at her. She wore baby oil on her face and chest. Her cleavage glistened as it slowly heaved up and down. She placed her leg over his lap and talked in his ear. "I am having a little last day of school get together at my house tonight. Why don't you come over? Leave Shaine at home and I will make it worth your while." Tony nodded his head. She kissed his ear lobe gently three times. At the end of each kiss her bare cleavage touched his arm. His penis instantly became erect. She placed her hand on his lap to swing her legs over the bench and purposely touched his dick and smiled as she stood. "Even if you don't want to come, I think that man in your pants does. Think about it. Here's my address and phone number again. Just in case you lost it. Later."

"Can Kahmelle come?" Tony placed her number in his pocket.

Latonji licked her lips and shook her head. "This is a personal invitation for you Tony, unless you're scared." With that she waltzed out of the lunchroom.

"Dag, you don't know how bad I want that!" Tony said.

"So hit it. Shaine won't find out," Kahmelle replied.

"Shaine look better than Latonji, right?"

"Yeah, she actually does. Your ass made her the best looking girl in the school," Kahmelle said.

"How you figure that? She look exactly the same."

"Yeah, but now that we Finest and shit, everybody is hanging on the scrotum, and she ain't Shaine no more— she's Tone's girl. Nobody knew who she was, or how bad she was until you started fuckin' with her."

"So my broad is bad, huh?"

Kahmelle shook his head and smiled. "Yeah, Tone, she's bad."

"I'm going to make my farewell rounds across the school. I got straight A pluses and two A's. You know how I do. Did you pass Spanish?"

"Yeah, nigga, I got a D+, I made it to senior year, Tony. I'm graduating next year."

"That's what the fuck I am talking about. One, son."

"One."

Tony walked out of the lunchroom and walked around the school talking to teachers and friends. Teachers loved Tony because he was a model student. Students loved him because not only was he down with Brooklyn's Finest, but he was also smart and approachable. Most of the kids that were down with gangs only associated with other gangsters— Tony respected everyone.

He approached the very last classroom he planned to visit. He knocked on the door gently, and Mrs. Simmons jumped in her seat. She wore dark eyeglasses, and sat at her desk packing things into a shopping cart. "Boy, you scared the you know what out of me," Mrs. Simmons said trying to catch her breath.

"I didn't mean to scare you Mrs. Simmons. Check out my report card."

As he walked over to her she noticed huge diamond studs in his ears. Then she looked at his clothing. He gave her a hug, and she looked at his report card. "Two A's you can do better than that," she joked. Have you thought about college yet?"

"I want to go to Howard, for Pre-Med."

Mrs. Simmons placed his report card on her desk and took her glasses off. Tony noticed that her left eye did not open all the way, but aside from that she looked like her old self.

"Is there anything you want to tell me, Tony?"

"No. Why?"

"Where did you get those earrings from?"

"Right up the block at Brooklyn Jewelry Exchange." Tony saw where she was going with her line of questioning and thought fast. "These aren't diamonds. They're cubics. I couldn't afford real ones."

"You are wearing Prada sneakers and official throwback jerseys. Come on now. You wear green and white almost every day."

"Green's my favorite color. I'm out of here, Mrs. Simmons."

"Stay out of trouble over the summer, you understand me?"

"I hear you loud and clear."

As Tony reached the door Mrs. Simmons called to him. "Wait, Tony. You don't have to be like your brother, or anyone else in the streets. You are different. Your brother never got the grades you get in school, and he didn't want to either. Your brother made it by the skin of his teeth. You might not be so lucky. Brooklyn's Finest is not the way," Mrs. Simmons pleaded.

"I don't know what you're talking about, Mrs. Simmons."

"You know exactly what the fuck I'm talking about. Don't do it."

Tony opened his eyes wide. He had never heard Mrs. Simmons raise her voice, and now she was cursing. Tony ran down the steps and left the school. He inhaled deeply, and exhaled freedom. *Two months of absolutely nothing to do, boy am I going to enjoy this*," he thought. Tony walked toward the corner and waved at Officer Nuñez.

"Hey, kid, wait up. Let me talk to you for a second," Joann said.

"Oh shit! Fuckin' Kahmelle done got us in trouble with po-po," he muttered under his breath. He stopped and tried to mentally prepare himself for what was about to happen as Joann approached him.

"Last day of school, huh? What's your report card looking like?" Tony pulled the report card out of his pocket, unfolded it and handed it to her. "What do you have planned for the summer?" Joann asked.

"Nothing much, I plan to hit the books, Officer Nuñez. I'm trying to get into the Pre-Med program at Howard University. This is my senior year coming up."

"Whoa, now this is a report card!"

"Thank you, Officer Nuñez."

"What about your friend?"

"He didn't do too good, but he passed most of his classes."

"Watch out for him, you hear me? I don't trust him," Joann said.

"He didn't mean anything this morning, he's just got a lot of things on his mind."

"I don't trust him in general. Anyway, I just wanted to tell you to stay out of trouble this summer."

"Thanks, Officer Nuñez. You be safe," Tony said as he started to walk.

Is this shit written all over my face? First Mrs. Simmons was like stay out of trouble. Now Officer Nuñez called me over here to tell me to stay out of trouble. I hope we pull this shit off tonight without getting caught. I don't want anyone to get hurt, and I definitely don't want to get locked up. Maybe I shouldn't go. But this is the start of exactly what I wanted. I guess I have to finish what I started. Tony exhaled as he completed his thoughts.

Malik stepped into his hotel room and was in awe. Not only was it enormous, but it had a private patio that led right to the beach. He dropped his luggage on the floor and flopped on the bed. He clasped his hands behind his head and smiled.

Just think, last month I was fantasizing about her with the rest of my co-workers. Now I am spending the weekend with her, in fuckin' Jamaica at her expense, he thought. He looked at the clock. It read four o'clock. *I'm not going to let the rest of my day go to waste. I'm going to throw on my trunks and take a swim.*

Malik went through his bag and pulled out a pair of dark red swimming trunks. He walked into the bathroom, grabbed a towel from a brass rack then slipped into his trunks As Malik was about to walk out of the bathroom he noticed two heavy, terry robes hanging on the back of the door. He grabbed one, put it on, placed the room key in its pocket and stepped onto the patio. "Wow, this is like a fuckin' postcard."

The sand was a pearly white. The water was a crystal clear blue. As he approached the water he felt warm inside. He shed his robe and towel, stood at the shore and let the cool water slap his knees and ankles. As he inhaled deeply everything felt light and clean. He looked around him and saw several people lying on the beach taking in the sun. He walked straight ahead and his knees were submerged, then his stomach, his chest –and he suddenly dived in. He opened his eyes wide under the water and viewed nothing but plant life and small fish. He felt fully relaxed for the first time in years.

He swam and floated in the ocean water for over two hours. Fatigued, he decided to lay down. As he approached the shore the hot sun caressed his chilly skin. He spotted an empty beach chair a few feet away and within seconds he was sleeping under the hot sun.

Malik awoke to a beautiful sunset. He felt like he swallowed a cup of sand. His lips stuck together and he tried to moisten his mouth, but to no avail. He inhaled deeply and sighed.

"I have a camera in my bag. I have got to get a picture of this. It is breath taking, isn't it?"

Malik was startled. He turned toward the mysterious voice. To his surprise there was a beautiful young lady lying on a beach chair inches away from him. He wiped his mouth with his hand, cleared his throat and took a long stretch. "Yeah. It is nice."

"I thought you would never wake up. I'm Laneice." She extended her hand and smiled.

Malik sat up and shook her hand. "Where did you come from? I'm Malik."

"I was watching you swim earlier. Are you here by yourself?"

"For now, my lady friend is arriving tomorrow. What about you?"

Laneice used her towel to rub some of the tanning oil off of her body. Malik was impressed. She had a six pack, and sat on twelve gallons of ass. Her arms were cut. Her complexion was golden brown, and her eyes were the darkest of brown. Her hair was jet-black and cut short.

"I am on vacation with two of my girlfriends. We're staying in the suite right next to yours. Would you like to join us for dinner tonight?"

"Has anyone ever told you, you look just like Halle Berry?" Malik asked.

"Pleeease, we have the same complexion and similar haircuts, but I look better. Now, how about dinner?"

Malik laughed. "I don't know—"

"I've been mustering up the courage to ask you all day, "Laneice said.

"Where are your friends?"

"They went jet skiing about two hours ago. They should be back any minute."

"How come you didn't go jet skiing with them? Let me find out you're the prude in the crew?"

"Ah ah. No, you didn't," she laughed. "We just got here today. I wanted to relax, unwind, and then start all of the fun shit tomorrow."

"Where are you from?"

"Newark."

"Newark, New Jersey?"

"Yeah."

"I am from Brooklyn."

"I should have known."

"Why do you say that?"

"I was looking at your scar. Do you mind if I ask how you got it?"

"That's a touchy subject, and a life that I left behind."

She pulled her chair closer to his and used her finger to outline the scar on his back. "It's just so big." Malik leaned back on his chair and flattened her hand. "Ouch!" she said loudly as she pulled her hand back and shook it.

"Don't touch me, yo! Are you always so forward?" Malik snapped.

"I had a good feeling about you, but maybe I was wrong." Laneice had an attitude ringing off her words.

Malik watched her shape as she walked off. He got up, jogged behind her and gently grabbed her hand. "Listen, I didn't mean to snap at you, but the scar thing, I don't like to talk about it. And you shouldn't have touched it. So how about you follow me to the bar, and we start this conversation over. I am so thirsty right now."

"Okay. I'm a bit parched myself," Laneice confessed.

As they walked and talked the chemistry between the two could not be denied.

"Is this your first time in Negril?" Laneice asked.

"This is my first time on a Caribbean island," Malik said.

"Really? My girls and I go away at least twice a year," Laneice said.

"So Malik, what do you do for a living?"

"I work at a law firm. What about you?"

"I'm a registered nurse."

"Really? So is my mother."

"So this *friend* of yours that's coming who is she?"

"It's complicated— she's married."

"Word? You know how many women out here would be dying to be with someone like you?" *I wouldn't mind my self*, she thought with a smile on her face. "Wait, wait, wait. Do you have multiple children by different women?"

"I don't have any kids."

"Are you sure you have a job?"

"I work in the mailroom at a law firm— but I just got accepted to NYU Law School, so that will change soon."

"Athletes foot?" Laneice asked with raised eyebrows and a smirk on her face.

"Look for yourself." Malik wiggled his toes as Laneice looked down. She was surprised to see a handsome, pedicured set of toes.

"You have one nut?" Laneice asked and they both laughed out loud.

"None of the above," Malik said.

"You don't want the responsibility of a girl. So you just—"

"I was engaged to be married, but my fiancée died in the attacks on the World Trade Center, and I just started dating again. I'm not even dating her— it's strictly a physical thing."

"People don't do 'strictly physical' in another country. You do 'strictly physical' in the local Ho Jo."

"When you have money you can do strictly physical in any country you want to. She is one of the top attorneys at my firm, and her husband is loaded."

"You have a point there. Can I ask you another personal question?"

"Shit, you haven't stopped yet," Malik said sarcastically.

"She paid for all of this?"

"What can I say? When you got it you got it."

"Is she White?"

"Yes."

"How could you?"

"I don't know. I always wanted to try it once, and this is my one time."

"That is so fucked up."

"Why?"

"Because there are plenty of single BLACK women out here looking for good BLACK men."

"Who said I was a good man? What are you drinking, Latreice?"

"It's Laneice and I am drinking a Piña Colada with a double shot."

Malik approached the bar. "I will have a Jamaica Me Crazy, and a Piña Colada with a double shot."

"Are ya' sure ya can tek dis drink? It's potent mahn," the bartender said in a heavy accent.

"I got this duke, I'm from Brooklyn, what? Hey, what is this thing here?" Malik pointed at a rectangular container with a thick string on it.

"It's like a waterproof wallet. People put dem keys, credit cards and money in it while dey're at the beach." The bartender made the drinks as he spoke. Malik checked it out. He opened it, and closed it several times.

Satisfied he slipped it into the back pocket of his trunks and sealed its Velcro patch. "I'm going to take one of these along with the drinks."

"That's eight US dollars," the bartender said.

Malik pulled out a soaked twenty and laid it on the bar. He and Laneice took their drinks over to their chairs by the shore. They laughed and talked about everything from interracial dating, to rap music, to the war on terrorism. In the middle of a conversation on whether or not Eminem was raping the rap industry two ladies interrupted them.

"Girl, you missed a good time," one of the ladies said to Laneice.

"Tricia, Monica, this is Malik. He is staying in the suite next to ours."

"Nice to meet you, ladies."

"Likewise," they said in unison.

"Where are your boys?" Monica said.

"I am here for self until tomorrow. Then I have a lady friend coming in. Nice to meet you all, but I think I am going to take it in." Malik started toward his room.

"So what is it looking like for tonight? Do we have a dinner date or what?" Laneice called out as Malik walked toward the hotel.

"Call me, neighbor," Malik replied over his shoulder.

"It's not like you have to pay, it's part of the 'all inclusive' thing," Laneice added.

He waved his arm in the air, tied the belt to his robe and entered his room. "Why is there always one pretty one in the crew and the rest are always beastin' or cock blockin'?" Malik asked himself.

"Damn, Laneice, he is fuckin' gorgeous," Monica said.

"And he doesn't have a girl!" Laneice replied.

"Are you serious?" Monica was incredulous.

"Did you peep those eyes though?" Tricia sighed.

"Fuck the eyes, did you see those dimples?" Laneice asked.

"And he doesn't have a girl?" Monica repeated.

"That's what he says. Anyway, he is fuckin' some married White broad," Laneice said.

"It figures," Tricia added.

"Maybe he is some kind of gigolo. Shit, I would pay for his fine ass to work me out," Monica said.

All three girls laughed and walked over to the bar.

"Honey, are you there?"

Susan received no reply. She pulled out her cell phone and itinerary from her purse and dialed out. "Darn, there's no answer. Malik, I just called to see if everything was satisfactory. I will see you tomorrow.

Enjoy." She folded up her itinerary and fit it in between two checks in her checkbook. She dumped it into her purse with the calling card. She peeled off her clothes and looked at the clock. It was ten-twenty. "If I go out and jog now, I won't feel bad about missing my morning exercise tomorrow."

Susan went into her closet, changed into her workout clothes, placed a fanny pouch around her waist and ran down the steps of her loft.

"Good evening Mrs. Eden. Going out for a jog?" a doorman asked as he opened the door.

"Yes, Earl. I'll be back soon, if my husband comes in tell him I am out jogging and will be back in a half an hour."

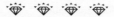

"Kahmelle, it's almost ten-thirty, ain't nobody in their right mind going to come out here to jog this late. And if they do, they definitely ain't going to be by themselves."

"I'm telling you there always be people out here, and there don't be no cops. Let's just wait a couple more minutes, at least fifteen, aaight."

"Yo, son, bust how Shaine found Latonji's number in my pocket and started trippin'. She was yelling and crying that I was fuckin' her and shit."

"There you go. She thinks you're fuckin' her already so you might as well do it, son. Let's go over there and tap that together tonight."

"Ain't nobody fuckin' after your ass and shit. You run up in her. I will go there and chill."

"So, Shaine still ain't come up off her ass yet?"

"Nope. She says she wants to wait until she is in love."

"Couldn't be me, son."

"I know. That's why you got old nasty-ass Camille pregnant."

"Stop callin' my bitch nasty, Tone."

"See even you know she ain't nothing but a bitch. Did you talk to her about having an abortion?"

"She told her mother and everything. Her mother had her when she was fifteen, and said that it is up to her. She told her that it ain't no joke, but that the decision was hers."

"My pops said that bitches do that to try and trap niggas. Tell her that you will leave her if she has the baby, but you will stay with her if she has an abortion and maybe she won't keep it," Tony said.

"I'll try anything. Don't nobody want no fuckin' crying baby around them all the time and shit. Oh shit, look. There goes somebody right there." They peered through the bleachers at the female jogger. "And she is by herself."

"Now we have gone over this at least ten times today. I will jump out and grab her and you know the rest. Don't do no stupid shit, you hear me, Kahmelle?"

Kahmelle held the gun in his hands and pulled the drawstring to his hoodie tightly. Tony yanked his hood on and pulled his drawstring so tight that only his nose and eyes showed. He and Kahmelle looked identical. Tony looked at Kahmelle as Susan approached the opening a second time. He shook his head once. Just as she passed the opening Tony sprung out and yoked her into his arm. He muffled her loud scream with his other hand and dragged her kicking and wriggling body into the opening in a mild chokehold. He pulled her under the bleachers withstanding her constant scratching and biting. Kahmelle stuck out his foot and tripped them.

Susan and Tony went tumbling to the ground. On the way down, she was able to free one arm, grab at Kahmelle and pull his hoodie off his head. She stared into his eyes momentarily as she and Tony hit the concrete. Her eyes shut tightly upon impact, but the sound of a cocked gun reopened them.

"Stop all that muthafuckin' moving before you get hurt!" Kahmelle said. Susan stopped moving. Tony turned her over, pushed her face into the dirt and held both of her hands behind her back. He had his knee pressed down on her spine.

"Take off her bag, and those big ass rocks on her finger," Tony said.

Kahmelle worked quickly but Tony couldn't bear to watch. He closed his eyes tightly and prayed silently. *God, please forgive me. . .*

Kahmelle slid the rings off her finger. He easily unclasped the pouch, then stuck his hand underneath her body and fondled her breasts. He grabbed the waistband of her shorts and yanked them down, revealing her bare ass. She began to whimper and squirm underneath Tony's grip. He opened his eyes to the sight of the barrel of Kahmelle's gun being rubbed on Susan's ass, while he pulled his dick out of his jeans.

"Please, no. Please, don't," she sobbed inhaling a mouth full of dirt.

Tony shoved Kahmelle. "What the fuck are you doing?" Tony yelled.

"Shhh. Why are you yellin'? Hold her down and—"

"Get the fuck out of here— you are not going to rape this lady."

Susan started to cry.

"Do you see the body on this cracker?" Kahmelle asked.

"Miss, don't worry. I'm sorry about—"

"What the fuck are you apologizing to this White bitch for?" Kahmelle said angrily in a coarse and heavy whisper.

"Let's just go before we get caught," Tony said.

Kahmelle sucked his teeth and fixed his pants.

"Now, listen miss if you try anything funny, I am going to let this animal violate you. But, if you just relax and do what I say, I won't let anything happen to you, okay?"

Susan sniffled and nodded her head just as Kahmelle placed the pistol on the back of it. Tony released his pressure, and slowly freed her hands.

"Pull up your pants, miss. I am going to count to fifty. You count with me. Do not pick up your head until you're finished," Tony said.

"Or I will shoot you and then rape your dead ass," Kahmelle added.

Tony was disgusted. "Yo, there is something seriously wrong with you nigga," he whispered.

"Count, bitch," Kahmelle snarled. Susan started to count. "Ah ha, keep it up," Kahmelle said.

Tony and Kahmelle removed their hoods and casually walked out of the park. As soon as they crossed the street they tore their hoodies off, shoved them into a back pack that Kahmelle carried and picked up their pace.

"I can't believe we did it. Did you see all that ice?" Kahmelle said.

"I was the one who told you to take the shit."

They walked briskly for three blocks, and they reached a huge outdoor parking lot. Kahmelle rummaged through the pouch and found nothing but a twenty-dollar bill, a small, water bottle, and a cell phone. He removed the twenty and the phone and placed them in his pocket.

Tony walkied Sweat. "The party's over, yo," he said.

"Go into that McDonald's on Fulton Street, order me a Big Mac, eat, and I'll be there to pick you up in less than twenty minutes," Sweat said.

Tony placed his phone in his pocket and looked at Kahmelle.

"Put the pouch in the back pack and throw it into that dumpster over there, Kah." Kahmelle opened a huge, green dumpster and took off the back pack. "If there is a garbage bag in the dumpster put the bag inside it. Did she have any ID?"

"Yeah."

"Let's gutter that on the corner, yo."

They were out of the parking lot within four minutes. They walked to McDonalds, which was four blocks away. They didn't talk much until they got closer. Both of them replayed the robbery in their minds several times. With each replay, Tony felt more sick inside, and Kahmelle felt more like the man.

"Yo, we could take this shit to the Brooklyn Jewelry Exchange and find out how much it's worth. We could probably sell it there, too," Kahmelle said.

"Are you fuckin' crazy? They'll probably ask where we got it and turn us in!" Tony said.

"Look at the body on that bitch— the one coming across the street," Kahmelle said. Kahmelle and Tony stared at the two women who were crossing the street.

"Which one?" Tony asked.

"The light skinned one."

Tony zeroed in on the women. "Kahmelle, that's Officer Nuñez— the cop from around our school."

"Yeah, and she is with that same bitch she was with in front of Junior's that wouldn't give me no shine the day we did the college. You know what? They pro'bly gay."

"I don't think so, Kah, they are both too hot for that. You think she lives around here, yo?"

"Nah, they probably going around the corner to Applebee's. That's where they went the last time we saw them."

"Come on, before she starts asking us questions," Tony said.

"Nigga, she's off duty, she ain't even thinking about us. She probably thinking about how she's going to rub her pussy up against that girl when she gets home tonight," Kahmelle said.

"That's word to everything I love that cop isn't gay. If I wasn't with Shaine, I could probably bag that, yo," Tony said.

Kahmelle laughed obnoxiously. "That chick wouldn't want your ass, school boy." Kahmelle pulled out the twenty dollars he had retrieved from Susan's pouch and surveyed the menu that was posted above the cash registers. He waved the twenty in Tony's face and whispered in his ear. "The food is on the White bitch with the big titties."

"Ever since we got into the gang you really acting funny style."

"What you talking about, Tone?"

"I can't believe you wanted to rape that woman."

"I'm saying— the bitch was hot."

"Yeah but—"

"Tony, let's not talk about this shit in McDonald's. Let's just chill."

Susan lay crying with her face in the dirt, for fifteen minutes. She was shaking with fear. When she heard laughter she turned around slowly. Four young women and two men running together came into her view. She sat up and cleared her throat. "Please help me. I have just been mugged," she called out.

The group continued to jog. They passed by her without even noticing her. "PLEASE HELP ME I HAVE BEEN MUGGED!" she screamed frantically.

One of the guys in the group turned around and looked down at Susan. "Yo, D'von, do you have your cell? Call 911."

The group stood around her. One of the women helped her to her feet. Susan told her story to the group as they waited with her until the police arrived.

"You know, Yanick, you really need to give this Applebee's thing a rest. I try to take you some place different and we still end up here."

"I don't do Sushi. Raw fish just doesn't agree with me."

They walked into Applebee's and looked around. It was crowded. Yanick gave her name to the hostess and sat on the lounge chairs at the front of the restaurant.

Joann's cell phone rang and she picked it up laughing. Yanick stared at her face as she talked. *I don't know if I can do this shit, she thought. Kissing and feeling up is one thing, but once I lay down with her its official, I'm gay. Well she is pretty, and attentive. She spends money and time with the baby and me. Maybe I should just do it and get it over with. This is no different from having a good man.* She continued to stare at Joann as she spoke on the phone. Joann smiled.

"Listen, Monique, my baby is getting frustrated with me being on the phone. Let me see what she wants." She closed the phone and smiled. "Now you have my undivided attention."

"Can I ask you a question, Joann?"

Yanick slid closer to Joann and Joann smiled. "I think I'm going to like this question already."

"When did you know that you were gay? I mean how old were you? Were you always like this, did you ever have sex with a guy before— if you did, when did you first become intimate with another woman?"

"Slow down ma, one question at a time. Let me see I was always kind of a tomboy, but I had no interest in boys or girls until I got to high school. I played on my school's basketball team, and there was a girl on the team that was drop dead gorgeous. I mean she was all of that and a bag of chips. Sheila. She went with the star quarterback and was straight. As far as I knew I was straight too. But, I couldn't stop looking at her. We would change in the locker room, and whenever she would catch me looking at her, she would smile. I would get butterflies every time she would drop her jersey and her perky ass titties would be— anyway, one day she asked me to help zip up her dress in the back of the locker room. When I went back there she touched my titties and we started kissing. I was with her for three years."

Joann touched Yanick's hand gently, placed her lips close to her ear and kissed it softly before she began to whisper. "Nobody, can make love to a woman like a woman. Nothing comes close to it, you heard. I keep trying to tell you. It's time you let me show you." She paused momentarily and flashed a seductive look at Yanick. *You don't know what I would do to that ass*, she thought.

"So that's it, huh? You weren't born that way or—"

"To be honest I don't know, but I am that way, I'm not ashamed, and if you let me, I'll show you that there is nothing to be ashamed of. There is nothing more sensual, beautiful or natural than two women."

Yanick sensed people staring at them. She felt as if they were sitting too close together. She slid to the opposite end of the bench. "I'm going to check to see if they called our name." As she walked to the counter, heads turned. She didn't know if they were staring at her because they thought she was gay, or because she looked good. She held her head high and walked to the hostess' station.

Malik woke up and looked at the time, it was eleven o'clock. He noticed the red light on his room phone blinking.

"Wow, I wonder who left me a message?" He pressed the button on the phone and listened to Susan's voice. He smiled at her thoughtful message and lay down. As soon as his head hit the pillow the telephone rang.

"Hey."

"Malik? I can't talk long. My husband went out to get us a bite to eat. I was mugged on Brooklyn High School's field."

Malik sat up in the bed. "Oh shit! Did they hurt you?"

"No. Not at all. They threw me on the ground, held me up by gunpoint, and stole my wedding band, engagement ring, and my fanny pouch."

"They? How many were there?"

"Two. One wanted to rape me, but the other one talked him out of it."

"Damn, I can't believe it. At least you weren't hurt."

"I'm not going to be able to come out there and meet you. So enjoy the vacation. Are you good for money? Do you need me to wire you some?"

"No. I am going to fly home tomorrow."

"Nonsense. My husband is going to stay home with me for the weekend. I promise you there will be other trips. Besides, I don't want all of my money going down the drain."

Susan heard her husband's keys jingling as he ascended the stairs. "My husband is coming, miss you." With that she hung up the phone.

"How is my little 'Suzy Q' feeling?"

"I am just fine. I was just calling the hotel to cancel my trip for this week."

"Are you sure you want to do that baby? I can book a flight and we can go together."

"No honey. I just want to stay here with you."

Susan loved the attention she was receiving from her husband. He fed her dinner and ice cream, and gave her a massage. When they made love, she came the closest she had ever come to climaxing with him— ever.

Malik lay down on the bed with his hands clasped behind his head and stared at the ceiling. The phone rang once and he snatched it up quickly.

"Susan?"

"No, it's Laneice. Are you coming out to the restaurant with us?"

"Yeah," he said in a disappointed tone.

"What's wrong?"

"Nothing. Looks like we will be hanging out all weekend. My friend isn't coming after all. So how about jet skiing tomorrow?"

Laneice smiled, looked up at the ceiling and mouthed, 'Thank you, Jesus.' "Dress casually we're going out to the club after dinner. Be outside in fifteen minutes," Laneice said.

"I hope they don't play that sun splash shit all night. I'll see you in fifteen." As Malik hung up the phone he could hear the women screaming on the other side of the wall, and then it suddenly stopped. He laughed, shook his head and got up to get dressed.

"The married chick isn't coming and he is coming to hang out with us tonight and tomorrow."

All three of the girls fell on the bed screaming and laughing on top of their lungs. Suddenly Laneice grabbed both of her friends by their arms.

"Wait, he probably can hear us. I don't want him to know it's like that. I have to change into something a little more sexy, then we can go to his door and pick him up."

"Neicy, you going to give him some ass? Are you going to pull a one nighter out this bitch?" Tricia asked.

"I don't know. If he is an asshole, maybe I will. But if he is a gentleman, he's a keeper, and you know you can't keep no man giving it up on the first night."

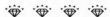

Kahmelle devoured two Big Macs without opening his mouth fully. Tony fiddled with his French fries and ate a quarter of his Quarter Pounder and Cheese.

How could you rob that innocent woman like that? She's probably traumatized, and this fool right here. Tony set aside his thoughts and looked at Kahmelle who had a mouth full of fries. *He has no fucking conscience. If I wasn't with him he would have run up in that lady raw.*

"Yo, you going to eat that? 'Cause if you don't, I will," Kahmelle said, pointing at Tony's tray.

"You just ate two Big Macs, and your ass is still hungry? You muthafuckin cock-a-roach."

Kahmelle looked up at Tony with a mouth full of Big Mac. "I don't know why you actin' gay, but you need to stop that shit."

"Yuck. You got food flying out your mouth all over the place. You sure *your* ass ain't pregnant."

"You know, it's probably a sympathy pregnancy. My aunt said she had that when I was born. She was sleepy all the time and had cravings, when my moms was having me. It's probably the same thing. Camille's ass lost twelve pounds since she's been pregnant."

"Is that good?"

"I don't know? Look, there goes Sweat now. Come on."

Kahmelle picked up a handful of fries and the remaining piece of Tony's Quarter Pounder and shoved it down his throat. Tony threw his tray's contents in the garbage can. They exited the restaurant and stepped into Sweat's car.

"Yeah, yeah, what up Sweat?" Kahmelle said as he extended his arm for a pound.

"What that green be like, Tone?"

"Chillin'." Tony got into the back seat of the car and pulled the brim of his hat over his face.

"Yo, check this shit out," Kahmelle said as he dug deep into his pocket.

"Don't pull that out in here, the streets is always watching, remember that. Where's my burger?"

"I kind of ate it, my bad," Kahmelle said.

Tony looked out of the window at the dark streets. People lined the corners as if it was the middle of the day. Girls in short shorts and tight minis, guys walking bare back or in wife beats in the heat of the night. Johnny pumps spat water, but no children ran through them, they circled the sidewalks and corners with their friends instead. Bright white lights illuminating the sticker-filled windows of ice cream trucks, on what seemed like every other corner shone down on kids and adults.

The brightness of tall white streetlights tinted the dark streets with hints of orange. Different lights allowed him visual access to people's homes as they drove down Fulton Street. Lights were everywhere, and they taunted Tony.

The traffic lights were in their favor, too. Tony could see a streak of green lights ahead of him as Sweat zipped down Fulton Street. When cars passed them big streaks of white lights shone from the headlights and illuminated the streets like big stars. Tony shut his eyes, but the lights wouldn't go away. They looked like a dozen shades of oil paint splattered across a black canvas. The lights were a constant reminder of the dark field. Their radiant beams from each source seemed to ask him, 'Why do this? Why?'

"You heard that, Tone? Kahmelle asked.

"What?"

"The Bat Cave is hot. Look," Kahmelle said pointing out of the window. Tony looked, and two blocks ahead of them were the red and blue roving lights of cop cars. Orange and white hazard lights blinked relentlessly. He shut his eyes and sat back reviewing the floating oil painting in his head.

"There's a lot of cops over at the Terminals right now, so I am going take you to my house. Only three of Brooklyn's Finest know where I live, feel me, and I want to keep it that way, dig?"

Tony nodded his head. He couldn't take his mind off of how the lady whimpered when Kahmelle pulled down her shorts and let the barrel of his gun caress her ass. He thought about the floodlight that peered through the bleachers and covered him and the woman he pinned down. *Who gave me the right to do that to her?* he thought.

"Yo, Thugglemen, you alright, duke?"

"I'm good," Tony answered.

"You kinda quiet back there. We here," Sweat said.

"That nigga is just mad because I wanted to fuck the bitch, yo. Her fuckin' titties was like BOW! She looked like a model," Kahmelle said.

"You need to slow your young ass down, Kah, you buck wild. That's exactly what the fuck I am going to call your ass too— Buck," Sweat said.

Sweat pulled up into the driveway of a brownstone. As they walked up the steps, Tony felt a chill of deja vu . . .

A much younger Malik, Tony and Sweat walked up the steps of this very house and entered. As soon as they stepped foot inside an old shaky voice filled the hall. "SWEAT, is that you?" The voice frightened Tony and he began to whimper.

"Damn Malik, why you always gotta bring your little brother with you? Yes, Slim, I got Malik and his little brother with me." The trio walked into the living room where Sweat's feeble grandmother sat.

"How are you doing Malik? Little Malik."

"My name is Tony, Miss," Tony sniffled.

"I'm Slim. Malik, he is the cutest thing. Don't be havin' him running them streets, you hear?"

"Why did you name him Sweat, ma'am?" Tony asked.

The old woman stuck out her frail and bony hands to affectionately touch Tony's face and he jumped back. "Don't be scared. Come and give me a hug." Malik pushed Tony into her arms. "When Sweat was a small boy, like you, he used to sleep in the bed with me. By the time we woke up in the morning the sheets would be wet from his perspiring. So I have called him Sweat since he was a boy."

Tony giggled in her arms and looked up into her tired eyes. "Because he peed the bed all the time?"

"No, because he used to sweat up the sheets," Slim replied with a smile on her face.

"Oh, I get it," Tony said laughing.

Malik laughed, too. "I thought it was because the girls be sweatin' you," Malik said.

"You boys go on upstairs. I need to get my rest."

"Yo, Sweat, Slim is getting old quick. Is she sick?" Malik whispered as they walked upstairs.

"Yeah, but she'll be okay."

Tony left the memory behind and tapped Sweat on the shoulder. "Sweat, is your grandmother still alive? This is the same crib, right?"

"My Slim passed away four years ago. She left me the house," Sweat said solemnly.

All three of them walked into the same room Tony had just depicted in his mind. The furniture was changed, with the exception of that Lazy-Boy chair that his grandmother sat in. Kahmelle jumped into the tattered recliner.

"Get your ass out of Slim's chair," Sweat yelled.

"My bad, Sweat. I ain't know."

"Nobody sits in that chair." Sweat pulled off his hat and sat on the couch. "Now, let's see the ring." Kahmelle dug deep into his pocket and pulled out both of the rings. "OH shit! You little niggas did good. Look at the diamonds on this shit, and the wedding band is blingin', too."

"I'm saying, can't you take it down to the Brooklyn Jewelry Exchange and pawn it?" Kahmelle asked.

Sweat stopped looking at the rings momentarily and shook his head. "Hell no. You said you stole this shit from a cracker, right?"

"Yeah," Kahmelle answered.

"You can bet that bitch has all kinds of insurance on this shit, and she lives around here too. For all I know she could have bought that shit from there, and Whitey sticks together. The dude that owns that spot knows a lot of people, word gets around, that shit could fall right on me. I'm going to take this out to my man in the diamond district, that nigga will fence this shit for me. We gonna eat off of this shit right here. You guys should see at least six or seven grand off this shit alone. I don't even know how much this band is worth."

Sweat stuck his hand out and gave Kahmelle a pound. He got out of his seat, walked over to Tony and gave him one too.

"This place looks really nice. I didn't expec—"

"What, Kahmelle? You thought I lived in the Bat Cave, huh? That's exactly what I want you muthafuckas to think. And dig nig, hardly anybody knows where I live. If some funny shit goes down, I am coming for you and yours." Tony laughed. "What you laughing at?" Sweat asked.

"I thought my brother was the only person alive that still says dig."

Sweat smiled. "Yo, you remember when we used to be at your crib back in the day?" Tony nodded his head. "I couldn't stand your fuckin' little ass. You were a fuckin' brat, always tellin' on us and shit." Sweat was silent for a few seconds. He placed the rings on the mantle piece. "Me and your brother was like you and Kahmelle. Nothing could tear our asses apart. And the fuckin' fish, they loved your brother. He was a pussy magnet."

"So what happened between y'all, man?" Tony reluctantly asked.

Sweat touched the scar on his nose gently and shrugged his shoulders. "I still got mad love for your brother, but we grew up and got into different things, you know? We both went down to Maryland. When we came back he continued school and I started Brooklyn's Finest, that's all."

"I'm sayin', ain't nothing going to stop me and Tone from being friends, you heard?" Kahmelle said.

"I got some shit for you next week, Buck. If it goes off good, you'll be eatin' well for a long time. You could come off with about fifteen grand for this next job." Sweat looked at Tony and smiled. "The Thuggleman ain't ready for that shit yet."

"Yes, he is, yo. He came up with the whole plan for tonight. Well, it was my idea but he put it together. He even pulled the bitch down, yo," Kahmelle insisted.

"Exactly, when I have jobs that need thinking, he'll be the one on call, but this shit right here is strictly fast feet, and instinct. You can't think about this one, you just got to do it," Sweat said.

"What is it?" Kahmelle asked.

"You will find out next week. And one more thing, you need to make Camille get rid of that fuckin' baby. A kid is not a good look for you right now. Take her down to the butcher and let them bake that."

Kahmelle's face fell apart, and his heart sank to his balls. "How did you find out?" he said softly. Sweat raised his eyebrows. "I tried to get her to have an abortion," Kahmelle continued.

"Try harder. Make sure you take care of that. I have some calls to make. I'll get at you," Sweat said.

"One," Kahmelle said as he stood up and embraced Sweat.

"One," he replied.

"Later," Tony said and extended his hand for a pound.

"One." Sweat escorted both boys to the door. As they reached the bottom of the steps, Kahmelle stopped. "Yo, let's head over to Latonji's house and see what's going on over there."

"Damn, Shaine got the address, yo. I don't know where to go," Tony said, trying hard to be convincing.

"Stop playin' like you ain't been stalking that bitch for the past three years, Tone. Every time we pass her house on the way home from school you be like, 'this is my wife's spot son'."

Tony sucked his teeth. "You got that, but I don't know what floor."

"Shit we'll figure that out when we get there."

Latonji opened the door and her smile revealed every filling that was in her mouth. "I knew you would come." Kahmelle walked in behind Tony, and her broad smile shrank. "I knew you would bring him, too. Come in. You guys want some Hypnotiq?"

"I've never tasted that before," Tony said.

"That shit is the pain, yo. I want mine with Hennesy," Kahmelle said.

"That's eight dollars for the Incredible Hulk and Tony, that will be four dollars for you, if you ain't gonna get your grown man on," Latonji said.

"I'm saying. I'll take mine with Hennesy, too. Here's twenty for the both of us, keep the change," Tony said as he retrieved the money from his pocket. "What's up, Latonji? You don't have no liquor license. Why you selling drinks up in here?" Tony asked as he looked at several quarts and pints of liquor standing on a card table.

"Shit. I ain't got no man to help me out, so I have to get money somehow. I'm starting college in January."

"You already got accepted?" Tony asked.

"I'm gettin' up out of here, I got accepted to Buoy State. I know your smart-ass is going to college. How does it feel to be so smart? Your ass is even in honors Chem." Latonji stared at him when she spoke; it made him feel uncomfortable.

"Well, I ain't no smarter than the next man, you know? I just read, and do all of my assignments. Niggas can't just pass class by sitting there. You have to do the work. I want to go to Howard, for Pre-med."

"Mmm hmm," Latonji placed her hand on his leg and rested her head on his shoulder. "I see you left Shaine at home. You know, I always thought you were cute. I don't understand why you got at Shaine before you even looked my way."

Tony sucked his teeth. "Yeah right! You ain't think I was cute until I started rollin' in green. Once my 'Finest' status was right then you started looking a niggas way," Tony said. He guzzled half his drink.

"Now you know that ain't true. Every time you would stare at me, I would look back at you AND SAY HELLO. I don't even speak to half the niggas that be saying hello to me. Besides, your AP Math class was directly across from my Spanish class last year. I used to see you every time I went to class."

Wow, I don't believe she remembered that, he thought.

"I ain't gonna front. I always thought you was a nerd and shit, but I thought you were a cute nerd." Latonji grabbed his wrist as he put the drink to his mouth, moved the cup away and kissed him gently. "You were a cute nerd with style. Your gear was always game tight."

Tony sat at the arm of the couch. There wasn't any more room for him to slide. He sternly pushed her away and drank down the rest of his drink.

"Let me get you another one, on me," Latonji said.

Tony felt a tingling sensation rush through his head. He hiccuped abruptly, and he could feel the brown and blue come up in this throat. He walked over to Kahmelle, sat next to him, and whispered in his ear. "Yo, son. That shit right there, got me fucked up. I'm straight."

"You? I already got my buzz on," Kahmelle said.

Three guys and two girls appeared from the back of her apartment giggling and clinging to each other. "Yo, Tony. What's up?" one of the guys said.

"Ain't nothing, son."

They all exchanged greetings. For the first time since he'd arrived he noticed other people in the room besides him, Latonji and Kahmelle. There were at least fourteen people there and they all attended The High. Latonji pulled a folding chair right next to Tony's and passed him his drink.

"Yo son, where did you get that fuckin' shirt from, duke? You borrow that shit from your baby cousin? It's mad young," Kahmelle yelled toward one of the guys that just entered the room.

All the teens in the room roared with laughter. Kahmelle was loud and obnoxious in his drunkenness. He was the king of the dozens in the lunchroom, and he was just heating up.

"Nah, I got this from your moms last night," the teen replied.

"What about your fuckin', moms duke? That bitch is so ugly if she was a brick she'd be the projects. Yo, y'all remember that movie 'Gorillas In The Mist'? Why they filmed that shit in his mother's shower." Kahmelle's jokes continued non-stop for at least twenty minutes. He gave his opponent no time to retaliate, and no one else time to breathe they all laughed so hard. Just as he was calming down the house phone rang. Laughter filled the room and Latonji screamed into the phone. Tony was bent over laughing.

"HELLO?"

"Latonji?" Shaine asked, her voice dripping with attitude.

"Yeah?"

"Tony there?"

"Yep. He's lying on my lap right now. Here baby, it's for you," Latonji said. She passed Tony the phone, and he could not stop laughing.

"TONY?"

"Shaine, what's up mama?"

"I can't believe your ass. What are you doing over there?"

"Drinking and listening to Kahmelle heat up on these niggas."

"I thought you weren't going to go— you promised."

"It's all good, besides, ain't shit in here I want. I'm just chillin' with my mans and them from the High that's all. You don't have to worry about me fuckin' this broad. I'll be over there later."

"You better not be fuckin that bit—" Tony hung up on her in the middle of her sentence.

Latonji got up and walked to the drink table. *He'll be mine before I leave school,* she thought.

Yanick stumbled into the house, laughing loudly. Joann came in behind her, locked the door and watched Yanick flop on the couch. As soon as she sat down she sprang back up, as if she had sat on a trampoline. "One more drink, and I would have been done. Come here Joey Crack."

"Let me find out that all this time all I had to do was get you drunk?" Joann said.

Before Joann could make her way across the room, Yanick walked over to Joann and kissed her passionately. Once they unlocked their lips, they both breathed heavily.

"Take off that sundress, and leave those heels and thong on," Joann said.

Yanick slipped out of her dress, they walked to the bedroom and Joann lay on the bed. With little hesitation Yanick climbed onto the bed, but Joann stopped her. "Nah, stand on the end of the bed and dance for me, sweetheart." Yanick's thighs and ass wiggled as she slithered and shook her body for several minutes. "Now, open your legs and bend over in my face."

"Joann, that's nasty." Yanick assumed the position anyway.

Joann inhaled deeply and hot flashes rushed through her body, causing the air she released to come out choppy instead of smooth and relaxed. "How can something nasty look so fuckin' good, Ma? How did your ass get like that?"

Joann stripped down to her brown skin watching Yanick bend and wiggle. "Talk to me in Spanish baby," Joann said.

Yanick stood upright and looked at Joann. "What do you want me to say?"

Joann reached into her dresser and pulled out a long brown dildo with a strap attached to it and a small silver vibrator. She placed them both on the pillow next to her.

Yanick reassumed her position and looked at Joann, upside down through her open legs. She stuck her finger in her mouth and pulled it out slowly then whispered, "¿Soy bella? ¿Te gusta lo que ves?"

"Sounds sexy, now say that shit in English."

"Am I beautiful, you like what you see?"

"Fuck yeah," Joann said in a coarse whisper. "Tell me what you want me to do to you."

Yanick looked at the dildo sitting on the pillow next to Joann. She turned to face her, knelt and stuck her middle finger in her vagina. As she fingered herself she provocatively licked her lips. "Meteme ese bicho." Joann breathed heavily and talked under her breath. "What?"

"Stick that dildo in my pussy."

"Talk some more."

"Come mi chocha ahrora.

"In English, baby, in English."

"Eat my pussy now."

"Ven, Yanick," Joann said.

"Come," Yanick panted out in English.

Yanick lay down, and before she could hit the mattress, Joann pulled off her thong. "Damn, your mother definitely blessed you," Joann said.

Yanick smiled as Joann kissed her body from her thighs down to her ankles and spread her legs open. Joann took the small bullet shaped vibrator from the pillow, clicked it on and placed it on her lover's clitoris. She kissed her passionately, then situated herself on top of Yanick, so that the tip of the vibrator buzzed on her clitoris as well. She humped softly on top of Yanick not wanting to lose her position on the vibrator.

As the vibrator buzzed both women both felt extreme pleasure. Yanick's was more intense. She couldn't believe all the different sensations that were taking place all over her body. Warm quivers tingled through her breasts, sensual tremors radiated around her pussy leaving her helpless and unsure of what to do. When it became too much for her to handle, she screamed loudly and grabbed Joann's back.

"What's wrong, baby?" Joann panted.

"It just feels so good," Yanick replied.

Joann got up, and lay by Yanick's side. "Turn around and get on your hands and knees."

When Yanick moved to comply Joann smacked her ass, palmed it, and moved her thick cheeks around several times before strapping on her dildo. She stuck her finger into Yanick's vagina and pulled it out quickly. Then she eased the dildo between her huge, round cheeks. Yanick exhaled and clutched the sheets tightly. Joann spread Yanick's cheeks open as she eased the dildo in and out of her ass with soft humps.

Joann pumped faster and faster leaving the dildo sticky and wet. She grabbed Yanick's ass tighter and tighter as she began to climax. "You still scared, Yanick?" Joann puffed.

"No," she panted.

"I want you to cum all over this dildo so I can rub it all over your ass." Yanick began to gyrate faster.

Joann felt moisture oozing down her inner thighs, but she continued to slide the dildo in and out of Yanick's vagina. "You gonna cum for me, baby?"

"I'm trying. This feels so good, but I have never had an orgasm before," Yanick said.

"Lay down on your back."

Out of breath, she lay down and spread her legs. Joann carefully mounted her and slid the dildo into Yanick's vagina slowly. She watched Yanick stare up at her. Joann reached for the vibrator and placed it on Yanick's clitoris, continuing her long, slow strokes. Within minutes Yanick was moaning loudly. "Oh God!"

"God's not doing this sexy, I am."

"Oh God, Joey! I think I'm coming."

"Come on."

Yanick released several high-pitched moans as she achieved her sexual peak. Out of breath and past the ultimate point of pleasure she relaxed her muscles, smiled and covered her face. Joann removed Yanick's hands from her face, kissed her fingers and played in her hair.

"So, how was it?"

Yanick lay as still as possible, but tremors shook her thighs as she inhaled and exhaled deeply several times watching her breasts rise and fall. After a few minutes she turned over and smiled at Joann.

"It was wonderful, Joann. I never imagined it could be so good, and believe me I imagined us having sex lots of times. Who would have ever imagined my first orgasm would be with a woman? I mean, when I masturbate I get them, but I have never had one with anyone else."

"And there will be many more where that came from," Joann said as she kissed her lips and played in her hair. "I'm going to sleep, you know I have work tomorrow."

"You know, we make a good pair— I am all ass and you're all titties." They both laughed and Yanick kissed Joann's plump breasts. She balled up in a fetal position and put her thumb in her mouth.

"I know you are not sucking your thumb?" Joann asked.

She nodded her head and spooned herself further into Joann's arms. "I am just trying to relax. I am a bit overwhelmed right now. Joann?"

"Hmm?"

"Please don't hurt me. I feel secure when I'm with you." She paused to take a breath. "Like I know you would never do anything to hurt me."

"That's not why I am here. I'm here to make you stop sucking your thumb. Now let's get some sleep, I have to go to work tomorrow."

❖   ❖   ❖   ❖

Malik grabbed onto Laneice and Monica as he missed the top step of the hotel's patio, and nearly went down face first.

"That club was hot it didn't even feel like we were in Jamaica and I got two numbers. They both talking about coming to the resort and checking me tomorrow," Monica said.

"Word, they were playin' Jay-Z and everything. I got one number and he said he is going to show me the town and shit," Tricia replied.

"You want to watch out for these native muthafuckas out here. They might try to rob you and shit. Let them come here, or we all go out together. OH SHIT!" Malik tripped. He tightened his grip on the ladies as his staggers became more pronounced.

"Are you all right?" Laneice asked.

Malik sat down in front of his door and laughed. "Alright Michelle and Kelly, Beyoncé is coming in here with me tonight. She has to make sure I don't choke on my vomit in my sleep. You are a nurse, right?"

"I know you have fantasized about having intercourse with a woman in a nurses uniform. Well, go shorty, it's your birthd—"

"Yo, did you hear that shit in Jamaican? I can't believe they did that shit over," Malik interrupted.

They laughed loudly at their shared initial reaction to the reggae artist that had mutilated Fifty Cent's song.

Laneice helped Malik to his feet. He tried unsuccessfully three times, to unlock the door. Laneice grabbed the key from him and opened it on the first try.

"I'll see you two lovebirds later," Monica said.

Tricia sucked her teeth and rolled her eyes. "We came together, we stayin' together," she said.

"I didn't even know she could talk. That's the first thing I heard her say all night— oh shit, excuse me." Malik ran into the room and grabbed the ice bucket and vomited.

"Laneice, you don't have to stay with me, I'm good." Malik said.

Monica grabbed Tricia and yanked her towards their door. Laneice walked right behind them "Why you hating, Tricia? We talked about this on the plane and shit. We all wanted to have a one-night stand and said if the opportunity knocked out here, we would answer the door. This dude is super fine and I think Laneice should go for hers. Just make sure you tell me how it was in the morning," Monica said.

Laneice walked up the spiral staircase in the corner of their room. She pulled out two condoms, a sheer nightshirt, and thong slippers from her suitcase. The slippers made a loud smack as they hit the bathroom floor. Looking in the mirror she fingered her hair and moistened her lips, then she slipped into her slippers. She walked out of the bathroom and descended the steps waving her condoms. Before she left the room the phone rang loudly. Tricia answered the phone and within seconds she was smiling. "Hi Delroy, this is me."

"The hater is coming up in this bitch. Tomorrow she will be waving her condom in the air," Monica said.

Using Malik's key Laneice let herself in. He lay in the same spot she had left him in, fully clothed. "Malik?" He didn't budge. Laneice yelled, "MALIK!" This time he grunted but didn't move. She slid out of her dress and into her nightshirt. She removed Malik's shoes. As she touched his belt buckle he sprang up in the bed. "Ah, my head," he groaned. He stumbled around the room, shoved his wallet into the inside pocket of his bag and made sure it was locked. When he sat next to her on the bed, he barley noticed she had changed. He stared at her fitted nightshirt that was almost her complexion. Then he took his three middle fingers and trailed them straight between her breasts. "No bra? Impressive," Malik said.

He lay down and before his head hit the pillow, he was knocked out. Laneice lay next to him. She traced the scar on his back, and kissed his neck, but he didn't move. She reached over him, picked up the phone and then dialed her room. "He is knocked the fuck out. No dick for me tonight," she said in an aggravated tone.

"Girl, don't rush, we ain't leaving 'til Monday. Now get off of the phone, I am on the other line with Delroy. We're making plans for tomorrow," Tricia said. Laneice placed the phone on the receiver and looked at the clock. "Damn, it's four already."

She snuggled close to Malik, and stared at his scar. She composed several stories of how his scar came to be. When her eyelids grew heavy his scar was no longer in her view, but was vivid in her dreams.

The next morning Laneice shook him violently. "Wake up, Malik! We have eleven-thirty appointments to catch the tour bus to Dunns River Falls and it's already minutes after ten."

"My fucking head is killing me? I wish I could call Susan."

"What?" Laneice asked.

"Nothing. You eat yet?" Malik sat up in the bed and stared at Laneice. "How long have you been up?"

Laneice sported a sheer hot pink sarong with flowers all over it. Underneath was a thong, which revealed her smooth rear end. Malik dragged himself to the edge of the bed, grabbed the end of her sarong and with one pull untied it. "Shit, is that all you?"

"Yep."

"Damn, do you work out every single day?"

"Not even. I played volleyball in high school and college. I still play in summer tournaments on the weekends, but that's pretty much it. And I do twenty minutes on my treadmill and a couple of crunches every night."

"You must be psycho."

"What?"

"I don't understand why you don't have a ring on your finger."

"My standards are too high. I have had several proposals, but—"

"But what? They didn't have enough money." Malik got out of the bed and palmed her behind. He grabbed it, rubbed it several times, then pulled her close to him. She pushed herself free and snatched her sarong.

"None of that. You missed out last night. Now I am going to enjoy my vacation."

Malik went into the bathroom and turned on the shower. He stepped out of his boxers, stood over the toilet and took a long piss.

"That's all those Jamaica-me-crazies your ass was drinking last night," Laneice said loudly.

Malik laughed as he shook the tip of his penis. "Where are we going to—" The phone rang cutting him off. "Don't answer that!!" he yelled. Malik grabbed the phone that was inside of the bathroom and turned his back on the door. Laneice suddenly felt ashamed and a bit jealous. She walked close enough to the door to hear, but far enough to be out of his sight.

"I was so worried about you— How are you feeling? Did the cops catch anyone— Yeah, I am enjoying my self immensely, wish you were here though— You're going to pick me up from the airport? You sure? I'll see you then— bye." Malik hung up and continued talking like he hadn't been on the phone. "Where are we going to eat?"

"I figured you might want to wait to go home and eat with her since you wish she was here," Laneice said jealously.

Malik shook his head and laughed out loud. "Whatever."

Laneice threw his key on table and slammed the door on her way out.

"I ain't even fuck that bitch and she open already? At least I don't think I did." Malik picked up his dick and looked at it. "Shit, I was fucked up last night. I don't even know how my ass made it back to the room."

He stepped into the shower and placed his hands flat against its white walls. He stuck his head directly underneath the nozzle. He bent over and let the water beat down on his head. Streams of water trickled down his face and caressed his neck. He stood there thinking about Laneice.

As Tricia sprayed Oil Sheen directly onto the tracks of her wet and wavy weave in the next room she talked to Laneice through her reflection in the mirror. "Fuck him, Neicey. You can meet another dude out here. You know you're a dime. Plus, that nigga work in the mailroom and he is young," Tricia said.

"You know that chick paid his way out here. That's probably his sugar mama. Out of respect for her he had to do that. I say we go scoop his ass up on our way out. It ain't like you fucked him. He really don't owe you shit," Monica said, shoving her triple D's into her bathing suit. After a moment of silence, Monica continued. "Laneice, if your ass keeps overreacting about small shit, he ain't gonna want to talk to you when we get back home."

"I guess you're right, Monica," Laneice said.

"And?" Monica said.

"And we'll scoop him before we leave. Let's go," Laneice said.

Malik was standing outside the door when Laneice swung it open. "I'm ready to go, but a nigga has to get some food before we leave," he said.

"Me too, I have to feed my twins," Monica said readjusting her swim suit top.

Malik laughed. "I like you. We're going to have to keep in touch and hang out when we get back home." He smiled at Laneice as he said it.

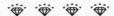

"Ma, I'm sorry, but I had a little bit too much to drink, and I spent the night at Shaine's."

"Tony, it's eleven-thirty, you couldn't have called me last night? Is her mother there? I would like to have a word with her— what the fuck were you drinking that made you forget to call home?"

Tony could barely get in one word, much less an entire answer. His mother kept cutting his answers off with more questions.

"Jonathan, you better come talk to Tony. I'm going to kill him." Tony's father tried to take the phone from his wife but she wouldn't let it go. "You have been acting real strange lately. Coming in late all the time, new clothes that I know you can't afford on your allowance. You better not be selling no drugs. Jonathan, I am going to kill him, you better talk to your son," Millicent said again before finally handing Jonathan the phone.

"Tony. You had your mother worried sick last night. I can't believe you are just getting around to calling."

"I know Dad, but—"

"No buts. Bring your ass home right now and we can talk. You're going down south to your grandmother's for the summer."

"Dad, this is the first time. Hello? Dad? Shit, I knew he was going to be mad, but I didn't think he would hit the roof. They only threatened to send me down south for the summer once before."

"The whole summer! I don't think I could live without you that long," Shaine said.

Tony walked into Shaine's bedroom and picked up his pants off of the floor. As he was tying his shoelaces he heard a key in the door.

"Oh shit! That's my mom. You better hide. If you think your moms be flipping, let her see you up in here. Quick, get under my bed. HURRY UP!" Shaine said nervously.

Tony slid underneath her bed and lay still. Within seconds her mother came shuffling into her room. He could see her high heels right in front of him. He shut his eyes tightly and prayed.

"Hey, Shaine, how are you feelin' baby?"

"Fine, Mom."

"Did you clean the house and do the wash like I asked you to?"

"I cleaned, but I ain't do the laundry yet."

"Shaine. You know I like to do the laundry first thing in the morning so I don't have to wait around for the dryers."

Shaine smiled at her mother. "But mom, *I'm* doing the laundry so it really shouldn't matter what time I go."

Shaine's mother laughed. "You know, you're right. Listen, Shaine, I don' t think we're spending enough time together. So I have arranged for you, me, Frank and his kids to go to Miami next month for two weeks."

Shaine sucked her teeth and jumped off the bed. Tony could see her bare feet land on the floor. "That's not us spending time together, that's more time for you to spend with Frank. His children and I don't get along. I don't know why you can't see the only reason he is with you is so you can take care of those two brats, 'cause their own mother won't."

Her mother calmly walked out of the room. "You're still going," she called back.

"I am going to do the laundry now, Mom." Shaine knelt on the floor and extended her arm to Tony. "Come on, she is super tight with me. She ain't going to come out of that room," she whispered.

The two crept to the front door. Shaine pushed a shopping cart filled with clothes and Tony followed her. Just as they were about to exit Tony's phone went off.

"YO, pick up nigga," came through the speaker loudly.

The door to Shaine's mother's room swung opened and slammed against the wall. Tony shoved Shaine out of the way, swung open the front door and positioned himself outside of it.

"Shaine what was that? her mother asked as she rushed to the front of the apartment.

"Good afternoon Ms. Lewis, how are you today?" Tony grinned. Ms. Lewis looked at her watch.

"It's barely afternoon. What are you doing out so early on a Saturday, Tony?"

"I was on my way to the library, and I wanted to stop by and see Shaine if you don't mind." Tony looked at Shaine and smiled. "Hi, Shaine, what's up? Feel like going to the library?"

"I have to do my laundry. Maybe we could go to the movies later."

"Sure, that is if it is all right with you, Ms. Lewis."

Shaine's mother smiled. "As long as Shaine finishes her chores."

"Come on Shaine, I will walk you to the laundry mat."

"Yo Tone pick up! You blaze that or what?" Tony turned the walkie off. Shaine's mother looked at Tony's hip as he clipped his phone to it.

"Blaze what?" Shaine asked.

Ms. Lewis walked back to her room and shut her door. Tony and Shaine left and started down the steps with the shopping cart.

"Blaze what? Latonji?"

"You still stuck on that shit? I thought the two-hour conversation we had about her when I got here last night was enough. You really want to know what Kah is talking about?" Tony unclipped his phone and turned it back on. Before he could push the buttons Kahmelle's voice blared over the speaker.

"Yo, did your girl give up the ass last night? You better had hit that, after you turned down Latonji's fat ass last night."

Shaine grabbed the phone and yelled. "No, he did not blaze me."

"Shaine? How you doing, ma? You better come off of that cat, ma. I don't know how long my man can hold out."

Tony grabbed the phone from Shaine and beeped in. "Yeah, yeah, what up, Kah?"

"Sweat wants us to meet him downtown."

"Where are we going to meet at?"

"I'll meet you in front of Junior's in an hour. One."

"One."

"So, if I don't give it up you gonna start fucking with that bitch?"

"Since when you listen to Kahmelle? You don't even like that nigga."

"Whatever."

They stepped out of her five-story building and started down the street.

"I will call you later. Stay in the crib, dig."

"Dig? Where you get that country shit from?"

"My older brother always says that. You just make sure you keep your ass in the house until you hear from me." Tony walked off as quickly as he could.

Damn, Tony thought, *should I go home and face the music, or check Sweat and them, first? Maybe I should just go home first— nah. If I do that they might try to keep me in the house. I'll just go deal with this shit first then I'll go home.* Tony changed his direction four times. *I don't know what to do, I wish I could ask Malik*, he thought.

Tony was in front of Junior's restaurant within forty-five minutes. He went inside and ordered a slice of strawberry cheesecake and a glass of milk. He sat on a barstool near the front of the restaurant so he could see Kahmelle when he walked in. An old, tired-looking waitress placed the cake, milk and bill in front of him. As the plate hit the counter he scooped up a generous piece with his fork and sank his teeth into the rich thick and creamy treat. A big strawberry fell off of his fork before he began to chew. He picked it up with is fingers and shoved it into his mouth. His phone went off as he finished his milk.

"We in front of Junior's, where you at?" Kahmelle asked.

"I'm inside. I'll be right out." Tony took a crumpled ten dollar bill out of his pocket and tossed it on the counter beside his plate. "Excuse me, miss," he said loudly.

She looked over and noticed him pointing at the money. He picked up a huge orange and white napkin, wiped his mouth and walked outside to find Kahmelle sitting in the passenger's seat of Sweat's truck.

"What up, what up?" Tony asked.

"That green, baby," Sweat said. Sweat scratched the scar on his face and looked into his rear view mirror as Tony situated himself into the seat.

"How's Leeko? He be asking about me?"

"He's chillin."

Sweat pulled off and continued to finger his scar as he drove. "What is he up to?"

"On the real, yo, I can't let that nigga know that I fucks with you, he would fuckin' kill me, and that's my word. You know he don't get down like that no more."

Kahmelle turned around so his upper body faced the back seat of the car. "Ten G's, son. Next week this time we will have ten thou'."

"Word, so what are we splitting that in three?" Tony asked.

"Nah, we get ten-thousand a piece!" Kahmelle exclaimed. Tony sat silently in the rear. "And that's with Sweat's cut."

"Duke, y'all picked a hot one, and Buck when you run this next job in about two weeks, you might be able to double that shit, you heard?"

"I thought the job was next week."

"Be easy, I pushed it back a week."

What am I going to do with all of this money? I can't come in with too much shit cause my moms is going to sniff that shit out right away. I guess I will put away eight and blow the rest, Tony thought.

"You with us?" Kahmelle asked Tony.

"Buck, I told you, I don't think this is Tony's kind of job, he could sit this one out. This is all you, son. It's definitely your speed. Do you bowl?" Sweat asked sarcastically.

Sweat drove them around the block and dropped them back in front of Junior's ten minutes later. Kahmelle and Tony walked up Flatbush toward Fourth Avenue deep in discussion.

"Yo, if that nigga gives us that much imagine what he's taking out for himself. I don't know, the next time we knock someone off I say we push mute, son. We could have sold that shit ourselves and cut his cut," Kahmelle said.

"The next time? You must be shitting me. I am going to do the last robbery and I want out kid. I mean that shit."

"That little snotty bitch got you wile'n, yo," Kahmelle snapped.

"What you mean?"

"You know damn well you wouldn't want to quit if she had made it in. She's just jealous because she ain't get blessed, now she wants you to quit," Kahmelle yelled.

"What are you talking about? She ain't got nothing to do with this. I just don't dig this shit the way I thought I would. But you, dun, you playin' a whole different ball game," Tony said.

"Yo I feel this shit. You know it's in my blood!" Kahmelle said.

"In your blood? Your father got killed robbing a fuckin' bank, and your mother's down south on welfare! Is that what you're trying to live up to?" Tony asked, his temper gone out of control.

"Fuck you, Tone! Kahmelle said coarsely, his angry emotions peppering his words. "I feel powerful when we do shit. When we was robbin' them cars and shit, I felt above the law, and when we robbed ole girl, my dick got hard."

Tony inhaled in an attempt to calm down. He cracked half of a smile and raised his brows. "Your shit is always hard, plus she did have some tig ol' bitties," he said lightly.

"No, I am dead ass, that shit gave me a muthafuckin' rush."

"Listen—"

"No, you listen, for once. If you want to drop out after initiation, fine but don't shit on me now, son."

"I think we should both drop out, pa," Tony said.

"Nah, not me. I like this shit. I'm Finest for life."

6

Rock the boat; work the middle, new position

"How far is this place? I am so hungry," Malik said.

"I don't know," Laneice replied.

"Why we didn't eat before we left?" Malik asked.

"'Cause this is the last tour bus leaving from our hotel."

"This is a fuckin' van!"

"Whatever, but this was the last tour leaving from our hotel."

"All I wanted to do out here was jet ski, swim and fu-" Malik cleared his throat.

Laneice smiled. "And what?" she asked.

"And forget about life for the weekend. You know, I just wanted to chill."

"You could have done that last night, Sleeping Beauty." All three girls laughed. Malik smiled.

A voice with a strong accent blasted throughout the van. "Dunns River Falls. We'll meet right 'ere at tree forty-five and we leave at four sharp."

The passengers exited the van and followed the van driver.

"This is it? You dragged me out my bed to see the Niagara Falls of Jamaica? I want to do some real live shit while I am out here. I want to go jet skiing as soon as we get back to the hotel."

Malik smiled as he walked closer to their destination. Beautiful clear water slid down mountainous sized rocks, and dozens of people were climbing them. "Yo, dig, this might be fun after all," he said, and Laneice squeezed his hand.

As Malik climbed to the top of the water spurting rocks he had not a care in the world. The falls were scenic. Malik looked down at Laneice, who was on his heels. He spotted Tricia at ground level, sipping a drink in a cup carved from a coconut, taking in the sun. Monica was several feet below Laneice.

Out of breath, Laneice struggled to pass Malik. She called out to him.

"I am right behind you now." She reached for a rock close to Malik's waist. She pulled herself up and was a torso's length away from him.

"OUCH!"

Both Laneice and Malik looked down to find Monica sitting on a rock that was a considerable distance between them frantically shaking her arm. "I fuckin' cut myself— look at this shit."

She had a small cut on her chest, and her finger was dripping deep, dark blood, into the gushing water.

"Girl, that looks like a little ash to me, come on," Laneice said.

"Fuck that. You two go ahead. I am going to get something to eat, and catch some sun with Tricia."

"I'll take a look at your finger when I come back down," Laneice said.

Malik looked up and Laneice was almost at the top of the falls. "You little sneak! How did you pass me?"

"I was going to beat you anyway, even before Monica's little mishap." Laneice struggled with the last stone and grunted hard. She could barley reach it and now Malik was at her heels. She looked below her and spotted a nice sized stone a few feet above where both of her feet were planted. She stepped on it and reached up. "Got it," she breathed heavily.

Laneice jumped to the top and pumped her fist in the air like she had just won the heavyweight title of the world. Seconds after Malik effortlessly reached her side. "Not bad. Do you do a little rock climbing at the mall between shopping?" he asked sarcastically.

"No, I just stay in pretty good shape."

"I can see that. Let's go eat, and see if we can rent some jet skis."

After eating Malik and Laneice rested for an hour and rented a two-seater jet ski. She sat on the back and held on to his waist lightly. Malik gripped the gears.

"Hang on tight!" he yelled.

Laneice gripped Malik's waist and rested her head on his scarred back. They sped full throttle into the clear blue waters. She thought about nothing at all, besides the warmth of the sun on her back and how good it felt to hold someone.

"Let's follow them," Malik said.

"WHAT?"

"Let's follow them, they look like they're going on a tour." Malik made a sharp turn and pulled up behind fifteen jet skiers driving in a row.

They followed them for about fifteen minutes before they came to the most exotic looking plant life they both had ever seen. It looked like a small jungle surrounded by water. Trees seemed to tower from the very bottom of the ocean all the way up into the sky blue sky. Flowers were in full bloom hanging off of branches that bent in the air like a willow tree. Bright reds, yellows, pinks and oranges were among the greenest leaves. The trees were tall and blocked the sunlight. Some vines hung down close enough for the jet skiers to touch. Even the big insects that flew around were beautiful. Bright flashes illuminated the dimly lit area.

The tour entered the shaded area slowly. The shade was a cool break from the sun. Malik was caught up he had never seen anything like it. Laneice hugged him tightly as she took in the sights with a great deal of appreciation. The tour had stopped and the guide began to name the exotic plant life that surrounded them.

Malik tapped Laneice's arm so she could release him from her tight grip. He carefully swung his legs to the side and she gripped the edge of her seat. Facing her fully, he smiled. "This is really nice. I have never seen anything so beautiful, besides you."

Laneice blushed. Malik kissed her lips gently. Then he kissed her again, more forcefully and started to unsnap her life vest. He caressed her scantily covered breasts and continued to kiss her.

"Stop," she whispered. "There are other people here, you know?" Malik stopped momentarily and looked around. As the tour started to move forward he swung back around and shifted the jet ski into reverse. He backed out of the dimly lit area to a pathway of thick hedges a couple of feet away.

"Malik!" she shouted.

"We aren't out here with them anyway. Besides, I know the shore is that way. I just want to enjoy all this beauty a little more. When I lived in Maryland, I used to go to Ocean City and jet ski almost every day in the summer. It was me, my man Sweat and his girl, Tasha."

His head began to pound as he thought about Sweat and Tasha and he paused for a few seconds. He shut his eyes and spoke under his breath. "Damn Tasha," he said sympathetically as he shook off the memory and faced her again. Malik kissed her lips and rubbed her breasts.

"Don't do this. You are getting me worked up, Malik."

"That's what I want, since I missed out last night. Before you say no, just listen. We're out here all by ourselves. This is some real Dexter St. Jock shit. When I jump off, lay on the wave runner with your head close to the edge of the seat, and let me give you what you came out here for."

"What you know about Dexter St. Jaques?"

"Are you serious? Eddie Murphy's 'Delirious' and Richard Pryor's old joints make them comic view niggas look like River Dance on stage. Now, just lay down."

"Uh-uh, I can't do that."

"Get ready to shift your weight to the middle when I jump off." Malik jumped off. "Just lay down. We are two horny consulting adults, there is no one here judging us."

She hesitantly lay with her head resting on the back end of the wet leather seat of the jet ski. Her knees were bent and her feet planted on the foot rails. She clasped her hands together, rested them on her chest and closed her eyes tightly.

He planted kisses up and down her calves. He massaged her inner thighs. She enjoyed the feel of the sun and his kisses on her body making her feel warm inside and out. He stuck his hand into the top of her thong and petted her throbbing cat. He watched her golden torso move up and down under the beaming sunlight as he bobbed in the water. He unsnapped her vest completely and fondled her supple breast. He stuck his finger in her mouth, and she sucked it like it was peppermint flavored. He looked around them. They were surrounded by nature.

When he stopped she felt good. Suddenly her heart dropped as she felt the bottom end of the jet ski tilt downward. She grabbed the foot rails on both sides, and before she could sit up she was looking up into Malik's crotch. He carefully walked directly over her face and she inhaled deeply several times sniffing for any unpleasant body odor, but she found none. He sat down and rested his back against the handlebars as he slid his middle fingers underneath her swimsuit.

"Malik, stop! We don't have any protection or anything. We can't go any further than this."

"Don't be sc'ered? You don't have any protection, but I do." Malik went into his pocket and pulled out the purple plastic waterproof container he had purchased from the bar when they had met. Laneice laughed as he removed the condom then snapped it tightly closed and placed it back in his pocket. "And it's dry, too."

He opened the condom and rolled it onto his penis. He pulled one leg out of his trunks then stroked his dick and fondled her clit. "Pull off that thong, grab your knees and pull them up toward your chest," Malik said

She cautiously pulled them off and clutched them in her hand. Then she grasped her kneecaps, spread them apart, and pulled them toward her chest, leaving Malik's furry target wide open. He continued to strum her with his fingers. The delightful sound of her wet pussy was music to his throbbing head. He stopped and prudently made his descent. A flush of adrenaline rushed through Laneice's body.

Bending awkwardly, he pushed the tip of his penis in until he was able to slide in and out with ease. Laneice closed her eyes and gripped her bikini bottom tightly as he thrust his big dick into her. He paced himself with short, hard strokes trying not to upset the jet ski's balance. Laneice was open, the painful pleasure felt so good. Once he caught his equilibrium he pulled all the way back and hit her with a long stroke. A moist fart sound escaped her vagina. She squirmed to the side to alleviate the stabbing pain, and the jet ski toppled over on them.

Laneice came up first and blushed as a cruise filled with tourists applauded as they slowly sailed by. The boat passed very close to the hedges that Malik thought had so cleverly hidden them. Mothers covered their children's eyes, and looked at her with disgust. Men stamped and whistled. Some wives rolled their eyes or gave their husbands quick jabs in the side. Others wished their marriages were as sexually adventurous. Malik surfaced and was startled by how close the boat came to them. He gave an embarrassed smile, looked around for Laneice, and quickly swam over to her. Her breasts hung over her top. He shoved them in and gave her a warm embrace, shielding her from the gawking cruise ship passengers.

Suddenly she started laughing loudly.

"You okay?" Malik said.

"Yeah, I'm okay. A bit embarrassed, but definitely okay," she smiled.

As soon as the ship passed Malik let Laneice go and right-sided the jet ski. When he jumped back on it he noticed his trunks floating in the water next to it. He could hear the passengers commenting and when he looked up, half of the people were running toward the stern of the cruise liner to get another glimpse of them. He stood upright on the jet ski, grabbed his balls and stuck his middle finger in the air.

Laneice handed him his trunks and he pulled them on. She climbed back on and they started off toward the shore. Laneice kissed his back, and hugged him. She had her dream man, minus a couple thousand dollars in her arms. If only for a short weekend, she would enjoy him for the moment.

Malik walked out of the airport Monday morning with Laneice on his mind. Holding his duffel bag, he waited patiently at the curb searching the bumper-to-bumper traffic for Susan's car. He checked his watch. His flight was due to come in at three o'clock, but it landed a couple of minutes early. Within five minutes the '97 family car pulled up in front of him.

"Shit, Mom and Dad. I forgot to call them and let them know that Susan was coming to pick me up."

As soon as he stepped off the curb to greet his parents, Susan pulled up three cars behind them. His parents got out of the car, and Susan came scurrying up the block in a high heel pair of Candies. Just as his mother released her grip Susan stopped in front of the threesome. She looked confused.

"Hey, honey. I'm sorry. You weren't waiting long?" she asked.

"Susan. These are my parents." His voice was monotone.

She extended her arm smiling. "Pleased to meet you."

"Likewise," Mr. Hendrickson said.

"I got my signals crossed. I was expecting you to be out there with me, and well— I asked my parents to pick me up," Malik said.

"I have never heard Malik mention you. You guys traveled together?" Mrs. Hendrickson asked.

"This is a friend of mine from the firm. Her travel arrangements were unexpectedly cancelled, Mom."

Susan smiled and shook Malik's hand. "I think I should go. I will catch up with you at work."

"Okay, let me walk you to your car." Malik handed his duffel bag to his father.

"Again, it was very nice to meet you, Mr. and Mrs. Hendrickson." His parents waved. "That was so awkward. I wish you would have told me they were coming to pick you up," Susan said.

"I totally forgot. I haven't spoken to them since I left. I'm sorry."

Susan put her arms around his neck and kissed his face as they reached her car.

"Jonathan, who the hell was that? Is that who he's been out with lately? She has wrinkles around her eyes. That bitch is probably my age," Millicent huffed.

"Millicent, your guess is as good as mine. Get into the car."

"SHE IS WHITE."

"And so are our eyeballs, what difference does it make, Millie?" Through the rearview mirror Jonathan looked at his son and watched the couple share a passionate kiss. "He just tongued her down. That answers your next question, they are fuckin'."

"Susan, I don't think we should be out here kissing in public like this," Malik said looking around.

She backed away from him. "You're so right. I just miss feeling your strong arms wrapped around my body. You look so hunkish. You're golden, look at you! Did you enjoy yourself?"

"Yes. I had a wonderful time, thanks. Any leads on those guys who robbed you?"

"No, I haven't heard anything yet. We'll definitely schedule another vacation together, my treat. You want to meet up tonight?"

"No, I really can't Susan. I need a rest from my vacation before I go back to work tomorrow."

"Okay. I'll call you tonight."

"Later," Malik said. He squeezed her hand, then walked to the car.

"How was Jamaica, son?"

"It was really nice, Dad." Malik sat up and kissed his mother's cheek. "Go ahead, Mom. I know you have twenty-one questions."

"Millie, leave him alone," Jonathan warned.

Malik looked at his father through the rearview mirror. "No Dad, it's alright. What do you want to know, Ma?"

"How old is she, Malik?"

"She is in her forties."

"I told you she was about my fuckin' age."

"Early forties, Ma."

"I just don't have all that plastic shit pumped into my body like her."

"And you don't need it either, baby," Jonathan said with a wide smile.

"Did she pay for the trip?"

"Yes."

"What are you, some kind of gigolo? Where did you meet her—"

"She is getting ready to make partner at my job. So she is a good friend to have."

"With all the beautiful, YOUNG, BLACK women out here why would you date her? What do you see in her, besides implants and makeup?"

"Oh, I see what you see, son," Jonathan smiled.

"Jonathan, you better quit while you're ahead," Millicent said sharply.

"Ma I am just—"

"What about Mrs. Felix's daughter. She is beautiful and she has no kids. I set you guys up on that date and you never went out again. No offense, but she's to old to be having kids."

"MILLIE!" Jonathan shouted.

"Ma! Nobody is having any kids by Susan. I am just having a good time, and getting out again. I'm not going to get serious with her. Besides, I couldn't even if I wanted to."

"Why? That bitch is married, isn't she?" Millicent yelled.

"Could you turn on the radio and pass me my phone from the glove compartment, please?"

Malik turned on his phone and sat back. The sultry sounds of Luther filled the car. His messages came over the music and into his ears.

'Hey Malik it's Tina from back in the days— Tina Simmons— Tony's teacher. Give me a call when you get a chance. Bye.'

'What's poppin', it's me, Mike. Just callin' to see how Jamaica is doing, because I know you're straight chillin'. Give me a holla when you get a chance. One.'

'Hey Malik, it's Laneice. What's the deal? I just made it in. Was wondering if you got home? I had a great time this weekend. Call me tonight, bye.'

With a smile he disconnected the call. "She's sweating me already."

"What you say, baby?"

"Nothing Mom. I was just talking to myself."

Malik pulled a piece of paper out of his pocket. He looked at it for a while and stared out of the window. He mentally recapped his adventurous weekend that was straight out of the pages of a novel, and smiled. He soon realized they were off the Belt Parkway and in Brooklyn. He looked at the paper, dialed the numbers on it, and waited.

"Hey, Laneice?"

Laneice shook Monica's arm and pointed at the phone. Monica mouthed the word Malik, Laneice nodded and they all smiled.

"Hey to you," Laneice said. "How was your flight?"

"It was average. I am just getting to Brooklyn. I got your message. I had a nice time with you this weekend. Why don't we get together this Saturday?" Malik said.

"That would be really nice." Laneice was deceptively calm.

"I was just sitting here thinking about the jet ski/cruise incident and the romantic dinner in my room last night, when I got your message. Laneice, I am glad we met. We could be really good friends."

The smile on her face dried up. "Okay. I look forward to seeing you this weekend, goodbye, Malik."

She ended the call and flopped on to her bed. "FRIENDS!?" she yelled. Laneice sucked her teeth and folded her arms. "Fuckin' men make me sick. You can't live with them—"

"But you can't live without their dicks," Monica interjected.

All three women collapsed in hysterics.

"After he fucked the shit out of me, over dinner last night, I would love to live with that dick."

"I know that's right," Monica laughed. "We could hear the both of you through the walls."

Malik smiled in the back of the car and looked at his phone.

"Who was that? I thought you were spending the weekend with over forty Barbie?"

Malik laughed hard. "Excuse me '007', that was someone I befriended while I was out there."

His mother paused for a second, and both Malik and his father laughed. They both knew what Millicent's next question would be.

"Is she under thirty and Black? And what's so funny?"

"She's Black and I think she might be thirty," Malik laughed.

"At that age she's going to want some kind of com—"

"Millicent, that is enough! When did you get so nosey, baby? You are starting to act like an old nag hag. Stop interfering with his business. I can't believe you." Mr. Hendrickson slammed on his brakes in the middle of their driveway. He got out of the car and slammed his door. He opened the front door to their house and his wife walked close behind him. "Millicent. You are really starting to get on my nerves with this shit. Leave the boy alone, he's a grown-ass man."

"But Jon I was just—"

"But Jon nothing. You're way out of line. You never act like this."

"But it's almost—" she looked back at her son and whispered as they walked into the house. "It's been some time since the World Trade Center attacks and he's very vulnerable. I just don't want him hurt, Jon."

"I understand that, Millicent, but he has to live his own life."

7

In Vegas front row to all the fights

Rocky looked at all of the people who filled the carpeted lobby of the MGM Grand Hotel and Casino. There were TV celebrities, politicians, hustlers, rappers and everyday ordinary people, like herself. She smiled at Donald Trump and licked her lips at Nelly. This was the type of life she wanted to live. She marveled at guys whose hair was as long as hers styled with either finger waves or Shirley Temple curls. They wore bright suits in a variety of colors: orange, pink, yellow and lime green with matching crocodile, or gator, shoes, and gaudy jewelry. What was even more amazing to Rocky was the beautiful women these men sported on their arms.

These niggas ain't got no business wearing those color suits. They look just like the men that shop in Mauri's clothing stores, she thought.

She saw ghetto chicks dressed in the best couture their money could buy, their hair weaves tight and make-up glowing. She noticed a pack of scantily dressed young Black girls with their guts hanging out, and stretch marks showing. She was immediately disgusted. *How come it's always us that have to run around looking like that*? she asked herself.

With two hours left until the fight she walked around the casino floor and continued her watch. She made way to a Blackjack table located at the very rear of the casino. She sat down and placed four thousand dollars worth of chips in front of her. There were two haggard looking drunk men at the table with her. They both looked to be in their forties. One was White the other Asian. Both of them wore long-sleeved shirts buttoned up to the collar that clung to their backs with perspiration.

They must have lost a lot of money in here and are trying to win it back, she thought.

She looked around and noticed it was the only Blackjack table with a hundred dollar bet minimum with vacancies. She shoved three chips toward the center of the table's felt green top. With her first hand she hit Blackjack and won six hundred dollars. She was off to a good start. People came by and watched her gamble. She had several rows of chips stacked in front of her and she was doing well.

"Hit me," Rocky said in a serious tone.

"I don't think you should do that, miss. Look at the card the house has up." Rocky looked to her left toward the voice and sitting in the chair right next to her was Marcus Best, the starting point guard for the Indiana Pacers.

"Hit me," she said again.

"House wins."

"Ouch. Was that one thousand dollars you just lost?" Marcus Best asked.

"I was on a serious streak until you came over here and jinxed me."

Marcus looked her up and down. "What does a pretty woman like you know about gambling?"

Rocky gently tugged him by his shirt, cupped her hands around his ear and whispered softly. "You better recognize; I play Blackjack and Roulette on my computer at work at least two hours a day. I'm a pro." Marcus laughed and placed a one hundred dollar chip on the table.

"Watch how fast I get that thousand back." Rocky placed seven hundred dollars in chips on the table in front of her. "I want a split." She instantly made fifteen hundred dollars. She counted her chips and smiled at Marcus, who lost his hand.

"Well, I have seven thousand five hundred, and I started out with four thousand. I would have had more if you didn't bring your bad luck behind to my table." Marcus laughed. "I am going to cash out. Catch you later," Rocky said.

"Why don't you hang out for a while? I'll show you how to play some real cards," Marcus said.

Rocky reluctantly sat back down. Marcus Best wore a royal blue Giants throw back Jersey with white numbers on it and the matching hat. He had on loose fitting jeans and white Nike- Air Force One sneakers with a royal blue swoosh. One rolled up sleeve revealed how muscular his biceps were. He was dark brown and six foot four. He had dark curly hair, which he kept cut low. Rocky always thought he was mixed with East Indian or from Trinidadian heritage. He had dark brown eyes and white teeth that were slightly crooked. But for sixty million, she could look past that.

"I'm going to play these five chips, and that's it for me," Rocky said. A barmaid came to the table with four drinks on a platter. "The Hennesy and Alizé is mine. I ordered it over an hour ago. Thank you."

"Wow, she gambles hard and drinks hard. What you know about Thug Passion?" Marcus asked.

"A lot more than you know about Blackjack," Rocky said as Marcus lost another hand.

"Where ya' girls at? I know you ain't out here alone?" Marcus asked.

"I sure am. I got a lot of shit on my mind. I need to iron out some issues. Besides, none of my girlfriends have a real interest in sports like I do. Well, not enough to fly out to Vegas and pay for a fight. What about you, where your peeps at?" Rocky asked.

"Here and there— but I am doing some soul searching this off season. I just lost my dad two months ago and I've got a lot of issues I need to come to grips with myself," Marcus said softly.

"I'm sorry to hear that," Rocky replied.

"What's your name?"

"Raquel, but everyone calls me Rock Candy."

Marcus placed three chips on the table. "How did you go from Raquel to Candy? Are you that sweet?" Rocky laughed. "What's so funny?"

"Nothing," she replied. *Shit nigga,* she thought, *you gotta taste this to find that out. I can't believe I am so calm. He just renegotiated his contract. He'll be making sixty million over the next four years if he stays with the Pacers.* Rocky quieted her wild thoughts, placed four chips on the table and smiled.

"My name is Marcus."

"I know who you are, nice to meet you. Where are you from talkin' like that?" Rocky asked.

"I grew up in Englewood, New Jersey. Where are you from?"

"Brooklyn, New York. Well, that's it for me. I just lost five hundred dollars and am cashin' out like I had planned," Rocky said in an agitated tone. *Rocky this is do or die. You either reel him in now, or that's it for your weekend. It gets no better than Marcus Best,* her head screamed.

She straightened her dress and opened up the matching clutch. She scooped all of the colorful chips into it and walked away. She walked as sexily as possible, without looking back. As she reached the cashier she felt someone tap her arm.

"You dropped two chips."

She turned around, and looked up into Marcus' eyes. She stepped up to the cashier, took the chips from Marcus and dumped them in a large cup along with the ones in her bag. She handed the cashier the cup.

"Seven thousand, two hundred dollars. How would you like that, ma'am?" the cashier asked.

"It doesn't matter."

Within moments she received a wad of crisp bills and placed them in her purse. She snapped it shut but quickly reopened it and removed two hundred dollars.

"I think this belongs to you, Marcus. I didn't drop anything."

"Hey, you goin' to the fight?" he asked.

"That's why I'm here."

"I could use some company. Let's go together."

"Sure. Are you going to take this money, Marcus?"

"Why don't you hold on to that and use it to treat us to something to eat after the fight."

Oh my fuckin' goodness. I am spending the evening with Marcus Best. I am going to die right here on the muthafuckin' spot. Stay calm, be nonchalant and think of a plan, she thought. "Cool," she said.

"How old are you, Rocky?"

"I just made twenty-five. How about you?"

"I'm twenty-eight." Marcus looked her up and down. "That dress wears you well. You look very nice tonight."

"Thank you. Let's hurry, the fight starts in ten minutes and there's no under card. The main event is the only bout— let's go."

Hmm, she knows her boxing, I'm impressed, Marcus thought. As they walked through the lobby Marcus gave several pounds and autographs to people. He stopped for the paparazzi and insisted Rocky be photographed with him. Rocky felt warm inside as they made their way to the arena. How she wished Marcus was her man and she could live this kind of lifestyle every time they went out. They stopped so many times and Rocky met so many industry people she almost didn't realize it was already twenty past the hour.

"Excuse me, Marcus, let's go right now. The fight might have already started." That being said, Rocky grabbed his arm and yanked him out of the crowd of people he was talking to.

"I'll have my agent call you," Marcus called back into the crowd.

"Marcus, don't worry about it just make sure you do that. Wifey knows best," a man from the crowd smiled at Rocky.

"Thank, you sir," Rocky said.

She walked through the hotel lobby, and Marcus walked directly behind her, holding her hand. Suddenly he stopped. "Hold up, you know who that was?" he asked in disbelief. Rocky released her grip, and continued to walk three feet before she stopped.

"Look, I paid one thousand dollars for my ticket, and I am not a ball player or a baller. I am a single college student who saved for three months to make her way to this fight and enjoy herself. You can go and catch up with your people and I'll catch you later. It's been fun."

Rocky walked faster and didn't turn around. Guys blew kisses at her and grabbed at her wrists, but that made her walk even faster. She yelled at herself inside. *Oh my God! I can't believe it. If I fucked this shit up I will kill myself. That's it! I'm just going to go shopping tomorrow, relax, fuck the parties, the passes— I'm just going to keep my two little boyfriends and weigh out which one will benefit me the most.*

She felt as if she were going to cry when she reached the arena. She opened up her clutch and searched for her ticket. There was no line and she walked straight up to the usher.

"Rock Candy— wait up," Marcus called. Rocky turned around and watched Marcus sprint across the floor. He looked like he was running to the other end of the court to play defense.

"Why you trippin?' I ain't mean nothin' by it, but that guy was a top exec at Nike and he's supposed to be endorsing me. I thought you were going to watch the fight with me? Come on, I have two ringside seats. My agent got them for me."

"You have two? I'd be a real ass if I turned those down, huh? Let's go. Oh— wait a second."

Rocky ran toward a cluster of slot machines where three girls stood talking on cell phones. One of the girls had smiled at her and Marcus as they were taking pictures in the lobby minutes before. Her companions rolled their eyes at her. Rocky remembered their faces from a previous function, but couldn't remember where.

"Excuse me, you need a ticket for the fight? Marcus and I have an extra. It's a thousand dollar seat, you want it?" Rocky asked.

"Hold on. The girl put her cell phone down. "How much do you want for it?"

"Girl, you can have it."

"For real?"

Rocky nodded her head and ran back towards Marcus.

"Thanks, thank you so much. You look really familiar to me, what's your name?"

"Rock Candy. You look familiar, too," Rocky called back.

The girl shoved the phone in her bag and jumped around. She waved her ticket in her friend's faces. One of the girls snatched the ticket out of her hand and surveyed it closely. "It's probably fake. Don't you remember that girl from the plane when was flying home from New York Memorial Day weekend? She was sitting in first class and when we reached the D a limo was there to pick her up."

"THAT'S RIGHT! Now I remember. Your ass was straight up hatin' on her too." The girl said a couple of words to her friends and entered the arena moments after Marcus and Rocky.

The place was packed. They walked down the middle aisle and stopped in the second row right behind Holyfield's corner. Rocky could barely watch the fight. She spotted Don King one row in front of her and a few feet away, Jack Nicholson. She turned around and Ben Affleck was a row behind her, sitting next to Jennifer Lopez.

Rocky was sick. Her palm itched to pick up her phone and call Kay, but she resisted the temptation. She tapped Marcus and he leaned toward her." Find out what round this is?"

"It's the second."

"See, we missed some of the fight. I love to see what music they come out to".

Marcus turned around and smiled at her. "Me too. Sorry about that."

"Oh, my God, there's Robert De Niro and Brad Pitt," she almost shrieked.

"What did you say? I didn't hear you."

"Nothing."

As the third round began Rocky stopped stargazing and fashion policing and focused in on the fight. She really did love boxing, basketball and football— her favorite past times aside from shopping. Two minutes into the third round Holyfield made a swift right to his opponent's eye. Beads of sweat flew in the air and a big splash of blood flew out of his nose and momentarily painted the air, then the canvas went bright red. He hit the ground twice as hard as he was hit. He tried to get up, but landed face down on the canvas. The referee swiftly kneeled; his black and white stripes hovered over the boxer as he counted loudly to ten. Holyfield threw his arms in the air.

"I know this ain't over," Rocky said.

"This is a bust," Marcus said.

"A KO? This was a joke."

"You know if I was home watching Pay-Per-View, this fight would have gone the entire twelve. Candy, I know you're no baller, and you paid good money for your tickets but do you mind if we leave before the crowd gets going?"

As they made their way through the crowd he stopped at the doorway to converse with Jack Nicholson, and Bishop Magic Don Juan. Rocky heard her phone ring and stepped away from a conversation between Shaq and Marcus.

"Rocky, I just saw you and the dress on TV— you look good." Kay said.

"I was on TV? You lying, Kay!"

"I swear to God, I saw you stand up as the doctors came out! You were behind Holyfield's side!" Kay screamed on the top of her lungs.

"Kay, hold on that's my other line. Hello?"

"Sweetheart, I could have sworn I saw you sitting ringside at the fight. Was it you?" Thomas asked.

Rocky turned around and watched Marcus watching her as he talked to Shaq. She turned and continued to talk. Yes, booby, that was me."

"How the hell did you get that seat?"

"This guy I was gambling with gave it to me."

"My father and I were sitting here and I almost lost my beer."

"Thomas, I miss you. But you are starting to break up. I'll call you when I get to my room." Rocky hung up and her phone rang.

"How long were you going to keep me on hold? Who did you get up and leave with?" Kay asked.

"You could see that on TV?" Rocky asked, horrified.

"Yes, Rocky, but his face was blocked. Who was it?"

"That's Marcus Best from the Indiana Pacers. Sixty mill, fine as hell and has been with me for the past hour. He's talking to Shaq right now and I met mad people. I WAS TALKING TO SHAQ! Kay, I was sitting behind Don King!"

"I've never known you to be so star struck. I mean it's not like you never dated celebrities before."

"I'm not star struck. But when you all up in it like this—I met Bishop Magic Don Juan and—"

"That man from 'Pimps Up Hoe's Down' that be with Snoop?" Kay shrieked. "Are you serious? Did you take a picture?"

"Ah-ha, who's the groupie now? Tell Audrey I will call her tomorrow. She left me a message."

"I want details as soon as you get to the hotel."

"You know there's a three hour time difference?"

"Who's that?" Marcus asked. Rocky turned around and Marcus was right behind her. "There you go, eyewitness newsin' it. It's Kay."

"Who's Kay? Your man?" Marcus asked with an attitude. Rocky passed Marcus the phone. "I don't want to talk to your man!"

Rocky held her arm out. "This is my best friend, Kay." Marcus still looked suspect. "My best *female* friend, Kay."

He took the phone from her. "What's up?"

"Hi, you better take care of my girl out there."

"She better take care of me. We're getting ready to get something to eat— her treat."

"Whatever. Put Rocky back on the phone."

"I thought you said everyone calls you Candy," Marcus said as he handed Rocky the phone.

"Shit, you can't even decide what you want to call me. You introduced me to your teammates as Rocky Candy, and you've been calling me both names at the same time." Rocky put the phone to her ear. "Listen, I'll call you later."

Marcus grabbed the phone. "She'll call you tomorrow afternoon. She's going to be out late tonight. Bye, Kay." He hung up. "Let's catch a cab right in front of the hotel," Marcus said.

They quickly made their way through the crowd. While they waited to grab a cab at the glass front of the hotel Rocky strategically went over her plan of entrapment for the man at her side. *So far so good. He's eating up all your bait. You turned him down twice and he's still around. You can't let him feel like you're sweating him. But now what? I've got it! Family— that will work*, she thought.

The bright lights surrounding them made her feel like a star. People crowded the front of the hotel waiting to make their next move. They stared at her and Marcus. She saw girls commenting on her attire. She knew they were wondering if she was his wife, girl or whore – she loved it.

"Marcus, where are you from?"

"Girl do you have Alzheimer's? Englewood."

"No, I mean what's your nationality?"

"Oh, my mother is a Jamaican coolie, and my pops is— was Black."

"What about you? Look at all of that pretty hair." He placed his hand in her hair and checked the back for tracks. She swung her hair to the side and placed her hands on her hips.

"Yeah, it's all me, and your ass would have been extremely embarrassed if it wasn't."

"Nah, I am all for enhancements. Not that you need any. You got mad attention in there. You're definitely breathtaking."

"Thank you," she blushed. "Anyway, all my family is from the south. I'm just a regular Black girl with a good perm. Although, my great-great grandfather was White so my mom had dirty blonde hair, and I got this red stuff."

Had dirty blonde hair, Marcus thought. *I wonder if that means her moms is dead. That's touchy ground I ain't goin' there.*

"Your family still out in Englewood?"

"They sure are. I was thinking of moving my moms and my little sister out to Indiana with me since my dad died, but my mom doesn't like that idea at all. Your family's still in New York?"

"I have none. My mom died when I was a kid. My aunt lives overseas, and my grandmother passed away two years ago."

"Wow. I'm sorry."

"Hey, I've learned to live with it after all these years. My grandma took good care of me."

"What about your father?"

Rocky's lips were silent but her thoughts were loud. Her brain flooded with different lies she could create to dramatize her situation. *I could say he died of an over dose. Nah, that's too much. I could tell him the truth, that I've only seen him two or three times in my life, nah that's too little. I've got it!*

"Candy. Are you all right? I didn't mean to intrude. You don't have to tell me—"

She took a deep breath held his hand. "It's okay. He passed away last year. He had kidney problems. We never really got along that well. When he called me out of the blue and asked me for a kidney, I refused. My grandmother died that month, and he died a year after in the same month— May."

"My father died in that month, too."

Shit, in my eyes he is dead. I ain't see or hear from him in nearly twenty years, she thought.

Marcus bowed his head and was silent. Rocky tightened the grip on his hand, grabbed the bottom of his chin with her other hand and lifted up his face. She rubbed the back of her hand gently along the side of his face. As the cab pulled up he opened the door for her and helped her in.

Mauri would never put me in a cab, but Thomas would, she thought.

Marcus' knees were pressed up against the back of the front seat. He looked at her and slowly shook his head.

"My pops was my best friend. We did everything together. He taught me everything I know, Candy. How am I supposed to let all that go? I can't forget."

Rocky turned towards him with an empathetic look. "Listen, I deal with my loss everyday, you aren't supposed to forget. Marcus, I had a lot of bad times with my mother when she was alive. She would fight with her boyfriends— I mean, head up, like Holyfield. They would black up her face and she would fuck them up with whatever was in her hands, and it always seemed like I would be standing there. One time I tried to help her and she hit me. Sometimes she would rob them for everything, and then we would move to another state, stay with my grandmother or a lot worse. Those are the type of things I had to let go to commemorate my moms." Rocky inhaled deeply and paused.

"I try to only remember the good things; and even though we were together for only eight years, those are a lifetime's worth of memories for me. That's all I have, and I know she is in this cab with us right now. She looks out for me. If your dad and you were tight, remember the good things and keep them with you. When you're playing a tight game, tell your dad you're playing it for him and do the damn, thing. Laugh at all the good times you had together. Discuss them with your sister and your mother. But never forget. You understand me? If you do, you'll drive yourself crazy. Take it from someone who did. I had to forgive my mom and remember the good times. Our matching fur coats, our vacations to Disney World and how she would let me help her cook."

They stared at each other silently. His eyes seemed to long for more. So Rocky continued.

"It won't happen tomorrow either. It takes time. It took me a while to stop mourning my grandma, but she's the reason I'm who I am and I love her every day for that. Dag, I ain't mean to talk you to death, but you have to believe me, it will get better." Rocky put her arm around his shoulder and placed his head on her chest. He moved in closer to her. Marcus felt good.

"I guess that makes sense," Marcus said.

"Tell him you love him right now. He can hear you." Marcus lifted his head and looked at her like she was deranged. "I'm serious Marcus, go ahead."

"I love you, Pop," he whispered. "You gonna fuck around and have me cryin' in here girl— and I don't even know your ass. But right now, I feel like I have known you all my life."

The cab driver looked through his rearview mirror and watched the couple embrace. He smiled.

"Cabby, could you drop us about a mile up the strip?" Marcus asked.

At their destination the pair got out and walked. They stopped in front of the Mirage and watched the fire filled show on the hotel grounds. They walked further down the strip to Caesar's Palace and ate. They talked like old classmates for hours, sharing their memories.

"It's getting late Marcus, and I am extremely tired."

"I've got passes to the official after party inside the MGM Grand. Wouldn't you like to escort me?"

"I love hanging out with you, but I don't feel much like partying. After walking the strip in these damn shoes for three hours I'm ready to sleep."

"Where are you staying? I'll walk you there."

"At the Venetian."

"Excuse me, what do you do for a living?"

"I am a recruiter for my college, and I graduate this coming January. I got accepted into Columbia where I am going to obtain my MBA."

"That's hot. You have a man— kids?"

YES, she thought. *No one asks this question if they don't have any interest. I have to watch how I answer this.*

"No. I do date, but I don't have one steady." *Because I have two*, she silently joked to herself. "What about you?"

"No kids and no girls. I date when I feel like it and that's it. Do you have kids?"

"Nope. I don't even own a pet."

"The Venetian, huh? I'm staying at the MGM Grand. I don't have Venetian money," Marcus joked.

"Well, I saved all semester for this trip and I wasn't going to stay at Motel 6."

He laughed.

They stopped in front the Bellagio en route to her hotel and watched the extravagant water and light filled show. Fountains, colorful lights and music illuminated the night sky. Dozens of people stopped to watch the show. As they watched, a bird flew by and Rocky jumped into Marcus' arms.

"What's wrong?"

"What the fuck are they doing flying around at night?" she cried.

"Don't worry they can't hurt you."

Rocky breathed heavily and wiped a small tear from beneath her eyelid. Marcus slipped his big hands around Rocky's small waist and pulled her to him. "Are you all right?" Marcus asked, concerned.

"You have to excuse me. I hate birds, I fuckin' loathe them," she said out of breath.

He bent over and placed a long soft kiss on her lips. When he met no resistance, his hands dropped from her waist to her round behind. She pulled away, grabbed his hand and started to walk. Their conversation flowed smoothly the twenty-minute walk to her hotel. Although Rocky's feet were at the point of blistering, she felt like she was on cloud nine. When they reached her hotel grounds, neither wanted the night to end.

"You don't want to get into something else? The night is young. It's only twelve." Marcus asked.

"No, thanks. I'm really tired. I haven't adjusted to the time difference yet and I need to get up early and work out. I missed two days as it is."

"This shit is off the hook. I have never been so close. Can you swim in that shit?" Marcus jokingly pushed Rocky toward the water. They laughed and playfully pushed each other around. Marcus gently grabbed Rocky's' hand and they stared in the calm waters of the tremendous manmade lake in front of the hotel. Men in stripe shirts and matching berets paddled couples in gilded gondolas. It looked like a scene straight out of Venice.

After a while they walked inside, hand in hand, toward the elevator. He stared upwards at the ceiling as he walked. *Is this a replica of Michelangelo's Sistine Chapel on the ceiling of the hotel?* Marcus thought. *This shit is banging. There must be thousands of feet of artwork up there. I wonder how long it took to complete that?*

At the elevator he looked at Rocky.

"Candy, I appreciate your kind words and you letting me into your personal like that."

"Don't mention it."

Rocky's phone rang. She ignored it until it stopped, but it immediately started again.

"Why didn't you answer it?"

"Because I know it's Kay harassing me again. She's already called me three times today. Ever since she's been married, she's been living vicariously through me."

As they reached her door Rocky stopped and gave Marcus a light embrace. He grabbed her behind and kissed her nose. He lowered his head a little, kissed her passionately on the mouth and pushed her up against the door. Rocky felt light headed from sudden hot tingles that flashed through her breasts and clitoris, but was still able to push him away. She placed her key into the slot and opened her door. Marcus followed her. "I had a fantastic time tonight, Marcus— don't fuck it up. I think you should go to your party now."

"If you're feeling the way I'm feeling— and that kiss shows me you do— let's just stay here and chill."

"I'm sure there are going to be at least one hundred groupies that will be more than happy to fuck Marcus Best at that party you're getting ready to hit up. Go hit them with your pipe game. I ain't come to Vegas for that. I came to chill and iron out some issues. If we get it on, that will just get me more wrinkled up. Shit, I'll have more issues to deal with than before I came down here."

"I respect that."

Rocky stood in the wide-open doorway. "It's been a pleasure."

"You ain't even going to hit me with your math and shit. How am I supposed to contact you?"

"I'm registered here under Raquel Jones, Room 518. Call me tomorrow. Maybe we can hook up."

"Later, Candy." Marcus walked out the door with his tail between his legs. Never had he been turned down in that matter. Well, not since he'd been playing professional ball. He went to the party, drank and mingled for a couple of hours, but not one hour was spent without thoughts of Rock Candy. Even when he took the 38, double D, blonde with the sky blue eyes from the club to his room, Rock Candy stayed on his mind. As he sat in a chair and looked out at the Vegas skyline, and the blonde bombshell's head bobbed between his legs he smiled at the countless laughs and conversations he had shared with Rock Candy on the strip. When the blonde bombshell let herself out of Marcus' room at eight a.m. that morning, he picked up the phone and called Rocky Candy. Her voice was on the hotel voicemail, and he left her a detailed message.

Rocky returned to her room at ten a.m. drenched from the hotel sauna. She always felt so good after her early morning jog. This morning's run was even more refreshing because she had run the same route she and Marcus walked the previous night. As Rocky dropped her jogging suit at her bedside and peeled off her wet swimsuit she noticed the flashing red light indicating a phone message.

"Damn, that fuckin' Mauri, calling so early. He must have called six times while I was with Marcus last night. I better call him back."

Rocky picked up the phone and dialed Mauri. "Good morning, sweetheart – did I wake you?"

"Yeah, but what up though? Why you ain't answer my calls last night?"

"I didn't hear my phone. I was in that loud ass casino until about twelve a.m., and you know that is three my time, so I was exhausted."

"How was your seat for the fight? Was it close?"

You better doctor up your shit just in case he saw you last night, she thought. "I didn't even use it, babes— I was killing niggas at the Blackjack table, and this White dude— I think he was an executive from Nike— he gave me his ringside, and I gave him three hundred dollars in chips and my ticket."

"Yeah, right."

"I'm dead ass. Kay ain't believe me either."

Rocky sat on the bed with her fingers and legs crossed. She hated getting caught in lies.

"That's my boo, take the shirts off they fuckin' back. You got a little hustle in you."

"I miss you, and I can't wait until I see you, so we can make up. It's been a long time. Mauri, I need some."

"If I ain't have business in Chicago this coming weekend I would send for you this week instead of the week after."

Rocky uncrossed her fingers and smiled. "Damn, I hope I can wait."

"You better. I am going to h'rup my ass and get ready for my meetings. I'll talk to you later, baby girl."

"I love when you call me that, Maur."

He laughed. "I know. Later."

"Bye." She hung up the phone and threw herself across the bed. *He has so much potential,* she thought. *I love the way he talks and dresses but his dick game is just so whack. It's not even that it's that small, he just don't work it right.*

Just as Rocky got up to shower and change, she noticed the red light again. Her curiosity caused her to withstand her sticky sweat filled body and check her messages. She listened carefully, and her face began to glisten like the rest of her shiny body.

'Hey Candy, it's Marcus. I figured I'd catch you before you went to workout, but I guess I missed you. Umm, I'm sorry if I offended you in anyway last night and, um, if you want to, let's go get something to eat around twelve or so—"

Rocky let loose a hi-pitched squeal and fell back on her bed. When she replaced the phone back by her ear she was just in time to get his two-way and cell phone numbers. She rummaged through the night table drawer and pulled out the hotel pad and pen. She listened to his message a dozen times before she hung up and got into the tub.

Once dry she clasped her strapless bra at the third row of clasps so her cleavage would have just the right look. Then slipped into a stretch denim tube top. She lay down to squeeze her thighs and behind into her jeans. Rocky admired herself in the mirror. "What am I going to do with my hair?"

She ransacked her luggage for her blow dryer then brushed and dried for an hour. She used the cylinder shaped bristles to curl her ends. Her make-up case was on the sink. She removed a bubble gum pink colored lip-gloss and began to apply it. Before she could finish her bottom lip, the hotel phone rang. She immediately dropped her lip-gloss into the sink and sprang from the bathroom to the bed before the second ring was completed. She let it ring once more before she picked it up.

"Hello?"

"Hello, Rock Candy, what's up?"

"Hey, Marcus. How are you?"

"Chillin' I called you this morning. Did you get my message?"

"Yeah, but I just came in from my workout about an hour ago. I wanted to freshen up before I called you back. I was sticky and funky."

"You're too fly to be sticky. Maybe funky but not sticky." Rocky giggled. "It's almost twelve. You up for grabbing a bite?"

"I ate before I got into the sauna. Besides, I am going down to Caesar's to check out their mall. I'm going to spend a little of what I won last night."

"You want me to roll? Then we could go eat?"

"Nah, I like shopping alone."

Marcus was disappointed. *I ain't going to beg this chick to eat with me. Fuck it,* he thought. "I guess I'll check you later."

"I do have some fun shit planned a little later. You wanna come with?"

"What's fun to you?" he inquired suspiciously.

"Don't worry about that. You're either in or out. Besides, I have to make reservations for one spot, so if you're down let me know and I'll meet you in your hotel lobby at three."

"You're coming to get me? Wow, I can't beat that."

"Call me if something comes up. If not, be downstairs. Don't be late."

"Trust me, I won't. Bye."

Rocky smiled so hard her fillings should have popped out. As she waltzed back to the bathroom, her cell phone beeped. She had voice mail messages. Kay had called her twice and to her surprise, Marcus had called an hour before she spoke to him.

"I didn't give him my number," Rocky recalled.

It took her fifteen minutes to realize that she had placed her cell phone number on the hotel voicemail the day she arrived. She slipped on a pair of pink Prada sneakers and moved her money and ID from her clutch to a pink Prada bag. Afterward, she removed a pair of pink Chanel shades from a large black eyeglass case. She went back into her luggage and fished out a neutral tan Christian Dior bag that had several pockets attached to it and a matching pair of high heel mules. She placed them on her bed.

"These will be for later. I'm famished. Let me go grab a bite and then I'll hit the mall." She placed the 'Do Not Disturb' sign outside her door, and hit the streets.

Later that evening Marcus and Rocky were enjoying the Vegas sights.

"I haven't been to a magic show since I was a kid. I ain't gonna front, at first I was like, she's buggin', this shit is going to be whack. But that shit was poppin'."

"Wait until we hit the second spot and shit. We can walk. It's only about six blocks."

"Before yesterday I just tried to forget. After I called you this morning I laughed at some of the times my pops and I shared. It really felt like he was here laughing with me. I feel a little better. I don't know how to thank you."

"Thank me for what?" Rocky asked.

"Thank you for opening that side of me up."

"Listen, I've come up with several ways of adapting to my many losses over the years. We could discuss them from time to time whenever you feel like it."

"I'd really like that."

Although there were hundreds of tourists walking up and down the bright strip, Rocky felt like they owned it and closed it to the public for a private party of two. They spoke about everything from A to Z.

"We are getting on that?" Marcus said.

They stopped in front of the New York, New York Hotel and Rocky pointed up in the air at a speeding roller coaster. It twisted and looped around replicas of New York City skyscrapers. There was also a replica of the Statue of Liberty and the Brooklyn Bridge. Although these replicas were far less than the size of the actual structures, they still stood high and tall. The couple looked up and watched, mouths open, as the roller coaster made its twisting entrance through the buildings again.

"Are you scared?" Rocky smiled.

"NO! But we can't get on that ride. You got those high-ass heels on."

"Why not? You chicken?" Rocky joked.

Marcus grabbed Rocky by her waist, lifted her off her feet and planted a kiss on her forehead. "Who you callin' 'chicken'?" He said as he flung her over his shoulder.

"Put me down," she yelled amidst a fit of laughter. She playfully punched his back and kicked her feet. One of her shoes fell off in the process. "Marcus! My shoe!"

Without setting her down he picked up her shoe and playfully hit her on the behind with it. "Let's get on," Marcus sighed.

They entered the hotel and got on the short line. Rocky paid for the tickets and they boarded the ride. They secured the ride's harness over their shoulders and strapped on their seat belts. As the ride started to move Marcus grabbed the harness so tightly the insides of his palms were crimson. Rocky just smiled.

"Let me find out you're scared. This ride is only a couple of feet taller than your ass."

Suddenly the ride plunged down and looped, twisting all of the passengers upside down. She giggled and laughed uncontrollably. Marcus kept his eyes closed, gritted his teeth and tightened his grip. He felt like he left his stomach at the very top of the steep drop.

Once they were off the ride Rocky rubbed his back. "Next time I'll take you to the carousel or the Ferris wheel or something."

"Very funny. I never liked shit like that. Not even when I was a kid."

"So why go on?" Rocky asked then dragged him over to a small booth directly under the ride. "They take pictures of you while you're on the ride. I want the photo of us."

"I don't even want to see that shit. I probably look bananas."

Rocky watched as the person who was running the booth scrolled through the pictures. "Right there! That's us right there. You don't look bananas— you look like you're taking a shit," she laughed.

Rocky's mouth was open in the photo. It looked as if she was having a hardy laugh. Marcus on the other hand, had his eyes tightly shut. His teeth were clenched and he looked as if he was in excruciating pain.

"Do you think you could sign a copy for me?" The young girl behind the booth asked.

"Oh, hell no. I can't put my signature on anything that looks like that! But I will give you my autograph."

Rocky purchased their photo and Marcus agreed to pose for a picture and sign it as long as the girl agreed to erase their photo from the computer. They played three carnival-styled booth games and Marcus won a stuffed animal for Rocky by shooting hoops. Outside the hotel, Rocky wanted to walk over the 'Brooklyn Bridge'. Two pigeons waddled nearby as they reached its end. Rocky stopped dead in her tracks and redirected their course. Marcus grabbed her by the wrist and turned her toward him.

"You have got to be kidding me! I know you're not scared of those two little-ass birds."

"Those, my friend, aren't birds. They are rats with fuckin' wings. I can't stand birds!"

"Last night when you jumped into my arms when that pigeon flew by, I thought it was cute. But today when the magicians let the doves out into the audience and you spilled all the drinks at our table trying to get under it, I knew you had a problem. Now this? All you have to do is stomp your feet and they will go away— look."

Marcus released her hand and ran towards the birds. He stopped running when he came within a few inches of the birds and jumped up and down in place. The birds immediately took off into the Las Vegas heat. They both watched the birds fly over the hotel.

"See? You definitely need to seek some kind of counseling about that shit. Now, I know you're not going to be too thrilled about this— but I'm hungry."

"I didn't say I never eat, but I can't be eating all day and shit. You know I've got to watch my figure."

"Why don't you let me watch that for you? You are a fuckin' dime, Candy."

Marcus placed his hands around her waist and kissed her forehead.

"Thanks. I have one more thing planned for us this evening. I wish this weekend would never end. I am really enjoying your company."

"Ditto, how long are you out here for? I'm leaving on Tuesday, the 8th." Marcus said.

"I got here on the 4th and I leaving tomorrow afternoon."

"Marcus, if you ever want someone to talk to, let me know. I'll give you my numbers at home. And I'm going to tell you right now, the first time you play New York I want courtside."

"You got it. I have an exhibition game at the Garden in October; I could definitely make that happen. I *was* hoping that I could see you before that, if that's at all possible."

Oh my God. He wants to see me after this. My shit is working. Wait until I fuck this nigga. She completed her thoughts with a seductive smile. "I think I would really enjoy that."

Rocky stood in the baggage claim area and stared out of the glass window. When she saw the black Range pull up outside she smiled and walked as swiftly through the exit as her heavy luggage would allow. Thomas stepped out of the truck and onto the sidewalk.

"Hey, baby. I've missed you so much," he said as he extended his arms for a hug.

Rocky dropped her bags and ran up to Thomas. She embraced him with all her might and planted a soft kiss on his mouth. Then she slid her tongue across his lips, slipped it inside his mouth, and killed him with a steamy kiss. "Thanks for coming to get me, my Tommy boy."

"You know I hate when you call me that. Did you enjoy the fight?"

"It was good, but there was not that much to enjoy, it ended so quickly."

He grabbed her bags and placed them in the back seat. She stood right behind him and watched as he situated the luggage.

"You know, my father is the one who saw you in the audience. He can't stop talking about it."

"Your father is still staying with you?" Rocky asked. The thought made her uncomfortable.

"Yes, he is. Why do you ask?"

"Something about him . . . you want to come to my house? I'll make your favorite," Rocky smiled.

"You only have to ask me once. Let's go."

Rocky got into the passenger seat and let her head drop back onto the headrest. She exhaled and adjusted her seat. As soon as Thomas sat in the car he looked at Rocky and smiled.

"You look well rested. How did you manage to get ringside seats?"

"Kay said that she saw me, too. I won the ticket in a card game."

"Wow. What you can do with a pretty face," Thomas said sarcastically.

"What do you mean by that?" Rocky asked.

"I couldn't go down there and win a three thousand dollar fight ticket in a game of Blackjack. If *that is* how you got it."

"What are you implying, Thomas?"

"Nothing. I need to stop at the grocery store so I can pick up the ingredients for the lasagna," Thomas said. "I don't keep those kinds of goods in the house."

Okay," Rocky replied blandly.

"So, tell me about your trip."

"Well you know the shopping thing goes without saying. I went to the spa and got a massage and sat in the sauna. I caught the magic show with the two fags and the white tigers; they were off the hook. We should really go down there and catch that together. I won about seven G's playing Blackjack, AND WON A RINGSIDE TICKET TO THE FIGHT!!!! I went to an amusement park and that is about it."

"That's it, huh? Sounds like an awful lot to me." Thomas pulled in front of a Pathmark. He looked at Rocky and ran his fingers through her hair. "What do you want me to buy?"

"Don't worry, I'll run inside because I know what to get. What do you want to drink?"

"Buy some brew-skis."

"Alright, Thomas." As soon as she stepped away from the car her mobile rang. "Wow. I timed that perfectly. I know my Mauri like a book," she looked at her caller ID and the prefix, to her surprise, was not 313.

"Who the fuck is this? 702— 702— oh shit, that's Vegas." She stepped into the grocery store and answered the phone. "Hello?"

"I was just getting ready to hang up. How was your flight?"

Rocky could not place the voice. "Fine, thanks. What are you doing?" *Who is this? She thought, I better play it mad vague until I figure this out.*

"Chillin'. Roy Jones is havin' a party tonight and I'm going to check that out. Otherwise, I'm just thinking about your sexy ass. You must have put somethin' in my drinks 'cause you're heavy on my mind."

Rocky placed Marcus' voice and became instantly horny. Her heart began pounding faster.

"Candy? CANDY?"

"Sorry, Marcus. I'm buying groceries— I was comparing prices."

"I said you've been heavy on my mind. I can't stop thinking about you."

"You were the first thing on my mind this morning and I thought about you the entire flight."

"Word? I was just callin' to make sure you made it home safely. You have my numbers right?"

"Yep. I saved them in my phone. I'll call you tomorrow when I think you're home."

"Yesterday was the best. Driving through the mountains and watching the sunset was hot, yo. Not to mention the amusement park and magic show it was straight out of the movies. That was some real Ronnie Romance shit," Marcus said.

Between throwing tomato sauce and pasta into her cart, Rocky laughed. "I ain't gonna front, I felt like we was Thelma and Louise. Nah, Thelma and Louis."

"I never met anyone like you before, Candy."

Rocky picked up a bag of tossed salad and rushed toward the beverage aisle. *Mauri likes Heineken and Thomas drinks Corona*, she thought. "Stop, you are making me blush," Rocky confessed.

She picked up her last items and walked toward the register. She looked out of the window and waved at Thomas who was looking at her as she approached the line. There were two customers ahead of her.

"Well, I'm going to jump in the shower and order some room service. I'll call you before I go to the party."

"Don't forget the time difference. I've got to go to work tomorrow. So if you're leaving your room at twelve— it's three here. I look forward to hearing from you. Talk to you soon, Marcus."

"Later."

Rocky saw that there was one person in front of her, and she had two phone calls to make. She cut it down to one and dialed. "Hey, Mr. Maurice, what's going on? I am home and safe."

"I was just getting' ready to call you, girl. You had fun?"

"Yes, baby, and I relaxed, too."

"My man said he saw you gambling at the MGM Grand and you were caking off, cuz."

Rocky panicked. "What man?"

"Don't worry about that. How much you brought back?"

"Well, I didn't lose any, and I already told you I won the fight ticket."

"I thought you might have been hittin' the tables yesterday, too since I ain't hear from you and shit. I figured you was alright 'cause you ain't call me to wire you no cash. You ain't have nobody out there strokin' my cat, did you?"

"Mauri, come on now. Why do you have to talk to me like that?"

"Well, as long as you know it's you and me to the end. Better not be nobody else in my shit, you heard? I gotta run. I'm in the middle of something. I love you."

Before Rocky could fix her mouth to reply he hung up. "Shit. Now he's starting that love you shit again— forty dollars! For what? Let me see my receipt, please." Rocky scanned her receipt and paid the cashier. She grabbed the three plastic bags and walked out of the store.

Thomas was waiting with the car door opened. He took the groceries from her and helped her into her seat. "I have to be at work tomorrow for ten so I will be leaving your place around seven," Thomas said.

"Well, I am out bright and early for my morning run. So you can leave with me or I will wake you up when I get back."

"Can I ask you a question without you jumping down my throat, Rocky?"

Rocky turned to stare at his profile, as she often did when they were driving. She tried to guess what was on his mind. "It depends," she finally answered.

"How many men tried to pick you up out in Las Vegas. Be honest."

"The same amount that try to talk to me every day. What kind of question is that?"

"Give me a ball park figure," Thomas said sternly.

"People who actually said something to me or just looked?"

"Those who actually approached you."

"I don't know. About eight or ten, why?"

"Inquiring minds want to know."

"Do you think I am attractive, Thomas?"

"That goes without saying."

"Well, so do a lot of people. Every day that goes by people approach me. I cannot help that. Maybe you should start dating ugly women and you won't have this problem," Rocky said.

Thomas was annoyed and stayed silent during the car ride. He wasn't even sure why he felt that way. He looked at her and she didn't seem the least bit affected by his demeanor. Rocky thought of Marcus. Thomas thought of Rocky's possible infidelity. *I'm not sure, but I'm beginning to think her trips out of town aren't for the purpose of a family business.*

She looked at him as they pulled up in front of her apartment.

"What's wrong baby? Is something bothering you?"

"No. I'm just hungry. You grab the groceries and I'll bring your luggage upstairs."

Rocky went up the steps and opened the front door. She climbed another set of steps and let herself into her apartment. She turned on the lights and everything was sparkling and in order, just as she had left it. She dropped her bags, ran into her bedroom, turned off the ringer on her phone and muted the volume on her answering machine. Then she hustled back to the kitchen. Moments later, Thomas came into the apartment and locked the door.

"If you would like to join me in the kitchen come on in. Your sweats are in the bottom drawer of my dresser on the left-hand side. The remote is by my phone."

Rocky prepared the meal. Her grandmother had taught her how to cook. She thought of her grandmother's words as she placed the pan in the oven: ' *Start a man off with this secret recipe for lasagna, and you will open up his heart'*.

Rocky went into her bedroom, stripped down to her underwear and joined Thomas on the bed. "Did I do something wrong?" Rocky asked. She rubbed her half-covered breast against his cheek and lay next to him. *Boy, is he going to get it, she thought. Between those panty-drenching kisses from Marcus, and riding my rabbit in Vegas, I've been waiting for this shit.*

Thomas did not answer.

"Come on, you can tell me. Everything was cool before I went into the grocery store. When I was picking up the groceries I was telling Kay how happy I was to see you. She thinks we are going to end up together. She really likes you for me."

Thomas looked into Rocky's eyes. "How about you? Do you like me for you?"

Rocky slid into his arms and kissed his nose. "Of course I do. Do you think I would call you every day, and be with you as much as I am if I didn't. I love the time we spend together."

"You never define the lines of our relationship, and you've never really made it clear how you feel about me. You know I love you, Rocky. There is no one else, is there?"

There must be some shit in the air. Mauri just hit me with the same shit in the grocery store, she thought. "Listen, you are already established in life. I am trying to get my shit together. I graduate in January and I want a family and a husband. After I get my degree I seriously want to think about that— and you're the only man I would even consider starting that kind of life with. I have deep feelings for you, but I have a hard time expressing them. My mother told me to love hard."

Thomas paused. *What the hell is she talking about*? he thought. "Love hard?" he finally asked.

"If I fall in love easily or too quickly the outcome is me getting hurt. I abide by that rule with you and every other man I have been with in life. So, just because I don't always say things, it doesn't mean I don't feel them. I thought my actions spoke louder than anything I may or may not say."

Thomas felt bad. *How could I have ever doubted her*? He thought back to the night of the fight . . .

"Hey, Junior, come here and look at this shit!" Thomas' father yelled.

"I have tons of paper work to complete. What is it Thomas?"

"That hot little number you be havin' up in here just flashed across the TV— at the fight!"

"What?" Thomas asked.

"Come look! They will show her pretty ass again. They always show the celebs and the good-looking people over and over. Besides, she's sittin' a couple of rows behind Don King and next to the guy that plays for the Pacers."

Thomas got up and ran down the hall to the guestroom, spilling beer along the way.

"Shit, they just showed her face again. Hurry up, son."

Thomas took a seat next to his father and within seconds the fight was over. *"Are you sure it was her?"* he asked looking at his father.

"Look, there she goes."

Thomas' mouth dropped as he saw the dress and matching clutch he had purchased for her birthday. She was exiting the aisle, and he couldn't see her face.

"I never forget a pretty face. What does she do for a living?"

"She's in college, and is a recruiter for her school."

"You buy her that BMW she be coming over here in?"

"No, it's a Benz, and she had it when I met her."

"She ain't recruiting no students, she recruiting for the Indiana Pacers. That's what her ass is doing. Never trust a big butt and a smile. You say she travel a lot, too?"

"Pop, she's not—"

"Your ass too pussy whipped to tell. What the hell a college recruiter doing with a ringside seat to a main event and a brand new Benz?"

Thomas ran back to his study and dialed Rocky's cell number . . .

His fingers submerged in familiar soft warm and wet flesh, pulled him away from his thoughts and back into Rocky's bed. She gently forced his fingers in and out of her vagina. "Your Rock Candy misses you. She wants some as soon as you finish eating." Thomas kissed her lips and placed his mouth around her breasts. He kissed and gently bit her nipples. "Lick it, please," Rocky moaned.

"Let's eat first."

"Eat me first. We could do it now and then again after dinner."

Thomas placed small kisses and bites all over her body during his descent. She wiggled out of her panties and struggled with them around her ankles. Thomas reached down and took them off. He placed them on his face and inhaled deeply. Rocky's natural body scent made his dick throb harder. He dropped the panties and dove between her legs. He could taste the smell from her underwear— now his dick was fully erect. The straight, thin red hairs that covered her vaginal area stuck together as his saliva moistened them. He sucked her unusually large clitoris and she gyrated against his face without a sound. He pulled the skin surrounding her clitoris back and licked it with the tip of his tongue. Then he used the middle of his tongue and stroked her clit with long wide licks.

She screamed inside and soft moans escaped her lips. At the point of climax she gently shoved him off of her. She always felt cheated if she had an orgasm without any penetration. She pulled a prophylactic out of her top drawer and placed it in his hand. He fumbled to remove it from the wrapper then put it on in one motion. She lay on her stomach and raised her behind slightly off the bed. He forced his penis into her vagina through the back entrance and bent his body over hers. She moaned loudly and grabbed the headboard. With each thrust she raised her ass up.

"Oh God, It hurts so good," she panted. She closed her eyes and bit her sheets as she released on him. She felt lightheaded as her juices flowed onto the rubber that clung to his penis.

He humped harder and deeper. She continued to meet his strokes with a raised ass. "Get on your hands and knees, Rocky," he whispered.

She went up on all fours. He stood on his knees and he pushed his penis back in. He grabbed her waist tightly and began to pump. "I can feel your balls smacking my ass." She felt herself rising to another climax.

He held her waist tighter and made shorter strokes, but he pushed harder. Rocky pushed her ass into his groin with all her might. She rotated her backside on top of his dick and she contracted the muscles in her vagina. He matched her move for move.

"Ooh you gonna make me cum," Thomas snarled.

"Choke me, Thomas. Please."

Thomas made a few awkward noises, grabbed a handful of her hair, pulled it gently and then rang her neck with his free hand, pumping forcefully. With one last hard thrust, he stopped and clutched her air. He slowly pulled his manhood out of her vagina and surveyed his condom. She dropped, her eyes momentarily rolled into her head then she began to cough. Thomas breathed heavily and watched for her smile.

"Now that's a load. It looks like you got the Brady bunch up in that bitch," Rocky said winded, trying to come back down. She was gone. Just as she regained her breath and full consciousness the timer on the stove went off and startled her.

"I guess that was our appetizer, now I get my main course." Thomas forced a smile. "Rocky honey, your urges to asphyxiate scare me. Let's give it a rest."

Rocky slowly nodded her head. "I think you're right. It just feels so good." She got up and stood still with her eyes closed for a while. Then she grabbed a see through nightie out of her top drawer. She picked up his boxers off of the floor and tossed them on the bed.

"I'll be back in a flash," Rocky said.

That was some good love making, he thought. *I hope she isn't messing around on me. If we keep going at this pace, I am going to propose to her by the end of the year.* He got up and walked to the bathroom. En route he squeezed her ass softly. In the bathroom he pulled off his condom, threw it into the toilet and flushed. "Rocky, can I use the wash rag that's hanging in here?"

"Yes."

He squeezed pearly white hand soap onto the rag and began to wash off his penis. He rinsed out his mouth and made his way back to the bedroom. Rocky had already set up a tray with an ice-cold beer, two bowls of salad, a steaming plate of lasagna and warm garlic bread. "This lasagna is better than my momma's," Thomas said before he started to eat.

"Now that's a compliment, you know I have to keep my man healthy and strong," Rocky said.

8

Five 0 said 'freeze' and I got numb

Joann entered the police station. She walked blindly past the dozens of black and white wanted posters that lined the walls. She waved at the TS operator at the front of the station house behind a bulletproof window and noticed the phone lines were lighting up already. She stopped momentarily and shook her head.

"It's not a game, huh? I guess the city doesn't sleep for real. It's barely seven, and your lines are busy already?"

"Tell me about it," the TS operator called back.

The dark and light blue tile of the station house always killed Joann's mood in the morning; the colors were so dreary. She slowly walked down the steps to the locker room where dozens of lockers stood. She passed lockers with worn stickers and/or magnets on their doors. She stopped in front of hers and removed a stiff navy blue uniform shirt from it. She changed quickly and walked to the bathroom. "Qualles, how the hell you take showers in this nasty-ass bathroom?"

Another female officer emerged from the dull white plastic shower stall fully dressed. "You know damn well I ain't take no shower in that bitch. I was just trying to clean it out." The officer ducked into another stall, boots and all, and began to scrub its tarnished yellow walls. "Last week I pulled a triple. I left this bitch sweaty as fuck! These are the only two showers we have down here. I am just trying to make them fit for human use."

Joann splashed water over her face. "What's the use, girl? This place hasn't been remodeled in eons. It's six fifty-three, Qualles. Hurry up before you're late for call," Joann said.

Joann ran up the steps and into the Muster room ready for roll call. She took off her hat and wiped her forehead. She looked at the huge iron floor fans that stood over five feet tall in each corner of the room and fanned herself with her hat. "When are they going to put some AC up in this piece?" Joann asked no one in particular.

"Right after they remodel the bathrooms," Qualles laughed as she joined the line.

"What's up, D?" Joann said to an officer who took a place in the line.

"Shit."

"Same here," Joann replied as she looked at her watch. It was six fifty-seven. She smiled at the thought of several tardy cops running in with their uniforms half done. She looked around the room at the dusty, dimly lit old age-beaten wooden desks that lined it. She watched the sergeant come into the room with a Styrofoam coffee cup and his paperwork ready to take call. Three cops ran up to join the end of the line. Promptly at seven the sergeant pulled up an old wooden podium and stood behind it. He called all the officers on the tour by their last names, and inspected their uniforms. As he called their names he assigned them each a post. When he called Officer Joann Nuñez, she passed inspection and as always, was assigned Post Two.

Minutes later, Joann was dropped to her post in a squad car and stood in front of the bodega. As they pulled off she started to walk her post. She walked passed Brooklyn High, which seemed still and lifeless without its students lurking the halls and the surrounding streets. *Work is so boring since school is out. Nothing hardly happens on my post without the kids around,* she thought. She circled her area nine times within three hours, and ended up in front of her comfort zone— the bodega. She looked at her watch, it was nearly ten thirty. As she leaned against the side of the building she looked down at her black, timberlands.

"I think it's time for a new pair of Chucckas."

Her radio blared loudly, "Post Two, Post Two pick up."

She was surprised to hear her post being called so early during her tour. She grabbed her radio and talked into it. "This is Post Two."

"There's a 31 in progress at 3467 Fourth Avenue. Perp seen running south on Fourth. Caucasian male, blonde hair, blue jeans, yellow top, approximately 5'8". Copy?"

"Four," she said looking up and down the block quickly before she made her move. *Damn, 3467— 3467— that's Whole in the Middle the donut spot right across the street*, she thought.

She looked in the direction of the donut store and saw the suspect running parallel to her. She began to run in the same direction on her side of the street. When the suspect spotted her, he ran into a building. Joann darted across the street. A red Honda Civic came to a screeching halt, piercing her eardrums and leaving dark tire marks on the black pavement, but she didn't stop. A Range Rover stopped short, violently jerking, causing an unbuckled child to bump his head into the back of the driver's seat. The uniformed boy, no doubt, on his way to school, rubbed his forehead and stuck his head out of the window to watch Joann in pursuit. In awe, he sat with his mouth open as she zoomed across the island and weaved through traffic. Tires shrilled, as she continued to run. She stopped only once, for a split second, as she put her hands on the grill of a huge soda delivery truck that came within an inch of hitting her.

Seconds behind him, Joann followed the suspect into the brightly-lit Department of Social Services building with her gun pointed straight ahead and clicked on her radio. "This is Post Two. I have followed the perp into 3423 Fourth Avenue."

"That's a copy."

People gasped, yelled, covered their mouths, put their hands up or dove straight for the floor as Joann walked the crowded room looking for the perp's bright yellow shirt. She walked slowly around the large room searching, while watching her back front and sides. She could hear distant sirens approaching. As she walked further into the room she saw the suspect sitting in the middle of a row of people. She walked toward him like she didn't know he was there. Suddenly, he stood with a small toddler dangling under his arm and headed for the front door.

"Get the fuck off my baby," the toddler's mother screamed. The mother jumped holding an infant in her arms and tried to follow them. A security guard stopped her. While the mother screamed and pleaded for the suspect to let her child go Joann followed quickly behind. "Sir. Put the child down, and nobody will get hurt," she said prudently.

The suspect stopped, gun in one hand and the child in the other. Joann looked at the toddler who smiled from ear to ear revealing her small white teeth. Her innocent deep dark eyes brightly stared back. "Cop? Cop?" The toddler said laughing.

The room was quiet, with the exception of the sobbing mother and her laughing child. Joann held her gun tightly and the suspect darted into the outer hall. Joann followed close behind.

Rocky sat in her cubicle and stared into her computer screen. She ignored the huge pile of work that sat on her desk, and pictured her and Marcus on the computer screen. Smiling, she clicked on a radio.

I cannot believe we had so much fun. And he called me twice yesterday. He should arrive home in about fifteen minutes, and I am going to make sure I call him as soon as he touches down, she thought. She picked up her phone and dialed out. "Kay?"

"Tell me everything— wait let me close my door. Okay every detail."

"We had such a fuckin' good time. I spent the entire weekend with him. I let him do the sweating. I turned him down twice, and he's called me a since I've been home."

"Turned him down for what? He wanted sex? Rocky, did you fuck him?"

"NO! I turned him down to hang out, and party. I didn't want to run into any of Mauri's people."

"You have to wait for three months before you give him a taste. Where did y'all go?"

"We went to a magic show, the fight, an amusement park, walked the strip, drove through the mountains, and out to eat. We even kissed, and oooh, he can kiss. This is the one. I can feel it."

"Well, he looked cute as hell on TV, and your dress was banging. Y'all sure did look like a couple."

"WE DO, RIGHT? she exclaimed happily. "That's the dress Thomas bought me for my birthday."

Tony walked slowly around the insides of the Brooklyn Jewelry Exchange— casing it. He counted six strategically placed cameras, that he could see, and one big bodyguard at the door. He could not tell if he was armed. A salesman in a cheap brown suit approached him.

"May I help you, young man, or are you just browsing?"

"I want to buy a name plate and a pair of earrings for my girlfriend."

"Sure, step this way. I'll show you the different styles of name plates we carry."

As they approached a large display case Tony looked through the glass and instantly saw the nameplate he wanted to purchase. He looked around the store and noticed a senior from The High at the counter across from him.

"Well, do you see one you like?" the salesman asked.

"That one right there. I want that one, with the kissing doves underneath it."

"Do you like the chain it is hanging on or would you prefer something else?"

"I like it just the way it is." Tony looked back toward the senior from his school and called out to him. "Yo," he said quietly. "YO." The guy turned around and looked at Tony. "Come here for a second."

The senior a Latino teen, walked over to Tony. He was 5'9" with a very fair complexion. He had brown curly hair, which was moussed stiff, and a few freckles sprinkled across his cheeks. He wore a pair of jeans, Timberlands, and a white T-shirt. He indicated for Tony to wait one second. He gave the clerk some money and placed a yellow slip in his pocket. Then he walked over toward Tony and gave him a pound. "You go to The High, right? I'm George," he said.

"Yeah. We had Mrs. Simmons together last year. I'm Tony." Tony pointed at the nameplates after they gave each other pounds. "What do yo think about that one over there? I'm copping one for my girl."

"That's hot, I'm feeling the diamonds on the birds."

"Good lookin', son," Tony said.

"One," George replied.

"Yo, you graduated?"

"I start Hunter in the fall."

"Now that's what's up."

The salesman cleared his throat, and Tony looked.

"Alright be easy, George."

"One."

When George walked away the salesman removed the nameplate from the case. "This name plate is going to cost you thirty dollars per letter to make, and an additional three hundred for the chain and kissing doves."

"That's a lot of money. I need something less expensive. I'm putting both of our names on it."

"I could probably do it for twenty-five a letter if I talk to my boss— and if you are buying earrings."

"Talk to your boss, and then come back," Tony said and he continued to look around the store.

After George exited Brooklyn Jewelry Exchange, he stood on the corner of Fourth Avenue, picked up his cell phone and dialed Yanick's number.

"Hey, George, what's up?" Yanick asked pleasantly.

"Nothing. I was just thinking about you," George said.

"Really? Where are you?" Yanick asked.

"I just left the Brooklyn Jewelry Exchange," George replied.

"I hope you didn't buy another piece of jewelry for little Seven."

"No, I didn't. You feel like hanging out with me tonight?"

"Nah, I have plans with Joann."

"What's up with you and that fucking dyke, yo? You're spending a lot of time with her. We don't even hang no more. We need to talk."

"I know. Come by my house."

"I went to your house last night, looking for you, and your mother was breaking. She knows that chick is gay, and she thinks you're freakin' off too."

"Are you serious?" Yanick shrieked.

"Yep."

"I guess I better go home and straighten things out. Meet me there later— then we could talk?"

"Okay. Later."

"Bye, George."

Inside Brooklyn Jewelry Exchange the sales person came from the back of the store with a smile on his face. "Twenty-five dollars a letter won't be a problem as long as you purchase a pair of earrings."

"I want the earrings in the same shape that I have on but I want the diamonds to be smaller."

"Sure, step this way, sir."

They walked over to a display case that had nothing but diamond earrings in it. Tony looked at the selection for a while, then he smiled.

"How much are the ones that are shaped like teardrops?"

"You want the price of the smallest size?" The salesman asked.

"Yes."

"Okay, these are one quarter of a carat and they cost two hundred dollars."

"How much is the next size up?"

"Those are three hundred and fifty dollars."

"I have nine hundred cash. Can that get me both items?"

"Nine hundred cash, right now?" Tony nodded. "They are yours. Now all you have to do is spell out the names for me on this receipt. If you come a week from today your jewelry will be ready. You can take the earrings now."

"Nah, I will pick up both items next week." Tony jotted the names down on a piece of paper. He counted out nine hundred dollar bills and placed them on the counter.

"You're all set, I'll see you next week," the salesperson said.

Tony walked out of the store smiling until he looked down the block at the State building. Police had surrounded it. Tony shrugged his shoulders as he walked in the opposite direction. "Somebody probably went postal because they ain't get their food stamps or something," he murmured.

The suspect saw several cop cars in front of the building. He ran into a nearby stairwell ascending the steps backwards. Joann ran three steps at a time, and was within reach of him. As he turned up the steps he peered down through the banisters and shot at Joann. The bullet missed by a long shot hitting a distant wall. The loud proximity of the shot temporarily clogged her hearing. Instinct told her to let him go up another flight. She aimed between the banister bars, and got a clear shot to his leg.

Joann didn't know what was louder the strident shot in the hollow, stone stairwell, or the ear splitting wails of the toddler and her distant screaming mother as the shot went off. She saw both her suspect and the toddler hit the floor. Her heart fell to her stomach and nausea overtook her body. She nervously ran up the steps, not knowing who had been shot.

The suspect lay awkwardly, face down, with his weapon thrown clear, and the crying toddler rubbing her side. Joann placed her knee in his back, and cuffed his hands behind him. She could see smoke coming out of the whole in his leg. The toddler began to scream at the top of her lungs. Joann picked her up, and bounced her in her arms. Then she handed the baby to one of several officers that had just arrived in the stairwell. Joann sat momentarily, caught her breath then thanked god.

As she emerged from the stairwell clutching the wounded suspect, dozens of people stood in the building's lobby cheering. The toddler hostage's mother was at the entrance. She smiled through tear-filled eyes.

"Thank you for saving my baby, and not hurting her. God bless you, officer." The woman hugged Joann. She released the arm of her suspect, to the custody of the same officer who had dropped her off that morning and hugged the toddler's mother. Joann took the toddler into her arms, hugged her tightly and kissed her cheek. The toddler, smiling once again touched Joann's badge and said, "Cop, cop." The crowd cried 'Awww'. TV cameras shone in her face, as she handed the baby back to its mother.

"Officer Nuñez, what was going through your mind in the stairwell? Were you frightened you would wound the child? " One reporter asked.

"Once he took that beautiful baby girl hostage, I just wanted to make sure she was safely back in her mothers arms, unharmed. If I wasn't absolutely sure that I had a clear shot, I wouldn't have taken it."

A sergeant stepped in front of the camera and Joann read the suspects his rights.

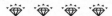

"Can you hear the radio through my phone?" Rocky asked Kay.

"Not really, why?"

"Yo, someone got shot at the state building, not too far from where I work out. I hope it wasn't anyone I know."

"Shut UP!"

"I'm serious. Kay, do you realize we've been on the phone for a half an hour?" Rocky asked.

"I know. I have a lot of work to do, I'll call you at home."

Rocky's cell phone rang. She shrieked as she saw Marcus' name flash across the screen. She quickly covered her mouth, and looked around her office.

"Dag, that was my ear girl," Kay said.

"It's him. Marcus is calling my cell. I'll call you at home." She simultaneously disconnected the call, and answered her cell.

"Hi. I was just thinking about you," Rocky said with a calm she didn't feel.

"Yeah right? I thought you would have called to see how I made it in."

"I swear I was going to, but you beat me to it. How are you?"

"I'm chillin. What about you?"

"Chillin'. I'm trying to figure out what your ass did to me out there. I have been thinking about you since we left each other," Rocky said.

"Same here, well, I just called to let you know I made it home. Call me tonight," Marcus said.

"I will."

"Bye."

"Later." Rocky squealed and spun around in her chair.

Tony reached home and walked quietly through the side entrance to find his father standing in the kitchen on the phone with his wife.

"Guess who just walked in?"

"Jonathan, you better talk to that nigga," Millicent said and hung up.

"So, you just walk out the house in the middle of the night and don't say nothing?"

"Daddy, I—"

"Daddy nothing. This is the second time. Now I don't want to send you down south, but your ass is too old to be sitting in the house all summer. If you're going to be doing this grown man shit, you need to get the fuck up out of my house. You got me, son?"

"Yes, Daddy."

"If you gonna stay the night at you girlfriend's house, you have to ask first— or at least call. You either gonna cut this shit out, or work with the P.A.L. this summer at my precinct."

"Yes, Daddy."

"Stay out of trouble, and if you and Cheryl are fucking—"

"Dad, her name is Shaine and I swear to god we are not doing anything. She won't let me."

"Remember, put a rubber on your meat— you don't want to bring home no BD."

"BD?" Tony looked at his father.

"Babies or diseases." Both father and son laughed and embraced each other tightly.

"Thanks, Pop."

"OH, now that you are off the hook I'm not Daddy any more, it's back to Pop."

Tony smiled, walked up the stairs into his room, closed his door and pulled out a shoebox from underneath his bed. It contained a bunch of scattered bills. He went into his pocket, pulled out a wad of money, dumped it into the box and slid it back under the bed. Then Tony reached beneath his pillow and grabbed a copy of 'Black Tail' from underneath it. He lay back and thought about all the things he could do with his money.

As he flipped through the pages he thought about fuckin' Latonji, and giving her money to keep her quiet. He stopped in the middle of the magazine. There was a two-page centerfold of a young-looking naked girl who was the spitting image of Latonji. She lay bare on a pile of hundred, fifty, and twenty dollar bills. She held a wad of money with one hand and spread the lips of her vagina open revealing pink flesh, with the other. He pulled his pants below his behind and began to stroke his penis.

He pulled on it harder and faster as he thought of how much he wanted Latonji and Shaine. He licked his lips and continued to jerk it. Suddenly he stopped.

Tony jumped out of his bed and shuffled to his dresser with his pants around his ankles and dick in his hand. He grabbed a bottle of cocoa butter lotion and moistened his hands with it. Still tugging on his dick he dashed back to his bed, looked at the picture and tried to remember the warmth of Shaine's body next to him just hours before. As he began to stroke, he pictured Shaine's pretty face in the magazine. He stroked faster and faster then . . .

Tony sprang up when he heard his door open. He scampered to put the magazine under the covers, but decided to cover his privates with it. "Don't you knock, muthafucka?"

Malik turned on the lights and laughed. "I'm sorry. DAMN, am I sorry." Malik laughed at his brother, and laughed louder when he noticed the open bottle of lotion.

"Why are you home so early? What time is it?" Tony asked.

"Early? It's a little after six," Malik said.

"I can't believe I've been sleeping so long. What do you want, Malik?" Tony snapped.

"Listen, Tone, I didn't mean to bust in here or nothing, I have just been meaning to speak to you. You're always with your girl or running out the house after dinner and we haven't really been talking."

"Can I finish sleeping?"

"I really have some things I would like to talk to you about, and it seems like your little ass has been avoiding me."

"Nah, why would I be doing that?"

Tony grabbed the sheet off of his bed, wrapped it around him and dropped the magazine on the floor as he was covered. "What the—"

He felt a wet, cold substance on his waist. He unwrapped the sheets and grimaced in disgust. There was a pool of cold semen on the sheet. "Oh fuck! Ewwww, I'll be right back, Leek."

"Damn," Malik said. Tony ran past him and heading for the bathroom. "Tony, make sure you wrap that shit up when you diggin' out your broad, cause you droppin' heavy loads. Come downstairs when your done, I really need to talk to you," Malik said.

"Why you gotta be all loud and shit. Mommy can hear you."

Malik ran down the steps, and into his room. He was a bit disturbed by the sight of his baby brother's penis, but couldn't help but smile. *We've all been there*, he thought. Just then his cellular went off.

"Yeah?"

"What up, Malik. This is Mike."

"What the deal, yo?"

"I forgot to tell you, we have dates tonight."

"Nah, I am going to have to pass on that one, son."

"Come on. I am going out with this broad that I met in Miami. She won't come out here, unless she brings a friend. Come scoop me. I already said that it was a date."

"Why are you always doin' that shit? I'll pick you up from the train station."

"I'm sayin', you gonna make me step on the train in my Scooby Doo's and shit? Come scoop a brother and I will take a cab home."

"Alright, ALRIGHT!! What time are we supposed to meet them?"

"Eight o' clock in the city."

"It's minutes after six. Why you ain't tell me at work?"

"I forgot, and she just called to confirm."

"Alright I'm getting dressed."

Tony increased the water pressure in the shower to its maximum, and let it beat all over his body. Thoughts dropped in and out of his mind like the beads of water that jabbed him. *What the fuck does this nigga have to talk to me about? I can't believe he just saw my dick! I wonder if he knows, nah, he can't know. I really need some pussy man— this jerkin' off shit is the pits.* Just then he heard a knock on the door.

"YEAH?"

"Your brother's on his way out, and your father has to go to work. We need to eat dinner right now, so hurry up."

"But ma, it ain't even seven yet."

"Just come on."

Tony let the shower run for a few more minutes before he stopped it and dried off. When he was dressed he ran down to the table. Everyone was seated, except Malik. "Ma, where did Malik go?"

"Out with Mike, but at least he had the courtesy to let his parents know," Millicent said sarcastically.

Joann wearily turned her key in the door. Before she could push it, it swung open.

"Baby, I am so proud of you. I saw you on New York One three times today. I know you must be tired." Yanick gave Joann a peck on the lips and ran into the kitchen.

"That sure does smell good. What are you cooking?" Joann asked.

"I am not telling. It's a special surprise. What you did today was amazing, Joey."

"Tell that to my captain. I was almost suspended for taking that shot— the perp had an infant hostage."

Joann walked sluggishly into the bathroom and turned on the shower. She stripped out of her clothes and then walked into her bedroom. She opened the door to find the room filled with white candles. They were glowing on her dresser, across the top of her bed head and on her nightstand. As she walked into the room she noticed the candlelit walkway that led to the bed. There was a negligee and a note lying on it.

Joann smiled as she sat on the bed. When she picked up the negligee and rubbed it's soft satin against her face the piece of paper fluttered to the ground next to her feet. She picked it up and read it aloud;

'To my Super Cop: Congratulations on being so good at what you do. I am so proud of you. Your prisoner of love, Yanick.'

"Prisoner of Love, come in here," Joann called loudly. Yanick was already peeking in the bedroom from the door. She entered smiling and sat on the bed. "Prisoner of Love?" Joann smiled.

"Yeah, I thought that was cute. So you like?"

"I love all of this. Put this shit on now."

"Nope. Not until you let me rub you down in the tub and feed you your deluxe dinner."

Yanick began to undress. "I have some special oils I want to rub you down with."

"Where's Seven?"

"I dropped her off at my house today. I had a talk with my parents. My mom is really buggin' lately. Anyway, let's get into the tub, so we can eat."

After two hours of romance including a dinner, a soothing bath, massage, some erotic dancing and sex Yanick and Joann lay free of clothes, side by side, watching the news. They flipped through several channels and watched Joann on the screen.

"I am glad you enjoyed the night. And I am so glad that we are together." Yanick kissed Joann's shoulder, and then turned over.

Glad we're together? What does she mean by that? Joann thought.

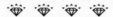

Rocky lay in her bed looking at her phone, deep in thought. *I don't want to seem too thirsty maybe I should call him tomorrow. But, if I call him tomorrow he might think I'm playin' games and be like fuck her. Besides, he did say call me tonight.* She debated this point for fifteen minutes before she finally decided to call.

"Hello?"

"Hey, Candy! What are you doing?"

"Nothing much, just relaxing."

"I'm glad you called. I was just thinking about you. What are you doing this weekend?"

"Nothing, why?"

"I have to make an appearance at a party at the Millenium in Miami, why don't you fly down there for the weekend? We can hang out or something."

"Marcus. I would love to, but I am a little strapped for cash right now. Maybe next weekend—"

"Candy, don't insult me like that, girl. I'm going to give my travel agent your information."

<u>9</u>

Wave your Rollie's in the sky

"Sweat, are you sure this shit going to work?" Kahmelle asked as he got into the car.

"I got you, Buck. Yo, this is my little man right here, yo," Sweat addressed the other guys in the car.

Kahmelle recognized two of them as Finest, but the other two were unfamiliar to him. Kahmelle looked out of the window as they were just about to cross the Brooklyn Bridge. He didn't recognize the little black car they rode in, but the paper temporary-resident license on the back window was very familiar to him. Kahmelle started to perspire. The car had no air-conditioning, and although warm air blew in through the windows, it didn't help the way he felt. His nerves were bananas. He couldn't decide if he was excited or frightened. He just sat quietly.

"We're going to do everything according to plan, and Buck, I do things like this all the time. I got a man on the inside that has my back. He's security and knows exactly when we strike. Get it, when we strike?" Sweat joked. Everyone in the car laughed loudly.

As they sped up the FDR Drive, Kahmelle looked at the Brooklyn Bridge in the distance over the water. He looked at the tall building with the clock on Atlantic Avenue that housed a bank. He thought about the stories his mother told him about how his father had died robbing that big bank. He couldn't help but wonder if he would get killed on his first armed robbery, with Brooklyn's Finest, just moments away. . .

Tony stood at the door of the Brooklyn Jewelry Exchange and waited to get buzzed in. Within seconds he was inside the store. He looked for the salesman that helped him, but he did not see him. He walked over to a different salesperson.

"Good afternoon. I am here to pick up some jewelry."

"Do you have your yellow slip?"

"Right here." Tony took out the slip and handed it to the clerk.

"I'll be back in a minute."

Tony stood in his place and looked around the store. He rechecked the cameras, then looked at the front door and noticed there was no security guard. He slowly walked around looking at the jewelry in the cases. *I wonder how much money we need to snag initiation, or if we just have to tote toast and rob something. Well, whatever the case I'm out after initiation,* he thought.

The salesman that sold him the jewelry came out with a small manila envelope and two gold boxes. "It's been a week already? The salesman looked at his watch. "It sure has. Anywho, here are the earrings you purchased and your nameplate. I think she'll love them."

There was a sudden bang on the glass that startled them both. There were eight boys around his age standing at the door. No one buzzed them in. The salesman turned his attention back to Tony. The guys banged on the door once more and walked off cursing and yelling.

"I don't remember there being a buzzer on the door when I paid for this," Tony said curiously.

"On Tuesdays, Wednesdays and Thursdays the manager in charge buzzes people in, and the following days, the door's unlocked and we have an armed security guard. It's solely for security purposes."

"Oh, Okay."

"Thanks for your purchase. Come again, please."

"Later." Tony looked at the clock on his phone and picked up his pace.

Damn, it's one already. I have to spend some time with Shaine. She leaves for Florida tonight, he thought.

Sweat drove down Fifth Avenue. "That's the store right there. I'm going to circle the block to look for cops. I'll be sitting right here. Grab as much as you can and bounce."

Everyone was quiet as Sweat passed the Rolex store for the second time, and checked his watch. It was one p.m. sharp, and they all knew exactly what they had to do. The car pulled around the block and the 'Finest's' members pulled their green hoodies tightly around their faces. They jumped out at the corner and Sweat drove to the designated spot. All five guys ran up to the Rolex storefront. Kahmelle counted to three loudly. On three, three bowling balls were thrown into the window with all of their might. As expected, the balls went crashing right through it. Shattered glass chips of all sizes instantly covered the street and the five pairs of sneakers that stood in front of it. A loud alarm sounded and people watched in disbelief, or just kept it moving down the busy city sidewalk.

Their sneakers crunched through the glass as each of them scooped as many pieces as possible out of the display. Kahmelle shoved watches in his hoodie pocket and went back for more. Thirty seconds later they ran around the corner. The security guard came running out of the store with his pants unbuckled, and ran in the opposite direction.

Bystanders yelled loudly at him, "They went that way!" But before he could get to the corner, all five of the 'Finest' were already in the car and speeding up Sixth Avenue.

They pulled off their hoodies and threw them in a plastic shopping bag. Sweat slowed down and drove at a moderate pace. He turned the next corner and parked the car at a hydrant on W. 54 between Sixth and Seventh Avenues. They all walked over to Seventh Avenue as planned.

A police car drove by slowly, but the cops didn't look their way. Once the Finest got to Seventh Avenue, Sweat's green truck was idling at the corner, with Webb behind the wheel. Kahmelle sat in the far rear with Sweat and everyone else got in where they fit in. The car drove down Seventh Avenue within the speed limit.

"Right here, Webb, turn right here," Sweat said.

Webb turned down 28th street and stopped the car in the middle of the block. When the car came to a halt the guys emptied their pockets. Sweat quickly tossed each watch into a book bag. He stopped once to show Kahmelle the price tag on one.

"Look at this Buck," he whispered." The price tag read forty-five thousand dollars.

"Get the fuck out of here, yo," Kahmelle said. Kahmelle went into his pockets and pulled out watches. He had stolen more than anyone else and turned them over to Sweat— with the exception of one.

"That's my little man— six watches," Sweat said.

Sweat got out of the truck carrying the book bag and opened the trunk. He lifted the cover to the hidden compartment that contained a spare, and stuffed the watch-filled book bag into the middle of the tire. He closed the compartment and jumped back into the truck.

Without a word they headed back to Brooklyn. No one spoke again until they reached the corners of Atlantic and Washington Avenues.

"I have some important people coming to meet me in a bout an hour or so. You will hear from me in a couple of days, keep your walkies on." Kahmelle went to give Sweat a pound but he refused it. "Nah, little man, I want you to roll with me. You drive?" Sweat asked.

"Nah," Kahmelle replied.

"Get in the front, son," Sweat said.

When the car was finally empty Sweat looked at Kahmelle. "So, how many watches you got in your pocket, Buck?" Kahmelle shook his head and bowed it in shame.

"One."

"You could keep it but if you try to sell it in a store your ass will get arrested. These watches ain't your speed. You need like a Locman, a Techno or even a Jacob."

"How did you know man?" Kahmelle asked softly.

"Because you like a mini-me. I bet you wonder how I know if them dudes are stealing from me or not, huh? Or why everyone just hands over their bread to me, right?" Kahmelle nodded. "Ask Thugglemen the type of shit me and his brother used to have poppin' off when we was your age. Niggas know me and they don't cross me 'cause I'm muthafuckin' thorough. The Finest run on trust, dig?"

"Yeah."

"Now, if I didn't like your ass you would have definitely been cut the fuck off, or cut. Truth be told, Buck, I would've done the same shit at your age. But don't fuckin' cross me again," he ended firmly.

Kahmelle took the watch out of his pocket and handed it Sweat. His stomach tied Boy Scout knots and he moistened his mouth.

"Don't be scared now, son, we good. My word is all I have in this world, nigga." Sweat extended his arm and gave Kahmelle a pound.

"I'm sorry. But that's exactly what I was thinking," Kahmelle said.

"I wouldn't cheat you little niggas. Y'all like my brothers. I got ten thousand dollars off of that ring shit, you heard?"

"Yeah," Kahmelle said.

"Listen, family, I want to talk to you about Camille. You need to make her get rid of that shit, Buck."

"I told her I would pay for an abortion, but she don't want to do it. She's talking about getting married and shit like that. I'm only eighteen— I even stopped speaking to her."

"You need to make her do that shit, son. Stick a hanger in that shit while your fish is sleeping or something. A baby is not a good look for you. Especially with the type of life you are trying to get into. Why you think I ain't got no girl or baby or no shit like that? What if we got caught for that shit we did today? Her ass would be out here in the streets by herself— well, her and the baby. She is a fuckin' chickenhead. Look how you met her!"

"You're right, Sweat. But I can't talk her out of that shit."

"Punch her in the fuckin' stomach. I'll take care of that shit."

"Nah, I got myself into this one, and I will get out of it. Trust me."

"I'm fuckin' starving, you hungry?" Sweat asked.

Kahmelle was disgusted. He couldn't believe everyone knew about Camille. And so far everyone agreed on her not having the baby. "Shake it off B, we'll figure something out. Let's grab some food," Sweat said.

"Yo, Tone, come here and give your big brother some love, nigga."

Nobody answered. Malik tossed his bag down and walked up the steps.

"Malik," Millicent called from her room. "I can't believe you stopped in for dinner— anyway, I don't know what's gotten into Tony but I would appreciate it if you talked to him for me."

"Millie, I already took care of that," Jonathan whispered.

"I have been meaning to talk to him anyway, Ma," Malik said.

Malik headed straight for Tony's bedroom. He looked around at the faded posters on the wall walked over to his desk and opened the drawers. There was some loose change, a few condoms, pens, pencils and some scattered papers in it— nothing out of the ordinary. Malik looked at the papers and shoved them back in the drawer. He walked over to Tony's bed and sat on it. On the nightstand was a photograph of Tony, Kahmelle, and two girls. He picked it up and smiled. "That must be Shaine— wow, she is a dime," he said under his breath. "He gets his taste from his brother."

He reached under the bed and pulled out a box. He opened it up and it was filled with pornographic magazines. He flipped through a couple and laughed. Underneath the magazines he found scattered dollar bills. He reached for another box and opened it up. The box was filled with hundreds and twenties. He jumped when he heard the downstairs door slam. He shoved the box under the bed and quietly exited his brother's room. "Tony, is that you?" Malik called out.

"No son, it's me," Jonathan said.

Malik went down to his room, dropped is duffel bag on the floor and stared at the ceiling. *Where could he have gotten that bread? He thought. Could Tina be right? I don't believe this. I can't tell Pop until I find out what's going on.*

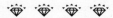

Shaine and Tony sat on the couch. She fingered her chain and gazed into his profile as they watched the Mauri Povich show. She touched her earring backs several times. "I love my chain and my earrings. Thank you so much, baby." Shaine gently kissed his cheek.

Suddenly Tony jumped up, pointed at the TV and looked at her. "You see that shit? He ain't even do nothing. Yo, if you ever fuck Kahmelle! How these cats go on TV to air their dirty laundry is beyond me. I don't understand it. This nigga slept with his best friend's wife and shit."

"Don't you know that this is fake? Besides, you don't have to worry about me sleeping with that clown. Camille said that he don't even be checkin' for her that much since she been pregnant."

"Yo. Can't you tell her not to have that fuckin' baby? It ain't right."

"I tried. I think Camille thinks the baby will make him like her more."

"That shit is just pushing him away? He'll take care of the seed, if it's his—"

"Wait a minute. You can't be for real. Of course that baby is his. What are you tryin' to say?"

"That nigga fucked her within the first minutes of meeting her. That baby could be any of the 'Finest's', except mine. Shit, remember she ain't make initiation the first time. What you think she had to do to get in the second time?" Shaine looked at Tony in disgust.

"Yo, Tone pick up, TONE, PICK UP, IT'S ME, BUCK," came blaring through Tony's phone.

"What's up, Kahmelle?"

"It's Buck now, nigga."

"What do you want, Kah? I am busy."

"I got something for you. Where you at?"

"I'm at Shaine's." Shaine slapped him on his thigh. "Ouch, that hurts."

"I knew you was there. Tell her to throw down the key."

Shaine lifted the window and threw her keys down. She kissed Tony's lips and looked into his eyes. "I love my gifts, baby. And, I love you."

"I am glad you do. They cost me some cheddar."

She kissed him again and smiled. "I love you, Tony. Do you love me?"

Tony hesitated, and Kahmelle came through the door.

"Don't you knock?" Shaine yelled.

"Not when I have your keys right here. How you doin', Shaine?"

"Good before you got here," she said with an attitude.

"Why you trippin?" He looked at Tony and pointed at Shaine. "Why your fish trippin'? Since when she come at me like that? I thought we was cool."

"We was, before you got my girl pregnant, and started shitting on her."

"Man, she got herself pregnant. She told me she was on the pill. You need to talk to her, yo."

Shaine jerked her head back, rolled her eyes, and twisted her neck with each syllable she spoke. "YOU need to talk to her."

"I do, but she doesn't want to hear me. Shaine, I ain't no kind of father. I can barely take care of myself."

Shaine dropped her guard, relaxed her arms and walked toward Kahmelle. "I know, Kahmelle, but she won't listen to me either. I told her to have an abortion but she won't."

"Can't you talk to her moms, or get your moms to talk to her?" Kahmelle asked.

"Her mother said it's her choice and my mom doesn't like her," Shaine replied.

"What about your aunt? Why don't you get Seepia to talk to her? She will set her ass right," Tony interjected.

"Thanks, I'm going to do that. Anyway, I need to talk to Tone alone."

"One more thing, Kahmelle," Shaine said.

"Yeah?"

"Ignoring her isn't going to make her get rid of that baby. Talk to her, She's miserable."

"I don't know what else to do. She doesn't want to talk about what I want to talk about. I'm going to go over there with my aunt."

"Tony, come here, man. Shaine think fast!" Kahmelle threw Shaine's keys toward her, and they hit the wooden floor with a loud clank. She scooped up her keys and walked to the back of the apartment.

"Yo, you wouldn't believe what the job was?"

"What?"

"We hit up Rolex on Fifth Ave. with bowling balls. Some White—"

"Bowling balls? How the fuck you hold up the Rolex store with a bowling ball?"

"Nah, son, we broke out the front window with those shits, and took all the joints out of there."

"You lyin'?"

"I'm for real, duke. I took seven and there was four other niggas with me. I think they got at least nine or ten between them. Sweat said there were eighteen watches on display."

"That is some shit right there."

Kahmelle laughed. "Oh, you ain't hear shit yet. These two young lookin' White niggas came to the Bat Cave and paid him three hundred and fifty grand in cash for them shits. When they opened that briefcase I thought I was in a muthafuckin 50 Cent video and shit. He gave me forty-five thousand dollars for that shit— everyone else is getting thirty-five grand a piece— plus he gotta hit off the security dude from the store with fifty grand. He sent five grand for you and said put that up for college. Plus I planned to hit you with a G just because you ain't come on this run. Here." Tony stared at the money Kahmelle was trying to give to him. "Here, take it."

"I- I- don't know. You don't think we in over our heads?"

"You ain't in over shit, and I am just going with the flow. I am blowing most of this shit before I go down south."

"You better start saving for that baby, nigga."

"Fuck that. Once my aunt gets through with her, she is going to give that shit up. Now this shit is on the low so don't be blabbing off."

"Who am I going to tell besides you?"

"Your girl or Leeko?"

"Malik don't hardly be around no more. Ever since he went on vacation a couple of weeks ago, he be shackin' up with some broad from Jersey. He's been there all week. I only saw him once. Plus you know I can't talk 'Finest' business with him."

"Well, I spoke to him like an hour ago when I called your house."

"Oh, yeah, I was in Brooklyn Jewelry Exchange and I came up with a plan for our initiation." Kahmelle had a surprised look on his face. "Yep. All I have to do is work out the finer details, but I think I got it."

"I knew you could do it."

"Shaine, I'm out, baby. I have to run," Tony shouted.

Shaine ran into the front room just as the boys made their way out the door. She grabbed Tony's arm. "Wait a minute. You know I am going out of town tonight and I start my summer job as soon as I come back. I wanted us to spend some time together."

"I have been here all day, plus it's almost seven-thirty. I have to go home for dinner. You ain't leaving until twelve I'll come back before you leave."

"Yeah, but my moms will be home by then."

"What's the difference if your mom's here? It's not like you gonna give it up anyway," Kahmelle said.

"Tony. You better keep this nigga out of our business!"

Kahmelle looked at her chain. "Let me find out you shinin' compliments of my nigga over here. Name plate with a little diamonds on that shit, and earrings."

Tony laughed. Shaine rolled her eyes. "Bye, baby." He kissed her on the cheek and shut the door. They walked down the steps and out of the door laughing.

"So that is what yo' ass was doing up in the BK Jewels, huh? Trickin' on Shaine."

"If she been down from day one, man, trick on your wife."

"You fuckin' Jay Z groupie," Kahmelle said. "I miss Camille, yo. I want to go see her, but I ain't tryin' to hear that baby shit."

"It's hard to tell. The way you was all up on Dulce at Latonji's house."

"You know I blazed that shit, right?"

"WORD? You suited up? Is the hair on her pussy straight like it is on her head or nappy? She looks kind of black."

"That shit is straight as hell, duke and a nigga was a Trojan man. Not for nothing Latonji is on your shit! Fuckin' Dulce's ass is always talking about how much Latonji be sweatin' you."

"Why you ain't call me after you hit that? You ain't even hit me after you hit up Rolex?"

"I'm here now. What you gonna do with your bread?"

"Shit, I still got money to blow from our first run. I haven't even touched the money from the ring yet. I can't believe that this shit is so easy." Tony stopped and looked at Kahmelle. "You know that nigga got paper right?"

"Do I? Look at the type of shit he into."

"Nah I mean paper, paper," Tony said as he started to walk. "When him and my brother used to hustle, they were both caking off big time. But my brother got caught and had to shell out mad money for a lawyer. Malik still has a lot of money saved. How you think he pay for NYU? Not by working in the mailroom!"

"Word?"

"Word, and that nigga's grandmother left him that house on Clermont, and she had two houses down south that I am sure he gets paper from every month. That nigga don't need this shit."

"So why risk it? Why risk being in the bing for this shit?" Kahmelle asked.

"That nigga is in it for the thrill, just like you. My brother told me that the streets give the best head. Once the streets give you good brain, you never get it off your mind. You always want to go back for more. Even when you have a good job, or a boojy broad, neither get down and dirty like the streets. A nine to five can't satisfy a real street nigga."

The two walked down the street and digested the same statement silently for a couple of blocks.

Dulce is a dime, classy and looks three times better than Camille, Kahmelle thought. *But, I can't get Camille of my mind. I really like her, and her head game is sick.*

Tony associated the statement with a vivid memory of himself at twelve years old— one year before Malik started college. He had just come home from jail. Malik hadn't been back for a week before he burst into his room at three in the morning and woke him up . . .

"Lil' Tone, wake up and go get the peroxide and some Band-Aids out of the bathroom!" Malik said stripping off his leather jacket.

Tony stretched, flicked the nightlight on his dresser and rubbed the sleep out of his eyes. He stretched long and hard as he spoke.

"What's wrong with you?"

"I just had a fight, that's all."

"Why don't you call Sweat?" Tony yawned.

"He was there. Just go get the fuckin' alcohol— and don't wake up Mom and Dad either. I don't want them flippin'."

Tony ran into the bathroom, pajama bottomed and bare on top. From the cabinet over the sink he grabbed cotton swabs, alcohol and a first aid kit. On white tube socks he slid back into his room, flipped on the bedroom light and began to scream as he looked at his brother's bare back. It had a gaping gash that ran from above his right shoulder blade all the way down to the top left side of his waist. There was bumpy, red flesh and tissue along the sides of it. The laceration leaked thick blood. His red vital fluid oozed out over the flesh and onto his golden brown skin.

"Shut the fuck up! It's just a little blood. You're going to wake up Mom and Dad."

"What happened?" Tony cried. "You just came back from jail! You want to go back in!" Malik didn't answer. He used his shirt to mop up the blood on his brother's chair. "Why you still be out there? You ain't going to do nothing but get into more trouble."

"Pour that shit on my cut and let me tell you something— is there medical tape in that box?"

"Yeah."

"Put the tape on top of the Band Aides."

"But there is gauze in here, too," Tony sniffed.

"Good. Pour peroxide and alcohol on it, then put the gauze on with the tape."

Tony did as he was told. As he poured the peroxide onto his brother's back thick white foam instantly permeated the wound. He could hear it fizzle. Malik didn't flinch, but Tony squeezed his eyes shut, and turned his back as he continued to pour. *"That doesn't burn?"* Tony asked.

"Tony, it stopped hurting me like twenty minutes ago. It hurt so much that it doesn't even hurt anymore. Pour some more on there."

"I used it up in one pour and it was brand new."

"Well, use the alcohol until it stops bleeding."

Tony threw the empty brown bottle on the floor and it rolled underneath his bed. He unscrewed the cap to the alcohol with his teeth and held a clean gauze pad in his hand. He poured it on and there was no white fizz, but Malik winced loudly in pain. Tony patted the wound with the gauze, pink spread through each threaded weave quickly, until it the gauze was a deep red hue, then he used another and another, and another—

"Malik, why? Mommy and Daddy are sick with you. Mommy cried every night that you were in jail. She wouldn't even take me to see you. Do you know how much I missed you, while you were gone?"

Tony paused for a minute then doused Malik's back with all the alcohol and threw the bottle against the wound as hard as he could. Malik got up and looked at him. *"What's wrong with you!?"*

"NO, what's wrong with you? You got off clean— no record. Why would you want to ruin all of that? You got a pretty girlfriend with a good job, and she's in school. Why don't you go to school?"

Malik sat down and Tony continued to try to stop the bleeding with the gauze, but it just kept flowing. Tony put the gauze inside of the cut, then taped it on there. *"Let me tell you something. The streets give the best head. Once the streets give you . . ."*

It all came into play for Tony right there. He never truly understood Malik that night, but a ten thousand- watt billboard went off in his head as he gave Kahmelle an explanation for something that he finally began to understand just minutes ago.

10

In Brownsville that you rolled dice with

Rocky rolled over, looked at her clock and sat up slowly. She slid gently off the side of her bed and into her slippers. She looked at the answering machine and the red light blinked four times. "Four messages? Probably Kay and Mauri, I will call them when I get back," she whispered. She stretched and quietly hopped out of her bed not wanting to wake Thomas. She threw on her pink sweats, grabbed her pink water bottle from the fridge and jogged out of her apartment.

As she jogged down Fourth Avenue she looked over at the Brooklyn Jewelry Exchange and thought about her Great Nahnan's broach. *Shit, I spent most of the money I won in Vegas. I think I can scrape up two G's. But that's not enough to pay my pawn off. I guess I'll hit Mauri up for some dough when I get down there next weekend and pay it off as soon as I come back.*

She jogged passed Brooklyn High School. Several blocks later she slowly began to approach the familiar surroundings of the school's field and her little park, which she deemed her personal gym. She edged over to the curb as she passed the green benches in front of the park where several pigeons poked around on the bread crusts that surrounded the area, for fear of one of them flying in her face. Pigeons held spaces for the senior citizens that would be occupying them in a few hours. Rocky shuddered as she watched the birds pecking away at the checked spaces on the stone chess tables in front of the park benches. She sprinted into the park and straight over to the adjoining track.

To Rocky's surprise Susan was there doing jumping jacks. She decided that she wouldn't start a conversation with her until she completed ten laps. Eight was her norm but she felt she needed to burn any extra fat she gained over the weekend past. She sat on the track and spread her legs apart stretching both of her arms above her head. She stretched hard and leaned to both sides with her arms extended above her head. She stood up and rolled her neck around several times. After completing a series of stretches she snapped her water bottle shut, placed it down and took off.

She paced herself as she went around and around. On her eighth lap she felt fatigue setting in but she ignored it and kept going. She adjusted her pace without stopping and her breathing pattern became short and harsh. The small beads of sweat that permeated her forehead were now dripping down her face. Her cleavage was glistening in her sports bra and her hair stuck to the side of her face. Suddenly she stopped, bent over and cupped her kneecaps. She coughed, spit and walked towards her water bottle. As she approached it, she noticed it was missing. She spun around and it was placed in her palm.

"Good run," Susan said as she handed Rocky her water.

"Thanks. I almost did not make it."

"How many laps was that?"

"Ten," Rocky looked at her water bottle. "Ten laps in twenty-five minutes."

"That's not bad at all."

"God, I feel like my head is going to explode."

Rocky took the water head up. She guzzled it like she had just eaten a pound of pretzels and only stopped when her stomach began to cramp. Then she poured the remaining liquid on her face. Rocky inhaled deeply before she began to speak. "Would you care to join me as I work on my butt and thighs?"

Susan looked at Rocky's shape and smiled. "I could always use some extra work on my behind. "What are you going to do— some squats?"

"No. I am going to run up and down the steps of the bleachers. Four sets of twenty-five. I do knee lifts for my stomach as well. It only takes fifteen minutes, then I'll jog home," Rocky said as she stepped up on the seat of the bench.

"Do you do the gym?" Susan asked.

"Rarely," Rocky answered still winded.

"You are in such good shape, Rocky. I envy you. I'm in the gym three times a week and out here five times a week."

"Please, I hope I look half as good as you do when I'm your age. Let's go."

As the two women approached the bleachers anxiety overtook Susan's body. As she stood at the foot of the bleachers, Susan thought of her attackers. She placed an open palm on her chest, inhaled deeply, closed her eyes and began to sprint upwards. Rocky followed soon after.

"Are you okay? Rocky asked

"Yes I am fine." They completed the work out in ten minutes flat. "Before I forget my husband is going to own that broach if you don't start making the payments on it. He keeps asking me to remind you, but I haven't seen you out here in over a month. He showed me the piece. I couldn't believe you'd pawn something so priceless. I don't mean to be nosy, but you don't look like you needed the cash. You could have easily pawned those earrings, or sold a pair. I can tell you have a couple."

"I know you're not going to believe me but I was just thinking about that on my way here. I will take care of it like yesterday."

As they began their last set Susan looked at Rocky. "Are you going to be here tomorrow? I always feel safer when you're here. Did you know I was mugged here last month?"

"Are you serious? Oh my God! I am so sorry. Were you hurt?"

"No. They made off with my engagement ring, wedding band, phone and a couple of bucks."

Not the fuckin' ring!! Rocky thought, as she stared at Susan's finger. "Here at the park," was Rocky's second reaction, but the first one to be heard.

"Yes, but it was nighttime."

"I can't believe you are out here again— and no offense Susan, night is no time for you to be jogging out here by yourself."

"Well, I'm no therapist but I didn't want to become frightened of going out for my run and there's generally squad cars and cops by here in the morning, especially since my mugging. I just won't come back out at night. Not to mention I haven't been out here for weeks. This is my first week back."

"Well you can count on me being here. You need to get one of these." Rocky pulled a can of pepper spray from her pink fanny bag. "I never run without it. I'll be here tomorrow at six. As a matter of fact take this one." Rocky tossed the can at her.

"I'll see you tomorrow. Thanks for the spray."

Rocky sat at the front desk of the admissions office. When students had a problem getting into a class, Rocky was the person to see. She always hated registration. It was the most strenuous time of the year. There was pre registration, early registration, registration, and late registration. She debated with her boss frequently that most of the duties her job entailed were the responsibility of the registrar's office and she needed to be paid double, but her boss would not even consider giving her a raise. However, eighty percent of her tuition was paid through her job, so it wasn't' a complete loss.

"Good afternoon, this is Ms. Jones. I am calling to see if you're still interested in attending our fine university this year. If you are please call me. There is still time to register. I can be reached at 7-1-8- 2-5-5-5-5-5-5, have a nice day." Rocky picked up a three-page printout. "I could probably have this list finished by the end of the day if I get some of the work study students to help me," she muttered.

"Talking to yourself again, Jones?" Rocky swiveled her chair around to face her boss.

"Sure am. I give myself the best conversation in this joint. And I answer myself, too." They both laughed. "Do we still have those work studies?" Rocky asked.

"Yes."

"Could you send me two? I really want to finish this list today."

"I will make that happen. How's it coming along? Are you going to make your quota?"

"I already did."

"Very good as always. Don't let me deter you from your work. I will see about the work studies."

Just as she dialed the next number on her list, her cell phone rang. "Hello? Hold on for a second, please, I'm wrapping up a business call." Rocky looked at the number on her caller ID, but did not recognize it. She held her cell phone up to one ear and the office phone up to the other. "This is Ms. Jones from Brooklyn College. Is this Mike?"

"Yeah, what up?"

"Are you still planning to attend school this year?"

"Nah, my pops said he ain't paying. He ain't got it right now, you know what I'm sayin'?"

"When he gets some loot, holla back," Rocky hung her office phone and spoke into her cell phone.

"Hello? Who is this?"

"You better recognize. Bitch I have not spoken to you all week!"

"Kay. Where are you calling me from?"

"The conference room at my job. I haven't heard from you in a minute. What happened with Marcus?"

"Well, you know he flew me out to Miami for the weekend, and Thursday I was going crazy looking for things to wear, because we left Friday morning. I didn't have any time to call you. We shopped and took a cruise to the Bahamas for two days and I didn't get back until Tuesday night."

"You didn't give him none, did you?"

"Nah, I got my period on Saturday, thank God, because I don't know if I would have been able to keep my pants on and shit. He can kiss his ass off. We slept in separate beds and he didn't press me for shit. Oh yeah— he hosted this party and the shit was off the hook. His flight left early Tuesday morning mine left around six and Thomas picked me up from the airport at seven-thirty. After holding out on Marcus all weekend you know I tore Thomas up Tuesday and last night. I left him asleep in my bed this morning."

"I thought you had your period— forget it I don't want to know. What did you tell Mauri?"

"He thought I was home, I spoke to him periodically."

"And you couldn't call me from Miami?"

"I could only squeeze a few calls in because I told Marcus my phone was acting up and I left it home."

"So far so good, huh?"

"I have spoken to him every day since we met, but I couldn't call him when I got in because of Thomas. My boss is watching me as we speak. I'll call you as soon as I get in the house."

❖ ❖ ❖ ❖

Tony lay across the couch watching 'The Five Heartbeats'. He wore a pair of boxer shorts and a white tee. Just as he drifted off for the third time, his phone went off.

"Yeah, yeah, nigga! It's me, Buck, pick up."

"What up, Kahmelle? What you into?"

"Chillin.' Sweat's walkien' us for a job. I suggest you get your ass off that couch and bring your ass on, duke. You watching the Five Heartbeats, nigga?" Kahmelle broke into song. "Nights like this I wish— Tony joined in. "—that rain drops would fa-a-a all." They both laughed.

Kahmelle cleared his throat, "Eh-em, Eddie Cane is back."

"You know that's my favorite movie?" Tony sat up and stared at the bright red digital numbers that ran across the face of the cable box. "What kind of job? It's four-thirty, nigga. What kind of job we doin' in broad daylight?"

"Just come on, Tone. Meet me on the corner of Atlantic and Fourth in a half. You know I'm leaving for down south Friday?"

"Word?"

"Yeah, son. One."

"One."

Tony stood up and stretched. He looked down at the couch and at his phone with a puzzled look on his face. "Does he know me or what? He definitely called it," Tony laughed.

He ran up the steps and threw on a pair of stone washed green denim shorts, a green New York Jets jersey, and a Jets fitted cap. He slipped on a green and white pair of Stan Smith Adidas. He removed forty dollars from his dresser, and a dark green sleeveless hoodie that he let hang out of his back pocket. He looked in the mirror, inhaled and shook his head. "Here we go again." He put his phone inside of his pocket, ran down the steps and was out of the crib.

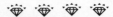

"Listen Kahmelle, I talked to the bitch but she refuses to get rid of that baby. I was about to punch her stupid ass in the stomach. How did you run up in that raw, in THIS day and age?" Kahmelle's aunt said.

Kahmelle looked at his aunt like he had lost all hope. "Seepia, she told me she was on the pill. Oh well, I guess I am really going to be a dad."

"What's wrong with you? The pill don't stop the muthafuckin' monster! You better go get tested."

"But Seepia, she—"

"Don't but me, nigga. I done raised your ass, and I am not raising your kid. I ain't got no fuckin' kids, you heard? You better daddy your ass up and be a man about this shit. Don't be avoiding her no more either."

"I don't be avoiding her, Seepia, I—"

"I SHIT. I just left that girl. She hasn't seen you in weeks!" Seepia sucked her teeth. "I have to get ready for work. You better figure this shit out." Kahmelle's aunt stormed out of the room.

Kahmelle looked at the time on his phone. He had fifteen minutes to meet Tony and Sweat. He'd be on time.

Tony stood on the corner of Atlantic and Fourth for ten minutes before an old, burgundy Nissan Stanza pulled up in front of him. He pretended to look in the opposite direction.

"Thuggle, get your ass in the car, son!"

Tony smirked when he saw Sweat and Webb sitting in the car. They all exchanged pounds after he got in.

"Nigga, if you pullin' up in a do-dirty, that means you going to get your fingers wet, huh?" Tony asked.

Webb and Sweat laughed loudly.

"OHHHHH! What you know about do-dirties?" Webb asked.

"Enough to know when you got them temporary tags and an old ass do dirty car, you getting your hands dirty in a job with us. What we got going on?" Tony asked.

"Let's wait for Buck to hop in. I see him running down the block now."

Less than a minute later Kahmelle hopped into the car.

"Sorry, I'm late. What's poppin'?"

"I got a dice game we gonna jooks."

"That shit sounds petty. How much we really going to get robbin' niggas shooting dice?" Tony asked in a disgusted tone.

"Where is this going down?" Kahmelle asked.

"Brownsville," Sweat said.

"BRONWSVILLE? At the Arizona?" Kahmelle asked.

"I don't even think that spot is still live. How you know about the Arizona, son?" Sweat smiled.

"My aunt used to fucks with this cat that spent all of her and his checks in that bitch," Kahmelle said.

Sweat nodded with a look of approval. "Buck, what's my muthafuckin' name?" Kahmelle looked confused. "Sweat?"

"You think I would send y'all out on a job if there was no real paper involved? I got y'all, this is how it's going to go down. . ."

Fifteen minutes later Sweat parked on the corner in front of the projects.

"Y'all niggas stay in the car for now. Let everything go according to plan. We going to bust they asses one good time, see if the bank is worth the jooks and leave. After we gets a G out of these niggas, we'll bounce. The nigga in the yellow has a lot of bread."

Tony yanked the hood to his sleeveless hoodie out of his pocket, and began to take off his throwback.

"Nah, go over there just like that."

"I don't want these niggas rollin' up on me later on in life. If they can't see my face then they—"

"I got this. After y'all jooks them, the Finest is going to be all over this shit. They'll come looking for me. Now, these niggas play hard. When you see me walking toward Livonia, get out the car and stick them niggas up, dig?"

"Got it."

Kahmelle and Tony sat in the car and patiently watched Webb and Sweat walk into the park. There was a group of seven guys standing on the corner, by the handball court, shooting dice. They formed a horseshoe around a bunch of bills scattered on the ground and whoever was up let the black and white cubes hit the ground.

"What's the name of those projects across the street?" Tony asked.

"Tony, you don't know nothing about Brooklyn, huh? Nigga, that's Sethlow."

They sat for at least twenty minutes, watching and talking very little.

"When are you leaving to go down south?"

"Friday, nigga!"

"Friday when?"

"Friday the 18th, like the day after tomorrow on Grey Hound."

"How long are you going to be down south?" Tony asked.

"The entire summer. I probably won't come back until the first day of school— LOOK! Webb just stepped away from them dudes," Kahmelle said excitedly.

"Yeah and Sweat just gave the dude in the yellow a pound. I don't know about them but I would be type mad if a nigga tried to step from my dice game before I could win my money back. They gonna be tight by the time we get over there," Tony said.

Kahmelle sucked his teeth. "That's Sweat! Nigga's don't want none of that. They headed for Livonia, that's our clue. Come on, Tone."

"That's our cue, not clue, stupid ass." Tony touched the pistol that sat in the waistband of his jeans and hopped out of the car. They both stepped quickly. Tony was nervous. *Damn, I wish I could turn around and run but I'm here now*, Tony thought.

They walked straight into the dice game. Kahmelle drew his pistol and Tony mimicked him.

"Yeah, yeah, niggas what you steppin' on?" Kahmelle said watching the bank on the ground, making his pistol even more visible by pointing it in the direction of the cash that was scattered in the center of the small crowd. Kahmelle looked at the guy in the bright yellow. "Yellow, do me a favor, collect that bank and drop it in this bag right here. Make sure you get everyone's cash. Do that shit for me right now, son."

"Nah duke, I'm sorry I just can't do that," the guy in the yellow said nervously.

Kahmelle looked at Tone then back into the face of the guy wearing yellow. Tony's pistol cocked.

"Just do the damn thing!" Tony shouted.

The guys dug into their pockets, pulled out cash and dropped it into the bag Kahmelle held open. The guy in the yellow shirt bent over, scooped up the bank off of the ground and dumped it into the bag. Kahmelle stared at him. "I knew he looked mad familiar. Pull out your chain, yo."

He reluctantly pulled out a platinum chain with a diamond-encrusted pair of 'Air Force Ones' hanging from it.

"Yo, it's that dancin' ass nigga that be in all the videos and shit. Son, give me the chain and then do the Harlem."

He did not move an inch. He stared at Kahmelle and pleaded with him through eye contact.

Tony stepped in closer and said, "You heard the nigga, dance, bitch."

"Come on nigga, pon the river, pon the bank— do something!" Kahmelle yelled.

He took of his chain and dropped it in the bag. Streams of tears rolled down his cheeks. The guy began Harlem shaking violently. Tears flew out of his eyes like sprinklers as he danced. Kahmelle started laughing, and Tony's tight screw face loosened up into a big grin.

Suddenly Kahmelle squeezed the trigger of the gun, shot once at his foot, and purposely missed it by a half an inch. Tony tensed up. His ears were clogged and pained him momentarily. All of the guys scattered including Tony and Kahmelle. The park was in a frenzy. Everyone dropped what they were doing and ran in different directions. Children scattered, but smiled at each other as they ran like it was all a game— and just another sunny day of playing and shooting in the park.

Tony and Kahmelle heard cop cars coming. The sirens blared loudly at the other end of the park. By the time the cops arrived, Tony and Kahmelle were in the Stanza and heading down Livonia Avenue.

"What the fuck was that?" Sweat asked angrily banging the steering wheel.

"The nigga ain't want to give up the money," Kahmelle said blankly.

"So you shot him?"

"I shot at his foot, and missed."

"Sweat, this dumb ass nigga stole his chain and made that nigga dance," Tony said.

The sound of Sweat and Webb's laughter occupied all the space in the small car." Buck, you a wild ass. You think you a good fella?"

"You should have seen him dancing and crying at the same time," Tony laughed.

"Let's go count this change and split it up," Sweat laughed.

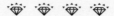

Once she got home from work Rocky walked straight into her bedroom with her cell phone glued to her face. "Kay, Mauri keeps on talking about proposing to me. He said he would start my own chain of clothing stores."

"You don't even like him anymore— I know you're not going to marry him."

"Hell no, but the chain of Rock Candy urban wear is definitely doable. If I marry Marcus, and use his money to do it— that could be my calling. Maybe I could put this damn degree to use. You know I've only stayed in school to have niggas pay my way. I'm getting ready to graduate. What do I do now?"

"I don't know. That's a decision that you're going to have to make on your own, sis. I can tell you what to wear on a date, and what not to spend, but you have to start making life decisions by yourself. You are starting to get old, bitch."

"Whatever. I'm going to be alright. Anyway— hold on, it's my other line." She looked the caller ID and screamed. "It's Marcus. Shit! I didn't even get a chance to call. I will call you back when we're finished." Rocky clicked over quickly. "Hello?"

"Hi, Candy. What are you up to?"

"Nothing much. I just got out of the tub and I was thinking about you."

"You have a funny ass way of showing it. I called you last night."

"I was worn out from the weekend. I went to sleep as soon as I got home."

"Did you enjoy yourself."

"I must have thanked you ten times during the weekend. I had a wonderful time."

"Yeah, but it didn't compare to that shit you cooked up in Vegas."

"What can I say? I just put things together well. Truth be told most of it was already planned."

"I start practice really soon. You want to meet up the weekend of the 25th?"

Damn he's cutting into Mauri time. How am I going to get out of going to Detroit? Rocky thought.

"Candy, don't worry about dough. Once my season starts I'm really hectic. I want to spend as much time with you as possible before then. And I am putting together a trip for us Labor Day weekend that will top that shit you put together in Vegas."

"You coming out here?"

"Nah, let's go back out to Miami next weekend. Give me your information so I can give it to my agent."

"Doesn't your agent have my information from Miami?"

"Just give me your information again."

"My name is Raquel C. Jones. My address is 112 Butler Place, Brooklyn New York 11201. I'm really excited, and am really looking forward to seeing you. I had fun this weekend, but Vegas *was* special. Anyway, how are you feeling?"

"I'm good. You know I have really been doing some soul searching. I am finally coming to grips with my loss and I really want to thank you for it—"

God, damn! Rocky blocked out his words with her thoughts. *Alright alfuckin'-ready. If this nigga thanks me for this shit one more time. Enough with this shit.*

"—weeks that have passed. I really feel comfortable for the first time since he died. I am grateful."

"It's going to take some time, but you will feel as normal as you did before he passed, trust me."

"What are you wearing right now?"

"Nothing. I just got out of the tub." She looked at her suit and pumps through the reflection of her mirrored closet and couldn't help but smirk at her lie.

"Your body, girl, is something else. That dress you had on the night of the fight is something else. All my man's and them that was at the party was sweatin' you over the weekend in Miami. I imagined you without your clothes in Vegas and Saturday night, so I know you look good now. Did you work out this morning?"

"Of course. That goes without saying."

"How was work?"

"Same old, same old. I have to get at least three hundred students to enroll for the fall."

"So who do you have in New York?"

"It's just me and Kay. She gets in my ass like a mother would whenever I need it. But that is it. I do have a couple of close friends, but none as close as her. My grandma was all that I had, and she's gone."

"I'm talking about male friends."

"I have a few. Nothing serious."

"I know there is some nigga out there wifen' you. Anyway, I'm going to watch a little TV." At that moment Marcus pictured her naked in the tub. "You caught a lot of eyes this weekend, and in Vegas."

"I caught yours didn't I?"

"Actually, I wanted to play Blackjack."

"Ah-ah," Rocky's mouth fell wide open. She felt small.

"Nah, I did want to play, but when I saw you sitting there I came over to your table. When I saw it was a hundred dollars a hand, I was going to leave, until I noticed how fly you were."

"That was a good clean-up job."

"Well, I just wanted to holla at you. But remember this phone shit works both ways. If we gonna make this happen you have to call me too. I'll have your flight arrangements in a few."

"Later, Marcus."

"Later."

After two minutes of smiling into the phone she finally put it down. Rocky lay across her bed, grabbed a pillow, hugged it and talked into it. "If we're going to make it happen? What the hell could he possibly be talking about? Make what happen, a relationship? A friendship?"

Rocky picked up the phone and dialed out. "Hello? Kay, this nigga just said if we're going to make this happen, you have to call me too. What do you think he means by that?"

"I don't know?"

"And, he's sending for me again. Your girl Rock is up in there. If he would have gotten a taste of my sugar walls he might —"

"Quit now before I throw up. You're really smelling yourself. What are you packing?"

"I'll call you back when I figure that out."

Rocky disconnected the call, got up and pulled a pink and beige dress out of her closet. She shook the dress and laid it across the side of her bed that she didn't sleep on. She walked into the small hallway and opened a closet. She pulled a dingy white cord that hung from a bulb and one hundred watts instantly illuminated skyscrapers of shoeboxes. Each box was labeled with either a Polaroid of the shoe it contained or a Post It describing its contents. The pictures and Post Its had their dates of purchase printed on them and they were arranged by color. Dress shoes were on the bottom of the pillars and her more casual shoes were on top. She removed ten boxes of blue shoes from the top of a row of twenty. Behind that row she had boxes of pink shoes on the top and beneath those boxes of red shoes showed. The front row of blue shoes blocked the remaining red shoes that grounded that row. Using her index finger she scanned the labels on the boxes. She smiled as she scrolled by the D&G Stilettos Marcus had purchased for her on Saturday. The photo was dark, but the shoe could still be made out.

"Ahh, here they are! My pink Gucci shoes with the wooden heel. I'll be taking these with me next weekend. And I have the entire week to think about it." She grabbed the dress off of her bed and placed it and the pink shoes in a small piece of luggage. "I'll continue to pack as I think of more fly things I can take with me." Rocky walked to her chaise lounge, removed a book from on top of it and looked at its cover. " Big Cess, by

Meisha C. Holmes. I hope this book is as hot as her last one, I couldn't put it down. My moms used to date this guy with a daughter named Cess." As she lay down to get into her novel, Rocky's telephone rang. She looked at the caller ID.

Shit, it's Mauri! How am I going to get out of this one? She thought. I haven't seen Mauri since last month, but I can't let Marcus down. Well, she thought, *here goes nothing.* She sat up and inhaled. "Hey, Mr. Maurice. How are you?"

"What up though? What you doing?"

"Missing you. Uhh, did you make my arrangements for next weekend?"

"Nah. I made them for this weekend. I can't go another week without seeing you, baby girl. It's been a second. I pushed my meetings back."

"I am so glad. I thought I was going to have to wait until next week." A feeling of relief rushed up her body and flushed her cheeks. *Thank you Lord Jesus! That was too easy,* she thought. *I thought this nigga would be going off on me right now. This shit is too good to be true. I just—*

"You had to work today?" Mauri interrupted her thoughts.

"Yep."

"I wish you would quit that bullshit and come down here with me."

"I need to finish school, Mauri. Then—"

"I don't want to hear shit. After you finish school you gonna bring your ass down here and marry me for sure. Yah heard?" The line was silent. "Well, I'm going out with Kev to go chase some tail."

"Your tail is right here, in bed, in Brooklyn."

"Yeah, you heard that shit. You keep on runnin' me around the maze and I will be chasin' tail."

"I beg your pardon? You just hit me with this shit. Give me some time, Mauri. I don't want to be with nobody else but you. I have to get myself together— just let me finish school first. A masters is only a year and a half." She rolled her eyes.

"What the fuck you need a masters to run businesses for when you got me?"

"What if you leave me for some model bitch? I have to be able to support myself. Look at my moms. We went from house to apartment and from apartment to house because she couldn't take care of hers when my father split. I'm going to take care of me and mine."

"As long as I know you ain't playin' no games. I miss the shit out of you, baby girl."

Rocky said goodbye to the dial tone and stretched out on her lounge. She ran her fingers from the front of her thigh to a small scar on her shin. She suddenly started to remember, as she stroked her scar, who her mother dated that had a daughter named Cess. Rocky thought back.

"Rock Candy! Wake up! Wake up!"

Rocky tasted her mother's cheap perfume on her own dark, morning breath. She turned over and looked out of the window, then sat straight up and looked at her mom. "Mama, it ain't daytime yet."

"Yes, it is. We got to get out of here before Shorty comes home. I got his card and I found his stash. We got at least twelve thousand dollars here. We can get far. I packed your important shit. Wear your pajamas and let's go now! The cab is downstairs."

"Mom, I like it here, and Cess is like my big sister!" Rocky said as she got out of her bed and was startled when she heard glass shattering. She picked up a Bible off of the nightstand and turned to run and defend her mother with it. As she took her first stride her shin went head up with the nightstand, and she fell to her knees in tears.

"Rocky Candy! What's wrong, baby?"

"Is he in here?" Rocky cried. Rocky fought hard to stop her burning tears, so she could focus on her mother. "I thought he was in there hurting you. See, I had this," Rocky said holding up the Bible.

Rocky's mother helped her up, removed the Bible from her hand and looked at it. "What were you going to do hit him with some scriptures?" Her mother took the Bible, and with a Warren Moon arm, flung it through the glass coffee table. The Bible crashed into the top of it. Shattered glass chips covered the floor and couch.

Her mother rubbed the lump in her bra, which was a small wad of toilet paper wrapped around a rubber band, full of money. Rocky ran through the hallway with the white bottoms of her pink, footed pajamas swishing unevenly due to her painful shin. The cold air outside penetrated the warmth of her furry fleece. She had never thought there was anything warmer than those pajamas, until she hit the cold.

With the hand in which she presently held the novel she ran her fingers over the tiny scar on her shin.

Fuck it. I'm riding this shit out to the end. Who ever I end up with is who I end up with – shit I might be by myself, I'm young. I ain't got to commit to shit until I get what I want. I am going to follow my mom's ABC of relationships— my own Apartment, Bank account, Car and College education if I don't have a ring on this finger. And it's going to be a ring from someone I want to marry, I ain't settling for shit.

Rocky exhaled and a tear rolled down her cheek. I wish my mom had followed her own wise words.

She stretched out and let thoughts about her and her mother's lifestyle run through her mind as she clutched the novel in her arms like a pillow. Suspense muscled her back to the present. I can't wait to find out what happens next. This little chick Cess is a mess. Wait. It couldn't be the same girl— nah. She situated herself comfortably and quickly dismissed that thought. Just as she reached the climax, her phone rang.

" Damn! Hello?" Rocky said annoyed.

"Hey, baby. What are you doing?"

"Nothing, Marcus," Rocky smiled.

"Marcus? Who is Marcus?" he said calmly.

Rocky read one more line of her novel, placed the bookmark in it and continued to talk.

"So, do you have my information, Marcus?"

"This is not Marcus!"

Rocky's heart dropped to her feet. She was so wrapped up in her book she hadn't caught her caller's voice. She quickly looked at her caller ID.

"Oh I'm sorry Thomas. What's up, baby?"

"Who is Marcus?" Thomas demanded.

"You know, Marcus from job? He is my co-worker, he is supposed to be calling me with some information about my new schedule."

"I'm on my way out for a bite. Would you care to join me?"

"I don't know. I really want to finish this book I'm reading. How about tomorrow?"

"Fine. I am going to stop by after I eat."

"Okay, then bring me a Caesar salad. And make sure you make up my bed if you're the last one out house. I don't like coming home to a sloppy bedroom."

"Yes, sweetheart. See you in a few." As they hung up, Thomas looked at his phone. *Marcus?* He thought silently.

11

But you said he's just a friend

School is about to start, its Labor Day weekend, nigga. When you coming home? Oh— guess what? I got into Howard University, Pre-Med, and I am getting a full scholarship. Can you believe that shit?"

Kahmelle sat back in his chair and closed his eyes tightly. *I can't believe this nigga is really going to leave me, Brooklyn and the Finest*, he thought.

"Yo, you ain't going to say congratulations, nigga? You know I have been dying to get into this school. This is the first acceptance letter that I got."

"Yeah, I am happy for you. But I'm sure Shaine is upset. What about her?"

"Nah, she understands, plus she applied for Howard, Morgan State, Norfolk State and Bouy. She started her applications a couple of months after me but— "

"Yo, you know Sweat was down here last week, right?"

"I know. He took me with him to pick up that slum shit you selling out there. I helped buy all that fake ass Prada, Gucci, Louy and Burberry shit. So once you flip that money, I'm still getting mine."

"This shit is selling like crack at the Carter."

"What?"

"That's what my moms been saying about these bags. That shit got something to do with some old 80's movie we watched while I was down here. But that shit can't touch 'The Five Heartbeats', nigga. I'm almost out of shit. Sweat has to come back out here and bring more bags soon. Why don't you come up here with him next time he comes?"

"My moms ain't tryin' to hear that, but I will put in my share so you can flip that money for me."

"Ain't you going to miss all this bread when you go away to school?"

"Nope. If I go to school and stick through it, my moms, pops and brother will give me anything I want. As a matter of fact, they are going to give me the family car when I go. I have had time to think and after initiation I definitely want out. I ain't messing up Pre-Med. I really thought I wanted to be down but this street shit, it ain't me."

"Whatever, nigga?"

"I'm serious. While you been out there getting your slum sales on, I got called on a few jobs. I witnessed these niggas beat somebody into a fuckin' knot. He was on super swole. Yo, Spam beat the nigga in the face and head with an iron meat tenderizer." He was momentarily silenced as he pictured the blood gliding through the maze of tightly zigzagged braids on the guy's head. He inhaled deeply then continued. "There wasn't one part of his body that wasn't swollen. And as he laid there knocked the fuck out, they wanted me to kick that nigga. I couldn't do it. And the fucked up shit is that he was down with the Finest. That nigga was pullin' jobs without giving Sweat his cut. I wouldn't even finish initiation if it wasn't for you. I threw up after that shit. I think that nigga was dead when they finished."

"I wish I was there," Kahmelle sighed.

"Most of them other niggas just be out thuggin', they don't make no paper. They come to the meetings twice a month, drink and wile out. I haven't seen them on a job since we robbed that fraternity party. It's the same guys all the time besides you and me."

"What are their names?"

"Webb, Juice, Spam and—"

"Darren and Gleason, yeah, I know. Those are the same guys that did the Rolex job with me. I guess Sweat just wants to put the youngest niggas on."

"Yo, Tone I need to talk to you for a second," Malik said.

"I'm on the phone, wait—"

"Nah, right now!" Malik ferociously demanded.

"I have to go, Kah, I'll talk to you later."

"Alright, one."

"One." Tony looked at his brother. "What's up, Malik?"

"You tell me," Malik said and walked straight up to Tony's room with Tony following silently behind. He went toward the bed, reached under it, and pulled out the shoebox.

"Get off of that, that's my personal business."

"You ain't got no business, Tony. Where the fuck you getting this money from?"

"I have been saving all my allowance."

"Don't play stupid with me. You told me your earrings were cubics and your watch was froze up with cubics, too. I believed you. Mom complained about you staying out overnight, you be missing seven-thirty and you got your little-ass girlfriend rocking jewelry, too. Not to mention I finally got in touch with Tina."

"Who?"

"Mrs. Tina Simmons. She has been trying to reach out to me all summer. After a little game of phone tag she told me she thinks you running with the Finest. Is that true?"

"Nah."

"So where are you getting all this money from? I know you're not fucking with that nigga Sweat?" Malik shoved Tony into his computer desk. His back hit its corner sending the books on it tumbling to the floor.

"Nah," Tony said rubbing his back.

"There is damn near twenty thousand dollars in that shoe box. You only get forty dollars a fuckin' week."

"Kahmelle and his aunt got this thing going on. See, they sell fake bags down south for real bag prices. So if we pay twenty dollars for a Gucci bag, Kahmelle sells it out there for two-three hundred dollars. I put four hundred into it the first time. That was my entire life savings, but they have been selling like hot cakes. Every other week his aunt buys more and last week she gave me three thousand dollars. Kahmelle made that in less than two weeks! He goes down to the university and the malls. You could call his aunt right now and ask her?"

Malik hovered over Tony and grabbed him. "You better not be lying to me. All it takes is one visit to that nigga Sweat, one. I am going to look into this shit. I swear to God if you fuckin' with that dude—"

Tony shook himself free of Malik's grasp and stood in his face. "What? What are you going do? Wasn't that your boy at one point? Besides, that ain't my style, you know that. I'm in the books and you were in the street. But now the tables have turned halfway. We both in the books now, right? You always have to have the spotlight, Malik. When your ass was running the streets all the attention was on you, and how I better not turn out like you, Malik. But now that you are in school and you got into NYU Law—"

"You sound super stupid, don't even say that. Mom and Dad are proud of us both. If anything they are proud that you never followed the wrong path like me. Don't let them down, you heard? Make them proud." Malik quietly walked out of Tony's bedroom. As soon as Malik was out of earshot Tony picked up his phone, and turned the speaker off. Then he walkied Sweat.

"Yo, Sweat, my brother might reach out for you. PLEASE don't tell him that I am down with the Finest. He will kick my ass. He is super tight with me right now."

"I got you, Thuggle."

"Seriously, my mother might send my ass down south and that might fuck up my Pre-Med scholarship."

"Don't worry about it, youngin'. You alright with me. Later."

"Bye." Tony disconnected his call, but Sweat sat still with the phone clutched to his face deep in thought. "Shit. It's been a long time comin', but I am ready for whatever." He closed his eyes tightly and shook his head. *Shit could get real crazy*, Sweat thought.

Tony lay on his back and looked at the ceiling. He dropped the phone on the bed next to him, and spoke in a low voice. "Just a couple more months. That's all I need. I could use the extra money for college. God, don't let them find out, please." He turned over on his side and fell fast asleep.

Malik picked up his cell phone and scrolled through the numbers. When he came across Sweat's name he inhaled deeply. Although they lived fifteen minutes away from each other, Malik hadn't seen him in years. He exhaled quickly and dialed; 'I'm sorry, the PCS number you have dialed is no longer in service. Please, check the number you have dialed and try again.'

"Fuck! Let me call Seepia," he said as he dialed Kahmelle's aunt. The phone rang for a long time. Just as he was about to disconnect the call someone answered in a coarse voice.

"Hello"

"Seepia?"

"Yeah, who's this?"

"It's Malik."

"Malik who?"

"Leeko."

"Hey Leeko, what's up, baby? Wow, it's been a minute."

"I know, I know."

"Are you looking for my nephew? He is down south with his mother for the summer," Seepia said.

"Nah, I want to talk to you. Are Kahmelle and my brother selling knock off bags down south?"

"Kahmelle's selling knock off bags down south and he is making a killing, too."

"Oh, alright. I thought my little brother was lying about money he claims he made off of some bags."

"Kahmelle made about six thousand dollars in the last two weeks alone. I gave Tony half of that myself. My AC is broken and I ain't got no energy, Leeko. Let me call you back later, when I wake up and maybe we could do some catchin' up."

"Okay." Malik hung up the phone. "Ain't nobody tryin' to catch up to her ass."

Malik walked over to his closet and started to flip through his clothes when his phone rang. "Hello?"

"Hi, Malik. What's up?"

"Nothing much, Laneice. How are you?"

"Fine thanks. Malik, I know this is short notice but Monica is having a little get together tonight for her birthday at a neighborhood club. I would love for you to come out here tonight."

"Why didn't you tell me that when I spoke to you last night? You know I would, but I already have plans."

"Pleeease. I didn't get to see you last weekend, and I thought I would see you this weekend. I miss you."

"Um, alright. I'll come out. Wait for me at your house— be naked?" Laneice blushed, "Okay."

Malik hung up the phone. *What am I going to tell Susan? She is going to be really upset*, he thought. *She already has the hotel room and everything. I'll just wait for her to hit me on my cell.*

Malik dressed quickly, ran down the steps and straight out the door. He sat in the Saab and put his seatbelt on. He drove silently— windows shut tight. He heard minimal noise from the streets he sped through. He paid close attention to the homes as he drove up Lafayette Avenue to Clermont. He stopped in front of the house, nodded, hopped out of the car and slammed the door. He lightly touched his coat pocket to reassure himself that his pistol was in it. "The house looks the same after all these years," he murmured.

He walked up the stairs, rang the bell and waited. He braced himself, for what he didn't know. He gripped his gun as he waited for the door to swing open. It had been a long time since he'd seen Sweat and the same amount of time since he felt the cool iron of heat in his hand.

Sweat sat in his bedroom and watched Malik standing outside his door on a small black and white surveillance monitor that hung from the middle of his ceiling, above his dresser.

"It's been five years muthafucka, and it will be five more years, too," Sweat said to the screen. He sat and listened to the bell ring. He gently stroked the scar on his nose and thought back. Malik walked down the steps and shared the same exact thought as his once left-hand man up stairs. A smile simultaneously darted across both of their faces. . .

"How the fuck do you run so fast?" Sweat said out of breath running up the steps of his house toward Malik who was already seated at the top.

"Just hurry up, and open the door."

Sweat opened the door and they ran inside. Out of breath, Malik and Sweat leaned against the wall, slid down and landed in a sitting position.

"I scuffed up my new kicks trying to catch up after your ass. Franchon and Stacey is going to be sweatin' us tonight with these new joints on," Sweat huffed.

"Yeah, but I loved my Timbs. I really wished I ain't have to leave them in the box".

Sweat looked at Malik and shook his head. "You didn't have to, but how else did you think we was going to get out of the store with these brand new Jordans and no cash?" Sweat asked.

Sweat stood and removed his shirt; Malik did the same. Both boys wore girdles that tightly gripped their ribcages. With one look they simultaneously started to yank clothing out of their girdles.

"You got two pairs of those Moschino Jeans?" Malik asked.

They pulled out jeans, shirts, boxers, and Sweat even pulled out a pair of shades.

"Why didn't you get me some shades?" Malik asked.

"Every man for himself, nigga." They heard the keys to the door and turned. "Shit, it's my grandmother— let's hide the gear quick."

Within seconds his grandmother opened the door to find Malik and Sweat scurrying around the foyer of her home. "What are you two shady little muthafuckas doing out of school at this hour?" She asked.

Sweat's grandmother had a fatigued look on her face. It glistened with a smooth coat of perspiration around it. She dropped four bags of groceries on the floor and looked at the boys who were bare-backed with girdles gripping their bony frames.

"Is that where my damn girdles have been disappearing to? Haven't I told you about stealing shit? Don't I give you enough? I'm tired of this!" She walked up to Sweat, and using her last bit of strength, punched him on his cheek. He dramatically slammed into the wall holding his face. Malik snickered under his breath. Without moving an inch, Sweat's grandmother stared at Malik. Her glare instantly ceased his laughter. She walked over to Malik and stomped on his foot as hard as she could, leaving a black scuff on the front of his sneakers.

"OUCH!" Malik yelled

"You probably stole those, too. I don't know what I am going to do with the two of you. I think I am going to have to call Millicent."

Malik looked up at the window where Sweat's room used to be. He smiled at the memory of the dozens of ass whoopin's Sweat's grandmother had given them both. He got into his car, and drove off thinking about the bond that was broken years ago.

Sweat stroked the scar on the front of his face as he watched Malik walk down the steps of his house, hop into his car and drive off.

"Every man for himself, no regrets, nigga. I ain't got no regrets."

Malik headed down Flatbush Avenue and once across the Brooklyn Bridge, dismissed the thought of Tony having any dealings with Sweat. *My brother is too square for that shit. He knows better,* was his final thought on the matter.

"I like this Negril better than the old restaurant, don't you, Thomas?" Rocky asked.

"The décor here is more appealing, but the food still tastes the same. Rocky, I never heard you mention a Marcus working with you before?"

Rocky sighed. "I thought we were done talking about that."

"You act like today was the first time you called me Marcus! This is the second time. Is there something I need to know, Rocky?"

"Thomas, calm down. People are starting to stare. You know I am really psyched about my class schedule. This is my last semester, Marcus handles student scheduling and I need this class to graduate. Why don't you come and pick me up for lunch one day? You can meet him. I have to use the restroom Thomas, excuse me." Rocky got up and walked to the restroom thinking hard.

I can't believe I did that shit again. I really fucked up. This nigga won't give this Marcus shit a rest. Let me call Marcus now, because this nigga is going to be playin' me close for the rest of the night.

"Hello, Marcus?"

"Hey, Candy. I was just thinking about you. I have your flight info for tomorrow right here."

"Do me a favor, I am going to hang up the phone and I want you to leave it on my voicemail."

"It's not much. Kennedy Airport, Continental Airlines, tomorrow morning— your flight leaves at 9:45 a.m. Go to the counter with your ID, preferably a passport, then you will find out where we're going."

"You got it. Listen, I am at Negril and my food is probably at the table. I'll call you as soon as I get into the house."

"That's that Jamaican spot down by Madison Square Garden, right?"

"Nah. Well, the same people own this one. You're talking about the one on 23rd Street. This one is in the Village. It's new. I don't even think it has been here for a year yet."

"Who you with?"

"A friend?"

"What kind of friend?"

"Just a friend."

"Alright, Lil' Mario. You better let him know that you got a new friend in town. Call me later."

"Marcus, would you think I was corny if I told you I missed you?"

"Not at all."

"I had so much fun with you. Now that I know we are going to see each other tomorrow I can't stop thinking about the times we've spent together."

"Wait until tomorrow."

"I can't. I'll call you later."

"Bye."

"Bye."

Rocky immediately hung up the phone and called Mauri.

"Hey Mr. Maurice."

"Hey baby girl. You calling your daddy to make sure he touched down alright? I made it into Cali about an hour ago. I already finished one meeting and I am on my way to the next. What are you doing?"

California? OH SHIT! I FORGOT! She thought. *He's flying straight into New York from there. I think he's coming in Monday, and I won't be home! What the—"*

"Rocky?" Mauri interrupted her thoughts. "Rock Candy, talk to me girl, are you still mad? You know I can see my boys anytime, but I got meetings. I touch down in your turf Tuesday night. I couldn't get a Monday night flight because of the holiday. "

A feeling of relief rushed up her body and flushed her cheeks. *Thank you Lord Jesus! That was too easy,* she thought. *Mauri would have been pissed if I wasn't here when he touched down. I wonder where Marcus is taking me? This shit is too good to be true.* "I was really looking forward to seeing you this weekend," she said in a somber tone. Rocky inhaled deeply before she continued. "Well, at least I'll get to miss you more. Make sure you leave your flight information on my answering machine."

"For sure, love you baby girl, bye."

Rocky flipped down the phone, looked at the bathroom attendant and washed her hands. When she was finished the bathroom attendant handed her a towelette. "Thank you," Rocky said.

The bathroom attendant smiled and lifted her head toward a glass jar that contained dollar bills. Rocky laughed and fished a wrinkled dollar bill out of her purse then dropped it into the jar. She grabbed two sticks of gum and rubbed lotion onto her hands. *I gotta get something for my damn dollar. All of the sudden every restaurant in the city has these damn attendants in the bathroom. It makes me sick. What if I didn't have any money? Does that mean I can't wash my hands? Shit!* Rocky thought and silently continued to haggle with herself all the way back to her table. By the time she reached it both the food and drinks had arrived at the table. As she sat Thomas placed his hand on top of hers.

"I'm sorry, Rocky. It's just that I have not felt this way in a long time. My feelings for you are really—"

"Thomas, my feelings for you are just as strong, if not stronger. I wouldn't do anything to jeopardize what we have. You are the only man that I ever imagined spending my life with. I'm just not comfortable with where I am in my life yet. I need you to be patient with me. Come on baby, eat up."

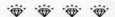

As Malik approached the Lincoln Tunnel he thought about his last meeting with Laneice and wondered what she had in store for him in the minutes to come. She opened the door to her condo wearing nothing but a smile. Laneice wasted no time getting him into bed, and turning their foreplay into a triple double. In the heat of the moment Laneice snapped the passion in half, with a sexual request.

"I don't know about that shit, Laneice. If you fuck a bitch in the ass then you will fuck a nigga in the ass. I ain't going there".

Laneice lay on her bare back next to Malik, holding his penis in her hand. "For one, I am no bitch. Two, I am all grown woman, and three I know you will like it."

"How many niggas you done let in through the exit?"

"Like I said, I am a grown woman and I do grown things."

She kissed his stomach and grabbed his muscular thighs. She placed his balls in her mouth and began to push his legs up in the air. Then his cell phone rang. He grabbed his phone. He looked at the number, sat up and grabbed her head firmly, stopping her movements at once.

"Shhh," Malik whispered. Laneice sat up and rolled her eyes "Hey, Susan, what's up?"

"My cunt and I are hot and waiting, big boy, where are you?"

"Bad news, Susan. I got tied up in Jersey and I am not going to be able to make it."

Susan looked at her phone. "No way. I am already at the hotel. I can't believe this. I haven't had you in a whole week."

"Last weekend should have held you down."

"You were with her last weekend? Laneice yelled. "You didn't even call me— and that's why? Over some—"

Susan heard a woman's voice in the background. She heard her every word but they were suddenly muffled. Malik cupped his hand over her mouth and rolled his eyes at her. Laneice managed to spit out her last words through his tight grasp "—White bitch."

Susan heard the voice again but this time she couldn't make out what was said. "Malik, who was that?" Susan asked.

"Just a friend of mine."

"Are you with a date? Is there someone else?"

"She's just a friend of mine."

"It's okay. Maybe next weekend?"

Malik could hear the disappointment in her voice. "I am sorry, Susan. Please forgive me. We can meet up in the morning or Sunday. Isn't your husband gone until after Labor Day? We could have the rest of the weekend together. "

"Sounds good. My husband won't be back until Monday night. I will just stay here. I'll be waiting." Susan hung up the phone and grabbed her pillow. "The nerve of him. I can't believe he stood me up for another woman!"

A flush of uneasy energy filled her body leaving her cheeks rosy red. Sitting upright she hugged her kneecaps tightly and rocked back and forth. Her unclothed body was wet with tears. They continuously ran down her arms to her thighs. Most dropped to her hands, then splashed onto her smooth kneecaps. She couldn't understand what she felt or why she felt that way.

When Malik disconnected his call he released his grip from Laneice by mushing her in her mouth.

"Neicey!" he yelled. "What the fuck is wrong with you?'

"That's why you didn't call me last weekend because you were with the White bitch! A friend, what am I, Biz Markie now? It's almost been three months and we are just friends I don't get—"

"Three wonderful months and don't fuck that shit up over her. You knew my situation from day one, Laneice. I never lied to you."

He tried to shove his tongue down her throat but she pushed him away and jumped out of the bed. He walked behind her and grabbed her by the waist. Malik caressed her gently from behind, massaging her breast with one hand; he dropped the other towards her vagina and fingered her clitoris. He gently kissed the small of her neck between his sentences. "I need her to get into law school, you know that. Besides, you wouldn't want to end up with someone that works in a mailroom for the rest of your life. Your standards are way too high for that. I am not trying to lead you on. I just want us to enjoy each other, learn each other, and get to know one another. When that is complete, then she will be gone. I promise you that."

"But Malik—"

He kissed her mouth and swallowed her words. He planted dozens of passionate kisses on her face as he coaxed her toward the bed. She knew what she wanted to say but the words wouldn't come out. He lay down on the bed, wiggled his dick in the air, licked his lips, and nodded his head towards his manhood. That was her cue. She licked her lips in response and assumed the position, sticking her ass out as she went down on all fours. She wanted to speak, but was overwhelmed with pain as he pushed his way into the tight walls of her rectum. After two minutes she had completely forgotten what she wanted to say. And the only thing Malik could think about was the tight warmth that caressed his dick and reruns of OZ.

Tony woke up and crept around his room. He dressed quickly and grabbed his acceptance letter off his dresser. He looked out the window and was pleased to find that neither car was in the driveway. Relieved, he left the house and walked toward his school.

The walk seemed different to him. Although it was the same twelve blocks, he passed none of his friends. When he walked past the field he hung his head in shame as he glanced underneath the bleachers.

Damn, that's the exact space where I held that poor jogger down and stole her ring. Who was I to do that? He thought.

Once he reached Fourth Avenue he looked toward Brooklyn Jewelry Exchange, wondering if he could really do what he had plans to do. *What if I get caught?* He thought.

He stood on the corner of the block for a few minutes, and noticed a lady dressed in a pink jogging suit jet in front of the Brooklyn Jewelry Exchange and instantly thought about the woman he mugged.

Rocky noticed the young guy staring at her across the street and automatically became tense. She continued to jog, but with her pepper spray held tightly in her hand. When she noticed the police officer approaching the thug from behind some of her tension was relieved and she jogged toward the field.

Tony felt a firm hand on his shoulder, jumped and swung around to find Officer Joann Nuñez standing behind him.

"What are you doing out here?" Joann asked.

"Officer Nuñez, you scared the shit out— I mean you scared the living day lights out of me."

"What are you doing here so early in the morning?"

"Actually, I came out here looking for you."

Joann looked puzzled. "For me? What for?"

"Well, I saw you on the news a couple of weeks ago. I have been wanting to come and congratulate you since then."

Joann looked skeptical. "Really?"

"Yeah, I was so happy you weren't hurt and I told my family that you were the cop that stays by the school, and that I know you."

"Well, thanks— what's your name again?"

"Tony."

"Thanks, Tony. I was just doing my job."

"Well, I have been wanting to come out here since then. Then I got this in the mail, I thought— well, I don't know, but I kind of thought you would be interested in seeing this." Tony pulled the acceptance letter out of his back pocket and handed it to her. She read it silently and looked up at him with watery eyes.

"I can't believe it! This is— I don't know what to say. I am so happy for you. I know your parents must be ecstatic." Clutching the letter, Joann gave him a tight embrace.

"I haven't showed them yet."

Joann released her embrace, and concern replaced her smile. "Why not?"

"I don't know. You're the second person I told. My girlfriend hasn't gotten accepted anywhere yet, so I haven't told her. I told my best friend, Kahmelle, and I think he was upset that I would be leaving him. I just feel so confused. This is what I have always wanted, but I think I wanted it because my parents wanted it. My older brother was a bad seed, so everything was always different for me. I don't know Officer Nuñez, I just don't know."

"Tony, you can be something. Even if this isn't your dream, it's your reality now. Go for it! Trust me, Brooklyn and what's his name will be right here when you graduate."

"But I don't even know if I will fit in. What if those D.C. cats are corny?"

"You are so intelligent and you're different from most of the kids that go to the High. You'll bring Brooklyn out there, your style of dress, the way you talk— just be yourself. And I happen to know that D.C. cats are just as live as New York cats. Besides, it's not where you're from that's important, it's where you're at." Joann gently tapped his arm several times. "Plus, this right here— it's hard for this skin tone to get into the doors that are already beginning to be open for you. We need doctors like you in this community and others like it. So go out there and get your degree, then come back here and set up your own practice."

Joann's radio went off. She stopped talking to listen then continued when it stopped. "Listen, Tony." she started as she handed him back the letter, "you accept that scholarship, and if you don't want to become a doctor once you get there so be it. But at least take advantage of this opportunity they are offering you. You do want to go to college, don't you?"

Tony nodded his head.

"Do the four years and decide your career path while you're in school. As for your girl, it might not seem like it now, but pussy comes a dime a dozen. There are other pretty girls out here. Let her come and visit you but don't miss out on this opportunity. And if that asshole can't be happy for you, then he really isn't your friend at all— fuck him, I told you I didn't like his ass before."

"Thanks, officer. I guess I'll see you around."

"Okay. Thanks for bringing me that wonderful news. Keep me posted."

"I will. You stay safe out here and keep cuffing them up."

Rocky stretched and thought about her upcoming day with Marcus. She expected Susan to be in the park with her, but wasn't surprised when she didn't show up. She stayed alert, looking for the guy that had been watching her as she made her way to the field, or anyone else that looked suspicious. As she sprinted she counted the hours until she could see Marcus again.

12

Got me looking so crazy right now

"I really appreciate you taking me to the airport like this and keeping my car, Kay."

"Who else were you going to ask? Besides, you know I am going to stick my flag on this bitch and drive it down the parkway on Monday. You have your passport and driver's license with you?" They both laughed.

"Yes."

"Where are you going?"

"I told you I don't know. It's a surprise. Why don't you wait right here and I'll run to the ticket counter and find out." Rocky jumped out of the passenger seat of her car and ran into the airport terminal. The line to the ticket counter was thick, so she ran to an E ticket machine. She pulled out a credit card and slid it through the slot. Her name flashed across the screen, and a series of questions followed;

'Please type in your destination and the number of passengers that you will be flying with.'

Rocky banged her fingers across the keyboard. "I don't know where I am going!" She looked at her diamond Choppard and it read eight fifty-five. She walked over to the end of a long line of suitcases, accompanied by travelers young and old, and waited. She periodically looked out the window at Kay and her car. After fifteen minutes she was in front of the line.

"Good morning."

"Good morning. Thanks for flying Continental. Are you going to be checking any luggage this morning?"

Rocky handed the ticket agent her passport. "No, I have one carry-on item."

"Has anybody asked you to carry anything onto the plane or have you left your baggage alone for any period of time?"

"No."

Rocky opened the zippered portion of her pocketbook and patiently waited for her ID and tickets. The agent looked at Rocky, then the photo on the passport. She punched several letters on her keyboard, printed her boarding pass and placed it with her passport on the counter.

"Go to Gate 67 and board direct Flight 765 to Cozumel. Enjoy your flight."

Rocky smiled, placed her tickets in her bag and sped toward the exit door. She quickly jumped into the car and smiled at Kay.

"I'm going to Cozumel!"

"Where the hell is that?"

"It's a very exclusive island in Mexico."

"DO NOT FUCK HIM!"

Rocky smiled at Kay. She looked over at her stern face and admired her best friend's beauty. They had always been opposites since junior high school. She was a pretty girl. Her brown skin was beautiful and flawless. Her complexion was smooth and even, one would think she wore a lot of foundation, but she didn't. She had shoulder length brown hair and big dark brown eyes. She was 5' 6" tall and relatively small on the bottom. She wore a double D cup and had been married to the same man since they graduated from high school.

"Don't stare at me like that. Do not fuck him under any circumstances. Make that nigga wait. You hear me?"

"I know the rules— I wrote them. But, this is our fourth meeting. I love you, Kay."

"Alright, you mushy bitch. Be careful. What time do you get in tomorrow?"

"Tomorrow?" Rocky spoke slowly. "I get in Tuesday September 2, at twelve thirty-five a.m."

"Dag. You always be fuckin' shit up. I got to be out here all late and shit."

Rocky gently rubbed and patted the dashboard, like it was a newborn pup. "Take care of my baby, Kaynai Bates. I don't want to see any scratches on her when you pick me up Tuesday morning."

"Whatever. Get out before you miss your flight."

She leaned over and kissed Kay on the cheek. Then she quickly removed a small Louis Vittuon duffel bag from the back seat and jumped out the car.

"Kiss the kids for me. And tell them I am going to take them to Chuck E. Cheeses next weekend."

"I'm going to tell them, too. You know they will harass you until you meet your Maker if you don't take them."

Rocky waved and went into the airport. She looked at her ticket and looked up at the signs.

"Gate 65 Gate 65— ah, here we go Gates 60 to 67 this way."

As she approached the entrance she dropped her bag to her feet. The line for her gate was wrapped around a corner. She sucked her teeth, picked up her bag and slowly walked to the end of the line. As she reached the line her phone rang. It was clipped onto the shoulder strap of her purse. Rocky looked at the caller ID and sucked her teeth.

"Hello," she said perkily.

"Hey. What are we doing tonight?"

"Why are you up so early, Thomas?"

"I have a big case coming up and I have tons of paper work to pan through. This is probably the only time I will have to call you today. I figured you would just be on your way back from working out."

Rocky was silent. "I miss you. After you dropped me off from dinner last night, I realized how much I care about you."

Thomas was shocked. *She rarely says things like that maybe she's loosening up, he thought.* "I miss you too. I have to be up early tomorrow. So I was thinking we would hook up between seven or eight tonight."

"Umm, that's fine. Just call me first. I have some things I need to take care of. Since I'm not flying into Detroit this weekend, I have some leg work to do out here," Rocky said as the line moved slowly.

"You know, I've been thinking . . . never mind."

"What? I hate when people do that. You have to tell me what you have been thinking, Thomas."

"Never mind, it was nothing. I'll talk to you about it when I see you later, okay?"

"No it's not okay, spill it."

"Well, if all goes right with this next case I am going to get a huge bonus. If you do your masters full time I could help support you. This way, you'd have an entire year to think about what it is you want to do with your life, and you can lose that low paying job you complain about. You are worth so much more. You practically run that office by yourself, fellowship or no fellowship. But, if I do pay your school bills and other living expenses— I want a commitment, Rocky."

Rocky looked at her watch. It was nine-ten and she was halfway through the line. She let out a soft but long sigh and shook her head. "Are you sure you're ready for that, Thomas?"

"Rock Candy, I've been ready for that the moment I laid eyes on you."

Here he goes with that corny bullshit again, Rocky thought.

"You are educated, beautiful and ambitious. I really want you in my life."

"I am in your life, Thomas. I just don't want to do anything rash, okay? When I settle down I'm settling down for life. Not any boyfriend and girlfriend bullshit, I'm talking man and wife." *That should shut his ass up. The marriage shit drives niggas away every time*, she thought.

"My sentiments exactly. You have enough time to think about it. Anyway, I am running late and looking forward to seeing you tonight. I'm going to tear that ass up."

"Oooh, Thomas, you know I love when you talk to me like that. I'll see you later."

"Have a good day, Rocky."

She looked down the line. *Good, there's only about fifteen people ahead of me. I will be out of here in no time.* She looked around as she thought about the conversation she just had. *I just don't get it. What's up with these fuckin' men of mine. First Mauri now Thomas. I hope I have half this luck with Marcus. Let's see— it took Mauri two years to want to marry me, and it took Thomas a little under a year. So at that rate I could get Marcus wrapped around my finger in about six months.* She checked her line status— she was fifth. *At least this line is moving fast. You know, it must be the fact that I keep on fucking with these men that have no kids. And they're successful, too. Once they have stacked their money, I guess they feel like they need the white picket fence and the two point one kids to go with it. If I got Marcus, I wouldn't need anyone else. I would never cheat or anything.*

"Excuse me." A female security guard startled Rocky back into reality. "You holdin' up the line. Step forward, please," the security guard said as she rolled her eyes.

"Alright, you fuckin' cow, I'm coming," Rocky muttered under her breath.

As Rocky walked toward the conveyor belt she watched the security guard approach her. The tall, thick woman placed her four-inch nailed hand on her hip. Her navy blue uniform pants clung tightly to her thighs and ass but loosened up at her knees. The blue stripe that ran down the sides of the pants looked as if they were about to burst from their seams and wrap themselves around Rocky's neck. She chewed a large green wad of gum loudly. Each smack ended in a loud pop, something Rocky had desperately tried to learn to do in her youth, but was disallowed by her grandmother. She held a beige metal detector in her hand and waved it around as she talked.

"Did you say sumpin'? 'Cause I ain't even hear you."

Rocky walked past her and placed her bag down on the conveyor belt. "I said I'm coming now."

"Oh, I thought so."

The security guard rolled her eyes and her head as she walked back to her post. She stood behind the belt and watched Rocky's bag from a black and white screen. Rocky didn't say a word; she stood at the far end of the belt and waited for her bag to come down. She watched as the security guard stared at the screen like she was hoping a dead body would appear. Finally she looked up at Rocky revealing a nasty smirk.

"Lake, come here. I need you to search this bag. There is somethin' in here that I ain't making out."

Two men dressed in army uniforms with large shotguns hanging from their shoulders approached Rocky as her bag came rolling down the conveyor belt.

"Please open your bag, miss. We need to check it thoroughly. The security guard has come across an apparatus that she could not detect."

"Yes, sir."

Rocky willingly opened her bag with a smile. She looked at her watch. It was nine thirty-five. She looked back at the security guard and hit her with the most pleasant smile she could muster up at that moment. The security guard rolled her eyes and continued to work.

I should go over there and smack the shit out of that bum bitch, Rocky thought. She smirked at how her dried out, black, Brillo roots became blonde and grossly contrasted with the smooth, straight, blonde, greasy horse hair that hung on her shoulders. When she noticed the initial rings on each of her fingers that spelled, Lisa, Rocky laughed out loud.

"Everything seems to be fine, ma'am. You may close your bag."

"Thank you, gentlemen, and you enjoy your day."

The female security guard smiled revealing a metallic gleam from the inside of her mouth.

As Rocky zipped up her bag she couldn't help but wonder if she wore platinum or gold in her mouth. Rocky smiled as the two, armed officers watched her walk away and waved. "Bye, Lisa, you tacky bitch," Rocky started her statement in a loud voice, but muttered the latter half.

She looked at her ticket and was hustling towards her gate when her cell phone went off, she unclipped it from her strap, put it to her ear and the loud ring startled her. She was rushing so much she neglected to answer the call. She flipped up the phone and waited to hear the caller speak.

"Hello, Rocky? Rocky, are you there?"

"Hey, Cheryl, what's up?"

"Nothing much. Kay told me you're on your way out of town with some new cat. I don't see what I am doing wrong. The other day I met this guy and I gave him my number. We were talking about us hooking up to hang out. Nice car, cute but—"

Rocky barely paid attention. Cheryl babbled on and Rocky counted the gate numbers as she sped through the airport. 'This is the final boarding call for Continental Flight 765 to Cozumel boarding at Gate 67.'

When Rocky heard the announcement, she broke into a run toward the gate.

"—then he said that he would buy some bottles and I could come over to his house, but his mother was really into church so I would have to come over early in the afternoon and I couldn't talk too loud because his grandmother would tell his mother he had a girl in the house. Can you believe that? Why do I always get the wacko cats?" Cheryl asked.

Rocky was out of breath, but she continued to run to the gate. Passing her boarding pass and passport to the ticket agent she spoke quickly. "It has to be the places you hang out. You are a very attractive lady."

"Did anyone ask you to carry something on board or did you leave your luggage unattended at any time?" the ticket agent asked.

"Hold on— no, sir."

"Enjoy your flight," the ticket agent said.

"How do you do it?" Cheryl asked.

"I don't know. I'm just lucky, I guess. Listen, I'm in a rush. Let me call you when we get back into town. I think it's my turn to host the next girl talk, but we'll talk before then."

"Alright, girl, you be safe."

"Later," she flipped her phone down, turned it off and shoved it into her purse. She pulled out a comb and ran it quickly through her hair as she walked across the bridge connecting the plane to the gate. She stopped at the entrance, applied some lip-gloss, moistened her lips and shook her head letting her hair fall on her shoulders. She walked to her seat and put her purse on top of it. She placed her slim fingers on the silver button marked 'push' on the overhead bin. As it popped open, a pair of hands firmly gripped her waist. She turned quickly and faced Marcus.

"Oh my God! I can't believe you're here!" She turned around fully and gave him a passionate kiss on the lips. *God, he is so fuckin' fine. Don't fuck this one up and don't fuck him,* ran through her mind.

"How did you get here? Well, when did you—"

"I landed here thirty minutes ago. I didn't have to change flights or anything. I just came from trying to call you. I was getting ready to get off the plane. Let me find out you have no sense of time."

"On the contrary. This big over-grown, over-jealous and over-zealous security-witch made the military spot-check my luggage. That took fifteen minutes over the hour I had to wait on line for the regular security check."

He picked up her luggage and placed it neatly in the overhead compartment. "I figured you would have some old fly designer luggage and shit. You look really good."

He looked her up and down from head to toe. She wore a cropped hooded jacket that revealed a flat stomach and small waist and pair of faded blue jeans that seemed to ride on her hipbones. She had pale pink fingernails that matched her luggage, toenails, glossy lips and pink and white shoes.

"So, what's good with you anyway? You're shoes are banging."

"Thank you." *I'm glad he recognized, these are Laboutin, these shits cost me some change,* she thought. Rocky countered his stares and made a mental note of everything that he wore.

"Would you mind if I sat by the window? I love the window seat."

"Not at all." He watched her sit down.

Rocky felt momentarily relieved that she had thought to straighten herself out moments before she entered the plane. "I was trying to figure out how we were going to hook up just before I got on the plane. I figured you would have a car pick me up once I got off of the plane,"

Rocky said as she smiled, slouched down in her seat and placed her head on his shoulder before finishing her statement—"but this is much better."

"Are you tired?" Marcus asked.

"No."

"Well. I am. And we have a busy day ahead of us. So if you don't mind, after we build for a few minutes, I am going to sleep. This flight is three hours."

As the flight attendant demonstrated emergency procedures the couple chatted away. The turbulent takeoff didn't seem to phase Rocky or Marcus. They smiled and laughed over the bumps and into the clouds.

"So, did you start practicing for the new season yet?"

"I start next week, this is my farewell weekend. But I workout everyday."

"Good we could exercise together in the morning. Finally, a man that can appreciate a good work out. So, what are we doing first? I am so excited."

"You'll find out when we get there. Do you swim? Did you bring your bathing suit?"

"Like a fish— I love jet skiing and I scuba dive."

"Say word."

"Yep, one more dive and I can get my scuba diving license."

"Hmm, I'm impressed. I love the water too. My mother sent me to Jamaica for two weeks every summer the day after school ended to see my grandmother. White-ass sand and clear blue water. We would eat fresh fish from the beach everyday. Then I would come home and my father would drive me upstate every morning to basketball camp. That was my nigga."

Rocky sat up, looked into Marcus' eyes and smiled. "Let's swap memories. I'll share fond memories of my mother and grandmother and you can share your father's. Tell me about basketball camp."

"Well, I started when I was six. I was really tall for my age. My father always wanted me to play ball. He built a hoop in our back yard. He would drop me off at seven and be there to pick me up at six. He shortened his summer hours just so he could take me to camp. Then, when I got older, he sent me to sleep away basketball camp. Everything that I am now was his dream."

Marcus gently placed his head on the headrest. He rolled it to the side and looked at Rocky. He thought about their conversations in Vegas. For the past few weeks, it seemed to help him. He silently thought about the jams his father had always seemed to pull him out of. Then he remembered a not so fond jam he had gotten his father out of. He closed his eyes tightly. Rocky seemed to infiltrate his thoughts.

"Hey, Marcus, I know how you feel. Remember, with every good time there is a bad time to go along with it. The most enjoyable times stand out vividly in our minds. The bad memories we consciously try to block out. We suppress them, but that doesn't help either. We have to let them all out to commemorate our loved ones. Living they might not have been perfect, but once they move on to the next element they're our guardian angels. You don't have to share them, but you have to let those go." She grabbed his hand and squeezed it tightly. "Let it go."

"Girl, are you a psychic? How did you know what I was thinking about?" Marcus asked.

"It doesn't take Ms. Cleo to read that look on your face," Rocky answered.

"So, what are you waitin' for, call me now," Marcus said in a thick Jamaican accent.

"Oh my God, you sound eight times better than that Jafaican bitch did. That was sexy, say something else."

"So what 'appen sweetness?"

Rocky laughed and shoved Marcus' arm. "You really are Jamaican!" After a few seconds the mood became less playful and Rocky ran her fingers through the thick curls on his head. "Let it out."

"On my sister's tenth birthday my moms took my sister and two of her friends away for the weekend. I came home from school and he had some young bitch up in the house."

"Was she White?" Rocky asked.

"No, what fuckin' difference does it make?" Marcus asked.

"I'm sorry go ahead."

"She was like twenty-four— anyway, I come home and they are butt-ass naked fuckin on the kitchen counter. My pops ain't have on no bag or nothing. The fucked up part is she looked just like my moms did when she was younger. He was too cool for me. She was all crying and shit. She pulled on her clothes, and my pops was acting like ain't nothing happen. He walked upstairs and left me with the bitch. And five minutes after I walk in my mother and the girls come back. They weren't having fun so they came home early. I'm down stairs with this bitch and my mother is all happy to see me, and wants to meet my new friend. Daddy came back down and was like, 'Son, when did you get here? And who is your friend?' She was crying and nervous. I introduced her to my family and explained that she wasn't feeling so well. I dropped her home and told her if she ever fucked with my pops again, or disrespected my home, my mother and I would fuck her up. My moms cooked stewed chicken, rice and peas, macaroni pie and spinach that night."

"What's macaroni pie?"

"You know, baked macaroni and cheese."

"Oh."

"I can still smell that dinner. That brown sauce and garlic, the cheddar from the pie. My pops pulled me to the side after dinner and smacked me

on the ass like I just made a play, and said, 'Thanks, son, I owe you one.'
My sister spent the night at a friend's house, and my father and mother
fucked all night. I could hear them. Do you know how disgusting it is to
hear your moms and pops smash? Their room was right next to mine. I
could hear her scream with pleasure. I could hear the bedpost against the
wall like a knock on the door. She said that he hadn't worked her out like
that in years. He said that he had missed her overnight— I had to leave.
The truth was that he hadn't bust off with home-girl and just wanted to
nut off in my moms."

"You know how you men do. Everybody is not perfect."

"But not Dad. . . I never thought that— they just seemed like the
perfect couple."

"You know I can still feel the sound of my mom's bedpost in my
bones. Every time it hit the wall anger burned inside me. My eyes burned
with tears and the tears burned my cheeks. I wanted to feel what she felt.
I wanted to be loved. I lived with my mother for eight years. In that eight
years she went through at least 12 boyfriends— that I knew of and I went
with her. They all loved her to death. You think I'm pretty, Marcus?" She
looked at him with watery eyes.

"What kind of question is that? You know you're gorgeous."

"Well, my mother was twice as beautiful and she knew it." She exhaled
and shook her head. "The bedpost. . ." Rocky wiped her eyes and looked
at him. "We all have memories. All that matters is how you choose to
keep them. I'm going to sleep now. I feel a little tired."

"Are you all right?"

"I'm fine."

He squeezed her hand gently and ran his fingers through her hair.
Rocky asked the flight attendant for a Hennesy and drank it straight— no
ice, no Coke. Then she drifted off to sleep, with Marcus' palm clasping
hers and the faint sounds of a bedpost knocking through the corners of
her mind.

Strong hands massaged Rocky's naked backside. He slid his hands up
and down her glutes. Her sweat meshed with the steam in the room.
"Marcus, how do you feel? Is your masseuse killing you, like mine is
killing me?" Rocky called out. She looked to the table on her left. There
Marcus lay, toweled in white, just like her. A slim shapely woman
massaged him, and a huge, muscle-bound man massaged Rocky.

"This is the pain right here! She is doing her thing. What about yours?"
Marcus called back.

"Wonderful. Fabio is doing his thing over here. It hurts, but it hurts
good. Can I tell you, when you busted your ass on those water skis I
thought I would pass out!"

"Yo, I never knew that shit was so hard. I only stayed up for like five minutes and my legs are killing me. I don't know how you did it. You stayed up for like fifteen, twenty minutes. You have some strong-ass legs, girl."

"This has been so beautiful. I really don't want this day to end," Rocky sighed. "The beach, jet skis, water skis, and ending our day at the spa. I don't know, I might have to lock your ass up and throw away the key," Rocky said then moaned loudly as the masseuse's hands went further down her back.

"It ain't over 'til it's over. Wait until tomorrow. I hope you brought something slinky to wear in that little bag of yours. We've got dinner tonight. I meant to tell you to bring that bangin'-ass dress I met you in."

"You think that's— ouch, that hurts." The masseuse slowed his pace down a bit. "You think that's the only nice garment I own?"

"Nah, I can tell you do your thing."

After the spa, the pair walked hand in hand to their room. Marcus periodically looked at her rear end. He admired her style. She wore a two-piece, beige and plaid trimmed string bikini with a huge straw hat with the same trimming. She had matching thong sandals. Her shades reminded him of something Jackie O would have worn. When they walked by, other couples smiled and looked at her like she was the star. She stood out and from when Marcus was in high school, he had been the star in relationships. He'd had women that were just as pretty, but there was something about Rock Candy.

When they reached the room Marcus sat on the bed. Rocky jumped on the bed and knocked him back. She kissed his forehead and then the tip of his nose. "Thank you for a beautiful day. Do you always do so much on the first date? Or am I special?"

"What do you think?"

"I don't know. Do you?" Rocky fingered his thick curls and kissed along his hairline. Suddenly she pictured Kay mouthing her last words, 'Don't fuck him', and she eased up. Marcus pulled her breast out of her bikini top. Just before he could lick her nipple she grabbed it and shoved it back in.

"Answer me."

"NO! The last woman I did anything like this for was my ex-girlfriend of four years and she didn't even get as much as you're getting. You must not understand what you did for me in Vegas. I was in the pits, Candy. I have not had a clear head in three months."

Here we go with this shit again. He's starting to get on my nerves, she thought with a sensitive smile.

"—you come along, insightful and irresistible. I even told my mother about you. I just wanted to show you a nice time, like you showed me.

And, most of all, thank you for helping me cope with my loss. Besides, the season is getting ready to start and I wanted to relax."

She got off the bed and pulled her bikini bottoms out the crack of her ass. As Marcus watched her motions, his penis moved in his trunks and became heavy. She reached into her duffel bag, pulled out a dress and quickly hid it behind her back. Then she picked up her entire duffel bag and backed into the bathroom.

"To be so small, you sure have a ba-dunk-a-dunk girl!" Marcus exclaimed.

Rocky smiled and rearranged her bikini bottom. "So you thought the dress I had on in Vegas was hot? I am wearing a Vera Wang tonight." She backed up a couple more steps, and then slammed the bathroom door. She slid off her swimsuit and turned on the sink. She quickly removed her pink purse and cell phone from the duffel bag. She turned the pressure up in the sink, and the shower. Then she quickly dialed out. "Please let this work out here. Please let this work out here— Hello? Hi, Mauri, what's up? I haven't heard from you all day. You go out to the West Coast and get amnesia on me."

"Nah, I called you twice today. I keep on getting a busy signal whenever I call your cell, and I just left a message at your house. Where you at?"

"I have my godchildren for the weekend. We are doing 'Six Flags' today— so I will be out until after twelve or so, and Chuck E. Cheeses tomorrow."

"What's that? Like 'Dave and Busters' or something?"

"Exactly, but this is exclusively for kids. They have pizza and the characters play music and walk around shaking hands."

"See, I knew my woman would make a good mother. I hope you have something hot for us to do when I come see you."

"I'll work on it, Mauri."

"Alright, I got to go. Love you, bye."

Rocky stared at her phone, "Love you? Again?" she mouthed. Then she dialed once more.

'Hey this is Rock Candy. Say something sweet after the tone and I might get back to you.' *Oh, I have to change my out going message*, she thought.

'Yo, where you at? Your fuckin' cell is busy. I'm in LA and I am stayin' at the La Meridian under my name call me.' A loud beep sounded between the first message retrieved and the next. 'Your cell is busy that's why I am leaving you this message at home. I guess you arrived safely and I dented the front of your car. I am so sorry— sike, just kidding. DON'T FUCK HIM, BYE!' A longer beep came next. 'Hey, Rock Candy. I really wanted to see you however I'm working really late tonight. If you're still up when I leave, I'll come over and get some. If not I will have to see you some time this week. Good night." An even longer beep came between that message and the next, and Rocky lost her patience. She flipped the phone closed, picked up the black dress and hung it on the back of the door. She placed a shower cap over her head, turned on a flat iron and entered the shower.

Afterward she put on the hotel's robe, unplugged her flat iron, zipped up her bag and walked into the cool air-conditioned room. Her nipples instantly became hard and began to hurt as they rubbed against the rough terry cloth of the robe. "I'm all done," she said perkily.

Marcus got up and walked toward her. He stuck his hand under her bathrobe and tried to fondle her vagina. She tapped his fore arm with the back of her flat iron.

"OUCH!"

"That's for dessert. Go get washed up so we don't miss our reservations."

Marcus rubbed his arm and laughed as he walked into the bathroom. He inhaled deeply and closed his eyes, as he took in her sweet scent. As he dropped his trunks to his knees, he grabbed his penis with one hand, and bent to scoop her bikini bottom with the other. He inadvertently stroked his penis a few times on his way back up. He looked at the tag inside of her bathing suit.

"Burberry. Everything's name brand, huh?" Then he looked at the door to make sure it was shut. He placed the crotch of her bikini under his nose. He inhaled deeply then dropped it on the floor where he found it. He looked toward the door again then into the mirror and almost laughed at himself. "Shit, I ain't running up in no stank shit. Everything that glitter ain't gold, right Pop?"

But Candy seems to be sweet inside and out. Maybe this is the gold I need to straighten me out and slow me down, he thought.

When Marcus closed the door she plugged in her flat iron again, and it was golden hot. Rocky covered her mane with oil sheen spray and began to straighten her hair out with the flat iron. She moved quickly in hopes that she would finish before Marcus came out of the bathroom. She went through her make up case and pulled out a small tube of liquid eyeliner. She slowly drew a thin black line across the bottom of her eyelids, and threw the liner back in. She removed the earrings Mauri had recently purchased for her birthday and placed them on the tip of her small lobes. She removed a small platinum chain with a solitaire diamond dangling off the bottom and fastened that around her neck. She removed two watches and pondered which one to wear.

"I'll be more traditional tonight. Cartier sounds like the way to go." She threw the Choppard into its case and placed the other watch on her wrist. When she heard the shower stop she quickly removed a simple black bra and thong set out of her bag and pulled it on quickly. Then she ran toward the bed and sat as if she had been waiting for hours. Marcus opened the door and was shocked. "I thought you would take forever to get dressed. You're quicker than me." He talked as he walked. "It's a good thing though. Our reservations are for eight. What time is it?" Marcus asked.

"Seven thirty-three," Rocky replied as she got up and walked to the bathroom. She removed her dress from the back of the door and shook it out. It was a simple black dress with a tube top. It clung to her every curve. Rocky always liked the compliments she got when she wore it. It had a split up the right side that stopped at her panty line. The dress stopped about an inch or two above her knees. She slipped it on and walked to the mirror. *Damn, I can't wear this bra with this outfit. I'll just have to take it off,* she thought.

Marcus paused in putting on his pants and watched the reflection of her body as she removed her bra. Her nipples were so round and pretty. He swallowed hard as he looked at her bare back. Not one scar. She was all smooth skin and tan lines. She wiggled up into the tube and her perky breasts shook with each move. In her opinion they weren't as firm as she would have liked them to be. As she contemplated getting implants Marcus spoke.

"Do you have implants?"

"NO, funny you should ask. I was just thinking about getting some."

"You do not need it. What are you? A, B or C cup?"

"C. The implant thing wouldn't bother you? It bothers most men, a friend of mine back home is dead set against me—"

Marcus' demeanor changed from easygoing to irritated. "I don't want to hear about any other niggas. *I* am all for enhancements, but you don't need any and that's that."

She walked to her luggage and Marcus could not take his eyes off her. The dress did more for her shape than her actual shape. Marcus didn't want to wait anymore. "Let's skip dinner and stay in tonight," he said as he walked toward her.

"Come on Marcus, I want to enjoy the island night life, we can wait until later."

Marcus exhaled and continued getting dressed. Rocky removed a pair of black patent leather Vera Wang sandals with a slim silver heel, and a black flower on the front outlined in silver. She fished through the bag once more and removed a black leather bag that had the same flower on the front. She pulled out a small bottle of baby oil and twisted off its pink top with her teeth.

"Marcus, could you put some on my back." She bent over and put oil on the front of her body. Don't put too much on, okay?"

He squeezed a few drops into his palm and caressed her shoulders with it. Then he went down her arms and rested his chin on her shoulder.

"I make you look good, you know that?" he said.

"I was just thinking the same thing," Rocky smiled.

"What? That I make you look good?"

"NO, that I make you look good."

"That dress is banging, girl. Fits you like a glove. You ready?"

"I sure am. Does this match up to the Vegas dress?"

He looked her up and down and smiled. He grabbed her by the waist and pulled her close to him. She felt her behind on his lower thigh. Rocky was flustered, and immediately became hot and bothered. He kissed her neck and her cheek, and then looked at her reflection in the mirror.

"I don't know. That dress was the pain, but this one is a close second."

As they walked out the door, Rocky heard Kay's last warning fading further and further away.

The restaurant was outdoors and consisted of eight intimate huts located on a beachfront in the whitest sand. Every dinner party had its own hut. They drank out of hard coconut shell cups and watched natives dance privately for them. Rocky drank piña coladas. Marcus drank Hennesy, straight. After her fourth drink she got up and danced with the natives. She seductively and slowly wiggled her hips and spun around. She wobbled over to Marcus and wiggled down to the ground in between his open legs. The dancers began to leave, as Rocky became more erotic. She pulled her dress up to the top of her thighs and sat on Marcus' lap. They were face to face and Rocky began to grind slowly. She grabbed the back of his neck and rode him slowly back and forth.

Marcus put his cup down, unbuckled his belt and unzipped his pants. He pulled them below his behind and removed his penis out of his boxers. Rocky smiled broadly as she looked at how thick and long his penis was. The veins popped out all over his rod like chocolate, licorice, shoestrings.

His shit is bigger than Thomas', she thought. Then suddenly Rocky jumped back and looked around. It was now that she noticed the singers with their guitars and trumpets and the dancers kicking up the red and white ruffles on their long fluffy skirts were no longer present. She hiccuped and the taste of refried beans started her sentence. "You have protection?"

Marcus quickly pulled up his pants and straightened himself out.

"I got caught up in the moment. You just looked so good, and the Hen rock got me going."

She kissed his forehead, scooped up a coconut cup and swallowed its contents. It scorched her insides as it went down. She turned the cup upside down and watched the thin brown liquid trickle to the ground. "This isn't my drink. Get me another piña colada."

Marcus watched her stumble to her chair. He could see that she had had enough. *Pissy and all she still looks good*, he thought. He removed the hair that was stuck to her lips from her face. He pulled the front of her dress down and started to laugh. "I don't think you need another drink."

Rocky flashed the sweetest and most innocent smile at Marcus. He smiled back. "Rock Candy, huh? I can see why. Come on, let's go back to the room."

Rocky wobbled as she stood and felt her insides turn over. She looked up at Marcus. "I must have looked really silly dancing with those Mexicans, huh?"

"No. You looked like . . . like you were enjoying yourself."

"No, I looked stupid." She grasped his waist and placed all her weight on him. "I feel sick, Marcus. I wanted to go to the beach and hang out but I need to lie down."

"Come on, it's okay. You need to get your strength up for tomorrow."

They walked side by side. Every time she opened her mouth to hiccup a small amount of vomit rose in her throat, and filled her mouth. She concentrated on walking as straight as possible and preventing herself from regurgitating all four of her piña coladas. She counted each step she took to keep herself alert. She kept her arms clutched around his waist and a smile on her face with a mouth full of vomit.

"Are you alright?" Marcus asked.

Rocky kept her lips closed tightly together, smiled and nodded her head. "MMM hmmm." Truth be told, she felt terrible. She finally swallowed the vomit, followed by three mouthfuls of saliva. "I'm alright. I need to get some water. I am not much of a drinker." She belched again and the same nasty taste of recycled Hennesy and coconut rushed up from her stomach and into her throat. She quickly shut her mouth. *I cant' fuckin' throw up in front of him. Stay focused, girl*, she thought.

The five minutes it took them to get from the restaurant to their room seemed like five thousand. Once there she walked straight into the bathroom and turned on the faucet. She stripped off her dress and vomited into the toilet. When she was done she washed her face and brushed her teeth. She didn't even realize she was nearly naked when she walked straight over to the bed where Marcus sat on the edge.

He marveled at her flawless body. As she got closer he probed for scars, but did not see one. She threw herself across the bed on her stomach. He smiled at two petite moles on her ass cheeks. Marcus kissed her back and she moaned loudly, but it wasn't a moan of pleasure— it was of a sickly nature. Before she knew it, she was knocked out across the bed. He rubbed her back, played in her hair and silhouetted her figure with his pinky. Soon, he was fast asleep, at her side.

Marcus awoke to an empty bed at seven forty-five in the morning and she was gone. He sat up and his head pounded a few times. "She is probably at the gym or something."

He slowly got up and walked into the bathroom to find her workout clothes in the doorway, and Rocky sitting in a tub full of bubbles. She jumped as he entered the bathroom.

"For someone who must be hung over, you sure are up early."

"Well, I figured I might as well try to sweat the rest out. I ran a couple of miles across the beach. It was so beautiful." She sat up in the tub and gestured for him to come toward her. "I made a real fool of myself last night and I just wanted to apologize. I can't hold liquor."

"You were okay. When you were kicking and dancing, you really looked like you were having a lot of fun. I enjoyed watching you. It was like you were putting on a show for me."

"I didn't get a chance to tell you, but that restaurant was gorgeous. I can't believe that you went out your way like this."

"You ain't seen shit yet! Today is going to be even better and tomorrow is our grand finale. We have reservations for nine o'clock, and it's already a quarter to eight. What time did you get up this morning?"

"Seven o'clock, I just can't sleep late. I tried not to wake you up."

"Trust me, you didn't. Um, let's hurry up. We need to get a cab to take us. It's a couple of miles away."

"You come out here often? How do you know about all of this stuff?"

"This is my first time here. I had my travel agent put this together for me. He gave me a very detailed itinerary, and all our expenses are already paid. So let's go because I ain't got no money to waste." He walked over to the toilet and started to urinate but he couldn't.

"Candy, turn around. I can't go with you watching me."

"You can't be serious?"

Rocky stood up in the tub and quickly grabbed a towel. She wrapped herself up and turned her back. "Well, I am finished anyway so you can have the bathroom," Rocky said.

"When you reach into your bag of tricks, don't pull out anything to extreme. We are going to have big fun today."

Rocky went into the room and rummaged through her bag. As soon as she heard the shower she repeated the same dance she had performed the night before at dinner. She hummed the same Mexican tune and fished out a pair of faded denim shorts with a gold coin belt. The shirt was a bikini top that had gold coins hanging from the bust line. She had a matching denim hat with a baseball cap brim, but it tied in the back. She slipped into a black bathing suit bottom, and then into her shorts. She had to suck in her stomach to close them, but once they were on she loved the fit. They practically cut off her circulation around her thighs, but curved her rear end just the way she liked. The top tied around her neck and accentuated her bust line. She had a small, navy, nylon, Prada knap-sack that she placed her bikini top and other little knick-knacks that she wanted to carry along.

In front of the dresser she brushed her hair back into a neat ponytail and tied her hat around it. She could imagine her and Marcus standing there the night before, his big ball palming hands anointing her back. She imagined him whispering slowly in her ear. I want you— I love you.

She removed a pair of flip-flops from her bag and slipped them on. She removed her cell phone from her bag, listened for the sound of the shower and flopped onto the bed. As soon as she finished dialing Marcus opened the door. She placed the phone on an end table and sat up. "Hurry up, slow poke. I'm hungry. Do you think we could get a bite to eat on the way to our destination?"

"Don't worry, you will eat once we get there." He looked at her outfit and shook his head.

She stood up and struck a model-like pose. "What's the matter? You don't like my duds?"

"That's just it. I love your duds— you stay fly. Someone must be hitting your purse."

Nothing annoyed Rocky more than comments like that. She went from super model to super tight in five seconds flat. "I work every day. I have not one dependent or family member to take care of. I live a very modest and solitary life. When I am down, I have no mother to learn life lessons from, no more grandma to tell me its going to be all right. I like to shop. It makes me feel good and gets me out of some tough depressions. I don't need no man to help me look or feel fly."

"Damn, Oprah, don't be so sensitive," Marcus returned.

She walked out onto the patio and looked at the dozens of people on the beach below her. Within seconds he was standing behind her.

"I didn't mean to—"

She turned around. "Don't worry about it. Did you go to Hawaii and buy stock in those fuckin' print shirts?"

"I caught these at Bergdorf's and I liked them, so I bought a couple. You don't like them?"

"You looked cute in it last night, but this one. . . "

"I'll go and change."

"No need to, you look just fine, but I'll tell you one thing. You will not walk out of this hotel room with me in those flip-flops and socks. It's either-or, brah, I ain't havin' it," Rocky said. Marcus had to laugh. "I don't care what your fuckin' toes look like. I will not walk out this room with you if you wear that shit outside. And here I am thinking you had a little finesse and shit," Rocky continued.

"But it's hammer time under my tubes." He bent over and removed his socks. Rocky laughed as soon as he peeled them off. He had the longest, ugliest toes she had ever seen. Most of his toes had two corns a piece and they laid on top of each other. "They soft as hell though," Marcus said and they both laughed the matter off.

Marcus called the concierge's desk and requested a taxi that arrived in five minutes. It pulled them up to a boat dock in fifteen minutes. They stepped out of the cab and into the crystal clear day. The few fluffy white clouds in the sky seemed out of place. Rocky was elated. She had no idea what they were about to do but she felt so special. Marcus pulled out a piece of paper with numbers and notes inked all over it. "We are looking for the 'La Santa Maria'."

The two of them walked side by side, along side of docked ships and yachts.

"Here she is, right here," Marcus said pointing at a big, beautiful, white yacht.

"Marcus, it's beautiful."

They approached the spectacular vessel. The fixtures were gleaming gold and in the very front of it, painted in gold cursive, were the words 'La Santa Maria'. A middle-aged White man stepped off the boat in a cap, blue jeans, and a white T-shirt and met them on the dock.

"Hi, I'm Sam. We are set to sail at nine a.m. sharp! The island is about two hours from here. We will stop at the halfway point where you will be able to scuba dive. I assume you both have dived before."

Rocky nodded her head.

"No, I've never been," Marcus replied.

"We are goin' one hundred feet below sea level, and will spend an hour down. This is one of the greatest locations! You'll be able to see a lot of sea life out there. Then we will continue out to the island. You must be at the drop off point by seven o' clock promptly for departure. As soon as we dock, my skipper will be there with whatever rentals you have requested and directions to where you need to go."

Sam looked at his watch and then removed his hat to wipe his forehead. "There is another couple due to join us, but if they are not here in fifteen minutes, we will have to sail without them. Breakfast is ready and waiting for you downstairs on the lower deck. You may go down whenever you're ready."

Rocky nudged Marcus' elbow as they entered the yacht. "Doesn't he look like that guy from 'Jaws'? You know the one who was always—"

"Oh, shit. You're right. He sure does." They both laughed. "I hope we don't see any sharks when we dive," Marcus said.

Rocky had never been on a privately owned yacht before. She was so excited. Marcus held onto her arm as they walked down a small flight of steps and entered a small cozy room. The floors were a shiny hard wood, and everything else was painted white. The windows were so clear it seemed as if there weren't any. There were three round tables covered with starched, white tablecloths. One table had four gold serving trays filled with pastries, pancakes, eggs, crepes and bacon. There were gold kettles and white plates and cups with golden trim. Rocky did not hesitate to go to the table and pile up her plate. Marcus followed right behind her. They sat at a table near a window and ate. When Marcus got up for seconds, he felt as if the boat was moving.

"We're moving?" Rocky asked as she stared out the window watching the beach slowly grow distant from the boat.

"Yep. We are moving. I guess the other couple got left," Marcus shrugged.

"That's terrible."

Marcus returned to the table and they both stared at each other. Their thoughts were on opposite ends of the block, but still on the same street.

Damn. This nigga can't possibly go all out like this for each chick he meets. He must really be feeling me. Then again he has mad cheddar. This could be the norm for him, Rocky thought.

I know this chick has a lot of dudes checkin' for her. She is fly, and spends a lot of chips. She's probably used to shit like this. "What's on your mind, superstar?" Marcus asked.

"I was just thinking about how nice this weekend is. I am really starting to take this personal. I feel so special. Should I?"

"Yes, you should."

"You know, my grandmother used to take me fishing right after my mother died. She said the serenity of the lake relaxed her. I remember her saying, 'Rocky, when the water is close to the sky, speak into it. Think real hard, baby, and pray right in between that line where the water and sky seem to meet. Your mother will hear you, and reply.' I can see that space. I am going up to the deck."

Rocky placed her empty plate on the serving table. Then she went upstairs and walked towards the yacht's stern. The beachfront looked like Barbie's beach party, and it's occupants looked like surfing Kens and Christies. Then she looked at the huge body of water that surrounded her and focused on the horizon.

Rocky thought about her grandmother and closed her eyes as the wind caressed her face. She took off her hat and untied her hair so her grandmother could breeze through it. She imagined the smell of burning hair and thick dark green pomade on the white stove next to the hot comb as the sun beat her brow and the wind fingered her hair. She remembered how her grandmother's thick caring hands would press her hair every other weekend for school. She let the wind blow memories through her mind. It blew her back— way back into time.

Marcus looked out the window and thought about his summer vacations with his father and the countless summer days they spent on the beach. He remembered being ten, and his cousins teasing him about how dark he was. His father immediately ran off to a concession stand and purchased him a chocolate ice cream cone and his favorite chocolate bar. He didn't buy one for the other kids. His father said, 'The darker the berry, the sweeter the juice. The only reason why chocolate tastes so good is because it was dark brown, remember that.'

He thought hard from the spot where he sat. He stared at the water and smiled at the thought of his father being there for him through every step of his career. He closed his eyes, inhaled and exhaled the word 'thanks' in his breath.

As he continued to gaze out the window, he saw a seagull that seemed to be chasing the boat. Its wings flapped quickly and as soon as Marcus took a good look at it, it hovered over the deck as though it was staring directly into his eyes for few seconds. Then it quickly took off. *No. It couldn't be*, he thought.

Suddenly he heard the loud claps and flops of Rocky's sandals as they came thundering down the steps. He looked at Rocky, her hair disheveled, as she cried with the look of horror on her face.

"Marcus, this big fuckin' bird swooshed by me on the deck! It looked so fuckin' disgusting, and his wings, I could hear them flapping by my ears." With that she shuddered twice and began to cry.

"Would you get a grip, girl? You need to seek therapy for that. Come here," Marcus said sympathetically.

Rocky walked toward Marcus and sat on his lap. She placed her head in the crook of his neck, breathing heavily, and wrapped her arms around his shoulders.

"Look at you, you're a wreck. Rocky let me let you in on a little secret. Not too long ago I was just like you— well, not to this extreme, but close enough. You couldn't get me near a horse. I was terrified of them throughout my entire childhood. About three years ago my therapist told me I should take some beginner riding lessons to overcome my fears, and guess what? I ride at least twice a month now. Start off by going to the pet store or the zoo or something. Then go to the park and feed them. Don't let this fear beat you."

Rocky looked out the window at the white bird flying into the sun at a distance. She knew Marcus was right. It seemed like the older that she became the more pronounced her fear got. "You have a therapist?"

"Yeah, my dad made me get one my first year in the NBA. He said he didn't want stardom going to my head."

"Well, I guess I could seek some therapy."

Marcus grabbed her by the waist and began to kiss her neck and neckline. She turned around and straddled him. His large chocolate hands fondled her tan supple breasts and caressed them gently. The coins hanging on her top jingled with each movement of his fingers. She inched up so she would be sitting right on his penis, and rotated her behind trying to appease her throbbing clitoris. They both jolted at the sound of someone clearing his throat and jumped up. As he jerked his hand from under her top, two of her coins went clinking to the floor. One of them rolled right to the steps where Sam stood with two life vests in his hand.

"Sorry to interrupt, but it's time to dive," Sam said.

Rocky kept her back turned until she shoved her breast back into her top. She quickly turned around and smiled. "An hour has passed already?" she asked.

"Yes, it has. There is a bedroom right through those doors. You can change into your swimsuits. Your tanks are up on the deck. Be upstairs in five minutes," Sam said then quickly returned upstairs.

"Why do I feel like I'm in military school?" Rocky asked stepping out of her shorts.

"Let's just do what he says so we can keep to our time schedule," Marcus said.

On deck they put on their scuba gear. They sat near the yacht's bow. Rocky hated having to go backward into the water. She pinched her nose, and fell back. The heavy oxygen tank plunged her right into the water. Once she gathered her bearings she adjusted her goggles and found the rope that anchored the boat. She climbed down and held her breath as she went. She filled her cheeks with air every few feet and blew with her mouth shut, to counter the pressure.

Up on the deck, Sam explained to Marcus the same movements and precautions that Rocky was presently taking under the water. Within a few minutes all three divers were on the ocean floor. They swam past schools of beautiful fish in vast arrays of exotic colors. They saw neon-colored fish, jellyfish and sea moss that squirmed and twisted like snakes. Sam led them to a sea cove inside of which were several baby sharks. Marcus felt tense when he saw the sharks, but he kept it moving. They periodically checked their gauges for oxygen levels and marveled at the sea life. Rocky went within inches of an octopus that was the entire length of her legs.

They swam for nearly an hour. Marcus looked up and noticed a pin of light way above their heads. He checked his gauge and noticed he had less than a quarter of a tank left. He tapped Sam, pointed toward his gauge, and the three of them began the swim back to the anchor and the rope. They ascended quickly. Back on the boat they helped each other remove their equipment. Sam provided towels and drinks.

"Oh my God, that was simply breathtaking. I nearly touched an octopus," Rocky said.

"But did you see the baby sharks? I couldn't believe I was so close and lived to tell it. I am open. You know we have to do this again," Marcus said.

"I can take you next time. I only need one more dive to get my license. I am a little winded. I really would like to lie down," Rocky said

"The room I showed you earlier is the bedroom reserved for the both of you."

"Your yacht is gorgeous, Sam. How many bedrooms does it have?"

"Two, and a small captain's quarter. Remember you only have about an hour."

"Okay."

"Candy, do you mind if I stay up here on the deck while you sleep?"

"Go ahead, baby. I am just going to catch some Z's. I was up early, and my stomach is still a little queasy from last night."

Rocky wrapped herself up with the towel and went down the steps. She looked at her lavish surroundings. She really wished she could live like this everyday. There was a small bed, sink and dresser inside the room. The bed was made so nicely it looked like it was straight off the pages of a catalogue. When she sat down she almost expected it to be fake. She combed through her wet hair and made six braids.

When she looked in the mirror she couldn't help but laugh at the fact that she looked like a cross between Ceilie and Beloved. She lay down, hugged herself tightly and stared up at the ceiling. "This is exactly where I want to be for the rest of my life," she sighed. "Not just on a yacht, but on a man that could do these things for me."

She felt open for the first time since high school. She inhaled deeply, but when she exhaled she felt mushy inside. She continued to stare at the ceiling. "Mommy? Grandma? I don't ask for too many favors, but I really want this one. So, if you have to pull some strings up there with You-Know-Who, make Marcus mine." She released her self-embrace and was soon fast asleep.

Late Monday night the couple sat on an airplane chatting away.

"Marcus, I really don't know how to thank you for this weekend. I have been many places and on plenty of islands but this was by far my best vacation yet. The scuba diving, the private restaurant, spa treatments."

"What about the moped rides across the island today?" Marcus added.

"That was hot, too. I really enjoyed my weekend with you."

"Ditto. I'm not going to front. When we came upstairs from the spa the first night I wanted you so badly, but when you gave me the lap dance— OH! And upstairs, after dinner, when you flopped in the bed drunk in that thong with all that ass, I thought my joint was going to bust. I was going to poke your ass, drunk and all— you were looking right. That would have topped off the weekend perfectly, but I can wait."

Rocky blushed. "Well, now that you mention it, when you were lotioning my back I was thinking, 'this nigga could get it.' Then when I was dancing on your lap? Oh, my goodness— you talk about getting ready to bust? For future reference; I am not much of a drinker."

"You've only told me that about ten times. What time are you arriving in New York?"

"Twelve thirty-five in the morning."

"I have to take a whiz. I'll be right back."

Rocky watched him walk up the aisle. *I should have given him something to remember me by*, she thought. A sudden smile invaded Rocky's face. She had no idea where the devilish idea that just popped into her head came from but she liked it. She looked around her furtively as if the other three passengers in first class could see her thoughts. She rummaged through her purse then power walked to the bathroom. The 'Occupied' sign was lit, but she still knocked.

"Someone's in here—"

"Marcus, open the door! Hurry, it's me," she whispered. As soon as Marcus opened the door she shoved herself into him and the small bathroom quickly. She slammed the door shut and clicked the lock twice, double checking the 'Occupied' sign.

"What are you doing?" Rocky kissed his mouth shut in reply. A wet tongue ceased his words. She gently pushed him against the door. He caught on quickly and ran his fingers through her wavy hair. She grabbed one of his arms and led it down to her vagina. He stroked her vagina as her hands made their way through his shorts to his penis and jerked it.

"Stay close to me and turn around," she said winded.

"You're fuckin' crazy," Marcus said.

"Crazy about you," Rocky smiled.

They turned around slowly, in an embrace, as if it was their last dance and the clock was about to strike twelve. Their 360 complete, Rocky pushed him back an inch or two and told him to sit on the sink. She just stared into his eyes and licked her lips. Marcus positioned himself on the sink, grabbed his penis and jerked it softly. Without warning she bent over and enveloped his dick with her mouth. Marcus jumped back and the faucet turned on. He reached back to turn it off, but only after his behind was saturated. She sucked his penis moving her head in slow, circular motions. She went straight down his shaft and rolled her head like a young chickenhead in an argument coming back up, but instead of mouthing off, she contracted her jaws around his penis. Marcus laid one hand down flat on the gleaming metal sink and the other flat against the wall, as if it was his strength holding up the bathroom.

She stopped suddenly and released the condom she had fished out of her purse. She clutched it so tightly that her palm was sweating. She pulled up her skirt and pulled her thong to one side.

"Shit. You have a mouth on you," Marcus said, out of breath.

He rolled the condom on. Rocky could see where it cut off his circulation; it was tight. It took less than one step for her to be close to him. She climbed on top of the sink— one foot on each side of him. He quickly followed her lead again and held his dick straight up. She positioned herself right above it and eased it in. The pain was hardly bearable. She moved slowly, and moaned loudly. There were three, sudden knocks on the door.

Damn, I just moaned, she thought as she looked at Marcus— they both turned pale,

"I-I am not feeling well. My stomach is very weak— I have the runs. Could you please go to coach?" Rocky said.

"Pardon me. I hope you feel better," the voice said.

"Thanks," Rocky said in a shaky voice. Then she went back to work. She was able to get his penis halfway in and she rode the tip. She held on to his shoulders and slowly gyrated up and down. Marcus pushed down on Rocky's shoulders forcefully. Her walls cracked as his penis was forced all the way inside her. She winced in pain. He covered her mouth and began to push. She could partially see herself in the mirror sitting in a frog-like position. Her face was red and tears rolled down her cheeks.

Marcus kissed her lips repeatedly, and her juices began to flow. His oversized penis didn't seem as painful as it had moments before and she continued to ride. She made long slow strokes and within seconds Marcus grabbed her shoulders again. She prepared herself for another hard thrust but instead he grabbed them and pushed them inward. He muffled his grunts by biting down on his bottom lip.

"That was a first," he said. "Now you get on the sink."

Rocky could barely move. She slowly put her legs down on the floor. They embraced each other again and awkwardly turned around in the small space. She sat on the sink and Marcus knelt in front of it. He pulled her legs over his shoulders, and moved her thong to the side. He teased her clitoris with quick flicks of his tongue. Then he licked and sucked, his mouth smacking as he ate his Rock Candy. She grabbed a handful of his thick black curls and let her head fall back against the mirror. The faucet jabbed at her tailbone but the warmth of his fine face between her legs dulled the pain. There was another knock on the door and Rocky tightened her inner thighs forcing Marcus to come to a complete stop.

"Is everything okay in there?" It was a flight attendant. Rocky released her grip and Marcus looked up. She opened her eyes wide, looking at him for directions.

"Um, my wife's stomach didn't agree with the dinner that was served. She made a mess of her clothing. I am just trying to help her out. We will be done in a second."

"Please, let me know if there is anything we can do."

"Okay."

Rocky slid down and Marcus stood up. He pulled off his semen filled condom, wrapped it in a tissue and flushed it down the toilet. They shuffled around each other like Siamese twins joined by the chest in a barnyard dance as they tried to make themselves presentable. Rocky wet the bottom of her shirt with some soap and water. She fingered through Marcus' hair and shook her head around. She sprayed the air freshener that was on the sink and kissed Marcus' chest through his shirt. She turned, faced the door and opened it. As she peeked out she grabbed her stomach. She was prepared for an audience outside the door, but no one seemed to be watching. She slid out the lavatory and looked ahead, but no one saw her exit the bathroom. Marcus came out behind her. As soon as they were both seated they busted out laughing.

"You looked like white chocolate when that passenger knocked on the door," Rocky said.

Marcus laughed. "I was scared to shit. But YOU! I can't believe you said you had the runs. I wanted to fuckin' die on the spot."

"You thought fast, too. My wife is sick? I bet you that flight attendant was scared to death when you said it was from their food," Rocky said.

"I never did anything like that in my life," Marcus said.

"Believe it or not, neither have I. But I wanted to put that cherry on top of your weekend. You said that would have topped your weekend off just right," Rocky said.

"Trust me, you did. Your wood peck is sick," Marcus said.

Rocky looked confused. "Excuse me? What's a wood peck?"

"You got mouth skills. I have gotten some skull but damn, girl!" Marcus exclaimed.

"Okay, okay. I got you now. It was the heat of the moment. Plus, I went at it a little harder than I normally would," Rocky confessed.

"Why?" Marcus asked with a skeptical look on his face.

"Never mind. I have said too much. I just want to be remembered. I am pretty sure you don't roll out the red carpet for everyone you just meet."

"Yeah and?"

"Nothing. I feel crazy right now. I feel embarrassed for the first time in a very long time. I can't believe I just did that."

"Neither do I."

"Thanks. I feel *a lot* better now."

"It's hard to find women like you to rock with. Intelligent and gorgeous hardly ever come together, but sometimes you can find that. Fly, intelligent, super gorgeous, street-wise, adventurous and freaky never come together. A chick is either fly, gorgeous and stiff— never willing to get loose. Or they're okay looking, fly, and too loose. Those types don't water ski or scuba dive, they be too fly to fuck up their hair. Roller coasters, magic shows— they don't do any of that. And the worst part is they don't understand ball. God forbid they follow my season. They want to date an NBA star, but they don't even know the game. Having a woman like you is a man's dream. I appreciate your realness and your beauty. Don't feel ashamed, Rocky feel good. I know I do."

He reclined his seat as far back as it could go and grabbed her hand. It seemed like he went to blink, and did not open his eyes until the flight landed. He was literally fast asleep. Rocky watched him sleep for an entire hour. She thought about her fantastic weekend and wondered if she would be the topic of locker room talk. *'Yo, this bitch I took to Cozumel, had good wood mouth,'* she laughed to herself. *Or will he feel me more after this.* She couldn't call it. She hoped for the best and fell asleep still gripping his hand.

Two hours later she awoke to find Marcus blocking her view of the aisle. He was retrieving his bag from the overhead compartment. As soon as he got it down he bent over and Rocky was staring at him. "Make sure you call me as soon as you get home," Marcus said.

"Okay, I will," Rocky said.

He leaned into the seat and she scooted over to meet his lips. Their kiss seemed to last an eternity. Neither of them wanted to stop. Rocky pulled back first. "Thanks for a wonderful weekend. I'll call you as soon as I get in," Rocky said.

Marcus kissed her lips quickly. "No— thanks for changing my life."

"Excuse me. I would like to get by," a passenger said.

"I have a fifteen minute layover. I'll sit for a few minutes with you. I have been meaning to tell you something. Earlier when we were on the boat and you told me that story about your grandmother taking you fishing I looked out the window, at the exact point where the sun seemed to touch the water and remembered vacations my dad used to take us on. Then I saw that bird. It seemed like he *was* sending me a sign. Like he could hear my thoughts. . . I wasn't even there— Rocky, I didn't get a chance to say good-bye to him. I've hung out with the fellas, I've run through some bitches—" He abruptly stopped speaking and looked at Rocky. "Talking to you is so comfortable. It's like talking to my mans and them. I feel so relaxed, I can't believe I just said that to you. You aren't offended, are you?"

Rocky smiled and shook her head, but inside she felt different. *Not this thanks for helping me cope with my pops shit again*, she thought.

"I've tried everything, but I haven't felt like my old self. Something was missing. I really miss him. I don't know if you realized it, but you closed the emptiness and taught me that missing him was okay. You showed me how to miss him the right way. And on top of that, you showed me a good time in the process. My therapist gets a couple of hundred every visit, and she couldn't teach me how to do that. This weekend is just the beginning of how I plan to thank you." With that he kissed her cheek and walked off of the plane.

Rocky sank in her seat and held her breath. *The beginning? I am so open right now.* She looked at her watch and checked the time. She had seven minutes until take off. She went into her purse and pulled out her trusty cell phone. "Kay, what—"

"Don't make me beat your fuckin' ass. You haven't called me all weekend."

"You know, no news is good news—"

"I know 'no news' is going to get your ass beat. Fuckin' Mauri called my cell like an hour ago. He said that he was having problems getting through to your phone and he wanted to know what time you will be dropping the kids back from 'Dave and Busters'."

Rocky didn't answer. She didn't have a care in the world besides Marcus.

"I told him that you dropped them by my grandmother in Mahwah, and that cell phones don't get good coverage in that area. ROCKY, am I talking to myself?"

Rocky let out a long sigh as she replied. "Oh, Kay. I had the most beautiful weekend. We rented— well, he rented a yacht, we rode mopeds on an island, we went scuba diving, we had spa treatments, ate at a private outdoor restaurant on the beach, we went water skiing, the hotel room was off the hook, and he didn't press me for no ass. I think I'm in love."

"So you didn't fuck him. I am so proud of you." Rocky was silent.

"Rock Candy! You did it, didn't you?"

"I just fucked him in the airplane."

"YOU DID WHAT!"

"I just fucked him in the airplane bathroom."

Kay laughed loudly. "You're serious. How did you manage that? Those bathrooms are like shoeboxes—"

"First I—"

"You know what, that is entirely too much information. I really don't want to know." Kay paused. "Well?"

"Yes, his dick is tremendous. *I* could barely take that shit, but once we started to get loose."

"Is his shit bigger than Thomas'?"

"Yes, but not much."

"How about Too Sweet's?"

"Shit. King Kong's shit ain't bigger than no Too Sweet's, but Marcus is probably just as big."

"Listen, I want details. I can hear the captain's announcements in the background. So you better cut that shit off, but first call Mauri. Remember you're out in Mahwah, and I will see you in a few."

Rocky did as she was told. She called him quickly and recited Kay's lame explanation. He reminded her that he would be in Brooklyn later that evening and that she was to pick him up from the airport. As soon as the captain mouthed his first syllable, Rocky disconnected her phone. She already had a foolproof excuse. She turned off the phone, adjusted her seat back and awaited take off.

As the plane glided upwards she looked down at the tiny lights, and wondered where Marcus was and what he was doing. How could she make him hers? This would have to be the plan of the century. She needed to come up with a strategic solution, just as she did with everything else in her life.

She thought about the bathroom episode and her emotions crawled through her like ants all over an unattended picnic basket. *He could either label me a freaky whore who turns ass all of the time or as what he mentioned, full of realness and beauty, willing to try new and different things. I hope he was telling the truth.*

13

She could make a bedspring sing a song of mercy

Joann stood on the corner of Fourth and Butler. The kids would be back to school the day after tomorrow, and she was looking forward to her tour being a little livelier. She looked at the clock on her phone and noticed she had three missed calls. They were all from Yanick.

"I just don't feel like being bothered today. I'll probably see her tonight so why she gotta call me all day?" she muttered. She double-checked the time on her phone with the time on her watch. "It's only one and she's called me three times she must be buggin." She flipped up her phone and dialed the number.

"Hey, Yanick, what's up?"

"I'm chillin'. Can I come by after class?"

"I'm sorry, baby but I am working a double. I will come and scoop you around ten for the fight party tonight. You and Seven can come by tomorrow as soon as I get off."

"You know I have a full day of classes, I don't get home from school until nine tomorrow and you'll be 'sleep by then. I won't be able to come spend time with you until later on this week."

Joann sarcastically snapped her fingers and stomped her feet. "Don't worry, we will make up for lost time at the end of the week."

Joann looked across the street at a group of boys standing on the corner around a street light. One was carrying a brown paper bag that contained a bottled drink. She recognized one of the boys from The High. *I hope that it's alcoho*l, she thought

"Okay, Joey, I love you. Call me when you get home."

"You got it, princess." Joann walked across the street in the direction of the kids hanging out on the corner. Before she reached the sidewalk she addressed the boys loudly. "Hey, guys, you don't have anywhere to go this afternoon? Go buy some school supplies, school starts Thursday. Get off of my corner."

The boys walked off without a fight. But a fight is exactly what Officer Joann Nuñez wanted that afternoon. "You, with the brown paper bag, come here. What are you drinking?"

Kahmelle sucked his teeth and slowly turned around toward the officer. The other three boys sped off in the direction of the school. Facing her fully, he answered with an attitude. "It's just something to drink."

"Let me see. Take the bottle out of the bag."

Kahmelle shook his head. "I just got back from down south today, and the boys was just welcoming a nigga home, that's all."

"LET ME SEE WHAT'S IN THE BAG, SON!"

Kahmelle pulled a fifth of Hennesy out of the bag.

The officer immediately retrieved her memo book from her back pocket and issued him a summons. "I could take your ass to jail for that stupid shit."

Nuñez looked at the boys Kahmelle was with as they headed toward the school, and was happy to see that Tony was no where in sight.

"Give me the bottle, and take your ass off of the corner and get ready for school." Kahmelle gave her an evil look, handed over the bottle and rolled his eyes. As he walked away he murmured a gripe.

"Excuse me? I can't hear you," Joann called out.

"I ain't say nothing, officer."

"I thought so."

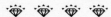

Rocky came in from work Tuesday evening smiling at thought of riding Marcus in the airplane bathroom earlier that dark morning and threw her keys down on the table. *Damn he has a dick on him,* she thought. After dusting, rearranging photos, straightening pillows and furniture she flopped onto her chaise lounge, picked up her briefcase off of the ground and removed one of two large textbooks from it. Just as she kicked off her shoes and placed her feet on the chaise her phone rang.

"Fuck. I just got in here!" she exclaimed. She answered the phone with an attitude. "Hello?"

"Hey you. What are you doing?" Thomas asked.

"Getting ready to do some reading for school. How about you?" Rocky replied.

"Sitting here thinking about how good making love to you is, and how I want some now."

"Thomas, I really can't come over right now. I have so much school work." She looked at her clock, it was already seven and Mauri's flight arrived at ten.

"I won't take no for an answer. This case has me stressed and I need to release some of this stress in you." Thomas knew she loved to be talked to in that manner, he just hoped it worked.

"Okay, baby as long as you're here in fifteen minutes and gone by eight thirty."

"Look out your window," Thomas said.

Rocky walked to the window, moved her blinds aside and saw his Range parked out front. The lights were on in his car and she could see him talking to her on the phone.

"Come on up. I'll throw the keys on the top step." She ran into her bedroom and quickly grabbed the pictures of her and Mauri that she just put out when she came in from work. She ran into the kitchen and shoved them into a cabinet, behind several boxes of cereal. She ran to her mantle and could hear the keys downstairs in her front door. She removed two pictures of Mauri and herself from it and put them in the same cabinet. She bolted to her bedroom and took three pictures of her and Thomas from beneath her bed. She placed one on her end table next to her bed and the other two on the mantelpiece in the living room. Then she stood against the wall. When Thomas opened the door she was hidden behind it.

"Rocky?"

She jumped from behind the door and hugged him tightly. "I'm right here."

"Hey, sweetie. I'm so sorry about this weekend. I wanted to make it up to you."

He presented her with two dozen yellow and white lilies, wrapped in white paper. Her mouth dropped open like she had a two-pound weight attached to her bottom lip.

"Thomas they are gorgeous."

"I'm glad you like them. Did you cook I am starved?"

"I just got in from work fifteen minutes ago. Now what is it you said you wanted to do to me on the phone?"

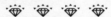

Kahmelle sat in front of the phone and stared at it for several minutes. He finally picked it up and dialed out.

"Hello?"

"Is Camille there?"

"No, she ain't. Who is this?"

Kahmelle didn't answer. He just sat and listened to Camille's mother yell into the phone.

"Hello? HELLO? FUCKIN' ASSHOLE!"

Kahmelle held his head in his hands and shook his head. "What am I going to do, yo? What am I going to do?"

"Thomas, what did you say you wanted to do to me over phone?"

As she spoke she performed a strip-tease letting her suit hit the floor. He grabbed his hard penis through his pants and shook it at her. "I want to release some of this stress in your ass."

"Ooh. Come and do it."

Rocky got on all fours and crawled backwards to him. "You want to stress me out? OR sex me out?"

"Both. Bring your fat ass over here." Thomas licked his lips and admired the tan line that covered her ass. "You look good. I love when you hit the tanning salon in Detroit." He dropped his pants and boxers to his ankles. He was barely three feet into her apartment. He reached into his pocket and pulled out a box of condoms. Fumbling, he opened it up. He savagely ripped the wrapper with his teeth and shoved the rubber onto his penis. He spread open her cheeks and began to gently push his dick inside of her. She squeezed her eyes shut, and grunted lightly. *God, my shit is still sore from the plane*, she thought as she bit down hard on her lip.

"Am I hurting you, Rocky?"

"Keep going," she said.

He continued to push and pull until they both came to a moist and steamy climax. They lay on the floor next to each other in front of her doorway. She thought about the slight size difference between him and Marcus and about how good sex between her and Marcus could be. He had came too fast on the plane for her to tell. She hoped it would get as good as this.

Thomas thought about how much he was really starting to feel for her, and how the sex was just a bonus. He caressed her back and rubbed his re-hardening penis against her bare behind. As he lay with her he couldn't help but hope that she would take him up on his offer. Just the thought of her being solely his aroused him once more. Rocky lay on the hardwood floor and watched his wood harden again.

"Thomas, I just came twice, you trying to put a black eye on my pussy?"

"I haven't seen you all week."

"It's only Tuesday."

"Plus, whenever I take my mind off my case, it goes straight to you."

He took off his cum filled condom, removed a fresh one out of the box, and laid the used one on top of the box. He almost gagged thinking of something dirty to say to her, but he aimed to please. He put it on and gently grabbed her hair. "I really love your fat juicy vagin— pussy. Just give daddy a little more. I'm not asking you. I am telling you."

He grabbed her with as minimal force as he could and placed his finger in her vagina. As he pulled it out he heard the sounds of wetness and he rubbed it on her back. He wished she would put his penis in her mouth, because he lived for that part of their foreplay, but he dared not ask. He had too much respect for her to do that. To him, that was crossing the line, no matter how much she loved to hear him say, "Suck my dick." He looked at his watch. It was already seven forty-five and he wanted to come quickly. He lifted her up, pants still dangling around his ankles and shuffled to her bedroom. He lay on his back and she quickly hopped on his penis.

"Rub your breasts and pull your nipples," he whispered huskily.

Watching her body go up and down— up and down— her hands cupping her plump breasts— her short trimmed finger nails squeezing her nipples— her beautiful face twist and contort with painful pleasure— the up the down— his name moaned out— it was too much. He even came quicker than their first round.

He quickly got up and slowly pulled off the condom. He walked to the bathroom and picked up the first dirty condom off the floor on his way. He placed them in the trashcan. "Rocky, could you please bring me a wash rag?"

Rocky opened her legs wide trying to let any bit of cool air pass between her legs as she spoke. "Why can't you ever remember that they are folded up on the shelves in the bathroom?"

"Thank you," he called back. Thomas stood in front of the sink and washed off his penis. Then he rinsed out his rag and wiped his face. He looked at himself and his thoughts were loud in his mind. *Do you feel any better? You still have a great deal of work to do before Friday and its Tuesday already. Stress wise, I feel the same, but that sure as hell felt good.* "Okay, baby. I'm out of here. Listen, don't be too upset if my calls are scarce this week. Saturday past I spent the night in my office. I was asleep headfirst in my files. So, if I don't call or I am not taking any calls, you know why."

"Okay. Don't burn your candle at both ends, Thomas!"

The door slammed, and it was twenty minutes after eight. She had work to do.

Rocky unplugged the telephone wire that led to her computer and hooked it into her cordless phone jack. Then she forwarded all of her house calls to her cell phone. She cleaned her floors, changed her linen and lit some scented candles. As she was about to leave her house the cell phone rang but the number was blocked. "Hello?"

"Hey miss lady, what's up? I thought I would hear from you today," Marcus said.

"I only slept for a couple of hours after the plane landed this morning and then I went straight to work. Not to mention I have a heavy duty paper due tomorrow and I have been working really hard at it," Rocky said.

"I remember my school days."

"Where did you go to school, Marcus?"

"I went to Georgia Tech. How was your day sexy?"

"It was cool. Would you think I was corny if I told you I missed you?"

"No. Why?"

"Because I do, that's why."

"Yeah, well I have been thinking about you a lot lately. I have an exhibition game out there in a couple of weeks. I'll give you my room key at the game and you could wait for me there."

"I'm dying to see you," Rocky said.

"I can't stop thinking about that boat ride, and how I felt like my pops could hear me. You don't think I'm crazy do you?"

"No. Why would I? When I was out on the deck I let my hair go and thought about how much I missed my grandmother. And suddenly I felt like she was there pressing my hair. I could smell it— it felt like her fingers were running through my hair. At that minute I knew she still loved me and was watching over me. Now do I actually think it was her body shaped by the wind? Not necessarily, but I felt her presence."

"That's exactly why I am feeling you. You know exactly what I feel so you understand me. You better get an 'A' on that paper. You had me checking my phone like a fiend. What are you getting ready to get into?"

"Well, I have to pick up my girl from the airport, and then come back to my paper."

"I've also been thinking about the flight home this morning. Every time I step into a plane bathroom I will think of you. I can't wait 'til we can really get into each other on the sexual tip. If it was like that on the plane, I know it's even better in the bed."

Rocky looked at her watch. It was already nine-fifteen. She rushed out of the house clutching her phone to her ear. She smiled and talked to him the entire thirty-minute ride to the airport.

"Every time we get on the phone I feel like I'm in grade school. Marcus, remember being on the phone when you were younger and being like, 'you hang up first' then the person you were talking to would say, 'no, you hang up first'. And you would do shit like that until somebody fell asleep or your grandmother would pick up the phone and tell you to get the hell off."

"Yeah, I remember doing that." Marcus laughed. "But did you ever play slow jams on the phone?"

Rocky laughed, "I sure did."

"Well, I am turning in. I have practice first thing in the morning."

"I'll call you when I get up to workout. Bye"

"Speak to you later."

Rocky checked the time, again. *Mauri should be out in fifteen minutes*, she thought. She prepared her self mentally. Then she suddenly remembered something.

"Hey Ty, is your better half there?"

"Yeah, Rock. Hang on."

"Thanks."

"Kay, you have my other number, right? Call me on that phone because I'm forwarding all of my house phone calls to my cell phone and I am turning it off. I need a couple of calls to come through that line. If I know Mauri, he will probably try some slick shit like answering my phone so give Lita and Audrey my computer line number and tell them to call twice a night for the next couple of nights."

"You really think you're a fuckin' pimp, huh? You always cover all angles. Anyway, did you speak to Mr. Best today?"

"Yes, he just called me. He asked why I didn't call him today. My fingers were itching too dial, but I am trying my best to regulate."

"That's good. At least you're on top of it. You know what you doin'."

"I never know. I just plan day-by-day. Anyway, did I tell you Thomas wants me to move in with him? He said he would hold me down until I graduated. I wouldn't have to work or nothing. The only catch is I would have to be with him and him only."

"You must have some Kool-Aid in your pussy." They both laughed hysterically. "Ever since high school niggas would be buggin' after they got a taste of that shit." Kay paused. "Thank you, baby. But you are one of two that have tasted my shit," Kay replied to her husband. "Tyrone just said that I have Kool-Aid pussy, too and he wanted some right now."

"You still telling him you only fucked one man besides him. We both know you're five strong."

"Shut up!"

"Don't tell your husband about me and Marcus!"

"I won't."

"Are you sure? When too many people know about shit, it backfires in your face. This shit has to be on the down low until I seal the deal. All I need is three more months. You've got to work fast with this type of shit. Oh look, here comes Mauri now. Kiss the boys for me and tell them that I'm coming to get them on Saturday. I'll talk to you later."

Rocky jumped out of the car and straightened out her clothes. She took a deep breath as she approached Mauri. *You have to stroke his sensitivity, girl. He's on this marriage shit, so humor him, but don't say yes just imply it. Oh shit I almost forgot.* Rocky turned back toward her car. She went into the back seat and retrieved the two dozen lilies that Thomas handed her a couple of hours ago. She walked up to him and hugged him tightly.

"Hi, baby, these are for you," Rocky said as she handed him the flowers and kissed his fore head.

"Hey, Rocky, I miss your ass real bad, girl. Give me some more sugar."

Rocky stuck her tongue directly into Mauri's mouth. For that minute she forgot about Thomas and Marcus. He always stayed dipped no matter what. Rocky always thought that Mauri dressed for the city he was in at the moment. Whenever she went out to Detroit he was never dressed like he was at that moment. He had on a pair of faded blue jeans. He wore a Jacob watch with an orange band. His earrings were as big as small prunes. He wore a Nuggets jersey with the matching warm up jacket and a pair of white uptowns with an orange swoosh.

She suddenly felt depressed. Was this the only thing she liked about him, aside from his money? How could she possibly consider marrying this man? But she vowed to go on with the charade until her final decision was made. Or at least until he paid off her car.

"Yo, I had a time out there in L.A. I was chillin' with Shaq and Koby. I might open up a Mr. Maurice at Beverly Center."

"Mauri, I am so proud of you. You really give me a reason to want to pursue my education."

"I got a flick to give you of me and Stevie Wonder. I know how much you like that old cat. Let me tell you how I met him."

Rocky could not hear one word he said. Her thoughts were sudden and filled the car like a booming system. *FUCK*! *That damn Kay jinxed me. Shit, I got one angle way uncovered. How could I forget to switch pictures?* She thought quickly. "Baby, I know you're hungry. Let's stop to get a bite to eat," Rocky said.

"Rocky, I just sat down for five fuckin' hours. I haven't seen you in forever. You know what the fuck I want? I want some of that fat pussy of yours on my dick—"

Rocky zoned out again. *What the fuck am I going to do? Kay has my key, let me call her*. She dialed out. "Hey, Tyrone, my man is here from Detroit. I really want us to double date Friday. I think I'm going to reserve a table at Negril Village. You're going to roll, right? . . . Good. Let me speak to Kay . . . thanks."

"I just told Ty about Friday," Kay said.

"Listen, don't forget I am having 'girl talk' this Saturday. Make sure you invite *Too Sweet's sister*."

"Oh, shit, what the hell is wrong? That is definitely code blue. What is wrong? Um, um, let me think. I know the whole school had naked pictures of her." Kay said nervously.

"Honey, why don't you tell Kay about your PICTURE with Stevie Wonder," Rocky said. She passed Mauri the phone.

He pushed it away. "Ain't shit to tell. I took a picture with Stevie Wonder!" Mauri said. Rocky shoved the phone into his ear. "Hey boo, what up, though? I don't know what's up with your girl but I took a flick with Stevie Wonder in L.A. I'll see you Friday," Mauri said.

"Alright, Mauri. I'll see you sometime this week," Kay said. Mauri shoved the phone into Rocky's hands—

"Hey, girl," Rocky said.

"Okay, I know it has something to do with pictures, but what?" Kay said excitedly.

"I am going to need your *spare key* for Mauri this week," Rocky said.

"Keys? Pictures? You have to give me more," Kay said.

"I did give them back to you after *you checked on my apartment* last time Mauri and I went away."

Mauri looked at Rocky. "That was around your birthday. She probably gave them keys back a long time ago," he said.

"You got naked pictures up in your crib and you want me to go move them before you get home."

"Yes. I used to keep them behind the *cereal boxes* in the kitchen."

"Girl, why are you yelling at her like that I am sure she can hear you," Mauri said.

Rocky looked at Mauri and rolled her eyes. "Mauri, my phone keeps on breaking up!"

"Say no more, I am on it, girl!" Kay hung up the phone and ran into the bedroom where her husband sat on the bed with the boys, who were fast asleep. "Ty, Rocky lost her keys and she wants me to go and bring her the spare. I'll be back in a half."

"You know I know about your girl? Remember she was my nigga first. Don't try no stupid Rock Candy shit, you understand. If you are not back in forty-five minutes or less me and the boys are coming after you."

Kay rolled her eyes. "If y'all were that tight, you would know that we are two totally different people." Kay grabbed her purse and Rocky's keys out of the top drawer of their dresser.

She jumped into her car. She thought about the clues Rocky had given her over the phone. "Cereal boxes, naked pictures? I guess I'll figure it out once I get there."

Rocky and Mauri drove slowly along the Belt Parkway.

"So you had big fun in L.A.? I can't believe my baby is going to be big time out there."

"If I'm big time, you're big time, remember that. Why don't we go to your crib and start making my son tonight."

Rocky looked at Mauri and rolled her eyes. "You always know how to ruin a moment. I was so happy to see you."

"And now you're not? You act like we ain't' gonna have no babies together."

"Of course we are. As soon as we get married and I finish school. Then I will be your baby-making machine."

"That's what I want to hear. Well, at least we could practice tonight." Rocky just smiled at him and continued to drive. "Why the fuck are you drivin' so slow? You ain't even doing fifty."

"That's because there are always cops up in the cut on this highway. I do speed limit around here. I don't need any unnecessary points on my license."

Kay pulled up in front of Rocky's house. She hopped out of her car and looked at the keys. "Let's see. I think this one is for the front door." She slipped the key into the lock, but it did not turn. She spoke softly. "That must have been the key to her upstairs door. Let's try this one." She slipped the key into the hole and it turned with a soft click.

She opened her apartment and the familiar aroma of lemon-scented cleaner greeted her at the door. She mumbled out loud as she looked around. "Cereal cabinet. Too Sweet's sister and naked pictures."

She walked over to the mantelpiece and saw two photographs of Rocky and Thomas in a tight embrace. "OKAY. No naked pictures but pictures of her other boyfriends."

She scooped those up and went into Rocky's bedroom. She spotted a picture of them tonguing each other down at Thomas' office Christmas party. She picked that up, too. Then she went into the kitchen and opened the cabinets.

"This bitch is so organized it makes me sick. I bet she has all her cans arranged in alphabetical order." She opened each cabinet, one by one, and took a mental inventory. "Pastas, rice, sauces, soups and spices." She closed that cabinet and opened another. "Canned beans, canned fruits, canned vegetables. She closed that cabinet and then reopened it to confirm her suspicions. "I was just playin'. She really does have her canned goods in alphabetical order. I can't believe she is so meticulous." She opened one on the top. "Here we go— cereal." Kay looked around the kitchen and spotted a step stool. She grabbed it and placed it right in front of the cereal cabinet.

There was a huge blue box of Frosted Flakes, then an orange box of Honey Nut Cheerios, and last was a box of Raisin Bran. On the side of those boxes was an empty box of Chex. She looked behind the Chex box and saw several framed pictures there. Rocky had at least six photos of her and Mauri. Kay retrieved all of them, and placed the pictures of Rocky and Thomas inside the empty box. She noticed the last photo was of her and a tall, dark brown guy.

"This must be Marcus. Rocky definitely means business."

As Kay arranged the cereal boxes in a neat row she laughed out loud. "I can't believe this chick. She changes pictures as different men come in here. Boy, I swear she's kin to Iceberg Slim or Goldie."

Kay placed two photos on the mantle between pictures of her own kids, herself and Rocky, A huge picture of Rocky's grandmother sat at the center. She looked at the single photos of Rocky and thought about how pretty she really was. She placed one on the chest in the center of the room, one on the bedroom dresser and the last on the end table next to the bed. She rubbed her hands together then wiped her hands on her pants.

"I can't believe the original Mrs. Clean let dust pile up on that mantle-piece." She rushed into the bathroom and turned on the faucet. Rocky's towels were neatly arranged on shelves by color. She dried her hands with a paper towel, and dropped it into the wastebasket by the sink. She looked down and noticed a blue condom wrapper and two used condoms in it. "Yuck, that is so disgusting."

She removed the white plastic bag from the can, knotted it closed and took it to discard outside. She looked around to see if there was anything else she needed to do and walked out the door. She grabbed her cell phone as she made her way down the steps.

"Hey, Rocky. Mission accomplished. Your keys are in the recycling can on the top. I switched the pictures and placed the other ones in an old Chex box. I even threw away the bathroom trash with the nasty cum condoms and wrapper in it."

"What would I ever do without you?"

"I don't know, but I have to hurry home. Tyrone probably has his stopwatch going."

"So you left the keys in the can? Alright, call me tomorrow."

"The fight is coming on tonight. Speed it up a little, so I can give you some before I watch it," Mauri said.

Rocky picked up the pace and stared at Mauri from the corner of her eyes. *He really looks good today*, she thought. He smiled at her, grabbed her upper-inner thigh and squeezed it. Rocky flinched. She was still sore from her episodes with Marcus in the darkness of that morning and Thomas just hours before.

"What's the matter with you?"

"Nothing you just caught me off guard."

"Damn, I want some of that plump shit right der, girl. As soon as we get up in your house I want mine."

He squeezed her thigh and grabbed his penis as he spoke. Rocky felt disgusted. She tuned him out and focused on her thoughts instead. Mauri's voice became a mere mumble.

I really don't understand myself. I can't stand when Mauri talks to me like that, I feel so disrespected. But when Thomas talks that shit, I love it. She looked at Mauri and smiled as he laughed. *Maybe it's because I know his shit is whack,* she thought.

Mauri kept to his promise; as they soon as they walked through Rocky's door, he was all over her. He'd stepped out of his jeans and draws in one motion. He lifted up his shirt and wiggled his dick on her clothed thigh.

"Can we get in the door?" Rocky asked.

"We up in here. Take them clothes off," Mauri said.

She removed her shirt and unclasped her bra. *There's only one way to get him off of my back.* She thought. *If I fuck him, I will so have a black eye on my pussy.* Rocky quickly dropped to her knees and grabbed his dick. Before she could open her mouth he pulled his dick back, bent down and rubbed it on her breasts. He lost his balance and his penis ended up skidding along the side of her cheek and in her ear.

"Sorry! Sorry! But I want some pussy first then you could give me some head."

Rocky forced a smile and walked back into the bedroom. "Let me freshen up a little first," Rocky said.

"Fuck that, I want you just like you are." He sat up and pulled her toward the bed. He lay down and went into her dresser drawer. He looked at their picture and smiled.

"I like that picture of us. Let me take that one home and put it on my dresser. I don't have any recent ones of you and me together."

"Yes, baby." Rocky watched sadly as he retrieved a condom out of the drawer and put it on. She kept her face but skin deep she was hurting. "Hit it from the back, Mauri."

"Nah, let me eat that first." She lay down and let Mauri spread her legs open.

I didn't have enough time to shower after Thomas left. Marcus called, and I had to clean up, she thought as he dove in, face first. She wondered if he could taste the remains of Thomas' condom covered dick. She shut her eyes. Mauri came up for breath and spit hairs from between his lips. "You like that? You want more?"

Rocky licked her lips and put on the most passionate voice she could.

"I love it, but your baby wants you to hit it from the back."

"Turn your fat ass around."

She quietly did as she was told. As soon as his penis entered from the rear, she squeezed her eyes shut and clutched the sheets. His moans, groans and name calling bounced off her ears. She rocked back and forth and thought about a million and one things. After five minutes, she was numb and the soreness was gone. She fingered her clitoris in an attempt to arouse herself. As soon as she got herself going Mauri started to groan louder. Just as she thought it was done he pulled his penis out quickly.

"Ouch. What happened, daddy?"

"I want you to suck it. Then I want to squirt all over them pretty ass titties of yours."

Rocky went to work quickly. She pulled off the condom and placed her lips around his penis. He tried to sit up and watch her but she rested her weight on his stomach. She took long strokes sucking in her cheekbones as she worked. With in minutes he started to groan again.

"Move back I'm getting' ready to cum." He rubbed his penis on her nipples and ejaculated on her chest.

"God, that was good. Was it good for you? Sorry you didn't cum, you want to do it again?"

"No, baby. You worked me out. I think we could both use some rest. You know I have work tomorrow." She went into her drawer and pulled out a flesh toned negligee. It curved over her body like a second layer of skin. Mauri looked at her body, and kissed her softly on the cheek as she lay next to him. He flicked on the TV and turned to the fight.

"I missed you so much, Mauri, I'm glad you came to see me. Are you here on business?"

"My business is laying right here next to me." The phone rang and Mauri stared at Rocky. After three rings he picked it up quickly. "Hellowho'sthis?"

"Hi, can I speak to Candy?"

"This Kay?"

"No, it's Audrey. Who's this— Mauri?"

"What up though, cuz?"

"Nothing much. How long you been here?"

"I just got in tonight."

"Is Candy available?"

"For sure, hold on. Here, its Audrey." Mauri passed Rocky the phone and silently stroked his own ego as he stared at the ceiling and drifted off to sleep in deep thought. *Better not be any niggas callin' here while I'm here, and her friends recognized what's going down. Shit, better not be any other niggas calling here, period.*

"Hello?"

"Hey, girl, don't forget this weekend. You said you were having girl talk at your house. Let us know what we have to bring and I'll call everybody."

"Alright. I'll talk to you later. I'm kind of busy. I haven't seen my man in a couple of weeks," Rocky said then disconnected her call.

"Hey babes, what do you have planned for tomorrow? I guess we could—" Rocky stopped, listened to Mauri's snores and finally relaxed the muscles on her game face. She felt like kicking herself. She turned over, clutched her pillow and a sudden burst of depression filled her body. At first only her inner thighs had ached, but after Mauri, her vagina was sore inside and out. She had still been sore from her episode with Marcus, not to mention her double session with Thomas hours earlier.

The more she thought the harder the pounding in her head became. She had had sex with two men in one day only two times before. Rocky had vowed the second time that she wouldn't be caught in that predicament anymore. But here she was again, sore and sorry. Today she had officially broken that record, she slept with all three of her men within a 24 hour period. She looked up and thanked God for His blessing, as she often did at night, then turned over and fought for sleep. She was defeated many times by thoughts of rough sex; interludes that each beat her down and kept her wide awake. She tossed and turned, squeezing her legs together to ease the pain but that didn't help her wounded body and soul. Finally, she let it go by reciting the most basic rule of baseball. Three strikes.

"Holla ma ma. ¿Que pasa?" Yanick said as she walked into her apartment to find her mother sitting on the couch.

"¿ Adonde estabas?" Yanick's mother asked.

"Fui con, Joann," Yanick replied.

"¡Di ablo! ¿No sabes que ella es una pata? ¡Coño!"

"Ma, no es verdad. Joann no es una lesbiana."

The loud arguing woke Seven up. Both women went to handle the baby. "I got it, Ma!"

Yanick's mother walked off into her bedroom yelling, "She's a fuckin' lesbian," in Spanish over and over again. Yanick ran into her room and called Joann.

Joann rolled over and looked at her clock as her phone rang in the dark. "It's one in the morning, girl. After I dropped you off you told me you were going straight to sleep. Why are you still up?"

"Joann, my moms was cursing at me when I came in and shit. She wants to know what's really going on between us. She was screaming, 'Lesbian' in Spanish, on the top of her lungs for an hour. If I tell her she'll kick me out. They will disown me and try to take Seven away from me."

"I told your ass to come back to my house after the fight."

"But I had to go back for Seven. What am I going to do?"

"Tell them they don't know what they are talking about."

"I did, but now she got my father in on this shit."

Joann cleared her throat and wiped her eyes. "Listen, all you have to do is get a cover."

"A cover?"

"What's that punk ass guy's name that's always in your ass?"

"George? We're just friends."

"Yeah, but I know he likes you. Bring him around your parents like you started dating. This way we can still do us and they won't think anything about it."

"That's not right, Joann."

"If you guys are just friends he'll understand, right? Make that happen, so I can go to sleep."

"I love you, Joann." Joann sat up in the bed and grabbed her head. "Did you hear me Joey, I love you so much. I think I should just tell my parents so we can be together forever."

"You don't want to do that. You need your parents right now. You are almost finished with school. Who's going to watch Seven while you go to school? I can't because I am working all the damn time."

"We could get Seven a babysitter."

"She has the day sitter and that's enough. We don't want the baby in too many hands. Fuck that, I have seen too much shit come through command to let my little angel be in the hands of somebody we don't know. Just talk to George."

"I can't— because he doesn't know about us either."

"Well, don't tell him, just string him along for a second until we see where this relationship goes. "

"I love you."

"Get some sleep, princess." Joann hung up before Yanick could reply and dialed out. "Simone? I didn't mean to wake you up. Can I speak to Monique," Joann said.

"You didn't wake us up, we are just coming in from Tru's fight party. Your girl is really nice. You better hold on to that one," Simone said.

"Thanks," Joann said.

"Here, baby, it's Joann," Simone said.

"You were right. She is definitely a dime piece and she is really sweet," Monique said.

"Monique, she told me she loved me tonight," Joann said.
Monique screamed in delight and looked at Simone. "They're in love, Simone."

"No, *she* is in love, I don't love her. Not yet anyway. I'm not ready to be tied down. I—"

"Don't you ever stop? I knew you were going to pull this shit. Stick it out— don't curb her. You will crush that girl. Especially after all she's been through. She sat and talked to me for a minute about how safe she feels with you and how she thought she would never be in love again after Seven's father left her. You preyed on her vulnerability and now you're ready to bounce on her," Monique said in disgust.

"I didn't say that, but I ain't no one-girl woman. I don't know what's wrong with me," Joann said.

"You just ruined a perfectly good night. Don't say shit to me about dumping that girl. Just lay low, promise me that you will do that," Monique pleaded.

"I ain't ready to give that up yet. I like her and all but—"

"But nothing. Be good to that girl. You my girl and all but you really make me sick sometimes, I have to go."

14

Mama said knock you out

Mrs. Simmons looked up from behind her book and smiled as Tony approached her. "It's already fourth period. I was expecting you to be the first person in here to see me. You let an entire morning pass without giving your favorite teacher a shout out? How was your summer?"

Tony sat on the edge of her desk. "Fine, thanks. Mrs. Simmons, why did you call my brother and tell him that I was down with Brooklyn's Finest?"

"I don't know— maybe because you wear green everyday, have more friends than I have ever seen you with in school, and although you've always been a nice dresser, you have been flossing a lot lately."

"It's not true but anyway I just came here to tell you that I got accepted to Howard University's Pre-Med program, on a full scholarship, providing I keep my grades up this year." He pulled out the letter and passed it to her. "That is wonderful! My baby is going to college to be a doctor. You're my first student since I have been teaching high school to go to college. I'm so proud."

"Thanks, Mrs. Simmons."

"What about you?" Mrs. Simmons said sarcastically with a disapproving look on her face.

Tony turned to the front of the classroom to see whom she was addressing and smiled broadly.

"Kah, I really didn't think you were coming back. When did you get home?"

The two embraced tightly and gave each other strong pounds.

"Tuesday morning," Kahmelle sighed. "I couldn't take it out there too much longer. Besides, my moms says I should finish school. I am going down there for Columbus Day weekend and Thanksgiving with more bags, and you are coming with me."

Tony looked at Mrs. Simmons and smiled. "Alright, Mrs. Simmons, I'll see you later," Tony said.

She looked at Kahmelle as he left out her classroom with his arm around Tony's shoulder, playfully punching him in the side. "Stay out of trouble, you understand me, Tony."

"Yes, Mrs. Simmons."

The two walked through the halls laughing.

"I think I could swing that. I think my mother would really let me go if I got my brother to talk her into it, and promised him a pound out the deal," Tony said.

"A pound of what?" Kahmelle asked.

"Five hundred dollars. You was only out there for the summer. You all countrified and shit. Plus, that will probably kill my brother's suspicions about me running with the Finest."

"You know that we still gotta get jumped in?" Kahmelle asked.

"We ain't got to get jumped in— Sweat blessed us. All we have to do for initiation is hold up something by gunpoint— Yo, you missed the blackout, son. Kah, when the power went off Spam and I were on line at an ATM waiting on the technician to replenish the machine. You know that nigga Spam replenished our pockets. He butted the security guard then held up the technician at gunpoint.

"I saw that shit on the news, tell me that wasn't you?"

"Son, yes it was, son, even though Spam did most of the work. He kicked the door to the bank in, went behind the machine, and I held the security guard down. I came off with five G's from that alone. The Finest caught two 'Rent-a-Centers', three 'Foot Lockers'— we had the entire Fulton Mall in the smash. I got a closet full of sweat suits and sneakers tags and all. I'm not even going to front, I was scared as shit."

"Sorry I missed that. Did you come up with the plan for initiation though?" Kahmelle asked.

"I got that in the smash, too. Which reminds me; have you spoken to Camille?" Tony asked.

"Nope. Not since I've been down south. I don't even know if she's still pregnant. Dulce came out there twice. I'm feeling her now, fuck Camille," Kahmelle said in an angry tone.

"How she get out there?" Tony asked.

"Amtrak, I paid for her to come down."

"Word? That's peace. But for real, for serious, you need to check on Camille."

"I called when I got home, but she wasn't there."

"We might need her. What is your schedule looking like? You got a lot of classes?"

"Nah, duke. I got four classes this time around. I might just be graduating with you in June."

"Well, I am taking a couple of extra advanced biology and chemistry classes. I got to keep my skills up for Pre-Med school."

"Whatever nigga. I am taking my ass to class."

"Kahmelle, I thought I would never hear you say that. I'm out, my day is done at one-thirty."

"I got p.m. home room, so my day ends at three-fifteen. I am going to Spanish."

"That's what I'm talking about," Tony smiled.

"Is it lunchtime already, Ted?"

"Yes, it is. Where are you going?"

"I'm not really that hungry. I do need to make a few phone calls, though. You go ahead without me."

"Alright, Rocky. I'll see you later. Oh and by the way, I finally got a phone call from a guy looking for Marcus this morning. He didn't leave a name and wanted to know when late registration was over. I wrote the number down from the caller ID. Here you go."

"Thanks, Ted! You're the best." Rocky looked at the message slip and smiled when she saw Thomas' work number on it. She crumpled it up, straightened out her desk and jotted down a few notes. She picked up her phone and called home only to get the voicemail on her cell phone. "Damn, I forgot," Rocky said. She disconnected her call and re-dialed.

"Mauri? Your still in the house?" Rocky asked.

"I was just getting ready to leave here," Mauri replied.

"What time is your appointment?"

"One."

"You better hurry up. It's already twelve."

"I'll be there on time. What time you coming in?"

"I'll be in at five— dinner's at six."

"I'm cool with that. I'm going to meet up with my people and them from New York tomorrow, okay?"

"Okay, bye." Rocky looked at the list of students she had to call and was disgusted. *This shit is going to take me all week to finish. Not to mention all the other paper work I have to finish up,* she thought as she sighed loudly and picked up the phone. She turned on her computer at the same time and began to write up a welcome letter for the present semester.

"This letter should have gone out towards the end of August," she said to the computer screen. "Hello, is Jason Framchuck in? . . . Is this his father? . . .Do you know if he plans to attend school this semester? . . . Although the semester started it's not too late to register . . . Okay, thanks. One down, three hundred more to go."

As she picked up the phone to make her next call her cell phone rang. She looked at the caller ID and a smile came up from her toes and quickly changed her face. "Hey Marcus. You don't know how pleasing this phone call is to me. I am buried in work and I needed a breather."

"What the deal? I was just going to leave a message on your machine, and I got you. Are you at work?" Marcus asked.

"Of course I am," Rocky replied.

"I could have sworn I just called your house and shit."

"Oh, that is because I forwarded all the calls from my house to my mobile. I am expecting a very important call from Detroit." Rocky smiled broadly as she spoke, "I really can't wait to see you."

"I cant' stop thinking about you— Cozumel, Miami, Las Vegas; you keep on creeping in my mind."

"When's that exhibition game at the Garden?" Rocky asked.

"We play the Knicks next month. Then New York comes to us the following week. So work is stressing you out, huh?"

"I'm just swamped with work and I think about you all the time." She paused momentarily. "I can't believe I told you that. I am slipping."

"You're tripping girl. Just go with what you feel. I think about you a lot, too. Anyway listen, my moms is having a little dinner party for me the first week in November— a few close friends and family right after a game. I have one day off after the game. It falls on a Thursday night. I told her about you and she wants to meet you."

Rocky sighed and rolled her eyes. "I would love to meet your family," she said with a disgusted look on her face.

"So what's up with your house guest?"

Rocky's mouth dropped open and she placed her elbow on the keyboard. Two rows of lower case e's went straight across her screen before Marcus broke the silence.

"Candy. CANDY?"

"I'm here."

"So why didn't you answer me?"

"I'm sorry I was typing up a letter to the students prior to your call and I was just looking at it. What did you say?" Her brain *screamed, "How does he know?"*

"What's up with your homey you got staying with you?"

"She's fine. I have to figure out where I am going to take her this week. She is leaving on Sunday morning. Saturday I am hosting a girl talk so I'll probably run her through Skyy on Friday. DJ Goldfinger is spinnin', so the music will definitely be bangin'. My cousin, Drew, is the head bouncer there. So he could run us up through VIP and we could mingle with the stars all night."

"I heard about that spot. Why don't we step up in there when I come to NY? I'll bring some of my boys and you can bring some of your girls."

"That sounds good. Let me ask you something? When you were growing up did you spend a lot of time in the city?"

"Yeah, I played ball at the Rucker and for Riverside Church all throughout high school. All of my peoples were from uptown, even my barber; my house was just five minutes over the GW Bridge. Why?"

"You sound just like you are from New York and shit."

"Jersey isn't down south. How I am supposed to sound?"

"I know this chick from East Orange she sounds straight out the Carolinas."

"That's damn near South Jersey, Boo. I'm from Englewood. All those from Brick City, down to Jersey City and on my side sound like y'all."

"I wish I could see you sooner."

"Fly down here this weekend. I'll spot your ticket."

"I'm hosting the monthly gathering of my women's group this Saturday or I would have been right there. What about next Saturday?"

"That's a bet. I'll call you with your flight arrangements later. I've got to get back to practice. I didn't even expect to talk to you. I just wanted to shout you out on your machine and shit."

"I'll call you tonight when I get in from work."

"Alright. Later, Boo."

"Please don't call me that. I hate it."

"My bad. Later."

"Later." Rocky flipped her phone down and looked at her calendar. She picked up her office phone and dialed out. Her slender fingers stroked the keyboard with the swiftness and grace of Alicia Keys. Before the person answered the phone, she was done with her letter. "Hey, Kay."

"Hey, mama, what's up? How was your first night with Mauri?"

"You know, it wasn't all that bad. For the first time in a long time I enjoyed his company and we weren't even shopping. What's up?"

"I am hanging in there. I've got work up the cazoo. I just acquired a new account, so you know I'm pissed off about that. Ever since I passed that test and became official my work load has tripled."

"Well, you did get a raise and your own office. I wouldn't do too much complaining if I were you." Kay laughed lightly. "Listen to this. Marcus just invited me to dinner. How am I going to get out of it?"

Kay looked at the handset on her phone like Rocky could be clearly seen and then pressed it gently against her ear. "What do you mean? Fly your ass down there! Bon appetite, bitch." Kay looked out her office door after her last statement to see if any of her co-workers had heard her. She swiveled her chair, lowered her voice and cupped her hand around the mouthpiece of the telephone receiver. "I thought you would be—"

"No, Kay. He has a game in Jersey in November. His mother is having a dinner party for him at her house. He wants me to meet his mother."

"Oh shit!" Kay squeezed her forehead as if she were suddenly struck by a migraine. "You just gave me a headache, Rocky."

"I know, I know. What am I going to do?" Rocky sighed.

"Calm down. Just go. Don't wear anything tight or suggestive. And definitely don't be your usual over luxurious self. You have to be a straight-up plane Jane, you understand? Fuck it, don't even talk."

Rocky nodded slowly and whispered," Her head felt light. "I can't go!"

"You have to. If you don't he might be insulted. Plus, it's usually a good thing when a man wants you to meet his mother. Don't talk much—don't say a word. Just move your head to indicate yes or no, and laugh when everyone else laughs. Don't worry we'll come up with a strategic plan before that day actually comes."

"I'll talk to you later, Kay."

Kay swiveled her chair around and hung up the phone. She couldn't help but laugh at what the two of them had affectionately titled the curse of 'Too Sweet' over the years. Rocky sat an entire borough away and brooded over the same topic, however, Rocky did not laugh. Both women let their minds take them back eight years as they shared the same memory at the same time— one with a light and humorous heart the other with a heavy and melancholy heart.

Kay and Rocky each visited his stocky frame in their mind. Too Sweet was one of the few boys in high school that worked out and owned a car. His chocolate skin was always smooth, shiny and clear, with the exception of a series of stitches across the top of his right eye. His big, deep, dark brown pupils were surrounded by painted on eye whites. Those eyes that never seemed to show any fear revealed trouble and nervousness that particular day. He wore a three-quarter length, army green, goose filled snorkel and a pair of beef and broccoli Timberlands. The three of them stood in the middle of his living room.

"Ma, I want you to meet my girlfriend, Rocky."

Rocky stuck out her arm and shook hands with his mother. His mother stared at Rocky's jewelry as they shook hands. She took a quick glimpse at the gold tennis bracelet that hung loosely from Rocky's wrist, and the gleaming T and S diamond rings Rocky wore on her fingers.

"It is so nice to meet you. This is my best friend Kay," Rocky said.

"Hello. Pleased to meet you," Kay said as she waved at his mother.

"So, you're Rocky, huh? My boy has been going on and on about you for about a year now. You are sure a pretty little thing. Why don't the two of you sit down?" Her tone was disapproving.

The three teens sat on the couch and his mother sat across from them. She looked totally different from what Rocky imagined. Too Sweet and his mother were literally like night and day. She was a light complexion with huge dark circles under her hazel eyes. Her short brown hair was pulled back into a ponytail that wasn't much of a tail at all. It was more like a small bush. Strands that couldn't reach the back of the pony bush stood out all over her head like she had just rolled out of bed, although it was three in the afternoon. His mother was slim, and had once been beautiful but at present it looked like a combination of stress, drinking and lack of sleep robbed her of her beauty. She clutched a glass of brown liquid and sipped on it as she stared at them silently. She smiled, as she finally polished off the remains of her drink in one huge gulp.

"Junior, go get me another one," his mother said. She spoke quickly and evenly. Too Sweet disappeared into the back.

Rocky noticed a southern accent bounce off of her words. This would be a good way break the ice, she thought. "Where are you from, Mrs. Howell? You sound like you might be from the south." Rocky asked. A distant door slammed in the back.

"Why? I ain't dressed fly enough for you, Pretty? I look backwards or something?"

Rocky looked at Kay. 'Did you hear that?' flashed through both of their minds. Rocky couldn't believe what Too Sweet's mother had just said.

"No it's not that. My family is from down south and I thought—"

"I am from Orangeburg, South Carolina." Too Sweet's mother's tone cut right through Rocky's courage like a knife. Although Rocky was wounded she decided to give it another go. She unbuttoned her coat and placed it next to her. She put her bag on her lap, took a deep breath and set sail once again. Kay looked over at Rocky from the corner of her eyes, hoping she would keep quiet.

"Really! My family is originally from Columbia, South Carolina. My mother's side is anyway. Do you get to go down there and visit?" Rocky said enthusiastically.

"That's a really nice bag you got there. What is it, Gucci? What did that run you? Around four—five hundred dollars. And your coat is gorgeous. Is that suede or shearling? Rocky did not answer. She stared at Too Sweet's mother in disbelief. "IS IT A SHEARLING?" his mother yelled. Spit and brown liquid flew out of her mouth and all over her loud yells.

"Yes, it is, ma'am," Kay blurted.

His mother directed her attention toward Kay and looked her up and down slowly. Kay's fingers, wrist and neck and were bare. She looked at her nylon bookbag and wool peacoat then quickly looked at Rocky who wore diamonds, a shearling and a Gucci shopping bag.

"You said your kin from Columbia?"

"Yes."

"They from money?" his mother asked.

Rocky looked at Kay for help. She was scared to ask his mother what she meant by that statement. Rocky swallowed the saliva that had built up at the back of her throat, and looked for Too Sweet.

"Are they from money?" She persisted. This time she sounded annoyed.

"I don't know exactly what town in Columbia they are from, I have only been there a couple of—"

"Don't play stupid with me, you little gold diggin' bitch. Are they rich? Where the fuck you get all that shit you waltzed in here with. Five hundred dollar bags, diamonds from your fuckin' ears to your fingers.

You got my muthafuckin' boy out on the street selling them cracks to keep your ass looking fly?"

Rocky grabbed her coat and started to get up. Kay copied her actions. "Sit down!" his mother yelled. Rocky continued to put her coat on, but Kay sat quickly. "Sit your fuckin' ass down," Too Sweet's mother said. Rocky did as she was told. "Did Junior buy you all that? Shit, I know he did. Don't you have any morals, little girl? Don't you know what the fuck he is doing to get you that shit?"

She shot out of her seat and started screaming on the top of her lungs. She walked closer and closer toward her as she spoke, until she was standing directly over Rocky. She stood up to leave, but his mother shoved her back down onto the couch.

"You need to stop him and it. And y'all better not bring any muthafuckin' babies in here either. I know y'all fuckin'. You got my little boy whipped and hustling in the street. I don't see him for days and weeks at a time. Then, when he comes back, he drops fuckin' money on the table, like—"

Rocky went to get up again, and his mother stopped dead in her words. "Get up like that again and I will knock your ass out right here, you little bitch."

"MA!! What's wrong with you?" Too Sweet yelled as he came running into the living room with a brown bagged bottle and a clean glass. He looked at Rocky who sat on the couch red-faced and teary-eyed. Then at Kay, who dared not look into anyone's face; she just stared at the floor. His mother walked over to him and snatched the glass and bottle out of his hand. As she opened it she spilled half the bottle all over his coat. He tried to jump back but the liquor seeped into the arm of his jacket. The brown bag leaked onto the floor. Before he could wipe it off his mother grabbed him by the wet spot and yelled in his face.

"It figures you would be out there trickin' on some pretty red bitch. You just like your father. You need to stop this shit, Junior. I know what you doin', and how you doin' it. And if you are doing all that for her it ain't worth it. She ain't worth it."

He roughly pulled his arm from her clutches and stared into her face.

"Ma, you need to ease up on that brown and stop trippin'. I love Rocky. As soon as she graduates we gettin' married and we're moving to Atlanta so she can go to Spellman. You would like her if you—"

"Like that money hungry little broad? No mother in her right mind would ever like her." Mrs. Howell looked at Rocky as Rocky sat on the couch crying, with Kay holding her hand. She plopped back into her chair and drained the glass. She put the empty glass to her lips and threw her head back. Then she peeked through the bottom of her glass at Rocky and quickly put it down on the floor next to her chair. "Junior, it's a mother's instinct. That bitch ain't' about nothin'. No mother in her right

mind would ever get to like her. Mark my words, Junior. Not one. Not now or ever."

Rocky's work phone rang. She picked up her mouse and dragged the toolbar down to the spell check icon. Then she picked up her phone.

"Hello, this is Raquel Jones. How may I help you?"

"Hey, my Rock Candy, what are you doing?"

"Working through lunch. What about you?" Rocky couldn't catch the voice.

"Finishing touches on this case."

It's, Thomas, she smiled to herself.

"I was just calling to say that I missed you, and tell you that last night was altogether marvelous. I slept the entire ride to work. How is your recruiting going?"

"So far, so good, but until mid-semester it will be hard to tell."

"Alright as soon as things ease up for both of us we are going to do something special. Maybe we can fly down to the South of France."

"I'd like that a lot."

"Remember, if I don't call you tonight, it's because I am really busy."

Got it, bye." Rocky hung up the phone and continued her spell check. *What the hell am I going to wear to this dinner?* She thought. *I'm so not ready for this. I will fake sick.* She looked at her calendar. "Let's see. There's three weeks left in September, and the dinner is first week in November. I can pull it together before then."

She thought back to Too Sweet's mom and Poochie's mom. Now, there was Thomas' mom and even Mauri's ghetto fabulous mom. Not one man she was ever close to had a mother who liked her. They were not as blatantly nasty as Too Sweet's mom, but none of them liked her. No matter how hard she tried. Even Thomas' mother seemed to come across nicety. She was cordial but always stared at her disapprovingly from above the rim of her eyeglasses. When Rocky asked Thomas if his mother liked her after their initial meeting he replied, "I really don't think she cares for you too much at this moment. But you know how most mothers are with their sons." Thomas confirmed Rocky's feelings after the next encounter with his mother. "Mom doesn't like you. She said you act phony and that you are probably out for my money." It was always the same thing no matter how well she thought things went they never approved of her.

15

But what's love got to do with a little menage

Rocky felt the fall air trespassing on the warm air. Soon, her morning routine would be a chilly one, but she didn't mind. There would be fewer birds for her to see in the streets and she could pull out her fall wardrobe. As she jogged toward the High's field the familiar figure of Susan came into her view two blocks ahead. She inhaled deeply then broke into a fast paced sprint, using Susan as her focal point. She kept a steady pace and within seconds, she was beside her.

"Hey, stranger, how have you been?" Susan asked.

"How did you see me? I was getting ready to slap your perfect buns," Rocky replied.

"Instinct. Ever since I was mugged I have been extra observant. When you reached the corner I turned around and saw you coming. Where have you been?"

"I have been coming out later than usual, so I have been missing you," Rocky said.

Susan stared at Rocky for a few moments and her thoughts ran deep. *Is it safe to ask her advice? She is young. Well, I guess it's alright.*

"Why are you staring at me like that? Do I look different? Have I put on weight?" Rocky asked.

"Rocky, come do some Cardio with me. I want to talk to you."

Her tone seemed concerned. Rocky didn't know what to think. "What's wrong?" Rocky asked.

"Follow my lead. Forty jacks, three reps, twenty squats, three reps and twenty leg lifts. Let's go!"

Rocky grabbed Susan by the arm and gave her an inquisitive look. "Really? What is the matter?"

"There is really nothing wrong. Umm, I want to try something new with my husband. You know sexually. Not that I think you— well— I wanted some pointers on oral sex and anything else that might add some spice to an old relationship. I hope I am not imposing on you by asking you this?"

Rocky laughed and started to do her jumping jacks. Relieved, Susan started as well. "What exactly is it you want to know?"

"Well, do you lick the tip for stimulation? How do you keep your teeth from grazing the penis?"

"Practice on a banana. That's how I learned. I can remember my moms driving men crazy with oral sex when I was smaller."

Susan looked at her apologetically.

"Yeah, I know. But that's just how it was until I moved with my grandmother. Anyway, I never understood what it was. I thought it was utterly disgusting. Then I realized what my mother realized so many years ago. There is power in pussy and cooking. She had men falling at her feet. The better I got regarding my sexual relations with men, the more they did what I wanted. Once I added the oral to my repertoire, I wore the pants in all of my relationships."

"Let's go with squats— so practice on a banana?"

"Yep. It also depends on the size."

"Oh it's—" Susan cut herself short and became flushed with embarrassment.

"Well, open your mouth wider. Keep your mouth on the upper half and jerk the bottom off with your hand. Why don't you come to my girl talk this weekend? We talk about things of that nature a lot. My women's group has them every other month and the months in between we do lunch, the spa, or the theater— it will be fun. There are a couple of older women who come. Woo, my legs are burning, Susan. I am not going to be able to run."

Susan seemed more worked up from the conversation than the workout. "Am I embarrassing you? I am very in tune with my sexuality. I aim to get pleased and then please. You don't have to be embarrassed around me. I will give you my information and we can talk if you don't want to join us this Saturday night."

"I might just take you up on that offer. By the way, my husband warned me last week to tell you you'd better pay off your loan on that broach. That is something you do not want to lose. If you don't make the payment in full I can't help you get it back."

"I have been so wrapped up in this new relationship, I totally forgot. I will stop by after work."

Rocky stopped and started to stretch. "How did you know you wanted to get married? And how do you stay faithful after the years start rolling by?"

"What do you mean?" Susan asked nervously.

Rocky smiled. It seemed as if a scarlet A suddenly stood out on Susan's chest. "Let me find out you are having an affair! Are those tips I offered you for someone else?"

"Of course not! Don't be silly I am very happy with my marriage. I love him to death."

"MM hmm. Well, it makes me no never mind. I have two different guys asking me to marry them. The trouble is that together they make the perfect man. I can't choose."

Susan seemed more interested in getting involved with Rocky's affairs than disclosing her own.

"Well?" She smiled broadly. "Stick with the one that buys you the jewelry."

Rocky stopped to pound out a cramp that was having it's own workout session inside her thigh. It was extremely painful. She punched her leg where she felt the most pain. "Oh God, a Charlie Horse!"

"The squats probably provoked it. Stretch your leg out," Susan said.

Once she was able to stop the pain, she reached into her bag and pulled out a pink pen and Post-it. "Here is my information. Call me if you plan to attend, because I do gift bags at my get togethers and I need an accurate count."

Susan took the Post It from her, folded it up and placed it in her sports bra. She watched as Rocky placed her pen and paper back into a pink Gucci pouch. She noticed that everything she wore was pink, including her track shoes, velour sweat suit, sports bra and socks.

"Did you purposely have pink Post-its in that pink bag?" Susan asked.

Rocky nodded. "Rocky, you are absolutely too much. When do you find time to do this?"

Rocky stretched and talked simultaneously. "I have Post Its in nearly all of my bags. When I purchase them, the first thing I do before putting them away is place a Post It pad, lip balm, hairbrush and wallet inside that best suits its color. I am very organized. I think that's one of my biggest flaws. I plan and arrange everything. I even alphabetize my food cabinets. My girlfriend was just getting on me about that."

"You're probably a clean freak too, huh?"

"Something like that," she said as she looked at her watch. "I have to go get my work out on. I am going to jog two miles around the track. Hopefully we will finish about the same time and we could leave together. If not, make sure you call me and let me know if you're up for this weekend, okay?"

"You bet. As a matter of fact, count me in. I will definitely be there."

After running Rocky hustled home and got ready for work. Oh, how she hated Thursdays, because they just weren't Fridays.

Later that afternoon at work Rocky felt at ease. She had finished a day's work by the middle of the afternoon. She leaned back into her chair and was about to pick up the headset on her phone when her boss called to her. "Rocky? Are you finished with that list?"

"Yes. I have made all of my contacts. Everyone that is in, is in. I am still calling the same list of people to see if they want late registration. I've mailed class schedules and late registration dates," she called.

Her boss swiveled his chair toward her voice and shuffled through some paper work that Rocky had left on his desk. "Rocky, make sure you stay on top of this for me. You know this time of year is always rough.

And make sure you give me a schedule of your classes for this semester. Are you taking any day classes?"

"Two. I have already revamped my schedule, so don't worry."

"I don't know what I am going to do without you when you leave us in January."

Rocky ignored him and continued her work. Just as she went to dial out the phone rang. She answered it. "Good afternoon admissions and late registration, this is Raquel Jones speaking. May I help you?"

"Hey, Rocky, what's up?"

"Work. What's up with you, Thomas?"

"Monday I am having a scheduling conference with the judge for my current case. This Saturday I'm meeting with co-counsel to make sure we are all on the same page. It will take all day, so can you do me a favor?"

"Yes, baby."

"I want you to be home waiting for me that night. I want you to cook a big dinner. I want West Indian food and I want one of your infamous massages. Even if you don't feel like cooking, I just want to come home to you, okay?"

"Well, I have my women's group meeting at my house this Saturday, but that is at seven. I could be there about ten, with dinner waiting."

"That's perfect, because I generally get in around that time after a long drudging day with my co-counsel. Afterward, I'm sure we will all go out for drinks. So, I probably won't come in until after ten-thirty. Your shit was so wet, god damn. I'll talk to you, if not later, mañana, sweetie."

"Okay, ba-bye. Corny muthafucka," she muttered under her breath as she slammed the phone down on its receiver. She looked at her list and began to dial out, again.

Joann leaned against the steel gate of the bodega and looked at her watch. She automatically looked down at her cell phone to double-check the time. It's Friday, it is almost quitting time and Yanick has not called me all day. She dialed out

"Hey, Yanick. How are you, princess?"

"I'm fine. What's up?" she said pleasantly.

"Let's go catch a movie after work today."

"Actually, I am going to hang out with George in a few."

Joann opened her eyes wide and forced a smile. "Oh, word?" she laughed. "Where are *you* two going?"

"We are on our way to the movies, and then we're going to stop downtown to get a bite."

"You have been hanging out with this guy an awful lot lately. You aren't fuckin' him are you?"

"What's wrong with you? Of course not I love you, Joann."

"Yeah, but why you with this guy all the time?"

"What are you talking about, Joey? I used to be with you all the fuckin' time. You're the one who suggested I start hanging out with him and it seems like you have been brushing me off lately. Every time I want to come over or go out you claim that you are doing overtime. Every time I tell you I love you, you change the subject. What do you want me to do? Plus, my parents stopped bugging me since he's been coming around."

"You know how freaky your ass is. Just don't fall and let his dick slip up in your mouth. Hello?"

Rocky left the campus at six and hustled down the block to Flatbush and Nostrand Avenues, otherwise known as The Junction. She stopped into the liquor store and came out with two big, light blue plastic bags. She stopped in the 99 cent store and came out with four huge, black, plastic bags. She was off of work at six, but did not reach home until nine o'clock that night. After helping Mauri pack his bags, for his seven a.m. flight, they immediately began to stuff gift bags and create an agenda for Saturday night.

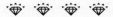

At the station house, Joann changed into a pair of jeans and a white T-shirt.

"Yo, D what time is your tour over?"

"I ain't out of here until ten, why?"

Joann threw her car keys to him. "Let me hold your car. I will have it parked out front. If you need my truck, it's yours."

"Bet," he threw his keys to her. "Yo, I am parked –"

"I passed your car when I came in. I know where you're at." Joann hurried out of the station house, hopped into his blue Toyota and headed straight for Applebee's. As she drove, her anger began to get the best of her.

Fuck that. Yanick hung up on me over three hours ago and hasn't called back yet. If I walk into that muthafuckin' restaurant and that fuckin' guy has his hands on my piece I am going to beat the shit out of both of them, she thought.

Joann screeched up to the corner of Dekalb and Flatbush and parked directly across the street from Applebee's. She posted a police department permit in the windshield, got out and slammed the car door.

She crossed the street and entered the restaurant. The hostess recognized Joann as a regular customer.

"Hey! How are you today? Where's your left hand?"

Joann smiled. "I'm looking for her now. Have you seen her?"

"No, and I have been here for about two hours. Should I get you a table while you wait?"

"No, thanks. I'll come back." Joann walked back to the car. Her phone rang as soon as she sat down. Joann picked it up on the first ring. "Yeah, where are you?" she snapped.

"I'm home. Where are you?"

Joann punched the steering wheel. It was Sammy, and Joann had been trying to avoid her call all day. "I'm in my car downtown. What's up?"

"You."

"Really? How come?"

"You haven't called me since I left your house last week. What's up with that?"

"Nothing. I have just been stressed out lately. You know how it is."

"I sure do, Joann. Why don't you let me ease some of your stress?" Sammy asked seductively.

"Why don't we hook up this weekend or something? Sunday is my day off, so maybe we could hang out tomorrow night," Joann replied in an uninterested tone.

"Call me when you're ready. She sighed. "Be safe, Joey," Sammy said.

"Thanks, good-bye." Joann disconnected the call then flicked on the car radio and adjusted the seat back in the car. She looked at her phone and smiled when she saw she had two missed calls. As she scrolled through, she became instantly depressed to find out they were Sammy's. When she looked up into the restaurant she thought she could see the couple seated near a window facing Dekalb Avenue. They stared at each other and were laughing. Neither saw Joann as she approached or entered the restaurant. She sat next to Yanick and placed her arm around her.

"What a surprise seeing you two here. Hi, I'm Jo, you must be 'Hor-hay'." Joann extended her hand and smiled. "So, how was the movie? Did you enjoy it? Yanick order me a drink, you know what I like."

Yanick tried to slide over trying to get as close to the window as she could, but the more she wiggled and squirmed, the tighter Joann's embrace got. She finally sat still and gave up. Her face became red from a mixture of embarrassment and anger. Joann stuck her face into the side of Yanick's head and inhaled deeply.

"I just love the smell of your hair. Especially when you sweat. So, 'Hor-Hay', is it?" Joann asked.

"George will do just fine."

"So, George, what do you do for a living?"

"I just started college, at Hunter, and I work part time at Macy's."

A waitress passed their table and looked at them strangely. Using her knee, Joann nudged Yanick under the table. "There's the waitress, order my drink," Joann said.

"That's not our waitress Joann," Yanick said.

"Excuse me, miss. Could you come here for a second?" Joann spoke loudly and tightened her grip on Yanick when she noticed how the waitress looked at them. "Do you think you can find our waitress so my girl can order me a drink?"

"Why don't you just let me know what you are drinking miss and I will bring that back for you."

Joann nudged Yanick's thigh with her leg and Yanick rolled her eyes.

"She'll have an Apple Martini," Yanick said flatly.

The waitress smiled and walked away. George watched the waitress walk toward the bar and gossip with other restaurant staff as she pointed at their table.

"How old are you?" Joann said as she broke his stare.

"I just turned twenty."

Joann was obnoxiously loud when she spoke. "Twenty, and you just started college? I don't have any competition over here."

"George, could you please excuse us? Joann, move over. Let's go to the bathroom, now!"

"She just can't get enough of me," Joann said as she smiled at George.

Yanick started to shove her off of the seat as the waitress came with the bright green drink. Joann collided with the waitress and the drink spilled on Joann and the table.

"Shit, Yanick, look what you did!" Joann yelled as she shook her shirt away from her body. It looked like she had been slimed.

"What I did? You're the one in here acting like a fuckin' fool," Yanick yelled.

"I'm sorry. I will clean this up quickly and get you another drink," the waitress said.

Within minutes there was a small busboy at the table with a large, dingy cloth. He picked up glasses and cleaned the table quickly.

While Yanick and Joann were in the bathroom George sat and thought. *What's up with that? I wonder if they are really involved. They prob'ly be burning rugs and shit. No way! After all these years of friendship she can't go that way. Nah, it can't be. Just when I thought I had her. Later for that, I ain't giving up that easy, I am going to make her mine. She's letting this dyke bitch get in her head. Once I get my head in her, it's a wrap. Hey, maybe they will let me watch— or maybe we could swing a threesome— fuck that, she's going to be my girl and my girl only.*

Yanick slammed the bathroom door and stood with her back against it.

"What's wrong with you?" she asked.

"Nothing," Joann replied.

"You come up in here and make a scene. This shit is cute to you?"

"I just wanted to see the guy that's trying to move in on my territory."

"I am not your fuckin' territory. You aren't trying to get serious. You won't even define our relationship."

"What are you talking about?"

Yanick folded her arms, rolled her neck and sucked her teeth to say one word. "Commitment."

"Commitment?" Joann asked.

"That's right, Joann. You have been avoiding me lately, and you told me to use George as a cover. This was not my fucking idea."

"Yeah, well now I am telling you to scrap him or else."

"Or else what, Joe?"

Joann looked away from Yanick and moved from in front of her. "Or else I walk."

"I ain't scrapping shit until you let me know something. Are you going to be my lover or what? I love you. Every time I tell you that you just brush me off. You hardly see the baby anymore. You've barely been around the past couple of weeks. You actin' like a regular nigga now. Fuck that. If you don't pay more attention to me maybe I will walk."

Yanick turned around to open the bathroom door and Joann pinned Yanick into it. She pressed her side up against her rear end and let the outline of her pistol rub against the crack of her ass. Joann grabbed a handful of Yanick's thick tresses and kissed her neck gently as she continued to rub the gun on her thick behind.

"Joann, stop it," Yanick whispered.

"Turn around and face me." Yanick turned around and looked into Joann's eyes. "I have only been distant because I haven't felt this way about a woman in a long time. I just don't want to get hurt. I always keep up my tough cop exterior, but the truth is, I think I am falling in love with you and I am scared."

Before Yanick could answer Joann kissed her passionately. Yanick felt a rush, poured her heart into that kiss and let all her weight hit the door. Joann placed her leg between Yanick's thighs and Yanick instantly opened them. She twisted her body to the side so the gun could gently rub her vaginal area. Yanick started to moan. Joann lifted her skirt, slid her thong to the side, and grabbed a handful of Yanick's warm skin. Yanick guided her hand to her vagina and pushed Joann's middle fingers inside.

At that instant someone trying to enter the bathroom thrust them both forward. "OUCH!" Yanick shouted. Her body jerked forward and Joann's fingers lightly scratched her insides.

"One minute," Joann called out.

Yanick stayed against the door and hurried to fix her clothes and adjust her thong. Joann fixed Yanick's hair and kissed her lips. Yanick darted into a stall leaving Joann standing at the door. She opened it, smiled and walked out. The woman shook her head and went into a stall. Yanick waited to hear the woman urinating, then ran out of the bathroom, and slowly walked back to their table. As she passed the bar all the waitresses stopped talking and looked at her. Yanick looked ahead and saw George's frame rise in front of Joann. Yanick sensed tension.

"Keep your dick away from my girl. I'm stroking that now, you heard?"

George stood up. "What if I don't, dyke? I've been dickin' that shit down for a–"

Joann cleared her throat making a loud 'hocking' noise. She threw her head back and quickly jerked it forward letting out a large wad of spit on George's face. The thick phlegm splat on his eyelid and dripped down his face. Without hesitation he harshly wiped the phlegm off and swung at her, but Joann jumped back and Yanick grabbed his arm.

"Lick that spit up, that's the only taste of Yanick's pussy you're ever gonna get."

"George, please no," Yanick cried. "Let her look like the ass, I'm beggin' you. She's being ignorant. Leave it alone," Yanick said as she placed her body in front of his and used every bit of her strength to hold him back.

"Smell this, son." Joann stuck the same finger she used to fondle Yanick's pussy in front of George's nose.

"Now *that's* the closest you will get to sniffing Yanick's pussy. We don't do menage a tróis." She looked at them with a vindictive smile as Yanick struggled to hold George back. "You know, I'll always take care of you, Yanick," Joann said as she tossed a fifty-dollar bill on the table and waltzed out of the restaurant.

Staff and patrons stared at Joann as she walked out. Once she was out the door, they turned around and gazed at George and Yanick.

"What's up? You're fuckin' her? Are you nuts?" George yelled.

Yanick was silent she looked down at her untouched plate. "Yanick, you tell me everything. Why wouldn't you tell me this?"

"I didn't know how to. I was embarrassed, I guess."

George ran his hands through his hair. As his hands raked his hair, it fell right back into place. They stared at each other. His small brown eyes had no expression. She extended her arm and rubbed the side of his cheek gently.

"I don't know what you are trying to pull here, but it's no secret how I feel about you. I know you know. After six years of friendship you have to know about all the feelings I have for you. When you started talking to Angel, I just knew I wouldn't have a chance to tell you how I felt. When he dipped, I wanted to step up. I figured you needed time to heal, but I never stayed too far away. I stayed close just waiting for that one moment. These past days have meant so much to me. Walking with

Seven in the park, movies, dinner, you helping me with my homework—
I thought you were coming around."

"George, these past weeks have been nice for me too, but—"

"Know this Yanick, I ain't givin' up on you. We are going to be
together. Come on, let's be out."

He got up, grabbed her hand and yanked her body into his. He grabbed
her face with both hands and forced a kiss on her. She pushed him off of
her and stared at him wildly. The waitress rushed over to the table as
George and Yanick stared awkwardly at each other.

"Are you ready for your check?"

"Everything is taken care of," George said as he pointed at the fifty on
the table and walked off.

She picked it up and ran over to the group of waitresses that had
assembled at the bar. "Their stuff came up to thirty-two dollars and they
left me a fifty. I think she's gay and old girl that just left is her lover and
caught her cheating with this guy," the waitress said.

"I think you're right. 'Cause they are always in here together," the
hostess agreed.

"And the chick that left was like, my girl is going to order me a drink,
and she smelled her hair," another waitress added.

"Yanick, I didn't mean to-" George began.

"It's okay, George. I didn't mean for you to find out about Joann and
me like that. I like you, too. I am just a little confused right now. Please,
don't be mad. I need you." She hugged him tightly and placed a gentle
peck on his lips.

*She said she likes you, and she's confused. I got something that will
knock the confusion out of her. I just have to wait until the right
moment— you see what happened when you waited for the right
moment? Someone stole your shine. You better make your moment, G.
Fuck that, take your moment George*, he thought.

Joann stared intently and motionless from inside the car as they kissed
and embraced each other tightly. She called Sammy and sped off.

16

I could teach you but I'd have to charge

"Welcome, everyone, I am glad that the entire group is here today and in good health. Okay, ladies, everyone open your bags. Inside you will find three Post Its. Two of them have the questions you are responsible for answering in accordance with today's theme that we all voted for via e-mail so don't point any fingers. You must answer honestly and to the best of your ability. Today's theme is how to please your man and yourself simultaneously. We also want feedback on last month's topic of the importance of friendship. Dues are due today and Andrea will collect those. Silver bags, your team is up first. Gold bag's go second."

Rocky walked over to the mantelpiece and placed four extra bags on the table. She joined the young women that sat in her living room, and rummaged through a bag she had set aside for herself.

"Oh, yes. The third Post-it contains what you have to act out for charades, and there are two paper dicks in your bag. The one with the safety pin needs to be worn. Now if anyone here says 'fuck', or crosses her legs, her pin is subject for removal."

"WHAT?" Susan said out loud as she pinned a penis onto her blouse.

One of the ladies on the opposite side of the circle called across to Susan. "Fuck' is the secret word. And crossing your legs—"

Rocky casually walked over to the woman speaking and grabbed the pin out of her hand before she could finish pinning it on.

"No fair!! I was just—"

"I know. I was just giving her a visual," Rocky laughed as she handed the pin back. "Continue."

"Crossing your legs is the secret motion. If you say it, anyone can take your dick— um your dick pin and the person with the most pins at the end of the meeting gets a prize."

"I get it," Susan said smiling.

"The second penis is for the last game we are going to play which I'm going to leave as a surprise. One last thing— I would also like to introduce a visitor and hopefully a new member to our group. Everybody give a warm welcome to Susan."

All fifteen women offered warm and friendly salutations. Rocky watched as everyone rummaged through their bag with excitement. They all felt like kids at a birthday party shaking down the piñata and filling their loot bags. Rocky had filled each of them with a banana, travel-sized shampoo bottles, perfume samples and small shot bottles of either

Hennesy, Alize or Tanqueray. Rocky placed bite sized chocolate bars, flavored condoms and miniature back massagers in each bag. She smiled at how cheerfully her friends and acquaintances reviewed each novelty. Each bag had cost her about twenty dollars to make, but the money didn't matter to her; she knew that whenever it was her turn to host their girl talk meetings, they were always the best.

"Ahhhh, the banana is in here. You know what that means," one of the women said holding it between her thumb and forefinger, laughing and stomping her feet on the ground.

The ladies loved when their women's group met at Rocky's house, twice a year. She always went the extra mile. Rocky had fun questions, fun games and everything was well organized. There were never any excuses made for the gatherings at Rocky's— she could always expect 100% attendance.

"Let's get this party started right! Everyone take out the question written on the pink Post-it. They are all numbered. Let's start with silver number one," Rocky said.

A slim, fair skinned woman in her early twenties stood up and walked to the middle of a circle of white folding chairs. She had a short, naturally curly haircut. She glanced at the small pink Post It she held between her fingertips and smiled as she read it out loud.

"What is the whackest sex you ever had and what did you end up having to do to satisfy yourself?"

All the women in the room commented among themselves. Some laughed, others clapped their hands and some sucked their teeth. Rocky stood up and cleared her throat.

"I'm sorry Audrey, I am going to interrupt you for a second. Remember, WHAT HAPPENS IN CANCUN . . ."

" . . . STAYS IN CANCUN," the entire room full of women replied, with the exception of Susan.

"We are not here to judge anybody or turn our noses up. We are here to learn from our experiences— and as women we often share the same ones. Finally, only ten of us have paid for our night out on Broadway, which includes a ticket for The Vagina Monologues and dinner at Carmine's. Thank you. And without further ado or any more interruptions, here's Audrey."

Audrey smiled at the women around her. She watched as Rocky took her seat next to the White woman with the extravagant jewelry and wondered, as did many of the other women, who she was.

"About two years ago I was dating this guy. He was the perfect gentleman, good job, decent family and a good kisser. Anyway he stuck around for the four month waiting period that I give myself for sleeping with someone I am dating, without a problem."

Andrea, one of the women in the group interrupted. "You should have known he was a whack fuck from that alone."

Kay and Audrey leaped over and grabbed at Andrea's pinned penis simultaneously. Kay ripped it clear off of the pin and attached it onto the one she was wearing.

"Damn, I can't believe you got me already. You better watch your back because I am going for blood, Kay," Andrea said as she touched the penisless pin.

All the other women laughed. Susan, who had been quite uncomfortable when she walked in, laughed until her face turned pink.

"On the first day of the fourth month, we went out to dinner and the movies and I suggested that I wasn't ready for the night to end. So he got us a room at the Marriott downtown. To make a long story really, really, short, he had a half of dick. I mean it was thick as shit, but it was a stump. It couldn't have been more than three inches long. The condom hung loosely off his dick like a pair of saggy socks. When he stuck it in, it was good for three seconds flat, but after that it was horrible."

Women laughed, slapped their thighs, hollered and giggled.

"Well, what did you do to please yourself?" Rocky asked winded from laughter.

"I told him to go down on me and that was decent," Audrey replied.

"Number two, silver," Rocky called.

Susan clutched her number and hesitantly stood up. She looked down at Rocky remorsefully. "I'm sorry, I don't think I could—"

"Please, girl. Go ahead," Audrey called out.

"There's no reason to be shy," another woman said softly.

The women in the room smiled because at one time they had all been virgins to the circle.

"Well, here we go." Susan said as she stood. "Where is a good place to take your man/husband out locally, that you can have just as much fun as if you were on vacation." After she read her question she let out a loud sigh of relief. "I'm married, and I often treat my husband for a day at the spa. Seriously, the first time we went he was really reluctant, but after his full body massage, he loved it. I even talked him into getting a pedicure and manicure. There are several around the city. Some of them are pretty pricey, but it is worth the money."

The women went on in this manner for about two hours or so. The entire night was filled with laughter and loud chattering. They enjoyed a game of charades with the eighties theme immensely. The silver team won by one point as they stunned the opposing golds with a reenactment of 'Purple Rain'. Near the end of the evening Kay was wearing eight pinned penises and won a chrome picture frame that had the word friends engraved all over it.

"Now it is almost time to close. Andrea will be collecting dues of twenty-five dollars right now. Our mission for this month's theme is to try something new with your mate that will stimulate you. I am not just talking in the sexual sense either. Is there anyone that made amends with a friend they have not spoken to in a while, after last month's theme?" Hands went up. "Good. Would you care to tell about it?"

Three women gave their account of how they tried to mend broken friendships. There were two successes and one failure.

"We have two activities left. The first is back by popular demand and was voted on eleven to three online. Since our topic dealt with sex, you guys wanted me to facilitate, as one of you called it via Internet, ' The Oral Sex Workshop'."

One lady stood up holding her banana by her mouth as she spoke." That would be my e-mail," Lita said.

"I'm going to start charging five dollars a head to teach you ladies. Get it a— head," Rocky said. Everyone laughed. "You ladies ready?"

"YEAH," they all screamed.

"Take your bananas out of the bag and peel them. Kay, go get the garbage can out of the bathroom and collect the peels for me, please. If you choose not to partake in this activity it's okay. The key is to open your mouths as wide as you can. If you skin the banana with your teeth that is no good. Now remember I am no expert."

"Yeah, right," Kay called out. Everyone laughed

Most of the women in the room sat and emulated performing oral sex on a banana, as instructed by Rocky including Susan, who got a kick out of the entire night. She planned to try out her new oral techniques as soon as possible.

The night ended with a game of Pin The Cock On The Jock. Each woman had a penis with a piece of adhesive on the back of it. Rocky pinned up a huge picture of Usher on the inside of the door to her apartment. The ladies were blindfolded, spun around and expected to pin Usher's dick on. The winner won a small wooden clock. When the games were over everyone scuttled around trying to help Rocky clean up the apartment. By nine forty-five everyone was gone except Susan and Kay.

"Rocky, you just threw a really nice party. I gave my twenty-five dollars to Andrea and am now an official member. Honestly I had an extremely good time, and those party bags, and prizes— you must have spent a small fortune on those items," Susan said.

"Actually I didn't. The bags cost me like twenty dollars a piece. Those prizes were all under ten dollars. I love putting together things like this."

"She sure does. You should have seen how she arranged my baby shower. My son is already six years old and people are still talking about it," Kay said.

"You have kids, Kay? You look so young. How many do you have?"

"One biologically, but my brother has custody of his son so my nephew spends a lot of time with me."

"What line of business are you in again, Rocky? You probably missed your calling. Perhaps you should have been a party planner."

"I recruit for a coll—" Rocky was stopped in mid-sentence by a broad smile that came out of nowhere. It was almost as she didn't produce it.

"I hope that the banana thing was a start for you," Rocky said to Susan.

Susan smiled. "I'm going to try it when I get home. I haven't done anything like that since before my marriage, and even then I only tried it once or thrice. I come from a different day. Is there anything else I can help you with here?" Susan asked.

"No, thank you," Rocky said.

"Then I'm off."

"Did you give your e-mail information to Andrea?"

"Yes, I did."

"E-mails from the next host will go out regarding the time and location of our next girl talk. And your vote is needed for the theme of our next meeting. If you want to join us for our night on Broadway—"

"I gave in the money for that as well. I guess I will see you in the park tomorrow?" Susan asked.

"Bye, Susan, it was nice having you," Kay smiled.

"Bye Kay. The pleasure was all mine," Susan replied.

"I won't be out tomorrow, but I will definitely be there Monday morning. Will you be all right getting home?" Rocky asked.

"I called a car while you were bidding your farewells. It should be outside," Susan said.

Rocky walked to the window and looked outside. There was a shiny black Town Car parked in front of her house. "It's there. I'll see you Monday," Rocky said. Susan waved and shut the door. Her footsteps could be heard all the way down the stairs. Way before she reached the bottom step Kay questioned Rocky.

"Rocky? Who the hell was that? I know she isn't one of your co-workers."

"I workout with her in the mornings— well, we workout in the same park. Her husband owns the Brooklyn Jewelry Exchange. SHIT! I forgot to pay off my pawn!" Rocky yelled.

"You fuck around and lose that piece of history, if you want to."

Rocky ignored Kay. She continued to pack up the twenty chairs she had rented and stack them outside her door. Kay helped her.

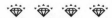

Pointy heels sank into Joann's mattress and she smiled as the ass wiggled in her face.

"Damn, Sammy, where did you learn to move like that? You sure you don't work nights at the club?" Joann asked.

Sammy bent down and spread her cheeks and Joann looked toward the dresser at the photograph of Yanick and Seven. Sammy stood upright.

"Joann. You are not serious? I am seducing you and you're not even paying attention to me. Maybe I should leave," Sammy said with an attitude.

"Samantha, don't do that. I'm sorry. Come here."

Joann kissed Sammy's neck, and rubbed her big breasts. Sammy lay straight on her back and pulled Joann on top of her.

"You know what, babes? You wore me out last night. Let's me get some shuteye, and we could pick this up in the morning. Okay, princess?" Joann said.

Sammy smiled and kissed her cheek gently, "Okay."

Joann turned her back and lay on her side thinking about Yanick. *Why won't she call?* She thought.

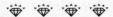

As Rocky placed the last four chairs outside her door she opened a closet and pulled out a big plastic bag. "This is a special gift bag I made for Ma," Rocky said.

"You know Rocky, she was right," Kay said.

"Who was right? About what?"

"Susan. You are an excellent party planner. Your ideas, packaging, decorations; you *should* think about opening your own business."

"Nah, this is something I like to do in my spare time. I wouldn't want to do this everyday, all day. You want to take some of this soda home for the boys? Tell them their Goddie sent it and she is sorry we missed Chuck E-Cheeses. Here, I bought these for them when I was shopping for the gift bags. I almost forgot."

She handed Kay two huge jars shaped like basketballs. They were made of a clear orange glass. She had filled them with the left over candy from the gift bags she had made. She also added pencils, erasers, a pack of markers and two twenty-dollar bills in each ball.

"Rocky, these are beautiful."

"Tell them I am sorry. The money is to buy their Halloween costumes. Are you hungry? I made some oxtails for Thomas, and you are getting ready to drive me over there before you get home."

"No, thanks. I have eaten enough here. I am ready to go whenever you are."

"Okay, let me change my clothes."

As Rocky was in the back changing her clothes, Kay thought about all of the things they had been through as friends. She laughed inside about the curse of Too Sweet and the first time Rocky came to her house for

Thanksgiving dinner. Her mother had served red snapper with the head on it, and Rocky nearly gagged. Kay was all the family that Rocky had. She looked inside of the gift bag that Rocky had made for her mother and there was bubble bath, prettily packaged herbal teas, a mug and a large sized vibrating back massager. Kay was suddenly warm inside. Anything the boys wanted, Rocky was there to purchase. Any emergency at school, Rocky would sometimes be there before Kay or Tyrone could reach.

"How do I look?" Rocky's entrance in garters and heels shattered Kay's tranquil thoughts. She wore a pink lace thong and bra set and a leather coat that reached her knees.

"You know, I don't understand how anyone so thoughtful could be so raunchy." Kay held up the gifts for her mother and boys as she made her last statement. "Look at you. Are you really going outside like that?"

"Yep. You would never know unless I unbuttoned my coat."

"How 'Boomerang' *is that*? We play a little eighties charades and you think you're Robin Givens."

"What? That's my muthafuckin' movie! Since you're driving I am going to have a little taste of this Hen dog right here to put me in the mood. And since Mauri has been here humping on me all week, I am really in the mood now."

"Put *you* in the mood? You are always in the mood, you fuckin' nympho. And you know you can't drink. After you sip that shit down, your ass might just pass out."

"Shut up," Rocky said as she guzzled the contents of the bottle and cracked open a second. "My man needs some healing. He had some attorney shit to do today and he wants me to be home waiting for him. Let me get my doctors bag out of the drawer."

As she went into the back the phone rang. She reached for it but the base stood alone. "Kay, answer the phone. It is on the coffee table."

"Hello."

"Hey, sexy. I can't wait until next weekend. I have your flight arrangements right here. You have me counting down the days and shit."

Kay giggled, "Really?"

"How come you didn't call me yesterday? That houseguest of yours is taking up all of my time, huh? Did she leave yesterday?"

Kay busted with laughter. "This is not Rocky, hold on."

"My bad."

Rocky hustled into the living room. "Who is it?"

"One of your concubines," Kay whispered.

"Shut up and give me the phone. Hey."

"Rocky Candy, how are you?"

"I'm fine, Marcus," Rocky grinned. "How are you?"

"I'm fine, I'm still in the gym and on my way home for a lonely night. You should have flown down here this weekend. I'm sitting here counting all the days I have not spent with you."

"That is so sweet, Marcus."

"Anyway, how was your women's meeting, and did your house guest leave, yet?"

"Nope, as a matter of fact, that was her on the phone, she's leaving tomorrow. Maurine, tell Marcus how the meeting was. I am putting you on speaker phone."

Kay smiled, and mouthed, 'You are a mess.' "Hello? It was off the hook. We played eighties charades and Pin The Cock On The Jock and Rocky gave out party bags with liquor and vibrators."

"What y'all do with those? Let me find out ya—"

"WAIT," Rocky interrupted. "Those were not vibrators, they were vibrating back massagers."

"Oh, sounds like y'all was trippin' up in there. It was fun, huh? I wish I was in there with all the ladies and all the vibrators."

"Ha-ha," Rocky said as she turned off the speakerphone and went into the kitchen. "I've been thinking. I'm not ready to meet your mother. Me and mothers don't get along."

"What? Where did that come from? My moms is mad cool, and my little sister is dying to meet you, too. You're not going to have a problem out of either one of them. Besides, my mother is always harassing me about having grandchildren and shit. At least if she thinks I have a girl— that might shut her up."

Rocky shoved her Tupperware bowls into a big canvas bag. *Now that might work. Maybe I could steer his mother toward my cause, that's if she doesn't curse me out first,* she thought.

"Well, anyway I need to get out of here and running my mouth with you isn't going to get me out of here any faster," Marcus said.

"And, I have some cleaning to do. Then I think I am going to crawl in with a good book. I have to get Maurine to the airport in the morning."

"Later, Candy."

"Bye, Marcus." As she disconnected the phone a frantic thought over came her. "Kay? KAY!" Rocky yelled.

"You are really funny— your houseguest is named Maurine?" Kay asked walking into the kitchen.

"Later for that, we forgot to come up with a game plan and I only have a few more weeks. What am I going to do? I just told him I couldn't come and he said that is mother and sister are anxious to meet me."

"We'll come up with a plan before then, don't worry, Rock."

"I guess," Rocky sighed. "I'm ready. That shot of Hen dog got me feeling right and on point. I'm going to finish the second one."

"You do use protection? Don't you?"

"I am shocked that you would even ask me something like that. Of course I do. Shit, I should have stock in Durex and Trojan. Didn't you empty my trash the other night," Rocky asked sarcastically as she swallowed the second bottle whole.

"Oh God, don't remind me," Kay said.

Rocky put her coat on and buttoned it up to the top button. "How do I look?"

"You look like you have clothes on underneath."

George and Yanick stood face to face in front of Yanick's building.

"I had a really nice time tonight, George."

"Me, too."

"I have never been to a comedy club before. This was hot. I can't believe I saw some of those comedians from BET."

"Well, I guess I'll see you tomorrow. Make sure you kiss Seven for me."

"George, I am really sorry about Joann's behavior yesterday at Applebee's. Can you ever forgive me?"

"I already have. Goodnight."

George leaned over and kissed her gently on her lips. Reluctantly at first, Yanick kissed him in return, and kept her eyes closed seconds after the kiss was finished.

"You want me to walk you upstairs?"

"No, I am cool from here. I'll talk to you tomorrow." Yanick walked into the building and ran up the steps. She opened and closed the door quietly. She tiptoed into her room, turned on the lights and looked into the empty crib. She automatically walked down the hall and opened the door to her parent's room. She smiled as she viewed her baby safely laying in the bassinet inches from the bed her mother slept in. She closed the door, walked into her room and lay on the bed fully dressed. Her tears hit the mattress before she did.

"I'm so confused," she sniffled into the air. "I love Joann, but George is really sweet, and I am beginning to like him, too. Am I in love, or is this infatuation?"

Yanick picked up her cell phone and began to dial out, but when she realized it was nearly ten-thirty she knew Joann would be fast asleep. She fell asleep trying to figure out who she should be with while Joann lay next to Sammy and waited for Yanick's call.

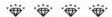

Kay and Rocky spent the short ride to Thomas' talking about the good old days and before they knew it they were there.

"Thanks, Kay. I'll talk to you in the morning. Kiss the boys for me."

"Okay." Kay sat and watched as Rocky made her way up the steps and into the house. As she pulled off she tried to figure out what it was that made her long time friend tick. She didn't even think Rocky knew.

Once inside Thomas', Rocky slammed and locked the door. Since the open door had been her only source of light, she stood in complete darkness. Rocky walked slowly and let her fingers gently probe alongside the wall. She stopped suddenly to listen carefully. She thought she heard a noise upstairs. She called out, "Thomas. THOMAS!!"

A deep, dark silence was her only reply. She began her search for the light switch once more. This time she was in a hurry, using both hands to feel along the wall. Her fingers glided over and past the switch. She froze then slowly retraced her movements and flicked on the lights. She took off her coat and placed it in his front closet. As she ascended the steps the cool air struck the entire back of her body. The chill trickled down her backside, danced off her round cheeks, and down to the top of her boots.

Delighted that she was able to beat him home, Rocky ran into the kitchen. She rummaged through his cabinets and made a mental note to rearrange his pots. He had a small radio on top of the kitchen counter. She flicked it on and let Doug E Fresh take her back to a place she wished she could be— with her mom. The heat from the stove blended with the prickles in her head and the tingles all over her body the shots of Hennesy left behind. Her memories and intoxication caused her to grow excited and elated. She pulled out seasoning and dashed it into the pot. With each sprinkle of salt she tried to make her butt jiggle and clap like the strippers she had seen on occasion at Mauri's strip club. She laughed at herself as she giggled and wiggled to the music. She could smell her ox tails warming up already. She pulled down an orange box of rice, retrieved another pot, poured water into it and placed it on the stove.

"Margarine," she thought out loud. As she turned to walk toward the refrigerator she spotted a man staring at her from the doorway of the kitchen. She froze in her place. Rocky opened her mouth, but fright seemed to freeze her voice as well. She didn't have enough hands to cover her smooth bare skin, so she just stood there and watched him smile. Once she recognized the face she felt a little relief, but it wasn't enough to stifle her blaring embarrassment. She backed her behind onto the door of the refrigerator. The cold white icebox seemed to melt her fear and release her vocal cords. "How long have you been standing there watching me?" she asked in a panicked state.

"Just enough time to watch you make it clap," he said as he walked toward her. With each sentence, he slowly walked closer to her. "I was sleeping and fancied hearing someone call my name. So I put on some clothes and came downstairs to see what was going on. But if I would have known it was this kind of party I would've left my clothes upstairs."

"I was calling your son, sir," she said in a timid voice.

"He's not here. Can I fill in?"

Thomas' father was within inches of Rocky. She could hear him breathing through his nose. She stared into his eyes and silently begged him not to. Using two fingers he traced her lips. Then he gently wiped the tears from her cheeks. When she did not stop him, he continued straight down the middle of her body. Rocky could feel the tingling effects of the Hennesy shots kicking in as he hooked the same two fingers inside her thong and rubbed her vagina.

Thomas Sr. removed Rocky's hand from her breasts and guided it inside his boxer shorts. His dick was large and hard. He kissed her lips, and she kissed back as she tightened her grip around his dick and stroked it. Her insides boiled as they both tugged his diamond hard piece out of his shorts and rubbed it against the front of her thong. Rocky opened her legs and her vagina followed his dicks every move. They started to ease off her thong, hand in hand. As they guided it past her thighs she began to moan loudly and her arm suddenly recoiled.

"STOP!! Are you fuckin' crazy?" Rocky asked, winded.

"Nah, just horny. Junior isn't here—"

"How old are you?" she screamed as she tried to cool off.

"Forty-seven. I started early. I can teach you a couple of things, if you let me," his father replied.

He grabbed Rocky's arm. She yanked her arm away, and using the back of her hand she smacked him dead across his cheek and nose.

"Get out of this kitchen. If I were you I wouldn't come down here again or you will have to find some where else to stay!"

Thomas Roland Sr. felt a sting across his cheek and a small pain at the bridge of his nose. But he seemed unmoved. He stared at her scantily clothed body and smiled as he rubbed his cheek with the same two fingers that had just outlined the front of Rocky's body. He backed out of the kitchen slowly staring at her and clutching his exposed dick.

"My dick is bigger than my son's and I can fuck you real good, too. But since I don't have that NBA money you don't want none of this, huh? Shit, I wanted your little ass since I first started stayin' here. You know where I am if you change you mind."

With that he was gone. She finally relaxed her muscles and knocked the back of her head into the refrigerator door. She slowly skidded down the front of the fridge onto the floor. Her butt made squeaking skid noises along the way. When she hit the floor his father waltzed back into the kitchen.

"Listen, sweet Candy. Do me a favor. Don't tell Junior. Because if you do, I will have to let him know that your ho ass let me feel your pussy up, and was tugging on my johnson, before you stopped me."

As he walked out the room he stuck the upper half of his body back into the opening. He stared at Rocky again and said, "Damn, you're fine."

"Fuck you and your old wrinkled ass dick," she yelled. She got up and wiped the tears from her eyes. She opened the refrigerator door and pulled out a half of a stick of margarine. Then she walked over to the sink sniffling and licking her lips. As she regained her composure she looked up towards the ceiling.

"Thank you Grandma and Jesus. I really thought that was a rapist and I just knew I was going to be violated. Shit, he might as well have been a rapist." She inhaled deeply and then smiled. "That motherfucka does have a big-ass dick, though— I can't even front." She laughed loudly and quickly turned to see if she was being watched.

She sniffled once more, wiped her nose and continued to talk softly over the sink as she washed her hands. The sound of the running water seemed to sooth her. She removed her hands from the gushing faucet, but continued to let it run. She felt her heart starting to beat at a normal pace again. She walked over to the pot and dashed the margarine and rice in it with one shot. She walked back over to the counter and began to chop up a big clove of garlic. She slammed a knife on the counter. "I can't believe what just went down."

Rocky replayed the incident in her mind. She thought back to the night of her birthday and how hot his father had made her feel then. She felt double those emotions when he stroked her vagina minutes ago. Then she quickly began to chop the garlic again. "Should I tell him what happened?" she whispered to herself. Her conscience stopped her from snitching. She felt guilty for masturbating in Thomas' closet the night they met when Thomas Sr. had fucked her with his stares and mind. She felt guilty for finding him attractive and enjoying their body contact minutes ago. Rocky felt bad for feeling so good.

Thomas entered the house one half of an hour after the incident to a plate of hot food and an even hotter girlfriend. On the verge of sleep, he silently acknowledged that although all of their sexual encounters were good, this had been the best by far. As they were having intercourse she thought of her could-be father-in-law's rough hands fondling her pussy. She even pictured his big, rigid dick penetrating her sugar walls. Three doors down, Thomas Sr. fucked the shit out of his hand as he listened to his son and Rocky's moans. He had wanted to taste Candy so badly, but would never have the chance. He packed his bags and left the next morning without saying a word.

17

Dying inside but outside
you're lookin' fierce

"Wow, Mauri. I didn't realize how much clout your name has in the fashion world," Rocky said.

"I ain't got no more clout than the next nigga with a pocket full of money. I just spend a lot of money with these cats. This merchandise moves quickly back home and shit. They just laid it on thick because I rarely make personal appearances. My buyer does it all for me. Only time I make trips down here is to see you."

Rocky removed a black jumpsuit from a clothing rack. It was sleeveless and revealed a little bit of cleavage. At the bottom of the pants were small slits and rhinestones.

"Do you like this outfit right here, Mauri?"

"That is kind of plain for you, don't you think? I mean it's nice and everything but it is not you."

"Would you buy it for me please?"

"For sure. But I'd rather see you in this." Mauri picked up a camel colored pony skin jean styled suit. The pants were low riders and the jacket stopped a little above the waist and had one button. "You could rock this with the button closed with no shirt or bra underneath. This right here is on, for sure. Excuse me?"

A woman dressed all in black with her hair combed out of her face came to his side. "Yes, may I help you, sir?" the saleswoman asked.

"Can you find these three items in a size six and take them to a fitting room for my wife, please?"

"Yes, sir." The woman quickly removed each garment from the rack and carried them to a fitting room. "We have some boots that reach the calf to match this suit. Would you like to see those as well?"

"Yeah, bring those to the fitting room as well. She needs a seven and a half."

Mauri sat outside the fitting room patiently waiting for Rocky, who sat down fully clothed clutching the jump suit in her hands. She could not get over the conversation she'd had that morning.

"Hey, Marcus I have some bad news," Rocky said.

"You have to show up at my mom's house. No ifs, ands or buts."

"I'm definitely going next month, but I can't fly down there today."

The phone was silent for a few long seconds "Why the fuck you wait until now to tell me?" I made all these arrangements and shit. Then you gonna go and back out. You did the same shit on the 3rd when I came to

New York for my exhibition game, talkin' bout you had to go to Detroit for business. Who you fuckin' in Detroit?"

"I'm truly sorry and I'm not going to Detroit this weekend I have a paper due first thing Tuesday morning. My syllabus says due Columbus Day, and I totally overlooked it. I need this three-day weekend to finish this paper. This is one of the classes that I need to fulfill the requirements for my degree, Marcus. If I come out there, there's no way I can finish this paper."

"I don't have money to be wasting like that. Whatever, I'll talk to you later."

"Rocky, I am going to walk further up the block to the Prada store. I want some black pants and some shoes to wear tonight," Mauri said facing the door of the fitting room

"No, baby. Why don't you wait? Let me pick something out for you. Plus, I want you to see this on me so you can tell me how I really look."

Rocky quickly started to undress in the fitting room and tried on the pony jean suit. It fit her really well. She slipped on the boots over the pants. They were camel colored with a neon green stiletto heel. She opened the door and placed her hands on her hips.

"That's hot! I want you to wear that tonight. Just like that. Nah, fuck that! You could wear that to the Cabaret I'm throwing next month. It's my fourth anniversary of my first store on Seven Mile. Wear that with your hair pulled back to the side like that White chick right there."

The saleswoman produced a smile.

Rocky talked in a whisper, "Maurice. What is wrong with you? Why do you always have to be ignorant? You always know how to—"

"—ruin a moment," Mauri interrupted. "I hear that fly shit. Just go in there, try on the black jump suit and come on."

She haggled with herself silently as she peeled off the pony suit. *If this asshole ever flies down here again on some sneak attack shit, I will definitely diss his ass, she thought, I can't believe he pulled this shit. Not a word, no warning just rings the bell. What if Thomas was there? And to make matters worse, now Marcus is mad at me. Last time I cancelled I had no choice, it was my week fly to Detroit to see Mauri. I couldn't keep on being lucky enough to get out of that. This time it's Mauri calling himself paying me a surprise visit. And why did he have to say that stupid shit in front of the saleslady?*

She slipped into the black jumpsuit and into thoughts about the upcoming dinner party. *I've got a few weeks left until I meet his mother,* she thought as she wiggled in the jumpsuit, and could already envision what boots she was going to throw on with her outfit. When she stepped out of the dressing room the saleswoman smiled and so did Mauri.

"You give that shit character— it looks really nice, doesn't it?" Mauri asked.

The saleswoman nodded her head. "That suits your shape. You look really nice," she added.

Rocky admired herself in the mirror. *This is conservative enough for his mother, she thought, but makes enough of a statement to catch Marcus' eye.* "Baby, this is perfect. I want this. Remember the Bottega Veneta leather shawl with the fringes and the matching boots and bag? Remember you bought it for me when we went to Italy?"

"Not really— surprise me. Ring up that pony skin outfit, the matching boots, and that black outfit, cuz. Here you go."

Mauri handed the saleswoman his credit card. "Thank you, sir," the sales woman replied. Moments later she handed him three bags, his card and the receipt.

"Thank you, and have a wonderful day," Rocky said.

"Likewise," the saleswoman said.

"I already know what I want to see you in tonight. Let's go to Prada," Rocky said.

Mauri held up his hand and put up one finger as he answered his cell phone. "Hello? What up though? I didn't think you was gonna holla at your dog while I was up top, cuz. Your ass ain't even call me when I was out here a few weeks ago— What's going down?— Word, tonight? I'm there, for sure. You gonna have a car come and pick me up? I'm stayin' by wifey in Brooklyn though hold on. Baby girl, what's your address? As a matter of fact I'm going to let my wife give you her math and I'll see you around ten. One."

Rocky gave her information to the guy on the phone. "Who was that?" Rocky asked.

"My man is having something at the Rainbow Room tonight, and then we gonna hit a club or something. You don't mind if I hang out with the fellas tonight?"

The sales associate seemed impressed with his last statement. She was even more impressed with the fifty-five hundred dollar sale she had just made. "He must be some sort of rapper or something," she said as she watched Mauri and Rocky walk out the door.

Camille clutched her necklace tightly in her hands. She walked to the front door of the Brooklyn Jewelry Exchange and took a deep breath. As she stepped in, she adjusted her top over her bulging belly and walked towards the counter furthest from the front door. Several sales people asked if she needed help but she continued to walk towards the back.

"Excuse me, can you tell me how much I can get for this?" Camille asked.

"Let's see what you have, young lady," Mr. Eden said.

Mr. Eden put a piece of jewelry down on a small desk and got up. He picked up the necklace, stared at it for a few minutes and placed it down on the counter before Camille.

"One hundred fifty dollars," Mr. Eden said.

"One fifty— that's it?"

"Yes."

Camille picked up the necklace, sucked her teeth loudly and walked out the door. She looked down the block, squinting through the sun at Brooklyn High. She thought she spotted Kahmelle and waddled quickly toward the school. She rolled her eyes at Joann, who was on the phone and decided not to trade insults with any of the kids today. Camille looked at the gun in Joann's holster and thought about grabbing it, running to The High and forcing Kahmelle into being a father.

It can't be that hard to get out. It's just sitting there, on her hip, all out in the open. Fuck it, she thought. She crossed the street and picked up her pace as she neared the school. She kept her eye on the back of Kahmelle's head as she drew closer and closer to the crowd of teens that stood outside. Before she reached, he turned around and to her dismay it wasn't Kahmelle. She exhaled and felt a bit relieved until she spotted Tony. He stood in the middle of five guys laughing and talking loudly. She tapped him on the shoulder and he quickly turned around. With eyes opened wide he stepped back and looked at her from head to toe.

"Yeah, don't look like you just saw a ghost, nigga," Camille said.

"Camille, you really are pregnant! Look at you," Tony said. He stared at Camille who sported a skintight pair of Ice jeans, and an Iceberg top.

"Where's your man?" she asked with her hands on her hips.

"*Whose* man? You mean *your* man?" Tony asked with a smile.

She sucked her teeth. "Where's Kahmelle?"

"I don't know. Why?" Tony answered.

"Tell him he can avoid callin' me, but he can't avoid this right here," she said as she tapped her stomach gently.

"Why you ain't at school, Camille?" Tony asked seriously.

"Don't worry about that. Just tell him that I am here," Camille said.

"He went down south for the summer."

"Yeah, and…"

"Well, he's been gone for a while."

"But he's back now. Shit he been back since school started. It's October!" Camille looked frustrated. She flinched, closed her eyes tightly and grabbed her stomach. When she opened them Tony could see the water surrounding her bright eyes, but she kept her head held up high. He inhaled deeply and put his arm around her shoulder.

"Nah, Meeley, the truth is, he went down south for Columbus Day weekend. He ain't come to school because he left last night."

Camille slipped from under Tony's arm and began to walk back in the same direction she had come from.

"Wait, come here for a second," Tony called. Camille stopped and Tony walked up to her. "You going to the doctor and all that shit, right?" he asked.

"Maybe, maybe not," she said with an attitude.

"Well, hold onto this," Tony said. Tony pulled out two crisp one hundred dollar bills and handed them to Camille. Without hesitating she removed the bills from his hands. Tony stared at her bulging belly as Camille placed the money into the pocket of her jeans. Her shirt stopped right above her protruding stomach and revealed a rubber band. One end of the thick, tan elastic went through the empty buttonhole and the other was fastened around the silver button on her jeans. The band looked as if it was pressed tightly against her stomach. He reached back into his pocket and pulled out his last hundred dollar bill.

"I hope this will help you out a little bit. You know— cab-fare to the doctor or perhaps you could buy some maternity clothes."

Camille tried to pull down her T-shirt, but as soon as she released her grip it just eased its way back above her belly.

"Thanks a lot. I'll see you later," she said as she removed the money from his hands and walked away.

"If you need someone to roll with you to the doctor, holla. I want to help you take care of my little godchild," he called.

It took everything she had not to break down in tears in front of Tony and The High. She kept her pace quick and her head up as she walked down Fourth Avenue. Tony watched her walk off.

Damn, this shit is real. I can't believe Kahmelle is getting ready to have a seed, he thought as he shook his head and walked back to the crowd of people in front of the school.

Later that night Rocky and Mauri sat in the living room of her apartment preparing for Mauri to go out.

"Mauri, you look so good right now," Rocky said, meaning it.

"You think so, huh?" Mauri said.

"I know so, baby. Don't give your number to any of them hungry bitches out there."

"Come on now."

The sound of a horn blowing filled the living room. Rocky fixed Mauri's vest and then walked to the window. A silver Rolls was parked outside of it. *Who the fuck is that in the Phantom with the suicide doors. And how come I never bumped into them on the streets*, she thought.

"Baby, I think your boy is outside. Come give me kiss," Rocky said. Mauri kissed her on her lips and walked toward the door. "Maurice."

He swung around and looked at her like she was insane. "That's the second time today you hit me with my government. What?"

"I am so happy you came out here and surprised me. Thank you. I'll be waiting up for you when you come in the house."

Mauri smiled and then walked out of the door. She peeked through her blinds, watched him climb into the car and grabbed her phone.

"Hey, Marcus, what's up?"

"Ain't nothing. How is the paper coming along?"

"I've been reading all day. Listen, I just want to apolo—"

"Nah, you apologized enough. I'm sorry. I was really looking forward to seeing you. I guess I spazzed out when you said you weren't coming. You can use that same ticket to come and see me another time."

"Thanks for understanding."

"Well, I am sure you have mad work to do. I'll call you in the morning, okay?"

"Okay, I miss you."

"I miss you. You better check your class assignments and clear your shit for next month. I'll never forgive you if you don't meet my moms."

"I'll be there."

"That's what your mouth says."

"I miss you so much. I'll be there, believe me."

"What up, what up?"

"Chillin', the bags are gone. We splitting up seven G's and I got orders for at least four thousand dollars more for Thanksgiving."

"But son, you just got down there yesterday. I can't believe they are gone already. And think about Christmas and shit," Tony added.

"You should'a came down here with us," Kahmelle said.

"I know, son. When you coming back?"

"This Tuesday."

"Listen, we have to talk. I saw Camille yesterday. She came up to the school looking for you." The phone was silent. "Hello? Kahm—"

"Yeah, I'm still here."

"She looked alright, but she is hurting, yo."

"What you mean, is the baby alright?" he asked anxiously

"I mean her feelings, and bust it, she had a rubber band holding up her pants. It was squeezing her stomach. Her stomach is like whoa."

Kahmelle exhaled and shook his head. "I don't know what I'm going to do, man. In January I am going to be a father, and I don't even want to. I guess I should have kicked that bitch down the steps months ago."

18

I'm fuckin' you tonight

"**I** am super proud of you. You aced all of your sciences. Look at our future doctor right here, Jon," Millicent said.

Mr. Hendrickson smiled as he stared at his son's report card over the kitchen table.

"Since I am doing so good, do you think I could go down south with Kahmelle and his Aunt for Thanksgiving?"

"Now you know I—"

"Mom, there's something I have been wanting to show you guys for a while. I wasn't sure if I wanted to go, but my deadline to respond is November 12 and that's just a couple of weeks away. I knew if I showed you, you would—"

"What is it? That girlfriend of yours isn't pregnant, is she?" Millicent interrupted.

"No, Ma. Read it," Tony said as he passed his mother the letter.

His mother read the letter and began to jump up and down. She passed it to her husband, looked over his shoulder and read it again.

"My baby boy is going to be a doctor. Who would have ever thought— a doctor, a lawyer, a police lieutenant and a registered nurse all under one roof!" Millicent said.

"A full scholarship! We are really proud of you, son," his father said hugging Tony.

"The letter was written in July. Why did you wait so long to show us?" Millicent asked.

"I told you. I wasn't sure what I wanted to do. Ma, please, can I go to North Carolina with Kahmelle for Thanksgiving to sell the rest of our bags?"

Mr. Hendrickson walked over to his wife and grabbed her from behind by her waist. He kissed her neck and whispered in her ear. "Millicent, I think we should let him go."

"But Jon!"

"He got all A's and A pluses— and this. Malik said that the bag thing is legit and he's making money off of it. He is seventeen. I'm saying yes."

"JONATHAN, it's Thanksgiving. And—"

"And this is the first year we are not having dinner at our house. Malik is going to the Caribbean and Tony should go with his friends."

Millicent sucked her teeth and walked out of the room.

"Thanks, Dad."

"You just make sure you don't get into any trouble out there. Is Shaine going?"

"Nope."

"Everything okay with you two?"

"Yeah."

"Listen, son. You don't want to end up like Kahmelle. Always protect yourself when—"

"DAD, I told you. She's waiting until she's married."

Jonathan nodded his head and muttered under his breath," Millie was waiting, but Malik came first."

"I am on my way to pick up Shaine. We are going to the movies."

"You have money, son?" Here hold on to this".

Jonathan pulled a worn hundred dollar bill out of a worn leather wallet and handed it to Tony.

"That's for this report card. This is the way to start your senior year. Your mother and I are really proud of you."

"Thanks, Daddy. I'll see you later."

As Tony ran out the side door in the kitchen, he could hear Malik as he walked in the front door of the house.

"Hey, Pop, what's up? Is Mom cooking tonight?"

"I don't know, but you've got to see this."

"MA! Come here please."

"Take a look at your little brother's report card and his acceptance into the Pre-Med program at Howard. You're not going to believe this," Jonathan said.

Millicent came running down the steps. Halfway down she stopped, grasped the wooden banister and called down the steps, "What's wrong, Malik?"

"I kind of invited my lady friend over for dinner tonight and—"

"The White woman?" Millicent said as she tried to catch her breath.

"No, Mom. Laneice is Black. This is someone that I feel you should meet. We're getting close."

A broad smile covered her face. "Say no more, baby. I will throw something a little extra together for you and your guest right now."

"Thanks." Malik took the sheet of paper from his father's hand. He looked over it and smiled. "Now that's what's up."

Later that evening Tony walked into Shaine's apartment and smiled.

"Hey, Shaine, why aren't you dressed yet? The movie starts in thirty minutes."

"I don't know. I have been thinking. I haven't gotten my acceptance to Howard yet."

"And? You have been accepted into Morgan State and that isn't that far from Howard. It's only November and with that report card, no one will turn you down. Stop thinking about it for now."

"I don't feel like going to the movies."

"You want to go out to eat?" Tony asked.

"Nah. I feel like staying in."

"Alright, whatever you say." *Yesterday she complained about not going anywhere and all of the sudden she wants to stay in. I just don't understand broads and shit*, he thought as he threw his jacket on the couch.

"Do you love me, Tony?"

"I guess. I have already told you. I have never been in love before. But I like you more than any other girl I have ever been with, so this must be it, okay? I love you, Shaine." Tony kissed Shaine gently on the cheek, continued to reach past her and grabbed the remote. "What's on HBO?"

"Tony, don't you notice anything different about me?"

Tony looked her up and down and pushed the power button on the remote control. "You always look good to me."

Shaine untied her see-through robe and let it drop onto the cushions of the couch. She arched her back so that her breasts were eye level with Tony who sat slouched on the couch. Tony looked at Shaine's breasts and sat up. She wore a see-through negligee, which stopped at her navel. Once Shaine saw that she had his undivided attention she stood up and turned her backside towards his face. Tony palmed her smooth brown buns with his hands. He ran his middle finger up and down the string of her pink thong. Once he noticed she didn't stop him he quickly placed his hand in the front of her thong and stroked her vagina. Shaine felt weird for a moment and she moved his hand out of her thong and stepped away from the couch. Tony quickly stood up.

"I'm sorry, Shaine. But that thing you have on and the thong— it was just too much for me."

Shaine inhaled deeply, "Sorry for what?" she asked. She pulled her thong down and seductively moved her hips so it fell to her ankles. She stepped out of them and walked toward Tony on the couch.

"Take off your pants," Shaine said. Tony fumbled with his belt and unbuttoned his jeans; he wiped his sweaty palms on them and then let them fall to his ankles. He stepped out of his jeans and his sneakers in one shot. He sat back on the couch with his white tee bright and his skinny legs crossed.

"Let's go into my room."

Tony followed Shaine staring at her behind the entire walk to her room. He thought about all of the honeys he'd fantasized about in his magazines and not one compared to this. As they reached her bedroom Tony extended his arm and touched her behind. It was soft, smooth and warm. She looked like a life-sized chocolate doll. She immediately laid down on her back and spread her legs.

"Shaine, are you sure you want to do this?" he asked, fumbling through his wallet for a condom.

"Yes, I am."

Tony jumped onto the bed, and placed his mouth on her breast and sucked it. He went back and forth from one breast to the other. He looked up at her face, which was expressionless, put his finger inside her vagina and yanked it back and forth.

"Ouch, Tony. Maybe we should stop."

Tony kissed her lips. "No, we shouldn't." He played softly around that area for a while watching Shaine hump his fingers. He removed his finger and wiped it on her thigh. He quickly slid a condom on, then poked his penis around her vaginal area searching for an opening.

"Tony," Shaine whispered in a panic.

"SHHH, just wait a minute," Tony said nervously.

Tony stuck his finger into her warmth again, slowly pulled it out, and pushed his penis inside of her. Shaine grabbed his forearms and dug her fingernails into them. He thrust his body into hers and sweat dripped off of his head onto her frilly negligee. His golden skin glistened. He looked up into the window at the white fan that sat there. The dust encrusted blade of the fan spun quickly, but served as little relief. He looked down at Shaine who closed her eyes tightly. "You feel it?" Tony asked.

She nodded her head vigorously.

"Does it feel good?" he asked.

"No, it hurts."

Tony slowed down, but didn't stop.

"It feels real good to me. You want me to stop?"

"Not if you don't want to. I love you, Tony."

"I love you too, Shaine. Oh shit!"

He slammed his narrow frame into hers once more before he yelled out and lay motionless on top of her.

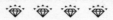

"Listen, Mom, don't overdo it, alright. Just be yourself. I ain't talking marriage, babies or no shit like that. But I am really feeling this woman, okay?" Malik pleaded.

"Yes, baby. I won't say much."

Malik gently grabbed his mother's wrist as she made her way to the door. "Please, mom?"

"Don't worry, Leeko, I won't embarrass you."

Malik sat on the couch and watched his mother shuffle to the door. She opened it and smiled as she looked at the young lady standing in her doorway.

"You must be Laneice. I'm Malik's mom, Millicent. Come in and make yourself comfortable. Leeko is on the couch."

"LEEKO? That is so cute. You look entirely too young to be his mother," Laneice said as she shook Millicent's hand. Laneice walked into the living room and looked around. Her denim skirt hugged her curves and stopped right above her knees. Her brown boots began where the skirt ended and fit perfectly over her calves. She wore a tan blouse that stopped above the navel. The light sent of her perfume reached the couch and caressed Malik's nose.

"You look nice, as always," Malik said.

"Thanks." Laneice said.

"Jon!" Millicent called.

"I'm coming, Millie," Jonathan answered. He jogged quickly down the steps in his uniform, smiling. Laneice stood up and extended her arm as he approached the couch.

"Pop, this is Laneice. Laneice, this is my father."

"Hi, Mr. Hendrickson. Pleased to meet you."

"Same here, and please call me Jonathan."

"Would you like something to drink? I have soda, iced tea, beer—" Millicent said.

"Ma, is it your homemade iced tea?" Malik interrupted.

"Yes," Millicent said.

"Laneice, you have to taste my mom's iced tea. It is the pain," Malik said.

"Then iced tea it is," Laneice said.

Millicent hurried into the kitchen and came out with a tray that held four tall glasses of iced tea. As she walked slowly into the living room the ice clanked loudly against the glasses. She placed the tray down on the coffee table and handed Laneice a glass.

"Here you go sweet heart. So, Laneice, what kind of work do you do?" Millicent asked.

"I am an RN." Laneice said.

Millicent removed the glass from her lips and swallowed what was in her mouth with a loud gulp. "Get out of here! So, am I. What department?" Millicent asked.

"The ER."

"Malik, did you know this? So am I. I have been a nurse for twenty years now."

"Well, I have been a nurse for ten, and I really love it."

"Where are you from? You have such a beautiful complexion."

"I was born here but my parents are from Belize," Laneice said.

"Millicent, is dinner almost ready because I don't want to be late for work." Jonathan asked.

"So, are you and Leeko going to Belize or another part of the Caribbean for Thanksgiving? I—"

"Ma, Laneice and I aren't going to the Caribbean for Thanksgiving. That's where I met her, remember?"

Malik stared at his mother with a plastic smile. Mr. Hendrickson placed his glass to his mouth and drank its contents down. Laneice cleared her throat and looked at Malik.

"Oh! Going to the Caribbean for Thanksgiving? With whom are you traveling?" Laneice asked.

Malik sucked his teeth. "My mother made a mistake. Tony is going away with his girl for Thanksgiving, I ain't going nowhere."

"Then you *can* go down to Florida with me to see my parents?" Laneice asked.

"Oh, your parents live in Florida? What part?" Jonathan asked.

"Pensacola and Miami," Laneice said with a forced smile.

"Laneice, why don't you come and help me in the kitchen?" Millicent asked.

"I would love to. Maybe I could steal some of your recipes Malik is always bragging about."

"No, I got this. You sit down and enjoy your drink, Neicey," Malik said.

Malik walked into the kitchen behind his mother and pulled down four plates from a cabinet.

"Malik I'm—" Millicent started.

"Ma, don't say one word. Just dish the food onto the plates and I will place them on the table."

"Really, I didn't—"

"Don't worry about it. No harm done. She'll be all right," Malik said.

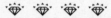

Tony rolled over onto his back and stared at all the dusty stuffed animals that adorned the shelves in Shaine's room. He smiled at the picture they had taken together at Coney Island at the end of the summer. He was dressed in green from head to toe. He stared at the posters and magazine snapshots of B2K and Mario that hung all over her walls. He heard her sniffle softly and shook her shoulder.

"Shaine, are you sure you're okay? You haven't said a word in hours."

"That's because when I was ready to talk, your ass was plopped on top of me fast asleep."

"My bad. So how was it?"

"Honestly? It wasn't anything like I imagined. It hurt like everybody says, but it didn't hurt good."

"You probably waited so long to do it that your shit don't work right. Maybe you got some dust up there that needs to be cleared out," Tony laughed.

"Or maybe you need to watch the Spice channel or something. Shoving your shit around in there like you knew what you were doing."

"Hey, I ain't the virgin, you are."

"Not anymore and you ruined my first time."

Tony sat up on the bed and placed his back against the wall. The glossy photo of Nelly was cool against his bare skin and stuck to his back. Shaine got up quickly but bent over clutching the lower end of her stomach even quicker. She shook her head and straightened herself out. Tony looked at her and a flush of guilt tingled through him.

"I love you Shaine and I know why you did what you did tonight. If you didn't have on that banging ass thong and nightie I would have made you stop. But I have been fantasizing about you and I doing it since I met you. I should have stopped you. I am not leaving New York for almost a year and when I do you don't have to worry about me leaving you for nobody else. I never wanted your first time to be like this. I'm sorry ma."

Shaine dropped her clothing on the ground and ran toward him. She kissed him passionately on the lips and they shared a long embrace.

"Hey, when I was leaving the house I overheard my brother asking my Mom to cook dinner for some chick he was bringing over. I think she made stew beef."

"You know I love when your mother makes that," Shaine said.

"Come on, ma, I want to see what this broad my brother's been with is about."

"Millie, I have to run. I don't want to be late for work. The dinner was delicious." Jonathan stood up, wiped his mouth, dropped his napkin on his plate and kissed his wife on her nose and mouth, then hurried toward the kitchen. He turned back and looked at Laneice.

"I hope I will see you again soon. It was really nice to meet you."

Mr. Hendrickson walked out of the house through the kitchen, and walked down the driveway. Just as he opened the car door he saw the dark silhouettes of two young people approaching the car from behind. Instinctively he touched his holster. He smiled as he saw his son's face under the glowing beam of a street light. He got into the car and turned it on.

"Hey, Dad, I thought you would be gone by now."

"So did I. I'll see you in the morning, son."

"Hi, Mr. Hendrickson," Shaine smiled.

"How are you, sweetheart?" Jonathan asked.

"I'm fine, thanks," Shaine replied.

"Tony, go in there and make sure your mother doesn't fuck anything else up," Jonathan said.

Tony smiled, "Dad, what happened?" he asked loudly.

"Shut up, fool! Just get in there and make small talk. You know how your mother can be."

"Okay, Dad, see you later."

Jonathan backed out of his driveway and sped off into the night. Tony and Shaine walked into the side entrance of the house.

"Hey, Ma. I smell food. Did you save any eats for Shaine and I?"

Laneice sat up in her seat and watched Tony and Shaine walk into the dining room. "Hi, Mrs. Hendrickson," Shaine said.

"Hello, Shaine," Millicent said with a smile.

"Hello, how are you? I'm Tony," he said as he tipped his fitted and extended his hand to Laneice.

Laneice stood up and smiled, "Your brother always talks about you. It's like I already know you."

"It better be all good," he smiled.

"Whatever, Tone. Come here, baby boy."

Malik and Tony walked toward each other. Malik reached for his brother's arm and yanked him into a long, firm embrace.

"These grades, yo, I don't even know what to say. I'm proud of you, and Pre-Med. I did a good job. Laneice, my brother is going to do Pre-Med at Howard on a full scholarship."

"That's wonderful."

"Thanks," Tony said.

"Hey, Shaina, what up?" Malik asked.

"I'm fine, thanks," Shaine said.

"It's Shaine, Malik," Tony said. Tony turned toward Laneice and grabbed Shaine's hand. "This is my girl, Shaine."

They smiled at each other. Shaine sat at the table next to Tony.

"Ma, what's for dinner?" Tony asked.

"I'm sure I have enough stew beef for the both of you. Laneice would you like some more?" Millicent asked.

"I'm going to take you up on that offer. This was delicious, Mrs. Hendrickson."

Millicent smiled as she took her plate off of the table and strolled into the kitchen. She thought of Laneice as she replenished her plate. *Hmm. That girl sure can eat. She'd better watch her back. In a couple of years that food is going to go straight to her stomach, sit there and spread those hips and ass. She doesn't have any kids either. Once she drops a load—*

"Ma, can you bring us some iced tea, too?" Tony asked.

Millicent walked up to Laneice and gently placed her plate in front of her. "You better get your behind up and fix your own drinks and plates for you and Shaine. So, Shaine, any news from colleges yet?"

Tony sucked his teeth and walked into the kitchen.

"I have been accepted into Morgan State, but I am waiting for my acceptance into Howard."

Millicent smiled. "Laneice, what school did you graduate from?"

"I graduated from Clark, in Atlanta," Laneice said.

"Really? I wanted to go away, but I got pregnant with Malik and that was all she wrote. So you live in Jersey. Do you live alone?" Millicent asked.

"Yes I do, and I have no children," Laneice said.

Millicent smiled and watched her son struggle to the table with two glasses under each arm and two plates piled high in each hand. "You couldn't make two trips?" Millicent asked.

"Nope. Shaine, come grab your plate and glass," Tony said.

"How old are you, Laneice?" Millicent asked.

Laneice had a mouth full of stew beef and rice. She picked the napkin up, wiped her mouth, looked up at Millicent and smiled as she answered, "Thirty-one."

"Ma, lay off Laneice for a while," Malik said.

"You go right ahead and ask me whatever you want to, Mrs. Hendrickson. By the way do you have any pictures of Malik when he was smaller?" Laneice asked.

"If she doesn't, I do. You want me to go and get them?" Tony asked enthusiastically.

"Don't do it, Tone," Malik said.

"I'll go get the photo album," Millicent said. Millicent's voice rose as she walked into the living room. She pulled out a step stool and looked on a high shelf in the hall closet. "You have any brothers or sisters?" she asked.

"No, I am an only child. Aside from a few cousins out here, all of my family is in Florida. My mom lives in Pensacola and has three sisters in that area, and my dad lives in Miami. I go and visit them three to four times a year. As a matter of fact, I am flying down for Thanksgiving. Malik, you coming with me?"

Laneice dropped her fork and knife then folded her arms as she made her last statement. The room was silent for minutes, aside from Tony and Shaine's utensils occasionally scraping their plates. She stared at Malik and her thoughts were clear and booming in her head. *I know he is going to Jamaica with that White bitch. He is probably staying in the same hotel we met at. How dare he fuckin' lie to me*, she thought as she suddenly got up from the table and broke the silence, "Tony," she said sweetly, "can you show me where the bathroom is?"

Tony answered with a mouth full of food, "Its right up the—"

"I got it. You finish your food, Tone," Malik said. He stood up and grabbed Laneice gently by her elbow. He guided her through the living room past his mother who stepped down from the stool and dusted off a big photo album. He led her up the steps and stopped in front of the bathroom. He rolled his eyes. "What the fuck is your problem?"

"You're my problem, Malik." She snatched herself free of his grip. "Are you and Susan going to Jamaica? Why didn't you tell me?"

"So you could act like this?" Malik yelled.

Laneice walked into the bathroom and slammed the door. The crystals and candles on the chandelier wobbled over the dining room table where Tony and Shaine sat. Laneice turned on the water. She quickly dialed Monica's number. "Hey, girl I am in the bathroom at Malik's house."

"So, are they Ben Stiller's 'Meet the Parents', 'Mommy Dearest', Big Dad-"

"Stop all the jokes— this is serious."

"What happened?"

"Everything was going fine until I found out that he is going to Jamaica on Thanksgiving with cracker barrel."

Monica exhaled and shook her head. "I know you just didn't call me with that bullshit again. Didn't he say she is paying his way through law school or some shit?"

"No, she got him into NYU Law and a scholarship."

"Same shit. He needs her to get his foot in the door. Look, the boy took you to meet his mama. Y'all spend a lot of time together and he is fine as hell. You said his pipe game is like a plumber's, so just relax and enjoy the ride; it is what it is. It hasn't even been a year yet, or six months. You gonna run the nigga out the fuckin' door. *You* decided to settle for a younger cat with a sugar mama from day one."

"But he lied to me!"

"And what was he supposed to say? I am going away with my married White woman for Thanksgiving— you can suck my dick when she's finished. You should be happy he had the decency to spare your feelings. Get out of that bathroom, give him a big kiss and forget about it. You have him where you want him, believe it or not, so try and keep him there. Don't push him away, Good-bye."

"Monica? Monica!" Laneice whispered.

Laneice quickly shoved her phone into her bag. She shut off the water and walked out of the bathroom door to find Malik sitting on the top of the steps. When she approached he looked up and caressed the back of her calves through her fitted boots. "Listen, Laneice, I—"

"Baby, don't say anything. Let's go down stairs and look at those pictures. I am dying to see what you looked like when you were younger."

19

My mom likes to show me off, of course

"Let's take it from the top. You walk in and wait for him to introduce you to his mother," Kay said.

"Uh-huh," Rocky said.

"Comment on how nice she looks, and how beautiful the house is—"

"Uh-huh."

"Be seated and don't speak unless spoken to. Play the shy role. When she gets up to go into the kitchen, or serves food, ask her if she needs any help."

"Uh-huh."

"Oh yeah and carry a bottle of wine."

"Uh-huh."

"Now, where is the food you set aside for me and the boys?" Kay asked as she walked into the kitchen.

Rocky yanked Kay out of the kitchen and pulled her through the apartment without saying a word.

"What is wrong with you?" Kay asked.

"You have to see what I am wearing to the dinner party tonight." Rocky fingered through her closet, pulled out a black jumpsuit and slipped it over her underwear.

"Turn to the side, let me see your profile. . . good, now turn your butt towards my face. . . bend over and let me see how far down your titties go. . ." Kay had Rocky turn around, suck in, poke out, bend and squat at least a dozen times before she gave her seal of approval. "You have only been telling me about this outfit for the past two weeks. When did you pick that up? It's really classy. You look sophisticated, and you still look fly."

"Me and Mauri picked this up last time he was here. Anyway Marcus says his moms is mad cool, but you know how that goes, especially when it comes to me."

"Tyrone is sitting outside with the boys waiting on me and our dinner. Now, did you cook for the boys or did you just say that to get me over here to see what you are wearing?"

"You know I would do that to you and Tyrone, but not my babies. The food is in a huge beige Tupperware container in the fridge. I will call you when it's time for us all to hook up. I'm going to start getting dressed."

"Girl, everything will be alright. It is already six-thirty— you better get out of here, if you want to get there on time."

"I'll call you as soon as I get to his mom's house. Later."

"Good luck girl."

Later that evening Rocky entered the huge arena and handed her tickets to a uniformed usher. She looked around and noticed the arena was a little more than half full. The game was already twenty minutes underway due to her indecisiveness on what jacket to wear. The usher smiled at her and stuck his arm straight out.

"Straight down these steps right here. You've got one of the best seats in the house."

"Thank you," she replied lightly. Rocky walked carefully down the steep steps. As she made her descent several pairs of eyes momentarily left the game and watched her. She received several smiles and she politely returned them. Her seats were courtside near the basket. She felt like a star. As soon as she reached her seat a friendly girl greeted her.

"Hey, you must be Candy! I love your jacket. I'm Missy, Marcus' little sister. He has told me a lot about you. I didn't think you were coming. Is this a mink? And ooh, what kind of boots are those, Chanel?"

The little girl seemed to hit her with twenty questions in twenty seconds. A genuine smile appeared across Rocky's face.

"Hey, Missy. I have heard a lot about you also. No this is not a mink, it's chinchilla, my boots are by Choo and it's really nice to meet you."

"You are pretty, and fly just like he said. Look there he goes right there but he won't look at us because he says that throws his game off. What's your real name?"

"Raquel, but everyone calls me Rocky or Candy."

"I think you look more like a Rocky. Can I call you Rocky?"

"Sure, most of my friends do. How old are you?"

"Sixteen," what about you?"

"Twenty-five. So that means you're in the 10th or 11th grade right?"

"Yep. And my brother promised to have a big sweet sixteen party for me in the summer. With water slides, rides and games. Well, I am not exactly sixteen yet. I turn sixteen in March. I just tell people that because it's less than six months away."

The crowd was silent as Marcus slammed the ball into the basket and opened up an eight-point lead. As he came down the court he smiled at the two young ladies and Missy and Rocky waved back. They talked about everything from boys to bags. They laughed and cheered against the crowd while eating junk food.

Three minutes before the end of the game a young male approached Rocky's seat with a smile. The smile seemed to be one of approval. He introduced himself as Bob. He gave her two laminates that read 'Guest Pass' and pointed out an exit they should meet after the game.

When the game was over. Marcus stood in front of an exit, talked to the press and signed about two-dozen autographs. Missy and Rocky stood behind the crowd and waited until he finished.

"Missy! Look at how big you've gotten! Give your brother some suga' smacks."

"Marcus! Please not out here in front of everyone," Missy said. She put her hand out so he could shake it but he pulled her into him and gave her a big bear hug.

"Eww, you are all sweaty and stuff," Missy shrieked.

Marcus looked at Rocky and smiled, "How it bees, girl?"

"I'm fine," Rocky replied.

"You look nice," Marcus said.

"Thank you," Rocky said.

" Did Bob come out and tell you where to meet?" Marcus said.

"Yep, he did. He is so cute— how old is he?" Missy asked.

"Too old for you. Just go where he directed you and wait until I shower. I'll be right out."

He kissed Rocky on the lips and walked through the exit. His shower went swiftly and the thirty-minute ride from the arena to his house seemed even swifter. She needed more time. She thought about her conversation with Kay and all the do's and don'ts they'd gone over for the night. Her stomach felt tight, like she suffered from gas pains. She drove her car and listened to Marcus talk to his sister the entire ride. At times she let her anxiety slip away to admire his sisters beauty and innocence. She was a light tan complexion, with a wavy long ponytail. Her teeth were pearly white and straight. Her wide eyes were the darkest of brown and the whites of her eyes were clear with no imperfections. When she spoke to her brother her actions showed her admiration. Her tone was full of affection. She marveled even more at their beautiful relationship.

Sure Rocky had Kay but she wondered what it would have been like to have a little sister. What would her and her sister's relationship have been like if her mother had not sent her away? Her next thought chilled her. *I probably would be dead.*

Before she had more time to stress about her upcoming introduction, Marcus instructed her to pull up into a long driveway. He hopped out of the car and let his sister out of the back seat. Then he ran around to the opposite side of the car. Rocky gave him her hand and he helped her too. Missy's cell phone rang and she took off in front of them telling a girlfriend about a cute guy named Bob, whom she had just met at her brother's game.

Rocky wanted to smile but she couldn't. As they walked up the steps to go into the house he grabbed her hand gently and pulled her close to him.

"Are you okay? You hardly had anything to say the entire ride."

Rocky looked up into Marcus' eyes. "I am just a little nervous about meeting your mother. Mothers and me never seem to get along to well. I really missed you."

He bent over and gave her a slow passionate kiss. Rocky felt all the blood in her body rush to her head. His kiss was so warm and wanted. He scooped her plump rear end in his hands and rammed his entire tongue down her throat. Rocky heard someone clearing their throat just behind where they stood, and she pushed him off of her.

"Mommy!! It's so good to see you," Marcus yelled.

"Come here and give me some of that love. That's if you didn't give it all to that young lady right there."

Marcus ran up the steps and lifted his mother off her feet. His embrace was stiff. He didn't want to let go. She kicked her legs and then kissed his cheek.

"There's a room full of people in there waiting to see you— put me down!" his mother said.

As he put her down she looked at Rocky and walked straight toward her.

God, please don't let her spazz out, Rocky thought.

"Good evening. I am Mrs. Best. Pleased to meet you." Mrs. Best's distinctive accent made her pleasant tone seem stern. Her smile revealed fresh, tiny wrinkles at the corners of her eyes. She was a little bit shorter than Rocky was and dark brown. She wasn't as dark as Marcus but they had the same hair texture and color. Her hair was pulled straight back into a bun. She wore a black jumpsuit similar to Rocky's, but not as tight or revealing.

"Hi. I'm Raquel— well, Marcus calls me Candy. Whichever you prefer, and it's nice to meet you*." Shut up Rocky, you're fuckin' yourself up already*, she thought.

Marcus' mother blatantly looked Rocky over from head to toe and smiled once more. "Won't you come in?"

Rocky walked up the steps and took off her jacket as they entered the house. She folded it and placed it over her arm. Marcus' mother ran the back of her hand over it.

"Your coat is beautiful. Marky, this is the kind of fur I want for Christmas. I think you should take Candy with you to pick it out." Marcus' mother tugged on the waist of Rocky's outfit and pointed to her own. "It's evident from her choice of clothing and man that she has style."

Rocky laughed. *Maybe this won't be so bad after all*, she thought. "Mrs. Best, this bottle of wine is for you," Rocky said as she handed her the bottle.

"Thanks, Candy. Come inside and let me show you off to our friends."

As they walked inside, Rocky checked out the décor. The house was medium sized and lavishly furnished. As soon as one walked in the door there was a white spiral staircase. Ahead she could hear laughter and as they got closer to the happy sounds she realized they were coming from the dining and living room area where the guests all sat waiting. Although the house was a medium size the dining room alone seemed bigger than Rocky's entire apartment.

About twenty people sat in the dining room and the living room, engaged in cheerful mini-conversations until Marcus walked in. Some clapped, some called out salutations, but they all looked happy to see him. He went around the room and gave everyone pounds or hugs. Marcus and his mother introduced everyone in the room to Rocky until he came up to a guest who was far removed from everyone, and with whom Marcus was not familiar.

"Honey, I want you to meet my friend Hubert. Hubert this is Marcus and his girlfriend, Candy."

Missy walked over to where they were standing, stomping her feet the entire way. "I can't believe he is here, Mom! Don't you even care?" Missy snapped. She spoke low enough so only the five people in that corner of the room heard her. She grabbed Rocky's hand and pulled her.

"One minute, sweet pea. Your brother is introducing me to the people in the room. Then we can go up into your room. I promise," Rocky said in a sincere tone.

Missy ran to the front of the house and up the steps sobbing. Marcus fought hard to keep his composure. He looked at his mother whose smile had left the room with Missy. The stranger stepped up and extended his arm.

"How are you, Marcus? I am so glad to meet you. There is not a day that goes by that your mother doesn't talk about you." Hubert held out his hand but Marcus just looked at it. He nodded and kept on walking. He followed his sister. He was stopped a couple of times along the way but he saved his face for the people who came to see him.

"Hue, it's going to take time for them to understand," Mrs. Best said.

"I know that, sweetie. I'm cool. What about you?" Hubert asked.

"I'm fine," Mrs. Best said.

Rocky extended her arm and smiled. "Nice to meet you, sir."

Hubert smiled at Rocky as he shook her hand.

Go ahead, ma. She got herself a little young thing. That's how I am going out when I get older, Rocky thought silently, even though the smile on her face said it all. She sized him up to about thirty-five.

Mrs. Best grabbed Hubert by the waist with two hands and he affectionately kissed her earlobe. Marcus stared at his mother's actions with disgust, but managed to uphold his present conversation.

"Listen, Hue, I am going to go upstairs and check on Missy."

314 - Brooklyn Jewelry Exchange

"If you don't mind Mrs. Best, I think I'll go. She talked about me seeing her pictures with B2K, and wanted some advice on clothes. I will try to talk to her. This way you can continue to host."

"Thank you, Candy. I'd appreciate that. It is so hard to understand her teenage mind sometimes. Did you notice the stairs as we came in?" Rocky nodded her head. "Missy's room is the first door on the left."

Rocky went up the steps and made her way to Missy's room. After opening the bathroom door to see how it was decorated, she walked in to find Marcus' sister laying on her back staring at a poster of B2K on her ceiling. "Hey, Missy. Do you want to talk?"

"I can't stand him, Rocky. He owns the gym my mom goes to. Since Daddy died he always comes here and spends the night after I am in bed, but I know when he comes. Or when I go to spend the night at Chasity's house, she goes over there to spend the night. He's always kissing on her and stuff. And what makes it really bad is I have seen him around before Daddy died."

"Well, Missy. I know things like this are hard to swallow. But your mom is going through a rough time, and Hubert is probably helping her get through it, that's all."

Missy sat up on the bed and looked at Rocky. "You think so?"

"I really do."

"Well, what was he doing around when Daddy was alive?"

"I can't answer that. But I think you should really take it easy on your mom. Losing your dad hurt her just as much as it hurt you, if not more. And you acting like this toward Hubert probably hurts her a lot. Try and understand that. Now, how about showing me some of your pictures."

After Missy had shown Rocky more than half of her wardrobe and dozens of pictures, Mrs. Best called them down for dinner. After her conversation with Rocky, Missy barely seemed to mind Hubert's presence and even held his hand during a group prayer before dinner.

The night passed smoothly. Marcus laughed with his friends and Rocky had a pleasant conversation with his mother. She even helped her clean up and after the masses left Rocky, Marcus, Missy, Mrs. Best and Hubert sat in the dining room. They discussed what a nice turnout there had been and how delicious the food was. The trivial conversation was awkward but it flowed until Marcus broke the pattern.

"Do you have any respect for the dead, Hugo?" Marcus asked.

"It's Hubert, and what kind of question is that?" Mrs. Best snapped.

"Ma, you're playing yourself! You think you're Roberta Kelly or something? You aren't Stella. He doesn't look any older than me. You were up in here in front of family and friends feeling up on that young-ass nigga and shit. Daddy hasn't even been dead for six months yet!!

Marcus was loud. His tone frightened Rocky. As he argued Rocky thought ahead to their future relationship and him possibly having abusive traits.

"First of all, watch your tone with me, Marcus. He's thirty-five and a lot older than some of the tramps your father rolled up in here with, yes, in my house, and I was still alive."

Marcus stared at his mother and sister. His mouth opened slightly. Then he looked at Hubert and rolled his eyes. "Mom, you knew about Daddy and—"

"Yes, of course I did. I even knew about him and that little tramp Melissa that I met through you and a host of other bitches."

"So why didn't you do anything about it?"

"I was protecting my children, marriage and home. The only way to stop your father from cheating would have been to leave him and I would never have hurt my children like that."

Mrs. Best got up from Hubert's side, walked over to Marcus and stood behind him. She hugged his tall seated frame from the back and rocked him back and forth.

"Marky, I loved your father, and no one will ever take his place, okay?"

Hubert stood up. "Listen, I think I better get going. Call me later on tonight when everything cools off."

"I will walk you to the door, sweetie," Mrs. Best said.

"Good night, Missy, I'll see you, and Marcus and Candy it was nice to meet you."

"Good night, Hubert," Missy said. Hubert looked at Missy in shock. The most he'd received from her in the four months he and Mrs. Best had seriously been dating were nasty glares, groans and sucked teeth. He smiled at her. Marcus, on the other hand, said nothing.

"Good night, Hubert, pleased to meet you," Rocky said.

As soon as they left the room Marcus stood up. His hands moved with his statements. He spoke loudly and paced around the dining room.

"I can't believe this shit! Mom is damn near fifty."

"She's forty-seven, Marcus," Missy said.

Marcus stopped in his tracks and stared at his sister. "Don't tell me you're co-signing this bullshit, sis. Fuck that."

"Your mother's not dead, Marcus. She has to live," Rocky said softly.

"He wants her for her money," Marcus said.

"I think he owns that gym Mommy goes to. He has a Lamborghini and dresses really fly. I don't like it either, but maybe he's helping Mommy get through rough times. And I didn't know Daddy and Melissa was getting' it on. Maybe it's Mom's turn now," Missy said.

Rocky smiled at Missy. She was happy that the young girl had really listened to her advice.

"Whatever," Marcus said.

When his mother came back in she walked past the dinning room straight into the living room. After a few minutes had passed she called them to join her. She had a cocktail glass in her hand filled with an orange-colored, fruity looking drink.

"Would you guys like a cocktail?"

"I do. I'll drink what you're drinking, Ma," Missy said.

Marcus stared at his sister and laughed. "You better take your little behind into the kitchen and get a glass of milk. Mom, you know I try not to drink too much during the season."

His mother looked at Rocky. "No, thank you," Rocky replied.

Mrs. Best pulled out three photo albums. They shared old pictures and stories. Rocky felt like she belonged as she listened to them laugh and talk. Missy sat on the floor directly in front of the love seat where Rocky sat, and Marcus sat by her side. Everything seemed so right. She almost didn't want to leave when it was time to go. Missy and her mother walked them to the door.

"Rocky, make sure you come and get me next time you go to Short Hills mall, like you promised."

"You got it, Missy." Missy and Rocky exchanged a short, warm embrace.

"Well, Marcus she seems like a winner to me. I hope to see you soon, and Rock Candy I was serious about you taking Marky to your furrier to pick out a chinchilla coat for me next month."

Rocky extended her hand, but his mother declined. "Get that little hand out of my face and give me a hug."

As they embraced Rocky could not believe it; it was too good to be true. She was hugging Marcus Best's mother instead of ducking a punch or being verbally abused by her.

"Marky, you gonna be home for the Holidays?"

"Not Thanksgiving. But I will have a couple of days off after Christmas. I will stop by tomorrow before I hit the road. I love you, Mom." He grabbed his mother and winded her with a tight embrace. "Be careful ma. I don't trust him."

"Marcus. I'm fine."

Rocky got into her car and started it up. She watched Marcus and his mother talk. After a few minutes he stepped into her car and pushed his seat back as far as it could go. She immediately pulled off.

"I can't believe it!" Rocky said.

"Neither do I. This dude is running up in my moms," Marcus said as he attempted to get comfortable in the seat. "She called him sweetheart and sweetie and all that shit. That nigga was actually nibbling on my mom's ears. In front of everybody! My boys were like, what's up with that? They all know him from the gym. But I didn't know he owned the spot. If that punk plays my moms, I'll kill him. I swear to God, yo."

Rocky could think of nothing besides the way she and his mother got along. She didn't care to talk about his mother's boyfriend. She was just happy to be accepted and liked by his mother. She tried to figure out if this could be a sign of them being together. Her cell phone rang just as she was imagining Marcus telling his mother he was going to marry her.

"Hi, Kay."

"So, how did it go?"

"Great. Really great."

Kay almost dropped the phone. A warm, tingly emotion ran through her body and she felt as if she was going to cry. "I can't believe it! His moms ain't curse you out? No frying pan, nothing?"

"Nope," Rocky said.

"I'm really happy for you. Anyway, what time are we going to meet up to go out?" Kay asked.

"Let me check. Babes, what time are we going to the club?" Rocky asked.

"Honestly? I was all down for that but my moms ruined my mood, yo. I just want us to lay up and chill. Next time I come to town we can roll. Who is that, Kay?"

"Yep," Rocky said.

"Tell her I really don't feel up to it."

"Kay, he said he doesn't feel up to it. Next game he plays out here we will all hang."

"Damn, Tyrone was dying to meet that nigga," Kay said.

"You told him!?"

"Yes, but only because he was coming to hang out. I'll call the other girls and let them know it's a dead issue. Audrey is going to be pissed."

"I know."

"Call me with details as soon as you get home tomorrow."

Rocky turned her phone off and it closed with a loud clap. She dropped it into her bag. "So, do you think your mother really likes me?"

"Yeah, I can tell. She is always cordial to the ladies I come through with but she never really takes to them like she did to you. It was probably that nigga she was with. He got her mind all fucked up."

Within minutes they were at a Marriott Hotel. She got out of the car and looked around her. As they walked into the hotel Marcus rummaged through a big duffel bag for his key. Once he found it he walked to the front desk to ask where the elevators were.

"Good evening, welcome to the Marriott Hotel at Glen's Point. How may I help you?"

"Where are the elevators?" Marcus asked.

"Go down to our gift shop and make a left, you will see them right there," the front desk person said.

"Thank you."

The two were silent all the way upstairs. In the room Marcus threw his bag on the floor and sat on the edge of the bed. He cupped his face with his huge hands and massaged his temples. Rocky walked over to him and sat by his side. She gently patted his lap and then rubbed his back.

"Marcus, I am going to tell you this as nicely as I can." She swallowed and cleared her throat. "When your father died, your mother did not die with him. I'm sure she loves your dad, but she has to live on."

"But I'm sayin', that dude is mad young. She is really doing the Roberta Kelly thing."

"Oh, yeah. You said that earlier. What are you talking about?"

"You know R. Kelly? Well she's the female version— Roberta Kelly."

Rocky couldn't help but laugh. "That is so corny! I wish people would give that R. Kelly thing a rest. He's a damned good artist."

"She's forty-seven years old and that nigga is thirty-five— so she says. He is probably younger than that."

"She is only forty-seven that means she had you mad young. And I bet you she was married to your father when she had you, right."

"Yep, they were fresh out of high school. My moms was only nineteen when she had me."

"You have to understand that your father was probably the only man your mother ever experienced. She is just trying new things. I bet you this thing with this Hubert man doesn't even last."

"You make it sound like she was waiting for him to die and shit."

"Marcus, I am not saying that all. If your father stressed her with the cheating shit, off and on, throughout their marriage, and she never experienced anything with another man she needs this to feel good about herself. She still has to feel like a woman, even if your dad isn't here."

Marcus turned over and pinned her down on the bed. He kissed her face and her neck.

"Why is it that you always know exactly what to say?" Marcus asked.

"I just call it how I see it."

"But why did he have to be so young and couldn't she at least have waited a couple of months— at least a year. It's like they fuckin' on my dad's grave and shit. Yo, she even purchased a new bed."

"Well, at least she had that respect for your pops and shit. And your mother isn't that old. Your mother is bad. I hope I am lookin' like that when I am her age. Shit, she was just a baby when she had you. Now it's her turn to have fun and do all the things that she missed when she was younger. Just be easy on her and Hubert for now. Okay? Ouch— you have all your weight on me, move over."

"You looked really good tonight. I got mad compliments from my family and friends on your behalf. They said you seemed nice, too."

Before she could reply he kissed her lips. Rocky couldn't stand sloppy kissers, but this saliva-packed kiss felt good to her. He unzipped her clothing and she stared up at him and smiled.

"I have been thinking about this since we were on that plane. Your wood peck is off the hook. As a matter of fact I want some right now."

"I come by it naturally."

He looked at her strangely as he took of his clothing. They both stripped down to nothing except for a pair of bright white tube socks worn by Marcus. She crawled to the head of the bed and Marcus followed behind her. Just as she was getting ready to lie down Rocky felt wet kisses on her behind and she let out a soft moan. The wetness moved to the crack of her ass and soaked her anus. She kept a doggy-style stance, and as soon as he spread her ass open and licked her clitoris she began to breathe heavily. Her body had taken her mind hostage. Her inner thighs began to shake and she begged him to stop. She could feel her own moist secretions dripping down her legs. Without warning she dropped onto her back and began to stroke her clitoris quickly. She let out a loud moan and clear thick cum came shooting out of her vagina. It gushed out like a water fountain and plastered Marcus' chin and chest.

"Oh, shit. I have never seen anyone cum like that yet!"

Rocky was momentarily embarrassed. That had only happened to her on four previous occasions. She bent over and took his penis into her mouth before he could ask anything. As she stroked it with her inner cheeks she thought about the last couple of times she had an orgasm so powerful. She quickly sucked herself back to reality and thought of her current situation. *Go for broke, Rock Candy*, her thoughts urged her on. *This is do or die. You have got to trap him.*

She followed her thoughts and tightened the grip on his penis with her jaws. It was so large that she couldn't get it all the way down, so she concentrated on what she could. She took it out of her mouth for a second to catch her breath. As she licked it like an ice cream cone she inhaled and exhaled deeply. Then went down under his nut sack. She sucked them whole like a jawbreaker, and released them with a kiss. He had a handful of her hair clutched in his fist. He pulled her head from the middle of his body to his upper torso. Loose locks of hair stuck out between each of his fingers as he placed her head to his lips and planted soft kisses on it. With the very last kiss he released his grip on her hair.

"You ready for this shit right here? " Marcus asked as he jerked on his dick. He stroked his penis with one hand and caressed her breasts with the other. Rocky did not answer. She felt disoriented. He squeezed her erect pink morsels tightly and then placed one in his mouth. He bit down on her nipple gently and she moaned out loud.

"That pussy is so wet, my dick is ready to go for a swim. You ready for this?" Marcus repeated.

She nodded. Marcus leapt off the bed and tore through his luggage. He pulled out a condom, ripped open the wrapper with his teeth and threw it on the floor. He quickly rolled the condom down his dick and got back into the bed. Rocky watched Marcus as he lay his body on top hers. She remembered how large his penis had felt inside of her in the airplane bathroom.

The corners of her mouth felt like she had cold sores in each of them. She had to stretch her mouth open wide to fit his penis in it. She was intimidated by his size— by him. She closed her eyes as soon as his hard body met hers. She could feel her legs being opened and his knuckles wandering around her vaginal area as they blindly guided his penis to her open insides. She closed her eyes tightly as he placed his long thickness inside of her then suddenly she opened her eyes.

His shit isn't any bigger than Too Sweet's. I can work this, she thought as her confidence boosted. She began to work her hips to meet his strokes. She curled her toes as she contracted the muscles of her vagina. Each time she tightened them, he bit down on his lips and she knew he was feeling it. Neither said a word. The room was silent aside from the sounds of Rocky's sodden vagina being pleasantly plunged. Marcus placed all his weight on Rocky. He kissed her earlobes and panted in them softly. She grabbed his ass and rammed his body into hers harder. It seemed as if both began to compete for sounds of pleasure. Rocky was dying to scream as her body did inside. She finally wrapped her legs around his body, squeezed his hips with her inner thighs and yelled. He grunted and groaned swears.

"OH shit," he finally moaned. Marcus dug his nails into her behind and she moaned in reply.

"Pull my hair, Marky, and bite on my collarbone."

He immediately did as he was told, and lengthened his strokes. As he pushed his throbbing piece in she lifted up her hips and pounded stiffly. They kept up this pace for a short time before Rocky wrapped her legs around his thighs again and squealed lowly. Her inner thighs shook and her vagina tingled. She felt good, relieved and relaxed. She was experiencing the kind of pleasure that she gave herself on lonely nights, with some soft jazz and her vibrating rabbit.

"Could you turn around and let me hit it from the back?"

She was submissive and waited on all fours. She felt his lips plaster kisses on her behind. He smiled and kissed two petite moles that rested on one cheek. She instantly became wet again thinking of how good his mouth felt in her ass. Soon the kisses turned into cold, wet spots and she felt his long rod slip back into her vagina. His groin smacked the back of her ass forcefully.

He enjoyed the greasy feel and the scenic view. "Damn! Your shit stays wet. You like this?"

"Yes! YES! YES," Rocky shouted and could not stop.

Something took over her as she repeated 'yes' over and over again. Each time his body struck her ass, Rocky responded positively. She stuck her ass out and waited to hear the loud smack his groin made against it. Her yes' got louder and louder. The pressure inside of her was too much to stand and was too good to bare. She wanted to stop saying yes. She became silent for a moment, then she started to scream 'no' and that very instant she exploded on top of his rubber coated dick. She could feel a thin stream of warm cum oozing down her inner thigh. He quickly pulled his penis out of her vagina and looked at it. He checked the condom and easily slipped it in again.

"Your shit is so wet, I feel like I'm hitting' this raw."

He grabbed her waist and pulled it toward him. Her moist insides created loud noises. He pumped harder and faster. Rocky was winded, she couldn't remember the last time she had three orgasms in one session, or one of that magnitude. She terribly wanted to lie down. She was so tired. "Marcus, you gonna cum for your baby girl."

"Yep. Keep on talking."

"You feel so good inside me, I came three times. You're the best, Mr. Best."

Marcus could feel the blood rushing through his body like millions of branding irons. "Say it again," he moaned.

Rocky swallowed and closed her eyes shut. As she spoke he thrust into her harder. "You're the best, Marcus Best. You're the best, Marcus Best. You got the biggest, best dick my juicy-ass pussy has ever had."

Marcus let out three choppy yells, forcefully pulled her by the shoulders and rammed her supple ass into him as he tightened his grip on her shoulders.

"OUCH, LET GO!" Rocky yelled.

He thrust into her once more yelling as he did so. Then he finally liberated her shoulders from his vice grip. She flopped on the bed, like Raggedy Ann and lay there, listless and red. Without knowing what to think or how to feel she just stayed still. Her face was smothered in the bright white pillow. Her hair hung loosely around it, like a fur sham. Marcus looked down at her. He had had sex with at least ten different women since his father passed and was unable to cum once. He needed that. He inhaled deeply and then glanced down at Rocky's body. If her back were not slowly moving up and down, he would have thought she was dead. He looked at how red her shoulders were. He could see pink imprints of his fingers on her left shoulder. He lay by her side and brushed her hair to the opposite side of the pillow.

Rocky did not move. Marcus got out of the bed and walked around to the other side where Rocky lay still. He gently picked her up, one arm underneath her head and the other underneath her knees, and carried her, like a baby, around the bed. After he kissed her nose and lips softly he placed her on the bed where he had pulled down the sheets and comforter. He crawled around her and got underneath the covers with her.

"Was I too rough?"

She still refused to talk. She did not know how she felt. She knew she was drained but didn't know what he was feeling and that made her very uneasy. He srtoked her hair from the top of her head down to the locks that were scattered around the pillow.

"Candy. Don't give me the silent treatment. What's wrong?"

"I feel weird," she replied quietly.

"Weird like what?" he asked as he sat up with his back against the wooden bedpost.

She sat up next to him and put her head on his chest. "I don't know whether to feel slutted, embarrassed or good."

"Why would you feel slutted? I introduced you to my family and we speak on the phone almost everyday. What's wrong with you?"

"It was like I wasn't even here toward the end of our little interlude."

At that moment the loud sound of the hotel phone startled them both.

"Hello?" Marcus said.

"Hey, baby. Are you okay?" Mrs. Best asked.

"Yeah, Mom."

"It was really good seeing you tonight, baby. I have missed you so much."

"I missed you too, Mom."

"I really wish you would give Hubert a chance— and remember I'll never love anyone the way I loved Dad."

"Okay Ma, but if he ever—"

"If I need you, you know that I will call you. By the way, Candy seems like a really nice girl. Your sister has not stopped talking about her since she left. She's a real knockout."

"So you like her?"

"From what I see, yes. Well, I'll let you two catch up. I love you."

"I love you too."

Rocky twirled her fingers around his dark soft curls as he spoke to his mother.

"She likes you, and Missy likes you. And Missy never likes any of my lady friends. Candy, I'm going to be honest with you— so don't laugh." He inhaled, took a deep breath and stared at her. "Yo, I haven't been able to cum ever since my father died. I mean I have whacked off a couple of good times and came, but not with a chick." Marcus began to blush. "Well, that is aside from the airplane episode. Sometimes I can't even get it up. I'm sorry if I hurt you but I guess I just lost control. I mean your shit is so wet and you should put insurance on that mouth."

"I'm okay. I just didn't know how to take what just happened but your explanation helps a little."

"Since we all up close and personal, what did you mean by, 'you came by your skills naturally'?" After he spoke he cupped his hand in front of his mouth and stuck his tongue inside his cheek several times. She laughed loudly.

"My moms was the best at what she did. I can remember hearing her performing oral sex on her boyfriends from my bedroom. Slurping noises and deep moans. I have even heard niggas asking her to marry them cause of her oral skills. Bedposts stayed clanking into my wall, yo. She used to boost. For as long as I can remember she never worked a day in her life and we stayed fly. She ran scams on the men she was with. Anyway, that's what I meant, she put it down with her mouth and so do I."

"How did your mother die?"

Rocky took a deep breath. "Well, she had just had a baby. I don't even think it was one year old. Rumor has it that Roger caught her sucking the next nigga's dick in their crib, and threw her and the baby out of the house after beating the shit out of my mom. Roger was my mother's last boyfriend. He couldn't stand me and he made my moms send me to New York to live with my grandmother. Anyway, somehow she managed to rob him for his shoe box money and stepped. He called my grandma later that same day and told her everything that happened. I remember sitting on the floor in between my grandma's legs as she did my hair during that phone call. I could hear him yelling and crying. I remember Grandma saying, 'Stop bawling and apologizing. It don't matter what she did you should have never hit her, Roger.' He said he only hit her because she was cheating in their house. He just wanted his girl and baby to come home. He asked if she had come up to New York or had called to say where she was."

"No one heard from mom for two weeks, until she called grandma and told her she and my baby sister were staying with the nigga Roger caught her with. Roger found her a couple of days after and tried to get her to move back in with him. She refused and said that she and the baby were moving to New York to live with my grandmother and me. That was the same night it happened. She let me hear the baby for the first time and told me she was ready to be the kind of mother she needed to be to the baby and me."

Rocky looked up toward Marcus' face and shook her head. Warm tears quickly filled her eyes and when she blinked the tears came somersaulting down her cheeks. They dropped onto the linen, his chest and her lap. As she looked up she sniffled loudly and wiped her face with the back of her hand. She continued to shake her head as she blurted out her first couple of words.

"I never got to meet my sister and I can't remember her name. I'm not really sure if I even knew it. Anyway, she never made it home. Old boy she lived with for those couple of weeks came home to find dozens of cops in his place and Mom dead on the floor of his apartment with her bus ticket clutched tightly in her hand. She had twenty thousand dollars cash in her pocket. The baby was in Roger's arms with a broken neck and Roger had a bullet hole straight through his head, that had gone into the apartment next door and through an elderly lady's side, killing her as well. There you have it. That shit was big in Philly. I'm talking like O.J. and Nicole big. Everyone knew Roger. I think he ran numbers."

"Wow, I'm so sorry. I really don't know what to say."

"Well, considering that I had only spoken to my moms six or seven times in the year that I had been living with Grandma, I tried to act like it didn't bother me and I kept it inside for a couple of days. But I freaked out at the funeral. The baby's casket was closed and so tiny. But my mother's was open. I knelt in front of that casket with my hand in her hair for the entire viewing. Three hours I sat in front of that casket and no one could move me, not even my grandmother. When people came up to pray and pay their respects, they had to kneel next to me. When the funeral director closed the casket, my grandmother finally lifted me up to my feet. Marcus, she was so beautiful. After she died I prayed to look and be like her every day. I mean I wanted to— never mind. I really don't want to talk about my mother anymore. "

"You've been through it, huh?"

Rocky didn't answer. She buried her head in his chest and fell asleep instantly.

Marcus caressed her head and stroked her hair. She looked angelic lying in his arms. Her mouth was slightly open and her bare skin was smooth and flawless. He looked straight up into the ceiling.

This might be it right here, Pop. I think she's the one. She's definitely wife material Candy is pretty, fly, educated and can fuck. I think I finally snagged one, he thought.

<u>20</u>

Take you out and buy that ring with a rock that will break your arm

Rocky tied her sneakers. It was really cold for the week of Thanksgiving. She jumped up and down in place and remembered Thanksgivings that had been even colder. She inhaled, exhaled and watched her breath appear and reappear, like a cloud of smoke. She looked around for her workout partner. When she did not see Susan she began to stretch. Just as she was about to start running she saw a small figure jogging toward the park. Rocky started to do jumping jacks instead. Susan came to her side, stretched and joined Rocky in her jumping jacks.

"Good morning. Is it cold enough for you?" Susan asked.

"I think it could be about ten degrees colder. What's up?" Rocky said.

"I have to tell you, my husband owns your broach, sweetie. You have not made one payment on it. I can't save you. When it comes to business, Edey will beat his mother for a buck. If you pay it off, in full, immediately, maybe he will let you slide. I am even surprised that he keeps urging me to remind you."

"No problem, I'll take care of it like yesterday."

Susan stopped jumping, and Rocky stopped as well. "What are you doing this holiday weekend?"

"I am leaving tonight for Detroit. I'll be out there all weekend. Why?"

"I told my husband that I was traveling with you and your women's group to the Bahamas this weekend. So if you do plan on coming to the store to pay off your debts, don't come today. I'll be back Sunday night and we are leaving Thursday morning."

"Let me find out you're creeping tomorrow?" Rocky's grin was so wide that her gums became instantly cold and her cheeks burned in the cold air.

"Will you be my alibi, or not?" Susan said in an agitated tone.

"Of course, I will. Why? What are you getting into?"

"Well, I guess it is safe to tell you. I have been seeing one of the guys from the mailroom at my job. Oh my God, he is so sexy, and his cock is huge. We have been sleeping together for the past five months."

"How old is he?"

"Twenty-seven. We are really enjoying each other."

"Don't get caught up. Cheat all you want but do not start catching feelings for this guy." Rocky nodded and smiled. "Twenty-seven? You got yourself a hottie, huh? Wait a minute, you little devil, is that who you wanted the oral sex tips for?"

Susan smiled and gently nodded. Rocky started to run, and Susan followed behind.

"My God, I can't believe I have forgotten about my great Nahnan's pendant. I will definitely take care of that first thing Monday morning. I have been so wrapped up in Marcus. I went to meet his mother a couple of weeks ago, and he has sent for me twice since then. Not to mention I still have been making my bi-weekly's to see my boyfriend in Detroit and the attorney I am dating here, has scheduled a trip for us to vacation in the South of France next month. I just have been tied up— did I mention my schoolwork?"

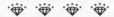

Tony hopped off the Greyhound bus and smiled at Kahmelle and Sweat.

"Hey, Donny, what the deal? Your ass finally left up top? We gonna get shit Crack-a-lack in North Caca-Lac, boy," Kahmelle said as he yanked Tony with all of his might and gave him a tight hug.

"I felt like I was on that bus forever. It left Port Authority at three p.m. Tuesday and its already eleven-thirty the next day."

"What up, Thuggle? Your parents finally turned you loose, pa?" Sweat asked.

Tony gave Sweat a pound and smiled. He dropped his large duffel bags on the ground.

"You got all the goods?" Sweat asked.

"Yep. I rammed fifty handbags into those duffel bags. I didn't even have enough room for my clothes. They're in my book bag."

"After we knock off these bags I'ma show your ass around Charlotte. We gonna go to the club and get fucked up, dog. Come on, hop in," Kahmelle said.

At first Tony was tense however Sweat's green Yukon eased his tension a bit. Sweat went to the trunk and arranged the bags. When Tony sat in the car he nearly shit in his pants.

"When did you two get down here?" Tony said.

Latonji smiled and looked into Tony's eyes. "We got down here late last night, Tony."

"Let's change seats, mama," Dulce said.

Latonji sat forward, let Dulce slip underneath her and slid next to Tony.

"You haven't returned my calls," she said.

"My fault. What's up?" Tony asked flatly.

"Me, you— this trip is what's up," Latonji said. Kahmelle hopped into the car and turned on the radio.

"Ow! That's the heat. Turn that up, daddy," Dulce said as she slithered and rolled her body like a snake in her seat.

Kahmelle pumped up the vibes and Sweat drove.

"D. and G. I am going to drop y'all down by the mall. I'm giving you ten bags. When you're done, hit up Kahmelle," Sweat said.

As the music played louder, the ride seemed to get longer to Tony. Latonji caught Tony staring at her several times. She, Dulce and Kahmelle sang every song on the mixed CD, from hip-hop to R&B, at the top of their lungs while Sweat cruised the streets of Charlotte like he owned them. When they finally reached their destination, Sweat spoke.

"We'll be picking you up right here."

The girls hopped out of the truck and Dulce grabbed a duffel bag from the trunk. There were three young women waiting alongside the mall. They had started walking toward the vehicle when the girls jumped out.

"Dulce, what took y'all so dang long?" one of the waiting girls asked.

Sweat slowly pulled off and Tony mushed Kahmelle in the back of his head. "What the fuck is that bitch doing out here, Kah?" Tony asked.

"I'm saying, Dulce is my piece and she wanted to bring her friend with her for the holiday weekend. Besides, Shaine won't come off of that ass but Latonji will," Kahmelle smirked.

"Nah, duke, that's a thing of the past."

Kahmelle turned around so fast he nearly fell out of his seat. "Don't be lying on your dick, son. You hit that?"

Tony nodded his head.

"Word? Nigga you ain't even tell me. I know that pussy's tight."

"You my man and all but I'm going to the grave with that shit."

Sweat laughed.

"What's so funny?" Kahmelle asked.

"My lil' mans is killin' me right now. You really like those fish, huh?"

"Dulce? That's my fuckin' wife right there."

Sweat laughed louder. "Think you're going to be with them fish forever, huh?"

"What? Me and Shaine are the new Bonnie and Clyde."

Kahmelle looked into the back and gave Tony a pound.

"What about you and Camille, Buck?" Sweat made a sharp turn around a corner and his tires swerved on the dirt-paved road, causing a cloud of beige dust to surround the car as it slid into a halt. He stopped in front of an old, small, white church. It had a tarnished copper bell hanging from its steeple. Its white wooden planks had started to chip, leaving black open cracks.

"Camille— remember her? The fish you knocked up?" Sweat asked.

"I'm saying. She wasn't me—"Kahmelle started.

"You was all up in that shit six months ago, you loved that broad, now 'that bitch isn't you'. Shit, she's all you. She's getting ready to have your seed, nigga. I told you to handle that. I got this fish pregnant once, Tasha, and I made her handle that, you feel me? Neither one of us was ready to have a seed so I forced her to get rid of it. Let me tell y'all something. Ain't nothing promised to you. Tomorrow will probably be here, but you may not."

Tony became tense and Kahmelle was dumbfounded.

"All I am sayin' is your life ain't promised to you, so what makes you think someone else's is? Be true to yourself, not no fish. They ain't worth it, because when the money is gone, they will be too. You think Dulce would be with you if you weren't Finest, nigga? How long have y'all been in school together? Three, four years, and she just decides that she wanted to be with you *now*? If I pull my dick out that bitch would suck it, 'cause she knows I have more money than you do. It's a paper chase baby boy— another hustle and I respect fishes' dig for the gold."

"I'm going to get my slum bag sales on, Sweat. You going to see Marva?" Kahmelle asked sarcastically.

"Yep, I'll be at her crib chillin'. Call me," Sweat said.

Kahmelle grabbed both duffel bags out of the trunk and stepped up on the curb next to Tony. Sweat scratched his scar and pulled off. As soon as Sweat's car was out of their view Kahmelle dropped both duffel bags to the ground and kicked one.

"Fuck that nigga, man. Yo, Tone, wait until you see this nigga's fish, Marva. She is banging. I know Sweat is sweatin that bitch for real."

"No pun intended, huh?" Tony laughed.

"What?"

"Sweat's sweatin'— get it?"

Kahmelle shook his head as if Tony had no idea what he was talking about and continued his conversation. "Who the fuck is that nigga to tell me that Dulce ain't in for the long ride? I think I love her."

Tony knelt down, placed his hands on the small curb of street and sat. He looked at his palms then clapped and rubbed them together several times watching the dirt from the concrete rise in front of his face. He looked up at his partner and patted the ground next to him, motioning for him to sit.

"Nah, these are brand new Evisu jeans nigga, fuck that."

"I'm sayin', Kah, Sweat made a point. When we first got down you was on Camille's dick. You my man and all but it seems like as soon as you got a little paper and found out that you could get a broad with good looks and an inch of class you dumped all over Camille."

Kahmelle sucked his teeth. "WHATEVER, NIGGA! Let's go inside and knock off these knock-offs."

"You can't get tight with me for tellin' the truth, duke," Tony called out as he got up and followed Kahmelle toward the church.

As Kahmelle entered the threshold Tony stopped. "Hold up, hold up. I know we aren't sellin' these bags inside the church! That shit ain't right."

"Just come on," Kahmelle said.

Kahmelle walked inside and went down a flight of narrow steps. Tony looked briefly at the pews that lined the small church's interior. As he rushed down the stairs, right behind Kahmelle, the picture of the fifteen or so rows of wooden pews stayed in his mind. He could still picture the red-carpeted church floor, all the way up to the small pulpit that was slightly elevated by a small platform. He couldn't remember the last time he had sat inside a church. They walked into a room filled with women, and very few men seated at long collapsible tables.

"B-28," loudly filled the church basement.

"Ma, come here," Kahmelle called.

I can't believe it. Tony thought as he watched a dark skinned woman approach from the far end of the church. *Six years of friendship and this is my first time meeting Kahmelle's mom. I have never even seen a picture of her.*

As she got closer Tony saw a slight resemblance. She had the most even dark skin that he had ever seen. It had a natural shine. Tiny, red, dark-colored veins crisscrossed her eyes like highways on a road map. Her pupils were nearly black, and were surrounded by a yellow hue. Her lips were the same complexion as the rest of her face. When she got close, she extended her hand. As she smiled her smooth dark lips revealed straight white teeth. Her hands were rough and wrinkled in comparison to the smooth appearance of her face. She had short, black hair that was plastered to her head with grease. Her hair was curled under tightly, and stopped just above her ears. She was 5'5" and very slim.

"So, you're Tony. Buck's partner."

As Tony stared past her face and shook her hand negative thoughts filled his head. *I wonder why she left Kah, with her little sister at that. Kahmelle said she was into the street but how could a mother leave her child? My mom would have never left Malik or I.*

"Tony, are you there?" Kahmelle asked.

"I'm sorry. I'm just surprised to meet you. You're so pretty. I always wondered what you looked like. Too bad Kahmelle didn't get his looks from you." All three of them laughed.

"Buck, set up those three folding tables right there in front of the stage. I am going back to my bingo game." She smiled at Tony and jogged lightly back to her seat. Tony shook his head.

"What you shakin' your head at my moms for?" Kahmelle snapped.

Tony responded quickly. "You got your mother calling you Buck?"

"At least she respects my gangster."

Truth be told, Tony could tell that Kahmelle's mother had probably been gorgeous before she hit the streets. As the two walked toward the stage Tony realized for the first time in his life how lucky he was to have been raised in a home with two loving parents. He didn't have to be out here doing this. What would they do if they found out about Brooklyn's Finest?

When Tony and Kahmelle reached the stage they connected two rectangular folding tables together. They both dumped dozens of bags on the table and categorized them by brand, price and size. Louis Vuitton, Gucci, Prada, Kate Spade, Yves Saint Laurrent, and Chanel. Wallets, hobo sizes, clutches, bowling bag shaped, drawstrings, and shoulder bags. All of the bags were spread out in front of them. After five minutes of silence between the two, Tony tapped Kahmelle.

"Kahmelle, you are much closer to Sweat than I am. Why don't you find out how he got the scar?"

"Why don't you ask your brother? They was tight like Shaine's cat, back then," Kahmelle said as he playfully punched Tony in the arm.

"You got mad jokes, huh?" Tony asked.

"You know that's right," Kahmelle replied.

"BINGO!!! I got Bingo!" A woman in her twenties jumped around and waved her card in the air. She smiled and ran up to the Bingo announcer who handed her an envelope. As she waved the card in the air other Bingoers clapped and cheered for her. The announcer knocked on the microphone with her fist, put it to her mouth and cleared her throat.

"Good afternoon. Due to the holiday tomorrow this is our only Bingo session today 'cause most of us have to get an early start in the kitchen, but for those of us who don't Thanksgiving dinners can be purchased in the back of the church. Also, the youth choir is selling refreshments to help fund their Black college tour and Nettie's son is selling bags to my left. Thank you."

Without notice every woman in the church with the exception of Kahmelle's mother, the Bingo announcer and two others were at the tables. Women haggled over purses; some purchased two or three while others placed orders and left down payments for the following month. The younger women flirted with Tony and Kahmelle trying to get the prices down or hoping to spend time with the boys from New York. After forty-five minutes, the entire table was empty.

"That was unbelievable. I can't believe we sold everything. Let's break down our profits," Tony said.

Kahmelle pulled a sheet of paper out of his back pocket and unfolded it. "I had 12 wallets, 10 medium sized bags and 15 large bags," he said.

"Let's see; I had 8 wallets with your 12 at thirty dollars a— piece thaaaat's six hundred in wallets," Tony said.

Kahmelle picked a pen up from the table. "You said six hundred, son?" Kahmelle asked.

"Yes. I had 20 medium-sized bags with your 20 at one fifty— carry the one— um, thaaaat's— forty five hundred in medium sized bags," Tony said.

After fifteen minutes, they had finished tallying.

"We've made nine thousand one hundred dollars. Now that's what's up. Split that three ways and it's three thousand thirty three dollars and thirty-three cents. I say we break the church off with two hundred and thirty three dollars. This way we donate seven hundred to the junior choir fundraiser. Do you sell in the church all the time?" Tony asked.

"This is my second time," Kahmelle replied.

"Have you ever donated money to them before?"

"Hell no."

"Well, we should do it today."

"I'm sayin'— I don't know if Sweat is going to go for that. If his money comes up short—"

"Later for him, let's give them three-fifty a piece," Tony said.

Kahmelle sucked his teeth and Tony shook his head.

"You're pathetic. I'll give them five hundred out of my stash," Tony said.

"How much do we all get again?" Kahmelle asked.

"Three thousand and thirty-three dollars Kahmelle, just give me five hundred. You and Sweat will cut it up later."

Tony took the money from him. Kahmelle folded up the tables and Tony walked to the back of the church where the youth choir sold refreshments. "Hey, how are you?" Tony asked a young girl behind the table.

"I love my bag. Thanks a lot," the girl said smiling. She pointed at a Louis Vuitton knapsack with the signature LV's all over it.

"How much are your donuts?" Tony asked.

"One dollar."

"That's a lot of money for a donut, don't you think?"

The young girl smiled, "We're trying to raise money."

"Alright, let me get five hundred donuts," Tony said.

"Excuse me?"

"I would like to donate five hundred dollars to the choir for your college tour," Tony said.

The girl smiled and revealed a mouth full of braces. She turned around and called to a woman who was serving dinners at the next table.

"Sister Rolanda, Sister Nettie's son and his friend want to donate five hundred dollars to us!"

Tony checked the girl out. *She's a cutie*, Tony thought. *Those braces, her accent and her ass. She can definitely get it.*

"Praise them! Come over here and get some of this food right here," Sister Rolanda said.

The girl smiled and batted her eyes at Tony. Tony smiled.

"You can hand that money over to Sister Rolanda. She organized the trip and don't forget to call."

"Call?" Tony said.

"I'm the girl that gave you my number when I bought the bag, remember?"

"I'm Tony. What's your name?"

"Saniya."

"Nice to meet you," Tony said.

Tony walked over to the next table. Kahmelle's mother was at the opposite end of it serving dinners next to Sister Rolanda. He handed the woman the money and she smiled.

"Thank you. Now what do you boys want to take home to eat?" Sister Rolanda asked.

"Can I have a barbecue turkey wing dinner with mac and cheese and yams, please," Tony said.

"You got it sweet heart. Nettie, fix your boy a plate," Sister Rolanda said."

"What do you want, Buck? Barbecue chicken and black eyed peas?" Kahmelle's mother asked.

"Nettie, you know I can't stand barbecue sauce. You don't remember that time I was little I got real sick after eating it and Seepia had to take me to the hospital? I never touch the stuff and I don't like black-eyed peas either. Give me fried chicken, collards and some of that potato salad right there."

She fixed his plate and smiled, "Here you go, Buck."

Tony looked at Kahmelle. *Nettie?* he thought. *My moms would backhand me if I called her by her first name.* Tony took his container then reached for his wallet.

"God bless. This plate is on us," Sister Rolanda said.

When they walked upstairs, and out of the church, Sweat was already parked outside. Kahmelle walked up to the window with Tony behind him and handed Sweat the cash. He counted it and looked up.

"Y'all sold all them bags?" Sweat asked.

"Yep, in forty-five minutes flat," Tony said.

"Buck, this shit is five hundred short," Sweat said.

"I donated five hundred dollars to the church's youth choir. So take that out of my cut," Tony said.

Kahmelle cleared his throat. "Nah, I'm going to go half with you so take two fifty out of each of ours."

Sweat looked at Tony and nodded his head with a smirk on his face.

"Only a Thuggleman, nigga." Sweat counted out the money and gave each of them their cut. He pulled two hundred and fifty dollars out of his pocket and gave it to Kahmelle.

"Run downstairs and give them my two-fifty. Hop in the front, Thuggle." Tony got in the car and Kahmelle jogged back inside the church. Sweat gave Tony the once over. "You not wile'n out with your money like Buck, are you?"

"Nah. I still haven't spent all the money from our first couple of runs. I I'm savin' mine."

"Good. Let me tell you how to hold on to that shit. Put all your money into thousand-dollar money orders so it won't be easy to spend. When they are about to expire, cash them and put the money right back into the money orders. Only get postal money orders or bank money orders, so you won't have a problem cashin' them."

"That's a good idea 'cause that money is burning a hole in my shoe box. I wanted to buy a new car to go away to school. But Dad is going to give me the Saab."

"How are your parents?"

"They're fine, thanks."

"Is your moms still fine as hell— and is your pops still all over her?"

Tony smiled, "Yep, nothing has changed."

"Remember Thanksgiving at your crib? Your mom used to put her foot and ass in each plate."

"Word, you would come every year with your grandmother. You were family."

Sweat looked at Tony then looked back down at the steering wheel and cleared his throat. "What up with Leeko?"

"He's chillin'. He just started law school."

Sweat smiled. "You know that dude came to my house. I hadn't seen that nigga in five years."

Tony's stomach dropped to his toes. "What did you say? When!"

"Nothin'— I didn't let him into the crib. He didn't even know I was home."

Kahmelle hopped into the car just as Sweat finished speaking. Sweat pulled off. "What's up with your grades and school?" Sweat asked.

"All A's and A pluses, and I got accepted into a Pre-Med college program. Why?"

"Just asking."

"Sweat, can I ask you something?"

"Sure, what up, Thuggle?"

"How did you get that scar on your face?"

Sweat's smile instantly dried up. He moistened his mouth, and let his tongue run over the portion of the scar that reached his lip. "Ask your brother how he got his. We got our scars at the same time," Sweat said.

"Who did it and why? I know they ain't breathing?" Kahmelle asked.

"Tone, didn't you say Leeko was chillin'?" Sweat asked.

"Yeah," Tony replied.

"So he's breathin', right?"

"Yeah." Tony replied in a confused tone.

"Ask him. He put it there," Sweat said and pushed on the radio.

The music was lonely; it was the only sound in the car until they reached the mall. Sweat pulled into the fire zone lane and the girls stood at the same spot they had been left. Tony sat deep in thought, and had a silent revelation. *Wait a minute, if they got theirs at the same time, did Sweat cut Malik? This shit is way deeper than I ever imagined.*

Mauri and Rocky sat in his car staring at each other. "I have missed you so much, Rocky. It feels like I haven't seen you in months," Mauri said.

"It's only been a couple of weeks. You've been so busy lately, I'm surprised you're here instead of Jack," Rocky said.

"I've been busy putting in all this extra work for you, baby girl."

Rocky leaned over and smothered Mauri's right cheek with kisses. Mauri smiled and stared at Rocky as she sat back and looked out the window.

"The light's green," Rocky said. Mauri pulled off and Rocky continued to look out of the window. "Where are you going? You've never taken this route home before."

"It's the day before Thanksgiving. You know I'm trying to avoid the airport traffic."

"Do you think you could get me tickets to tomorrow's Piston's game since you are leaving for Chicago right after dinner?"

"No sweat, baby girl. I'll make a call to my man tonight. What are you wearing to my mother's house?"

"I don't know, I was thinking we could go and buy something now?" Rocky smiled broadly at Mauri and he in turn looked at his watch.

"Your flight was delayed fifteen minutes and it's already eight o' clock. By the time we get downtown the stores will be closed. But you know I took the liberty of buying you something really nice for tomorrow."

Rocky smiled and threw both of her arms around Mauri's neck. "Stop!" Mauri shouted. "You gonna fuck around and make me crash."

They drove for another fifteen minutes. Rocky sat back listening to nothing but the thoughts conjured up by her conniving mind. Mauri slowed down. "Belle Aisle? What the hell is this?" Rocky asked with an attitude.

"Uh, we gonna drive through the park to cut traffic, you know like ya'll drive though Central Park."

"Okay," she said. Rocky saw a huge bridge in the far distance, that she'd never seen in the two-plus years she'd been coming to Detroit. "What's the name of that bridge over there, Mauri?"

"That's the Ambassador bridge, it takes you right into Ontario, Canada."

"Canada, the country?" Rocky asked.

"Yep."

"I never realized Detroit was so close to Canada."

Before she knew it they had pulled up in front of a very scenic area. She looked through the front window and continued to gaze at the Detroit skyline. Although it had a few small skyscrapers in comparison to the dozens that fill New York City's skyline, the sparkling stars in the Detroit sky were priceless. *This skyline can't touch mine,* she thought silently. She looked around the area.

Mauri parked the car. Rocky noticed two benches facing a small pond. She opted to look at the skyline in the reflection of the dark water. When she looked back up she saw a man standing in front of the bench with a violin case in his hand.

It's too damn cold out here to be beggin and shit, she thought. She tapped Mauri's shoulder. "Mauri, what are we doing here? We could be downtown now. Why did you stop?"

"Because I want you to open the box and see if you like what I bought you before we leave the downtown area. This way we can take it back if need be. We have twenty minutes. Besides, I have to take a piss. The packages are on the back seat." Mauri got out, walked and disappeared behind a tree."

I don't think we're anywhere near downtown. Oh, well, Rocky thought as she reached into the back seat and picked up a wrapped box. "Wow, he really went all out. He never wraps things," she said.

Rocky ripped the paper off the box like a six-year-old on Christmas morning. She removed an orange jumpsuit similar to the one she had worn to Marcus' house. She was impressed. As Rocky searched the jumpsuit for tags she noticed several people standing outside the car. They stood around the benches. She immediately directed her attention outside. When she caught the whole picture, she dropped the jumpsuit and covered her mouth.

Mauri was down on one knee in front of the benches. The beggar, Rocky had glanced at minutes earlier was accompanied by twenty men and women dressed in formal black attire holding instruments. Her tears seemed to weigh her down. They flowed freely down her cheeks into her lap. She could not move. The violinist walked to the car with his instrument under his arm and bow in one hand. He escorted her from the car and sat her on the bench.

As she sat, the small orchestra broke out into the most sophisticated rendition of Jagged Edge's, 'Let's Get Married' to date. Although she was breathlessly seized by the moment she stopped for a short thought.

How ghetto. He's got an orchestra playing Jagged Edge. All he needs is for P.Diddy or Rev Run to jump out and rap my proposal. She shook off her thoughts and seized the moment.

Mauri gave her a couple of minutes to take in what was happening. After which, he grabbed her right hand and held it firmly. He looked into her eyes and cleared his throat.

"Raquel Candace Jones, I've loved you for over two years now. I want you to have my seeds and I want you to have my last name. I want you to have this ring and be my wife. Will you marry me?"

He reached into the breast pocket of his gray and black, goose down, North Face and pulled out a cranberry, velour, ring box. When he opened it Rocky began to cry out loud. Her insides started to tingle and get warm. Strangely, she began to feel excited— sexually excited. When he slipped the ring onto her ring finger her clitoris started to pulsate and she became more aroused.

A bright flash illuminated the park. This caused the scene to momentarily look like a black-and-white snapshot. The diamond was enormous. For the first time in their two-plus years her horniness ran straight through her vagina and into her womb. From her womb it traveled through her digestive system and she regurgitated three words that she could have never mustered up under normal circumstances.

"I love you too. Yes, Maurice, I will marry you."

Bright flashes lit up that area of the park. The orchestra stopped playing their instruments. They clapped and threw white orchid petals on the happy couple. He stood, turned her around toward a huge fountain and within seconds its bright lights illuminated and it gushed water. Two photographers snapped shots of Mauri kissing his fiancée. Then, the orchestra played 'Differences' by Genuine.

"You make me responsible, Rocky. Sure, I was making money and had businesses when I met you. But, it's because of you that I am trying to take my franchise world wide. It's because of you that I want more than flashy cars and bitches. I want to build a family and a life and I want this with you."

Rocky suddenly felt cold all over. *What did I do? I don't love Mauri, I love Marcus,* she thought. "What about your mother? She hates me," Rocky bawled.

"But I love you and now that I know you love me, it doesn't matter. Baby girl, get in the car. I need to take care of some things out here."

She slowly got up from the bench, knelt and began gathering and shoving handfuls of orchid petals and into her coat pocket. As she stood upright she stared into the eyes of one of seven, large, white geese that had waddled over to the scene to check things out.

"UUUGH!!" Rocky shrieked. She threw the remaining petals at the geese and scurried in the direction of the car in hysterics. The members of the orchestra congratulated and consoled her along her way. She tried to smile and thank all that approached her but constantly kept her eyes on the geese. As she entered the car the loud ring of her cell phone filled it. She grabbed it from her bag and answered it. She stared at the huge white fountain and the white stone steps beneath it.

"CANDY!" Marcus shouted.

"Hey," Rocky said.

"You need a new phone. I said 'hello' like five times."

Rocky broke into tears and sobbed loudly, "Hold on, baby." She looked at Mauri. He was paying each orchestra member in cash, one by one. She had time. She reached into his glove compartment and removed some napkins. She blew and blew her nose until it was sore then she returned to her call without taking her eyes off Mauri.

"What's wrong, Candy?"

"Nothing, I am just having a moment."

"What kind of moment?"

"It's a woman thing. I'll be alright."

"Well, if you need to talk, you know I am here."

"I have a big surprise for you," Rocky sniffled.

"What?"

"You'll see. What hotel do you guys stay at when you're in Detroit?"

"The Townsend, why?"

Rocky smiled. She was very familiar with that hotel. That is where she went in Detroit for a day at the spa and Jack had driven her there after the cat incident, with Mauri. "Be expecting something after the game, okay?"

"Okay. I really wish you would say something to me. What's wrong? It hurts me to hear you hurting."

"It's nothing, really. I get a little emotional around the holidays."

At this point Rocky began to cry louder. She covered her eyes with her hand and used the other to clutch the phone to her face. She wiped her eyes with the tightly balled snot-filled napkin.

"Listen, just expect a surprise tomorrow. I really don't feel much for talking right now."

"Did I do something?"

"Nope. I'll talk to you tomorrow. Call me and leave your room number once you figure that information out."

"One second. I forgot to tell you. My mother invited you over for dinner, if you aren't doing anything for Thanksgiving tomorrow. "

Marcus' words seemed to instantly clear her nasal passage and her tears stopped. "What? Why?" she asked.

"Well, she asked what we were doing and I told her we didn't make plans because I was working. I also told her you didn't have any living relatives. That's when she suggested you spend Thanksgiving with our family."

"Tell her I appreciate the invitation, but I already have plans."

"Oh? Where are you going?"

Rocky watched as Mauri walked towards the car. "Just leave your info on my phone and call me tomorrow." She flipped the phone down quickly and reopened it faster. When Mauri entered the car she began to talk louder. "Yes. I am getting married, girl. The proposal was so romantic, too. It was straight out of a fairytale. Okay, my hubby is back. I'll talk to you later," Rocky flipped the phone down and looked at Mauri. "That was Kay. She said congratulations."

"What the fuck was you yellin' like that for?"

"Mauri, you know I hate birds and that goose was all in my face."

"Oh." Mauri paused for a second. "I thought you might be a little tight with me and shit."

She threw a puzzled look at Mauri, "Why would I be tight after that beautiful proposal?"

Mauri drove off. "I know you wanted to wait until you finished school."

"Yeah, and we are still going to wait. We will set our date after my graduation."

"I have dinner reservations for nine at—"

"Mauri, I am mentally exhausted. I don't feel like going out to eat. Let's just go home, start a fire and have cocktails in front of the fireplace. We could make our pre-wedding plans. Besides, we have a long day ahead of us, tomorrow. After you break the news to your mother, you have to make the four hour drive to Chicago."

"I want to have our wedding on a yacht, and . . ."

Rocky tuned Mauri out and as usual her thoughts ran wild. *My God, I don't have that much time*, she thought. *I have to make Marcus love me. I can't let these wedding plans get underway and then break them at the last minute. Tomorrow is do or die. I have to come up with a foolproof plan.*

21

After the party it's the hotel lobby and. . .

The five drunk teens came stumbling back into the hotel. Tony sported two girls on his side, and Kahmelle sported one.

"That was a bangin'-ass club. They did it real big for a Wednesday night," Tony said.

Kahmelle and Dulce followed closely behind.

"Kid Capri handled his business up in that joint," Kahmelle said.

They all stopped when they reached the rooms.

"Kahmelle, you got my key?" Tony turned and looked at the girls. "Ladies, the pleasure was all mine."

"This is my room, too, I have the key," Latonji said.

"Whatever. Open the door, I gotta pee," Tony said.

Latonji opened the door and Tony stumbled into the bathroom. He came out to find everyone in his room.

"Yo, let's blaze this shit right here before we turn in," Kahmelle said.

"Kah, I feel like shit. My head is throbbing and I am tired. Spark that shit in your own room!"

"Alright, son. Come on y'all."

As everyone left, Tony rummaged through his bag and took out a wad of money. He undressed down to his underwear and put on a pair of long shorts with an old nylon wallet pinned to the inside. When he opened it the sound from the Velcro enclosure sent a chill up his spine. He placed all his cash in it, pulled back the covers and got into bed.

Two hours later the door to his room opened and the light came on, but Tony was in a deep drunken slumber. Saniya and Latonji came in giggling and laughing. They toppled onto the bed opposite his.

"Look at Tone. That nigga is a dime," Latonji said.

"I tried to holla' at him in the church today. He donated some money to my choir," Saniya said.

"Well, he's spoken for," Latonji snapped.

Saniya seemed surprised. "That's your boyfriend?"

"Nah, but I got first dibs on that one. He was sweatin' the shit out of me for a second, but I had a man."

"Let's see if he wants a little company— come on." Saniya stood up and took off her shirt. As she pulled it over her head she spoke. "Take of your clothes."

"Listen, country, I don't get down like that. I know I said your outfit was cute and all but I stick to the dick."

"You get on one side of him and I'll get on the other. I got my buzz on. I ain't gay, I'm just horny. He can't turn both of us down naked," Saniya said.

Latonji smiled and wiggled her way out of her tight jeans. She untied her Timbs and kept her underwear on. Latonji couldn't help but notice how big Saniya's ass was. Her large butt cheeks swallowed a purple cotton thong. Her waist was tiny and her small A cup breasts were all nipples. One side of her blunt bob was behind her ear. The other side fluttered on her face as she bent over and rummaged through her purse. She pulled out a condom and laid next to Tony on the bed.

"Girl, you know you're crazy, right?" Latonji asked as she lay on the other side of Tony. Latonji kissed him gently on his lips. When he didn't move she kissed him again. Saniya nibbled on his earlobe and rubbed his back. Tony turned over and opened one eye. A blurry vision of bare skin came into his view. He shut that eye and struggled to open the other. The light was too bright. He cleared his throat, stretched, opened both eyes and Saniya came into view. He sat up quickly, covered his chest and leapt back to the other side of the bed, only to collide with a soft, warm body. He turned around quickly.

"What the fuck!" Tony exclaimed as he exhaled deeply and closed his eyes. *I love Shaine, I love Shaine, I love Shaine*, he repeated silently before he reopened his eyes.

It was then he noticed they were both naked. Saniya got up and walked slowly over to Latonji's side of the bed. Tony grabbed his dick and shifted it to the side underneath his shorts as he watched Saniya walk across the foot of the bed. He had never seen a more perfect ass in his life. He had seen bigger in his magazines, but they were always scarred up and filled with cellulite, stretch marks or scars.

"You know you want some of this," Saniya said as she crawled closer and wiggled her ass near Tony's face. "And this." Saniya fondled one of Latonji's breasts through her bra. Latonji tensed up but once she saw Tony pull his dick out and tear his wife beater off, she went along with it.

"Shit, I could hardly hold my liquor. As soon as y'all touch me I know I'm not going to be able to hold no nut. Sorry, ladies, but I can't."

Saniya sat on his lap with her back facing him.

"Latonji, go in my bag and get my disposable camera. I have to get a picture of this shit." He hiccuped and burped at the same time and could feel a wave of bile rise in his throat and tickle his tonsils. He grabbed three plastic cups from the hotel dresser and vomited into them. Latonji handed him the camera and sat next to him.

"Saniya, bend over and spread your cheeks." She bent over and he snapped a picture. Then she got up and spread her legs and ass cheeks in front of him. Tony snapped two pictures of that. He pulled his shorts and boxers down to his kneecaps, and started to jerk off.

"Now bend over standing up and let me take one more picture. Latonji, suck my dick."

"I don't do that, that's nasty and—"

Tony let out a monster load of sperm in the middle of her sentence. A little shot into Saniya's hair but most of it shot out in Latonji's face, and on Tony. Latonji screamed and ran into the bathroom. Saniya laughed. She kissed him gently on the mouth and grabbed his dick. Tony searched for his wife beater. When he located it on the floor, he picked it up, wiped his cum out of Saniya's hair, and cleaned himself. "Come here," he said.

Saniya followed him to the dresser. He faced the mirror and pushed her head down. Without hesitation she was on her knees.

"Nah, could you just bend over and suck it. I want to see your ass in the mirror."

Within seconds of the blow job, his penis was fully erect. He tapped her shoulder and she stood up. He pulled a condom over his penis then he opened a second and pulled that one on, too.

"Dang, I ain't got no AIDS or nothing. Why you put on two?" Saniya asked.

"Bend over," Tony hiccuped. "If I had another one I would put on three." She stepped out of her thong and bent over. Tony fondled and poked around for a minute or two, then watched himself pound his slim frame into her vast backside. Latonji snapped several pictures of them then covered her head with the spread. It took several minutes for her to sleep with nothing but the loud sounds of pleasure to lull her. Tony thought about Shaine and momentarily felt bad. But the infinite behind in front of him felt too good and over powered his remorse.

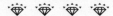

Susan sat on the tip of the thin barge and let her feet dangle over the edge. This was the first Thanksgiving she had spent without her husband since they were married. And here she was, with nothing but clear blue water beneath her feet and clear white sand with a few tourists spread over it in her view. Malik was whipping a jet ski in the far distance. She smiled as he attempted to do tricks and his jet ski toppled over and became aroused when he performed a successful trick. After forty-five minutes he buzzed over to the pier and returned his jet ski rental.

Susan could feel his shadow encompass her being as Malik approached. He sat down with his legs open wide enough for her to fit in between. His wet body sent a relieving chill against her hot and sticky bare skin. He inhaled deeply and let out a pleasant sigh.

"This is so beautiful." Malik squeezed her waistline from behind. "You know what? I didn't have half as much fun when I was out here alone."

"I hope you didn't showboat like that for any other women when you were here without me."

Malik smiled. *Shit, I fucked a bitch on that same jet ski while a cruise ship watched. Now that's showboating for your ass*, he thought. "Of course not," he chuckled. "I stayed on the beach, in the water, tanned and drank. I basically kept to myself."

Susan grabbed his legs tightly so that they caressed her small frame from the back. "Is there anything wrong? Are you getting tired of me, Malik? You seem so distant."

Malik faced Susan, stroked her long, golden hair and then passionately kissed her on the lips. "Why would you think that? My mind has been on my little brother. I'm worried about him, that's all."

"Didn't you say he got accepted into a Pre-Med program?"

"Yeah, but I think he's running with the wrong crowd, and instead of me trying to correct it I'm acting like it's not happening."

"As soon as you get back you need to address that issue."

"Susan, I have. I asked him. He told me he wasn't. I checked out his alibi and it was true, but I still feel like there is something wrong." Susan affectionately tightened the grip on his hand. "I know I'm not going all out because I really don't want to find out the truth. It would just kill my parents."

"I'm sure everything is okay. I wish there was a way I could help you."

"I was always the delinquent. Hanging in the streets, bad grades, fighting, selling drugs— I ran the streets for him. I don't want him out there. He is so smart. You should've seen his report card. I love him."

"I know you do, Malik. I've been thinking. Wouldn't you like your own apartment?"

"Where did that come from? You know I'm trying to save my money so I can pay for school."

"I've got an idea. I could put you up in an apartment, so I could be able to come and stay with you when my husband is out on business. He travels a lot and I will pay what ever your scholarship doesn't."

"I don't know, Susan. I would have to think about that. I love spending time with you, but where is this relationship going to go? I'm starting to have deeply rooted feelings for you. If we share that kind of time together, my feelings would get even deeper and that is not fair to me because you belong to someone else. For now, I think we should just keep things the way they are."

"Malik, something has been bothering me and I really don't know how approach the subject."

Susan paused for a moment and Malik kissed her neck as he stared at an attractive, young White couple. They stood a few feet away catching tropical fish off the barge with a string and a hook. They reminded him of a celebrity couple he had seen on the cover of 'People' magazine. An older local with thick dreadlocks, deep dark brown smooth skin, and the few teeth that remained in his mouth all capped in gold, was charging ten American dollars per person to fish off the barge for fifteen minutes. The couple flashed a huge smile at Susan and Malik as Malik kissed and caressed Susan gently from behind.

They probably think I'm a native, and Susan is getting her swerve on. I am going to make it my business to strike up a dummy conversation when we walk by, Malik thought.

"Malik, who was the girl you were with when you stood me up at the hotel a couple of weeks ago? Is she your lover?" Susan asked. Malik exhaled heavily but remained silent. Susan turned around and looked at him. "Seriously, are you intimate with her?" she asked.

"She's just a young lady that I met a couple of months ago— that's all. Don't feel threatened. She is just a friend."

"What's her name?"

"Please don't. I'm really enjoying my time with you out here. Don't waste our little bit of time together talking about something that does not concern our relationship. When I leave here, you'll remain for another seven days. I am not going to see you for a while."

"Is she the reason you don't want the apartment I'm offering to purchase for you? I'm sure she's the reason the time we spend together has been dramatically reduced," Susan said firmly.

"I don't know what you want me to do! I am there whenever you need me. I have done everything you have asked me to and I never get into your personal business. So please don't get into mine."

Malik stood up and stretched his arms. *I definitely did not see this coming,* he thought. He helped her up, kissed her neck and whispered in her ear. "Follow my lead and just go along with everything I am about to say," Malik whispered.

When they were within earshot distance from the couple, Malik started to talk loudly. "Sweetie? Do you think the twins are too much for your mother to handle for an entire week? Maybe we should shorten the length of our stay a couple of days?"

Susan smiled. "Honey, we have discussed this a dozen times. We need this time for us. The girls are okay and we are not going to spend our entire vacation worrying about them."

"I guess you're right, but I am calling home as soon as we get to the room," Malik said.

As they walked slowly by, the female in the couple looked down at Susan's ring and flashed a smile of approval. Both Susan and Malik smiled back and continued their idle chatter.

"Do you think we should ask them? The guy is Black. I always wanted a Black man," the woman said as she watched Susan and Malik.

"I guess we could try, sweetie," the man replied as he retrieved twenty dollars from his wallet and handed it to the native. They followed Susan and Malik who were analyzing the situation.

"You know, I sensed they were talking about us when you were on the jet ski," Susan said.

"I figured they thought you were getting your 'Stella' on," Malik said.

"Stella? Like the Stella Awards?"

"No, like the main character from that novel 'How Stella Got her Groove Back'."

"I saw the movie. You think I look that much older than you?"

"No, Susan. I'm making reference to the fact that Stella was fooling around with one of the islanders, like a one-night-stand kind of thing. And homegirl from the movie did not look old."

"I knew it was something. I figured they were discussing the race issue. Malik they're right behind us," Susan said as she and Malik turned around and faced the couple from the barge.

The couples stared at each other. The female looked at Malik and seductively licked her lips. The male stepped forward.

"Hi," the man said as he extended his hand to Malik. "Do you swing? My wife finds you very attractive and I think your wife is stunning."

"Excuse me?" Malik said defensively.

Susan smiled. She had recently viewed a program about swinging on the adult channel. *This could be the perfect time for me to try out my new oral skills,* Susan thought. Before the man could answer Susan whispered in Malik's ear. His face screwed up as she explained the concept and he sucked his teeth.

"Oh hell no. I am not fuckin' around like that. I don't want no one else tapin' my wife but me—" *and her husband,* he thought.

"Come on I want to show you something," Susan said to Malik. Then she smiled at the couple. "Won't you please come in?" she asked them.

As soon as the foursome walked into the room Susan dropped to her knees and pulled Malik's penis out of his trunks. She thought of Rocky's women's group and how she had practiced on a banana a few times a week since then. Susan closed her eyes and began to suck.

Malik looked down at her in amazement as she plunged his penis into her mouth. He groaned as she sucked it quickly. Her head bobbed up and down while she held the bottom of his dick and moved her wrist in a circular motion, just as Rocky had showed her. Malik looked at Susan and the perkiness of her big breasts bobbing up and down had him ready to explode. Malik looked at the couple. The wife had copied Susan's motions and began to suck her husband's penis. Malik caught the wife peeking at his dick. "Susan, swallow," Malik moaned.

Susan had never seen him so aroused. Her jaws felt numb. Just at the point she could not suck anymore his sperm oozed out the corners of her mouth and she gulped as much of it as she could. As Malik caught his breath he felt a pair of frail hands massage him from the back and lick his scar. He quickly turned around. "I'm sorry ma, I don't get down like that."

The woman approached Susan, bent down and began fondling and sucking her breasts. Malik could feel his dick getting heavier by the moment. Susan, overwhelmed, stepped back, and could feel the husband's rubber coated penis on her back. She quickly retreated back to the lips of his wife.

As the wife worked on Susan's erect nipples she gently stroked Susan's lips with her fingers until she parted them. Susan sucked on her fingers like it was Malik's dick and stared at him seductively as he tugged on his own. The wife eased her fingers out of Susan's mouth and slid them into Susan's vagina.

Malik's penis led him towards the wife who knelt in front of Susan as she stood spread eagle humping the fingers sliding in and out of her. The wife enveloped Malik's dick. "OH SHIT!" Malik exclaimed. The husband tugged his own rod faster and faster as he walked toward Susan and rubbed his penis on her behind. He fondled her breasts and began to push her shoulders downward. Malik pulled his dick out of the wife's mouth and pushed the husband off of Susan.

"The party's over. I'm sorry— I didn't even catch your names but I think you should leave," Malik said in an authoritative voice.

The married couple pulled on their swimsuits and walked to the door. Winded, the wife smiled. "If you would like to continue where we left off we're in Room 3214."

"Don't worry, we won't." The couple let themselves out. "Wow, Susan, I would have never thought you could put it down like that. The head was no joke," Malik said as he cleared his throat. "But that freak shit you just pulled right there— I did not like that at all."

Susan exhaled. "I really didn't want them to touch us. I was nervous about giving you head, and I figured if they were there it would take away from— you looked so excited when they were— I'm parched, I really need something to drink." Malik stared at Susan as she fixed her clothes. "Why are you staring at me like that? You think I'm a slut now, don't you?"

"No, I still can't believe I am with the baddest woman at the job."

"You're just saying that."

"Don't you know that every man at our firm has fantasized about what we just did. Why me? I just don't understand. Is it a Black thing? Did you want to see if the myth was true?"

"It was 30% myth, 60% your stunning looks— your eyes. The other 10 was the fact that you were in the mailroom."

"What did the mailroom have to do with anything?" Malik said.

"Very little, but if you worked anywhere else in the building, I would have never approached you."

"Aren't you going to get us some drinks?"

"Yes, but I don't want to go to the bar with cock breath," Susan laughed.

"Why don't you polish me off first?"

"Only if you promise to fuck my cunt really good. But I need something to drink first. Keep my cock hard, and I'll be right back."

He sat on the bed as Susan went to brush her teeth. When she left the room he rushed to his cell phone and dialed out. "Hey, Laneice. How was your flight?" Malik asked.

"I guess you would know if you called me last night when I got in," Laneice replied.

"I can't wait to see you," Malik said.

"Where's the Barbie doll?" Laneice said sarcastically.

"Laneice, don't start." He smiled as he thought back to his mother referring to Susan as 'Over Forty Barbie.' "You know that I really am starting to have deeply rooted feelings for you. I almost didn't want to come out here. I like you a lot."

"Really, Malik?"

"Really. Bear with me. Give me a year to do this, and I promise you can have me to yourself."

Laneice smiled. "Give me a kiss, Malik."

Malik rolled his eyes and puckered his lips loudly next to the mouthpiece of his phone. "See you soon."

"Goodbye," Laneice said.

"Well, that went well didn't it, baby?" Rocky said sarcastically as she stared at her ring.

"She'll get over it. I don't know what's up with my moms. She generally likes every body. She's a churchgoer and all that," Mauri said.

Rocky smiled as thoughts of the curse of Too Sweet danced through her mind. "I'm cursed, Mauri."

"I can't believe she was cussing and shit," Mauri said.

"She called me a yellow whore bitch. I knew she didn't like me, Mauri, but damn— she hates me now."

"That's word to everything I love, I ain't know she hated you like that." Mauri sucked his teeth and shook his head. "Don't worry, she'll get used the idea of you being my wife. Anyway, my shit is packed up in the trunk. The ticket to the game is at 'The Palace' in Will Call under your name so bring ID with you. You can take the Porsche. You know where the keys are, right?" Rocky nodded her head. "I'm sorry, I can't believe Ma carried on like that," Mauri said.

"It's okay— I have heard worse," Rocky said.

Mauri sat and visions of his mother yelling and crying over Thanksgiving dinner were clear in his mind. *Why would she act like that towards her?* He thought. He looked over at Rocky who was staring out of the window. *Maybe Mom is right. What if she is a gold digging bitch?* At that moment Rocky looked at him. She silently touched her ring then placed an open palm over her heart. Mauri refocused on the road and thought hard. *Nah, it can't be true,* he thought, *she's the best thing that ever happened to me. It's evident she's not creeping and she loves me.*

The last fifteen minutes of the forty-five minute ride were silent. Rocky was coming up with a foolproof plan to win Marcus and Mauri was trying to think of ways Rocky could win his mother over. Once they were in his driveway he kissed her passionately and promised to be home early Friday night so they could discuss plans for their future. As soon as she jumped out of the car Mauri sped off. Rocky went into the house and put her plan into action. She started by making the dishes that went straight to all her men's heart; oxtail stew; rice and peas, macaroni and cheese and spinach. She even baked a sweet potato pie.

She rummaged through her luggage and retrieved the uniform for her mission. It was the tan pony hair and leather, denim styled suit that Mauri had purchased for her during his last visit to Brooklyn, with the matching boots. She fretted in the mirror for at least an hour over the same outfit, as the aroma of her cooking flooded the house. She finally decided not to wear a shirt under the jacket and to keep her hair down.

When she was fully dressed she checked the time. It was already eight and the game started at seven. She placed all of the food into a large bowl, covered it tightly with aluminum foil and placed it in Mauri's Louis Vuitton duffel bag. As she walked out of the kitchen she backtracked, grabbed one of Mauri's many bottles of Cristal and one of three plastic baggies filled with orchid petals from her proposal. She placed these items in the duffel bag and struggled to zip it up. She checked the stove and waltzed out of the house.

She went into his garage and removed a set of car keys from inside a tall wooden toolbox that was mounted on the wall. She started the Porsche and its engine rumbled loudly. When she got into the car she sat on one of the mink balls that hung off the drawstring of her mink jacket. She shifted her behind to one side and managed to yank it from under her. Using the remote control she opened the garage door and backed out.

She glanced at her face in the mirror. *Am I over done?* She thought. *Everything is the same color— my suit and my coat. Shit, I got too many furs going on.* Finally she sucked her teeth and screamed aloud, "Fuck it!"

She sped off into the moonlit streets. Rocky parked her car in guest parking at the Townsend Hotel and casually walked through the lobby to the elevator. On the eighth floor she searched for the room number. When she reached it, she tried the door but it was locked.

"That would be too easy," she said softly. She gently placed the bag on the floor and looked at her watch. She thought of all kinds of plans, but couldn't come up with a good one even after fifteen minutes of standing in front of the door. As she picked up her bag to leave she heard knocking on a door from somewhere behind her. She quickly spun around to see a young maid pushing a cart.

"Housekeeping. You called for some extra towels?"

The door opened and the maid handed three towels and three wash rags to the person on the other side of it. "You're welcome, and enjoy your stay with us here at the Townsend. I am Sahbeen the evening housekeeper during your stay." The door closed with a slam and the maid switched down the hallway with an attitude muttering harshly under her breath. "These muthafuckas never want to give you a tip."

"Sahbeen, come here for a second," Rocky said inquisitively.

The young housekeeper stopped and placed her hands on her hips. "Do I know you?"

"No, but you can."

"So, how do you know my name?"

"I overheard you talking to those cheap-ass guests over there."

"They was cheap and shit. I can't stand this job."

Rocky thought fast as she listened to the housekeeper complaining about her job. She looked no more than sixteen and was slim and short. Her complexion was a little lighter than Rocky's. Sahbeen's hair was bleached blonde and streaked black. It was starched into several big bows on top of her head. She had so much gel and hairspray in her hair it looked as if it had white patches on it. Rocky smiled broadly.

"Girl, your hair is fly. Where did you get it done? I'm from New York and I am here to surprise my boyfriend, Marcus. But I need to get into his room," Rocky said.

"Thank you. That outfit you have on is tough. I could tell you from New York and shit. But I can't let you in there. I could lose my job," Sahbeen said.

"The only way you could get in trouble is if he reports it and that isn't going to happen. Check it out I got three brand new yards for you if you do," Rocky said.

"What's a yard?" Sahbeen asked.

Rocky had been trying so hard to be ghetto, she had dug too deeply into her vernacular. "Three hundred dollar bills."

"What? That's almost a week's salary," she whispered.

Rocky looked at her watch. There were still things to be done so she had to act fast. "How much do you make in a week?"

"Four hundred and twelve dollars."

Yeah right, Rocky thought as she went into her purse and pulled out five one hundred dollar bills.

"Here's five hundred dollars. Bring me two plates, two champagne glasses, a book of matches and open the door." Rocky extended her arm towards Sahbeen with the bills folded neatly in between her fingers, but she just looked at it. "Look, I'll be in and out. You can stay here and watch me if you want."

Sahbeen looked at Rocky's ring and smiled broadly. *She must be legit with a ring like that. It feels right. I'm going to do it. Shit, I can go buy me something to wear to the cabaret tomorrow*, Sahbeen thought.

"Dang! He bought you that ring? Shit you got a deal. I'll be right back with those plates and thangs," Sahbeen said. The young housekeeper turned her head slowly to the left and then to the right. She slid the white key she had hanging around her neck into the slot and the door clicked. Rocky pushed it open. Sahbeen took the money from Rocky's hand, shoved it into her apron pocket and scurried off.

The room had not been touched. The beds were neatly done. There was no luggage to be found and everything was nice and clean. Rocky walked toward a small table by the window. She dropped the bag on top of it and went into the bathroom. The room was silent, which intensified the sound of her urine hitting the water in the bowl. When she was half done there was a knock on the door. She tightened her muscles and immediately stopped her urine flow to listen carefully.

"Housekeeping," Sahbeen yelled from outside of the door.

Rocky relaxed her muscles. "Come inside."

She hurried out of the bathroom to find all the items she had asked for on the bed. "Good looking out, Sahbeen. Do you think you could fill my ice bucket with ice? I want to chill my Cristal."

"Not a problem. I hope you enjoy your stay here with us at the Townsend."

"I sure will."

As soon as the doors closed she went into action. She pulled a slinky, see-through negligee from her bag and placed it neatly across the bed. Then she retrieved the big bowl of food. She touched the bottom of it and was delighted to find that it was still very warm. She placed the bowl in the middle of the table. She ran to the bed, picked up the two plates and placed them on the table. Next she pulled out two slim candles attached to two silver-plated candleholders. She placed them gently in front of the two plates. She reached into the bag again and pulled out the bottle of Cristal. Startled, she jumped and nearly dropped the bottle as the door opened.

"Sorry. I ain't mean to scare you but here is your ice and bucket. Happy Thanksgiving," Sahbeen said as she placed the items on the table.

"Same to you sweetheart."

Sahbeen left the room pulling the door gently closed behind her. Rocky looked at her watch. She fussed around the table for a couple of minutes rearranging the plates, candles and glasses. When she deemed it perfect she pulled the petals from her proposal out of the bag. As she sprinkled them on the bed, she stopped short and touched her ring. She slid it off her finger, held it tightly in her palm and looked around the room. Rocky slid her hand into the tight inside pocket of her duffel bag scratching her knuckles as it went down. When she eased her hand out it came up without the ring and with a condom.

She carefully tore open the condom and took it out of its foil cover. She stuck her index finger in the tip of it without unfolding it. The fresh smell of rubber rolled into her nose and flipped her stomach. Rocky picked up a fork. She pressed the fork into her finger until she could feel its prong prick her through the rubber. Rocky examined the tiny tear and when she saw a slit of her pink flesh through the miniscule opening she smiled. She slid the condom back into the package and forced it back into the zipper compartment of her bag. She felt around for her ring and grasped it between her forefinger and thumb momentarily.

"Tonight's the night. I have to make him mine," Rocky thought aloud.

Rocky zipped up the bag and shoved it into a mirrored closet. She adjusted her coat and zipped it up. Her hair— perfect, her makeup— perfect. She smiled at herself in the mirror and began to dance seductively as she walked over to the bed and spread more petals on it. The few that remained she shook into a path from the bed to the door. Finally, she was on her way.

The man behind the thick Will Call window looked up at Rocky and then at his watch. "The game will be over in about fifteen minutes," he looked at Rocky strangely.

"Yeah and?" Rocky replied.

"Do you have your driver's license or some form of identification, ma'am?"

"Yes, here you go." Rocky showed her license to the gentleman behind the window. In return he handed her an envelope and smiled. Rocky rushed into the arena. The crowd had already started to leave. As soon as she spotted Marcus she felt warm inside. He was sweaty and running up the court towards the basket.

"BOOM, Baby!" Rocky screamed as he dunked the ball into the basket. She sat down and unzipped her coat. She didn't bother to take it off. She looked up at the scoreboard. *Marcus is whipping the Pistons down to the ground. We're up by twenty with four minutes left on the clock*, she thought.

As soon as she got into the game a buzzer sounded and a sub was put in. She watched as Marcus sat down and a young boy handed him a paper cup. He had covered his head with a white towel.

I love him. Damn, I really love him, she thought as she stared at him sitting on the bench.

It felt really strange for Rocky to be in love. She hadn't felt this way since she was with Too Sweet in high school, who was imprisoned for fifteen years under the Rico Statute. Within minutes the game was over and the disheartened fans started to pour out of the arena in droves.

◈ ◈ ◈ ◈

Yanick, George, Seven, and Yanick's entire family sat at the table. There was so much Thanksgiving food left on the table there was no room for plates.

"Yanick, fix George a plate to go home with."

"Yes, Ma."

"George, come into the living room and let's have some drinks," Yanick's father said.

George and the entire dinner party got up and went into the living room with the exception of Yanick, who was left to clear the table. She cleared it off quickly. In the kitchen she immediately picked up the phone. She dialed Joann's number and it rang . . . and rang . . . and rang. Just as she was about to hang up, the phone was answered. She heard a lot of laughing in the background.

"Hello?"

"Joey? What are you doing?" Yanick asked.

"Joey is busy right now. Can I take a message?"

"Who is this?" Yanick asked.

"STOP, Joann! Sammy did you see what your girl just did to me?" the girl replied.

"WHO IS THIS?" Yanick yelled.

"Hold on and I'll get Joey. Here, Joey, the telephone."

Yanick could hear Joann laughing in the background but she never came to the phone. Yanick was furious. She hung up the phone, immediately picked it back up and redialed. It was busy. She washed the dishes creating scene after scene in her head. She replayed the female voices over and over again in her mind. After she placed all of the food in the fridge and made George a plate to take home, she called back and the phone was still busy.

"Okay, George. You ready to go?" Yanick asked.

"Yeah, babe. Let me finish saying goodnight," George said.

"Okay. I'm going downstairs to warm up the car. Get Seven dressed she hasn't been out all day so she's going to ride with us." Yanick continued in a low voice, "I think we're going to pay Officer Nuñez a visit."

What she would do next, she didn't know. Rocky sat in the arena until the media was gone and both teams were out of sight. She sat until she could count the number of people in the arena on her fingers. Finally she stood up and straightened out her clothes.

"Damn, it's hot in here," she said quietly. *Maybe if you would have taken off your coat you wouldn't be so hot. Shit I have had this thing on all night. I hope I don't stink*, Rocky thought as she opened her jacket and sniffed inside of it. Then she laughed quietly to herself.

She went outside and approached the car. She turned on the radio, pulled out her cell phone and called Marcus. "Happy Thanksgiving," she said cheerfully.

"Same to you. You feeling alright? You was bugging on the phone last night, yo," Marcus said.

"I was just having a moment. What are you doing?"

"I'm on my way back to the hotel. I am dying to see this surprise you sent me," Marcus said.

Rocky smiled. "When you reach the hotel and get into the room make sure you call me."

"I'll be there in about twenty minutes. We could keep on talking until then. Tell me what it is, you done put a fuckin battery in my back. I'm not even going to front— I'm mad charged."

"You'll see when you get there," Rocky began to drive.

"I wish I was home with my moms, she can throw down. How are your skills in the kitchen?"

Rocky could hear a lot of deep male voices in the background. They were laughing and talking. "You'll see," she said.

"That means your ass probably can't cook. I knew it was too good to be true. Dope face and mind, dope body, dope sex, dope personality *and* dope in the kitchen? Nah, a man can't have it all."

"Damn, Marcus hold on for a minute that's my other line."

Rocky hit the talk button on her phone and cleared her throat.

"Hello."

"Bitch, you are not grown. How dare you not call me for two days? You didn't even call the boys back. They called you this morning to wish you a happy Thanksgiving. Don't make me fly down there and kick your ass!" Kay said.

"Kay, you would not believe what happened to me last night. Mauri proposed to me. Hold on let me clear my other line— hello, Marcus? That's Kay and my godson is on the phone wishing me a Happy

Thanksgiving. Call me as soon as you get out of the locker room. Rocky clicked over. "Kay?"

"He did WHAT!?" Kay screeched.

"He proposed to me in a park, equivalent to our Prospect Park, he had an orchestra play Jagged Edge—"

"Which song girl, which song?! Kay interrupted.

"You know, the one that goes, 'Meet me at the altar in your white dress we ain't getting— Kay began to sing along— "we ain't gettin' no younger we might as well do it'. That's 'Let's Get Married,'" Kay laughed.

"Yeah, that's it. The scene was right and the park was beautiful. It was on a lake, he had orchid petals thrown at our feet and an illuminated water fountain went off right after he proposed. Did I mention that he hired nearly half the members of the Detroit Philharmonic? His mother flipped and called me a whore bitch in the name of the Lord. The curse of Too Sweet 'Rocks' on. And Kay my ring is sick. I have to get it appraised and insured— SHIT! Don't let me forget about my great Nahnan's broach. It has to be paid off this week."

"Oh, my God. I can't believe he proposed to you! How did he take it when you turned him down?"

"Turned him down? It's about time that ho slowed down anyway," Kay's husband Tyrone said in the background.

"Shut up, Tyrone, and mind your business," Kay shouted.

"Anyway, I'm getting ready to surprise Marcus out here at his hotel room," Rocky said.

"Rocky? Have you lost your mind?" Kay asked.

"Yep. I sure have. Damn, there goes my other line. I'll talk to you later." She pressed the talk button on her phone and saw Marcus' name flash across her caller ID. "Hey," Rocky said. She pulled up in front of the hotel and had a valet park her car.

"Who are you talking to?" Marcus asked.

"I was just paying a parking attendant. Where are you now?"

"I'm right across the street from my hotel," Marcus said.

Rocky continued her conversation as she ran into a bar that was located in the hotel lobby and ordered a drink. It was about fifteen minutes after she reached there that Marcus actually entered the hotel.

"Come on, tell me what my surprise is."

"I am not going to tell you. Aren't you almost at your hotel?"

"I am here right now. I got my key and I am heading upstairs. Is my package at the desk?" Suddenly Marcus was cut off. Rocky smiled at how her once bumpy plan was moving along smoothly. She guzzled down her Hennesy and settled her bill. She called Mauri quickly.

"Hey, baby it's Mrs. Maurice. Happy Thanksgiving."

"Thank you baby girl, I am busy. I'll call you first thing in the morning. I love you."

Rocky closed her eyes and forced the words out as pleasantly as possible. "I love you too." Then she shut her cell phone off and placed it inside her coat pocket. She made her way to the elevator, waited patiently and pressed the eighth floor. She tried to fix herself up and the doors suddenly opened. Two White girls dressed in black dresses got into the elevator on the eighth floor and rolled their eyes at her. She smiled at them and walked off the elevator. She nervously approached Marcus' door and knocked firmly. Yelling, Marcus swung the door open.

"I told you bitches that my girl is on her way—" As he saw Rocky's face he changed his demeanor. "Oh my God, you just won so many points, Candy."

Why did he just open the door like that? Rocky thought. Then it hit her "Let me find out you was gonna spend Thanksgiving with Janet and Chrissy, Jack."

"Niggas always be sending chickens up to our room and shit. I am so happy to see you. How did you pull this off?"

Rocky was silent. Although she was angry she had mixed thoughts. *He did say 'I told you my girl was on her way up' so does that mean we are official? Bitches do come with the territory, if I have an NBA man there will be NBA bitches.*

"Candy, you know I hate when you give me the silent treatment. Come inside. My man sent them girls up here— I swear."

"I can't believe you! And they were White. How could you? But then again its not like I am your girl or anything like that? I think I should leave. Happy Thanksgiving, Marcus."

Rocky started down the hallway and Marcus was right behind her. "Honestly, Candy, Bob sent those girls up here. Don't leave. I was shocked when I opened my door to find the orchid petals and a home cooked meal. Let's call Room Service and ask them to warm it up. Put that sexy shit on that's lying across the bed and let's eat. How the fuck did you get into my room?"

"Don't sweat that," Rocky said as she finally broke down and smiled. They walked back to the room hand in hand. Marcus called Room Service and they came for the bowl. She changed into her gown and they laid on top of the orchid petals and talked. He held her in his arms and she felt like she was in the safest place in the world.

A knock on the door interrupted their conversation. Rocky got up and lit the candles.

"Candy, go into my pocket and pass me a twenty."

Rocky handed him the twenty and he in turn handed it to a smiling Sahbeen. "Thank you and enjoy your stay at the Townsend." Sahbeen smiled.

Rocky started to make their plates. He walked to the table and removed the champagne from the ice. "Ah, Cristal."

He popped the cork and they sat down and ate. They laughed through the entire dinner. When he was done he called home.

"Hey, Mom. You would never guess who came out here to surprise me?"

"Rock Candy?" Mrs. Best asked.

"How did you know? She cooked me Thanksgiving dinner. It's not as good as yours, but she definitely be getting her chef on."

"Marcus, tell her I said Happy Thanksgiving," Rocky whispered.

"Ma, Candy says 'Happy Thanksgiving'."

"Tell her I said thank you."

"So what are you and sis doing?"

"Well, your little sister is at a teenage club. The party is over at twelve, so Hubert and I are going to pick her up. By the way he says hello."

"Oh, he's there, huh?"

Rocky nudged him on the arm and whispered, "be nice, and remember what I told you about that."

"Tell Hubert 'Happy Thanksgiving', and Mom, enjoy the rest of your night. I love you."

"I love you too, Marcus. I'll talk to you soon. Tell Candy to call me. She promised she would take Missy out."

"Okay. Bye, Mom." Marcus hung up the phone. "My mother said to call her cause my sister wants you to take her out."

"I will."

"I can't believe you came all the way out here to see me. And you came with a home cooked meal. How did you manage to do that?"

"I've got people out here, I cooked at their house."

"How did you get up in my room?"

"You're fucking up the surprise. Are you upset?"

"NO."

She looked at the bottle of Cristal and smiled. "If you must know my friend's little sister, Crystal, works here and I paid her to do it. So please don't get her in trouble. I told her I was your girlfriend and she did it."

"Well, at least you didn't have to lie."

Rocky didn't know what to make of his last comment, but she knew it was a good thing.

"Get me another glass of Cristal, please," Marcus said.

As the two of them talked they drank the entire bottle down. When Marcus finished the last drop Rocky slipped out of her gown and he stripped naked and laid across the bed. She crept up the bed kissing his ankles and kneecaps as she ascended his lanky body. She spread his legs wide and stuck her tongue in his ass. She licked underneath his balls and swallowed his penis whole. She could hear him moan and curse under his breath as she continued to please him orally. She felt her mother's spirit take over her as she drank from his thick, chocolate straw.

In her mind she knew what she had to do. Rocky got up and went into her bag. She retrieved the condom and sat on the edge of the bed. She opened the unopened end of its wrapper and pulled it out. She saddled his mid section, with her back to his face and slid the condom down his stiff dick. Marcus took his hand and secured the rubber, rolling it all the way down. She sat on him and rode slowly up and down. Marcus sat up and viewed her silhouette. Her slender back and wide ass looked so good to him. She started to slam up and down quicker.

"Turn around so I can see your pretty face," Marcus panted.

She got up and sat back down on his penis. He grabbed her waist and pulled her down on top of him over and over again. She laid her head on his chest, still riding him fearlessly and fast. Suddenly he started making loud noises. She screamed in pain. He sat straight up and yanked her down one final time. "Goddamn, that shit was good."

Rocky rolled off of him and lay at his side. Just as her body hit the mattress Marcus yelled.

"The fuckin' bag bust! I knew you felt extra wet— no wonder I came so fast," Marcus said.

Rocky sat up in the bed and stared at his half limp, half-bagged penis. "So why the fuck didn't you stop, Marcus!?" Her angry voice filled the room.

"I don't know. You always feel wet like that. It just felt so good."

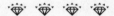

Yanick unzipped Seven's coat and straightened out her dress. She knocked on the door and Joann immediately swung it open. Yanick covered her mouth at the sight of Joann standing in the doorway with no top on, a pair of boxers and Sammy standing directly behind her wearing a pink thong. A girl wearing Yanick's princess cropped pajama top walked to the door. The girl was shocked when she saw Yanick's face, covered her hairy, bare bottom and ran to the back.

Yanick burst into tears and dropped a bowl of food on the ground in front of Joann's door. It broke upon impact and Seven cried as soon as the glass shattered onto the ground. She turned Seven's stroller around, picked it up in her arms and started to run down the steps. Joann grabbed a jacket from the coat rack and ran to the top of the steps.

"Yan, wait. Let me explain."

Yanick was already down the steps and out the door. Joann slowly shook her head, stepped over the food and walked back into her apartment. Sammy shut the door.

"Explain what? Who was that, Joey?" Sammy asked.

"This girl I used to mess with," Joann replied. "Crack open the bub, Thanksgiving has just begun."

As Sammy walked toward the kitchen Joann smacked her ass.

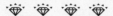

Marcus tried to grab Rocky's hand and she yanked her arm away.

"You are so selfish! I better not get pregnant, Marcus, I swear! Why didn't you stop!"

Rocky got up and searched the floor for her negligee. She found it, pulled it on and sat at the table. Inside she was elated. *I didn't expect the entire condom to break*, she thought. *I figured some would leak from the hole, but this is even better! Now I have a better chance of becoming pregnant, and it will be easier to prove.*

Marcus got out of bed and sat across from her at the table. "Rocky, it ain't my fault the condom broke. I'm sorry," he said.

"But you said you felt it and kept on going, now that's your fault."

"Don't trip. I said you felt mad wet. You ain't pregnant, and if you are, we will deal with it."

"I don't want to have a damn baby now, Marcus and I don't want to have any abortion either— let's just hope that I'm not. I want to sleep now." Rocky got into the bed and Marcus followed.

"Don't worry. Everything will be all right. I am so happy you're here. You surprised the shit out of me and we aren't even in New York. You the man, girl and you better surprise me again when I come home to play next month."

"You got it, baby. You whipped the shit out of the Pistons today," Rocky said.

"You were at the game, too?" Marcus asked.

"I caught the tail end of it. I was there when you dunked on old boy in the fourth quarter."

"You know, Candy, I'm really feeling you, a lot."

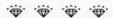

"Didn't I tell you not to call me anymore, Joann? You are so fucking pathetic. To think I ever fell for your bullshit. You got what you wanted— now leave me alone!" Yanick said.

"I didn't get what I wanted because I don't have you. Now, let me explain. You have been spending so much time with George lately, I got jealous. Sammy is always calling, and begg—"

"That's why you had that bitch answering your phone? Then when I get there you don't even have the decency to make her leave. You and the next two bitches were laughing at my expense. And the bitch was wearing my pajamas! I felt sorry for you yesterday because I thought you were spending Thanksgiving alone and you had two bitches on your plate. Fuck you, Joey. Shit ain't been the same since you showed your ass in Applebee's that night.

"Yeah? Remember I picked you up from school the next day? You can't deny that night. We bonded. We never had sex like that before."

"Joey, you are all about sex. Whatever little bullshit we had together is over. I am so out."

"But Yanick let me— Yanick! YANICK!!" Joann slammed the phone down on the receiver and pushed it off the kitchen counter.

22

Don't forget to put your ring back on

"Girl, I broke the news to Marcus last week," Rocky said. "I can't believe you're pregnant! You know you're a muthafuckin' mess. You can't be more than two weeks. What did he say?" Kay asked.

"He said that he respects any decision I make but he wants me to have it. His mother is having a New Years Eve dinner and we are going to tell her then."

"What are you going to do with Mauri and Thomas?"

"Don't try to act like you don't know what happened to Thomas, Kay."

"What?"

"His muthafuckin' father told him what happened, but he exaggerated the truth. I tried to deny it and shit but his father described my privates to a tee. He even mentioned the two moles on my ass."

Kay took her eyes off of the road and stared at Rocky for a brief second. "Rocky, you never told me that."

"It happened via the phone, the day Mauri proposed to me. I haven't heard from Thomas since."

"Why didn't you tell him the truth?" Kay asked.

"I tried to after the fact but me not telling him in the first place made me look suspect. It was all for the best. I was going to have to cut him off sooner or later. Not to mention I called him Marcus twice, and his father figured out that I was sitting next to Marcus Best at the fight. He put two and three together. I know I told you about that."

Kay stared at Rocky like she was from another planet. "I don't see how you are going to pull this shit off. What the hell are you going to tell Mauri? He will kill you— literally," Kay said in a worried tone.

"I'm not going to tell him anything until right after the New Year. I want him to pay for my first semester of grad school, or at least finish paying off my car, so I can get rid of it."

"Just be careful." Kay sighed. "Well, here's the airport."

"Why do you sound so sad? Everything is going to be alright."

Kay shook her head and smiled. "I hope so. This entire thing is crazy. You know Mauri is going to want some ass. It only December 12th, how are you going to keep him off of you until the New Year?"

"I'm only a couple of weeks. If I have to fuck him one more time, so be it. But the next time, I'm going to say I have my period or that I have a yeast infection or something and that will be my last trip to Detroit."

"No! Don't fuck him this weekend. Tell him you have your period now and the yeast thing will be for next time. Hurry, go catch your flight."

"Okay. I'll talk to you later." Rocky moved to get out of her car, but Kay grabbed her harshly by her wrist.

"Do not sleep with him. That's the lowest thing you could do. I mean it won't harm the baby but just the thought."

It was no surprise that Kay's last warning rang in her ears the entire flight. Off of the plane and out of the airport, she was happy to see Jack and Mauri. "Rocky you look hot. I have a surprise for you," Mauri said.

"Hey, Jack. I haven't seen you for a while. How have you been?"

"Chillin'. Congratulations, Mrs. Maurice," Jack said. Rocky flashed her ring and smiled. "You better start working on some kids," Jack said.

Rocky rubbed her stomach and shook her head. "Not until after the wedding. I'm doing this the traditional way." She turned toward Mauri and gave him a loose hug. "What's my surprise?" she asked.

"You will find out soon enough. Let's get married on an island."

"Which one? And how will your family get there?" Rocky asked.

"We'll pay for the wedding party to get down there. You thought about who is going to be in the wedding party?"

"Of course, Kay is matron of honor, and Audrey, Kika and Lita are the bridesmaids." Rocky snuggled next to Mauri and they discussed their plans for three and a half hours until they pulled up in front of the home of the Chicago Bulls.

"I have some business to tie up with a couple of players from the Bulls. I've got passes so we're going to meet some of the players," Mauri said.

Rocky smiled. "Oh, that's cool. Who are they playing?"

"The Indiana Pacers." Rocky's smile dried up. "Jack's man plays for Indiana and he wants me to style him as well."

Rocky's heart was in her throat. She just smiled at Mauri. "You know, I really don't feel so good. Can I just stay in the limo?"

"Nah, baby. I want to show off my wife, besides we're all going out afterwards and their ladies will be there. Just stick it out for me."

"But—"

"No buts, Rocky, just chill. If you don't feel like chillin' after alright, but I said my wife was coming and that's that. Don't fuck up my mood."

Rocky was stiff through the entire game. All kinds of thoughts dribbled through her mind. *I can't believe that all my planning is going down the drain. How the fuck am I going to get out of this one? I'll go to the bathroom and never come back. I can tell him that I fell in the stall and got amnesia. No, that won't work,* she thought. Rocky started to panic.

"OOOH shit! You saw that, Rocky? Marcus Best just dunked on my boy and shit," Mauri yelled.

"Oh, I saw it," Rocky replied blandly. She was there, but her words were empty. Her temples throbbed and her forehead beat like a bass drum. *Why me? Hopefully, he'll just head straight for the lockers and then straight out the arena. He won't be one of Mauri's peoples, peoples. It will work out just fine,* she hoped silently. Rocky let her thoughts carry her into the fourth quarter. When the buzzer went off she shut her eyes.

"I got these one day guest laminates right here and we are going straight to the tunnel," Mauri said.

"You know, you should give them about fifteen minutes to shower, then we'll go back," Jack said.

"Mauri, I am going to the bathroom quickly. I'll be right back," Rocky said.

Rocky walked aimlessly through the crowd and bumped into several fans. They either cursed her out or bumped her back. When she entered the bathroom she walked straight past the long line and into the first available stall.

"What the fuck you think you doin'?" Don't you see this long-ass line right here?"

"You gotta wait like everyone else. I beg your pardon but the line starts here."

Several women spoke but the words seemed to bounce off Rocky. She entered the stall, pulled down her pants and urinated without closing the door. Her tears streamed down, as fast as her urine. She looked at the women that stood outside and wasn't bothered that she was being watched. When she was done, she turned toward the bowl and vomited clear liquid with her pants at her ankles, and her bare ass smiling at the women outside the stall. She regurgitated repeatedly until she just dry heaved and nothing came out.

The women that were waiting to curse her out and beat her down silently empathized with her now. She walked out of the stall without flushing the toilet and washed her hands. Instead of drying them she wiped the remaining wet liquid over her face, and her body dragged her mind out of the bathroom and back into the arena.

Back at the seats, she tried to explain to Mauri how she threw up in the bathroom and how sick she was feeling. But all her excuses and explanations led her right to the back of the arena in front of six men. One of them, the father of her unborn child watched her walk toward him.

"Yo, man. That dunk was of the meat rack, Marcus," Mauri said as he held out his hand.

Marcus did not reply. He just stared at Rocky. The silence was disturbing. Mauri watched Marcus stare Rocky down. He felt proud. *These basketball niggas is sweating my broad up in here,* he thought.

Jack stepped up and cleared his throat loudly. "Yo, Jalen, this is my man Mauri."

Mauri extended his hand and gave him a pound. "Nice to meet you, Jalen," he said.

"Yo, you doin' your thing. Them Mr. Maurice's is poppin' up everywhere. I heard one is opening in Fairland," Jalen Chambers said.

"Thanks. It will be opening up next month. So you want me to style you?" Mauri asked.

"Yep. I really don't have the time to be out and shopping during the season, and my girl is always complaining that I dress like a NBA player. She said I am turning into a corn ball."

"So why doesn't she shop for you?" Rocky interrupted.

Jalen Chambers turned towards her and smiled. "Because she has a hard time finding my size," he replied.

"This is my fiancée, Rock Candy. Look out for a chain of those stores coming your way soon."

Marcus caught a sharp pain in his stomach as Rocky flashed apologetic looks his way. She extended her hand to Jalen and gave him a firm handshake. Marcus didn't know if he should open his mouth, slap her to the ground or punch out Mauri. She extended her hand toward Marcus. Her facial expressions were stiff as ice, but inside she felt feverish and weak. Her knees barely held her body weight and she fought hard not to break down. Marcus looked at her hand momentarily and walked away.

"Yo Jay, I'll catch up with you the next time I wop the Bulls. I have a headache— I'm going up to the room," Marcus said as he quickly walked away with his back to Rocky and the rest of the group.

"Dogs, we been planning to hang out all week. Stop playing, man," Jalen called out.

"Hit me on my cell. Maybe, I'll come out after I have a little nap and shit." Marcus walked away without looking at Rocky or anyone else. She felt extremely bad. But she smiled and saved face for the fifteen minutes the small group of people conversed.

"My girl couldn't make it after all, so it's just going to be us. I hope you don't mind being the only female here," Jalen said.

"Actually I do. Baby, do you mind dropping me back to the hotel? I really am not feeling to well and I don't feel like hanging with the fellas tonight." She turned towards Jalen and smiled. "Any other time, I wouldn't mind, but I really don't feel too sporty today," Rocky smiled.

"I'll drop her back to the hotel before we hit the town," Jack said.

The entire ride back she felt awful. She rubbed her stomach and thought about what it would be like to raise her baby by herself. She had to make things right. Once she reached the hotel room she stretched out across the bed. She hugged her pillow tightly and poured a bucket full of tears into it. She tossed and turned and talked out loud as if someone was in the room.

"I can't believe this shit. Why the hell did Mauri have to introduce me as his fiancée? I know he is mad and hurt he even looked at my ring . . ."

In the same hotel, three flights up, Marcus sat on the edge of his bed with his hands cupping his head.

"I can't believe she was playing me all this time. And she's pregnant? That kid probably isn't even mine. It's probably Willie Wonka's, and they getting married." Marcus turned his head to the side, and stared at the beige telephone. *Don't do it. Let her call you first*, he thought. No more than one second after his thought he jumped out off the bed and dialed her cell phone number. Rocky released her grip on the pillow, rolled over toward her bag and answered her phone.

"Hello?" Rocky said meekly.

"You fucking bitch! How could you? If that kid is mine you need to get an abortion like yesterday." Once Rocky realized it was Marcus she sat up and looked up at the ceiling. *Please let there be an ounce of hope*, she thought silently. Marcus continued to vent, and Rocky didn't say anything. Her tears just dropped from her eyes as if they were laced with concrete. She could feel them landing on her lap.

"You ain't got shit to say, huh and you are engaged to Willie Wonka?" Marcus yelled. Rocky sobbed loudly. "How do I know that that ain't his fucking baby, *Rock Candy*. You owe me some answers," Marcus said.

"Marcus, I haven't done anything wrong. I have been talking to Mauri for two years now. I'm very unhappy with our relationship. I told you in Vegas I was ironing out issues and that I wasn't looking for anything. I told you I had a friend that I see and that is him. He just popped the question this morning. I didn't want to turn him down because his mother was present. I flew out here to end our relationship. I have been hinting I want out for the past three months and I guess that is why he proposed. Besides, it's not like you don't be doing your thing, Marcus. We don't have anything steady, we have no commitments."

"How do I know that's my baby?"

"We haven't had sex in a minute," Rocky said.

"Yeah, right."

"I swear on my grandmother's grave."

Marcus was quiet. He thought about things. He really cared for Candy. As a matter of fact, he had revealed to his mother that he loved Candy and was thinking about making some kind of commitment with her.

. "Where are y'all right now?" Marcus asked.

"I'm at the hotel and Mauri and everyone else went clubbing."

"Where are you staying? We need to talk face to face," Marcus said.

"I am at the Four Seasons near the arena," Rocky said.

"So am I. What's your room number?"

"I'm in 236."

"Alright. I'll be there in a few."

Rocky flipped the phone down and straightened herself out. Within seconds, it rang again. "Hello?"

"What's up? How is everything? You didn't call me when your flight came in," Kay said.

"Girl, I am going to say this quick and fast before Marcus gets here."

"MARCUS?! I thought—"

"Mauri surprised me and took me to a Bulls game. You will never guess who they played."

"No! SHUT UP!" Kay said.

"Yes! We went in the back and Marcus was standing there with Mauri's man's man. He introduced me to everyone as his fiancée and Marcus rushed out of the arena. Now he thinks the baby is Mauri's."

"I don't know what to say. Marcus ain't flip on you in front of Mauri?"

"Nope."

"That means you could still get him back. Do what you do, girl."

"I told him that he knew I still had—" a knock at the door stopped her conversation. She hung up, walked towards the door and opened it.

"Get in here before some one sees you." She pulled him into the room.

"Candy, I swear to God I was going to fuck your ass up back at the game." Marcus walked inside and looked at her.

"You have to believe me," she cried. Rocky walked over to the drawers near the bed, retrieved a pad and a pen and began to write.

Dear Mauri,

I am really sorry but I cannot marry you. I don't want to be with you and you know I have been trying to tell you this for months. The fact is I love someone else. Here is your ring. Don't call me. I'm very sorry. Take care,

Rock Candy

She removed her ring and placed it on the dresser, leaving the light shining on the note and her ring. "Read that, Marcus. If you walk out this room with me right now, I promise you I will never speak to him again. But I need a commitment from you. I don't want to raise this baby by myself. It's not his, we can take a paternity test."

Marcus shuffled over to the drawers and read the note. "I love you, Candy. We can work this out. But if I catch breath that you're still fuckin' with this Willie Wonka nigga I am deadin' this whole shit."

He hugged her passionately. They went to his room and ordered the best room service she'd ever had. They lay down and gently made the best love she ever had. She had never felt so loved in her life.

She kept good to her promise. Marcus purchased her a new a ticket home; new numbers, a new location and he forced her to quit her job. Raquel Candace Jones had begun a new life with Marcus Best by her side.

23

Baby mama drama

"We are going to need her to pull off our last job for initiation. More importantly, your baby is going to need you to be a daddy. You have to go in there. I'll be waiting for you right outside this door. Now I will knock but you have to speak."

Kahmelle nodded his head. Tony knocked on the door and Camille's angry voice answered.

"Who is it?"

Tony nudged Kahmelle's arm. "It's me, Camille," Kahmelle said.

She lifted her peephole and saw Tony and Kahmelle standing in her view. Camille straightened her hair and fixed her clothes before she opened the door. When she opened it, Kahmelle couldn't believe his eyes. Camille stood with seven months of belly in front of her. Her face, arms and legs were still slim but her stomach poked out.

"Are y'all going to just stand there or are you going to come in?" Camille asked.

"I will wait out here," Tony said.

"You can come in Tony. It's okay," Camille said as she waddled to the couch. Both of the boys watched her. "Sit down," Camille said. Kahmelle sat next to her and Tony sat across from them. "Well? Aren't you going to say something? It's the middle of muthafuckin' December and I ain't seen or spoke to your ass since the summer."

Kahmelle shook his head. "I guess I am sorry for not being around. I can't believe my baby is in there."

"What, you thought I was lying?" Camille said.

"Nah, I just— I don't know. Camille, I ain't ready for this and neither are you."

"Well, it's here. You need to come and take care of your responsibility, Kahmelle."

Kahmelle stood up. "You told me you were on the pill! You lied to me. Everything was everything until you pulled this shit, Meely. I ain't want no girl but you. Now, I hate you for this shit. You tore us apart!"

"Why you ain't tell—"

"I fuckin' told you to have an abortion!"

"But I ain't want to do that."

"So what choice do I have? Where is my say? It's part of me too you know! You quick to say take care of your responsibility, but what about my pro-choice, huh? We ain't got no real money. It takes cash to have a baby."

Kahmelle sat down and looked at Tony. *That's the perfect segue*, Tony thought and he slowly nodded at Kahmelle.

"Look we have this big job. It's the last job we have to do to become official Finest. We could come off with mad paper. My cut would go toward the baby and you could do whatever you want with yours. This Thursday, we are going to jooks Brooklyn Jewelry Exchange and we need your help," Kahmelle said.

Camille rubbed her stomach and shook her head. "I don't know— JAIL isn't a good look for a pregnant girl," Camille snapped.

"All you have to do is go to the door holding onto your stomach and jump around like you have to use the bathroom. Once they let you in Tony and I will run up in the joint with our burners. You will lay on the ground with whatever customers are in there and be a hostage. We drop you some jewels and we let you go because you're pregnant. You run out and go straight home. We grab all the shit we can and then we bounce. No one gets greedy no one gets caught. We are out in five minutes— way before the police can catch up to us. We run up Flatbush to Fourth, turn down Butler and hide in the shed of the abandoned house. Sweat picks us up, and we are done."

"I don't think she could run."

"I'm down for whatever. Anything for the Finest," she looked away from Kahmelle and held her belly.

Kahmelle walked toward the door. Tony followed him.

"Don't worry, Meely, we will make this baby thing work. But we can't make this us thing work no more 'cause you played me. We are going to have practice runs at the Bat Cave tomorrow, Tuesday and Wednesday— Thursday is the big day," Kahmelle said.

"I definitely need the money for little Kahmelle," Camille said waddling to the door.

Kahmelle stopped in the doorway. "It's a boy?" Kahmelle asked.

"Yeah. I took two sonograms. You want to see?" Camille walked into the kitchen and removed the picture from the refrigerator. She walked back over to Kahmelle and handed him the picture. "This is your baby."

Kahmelle looked at the picture then showed it to Tony. "Can I keep this?" Kahmelle said.

"Yeah. I have another one in my room. That was the baby at five months," Camille said smiling.

"How many months are you?" Kahmelle asked.

"Seven."

"Can you feel him moving around?"

"Yeah. Put your hand on the side of my stomach."

Kahmelle gently placed his hand on the side of her stomach but he didn't feel anything. She took his hand and placed it on the top of her stomach but the baby didn't budge. She jumped up and landed softly. Then she quickly pressed Kahmelle's hand to the side of her stomach again. Kahmelle felt something hard press against the palm of his hand. "Tony, come here and feel this."

Camille placed Tony's hand in the same place and he felt movement too. "I am going to be a godfather," he said excitedly.

For the first time in months the three of them laughed together. As they walked out of the door Kahmelle looked at the picture. "This baby shit just might work," Kahmelle said.

Tony looked at his watch. It was well after seven-thirty. "Shit, I am late for dinner, again," he said.

"Isn't your moms going to flip?" Kahmelle asked.

"Not really. She's been easing up on that since the summertime, but I am still trying respect that time, son. I am going home."

"Yo, D! Let me hold your car," Joann said.

"AGAIN? What are you a loan shark or something? Nuñez, you better not be doing no bullshit in my car," D said.

"Whatever, nigga. I'll be back," Joann said.

Joann sped down Park Avenue and reached Bushwick Avenue in a record fifteen minutes. She parked across the street from Yanick's apartment and waited patiently for what she did not know. She looked at the small clock on the dashboard. It was seven forty-five. She thought about the hot summer nights they'd spent in her room and the long evenings they'd spent at Applebee's. Well into the second hour she thought about the first time they had been intimate. She pondered all the times Yanick had confessed her love for her and how she would ignore her need to be loved back. A little over two weeks had passed since she last saw Yanick. Hours had passed since she'd been sitting in the car and her toes were numb, her nose red, and her fingertips frozen. *How did it come down to this?* Joann thought

She peered across the street and recognized George's frame. George stopped in front of Yanick's building and looked at his watch. Joann slid down on the front seat of the car and continued to wait. Seconds later Yanick came running out of the building with Seven bundled up in a stroller. Joann put her hand on the door handle and started to push the door open until she saw them kiss. They walked toward the car Joann sat in and she ducked further down on the front seat. Joann was parked three cars ahead of Yanick's car. She waited momentarily and then peeked from behind the steering wheel. She watched them situate Seven in her car seat. She watched as George pushed Yanick's hair behind her ear and kissed her again. Within seconds they pulled off. This was the third time in two weeks that she had used D's car to stakeout Yanick.

"I have to do something. And I have to do it soon," she said as she pulled off minutes after Yanick.

"That was too slow, Tony. You need to shove as many things as you can into that bag in three minutes. Buck, keep your gun up and watch the employees so they don't get slick. Camille, you stay on the floor and don't do anything stupid. As soon as they run in behind you with their guns out, you lay down. Empty those bags and let's try this again," Sweat said.

"Do we have to wear these fuckin' spandex underneath our clothes?" Kahmelle asked.

Sweat did not answer. He simply lifted his arm and pointed in the direction of the hall. They all exited the living room and stepped into his apartment's hallway. Camille was the first in. She jumped around and wiggled as if she had to use the bathroom. Then Sweat waved his arm. Tony and Kahmelle rushed past her with black leather gloves clinging to their fingers and their black guns, drawn, in their hands.

"Everyone down— now!" Kahmelle yelled. He kept his gun pointed and covered the entire width of the apartment, as Tony ran to the kitchen counter.

"Open this display and those two right now," Tony yelled. Sweat pretended to unlock a counter, and then raised his arms above his head. With a gun in one hand and a large velvet pouch, Tony raked jewelry from a kitchen counter top into two velvet pouches. He ran into the livingroom which was connected to the kitchen and dropped one shoe bag next to Camille.

"Don't any of you bitches think about moving because I will blow a hole right through your legs."

As Kahmelle yelled out Camille slid the bag into the front of her maternity jeans and wept louder. Tony ran into the kitchen and raked more jewelry off a folding table. As he reached the kitchen, Camille slowly got up and ran towards the front of the apartment. Tony turned his body briefly in her direction with his gun aimed at her and Kahmelle did the same.

"She's pregnant— let her go," Tony yelled towards Kahmelle. Then he quickly raked all of the jewelry into the bag. "Go, open up those two right there. Come on, move faster." Tony ran to the television, opened a cabinet door and raked jewelry into another velvet bag.

"Cover me at the door," Tony yelled to Kahmelle as he backed toward the door. When he reached Kahmelle, Kahmelle opened Tony's pants and the spandex biking shorts he wore underneath and dropped all three bags of jewelry inside them. They bolted from the living room area to the front door.

Sweat looked at his watch. "That was six minutes. If you can pull that off the day after tomorrow we might have something here. Now Buckle, you have to watch all corners with that gun. I have been in that store three times this month. I've set this up in here as close to the real thing as I could. The counters with the most value that you guys need to hit at Brooklyn Jewelry Exchange are the same distances as the TV I dragged in here from the bedroom, that folding table and the kitchen counter top. He turned toward Camille. "Camille, you have to cry like you are really scared. You got that? As soon as Tony leaves that counter and Buckle creates the diversion, grab the bag and run out. We have been at this for over three hours. Yesterday we ran this for 5 hours straight. I don't think Camille needs all this excitement, y'all. It's getting late and I got other shit to do. Thursday is only 48 hours away. You think you can pull this off?"

"This ain't shit, Sweat," Kahmelle said.

"What about you, Thuggleman? Can you handle this shit?" Sweat asked.

"As long as you let Kah in, and let me out, I know I can do this," Tony said.

"Once you pass this final stage, if you want out, you got it— no consequences. You have my word."

"All I know is my baby is hungry. I have to go and eat. I'll see you the day after tomorrow," Camille said. She stood with her body half in and out of the doorway as she heard the sound of Kahmelle's voice.

"Camille, you going to be alright? You want a take a cab or something?" Kahmelle asked.

"Nah, I'm good. One, son," she said as she quickly waddled out of the door letting it slam shut.

◆　◆　◆　◆

Joann leaned against the wall of the bodega. She picked up her cell phone and dialed Yanick. "No longer in service? That bitch done changed her number on me. FUCK!" Joann exhaled loudly and walked across the street toward Brooklyn Jewelry Exchange. She stood against the streetlight on the corner in front of the store. Joann did a double take when she looked through the glass storefront and saw George standing inside talking to the salesman.

"You may pick up your ring the day after tomorrow. Congratulations, your girlfriend is very lucky," the salesman said.

"Thanks, man. I'll see you Thursday," George said.

George walked out of the store and flipped up his phone. He pushed the radio button on his phone and it beeped loudly. With a look of disbelief on her face she inched up to the front of the store and listened to Yanick's voice blare from the phone's speaker.

"Hey, George. What's up?" Yanick asked in a perky tone.

"Nothing, Ma. Come pick me up from work and we can get a bite to eat," George said.

"Sounds like a plan," Yanick said.

"Love you," George said.

"Love you, too," Yanick replied.

He flipped the phone closed and struggled to fit it inside its clip properly. When he got it in place he looked up to find Joann standing in front of him writing a summons.

"What's your last name?" Joann asked.

"What are you giving me a ticket for? George asked.

"Loitering, what else? Now what's your last name, George?"

George sucked his teeth. "Soto."

She ripped the ticket out of her book and handed it to him. "Isn't that cute. You two have walkies, huh? Let me get Yanick's new number," Joann said.

"You can't make me do that. I should report you to the cop's bureau for harassment. I didn't deserve a ticket."

"Hey, don't blame me, blame your mayor. Tell my wife I said to call me," Joann laughed.

George laughed harder as he held in one hand the yellow jewelry receipt that had Paid In Full stamped in red ink on it, and the summons in the other. "Who's wife?" he said in a loud voice as he walked away.

Joann waited until he was out of her sight and walked into the Brooklyn Jewelry Exchange, straight to the salesman George was speaking to. "Hey, Mel, how's it hanging?" she asked.

"Good after noon, Nuñez. I'm fine thanks. Do you have to use the bathroom? Need to make a call?" the salesman asked.

"Nah, that young kid that just came out of here what did he want?"

"Oh, he just made the final payment on an engagement ring. Why do you ask?"

"I just issued him a summons, that's all. I'll speak to you later." Joann walked out of the store and looked at her watch. "Fuck that, this has gone far enough," she said under her breath.

She looked in the back of her memo book where she kept a copy of Yanick's school program. She studied it for a minute or two. Then she ran to the corner of Fourth and flagged down a bus, as it was about to pull off. Joann walked straight to the back of the bus and stood at its back door. She held it open for passengers as they exited. People stared at her, some with admiration and others with contempt. She felt them looking, but she didn't care— it was part of the job. With four hundred arrests under her belt she could never quite tell if onlookers knew her from her helping them out or her locking them up. Most people downtown Brooklyn seemed to hold a very low regard for the police.

Thoughts of George's conversation with Yanick crept into her mind. *Love? Mere weeks ago she professed those words to me but I was too fuckin' stupid to let her hear what she wanted to hear,* Joann thought.

Within ten minutes the bus stopped on Flatbush and Tillary and she ran up the block and into New York City Technical College. Unarmed security guards dressed in blue and orange uniforms stood at the entrance.

"May I help you, officer?" one of the security guards asked.

"I need to find this student right here for questioning. Can you direct me to this class, please?" Joann said.

"Follow me," a security guard replied.

Joann followed the guards into an elevator and they rode up to the fourth floor. As they passed classrooms and lecture halls Joann peeked in on dozens of students, young and old. When they reached 427 the security guard stepped into the classroom.

"Pardon the intrusion, professor but can Yanick Garcia please step outside for a moment?" the security guard asked.

Shocked, Yanick stood up and walked to the front of the class. The security guard led her to Joann who stood outside of the classroom door with a solemn face.

"Ms. Garcia, can I have a word with you? Follow me, please." Joann turned her attention to the security guard. "Thank you, officer."

"Glad I could help out," the security guard replied.

Yanick forced a smile, trying not to create a scene. She quietly followed Joann with the frozen smile. They walked into an empty lecture hall Joann passed en route to Yanick's classroom. Joann closed the door behind them.

"Where do you get off changing your fuckin' number?" Joann said in a low, harsh voice.

"How dare you come up here like this! Are you fuckin' crazy?" Yanick replied in the same tone.

"Yes. I must have been crazy to let you go. I'm sorry. I want you back. Give me another chance."

"Back? You never had me. You didn't want a commitment and you don't even love me. You have Sammy and a bunch of other broads at your disposal. You caught me at a very low point in my life but I am not gay. I could never be gay I was just confused and you preyed on my vulnerability. It was something to try and it was fun while it lasted." Yanick moved to walk out the door but Joann pulled her.

"But I do love you. I am just realizing it. I have been super depressed these past couple of weeks."

Yanick sighed. "I am with George right now and very happy. I'm in the middle of taking a final. Don't come up here like this again."

Yanick tried to yank her arm free of Joann but her grip was extreme. Joann dug her fingers into her arm and pulled her closer to her. "Stop it, Joey," Yanick said.

Joann pulled her near and tried to kiss her lips but Yanick managed to push her back. Yanick looked up at the clock over the chalkboard and rolled her eyes. Anger rang in her tone. "It's only twelve fifty. How about I call dispatch and let them know Post Two is harassing me on Jay Street? Goodbye!"

Joann watched Yanick stomp out of the room and out of her life. She gathered her composure and walked out steps behind her. Once Joann reached the lobby she addressed the security. "Thanks for your help."

As Joann stepped outside the building she picked up her radio. "This is post two. Leaving post and coming back to command on public transportation."

"Four."

24

Ride or Die Bitch

Tony and Kahmelle walked several feet behind Camille. "This is it— ride or die," Tony said nervously.

"Who the fuck are you, DMX, Tone? We got this. Don't go gettin' nervous on me now. This is your ticket out and mines in, nigga," Kahmelle said.

"Camille, you up for the ride?" Tony asked, looking for an excuse to back out. She caressed her stomach and nodded her head.

"Let's do it!" Kahmelle said.

The boys slipped on their gloves and shades as they walked. When Camille crossed the street and walked to the door of the store the boys pulled on their hoods and tied the drawstrings so tightly, only their lips and dark shades could be seen. They walked to the corner and stood on the side of Brooklyn Jewelry Exchange. Kahmelle touched the gun on his waist and Tony placed his finger on the trigger of the burner, which coldly sat in the front pocket of his hoodie. They waited at the corner and watched Camille hop from foot to foot in front of the glass doors. "Please, I gotta pee," she yelled.

The salesman behind the counter was hesitant but felt sorry for the young pregnant woman at the door. He placed his finger on the buzzer, paused, then pushed the button and buzzed Camille in. She stood in the open doorway and continued to squirm. "Thanks, which way is the bathroom?" she asked calmly.

"The restrooms are straight to the back," the salesman said then he quickly turned back to his customer, "So George, you're finally picking up your ring today?"

The screech of the pregnant girl redirected the salesman's attention to the door. He watched in panic as she was pushed to the ground by two hooded thugs.

"Don't move a muscle, muthafuckas, or you will all 'say hello to my little friend'," Kahmelle said.

Camille sobbed loudly on the ground grabbing her stomach. Tony momentarily looked down at her wondering if she was acting or serious but quickly went on with the plan. His gun hand targeted the man who had buzzed Camille in. His free hand removed four, large, deep purple, velvet bags with yellow drawstrings from his pants.

"YOU—keep your fucking hands up," Tony said as he zeroed in on his target. His aim steadied as he walked closer to the salesman. When Tony got behind the counter he placed the gun on the salesman's cheek.

"Open up that display, right there, quick. Then keep your hands where I can see them."

The salesman did as he was told. Tony stepped behind the counter and raked all the rings, bracelets and chains from the display into two bags. Several pieces of jewelry missed the bag and hit the floor but he continued as planned.

"Open that case over there. Come on, let's go, HURRY UP!" As Tony quickly moved toward the other counters he hustled past Camille and dropped a bag inches away from her. It landed with a solid thud. As soon as it hit the floor Kahmelle took over.

"Don't do nothing funny, bitch or I will pop a cap in your faggot ass so fast you will turn straight! Open that shit up like your life depends on it, 'cause it does," Kahmelle yelled.

As Kahmelle mouthed off Camille nervously dragged the bag close to her, pulled its strings tightly and shoved it into the top of her pants. As Kahmelle yelled louder, a sharp pain seized her midsection. She quit maneuvering and grabbed her stomach, leaving the bag tucked halfway into her pants.

"Don't think about shit but tryin' to stay alive. As a matter of fact, you four, get your asses out here where I can see you and lay down with your hands behind your heads."

Camille closed her eyes tightly praying the pain would go away. Kahmelle paced in front of the three sales people and the sole customer as they assumed their positions— face down with their hands behind their heads. Tony grabbed the salesman by the nape of his neck and shoved him toward the final display counters. "Open these two, then put your hands behind your head," Tony said.

"No tricks, bitch," Kahmelle called across to the salesman as he cocked his gun.

Tony quickly emptied the cases with his gun gripped tightly in his hand. As he raked the remaining jewels into the bags he noticed the biggest diamond cross he had ever seen and an unusual diamond beetle in the neighboring case. "Open that one right there. Then hit the floor with your co-workers, bitch," Tony said.

The salesman hesitated and Tony reunited the gun with his cheek. The man fumbled, missing the keyhole but was quick to find it as Tony's gun hand followed his every move. He wasted no time in running to the middle of the store after opening the case and Kahmelle shoved him to the ground. Tony saw Camille get up and scurry toward the door through his peripheral vision as he grabbed the diamond beetle and shoved it into the front pocket of his jeans.

As he reached for the cross he heard a gun shot. Tony instinctively ducked for cover. The shot rang in his ears, clogging them. He looked up from behind the counter and watched Camille fall to the floor in the doorway of the store.

Tony stood upright and watched in horror as Kahmelle fired two additional shots to the side of her stomach. "WHAT THE FUCK IS WRONG WITH YOU? SHE'S PREGNANT!" he cried.

Without a speck of remorse Kahmelle looked at his watch. "Five minutes nigga, I said everybody down. I guess let go my prego did not understand that."

Joann stood against the streetlight on the corner of Brooklyn High's field. With no hesitation she removed her phone from her ear when she thought she heard a shot in the distance. Seconds later, her suspicions were confirmed when she heard two additional shots. They were muffled and she had no idea what direction they were coming from but she knew they were close. She stayed alert and ready to run looking for a sign of some sort.

Tears rolled from beneath Tony's dark shades as he backed towards the door. "Cover me," he yelled as they both pointed their guns down toward the floor, aiming at the four hostages who lay motionless. Kahmelle pulled the elastic waist of Tony's sweat pants and biker shorts at one time, and Tony dropped three velvet jewelry bags into his crotch.

Tony looked down at Camille, as she lay motionless on the ground. There was a hole in her shirt near her stomach. The hole was frayed at the edges and blood oozed from it. *That's exactly where we had felt the baby moving around,* Tony thought. He looked with horror at the bloody flesh splattered on the glass and ground of the doorway that Camille's lifeless body blocked. He froze and his partner rushed passed him. Kahmelle stepped over Camille, stopped, then grabbed the soggy blood soaked velvet bag that was lodged halfway into her pants.

"Let's go! LET'S GO," Kahmelle yelled.

"Post Two, Post Two, pick up. There's a 54 at 3665 Fourth Avenue. Two male perps, race unknown," Joann's radio blared loudly.

"Four," Joann said as she bolted toward her given address. She looked at the numbers on the buildings before she took off from 3522 Fourth Avenue at top speed, briefly checking the address of each of the buildings she sped past, block by block. Four blocks and two minutes later she cautiously crossed the intersection at 3661 Fourth Avenue. She drew her pistol, paused momentarily and stomped her foot.

"They got the fuckin' Brooklyn Jewelry Exchange," she murmured. Joann slowed her pace as she reached the beginning of its glass front. As she followed the glass front she noticed the people inside were helping each other to their feet. She quickly noticed her friend, the salesman. *Look at Mel*, she thought, *he's fuckin' trembling—*"

Her thoughts were disturbed by the gruesome sight of the bloody, stiff, pregnant body lodged in the doorway of Brooklyn Jewelry Exchange.

"Oh shit!" Joann exclaimed and instinctively aimed her pistol into the store. Everyone in the store immediately put their hands in the air with the exception of the salesman. She surveyed their frightened faces and recognized George. She aimed for his head, cocking her pistol.

"Nuñez, it's not him— they just ran that way!" Mel, the sales manager screamed.

Joann did not budge. She stared at George and he helplessly did the same. The seconds it took her to put her weapon down seemed like hours to George. He relaxed his muscles and released his breath as she took off in the direction the salesman advised.

As Joann turned the corner she saw a figure slouched down at the far end of the long block. When he stood up, Tony looked back, noticed the cop and continued to run. Joann ran after him. She could hear the screaming sirens filling the neighborhood. She saw him run into a backyard. She smiled. "The abandoned house," she whispered.

Kahmelle was a running a few feet in front of Tony, who had just stopped to vomit a third time," Come on, man," Kahmelle called back.

Joann ran at top speed down Butler. She slid in a lumpy pile of fresh vomit on the ground. She turned into the driveway of a home and began the shortcut toward the abandoned house. She saw one perp descending a fence. His vomit-filled sweatshirt was caught on it and as he tried to yank himself free his shades dropped off his face. Out of breath she caught up quickly and stopped dead in her tracks when she saw Tony. He looked at her, quickly freed himself of the fence, dropped down, picked up his shades and took off running.

Joann was petrified. After a minute or two the sound of her radio loosened her up. Ignoring it she shook her head and wiped her face so hard she dragged her eyelids down. She ran out of the driveway, clicked into dispatch and looked around to make sure no one noticed her.

"Perp ran down Butler and turned right on Third. I saw one perp, wearing all black about 5'9'." Clutching her radio, Joann ran in a different direction from the shortcut that she knew Tony was taking. Two squad cars met her at the corner of Butler. Out of breath she stopped and addressed the officers.

"He ran down Butler and turned right across the street. I lost sight of him he was about 5"9" wearing all black."

"Come on!" Kahmelle called back several times as they ran and jumped fences an entire block via back yards. When they reached the street they pulled down their hoods and walked quickly to the next block. They crossed six backyards, that put them in middle of the block and in front of the abandoned home's shed. Kahmelle broke the old rusted lock to the shed with the back of his gun and he and Tony entered.

Inside the cold and damp shed Kahmelle started to strip. They both wore black hooded sweatshirts with thick fleece jackets underneath and jerseys on their backs. The thick black sweatpants concealed their loose fitting jeans and spandex biking shorts. Kahmelle wore spandex biker shorts that contained a large garbage bag, and four bright yellow, grocery bags. He kicked himself free of the tight shorts and the bags fell to the ground. Tony grabbed the garbage bag and hurled. Aside from his sobbing and vomiting the shed was silent.

"It is cold as fuck out here, boy. Come on, change your clothes, Tony," Kahmelle said.

Kahmelle paced the cluttered shed in small circular motions trying to keep warm. He watched as Tony slowly peeled off his layers. He made it down to his Jets Jersey and biker shorts and suddenly Tony began to hurl, again, his insides gushing into the bag like a fountain of vomit. Kahmelle shook his head and walked to the window. It was small and covered with a thick film of dust and dirt. It let in very little to no light.

"Remember when we first discovered this spot, man. I got my first piece of ass behind this shed I was in the ninth grade. Hurry up and change," Kahmelle said.

Tony looked up. He executed a series of dry heaves with his face inside the bag but there was nothing left inside of him to throw up. He was pale and lightheaded. "How could you? This wasn't part of the plan," he whispered.

"Yes, it was. You just didn't know. Hurry, Sweat will be here to pick us up in—" he looked at his watch—"three minutes."

"Who the fuck are you, nigga?"

"B to the mutha fucking Buckle, that's who. Buck Wild."

"You plotted to kill your seed and Camille? That's a double homicide. I remember when you were scared to kill water bugs," Tony said softly.

"And? She didn't want to have an abortion, so I took the liberty. Now pull yourself together. Sweat is going to drop us off at school. That is going to be our alibi. Good thing you came up with that, Tone. We already signed into homeroom and made our first, second and third period classes. We got lunch right now and we just came in a little late so we could see what all of the commotion at The Brooklyn Jewelry Exchange was."

Tony's head boomed.

"Look around the shed for something to put our clothes in. You done hurled all in our trash bag and shit."

Tony just sat still.

"Fuck it, since we gettin' rid of the clothes it doesn't matter if you hurled in it."

Tony finally pulled off of his spandex shorts and let the velvet bags fall to the ground. He picked up his jeans and patted his pocket, then stepped back into them. Kahmelle placed all of the jewelry into the bright yellow plastic bags. Tony zipped his fleece and picked up the remaining clothes from the floor. He put them into the big vomit-filled garbage bag. Then he placed that garbage bag into another.

"Nigga, my balls was on fire in those spandex with all that shit in 'em. All you had to carry was those velvet bags. Shit, I had plastic bags, garbage bags and this extra set of clothes underneath my sweats. A nigga almost passed out in there. We did it man, we did it."

Tony was quiet.

"SHHH. Listen, you hear anything?" Kahmelle asked. He walked to the front of the shed, cracked the door and peeked through the small opening. A slither of light beamed into Tony's eyes momentarily blinding him like a deer in headlights. He closed his eyes and shook his head. Kahmelle smiled when he saw Sweat in an old, rusted white Honda Accord. "Come on and bring that fuckin' barf bag with you."

Tony looked around the shed, for what he did not know. Kahmelle looked around to ensure everything was in place and it was. The boys left shed. Kahmelle carried the four grocery bags and Tony followed with the big black garbage bag. He used his gloved hand and shut the door. He picked up the broken lock from off of the ground and dumped it into the vomit and clothes-filled bag then knotted it. They got into the car without a word.

They rode in silence. Sweat pulled up to the back entrance of the school. He turned back and stared at Tony. "Go into the bathroom and clean your ass up. You don't want to look suspicious."

They left all bags in the car and slid into the school through the side entrance without being seen.

25

Toss my bread and the pigeons come flockin'

"This shit doesn't work. I had this damn powder down for weeks and these fuckin' roaches is sniffin' this shit like cocaine," a middle-aged woman laughed. "I guess I shouldn't have put sugar in the bottle. But that was 'posed to attract 'em to it."

She vigorously swept the kitchen and opened her window, which overlooked the stone chess tables and benches of the playground neighboring Brooklyn High School's field. She shivered from the cold as she extended her upper body out of the window and shook out the dustpan. The thick, chalky substance filled the air covering the benches and the ground surrounding them.

"Damn the day I bought this 'Kill Your Roach n Rat'. All this shit is ammonia and boric acid. I ain't have to pay twenty dollars for this shit." She picked up the bottle and looked at its label, which pictured a few dead roaches lying on their backs in front of a stiff rat carcass. She struggled to unscrew the cap. The woman placed the cap under her housedress and tried to unscrew it a second time. "Got it."

Shaking the bottle out of the window she emptied its contents and a chilling breeze carried the 'Kill Your Roach n Rat' to the tops and fronts of the chess tables and playground benches. As she shut her window two pigeons flew down and began to peck around the benches. One picked up a small piece of bread between in its beak and gobbled it down. The second did the same. The woman looked up at the clock.

"Oh my goodness. It's seven already! I gotta get ready for work." She locked her window and headed toward the back of her apartment.

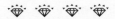

Rocky power-walked toward Fourth Avenue clutching a loaf of bread. She looked at her watch and walked faster. "I can't believe it's almost seven-thirty." Rocky looked at the bread and exhaled deeply. "Well, it is stale and I have to get over this fear sometime," she sighed.

At Fourth Avenue she squinted trying to glimpse at the corner of Butler Street, looking for Brooklyn Jewelry Exchange.

Damn, I miss that apartment on Butler but at least now I'm closer to Brooklyn High's field and I have much more space, she thought.

As she waited for the light she rubbed her hands together and blew into them. She continued struggling to make out the Brooklyn Jewelry Exchange, and estimated it to be six blocks ahead. She could only see as far down Fourth Avenue as the bodega, and although closed, its bright multi-colored lights still flashed off its iron gates.

If it's the last thing I do, I'll pick up my Nahnan's broach from there tomorrow. Besides, I'll probably be getting some really nice pieces of ice for Christmas next week and I'll take them there to be appraised and insured.

As she sped down the street she smiled at the thought of what gifts she would receive from Marcus. *I know he's going to pay off my Mercedes, I hinted that I wanted a new chinchilla coat, stroller length, when I took Marcus' mom to my furrier last week.* She smiled momentarily. *He is talking diamonds but his sweet-ass dick will be the best present of them all. Shit, it's only been five days and I am already about to bust.* Rocky clutched her stomach. "But I can't overdo it now," she whispered.

When Rocky reached the corner of Brooklyn High's field, she stepped up on the curb and noticed a dead pigeon. "Ewwww! Oh my God!" she shrieked quickly looking in the opposite direction of the stiff bird. She picked up her pace and chanted loudly as she rushed toward the park, "I am going to feed the birds. I am going to feed the birds." She repeated the phrase until she reached the benches outside of the park.

"As a matter of fact, I'm going to do it before I hit the track and get it over with," Rocky said.

She sat down on a bench and opened the bag. She removed one piece of bread, ripped it into several pieces and threw it down. Rocky reached into the plastic bag and pulled out another piece. As soon as she tore the second piece, three birds flew down, one by one, and devoured the bread on the ground. She heard more wings beating against the wind and cringed. Trying to relax, Rocky sat back clutching the slice in her hand. Small beads of sweat permeated her face. Nervously, she wiped her brow with the slice of bread leaving doughy crumbs on her forehead. When she dropped her hand to her side four more birds swooped down from behind her. Two of them dived at her hand pecking away at the bread in her clutched fist. Another dropped on her lap with a thud and began twitching violently. The fourth landed on top of the bag wedged between her legs.

Rocky let out a blood-curdling screech. Her legs would not carry her to safety; petrified by her fear and a severe pain in her chest, she sat motionless. Before she knew it countless birds flew down from all directions. Two big white and gray seagulls pecked away at the crumbs on her forehead and several pigeons pulled at her hair. Rocky felt a warm thick stream of liquid roll down her cheek. She lifted her free hand to wipe off the substance aimlessly, like she wasn't using her own fingers then looked at it. Her hand revealed a thick white substance streaked with red. This snapped her out of her trance.

"Bird shit and blood," she nervously stuttered.

Rocky felt as if she had walked into a cactus garden as the birds painfully bit and pecked away at her. She swung her hands around wildly in large circular motions, like a young girl in a catfight. She could hear them coming. Their wings fluttered and flapped against the cold winds from all directions. As each wing beat against the frigid morning air Rocky became more frantic. The pecking of the birds became more painful and more profound. She felt as if she was being jabbed by dozens of hypodermic needles.

A small, red car drove slowly by. The driver did a double take of the scene and sped off.

The middle-aged woman who neighbored the park didn't realize it was her carelessness that had caused the birds' frenzy. She sat on her windowsill and watched in horror as the birds reacted combatively to the 'Kill your Roach n Rat' and sugar mixture that she had emptied out of her window minutes before. She was amazed at what she saw. It seemed as if more than one hundred birds covered Rocky. And what was even more odd, the birds were not only eating away at her, they were eating each other. At least forty dead birds surrounded the bench.

"Help her!" the woman cried from her window.

People stood in their doorways and watched in dismay as Rocky flailed her arms about wildly. The sound of the birds began to push her to the brink of sanity. What was left of her distorted instinct told her to run and she did. Just as she took her third stride she slipped on a dead seagull and stumbled to the ground layered with her jerking and twitching feathered friends. She miraculously stood up and attempted to run again. With birds covering her like a multi-colored feather hat and matching coat buttoned to the neck, she fought back. Her arms began to flail with less vigor as she tried to swat them away, stumbling about like a drunken crackhead.

Rocky had left her home with a loaf of stale bread and the intention of overcoming her fears during her routine morning jog. Instead she ended up with her fears overcoming her. There was not one ounce of hope left inside of her and not one part of her body left uncovered by a bird or stray feather.

Just as the squad car pulled up to drop Joann and an additional cop off at their post a red Nissan screeched in front of them and a young man hopped out. "Officers, there's a woman being attacked by an army of birds. It's the weirdest shit I have ever seen, right beside the High's field. There are flocks of them!"

"Pop the trunk. Richie, you catch, " Joann said as she reached inside the trunk and grabbed as much gear as her hands permitted. She passed it to her new partner and he threw it into the car. It was like a small assembly line. Once the trunk was emptied she hopped into the squad car. Suddenly the sounds of their sirens filled the air. The police followed the little red car. All four officers jumped out of the car, in full riot gear, and took a moment to examine the situation at hand.

"Would you look at this shit, Nuñez!" one of the cops shouted from under his headgear. "It looks like we just drove into an episode of the 'Twilight Zone'."

Joann lifted the protective shield on the helmet an inch and shouted back, "Either that or a ghetto Hitchcock movie. Come on let's move."

All four of the officers ran to the sidewalk swinging their clubs at the birds in their path. Rocky felt a huge hand grab her arm and shake her violently. She tried to use her other arm to defend herself but she could barely lift it.

Joann's new partner picked up his radio. "This is Post Two. We've got a— I don't know— we need a bus like yesterday. This is the craziest thing I've ever seen. Female jogger attacked by out of control birds."

"Copy."

The officers used their gloved hands to fling birds off Rocky. Most of the winged creatures just dropped to the ground. A few were able to flap a few feet away, while others jerked on the ground for a few seconds like they suffered a fatal seizure— then stopped stiffly. A brown pigeon flew top speed at eye level into Joann's helmet and thumped on its glass. It quickly slid off to the ground leaving smeared feces and blood on it. She let out a rough, startled yell.

All four cops plucked them off Rocky's body as if Rocky was the fowl and the birds were her feathers. As they flung the remaining birds to the ground Rocky was stiff. Her face was covered in bird feces, dark bruises and blood. Some of the onlookers cheered as the last birds were removed. Others cried and shook their heads in disbelief.

The ambulance arrived just as the last birds were removed. The EMT technicians placed Rocky on the stretcher and the ambulance drove off. The cops stood amidst a flood of dead birds talking to bystanders. Lieutenant Cruickshank arrived on the scene as the ambulance pulled off. He walked towards the bench and picked up the tattered remains of the bread bag. He surveyed it and looked at his men, shaking his head.

"I'm going to call ESU on this one. This shit's way out of our hands," Lieutenant Cruickshank said.

"What's ESU?" Joann's partner asked.

Joann pulled the rookie to the side and smiled. "Emergency Service Unit. Welcome to Post Two, Richie. It might not be the most live post on the tour but something different is always bound to go down. After they robbed Brooklyn Jewelry Exchange yesterday, I thought this post wouldn't see any more action for a while but this shit is off the chain AND IT ISN'T EVEN EIGHT O'CLOCK YET!"

Joann looked at her new, rookie partner and toned her smile down.

"You alright?" she asked.

"Yeah, I am just a little shaken up," Richie replied.

"Come over here and let me show you how to fill out your paper work," Joann said.

Both officers stepped over a slew of dead birds. Joann could feel them crush underneath her feet. She was momentarily grossed out until she thought about the face of the young dead pregnant girl in the doorway of the Brooklyn Jewelry Exchange. *Nothing*, she thought, *is worse than that. But I know I did the right thing.*

She made her way to the benches and used her billy club to knock off some of the birds. Before her behind reached the bench she quickly got up. "You know what, Richie? Let's walk— these birds must be contaminated or something." Both officers walked in the direction of Fourth Avenue.

Rocky awoke to a fresh floral scent. Her head throbbed steadily as she made her first attempt to sit up. She found her joints stiff as she used her arms to push her upper body against the headboard. She opened and closed her eyes several times trying to focus and was instantly alarmed. *Where am I?* she silently panicked. She tried to swallow but her mouth was dry.

When she was finally able to focus, Rocky looked around with her eyes opened wide at the countless flowers that crowded the white room and at the empty bed next to her. Suddenly, she covered her head with both arms, like she was blocking a blow and ducked. She began hyperventilating and swinging her arms. "Bird! Bird! Bird! Bird!" Inside Rocky's head her deafening screams were continuous between each short breath she took but each cry hit the air in a soft, coarse whisper. The machine monitoring her heart started to beep faster each time she cried out 'BIRD'. Within seconds the beeping brought her to a sudden halt. It was only then Rocky began to fully realize where she was.

The task of sitting up was a bit easier this time around and she took in more of the room. A small, square-shaped TV hung to her immediate right and as she looked straight ahead Mauri and Kay sat next to each other, fast asleep in the wilderness of flowers. *MAURI!* she screamed inside.

On a tray located to her left was a salmon pink, plastic jug. Rocky turned to the side and reached for it and felt an immense pain in the middle of her head. When she touched it, she realized that her hair had been cut bluntly to her ears. She grabbed the jug and shook it around. The water swished and the ice hit the sides. The sound of the ice woke up Kay who in turn tapped Mauri.

"Oh my God. I thought I lost you," Kay said as she ran to the bed and kissed Rocky's forehead repeatedly. Tears slowly rolled down Kay's cheeks.

Mauri walked over to the bed and slipped Rocky's ring back onto her finger. Rocky tried to open her mouth but nothing came out. Her throat was extremely dry and her tongue felt like sandpaper. She pointed to the cup. Mauri grabbed the pitcher from her hand and poured. He fluffed and positioned her pillows so that one was directly behind her back and the other rested behind her head.

"Don't worry. Kay called and told me everything. I didn't mean to push the marriage issue and scare you away. I know you asked me for more time and I am sorry. I'm sorry about the baby, too. I wish you had told me. Excuse me," Mauri said as he walked out the room choked up and teary eyed.

Rocky gagged on the water as it went down. After a short coughing bout, she managed to speak, although her delivery was rough and raspy. "What happened to my baby?" Rocky asked.

Kay moved closer to her bedside and stroked her hair. "You have been here, in ICU, for three days now. You spent one day in isolation, because they thought you were contagious. You have not said one word. I have been at your bedside every night. Mauri flew in yesterday night. You were attacked by birds. Your doctor said that the area you were jogging in had been exposed to some kind of powder that contained pheromones, boric acid and sugar. The pheromones attracted them to that area and the combination of the three agents caused the birds to become combative. The doctors called it a 'freak occurrence'. They gnawed at your skin and pulled out a lot of your hair. Kiki was here and she cut it for you." Kay cleared her throat and inhaled deeply. "Anyway the doctors said that the boric acid entered your blood stream and the fetus was too weak to survive, I am so sorry."

Rocky banged her head gently against the pillow that was propped behind her head. Kay closed the door and began to talk quickly as she walked back to Rocky's side.

"I went through your phone and called Marcus. He flew in and was the first one to hear the news about the baby. I don't know if he asked your doctor or how it went down because he came while I was at work. He left a note that, you know, I read. To sum it up he doesn't trust you and wants out of the relationship. I called Mauri and told him you were in the hospital. I also told him that you didn't really want to leave him but you were not ready to get married until you finished school. I explained that you would have really felt trapped with no job of your own and without a completed education. And, when you found out you were pregnant you were scared to tell him because you thought he would rush the wedding date and wouldn't let you finish school. I told him that you basically raised yourself and are used to being independent. I told him that you cried every night but were scared to tell him and planned to tell him when you were showing. At least you have your health and a man that really loves you. Even though you don't like him, this situation has changed the way I feel about him. He has been at your bedside and beside himself with grief since the moment I called him. I am going to stall Mauri. I think you should read this letter and you will know that Mauri is the one.

Kay went into her pocket and unfolded a letter written on the hospital's letterhead. She handed it to Rocky and walked out of the door. Rocky reluctantly read the letter;

Dear Candy,

Since you like writing notes I thought this would be right up your alley. When I got the news, I rushed to see you. Your beautiful face is scarred, and our baby was gone. You don't look like the person I met, and I am not sure who you are. I'm unsure whose baby it was, but now that it's gone I am gone too. You helped me through a tough time.

Thanks,

Marcus

Rocky held the note to her chest and began to cry. She shook her head and looked out the window. Rocky saw a flock of birds circling around and around, far up in the sky. They seemed to have no direction; at least thirty of them flew in an arrow-shaped formation in the same circular motion, over and over again. She had seen birds doing this before. She used her fingertips to brush her face. She felt no scars. She slowly fingered her face a second time. When she reached her forehead a harsh pain went through her head and face. It was a long scar. She shuddered at the thought. As she dabbed it she began to cry harder.

Rocky watched the arrow of birds. She couldn't help but wonder if there was any truth to what she had told Marcus on the yacht in Cozumel that day. Perhaps his father had summoned those birds to attack her and rob her of his grandchild. She lay back and slowly placed the note underneath her blanket. Minutes later the door opened and it was Kay. Rocky handed her the note.

"Could you get me a mirror so I can see my scar?"

"It's not that bad. Nothing a little plastic surgery couldn't fix. I already had the resident plastic surgeon do a consultation." Kay sat on the edge of the bed and affectionately stroked her hair as she talked.

"Rocky, this is by far the toughest thing you have been through. But you have been through other tough situations and you always manage to come out on top. I will always be here for you. I just spoke to your doctor and you should be out of here it two days, just in time for Christmas."

Rocky sat motionless and watched the flock of birds flying around out the window. Kay grabbed her hand and smiled. Rocky turned towards her and continued to cry.

"Listen, you could have been left with nothing," Kay said.

Rocky heard Mauri's voice talking to another man outside.

"I think that's your doctor now. I lied and told him that you were my sister so I could get the information on your condition."

Rocky rubbed her engagement ring and forced a half of smile. "You are my sister, Kay. I guess I have taught you well," Rocky said.

"I learned from the best," Kay said.

"I could have been Mrs. Marcus Best, Kay!"

At that point the doctor and Mauri entered the room.

"Well, Ms. Jones, I am glad to see you are up and lively."

26

I never seen a man cry 'till I seen a man die

Malik walked into his brother's room and found him laying face down, bawling into his pillow. He sat on the edge of his bed and rubbed Tony's back.

"Tone, I know how you feel. This is really the first time you have experienced death so close to home, and it won't be the last. I mean— I don't want to sound fucked up or anything but it's probably for the best. I don't think that baby would have stood a chance with Kahmelle and Camille as its parents. I know Camille's mom from back in the day; it's a wonder Camille made it as far as she did. Besides, she's in a better place now. You haven't stopped crying since. Come on, sit up."

Malik patted his brother's back and pulled him up. His pillow was sodden with blood and spit. "What the fuck?" Malik said.

Tony jerked several times, hiccuped and threw up a small amount of blood.

"Dad—" Malik was silenced by Tony's hand over his mouth. He kept it there for a few seconds to see if there would be an answer to Malik's call. When none came he released his grip.

"Kahmelle and I— robbed Brooklyn Jewelry Exchange— Kahmelle shot her. That was our final initiation into Brooklyn's Finest. Sweat said he would let me out of the gang— that's where I've been getting all the money from," Tony stammered.

Malik stared at his brother. He was hoping that it was a joke but as Tony regurgitated more blood he realized it wasn't. He spoke in a harsh whisper.

"How the fuck did you manage to pull this shit off? Don't you know Sweat never gave a fuck about nothin' and he definitely don't give a fuck about you?" Malik said.

Malik ripped his shirt off his back and turned his back toward his brother. "Do you see what this nigga did to me! He turned me into the muthafuckin' police so he could go free. I did two years in prison, while he chilled and spent my fuckin' money. He ain't no fuckin' man. I done seen that nigga catch bodies, you heard? But I'll be damned if I let him catch yours."

"What happened between you two, Malik?"

Malik sighed. "As soon as I came home I approached him and he hit me with, 'it didn't make any sense for both of us to do time. Besides you're bigger than me.' I squared his ass dead in the chin and then the stomach. I hit that nigga so hard I can still smell him pissin' and shittin' his pants as he hit the floor like yesterday. He apologized, sincerely. He said he never really had family besides his grandmother and me, and he went on about how he taught himself how to be a man and still had shit to learn. I accepted the apology, helped him up to his feet and went to walk out of the door. That's when he butchered my ass, Tone. He stabbed me in the lower back using both of his hands and cut me upward. Reflex, turned me into his cut and I slashed him with my knife right across his face. That's why my cut curves up my neck, I turned into it and he didn't let go until the tip of the blade broke off in my neck; I went toward the door and he called out to me. I can still see him clutching the top half of his face; blood seeping between his fingers. He said, 'This ain't over, Leeko. I will kill your fuckn' ass for this shit. Look at my face.' I laughed at that nigga then I said. 'No you won't, remember Tasha? I know I do'. We stood there staring at each other for a long time. Then Sweat said 'You wouldn't man, I know you wouldn't. You still my man for life, I know you wouldn't. Then I said, 'Fuck me again, and you will see', and those were the last words we had."

Tony began to breathe easier. He clutched his stomach and dropped his face into his brother's bare chest. "I remember when you came in that night and I tried to doctor up the cut on your back."

"We have to tell Dad and I don't think we should take you to the hospital. There might be a way I can get you out of this— YOU, Tony, not fuckin' Kahmelle. I am going to fix you some toast and soup. Then I am going to tell Dad, before he goes to work and Ma comes home. No phone calls."

Malik held his brother tightly and gave him a firm embrace. "I ran the street for you little brother. I did time so you wouldn't have to."

"I just wanted to belong, to be down. I don't know."

"I'll work this out. Don't speak to anyone on the phone or on your walkie. Only speak to Kahmelle in school. You can't tell Shaine shit. Let me handle this, baby bro. You're going to graduate in February. Fuck the extra science classes. You have more than enough credits to graduate. I'm going to take you to D.C., and you're going to live there. Does Sweat know where you are going to school?"

"No. I just told him I got into Pre-Medical school."

"Let me handle that nigga."

"I feel a little better. But he wasn't supposed to shoot her Malik. That wasn't part of the plan I swear! I ain't never seen nobody die before." Tears ran down his cheeks.

"Trust me, I know you didn't. I'm calling Dad. Don't worry everything will be alright."

"Dad . . . DAD!"

27

It ain't where you from it's where you're at

Tony and Kahmelle sat in the lunchroom of Brooklyn High School two weeks after the incident. Tony had a smile across his face and Shaine in his arms. They sat with a group of seven teens. This being their first day back from Christmas vacation they discussed presents, what they did during their vacation and their upcoming senior trip.

"Oh, you know I'll be there for that, son, I wouldn't miss a week at Walt Disney World for nothing. Me and Mickey go way back," Tony smiled.

The teens laughed. Tony looked up and froze as he saw the school safety guards come down the steps with two cops. He stared hard as it was difficult to make the distinction between school safety and cops. Their uniforms were nearly identical with the exception of a gun in a holster and differently shaded blue shirts. Tony released his grip on Shaine and straightened up. He tapped Kahmelle gently on his fingers as both school safety and the police scanned the lunchroom from its main entrance. They both leaned across the table and Tony whispered in Kahmelle's ear. "Yo, po-po is coming up on us."

Kahmelle didn't say a word. He stopped smiling. The teens at the table continued to laugh, but Kahmelle and Tony sat solemnly. Kahmelle quickly placed his index finger over his lips. Then he moistened them with his tongue. He sat forward and began to whisper as he nodded his head. "To the end, nigga, you heard? Stick to the story. You my nigga for life," Kahmelle said.

"They about eight tables away, Kah," Tony said.

Kahmelle placed his finger on his mouth again and shook his head, "To the end nigga, to the end." Then he snatched Dulce from behind and kissed her neck. He hugged her tightly. "You think you can put on some ears and a polka dot mini skirt when we get to Disney World and dance for me in the hotel?" Kahmelle asked.

"Of course, Buckle. Shaine, you see the chain Buckle got me for Christmas," Dulce said.

Shaine rolled her eyes. Kahmelle kissed Dulce's ear lobe, loosened his grip and slid back several inches from her. Dulce continued talking and showing off her Christmas gift. Tony whispered into Shaine's ear. "I love you."

"I love you too, Tony."

As they closed in on them, Tony felt a big lump in his throat. He kept his eyes on the back of Shaine's neck as they finally stopped in front of the table.

"Excuse, me, guys, but I need Kahmelle Dunson to follow me," a school safety officer said.

Shaine looked at Kahmelle as he stood up and faced the police.

Kahmelle forced a smile at one of the school safety officers that he was familiar with. "What's the problem, Junior? I haven't cut class this entire school year."

Junior shook his head. "Nah, Kahmelle, it is a little deeper than that. I need you to follow me."

Kahmelle went willingly. His friends watched quietly as he walked off. Tony looked down at the black hard bottom shoes of the police officers, then at Kahmelle's dark green Timberlands. Then back to the feet of the officers as they walked away. The soles of one cop's shoes were so worn down his left shoe leaned over to the side as he walked. Tony watched the shoes get smaller and smaller until they weren't visible. Tony dared not look up, Kahmelle or one of the cops might turn around and he was sure his face would give him up. So he watched their feet. Kahmelle never looked back.

The cops, school safety officers and Kahmelle walked down the empty halls of the school. Kahmelle looked in through the windows at teens sitting down in their classes. He looked at the pistols that sat in the holsters of the two officers in front of him and temptation tingled through his body and sparked his thoughts.

Shit, I should just snag the two pistols, spray em, and run. But where am I going to go? Before he knew it they were at the main office.

"Hi, son, I need to take you down to the precinct for some questioning. I will allow you to call your parents, so they can meet you at the precinct," an officer said.

"What am I being questioned for? My moms is in North Carolina and my aunt is at work."

"We just want to ask you some questions about Camille, that's all."

Kahmelle bowed his head down and looked at the officers with tears in his eyes. "You know, I was going to be a daddy. I hope you guys hurry up and catch those punks that killed my babies."

The school safety officer placed his arm gently on Kahmelle's shoulder as the forced tears rolled down Kahmelle's cheeks.

"What was that about?" Dulce asked Tony.

"I don't know," Tony said.

"Well, I have class. See you guys later," Shaine said as she got up from the table.

Dulce looked at Shaine and rolled her eyes, "Tony, call me when you hear from my man."

Tony nodded his head then looked at Shaine. "Come on, Shaine, let's go to class."

Tony walked Shaine to class and then he walked straight to a pay phone. He went into his wallet and pulled out a royal blue and yellow calling card. He looked on the back of the card and dialed the numbers on it.

"Good afternoon, may I please speak to Mr. Hendrickson?" Tony asked.

"One moment."

"Hello?" Malik said.

"Hey, Malik, they came and picked that up at my school today."

"Where did they take that?"

"I don't know?"

"What time do you get out of school today?"

"One-fifteen."

"I'll meet you in front of the house at one-thirty. Where you callin' me from?"

"I'm at school, in a phone booth, on the card."

"Good. Go straight home."

Tony and Malik had gone over this day dozens of times in their home. Now that it was finally here, Tony didn't know what card fate would deal.

As soon as school was over Tony walked Shaine home and tried his best to dodge each question she hit him with.

"What aren't you telling me, Antonio Hendrickson? Why did they take Kahmelle? Did you guys run a job that you didn't tell me about last night?"

"Shaine I don't kn—"

"Don't tell me it was y'all that held up that token both on Dekalb Avenue last night— you promised you would stop."

"Trust me I have. Goodbye, I 'll call you later," Tony said.

As he continued to his house Tony thought about Camille's lifeless body laid out on the floor and her insides splattered against the door of Brooklyn Jewelry Exchange. Thoughts of Kahmelle fucking her during their initiation at Brooklyn High's Field waltzed through his mind as well. He could picture him smacking her ass, and everyone cheering him on in the background. He envisioned Kahmelle's remorseless face as they were in the shed after the incident. These thoughts flashed through his head over and over— back and forth like it was on advance and rewind in a DVD player.

As he approached his house, he noticed the big, green truck parked in front of it. He recognized it as Sweat's. He picked up his pace and looked at his watch. A ray of sunlight hit his stone-filled wrist. It caused him to squint in an attempt to refocus. It was one forty-five. As he approached the SUV, he suddenly wished he were staring into the face of his old black plastic digital Timex. He walked up to the door and it unlocked as he touched the handle. He opened the passenger door to the car. His heartbeat triple timed and took a hundred foot Six Flags drop to his balls when he saw his brother sitting in the front of the car next to Sweat. He stood, as if he were in shock, with his hand clutching his chest. He cleared his throat.

"Stop standin' there like that. Get in, Tone," Malik shouted.

As Tony went to close the door he noticed Sweat had dried up blood smeared on his cheek. He sat down in the back and shut the door.

"You've been doing the right thing by not checkin' for me, Thuggle," Sweat said.

Malik snickered under his breath and looked at Sweat with a twisted smile and slowly shook his head. "Thuggleman, huh?"

Sweat smiled. "The apple don't fall too far from the tree. So, they bagged Buckle at school today?" Tony looked at Sweat. "Stick to our story, Thuggle, and you'll be straight," Sweat said.

Tony looked at the back of his brother's head that turned slowly toward him. With a quick nod, Malik gave him a reassuring look.

"I will be in touch to find out what's going on. Your brother will know where I am at."

He inhaled deeply through his nose, wiped under it with the back of his hand and inspected it for a couple of seconds. Using that same hand he reached back and placed his hand underneath his seat.

"Hold onto this," Sweat said as he handed Tony a large-sized, shiny, blue gift bag with silver stars on it. It had blue tissue paper shoved inside the top of it. "There's sixty-five grand in that bag, Thuggle. Sixty-five. I have Kahmelle's cut right here and I want you to take that. I'm going away for a second," Sweat said.

"Yeah, we both thought that would be best," Malik cut in.

Tony began to shift things around in his bag but the tension in the air gripped him tightly and would not release him. He nervously fumbled around in the backseat as his brother and Sweat sat staring at each other.

What the fuck went down in here, yo? There's blood on Sweat's face, my brother's lip is swollen and my muthafuckin' brother looks like he is getting ready to kill him. The thoughts unleashed Tony's tears.

"Tony, don't start bitchin' up now, baby boy! Man your ass up. You wanted to get gansta nigga, and you got it," Malik said.

Malik abruptly looked at Sweat, palmed the middle of his face with his hand and forcefully pushed it back into the headrest. Then he delivered a blow to his temple. The car jerked violently as the sneak blows caused Sweat's foot to come off of the brake momentarily and quickly slam back down on it.

Sweat rammed his fist into Malik's headrest, purposely missing his head. "Don't get too fuckin' cocky, Leeko," he said breathing heavily.

"That's my little fuckin' brother, Reginald Watkins. What the fuck was you thinking, Sweat? You remember lil' Tone, that snot face little brat we dragged all over the place with us. You was family, baby. The only thing you two have in common is that he ain't ever gonna see the inside of a cell. I'ma make sure of that. If I got to bring you down Sweat, I will do it!" Malik started yelling on the top of his lungs. "Nigga you owe me every thing you got, you KNOW this. WHY would you drag him into this?"

Tony and his tears were scared stiff. He expected Sweat to pull out a gun and blow both his and his older brother's head off. Sweat just licked around his mouth removing some of the blood that trickled over his scarred lip. Then he wiped under his nose with the back of his hand, inspected the deep red blood that was on it, and quickly wiped it off on the side of his deep dark denim jeans.

"You right, fam. I still feel your loss every fuckin' day, nigga. You was the only family I had. I'll fix this shit and that's word to Slim, God bless the dead," Sweat said.

He made the sign of the cross and then kissed the diamond filled crucifix on his neck. Malik knew right there and then, Sweat would keep his word. He would never swear on his grandmother.

"We'll go ahead with the plan, Leeko. Thuggle, you go in the house, Leeko, follow me to my spot."

Sweat looked Malik in the eyes and initiated a tight embrace. They smacked each other's backs and didn't let go for a minute. "I'm sorry, son. That's word to Slim I'm sorry, I miss you, nigga. I'm only going out like this on the strength of us baby, one love, nigga," Sweat said over Malik's' shoulder.

"Malik, don't go with him," Tony said.

"Trust me on this one, Thuggle, you ain't got shit to worry about," Sweat said.

"Then I'm riding with y'all," Tony replied.

"Tony, go into the house. I will be back in fifteen minutes or so," Malik said.

Tony looked at Sweat and his brother then reluctantly got out of the car. He walked slowly toward the house and wondered if he would ever see his brother again. *How did I get my self into this, my brother into this?* Tony thought. As he walked through the door he found his father there waiting for him. *Shit, I even got my parents into this shit. What was I thinking?* Tony burst into tears.

"Pull yourself together, son. I have spoken to the sergeant at the precinct and I have filled him in on what he needs to know. I know him casually and am trying to pull a favor in on this one. You can't go down there crying and shit. You are going to look guilty. Now, here's the deal— come here boy."

Jonathan walked toward his son and hugged him tightly. Tony didn't want to let go.

"I never meant for anyone to die, Dad. I just wanted to be down, I really didn't think it would go this far. I know you're disappointed in me, Dad. I'm sorry. Did you tell Mom?" Tony looked at his father as he released his embrace.

"You're kidding me, right? Millie would fall out on this kitchen floor. I am not going to tell her unless I have to, and fuck yeah, I am disappointed in you. But that street shit is in your blood, son. You know what I was into before I became a cop, way before you were born? Your grandfather owned a bar, which contained one of the biggest Black owned number wholes in Chi-town. So, I am disappointed that you took a walk on that side, yes, but son, I am not surprised and I won't hold it against you. I went through it with your brother and now it's your turn."

Tony had never thought 'its in your blood' held any validity. Tony always believed a man was responsible for his own actions, but perhaps it was true.

His father retrieved a container of juice from the refrigerator and two glasses from above the sink. He poured them a drink and they continued their conversation. They spoke about Jonathan's childhood and Malik's childhood for at least a half an hour before his father touched the present situation.

"Listen, they called Kahmelle into the station to question him about Camille's murder. They don't have a clue that you two robbed that store and Kahmelle is performing. According to the sergeant he is clutching onto a sonogram of the fetus crying hysterically over the death of Camille and Kahmelle Junior— he had everyone won over until they placed his ass in the line up. The salesman from Brooklyn Jewelry Exchange did not ID him as one of the people who stuck up the store but they bagged him for attempted rape and grand larceny. It seems that Kahmelle robbed the owner of the store's wife for her ring and she I D'd him. Now they want to question you and place you in the lineup. He gave up your name. As Tony placed his head on the table, his brother walked in the door.

"You weren't his accomplice, were you? He's not telling the truth?" Jonathan asked with all hope fading from his eyes.

"It's true, I was. I held her down and Kahmelle took the rings. Then Kahmelle started talking crazy and wanted to rape her. We robbed her on the High's field this summer."

"WHAT? When was this, Tony? Was this in June?" Malik asked as he walked through the kitchen entrance of the house.

"Yeah, it was the last day of school."

"Dad, fill me in," Malik said as he walked to the table, sat next to his brother and drank juice out of the container.

"Kahmelle and Tony robbed the owner of the Brooklyn Jewelry Exchange's wife for her engagement ring and wedding band. They placed Kahmelle in a lineup. The salesman from the store didn't recognize him from the robbery, but the wife picked him as her assailant."

Malik smiled. "Talk about small worlds colliding. Don't worry, Dad, I can handle this."

"I don't know if I can get him out of this one. I called in a favor but I didn't know he was part of a robbery. They want him for questioning today. Kahmelle gave up his name as his accomplice. So it's up to the—"

Tony shook his head. "He snitched on me!" Tony shouted.

"Sang like a bird, son," Jonathan said.

"Dad, I got this. That's my— lady friend," Malik said.

Jonathan stood up and both he and Tony stared at Malik.

"Susan Eden is the White woman who came to the airport that day you and Mom came to pick me up. That was the same weekend you robbed her, she didn't make to Jamaica because you robbed her. I probably can get her to drop the charges against Tony but Kahmelle is on his own."

Jonathan shook his head. "The Lord works in very mysterious ways. I hope you can do it."

"I'm keeping Sweat close by, if you go down, he's going down. I have the deed to the house on Clermont, and the title to his Lexus, so I can keep him close. I'll bargain him for you or something."

"How did you manage that?" Tony asked.

"Mainly because no matter what differences we have, we are still fam. He owes me Tony and he knows I will take his ass down if he doesn't cooperate. He's still on the run in Maryland, for murder, I'll turn him in."

Mr. Hendrickson fell into his seat and grabbed his head.

"Now keep your mouth shut about everything else. You deny being with Kahmelle on the day y'all robbed her and I am going to run to the precinct and talk to Susan—"

"Son, are you sure you're going to be able to—"

"She's getting ready to make partner at my job. I will threaten to go public with our relationship, I'm sure she's not ready to lose her marriage and her job over this. I have nude pictures of her and me in Jamaica and I will blow up the picture of her sucking my black dick and circulate it from the mailroom all the way up to her corner office."

Mr. Hendrickson laughed. Tony wanted to but he couldn't. His nerves had his vocal chords in a knot. "What if the sales person ID's me?" Tony asked.

"Just let me handle this," Malik said.

"What about the jewelry? What if they want that shit back?" Tony asked.

"Listen, we'll cross that bridge when we get there. I will be at the precinct waiting for you."

"Malik, you can't take my car your Mom isn't home from work yet so there's only one—"

Malik dangled a set of keys in the air. "I told you I have Sweat's green Lex. He's going to lay low for a while just in case your boy Kahmelle starts snitching. I'm holding on to some of his shit so he won't lay too low for me to find him. I'm out."

The screen door slammed behind Malik. Tony looked at his father.

"Dad, I can't stop thinking about Camille's face at the wake. She looked so different and peaceful."

"That's what you have to remember son, how peaceful she looked. That baby is probably better off up there in heaven, than down here in the streets with such young and carefree parents. Don't think about that awful day. Think about how peaceful she looked in that coffin. Why don't you take a nap? We are not due at the precinct until five— and it's only two-thirty. You need to rest up before your mother comes home and sees you like this. Go on."

Tony gave his father a tight embrace. "Thanks Dad, for everything."

Tony took the money upstairs and neatly packed it into the large shoeboxes under his bed. He lay down and thought about how peaceful Camille looked in her coffin, with the pink teddy bear she clasped between her cold fingers. He was able to fall asleep without tossing, turning or having a nightmare for the first time in two weeks.

"Baby, wake up, it's time for school," Millicent said as she lightly tapped her son's shoulder. Tony sat up and stretched. He looked at his alarm clock it was nine a.m.

"Oh my God. I can't believe I slept that long." He looked at his shirt and pants. "And I slept in my street clothes."

"You needed it .You haven't slept like that since your friend was killed, I almost didn't wake you up. Your brother said not to call him at work he didn't go in today, and will be back soon. I am off to work and your Dad is here. I'm happy you finally got some sleep, baby. I love you."

"I love you too, Mom." Tony said.

He waited until he heard his mother walk out of the front door. He got up and ran into his parents' bedroom where his father lay on the bed, fast asleep. He tapped his father's shoulder lightly. "Dad, wake up. What happened?" Why didn't you wake me up to go in for the—"

His father opened his eyes, moistened his mouth and spoke without sitting up. "Where is your mother, Tony?"

"She just left for work."

"Your brother spoke to Susan Eden, the woman you guys robbed. She brought up the fact that you stopped Kahmelle from raping her and she didn't want any charges brought up against you. Malik will have to fill you in on the rest. I just got in here an hour ago and I haven't been right since you filled me in on this ordeal. Wake me up if you need me. If not speak to Malik."

"Yes, Dad."

Tony anxiously sat at the kitchen table for an hour waiting for Malik. He tried to imagine what words had been exchanged that would prevent him from having to show up at the police station. When Malik walked through the kitchen door, Tony wasted no time. "What happened, Malik? Tell me everything."

"Can I get in the door?" Malik said as he sat at the table next to Tony. "Well, you are definitely cleared of that attempted rape and grand larceny shit. She's not pressing charges against you. I even filled her in on your big job. She said not to worry insurance covers all lost, and if anything leads back to you we could work something out."

"All of that for you?" Tony asked

"I just left her in a hotel. I promised her that I would move into an apartment, where she has the keys to and break up with Laneice."

"Word?"

"Yeah, but I will work those kinks when I go back to the hotel, tonight. Kahmelle is locked up. Daddy and I spoke to him and warned him about anymore snitching. I let him know that Sweat is on my team now. I showed him the deed to Clermont and told him if he brings either your name or Sweat's name up to the cops, Sweat will definitely take care of his moms and grandmother in North Carolina and I will deal with his Aunt Seepia myself. I told him his forty grand is waiting for him from the last job, and will be safe when he comes home, as long as he keeps his mouth closed."

"It's sixty-five."

"Nah, son, I deducted twenty-five for your moving expenses next month."

"How long does he have to stay in there?"

"It's going to be up to the courts to decide that."

"So, that's it?"

"That's it for now. We just have to work on getting you ready for D.C., baby bro."

"I don't know what to say. I'm scared. I am not ready to leave Brooklyn. I don't know nothing else."

Malik placed his hand over Tony's and squeezed it. "You're too smart not to know anything else. I love you lil' Tone. Just promise me you won't leave school until you are Doctor Hendrickson. That's all you have to say and make sure you do it."

"No doubt, I promise and— I love you too— Malik? What do you have on this nigga, Sweat? How did you get him to go along with everything."

"Tony, it's a combination of respect and repaying his debts." Malik sucked his teeth and continued." I did two years, and he did not, when we should have both did them together. I came home, and after we fought, I never turned that nigga in. He owes me for that, and respects our past relationship."

"Turned him in for what, Malik?"

"Sweat killed his girl, Tasha, in Maryland, because she was pregnant and did not want to have an abortion. That's how I know he put a battery in that nigga Kahmelle's back. That shit had Sweat's name written all over it. I walked in on that nigga, after he put her in the ground bloody and all. That nigga respects me for keeping my mouth shut after all these years. Most of all that nigga went along with everything just on the strength of how tight we were back in the days. He still has mad love for me and this family, and believe it or not I still got mad love for that nigga." Tony gave his brother a firm embrace. "You better go to school today, Tone."

Tony ran up the stairs, went into the bathroom, took a shower, freshened up and walked into his room. It had been two weeks since he touched the small bag on the bottom of his closet that contained the clothes he'd worn on that day. He pulled the jeans out by its cuff and a small heavy object fell out of the pocket, hit the floor and rolled under his bed. He pulled everything out of the bag and balled it up. He walked to his bed, got on his hands and knees then retrieved the small diamond beetle broach from under it. He held it tightly, looked up at the ceiling and whispered, "Camille, live on, baby."

He fished out a shoebox from underneath his bed and opened up one that was filled to the top with money. He placed the broach on the top.

Tony took the clothing downstairs, grabbed his book bag from the side of the kitchen door and threw his clothes in the garbage can outside his house. In his mind he let go of that day by trashing his clothes. He went to school feeling like himself. At lunchtime he sat at the table with his friends and didn't have to force a smile. With Shaine at his side, and his books on his back, he knew everything would work out for the best.

❖ ❖ ❖ ❖

Joann stood in front of the closed gate of her bodega. Now she shared the gate with a rookie and another male cop. She watched as her breath clouded around her mouth. She rubbed her hands together in an attempt to keep warm.

"So Nuñez, are you married?" the rookie smiled.

"Nah, what about you?" Joann asked.

"I just got married six months ago," the rookie replied.

"I've been divorced twice," the third cop said.

"Let's walk and warm up," Joann said.

Just as they made their way to the corner they heard a voice calling in the distance.

"Officer Nuñez, wait up." Tony ran to the officers as they stood on the corner. Joann became tense. She didn't know what to expect. They looked at one another and greeted each other with an awkward silence.

"I saw you on the news with the bird lady. You were brave."

"Thanks, kid."

"Oh here, I bought you some cocoa." Tony looked at the other cops. "I didn't realize you had partners now, or I would have purchased you guys some, too. Anyway, I wanted to show you my report card." Tony handed it to Joann and she smiled broadly.

"Would you look at this fellas he's averaged straight A's since his freshman year, he's a senior now," Joann said as she passed the report card around to both her partners. They smiled and congratulated him.

"And I am the valedictorian."

"But it's January?" Joann said.

"I know I am graduating early. Can I have a word with you?" Tony asked.

"Sure, Tony. Go on ahead guys I'll catch up. Girl trouble, I'm sure."

"Keep up the good work son," the rookie replied.

The officers made their comments and began to walk slowly up Fourth. Tony stared at Joann for seconds before he said anything. He finally cleared his throat and said, "Thanks."

"Thanks for what?" Joann asked.

"You know?"

"I don't know what you're talking about. But thanks for the hot chocolate," Joann said as she sipped it down.

"Anyway, I am leaving to go to Washington D.C. right after I take my regents. These are my last days of school. I just wanted to say good bye, thank you, and let you know that I *will be* attending Howard's Pre-Med program."

"I'm proud of you, kid, and remember, you bring Brooklyn out there. Remember it ain't where you're from," Joann said.

Tony hugged Joann tightly and whispered in her ear. "It's where you're at. Thank you. I just had to let you know that I never intended for anyone to get killed. Kahmelle had his own agenda, I swear— I really didn't know. Thanks."

Joann looked around to see if her partners were watching and gently pushed him off of her.

"Tony, stay out of trouble. You've got doors open for you out there in D.C. But, I won't be out there to unlock any more cells, you feel me? The story won't end the same way next time. Don't look back," Joann said.

"I won't."

"What about your girlfriend?"

"She got accepted to Morgan State. It ain't that close, but it's not that far away," Tony said.

"What about—"

"He's has to do 3 to 5 for attempted rape and grand larceny. He's eighteen, so he will do time. But he can get out in about a year if he acts right."

"All right, kid. Whenever you come home, keep me posted."

"I will. Goodbye, Officer Nuñez."

"Goodbye Tony."

Tony ran to the Brooklyn Jewelry Exchange and took one last look. He made the sign of the cross on his chest and added carnations to a small shrine for Camille that sat in front of its closed gates. Joann looked across the street as Tony dropped the flowers and continued to run. He dropped the flower near the same space where Joann first laid eyes on Yanick. She thought about her momentarily. She recalled the day the store was robbed and her decisions not to shoot George and let Tony go. She knew she made the right decisions and moved quickly on with her thoughts running down the block joining her partners.

Moments after Joann and her partners turned the corner, Rocky's black Mercedes pulled up in front of the Brooklyn Jewelry Exchange. There was yellow and black caution tape hanging across its shut gates. Kay pulled up right in front of it. Rocky got out and stood on the corner.

"I still can't believe it," she cried to Kay. "It's been two weeks and they are still closed after all this time. I need my Nahnan's broach. I'm going to have to call Susan in on this one."

Rocky stood in front of its gates and shook her head. She remembered the day she had exchanged her broach for cash at Brooklyn Jewelry Exchange. She could remember the female cop who had given her the ticket right in front of those gates. She looked down the block toward the High's field and shook her head.

"Kay, I don't want to go."

"I think it's best. He really loves you and you need to be off your feet for at least three weeks while you are on this medication. He could have someone wait on you hand and foot 24 hours a day. Make the best of a not-so-bad-situation. Besides, Detroit can't be all that bad."

"It's not but Mauri is," Rocky said.

Kay shook her head. They hopped into the car, and as Kay drove past the block of Brooklyn High's Field Rocky stopped her. She got out of the car and looked down at the exact spot the dead bird was minutes before her attack. "If only I turned back," Rocky whispered.

"Let's go," Kay said.

Rocky stood there for a minute or two before Kay called her again.

"Rocky, you are going to miss your flight. Let's go," Kay said.

As they pulled off, she watched Brooklyn Jewelry Exchange disappear in the rear view mirror. She could still see the black and yellow caution tape in the distance. She closed her eyes and let the yellows and blacks swirl in her mind. When her cell phone rang, she ignored it and closed her eyes tighter. Mauri had already called her several times that morning. Rocky did not open her eyes the entire twenty-minute ride to LaGuardia Airport.

When they arrived she hugged Kay tightly. Kay wiped away Rocky's tears.

"I would exchange every piece of jewelry I own, every bag, fur and shoe just to be back in Brooklyn with you. I love you, Kay. I'll be back to visit as soon as I can." Rocky didn't wait for a response. She suddenly hopped out of the car and walked toward the entrance to the terminal with nothing but a purse on her shoulder and a ringing cell phone in her bag. She dared not turn around when she heard Kay's crying words.

"You act like Brooklyn is in another country, I'll see you soon."

As Rocky entered the airport she wiped her eyes and rummaged through her purse and sighed, "Mauri, I know it's you." When she finally caught hold of her cell phone the ringing stopped. Her mouth dropped as she scrolled through her Missed Calls menu and the word Marcus popped up across the screen three times.

End!

What's next from My Lyric's House Press?

Big Cess

By
Meisha C. Holmes

You enjoyed the situations the characters in Brooklyn Jewelry Exchange got themselves into and out of, didn't you? If you thought Rock Candy was an insatiable hot mess as an adult, could you imagine what her childhood was like with Denise—a drop dead gorgeous, twenty-two year old, boosting, pick pocket as a mother? Well, wait until you find out what happens in Big Cess, the story of Shorty Jones, a young, renown, Brooklyn drug dealer and single parent to, Cess, a beautiful and bold girl who carries the Jones name into the dealings of the next generation of drugs— Crack Cocaine. More sex, betrayal, lies and murder from cover to cover. Find out why Rock Candy is afraid of birds, why Susan needs to cheat on Edey, if Nunez was really born that way, and what turned Sweat to the streets as some of Brooklyn Jewelry Exchange's favorites make cameos throughout this novel. Check out the first few pages right now.

1

Smoked some nice Cess in the West

It was brutally cold for an August night, fifty degrees to be exact. As Barbara stood at the corner of Putnam Avenue, a strange feeling overtook her. Although sharp pains continued to rip through her stomach, liquid suddenly gushed from between her inner thighs. Her denim maternity pants were sticky down to her swollen calves, leaving her shivering cold. Barbara's water just broke, and the nearest hospital was twenty minutes away.

"Shit, it was just 80 degrees two days ago," she sobbed to the cold breeze as it smacked her in the face and stung her wet legs. The wind howled a deadly song in reply, and the rustling garbage on the streets added a lyric.

"Why couldn't you have come two days ago," she said as she caressed her stomach and painfully hustled to the opposite corner of Putnam Avenue. Barbara stopped and stood bent over in front of a bodega to flag down a cab where six guys were shooting a game of dice against the building's side. 'Bed Stuy do or die' was spray painted on its dull brown bricks in huge purple and white letters. Barbara looked up at the message, straightened herself out, then looked down at her stomach and whispered. "I'll get us out of here before you take your first step."

"C–lo niggas, give me my money now," a tall, lanky young guy yelled. "It's right here in black and white 4, 5, and 6 now give me my fuckin' bread."

"Fuck that, you ain't from around here. We ain't got to give you shit!" A shorter, younger guy shouted.

Barbara looked over in a bit of panic when she heard the guys starting to argue, but when she recognized the last voice as Shorty's, her ex-best friend, she knew she was safe and continued her search for a cab.

"That's exactly why you jive ass nigga's shouldn't fuck around. You don't know us, and you don't know how we roll, so if you know like I know you should just hand over the bread," the tall guy replied as he slid his left hand inside his jacket to indicate he was carrying a gun.

It seemed as if Shorty was the only one who noticed his motion, and as he checked out his surroundings, he noticed Barbara and changed his tone. "All right slick, he said smoothly, "—cool out, you'll get your bread," He said as he slowly lifted a beer bottle to his mouth and took a quick swig.

"Fuck that, they ain't getting' shit, Shorty!" A guy from the dice game yelled.

I just gotta make sure Barbara gets where she needs to go before any kind of beef breaks out, Shorty thought as he quickly glared at his boy who continued to argue.

Shorty and Barbara were best friends since grade school until she got pregnant by the neighborhood dopefiend and dropped out of high school. The dopefiend denied that the baby Barbara carried was his. He also denied the fact that he was on dope, but Shorty knew because Derrick was Shorty's biggest customer. Shorty's boys continued to argue.

"Yo, Shorty, fuck this jive ass cat. Where you goin'? These mo-foes think that we got some bread for them, let's show them what we do got."

"Layback, I'll be right back," Shorty said as he looked at the guy who put his hand inside of his jacket and thought, *them house niggas ain't got no piece, and if they do, they to home trained to know how to use it.*

As Shorty walked towards Barbara, they all watched him. His slim frame glided with a diddy bop, and his handsome light brown face wore a smirk. He stood five feet nine inches, had a sandy-brown curly afro, straight teeth and narrow and deep hazel eyes. It was his deeply set eyes that gave him a sinister look and in his opinion were the only things that kept him from being a pretty boy.

He stood in front of Barbara and shook his head at how damn fine she looked. Her skin was a deep chocolate. Her hair was straight, long, jet-black and danced in the wind. He pictured her walking the halls at school just before she dropped out. Barbara's motions were always melodic. Each step she took, her hips seemed to spread out like a symphony over sheet music. She was 5'7", thick on the bottom, and the envy of all women ages sixteen and above in Putnam Avenue Projects. Every man in school and the projects had wanted her, but no one would dare try to rap to her. She was like one of the guys, cussed like a sailor and her beauty was too intimidating. The few men who did approach her usually got their feelings hurt. Shorty wasn't scared, but he was only sixteen. She was a year older than him, and girls were always on that, "I ain't talkin' to no one younger than me shit."

"Shorty, you gonna stand there staring in my fuckin' face or are you gonna give a bitch a ride to the hospital? I'm about to drop this load right in the street."

"Yeah, Barbara, come on my car is around the corner." Shorty watched her rub the bottom of her stomach, and then looked up into her face. "Why ain't that fucking fiend taking you to the hospital, where is he at now?" He surveyed her round face, which was now bloated like the rest of her body, her nose spread clear across it but she was still beautiful in his eyes.

"Fuck you, Shorty. I don't want you to go anywhere except straight to hell. And for your information, I don't need him or anyone else to raise this baby, I been on my fuckin' own since I was fifteen; and I definitely don't need no sixteen year old trying to act like my father this late in the game. I rather hop on the 'A' train and get to the hospital my damn self," she said as she stormed off.

The pain started to kick in, but Barbara kept on walking at top speed against the sharp winds, sharp pains, and the world. She hated Shorty ever since she found out that he was pushing dope to Derrick.

So what Shorty had boo-koo money now that he was hustlin', she thought. *I could still toss that nigga up in a fight.*

An escalating jab began stabbing Barbara in her vaginal area. As it reached it's peak she threw herself against the hood of a parked car clutching her huge stomach and winced loudly. She took short coarse breaths trying to alleviate the pain.

"Just wait a minute baby, I'll get you there," she managed to force out between breathing.

Shorty walked past the guys to get his car. One of them called him. "Yo Shitty, what's up with our dough? These punk ass boys of yours don't seem to have any clout. Looks like you got it all, so what's happening?"

"The name's Shorty, and the game's over so split. Go back home to mommy and daddy, before you get hurt. I got other things to do. Yo, fellas, I'll be back around tomorrow, see y'all later."

Shorty's boys stood there with their mouths ajar. He never took to jokes about his name easily. "Alright, Shorty," "See you later," "Be easy greasy," Three guys replied and then shuffled away from the corner.

Without notice Shorty quickly walked up on the two remaining guys, lifted his beer bottle to the face of the taller one and swung it across his eyelid. It broke upon impact and shattered in his palm. Shorty gave him no time to retaliate. Clutching the neck of the broken bottle he rammed its sharp jagged edges into the guy's cheek, withdrew it, turned to the guy's partner then dragged it down the side of his face.

"The next time you choose to act like you have a gun you better use it or you'll get used," Shorty said as he wiped his bloody palm on his pant leg. Shorty jumped into the shorter guys face, and he turned and fled. The taller guy held the upper portion of his head, looked down at the trickles of blood dropping to the ground, and didn't make one sound. Tears of anger and embarrassment streamed from his eyes, and stung the open wounds on his face.

"See YOU later, shitty. You know me, and where I stay, if you dare try to do me some," Shorty said as he walked to his car.

"Dig that, man! That's the Shorty we know! Fuck them Canarsie living, house having, wanna be white boys up," Shorty's friends cheered from the stoop of a building.

Shorty got into his brand new Cadillac, and drove up the block to find Barbara bent over and slowly walking down the street. He pulled up beside her. "Get in and let me drive you to the hospital."

Barbara swallowed her pride and holding on to her stomach got into the car. "Hurry Shorty, this shit hurts really bad," she strained loudly.

Shorty made a U-turn and sped up to the top of the block where they were stopped by a red light. After a few seconds Shorty took his foot off of the brake and the car began to inch through the light. "Damn, why is this light takin' so long?"

"Don't run it Shorty. We don't need no police stopping you now. I don't know how you be riding around in this brand new hog, a black young ass nigga. You ain't got no fuckin' lic—" She inhaled deeply at the end of her sentence, and tears crowded her eyes. As she slowly exhaled, the rising pain stabbed her insides once more.

"I got a license," Shorty replied loudly as he sped through the light.

"No you don't, you only sixteen. Ahhhhhhh! she yelled. "Shorty hurry, please, you got to hurry! I can't take this pain too much longer," Barbara cried.

Shorty glanced at his speedometer, he was doing sixty-five. Barbara let out another loud bellow. As Shorty floored the gas pedal, the sound of glass braking filled the car. "Oh God Shorty, noooooo," she wailed hoarsely. "Please no!" she screamed grabbing the arm of the door with both hands. She squeezed her eyes shut as tears ran from between her lashes.

Shorty looked at Barbara and her chest was filled with blood.

"Damn girl, what the fuck you doing bustin' up my windows like that? I know you in pain but— how you get blood on your shirt? Are you having the baby now?"

Shorty looked up from her stomach then briefly glanced at the streets in front of him. There was a clear string of green lights, with no traffic ahead. He looked at Barbara again then over her and stared at the barrel of silenced pistol in the car next to them through his blood filled shattered window. It was then that he realized Barbara had been shot. His thoughts screamed inside, *It's those house trained niggas from the C-lo game*!! "Oh my fuckin' God Barbara, I'll kill those bitches!"

As Shorty swerved his car away from theirs they shot again, and hit Barbara on the side of her arm. Shorty reached under his seat and pulled a gun from underneath it.

Barbara cried in a barely audible whisper, "Just drive, Shorty. You can out drive them with your new car."

Against his better judgment he sat his gun on his lap, gripped the wheel and left the other car far behind. He looked at Barbara, and even with her face blood stained she still looked beautiful. Just as he laid his eyes on her she suddenly let out two short ear piercing gasps and tightened her grip on the door, snapping three of the nails on her right hand.

There was a sudden loud and deep silence in the car with the exception of Shorty's sobs. He kept one eye on the road and the other watched Barbara as she started to drift off releasing her hold on the door and lightly placing her bloody hands on her stomach.

"BARBARA!" he sobbed loudly. "Stay up. Please don't drift off. Don't worry, I'll get you there, you'll be alright."

As he spoke to her he watched her hands slowly slide off her stomach, leaving four temporary pink lines on her blood stained blouse. Within seconds her finger markings were quickly covered with blood.

"Ah– remember when we went to Satellite West, and– and we used to– ah smoke in the school's exit?" he stammered, as he gently rubbed the back of his fingers along the side of her face. She slowly tilted her head towards Shorty, and it dropped as if it were a free weight and whispered. "We smoked weed— Buddha and Cess."

"You used to love smokin' Cess," Shorty sobbed. "Remember we all got suspended when we got caught? Barbara— Barbara answer me!" he yelled frantically. Please answer me, do you remember. . ."

Shorty sat in the waiting room full of police answering questions for what seemed to be hours, crying beside himself with worry. He had not cried since he was twelve, when his mother died.

"Please God, don't let Barbara die." He hadn't prayed since his mother died either. A nurse and doctor came into the waiting room in blue uniforms and walked straight over to Shorty.

"Are you the father?"

Shorty hesitated, and asked himself, *Are you the father? That means Barbara and the baby are all right.* "Yes . . .Yes I am. Oh my God, she made it through, thank you so much, I don't believe she survived."

"Your daughter survived, but I'm sorry your wife died during labor, as soon as she was born."

Shorty palmed his face tightly with both of his hands as he shook his head. He looked up at the nurse and his hazel eyes were surrounded by fiery red. "When can I see her?"

"You can go in to see her as soon as you feel you are ready."

Shorty immediately followed the nurse and doctor into the delivery room, cursing himself inside for the death of his longtime friend whom he missed already.

Inside the room, the delivery staff was all crowded around the baby. She was exquisite; like a piece of art. Deep, brown in color with smooth skin and a head full of straight hair. Shorty watched them stare at the baby girl, kicking and screaming full of spunk already having traits of her mother. *Damn she's just like her mother,* he thought.

Shorty looked up into the bright lights in the middle of the room. They were shining down on the operating table where Barbara's feet were sticking out from under a green surgical blanket, which was soaked with blood. Was it the blood of new life or the blood of death? He walked towards the table, but before he reached it a nurse hurried to him.

"Would you like to hold your daughter? Have you decided what to name her?" the nurse asked.

Shorty continued to the table and lifted up the blanket. There she lay— still— naked— beautiful and peaceful. Her skin dark even and blood stained. To him, she still looked sweet like the middle of a chocolate covered cherry. Shorty tried desperately to remember the last words they spoke before those two house niggas took her life.

"Please sir step away from the table. Why don't you come and hold your daughter? She's precious," the nurse said.

Shorty looked at the nurse in the blue uniform as she talked to him but her words did not register. He thought desperately, trying to remember Barbara and his last words but all he could remember was watching the bullet strike her arm. He instantly looked at that arm, and his heart sank as he viewed the hole where the bullet sped through causing instant nausea to travel through his body. He walked closer to her and hurled a trailer load of vomit, which landed in loud splats when he saw where the bullet ripped through her arm and entered her stomach as she tried to shield it. As he went to touch yet another hole in her shoulder one of the doctors came over and yanked Shorty away from the table.

"Here she is. A healthy, beautiful newborn," the doctor said as he handed her to Shorty.

Shorty had never held a baby before, she fascinated him. He placed his pinky in the baby's wrinkled palm and he suddenly remembered Barbara's last words.

"Cess," he forced out as a tear rolled off of his face and landed on the baby's hand. He pictured Barbara's lips mouthing her last words as he held her daughter's warm soft body. "Cess," he repeated softly.

"My chocolate little girl. "I'm gonna name you Cess Chocolate Jones."

Also Coming Soon from My Lyric's House Press

Brooklyn Jewelry Exchange: The Grand Reopening

By
Meisha C. Holmes

Acknowledgements

I want to thank you, heavenly Father, for shinning your light on me and for giving me the gift. I would also like to thank:
You—for purchasing Brooklyn Jewelry Exchange. I really appreciate it. Tell a friend!

Carol Cruickshank, Audrey Qualles and Tracy Qualles—for believing in me and my pen's flow when no one else did. Audrey— for the encouragement, inspiration, staying on my back when I was slacking and being a true friend. Tracy—for your thorough critiques and giving me a walk-through of your station house (what up to the 84th precinct). Aunt Carol—there is no way to measure or put in words the thanks that you are owed. Your support, nurturing, and the time you spent on making both Brooklyn Jewelry Exchange and myself the best will always be appreciated. Sandra Holmes, for giving birth to the hottest/flyest author to date—I love you.

The members of my focus group— for the countless readings and critiques of Brooklyn Jewelry Exchange—get focused man! Charene Chapman, Judy Selmci, Franchon Prioleanu and Allison Lavalas for making the initial edits on Brooklyn Jewelry Exchange, we've come a long way baby! Ski, at Hot Spot Digital for bringing my cover back from the dead. Anré DaCosta and Haz for making my web site super hot!! Aunt Sandra DaCosta for taking the time. My people in Detroit: especially Verna Green and DJ G-Raw of WJLB—for showing me the 'D'.

Drew Campbell—for being on My Lyric's House's team and marketing the hell out of my project—love you. Lynn Scott—for being on my Lyric's House's team and taking the time. DJ Beetle—for being my mouthpiece, remaining my best friend after all these years and helping take my love of music from the pages of my novel to life on that hot mixed CD. Gordy Groove— for your help in putting together that hot mixed CD. Mr. Walt and Evil Dee for putting the finishing touches on that hot mixed CD. Shawn Tillman—for taking the Less Brown approach to my problems and pushing me when I was ready to quit—I love you. Chad, for reading out of your element—I love you. Uncle CC for being the best uncle/dad ever! My big brothers Isadore and Fresh Johnson— we are going to take this book thing to the next level! My cousin Jay for spreadin' the word— one love. Kiki for wash and setting me through three novels and sticking your neck out for me (smile). Kika Martin, for taking the time and remaining a close friend after all these years—love you. Teddy Latimore—for always taking interest in whatever I do. Nacole Powers for taking the time and coming through when I needed you, don't get lost again (lol) Lita, Ramcharan— for being my right hand and remaining my close friend after all these years — love you. Nikki Ramsey, Kobe Brown, Cheryl Cole, Stacey Barden and Velda Colthurst—for believing in me and taking the time. Aunt Carol Grinage—for the countless copies—see you in N' Owleans

Mrs. Weinstien, Ms. Jones, Professors: Paul Broer, Dr. Allen Kay, Gerri Deluca, Ronni Natov, Saul Galin and Marissa Flateau—for knowing your craft, sharing your knowledge, being exemplary educators, and expecting the best from all of your students—especially me.

My Co-Workers— for showing interest in my project especially: Adria Simmons, Dennis Herring Jr., Katrina Holder, Tonya Ingram, Cilon Wilson, Amoye Neblett, Leah Ross, Africa Conyers, Jelani Miller, Natalie Lawrewnce, Makeda McDonald and Sohndra Snead.

John and the boys at Riverside Copy— for giving Estos and I a place to work. Scott Morris of Morris Printing for your patience. Malik Cumbo— for snapping the perfect picture. Ken Simmons, Terry Colter and Doc Martin of X Radio Networks— for showing much interest and helping a sister out. Big Stacey, Sada Lewis, Marie, DJ Gold Finger, Nancey Flowers, Michael Saunders of Power 1051, Aiesha Bell, Tracy Gaither and Darrel Bunton—for showing much interest. Veroinca and Miranda Johnson— for your knowledge and taking the time. Marlon Rice (the apprentice)— for your time and effort. It is time for our pens to shine we did it! You're next.

My St. James family aka Club 21— for your interest and support. To the rest of my friends and family—for being there.

A special thanks goes out to Maurice 'Moe'Myers and Angelo 'Lo" Moreno, I know they're reading way up there, R.I.P...

Order Form

My Lyric's House Press, LLC
593 Vanderbilt Avenue
Suite # 135
Brooklyn New York, 11238

Brooklyn Jewelry Exchange $15.95
Shipping & Handling
Via US Priority Mail $ 4.00
Total $19.95

Purchaser's Information

Name_____

Address_____

City_____

State_____ Zipcode_____

My Lyric's House offers a discount to book clubs and retailers who purchase ten or more copies. To find out the available store locations in your area where you can purchase this novel, log onto:
www.Brooklynjewelryexchange.com